The Greatest
Short Stories of
LEO TOLSTOY

CLASSICS

Reprint 2024

FiNGERPRINT! **CLASSICS**
An imprint of Prakash Books India Pvt. Ltd

113/A, Darya Ganj,
New Delhi-110 002
Email: info@prakashbooks.com/sales@prakashbooks.com

⬛ Fingerprint Publishing
✖ @FingerprintP
⬛ @fingerprintpublishingbooks
www.fingerprintpublishing.com

ISBN: 978 93 8881 044 9

"Do in after life the freshness and light-heartedness, the craving for love and for strength of faith, ever return which we experience in our childhood's years? What better time is there in our lives than when the two best of virtues—innocent gaiety and a boundless yearning for affection—are our sole objects of pursuit?"

—*Childhood*

orn at Yasnaya Polyana, southwest of Tula, Russia, on September 9, 1828, Leo Tolstoy grew up to become a novelist, short story writer, essayist, playwright, and philosopher. He had four siblings and after their mother's death they were looked after by their aunt. A master of realistic fiction, Tolstoy had little interest in academics when he was young. In 1851, he enlisted himself in the Russian army and served in the Crimean War (1854-1856) as a second lieutenant in an artillery regiment. He records his experience in *Sevastopol Stories* (1855). He developed techniques of representing military actions and deaths which he later used in *War and Peace*. Tolstoy produced an autobiographical novel, *Childhood* (1852), followed by *Boyhood* (1854) and *Youth* (1857) which earned him literary acclaim.

He married Sofya Andreevna Behrs in 1862 and devoted most of the next two decades to raising a large family and managing his estate. *War and Peace* and *Anna Karenina*, two of his greatest novels, were also written during this period. Notable for its dramatic breadth and unity, *War and Peace*—serialised in *The Russian Herald* between 1865 and 1867 before being published in book form in 1869—is considered to be one of the greatest novels of all time. *Anna Karenina*, regarded as the zenith of literary realism, was declared "flawless as a work of art" by Fyodor Dostoyevsky. It was serialised in *The Russian Herald* between 1875 and 1877 and was published in book form in 1878. But for all the praise these two works received, they were rejected by Tolstoy himself as something not as true to reality.

Known for his paradoxical persona and extreme moralistic and ascetic views, he became a social reformer and a moral thinker in the 1870s. In his short autobiographical story *A Confession* (1882), Tolstoy reflects on his mid-life existential crisis. In his later works, he concentrated on Christian themes. *The Death of Ivan Ilyich* (1886) and *What Is To Be Done* (1889) led to his excommunication from the Russian Orthodox Church in 1901 for a radical anarcho-pacifist Christian philosophy. *The Kingdom of God Is Within You* (1894) expresses his ideas on non-violent resistance which have left a deep impact on figures as M. K. Gandhi, Martin Luther King, Jr. and James Bevel.

The Russian society in which he lived is depicted realistically in his fiction. Apart from drawing from his own life experiences, Tolstoy was very imaginative. Characters such as Pierre Bezukhov and Prince Andrei in *War and Peace*, Levin in *Anna Karenina*, and Price Nekhlyudov in *Resurrection* are memorable literary characters. His works include dozens of short stories and many famous novellas including *Family Happiness* (1859), *The Forged Coupon* (1911), and *Hadji Murad* (1912). He also wrote plays and philosophical essays.

In the last few days of his life, while his health was deteriorating, he separated from his wife and left home. He died of pneumonia at a train station in 1910, at the age of 82.

Contents

The Wood-Cutting Expedition

(Rúbka L'ýesa)

THE STORY OF A YUNKER'S[*] ADVENTURE

[Written and first published in 1855. Also translated as
'The Cutting of the Forest' and 'The Woodfelling'.
This version is a translation by Nathan Haskell Dole taken from
the collection *The Invaders and Other Stories* published in 1887 by
Thomas Y. Crowell & Co.]

---

* Yunker (German *Junker*) is a non-commissioned officer belonging to the nobility. Count Tolstoy himself began his military service in the Caucasus as a Yunker.

I

In midwinter, in the year 185–, a division of our batteries was engaged in an expedition on the Great Chechnya River. On the evening of Feb. 26, having been informed that the platoon which I commanded in the absence of its regular officer was detailed for the following day to help cut down the forest, and having that evening obtained and given the necessary directions, I betook myself to my tent earlier than usual; and as I had not got into the bad habit of warming it with burning coals, I threw myself, without undressing, down on my bed made of sticks, and, drawing my Circassian cap over my eyes, I rolled myself up in my *shuba,* and fell into that peculiarly deep and heavy sleep which one obtains at the moment of tumult and disquietude on the eve of a great peril. The anticipation of the morrow's action brought me to such a state.

At three o'clock in the morning, while it was still perfectly dark, my warm sheepskin was pulled off from me, and the red light of a candle was unpleasantly flashed upon my sleepy eyes.

"It's time to get up," said someone's voice. I shut my eyes involuntarily, wrapped my sheepskin around me again, and dropped off into slumber.

"It's time to get up," repeated Dmitri relentlessly, shaking me by the shoulder. "The infantry are starting." I suddenly came to a sense of the reality of things, started up, and sprang to my feet.

Hastily swallowing a glass of tea, and taking a bath in ice-water, I crept out from my tent, and went to the park (where the guns were placed). It was dark, misty, and cold. The night fires, lighted here and there throughout the camp, lighted up the forms of drowsy soldiers scattered around them, and seemed to make the darkness deeper by their ruddy flickering flames. Near at hand one could hear monotonous, tranquil snoring; in the distance, movement, the babble of voices, and the jangle of arms, as the foot-soldiers got in readiness for the expedition. There was an odour of smoke, manure, wicks, and fog. The morning frost crept down my back, and my teeth chattered in spite of all my efforts to prevent it.

Only by the snorting and occasional stamping of horses could one make out in the impenetrable darkness where the harnessed limbers and caissons were drawn up, and, by the flashing points of the lintstocks, where the cannon were. With the words *s Bógom*— God speed it—the first gun moved off with a clang, followed by the rumbling caisson, and the platoon got under way.

We all took off our caps, and made the sign of the cross. Taking its place in the interval between the infantry, our platoon halted, and waited from four o'clock until the muster of the whole force was made, and the commander came.

"There's one of our men missing, Nikolaï Petróvitch," said a black form coming to me. I recognized him by his voice only as the platoon-artillerist Maksímof.

"Who?"

"Velenchúk is missing. When we hitched up he was here, I saw him; but now he's gone."

As it was entirely unlikely that the column would move immediately, we resolved to send Corporal Antónof to find Velenchúk. Shortly after this, the sound of several horses riding by us in the darkness was heard; this was the commander and his suite. In a few moments the head of the column started and turned—finally we also moved—but Antónof and Velenchúk had not appeared. However, we had not gone a hundred paces when the two soldiers overtook us.

"Where was he?" I asked of Antónof.

"He was asleep in the park."

"What! He was drunk, wasn't he?"

"No, not at all."

"What made him go to sleep, then?"

"I don't know."

11

During three hours of darkness we slowly defiled in monotonous silence across uncultivated, snowless fields and low bushes which crackled under the wheels of the ordnance.

At last, after we had crossed a shallow but phenomenally rapid brook, a halt was called, and from the vanguard were heard desultory musket-shots. These sounds, as always, created the most extraordinary excitement in us all. The division had been almost asleep; now the ranks became alive with conversation, repartees, and laughter. Some of the soldiers wrestled with their mates; others played hop, skip and jump; others chewed on their hard-tack, or, to pass away the time, engaged in drumming the different roll-calls. Meantime the fog slowly began to lift in the east, the dampness became more palpable, and the surrounding objects gradually made themselves manifest emerging from the darkness.

I already began to make out the green caissons and gun-carriages, the brass cannon wet with mist, the familiar forms of my soldiers whom I knew even to the least details, the sorrel horses, and the files of infantry, with their bright bayonets, their knapsacks, ramrods, and canteens on their backs.

We were quickly in motion again, and, after going a few hundred paces where there was no road, were shown the appointed place. On the right were seen the steep banks of a winding river and the high posts of a Tatar burying-ground. At the left and in front of us, through the fog, appeared the black belt. The platoon got under way with the limbers. The eighth company, which was protecting us, stacked their arms, and a battalion of soldiers with muskets and axes started for the forest.

Not five minutes had elapsed when on all sides piles of wood began to crackle and smoke; the soldiers swarmed about, fanning the fires with their hands and feet, lugging brush-wood and logs; and in the forest were heard the incessant strokes of a hundred axes and the crash of falling trees.

The artillery, with not a little spirit of rivalry with the infantry, heaped up their piles; and soon the fire was already so well under way that it was impossible to get within a couple of paces of it. The dense black smoke arose through the icy branches, from which the water dropped hissing into the flames, as the soldiers heaped them upon the fire; and the glowing coals dropped down upon the dead white grass exposed by the heat. It was all mere boy's play to the soldiers; they dragged great logs, threw on the tall steppe grass, and fanned the fire more and more.

As I came near a bonfire to light a cigarette, Velenchúk, always officious, but, now that he had been found napping, showing himself more actively engaged about the fire than anyone else, in an excess of zeal seized a coal with his naked hand from the very middle of the fire, tossed it from one palm to the other, two or three times, and flung it on the ground. "Light a match and give it to him," said another. "Bring a lintstock, fellows," said still a third.

When I at last lighted my cigarette without the aid of Velenchúk, who tried to bring another coal from the fire, he rubbed his burnt fingers on the back of his sheepskin coat, and, doubtless for the sake of exercising himself, seized a great plane-tree stump, and with a mighty swing flung it on the fire. When at last it seemed to him that he might rest, he went close to the fire, spread out his cloak, which he wore like a mantle fastened at the back by a single button, stretched his legs, folded his great black hands in his lap, and opening his mouth a little, closed his eyes.

"Alas! I forgot my pipe! What a shame, fellows!" he said after a short silence, and not addressing anybody in particular.

---

* Ekh-ma.

II

In Russia there are three predominating types of soldiers, which embrace the soldiers of all arms—those of the Caucasus, of the line, the guards, the infantry, the cavalry, the artillery, and the others.

These three types, with many subdivisions and combinations, are as follows:—

(1) The obedient
(2) The domineering or dictatorial
(3) The desperate

The obedient are subdivided into the apathetic obedient and the energetic obedient.

The domineering are subdivided into the gruffly domineering and the diplomatically domineering.

The desperate are subdivided into the desperate jesters and the simply desperate.

The type more frequently encountered than the rest—the type most gentle, most sympathetic, and for the most part endowed with the Christian virtues of meekness, devotion, patience, and submission to the will of God—is that of the obedient.

The distinctive character of the apathetic obedient is a certain invincible indifference and disdain of all the turns of fortune which may overtake him.

The characteristic trait of the drunken obedient is a mild poetical tendency and sensitiveness.

The characteristic trait of the energetic obedient is his limitation in intellectual faculties, united with an endless assiduity and fervour.

The type of the domineering is to be found more especially in the higher spheres of the army: corporals, non-commissioned officers, sergeants and others. In the first division of the gruffly domineering are the high-born, the energetic, and especially the martial type, not excepting those who are stern in a lofty poetic way (to this category belonged Corporal Antónof, with whom I intend to make the reader acquainted).

The second division is composed of the diplomatically domineering, and this class has for some time been making rapid advances. The diplomatically domineering is always eloquent, knows how to read, goes about in a pink shirt, does not eat from the common kettle, often smokes cheap Muscat tobacco, considers himself immeasurably higher than the simple soldier, and is himself rarely as good a soldier as the gruffly domineering of the first class.

The type of the desperate is almost the same as that of the domineering, that is, it is good in the first division—the desperate jesters, the characteristic features of whom are invariably jollity, a huge unconcern in regard to everything, a wealth of nature and boldness.

The second division is in the same way detestable: the criminally desperate, who, however, it must be said for the honour of the Russian soldier, are very rarely met with, and, if they are met with, then they are quickly drummed out of comradeship with the true soldier. Atheism, and a certain audacity in crime, are the chief traits of this character.

Velenchúk came under the head of the energetically obedient. He was a Little Russian by birth, had been fifteen years in the service; and while he was not a fine-looking nor a very skilful soldier, still he was simple-hearted, kind, and extraordinarily full of zeal, though for the most part misdirected zeal, and he was extraordinarily honest. I say extraordinarily honest, because the year before there had been an occurrence in which he had given a remarkable exhibition of this characteristic. You must know that almost every soldier has his own trade. The greater number are tailors and shoemakers. Velenchúk himself practised the trade of tailoring; and, judging from the fact that Sergeant Mikháil

Doroféïtch gave him his custom, it is safe to say that he had reached a famous degree of accomplishment. The year before, it happened that while in camp, Velenchúk took a fine cloak to make for Mikháil Doroféïtch. But that very night, after he had cut the cloth, and stitched on the trimmings, and put it under his pillow in his tent, a misfortune befell him: the cloth, which was worth seven roubles, disappeared during the night. Velenchúk with tears in his eyes, with pale quivering lips and with stifled lamentations, confessed the circumstance to the sergeant.

Mikháil Doroféïtch fell into a passion. In the first moment of his indignation he threatened the tailor; but afterwards, like a kindly man with plenty of means, he waved his hand, and did not exact from Velenchúk the value of the cloak. In spite of the fussy tailor's endeavours, and the tears that he shed while telling about his misfortune, the thief was not detected. Although strong suspicions were attached to a corruptly desperate soldier named Chernof, who slept in the same tent with him, still there was no decisive proof. The diplomatically dictatorial Mikháil Doroféïtch, as a man of means, having various arrangements with the inspector of arms and steward of the mess, the aristocrats of the battery, quickly forgot all about the loss of this particular cloak. Velenchúk, on the contrary, did not forget his unhappiness. The soldiers declared that at this time they were apprehensive about him, lest he should make way with himself, or flee to the mountains, so heavily did his misfortune weigh upon him. He did not eat, he did not drink, was not able to work, and wept all the time. At the end of three days he appeared before Mikháil Doroféïtch, and without any colour in his face, and with a trembling hand, drew out of his sleeve a piece of gold, and gave it to him.

"Faith,* and here's all that I have, Mikháil Doroféïtch; and this I got from Zhdánof," he said, beginning to sob again. "I will give *you* two more roubles, truly I will, when I have earned them. He (who the *he* was, Velenchúk himself did not know) made me seem like a rascal in your eyes. He, the beastly viper, stole from

---

* *yéï Bogu.*

16

a brother soldier his hard earnings; and here I have been in the service fifteen years."

To the honour of Mikháil Doroféïtch, it must be said that he did not require of Velenchúk the last two roubles, though Velenchúk brought them to him at the end of two months.

III

Five other soldiers of my platoon besides Velenchúk were warming themselves around the bonfire.

In the best place, away from the wind, on a cask, sat the platoon artillerist[*] Maksímof, smoking his pipe. In the posture, the gaze, and all the motions of this man it could be seen that he was accustomed to command, and was conscious of his own worth, even if nothing were said about the cask whereon he sat, which during the halt seemed to become the emblem of power, or the nankeen short-coat which he wore.

When I approached, he turned his head round toward me; but his eyes remained fixed upon the fire, and only after some time did they follow the direction of his face, and rest upon me. Maksímof came from a semi-noble family.[†] He had property, and in the school brigade he obtained rank, and acquired some learning. According to the reports of the soldiers, he was fearfully rich and fearfully learned.

---

[*] *feierverker;* German, *Feuerwerker.*

[†] *odnodvortsui,* of one estate; freemen, who in the seventeenth century were settled in the Ukrafoa with special privileges.

I remember how one time, when they were making practical experiments with the quadrant, he explained, to the soldiers gathered around him, that the motions of the spirit level arise from the same causes as those of the atmospheric quicksilver. At bottom Maksímof was far from stupid, and knew his business admirably; but he had the bad habit of speaking, sometimes on purpose, in such a way that it was impossible to understand him, and I think he did not understand his own words. He had an especial fondness for the words "arises" and "to proceed;" and whenever he said "it arises," or "now let us proceed," then I knew in advance that I should not understand what would follow. The soldiers, on the contrary, as I had a chance to observe, enjoyed hearing his "arises," and suspected it of containing deep meaning, though, like myself, they could not understand his words. But this incomprehensibility they ascribed to his depth, and they worshipped Feódor Maksímovitch accordingly. In a word, Maksímof was diplomatically dictatorial.

The second soldier near the fire, engaged in drawing on his sinewy red legs a fresh pair of stockings, was Antónof, the same bombardier Antónof who as early as 1837, together with two others stationed by one gun without shelter, was returning the shot of the enemy, and with two bullets in his thigh continued still to serve his gun and load it.

"He would have been artillerist long before, had it not been for his character," said the soldiers; and it was true that his character was odd. When he was sober, there was no man more calm, more peaceful, more correct in his deportment; when he was drunk he became an entirely different man. Not recognizing authority, he became quarrelsome and turbulent, and was wholly valueless as a soldier. Not more than a week before this time he got drunk at Shrovetide; and in spite of all threats and exhortations, and his attachment to his cannon, he got tipsy and quarrelsome on the first Monday in Lent. Throughout the fast, notwithstanding the order for all in the division to eat meat, he lived on hard-tack alone, and in the first week he did not even take the prescribed allowance of vodka. However, it was necessary to see this short figure, tough as iron, with his stumpy, crooked legs, his shiny face with its moustache, when he, for example, under the influence of liquor, took the *balaläika,* or three-stringed guitar of the Ukraïna, into his strong hands, and, carelessly glancing to this side and that, played some love-song, or with his cloak thrown over his shoulders, and the orders dangling from it, and his hands thrust into the pockets of his blue nankeen trousers, he rolled along the street; it was necessary to see his expression of martial pride, and his scorn for all that did not pertain to the military—to comprehend how absolutely impossible it was for him to compare himself at such moments with the rude or the simply insinuating servant, the Cossack, the foot-soldier, or the volunteer, especially those who did not belong to the artillery. He quarrelled and was turbulent, not so much for his own pleasure as for the sake of upholding the spirit of all soldierhood, of which he felt himself to be the protector.

The third soldier, with earrings in his ears, with bristling moustaches, goose-flesh, and a porcelain pipe in his lips, crouching on his heels in front of the bonfire, was the artillery-rider Chikin. The dear man Chikin, as the soldiers called him, was a jester. In bitter cold, up to his knees in the mud, going without food two days at a time, on the march, on parade, undergoing instruction, the dear man always and everywhere screwed his face into grimaces, executed flourishes with his legs, and poured out such a flood of nonsense that the whole platoon would go into fits of laughter. During a halt or in camp Chikin had always around him a group of young soldiers, whom he either played cards with, or amused with tales about some sly soldier or English milord, or by imitating the Tatar and the German, or simply by making his jokes, at which everybody nearly died with laughter. It was a fact, that his reputation as a joker was so widespread in the battery, that he had only to open his mouth and wink, and he would be rewarded with a universal burst of guffaws; but he really had a great gift for the comic and unexpected. In everything he had the wit to see something remarkable, such as never came into anybody else's head; and, what is more important, this talent for seeing something ridiculous never failed under any trial.

The fourth soldier was an awkward young fellow, a recruit of the last year's draft, and he was now serving in an expedition for the first time. He was standing in the very smoke, and so close to the fire that it seemed as if his well-worn short-coat* would catch on fire; but, notwithstanding this, by the way in which he had flung open his coat, by his calm, self-satisfied pose, with his calves arched out, it was evident that he was enjoying perfect happiness.

And finally, the fifth soldier, sitting some little distance from the fire, and whittling a stick, was Uncle Zhdánof. Zhdánof had been in service the longest of all the soldiers in the battery—knew all the recruits; and everybody, from force of habit, called him *dyá-denka*, or little uncle. It was said that he never drank, never smoked, never played cards (not even the soldier's pet game of *noski*), and never indulged in bad talk. All the time when military duties did not engross him he worked at his trade of shoemaking; on holidays he went to church wherever it was possible, or placed a farthing candle before the image, and read the psalter, the only book in which he cared to read. He had little to do with the other soldiers—with those higher in rank—though to the younger officers he was coldly respectful. With his equals, since he did not drink, he had little reason for social intercourse; but he was extremely fond of recruits and young soldiers: he always protected them, read them their lessons, and often helped them. All in the battery considered him a capitalist, because he had twenty-five roubles, which he willingly loaned to any soldier who really needed it. That same Maksímof who was now artillerist used to tell me that when, ten years before, he had come as a recruit, and the old drunken soldiers helped him to drink up the money that he had, Zhdánof, pitying his unhappy situation, took him home with him, severely upbraided him for his behaviour, even administered a castigation, read him the lesson about the duties of a soldier's life, and sent him away after presenting him with a shirt (for Maksímof hadn't one to his back) and a half-rouble piece.

"He made a man of me," Maksímof used to say, always with

---

* *polushubochek,* little half *shuba.*

20

respect and gratitude in his tone. He had also taken Velenchúk's part always, ever since he came as a recruit, and had helped him at the time of his misfortune about the lost cloak, and had helped many, many others during the course of his twenty-five years' service.

In the service it was impossible to find a soldier who knew his business better, who was braver or more obedient; but he was too meek and homely to be chosen as an artillerist,[*] though he had been bombardier fifteen years. Zhdánof's one pleasure, and even passion, was music. He was exceedingly fond of some songs, and he always gathered round him a circle of singers from among the young soldiers; and though he himself could not sing, he stood with them, and putting his hands into the pockets of his short-coat,[†] and shutting his eyes, expressed his contentment by the motions of his head and cheeks. I know not why it was, that in that regular motion of the cheeks under the moustache, a peculiarity which I never saw in anyone else, I found unusual expression. His head white as snow, his moustache dyed black, and his brown, wrinkled face, gave him at first sight a stern and gloomy appearance; but as you looked more closely into his great round eyes, especially when they smiled (he never smiled with his lips), something extraordinarily sweet and almost childlike suddenly struck you.

* *feierverker.*
† *polushubka.*

IV

"Alas! I have forgotten my pipe; that's a misfortune, fellows,' repeated Velenchúk.

"But you should smoke *cikarettes,*[*] dear man," urged Chikin, screwing up his mouth, and winking. "I always smoke *cikarettes* at home: it's sweeter."

Of course, all joined in the laugh.

"So you forgot your pipe?" interrupted Maksímof, proudly knocking out the ashes from his pipe into the palm of his left hand, and not paying any attention to the universal laughter, in which even the officers joined. "You lost it somewhere here, didn't you, Velenchúk?"

Velenchúk wheeled to right face at him, started to lift his hand to his cap, and then dropped it again.

"You see, you haven't woke up from your last evening's spree, so that you didn't get your sleep out. For such work you deserve a good raking."

"May I drop dead on this very spot, Feódor Maksímovitch, if a single drop passed my lips. I myself don't know what got into me," replied Velenchúk. "How glad I should have been to get drunk!" he muttered to himself.

"All right. But one is responsible to the chief for his brother's conduct, and when you behave this way it's perfectly abominable," said the eloquent Maksímof savagely, but still in a more gentle tone.

"Well, here is something strange, fellows," continued Velenchúk after a moment's silence, scratching the back of his head, and not addressing any one in particular; "fact, it's strange, fellows. I have been sixteen years in the service, and have not had such a

***

[*] *sikhárki.*

thing happen to me. As we were told to get ready for a march, I got up, as my duty behoved. There was nothing at all, when suddenly in the park *it* came over me—came over me more and more; laid me out—laid me out on the ground—and everything . . . And when I got asleep, I did not hear a sound, fellows. It must have been that I fainted away," he said in conclusion.

"At all events, it took all my strength to wake you up," said Antónof, as he pulled on his boot. "I pushed you, and pushed you. You slept like a log."

"See here," remarked Velenchúk, "if I had been drunk . . ."

"Like a peasant-woman we had at home," interrupted Chikin. "For almost two years running she did not get down from the big oven. They tried to wake her up one time, for they thought she was asleep; but there she was, lying just as though she was dead: the same kind of sleep you had—isn't that so, clear man?"

"Just tell us, Chikin, how you led the fashion the time when you had leave of absence," said Maksímof, smiling, and winking at me as much as to say, "Don't you like to hear what the foolish fellow has to say?"

"How led the fashion, Feódor Maksímovitch?" asked Chikin, casting a quick side glance at me. "Of course, I merely told what kind of people we are here in the Kapkas."*

"Well, then, that's so, that's so. You are not a fashion leader . . . but just tell us how you made them think you were commander."

"You know how I became commander for them. I was asked how we live," began Chikin, speaking rapidly, like a man who has often told the same story. "I said, 'We live well, dear man: we have plenty of victuals. At morning and night, to our delight all we soldiers get our chocol*et*;† and then at dinner every sinner has his imperial soup of barley groats, and instead of vodka, M*o*deira at each plate, genuine old M*o*deira in the cask, forty-second degree!'"

"Fine M*o*deira!" replied Velenchúk louder than the others, and with a burst of laughter. "Let's have some of it."

---

* *Kaphas* for *Kavkas,* Caucasus.
† *shchikuláta id'yót na soldátá.*

"Well, then, what did you have to tell them about the *Esiatics?*" said Maksímof, carrying his inquiries still further, as the general merriment subsided.

Chikin bent down to the fire, picked up a coal with his stick, put it on his pipe, and, as though not noticing the discreet curiosity aroused in his hearers, puffed for a long time in silence.

When at last he had raised a sufficient cloud of smoke, he threw away the coal, pushed his cap still farther on the back of his head, and making a grimace, and with an almost imperceptible smile, he continued: "They asked," said he, "'What kind of a person is the little Cherkés yonder? Or is it the Turk that you are fighting with in the Kapkas country?' I tell 'em, 'The Cherkés here with us is not of one sort, but of different sorts. Some are like the mountaineers who live on the rocky mountain-tops, and eat stones instead of bread. The biggest of them,' I say, 'are exactly like big logs, with one eye in the middle of the forehead, and they wear red caps;' they glow like fire, just as you do, my dear fellow," he added, addressing a young recruit, who, in fact, wore an odd little cap with a red crown.

The recruit, at this unexpected sally, suddenly sat down on the ground, slapped his knees, and burst out laughing and coughing so that he could hardly command his voice to say, "That's the kind of mountaineers we have here."

"'And,' says I, 'besides, there are the *mumri,*'" continued Chikin, jerking his head so that his hat fell forward on his forehead; "'they go out in pairs, like little twins—these others. Everything comes double with them,' says I, 'and they cling hold of each other's hands, and run so *queek* that I tell you you couldn't catch up with them on horseback.'—'Well,' says he, 'these *mumri* who are so small as you say, I suppose they are born hand in hand?'" said Chikin, endeavouring to imitate the deep throaty voice of the peasant. "'Yes,' says I, 'my dear man, they are so by nature. You try to pull their hands apart, and it makes 'em bleed, just as with the Chinese: when you pull their caps off, the blood comes.'—'But tell us,' says he, 'how they kill any one.'—'Well, this is the way,' says I: 'they take you, and they rip you all up, and they reel out your bowels in their hands. They reel 'em out, and you defy them and defy them—till your soul . . .'"

"Well, now, did they believe anything you said, Chikin?" asked Maksímof with a slight smile, when those standing round had stopped laughing.

"And indeed it is a strange lot, Feódor Maksímovitch: they believe every one; before God, they do. But still, when I began to tell them about Mount Kazbek, and how the snow does not melt all summer there, they all burst out laughing at the absurdity of it. 'What a story!' they said. 'Could such a thing be possible—a mountain so big that the snow does not melt on it?' And I say, 'With us, when the thaw comes, there is such a heap; and even after it begins to melt, the snow lies in the hollows.'—'Go away,'" said Chikin, with a concluding wink.

V

The bright disk of the sun, gleaming through the milk-white mist, had now got well up; the purple-grey horizon gradually widened: but, though the view became more extended, still it was sharply defined by the delusive white wall of the fog.

In front of us, on the other side of the forest, could be seen a good-sized field. Over the field there spread from all sides the smoke, here black, here milk-white, here purple; and strange forms swept through the white folds of the mist. Far in the distance, from time to time, groups of mounted Tatars showed themselves; and the occasional reports from our rifles, guns, and cannon were heard.

"This isn't anything at all of an action—mere boys' play," said the good Captain Khlopof.

The commander of the ninth company of cavalry,[*] who was with us as escort, rode up to our cannon, and pointing to three mounted Tatars who were just then riding under cover of the forest, more than six hundred *sazhens* from us, asked me to give them a shot or a shell. His request was an illustration of the love universal among all infantry officers for artillery practice.

"You see," said he, with a kindly and convincing smile, laying his hand on my shoulder, "where those two big trees are, right in front of us: one is on a white horse, and dressed in a black Circassian coat; and directly behind him are two more. Do you see? If you please, we must . . ."

"And there are three others riding along under the lee of the forest," interrupted Antónof, who was distinguished for his sharp eyes, and had now joined us with the pipe that he had been smoking concealed behind his back. "The front one has just taken his carbine from its case. It's easy to see, your Excellency."

"Ha! he fired then, fellows. See the white puff of smoke," said Velenchúk to a group of soldiers a little back of us.

"He must be aiming at us, the blackguard!" replied someone else.

"See, those fellows only come out a little way from the forest. We see the place: we want to aim a cannon at it," suggested a third. "If we could only *blant* a *krenade* into the midst of 'em, it would scatter 'em . . ."

"And what makes you think you could shoot to such a *tistance,* dear man?" asked Chikin.

"Only five hundred or five hundred and twenty *sazhens*——it can't be less than that," said Maksímof coolly, as though he were speaking to himself; but it was evident that he, like the others, was terribly anxious to bring the guns into play. "If the howitzer is aimed up at an angle of forty-five degrees, then it will be possible to reach that spot; that is perfectly possible."

"You know, now, that if you aim at that group, it would infallibly hit someone. There, there! as they are riding along now,

---

[*] *jägers.*

please hurry up and order the gun to be fired," continued the cavalry commander, beseeching me.

"Will you give the order to limber the gun?" asked Antónof suddenly, in a jerky base voice, with a slight touch of surliness in his manner.

I confess that I myself felt a strong desire for this, and I commanded the second cannon to be unlimbered.

The words had hardly left *my* mouth ere the bomb was powdered and rammed home; and Antónof, clinging to the gun-cheek, and leaning his two fat fingers on the carriage, was already getting the gun into position.

"Little . . . little more to the left—now a little to the right—now, now the least bit more—there, that's right," said he with a proud face, turning from the gun.

The infantry officer, myself, and Maksímof, in turn sighted along the gun, and all gave expression to various opinions.

"By God! It will miss," said Velenchúk, clicking with his tongue, although he could only see over Antónof's shoulder, and therefore had no basis for such a surmise.

"By-y-y God! It will miss: it will hit that tree right in front, fellows."

"Two!" I commanded.

The men about the gun scattered. Antónof ran to one side, so as to follow the flight of the ball. There was a flash and a ring of brass. At the same instant we were enveloped in gunpowder smoke; and after the startling report, was heard the metallic, whizzing sound of the ball rushing off quicker than lightning, amid the universal silence and dying away in the distance.

Just a little behind the group of horsemen a white puff of smoke appeared; the Tatars scattered in all directions, and then the sound of a crash came to us.

"Capitally done!" "Ah! they take to their heels;" "See! the devils don't like it," were types of the exclamations and jests heard among the ranks of the artillery and infantry.

"If you had aimed a trifle lower, you'd have hit right in the midst of him," remarked Velenchúk. "I said it would strike the tree: it did; it took the one at the right."

VI

Leaving the soldiers to argue about the Tatars taking to flight when they saw the shell, and why it was that they came there, and whether there were many in the forest, I went with the cavalry commander a few steps aside, and sat down under a tree, expecting to have some warmed chops which he had offered me. The cavalry commander, Bolkhof, was one of the officers who are called in the regiment *bonjour-oli*. He had property, had served before in the guards, and spoke French. But, in spite of this, his comrades liked him. He was rather intellectual, had tact enough to wear his Petersburg overcoat, to eat a good dinner, and to speak French without too much offending the sensibilities of his brother officers. As we talked about the weather, about the events of the war, about the officers known to us both, and as we became convinced, by our questions and answers, by our views of things in general, that we were mutually sympathetic, we involuntarily fell into more intimate conversation. Moreover, in the Caucasus, among men who meet in one circle, the question invariably arises, though it is not always expressed, "Why are you here?" and it seemed to me that my companion was desirous of satisfying this inarticulate question.

"When will this expedition end?" he asked lazily: "it's tiresome."

"It isn't to me," I said: "it's much more so serving on the staff."

"Oh, on the staff it's ten thousand times worse!" said he fiercely. "No, I mean when will this sort of thing end altogether?"

"What! Do you wish that it would end?" I asked.

"Yes, all of it, altogether! . . . Well, are the chops ready, Nikoláief?" he inquired of his servant.

"Why do you serve in the Caucasus, then," I asked, "if the Caucasus does not please you?"

"You know wiry," he replied with an outburst of frankness: "on account of tradition. In Russia, you see, there exists a strange tradition about the Caucasus, as though it were the Promised Land for all sorts of unhappy people."

"Well," said I, "it's almost true: the majority of us here . . ."

"But what is better than all," said he, interrupting me, "is, that all of us who come to the Caucasus are fearfully deceived in our calculations; and really, I don't see why, in consequence of disappointment in love or disorder in one's affairs, one should come to serve in the Caucasus rather than in Kazan or Kaluga. You see, in Russia they imagine the Caucasus as something immense—everlasting virgin ice-fields, with impetuous streams, with daggers, cloaks, Circassian girls—all that is strange and wonderful; but in reality there is nothing gay in it at all. If they only knew, for example, that we have never been on the virgin ice-fields, and that there was nothing gay in it at all, and that the Caucasus was divided into the districts of Stavropol, Tiflis, and so forth."

"Yes," said I, laughing, "when we are in Russia we look upon the Caucasus in an absolutely different way from what we do here. Haven't you ever noticed it: when you read poetry in a language that you don't know very well, you imagine it much better than it really is, don't you?"

"I don't know how that is, but this Caucasus doesn't please me," he said, interrupting me.

"It isn't so with me," I said: "the Caucasus is delightful to me now, but only . . ."

"Maybe it is delightful," he continued with a touch of asperity, "but I know that it is not delightful to me."

"Why not?" I asked, with a view of saying something.

"In the first place, it has deceived me—all that which I expected, from tradition, to be delivered of in the Caucasus, I find in me just the same here, only with this distinction, that before, it was all on a larger scale, but now on a small and nasty scale, at each round of which I find a million petty annoyances, worriments, and miseries; in the second place, because I find that each day I am falling morally lower and lower; and principally because I feel myself incapable of service here—I cannot endure to face the danger . . . simply, I am a coward . . ."

He got up and looked at me earnestly.

Though this unbecoming confession completely took me by surprise, I did not contradict him, as my messmate evidently expected me to do; but I awaited from the man himself the refutation of his words, which is always ready in such circumstances.

"You know today's expedition is the first time that I have taken part in action," he continued, "and you can imagine what my evening was. When the sergeant brought the order for my company to join the column, I became as pale as a sheet, and could not utter a word from emotion; and if you knew how I spent the night! If it is true that people turn grey from fright, then I ought to be perfectly white-headed today, because no man condemned to death ever suffered so much from terror in a single night as I did: even now, though I feel a little more at my ease than I did last night, still it goes here in me," he added, pressing his hand to his heart. "And what is absurd," he went on to say, "while this fearful drama is playing here, I myself am eating chops and onions, and trying to persuade myself that I am very gay . . . Is there any wine, Nikoláief?" he added with a yawn.

"There *he* is, fellows!" shouted one of the soldiers at this moment in a tone of alarm, and all eyes were fixed upon the edge of the far-off forest.

In the distance a puff of bluish smoke took shape, and, rising up, drifted away on the wind. When I realized that the enemy were firing at us, everything that was in the range of my eyes at that moment, everything suddenly assumed a new and majestic character. The stacked muskets, and the smoke of the bonfires, and the blue sky, and the green gun-carriages, and Nikoláief's sunburned, moustachioed face—all this seemed to tell me that the shot which at that instant emerged from the smoke, and was flying through space, might be directed straight at my breast.

"Where did you get the wine?" I meanwhile asked Bolkhof carelessly, while in the depths of my soul two voices were speaking with equal distinctness; one said, "Lord, take my soul in peace;" the other, "I hope I shall not duck my head, but smile while the ball is coming." And at that instant something horribly unpleasant whistled above our heads, and the shot came crashing to the ground not two paces away from us.

"Now, if I were Napoleon or Frederick the Great," said Bolkhof at this time, with perfect composure, turning to me, "I should certainly have said something graceful."

"But that you have just done," I replied, hiding with some difficulty the panic which I felt at being exposed to such a danger.

"Why, what did I say? No one will put it on record."

"I'll put it on record."

"Yes: if you put it on record, it will be in the way of criticism, as Mishchenkof says," he replied with a smile.

"*Tfu!* you devils!" exclaimed Antónof in vexation just behind us, and spitting to one side; "it just missed my leg."

All my solicitude to appear cool, and all our refined phrases, suddenly seemed to me unendurably stupid after this artless exclamation.

The enemy, in fact, had posted two cannon on the spot where the Tatars had been scattered, and every twenty or thirty minutes sent a shot at our wood-choppers. My division was sent out into the field, and ordered to reply to him. At the skirt of the forest a puff of smoke would show itself, the report would be heard, then the whiz of the ball, and the shot would bury itself behind us or in front of us. The enemy's shots were placed fortunately for us, and no loss was sustained.

The artillerists, as always, behaved admirably, loaded rapidly, aimed carefully wherever the smoke appeared, and jested unconcernedly with each other. The infantry escort, in silent inactivity, were lying around us, awaiting their turn. The wood-cutters were busy at their work; their axes resounded through the forest more and more rapidly, more and more eagerly, save when the *svist* of a cannon-shot was heard, then suddenly the sounds ceased, and amid the deathlike stillness a voice, not altogether calm, would exclaim, "Stand aside, boys!" and all eyes would be fastened upon the shot ricocheting upon the wood-piles and the brush.

The fog was now completely lifted, and, taking the form of clouds, was disappearing slowly in the dark-blue vault of heaven. The unclouded orb of the sun shone bright, and threw its cheerful rays on the steel of the bayonets, the brass of the cannon, on the thawing ground, and the glittering points of the icicles. The atmosphere was brisk with the morning frost and the warmth of the spring sun. Thousands of different shades and tints mingled in the dry leaves of the forest; and on the hard, shining level of the road could be seen the regular tracks of wheel-tires and horse-shoes.

The action between the armies grew more and more violent and more striking. In all directions the bluish puffs of smoke from the firing became more and more frequent. The dragoons, with bannerets waving from their lances, kept riding to the front. In the infantry companies songs resounded, and the train loaded with wood began to form itself as the rearguard. The general rode up to our division, and ordered us to be ready for the return. The enemy got into the bushes over against our left flank, and began to pour a heavy musketry-fire into us. From the left-hand side a ball came whizzing from the forest, and buried itself in a gun-carriage; then—a second, a third . . . The infantry guard, scattered around us, jumped up with a shout, seized their muskets, and took aim. The cracking of the musketry was redoubled, and the bullets began to fly thicker and faster. The retreat had begun, and the present attack was the result, as is always the case in the Caucasus.

It became perfectly manifest that the artillerists did not like the bullets as well as the infantry had liked the solid shot. Antónof put on a deep frown. Chikin imitated the sound of the bullets, and fired his jokes at them; but it was evident that he did not like them. In regard to one he said, "What a hurry it's in!" another he called a "honey-bee;" a third, which flew over us with a sort of slow and lugubrious drone, he called an "orphan,"—a term which raised general amusement.

The recruit, who had the habit of bending his head to one side, and stretching out his neck, every time he heard a bullet, was also a source of amusement to the soldiers, who said, "Who is it? Some acquaintance that you are bowing to?" And Velenchúk, who always showed perfect equanimity in time of danger, was now in an alarming state of mind; he was manifestly vexed because we did not send some canister in the direction from which the bullets came. He more than once exclaimed in a discontented tone, "What is *he* allowed to shoot at us with impunity for? If we could only answer with some grape, that would silence him, take my word for it."

In fact, it was time to do this. I ordered the last shell to be fired, and to load with grape.

"Grape!" shouted Antónof bravely in the midst of the smoke, coming up to the gun with his sponge as soon as the discharge was made.

At this moment, not far behind us, I heard the quick whiz of a bullet suddenly striking something with a dry thud. My heart sank within me. "Someone of our men must have been struck," I said to myself; but at the same time I did not dare to turn round, under the influence of this powerful presentiment. True enough, immediately after this sound the heavy fall of a body was heard, and the "o-o-o-oï"—the heart-rending groan of the wounded man. "I'm hit, fellows," remarked a voice which I knew. It was Velenchúk. He was lying on his back between the limbers and the gun. The cartridge-box which he carried was flung to one side. His forehead was all bloody, and over his right eye and his nose flowed a thick red stream. The wound was in his body, but it bled very little; he had hit his forehead on something when he fell.

All this I perceived after some little time. At the first instant I saw only a sort of obscure mass, and a terrible quantity of blood as it seemed to me.

None of the soldiers who were loading the gun said a word—only the recruit muttered between his teeth, "See, how bloody!" and Antónof, frowning still blacker, snorted angrily; but all the time it was evident that the thought of death presented itself to the mind of each. All took hold of their work with great activity. The gun was discharged every instant; and the gun-captain, in getting the canister, went two steps around the place where lay the wounded man, now groaning constantly.

VIII

Everyone who has been in action has doubtless experienced the strange although illogical but still powerful feeling of repulsion for the place in which any one has been killed or wounded. My soldiers were noticeably affected by this feeling at the first moment when it became necessary to lift Velenchúk and carry him to the wagon which had driven up. Zhdánof angrily went to the sufferer, and, notwithstanding his cry of anguish, took him under his arms and lifted him. "What are you standing there for? Help lug him!" he shouted; and instantly the men sprang to his assistance, some of whom could not do any good at all. But they had scarcely started to move him from the place when Velenchúk began to scream fearfully and to struggle.

"What are you screeching for like a rabbit?" said Antónof, holding him roughly by the leg. "If you don't stop we'll drop you."

And the sufferer really calmed down, and only occasionally cried out, "*Okh!* I'm dead! *o-okh*, fellows!* I'm dead!"

As soon as they laid him in the wagon, he ceased to groan, and I heard that he said something to his comrades—it must have been a farewell—in a weak but audible voice.

Indeed, no one likes to look at a wounded man; and I, instinctively hastening to get away from this spectacle, ordered the men to take him as soon as possible to a suitable place, and then return to the guns. But in a few minutes I was told that Velenchúk was asking for me, and I returned to the ambulance.

The wounded man lay on the wagon bottom, holding the sides with both hands. His healthy, broad face had in a few seconds entirely changed; he had, as it were, grown gaunt, and older by several years. His lips were pinched and white, and tightly compressed, with evident effort at self-control; his glance had a quick and feeble expression; but in his eyes was a peculiarly clear and tranquil gleam, and on his blood-stained forehead and nose already lay the seal of death.

In spite of the fact that the least motion caused him unendurable anguish, he was trying to take from his left leg his purse,† which contained money.

A fearfully burdensome thought came into my mind when I saw his bare, white, and healthy-looking leg as he was taking off his boot and untying his purse.

"There are three silver roubles and a fifty-*kopek* piece," he said when I took the girdle-purse. "You keep them."

The ambulance had started to move, but he stopped it.

"I was working on a cloak for Lieutenant Sulimovsky. He had paid me two-o-o silver roubles. I spent one and a half on buttons, but half a rouble lies with the buttons in my bag. Give them to him."

"Very good, I will," said I. "Keep up good hopes, brother."

---

* *bratsuí moï.*

† *chéres;* diminutive, *chéresok*—a leather purse in the form of a girdle, which soldiers wear usually under the knee.—AUTHOR'S NOTE.

He did not answer me; the wagon moved away, and he began once more to groan, and to exclaim "*Okh!*" in the same terribly heart-rending tone. As though he had done with earthly things, he felt that he had no longer any pretext for self-restraint, and he now considered this alleviation permissible.

IX

"Where are you off to? Come back! Where are you going?" I shouted to the recruit, who, carrying in his arms his reserve linstock, and a sort of cane in his hand, was calmly marching off toward the ambulance in which the wounded man was carried.

But the recruit lazily looked up at me, and kept on his way, and I was obliged to send a soldier to bring him back. He took off his red cap, and looked at me with a stupid smile.

"Where were you going?" I asked.

"To camp."

"Why?"

"Because—they have wounded Velenchúk," he replied, still smiling.

"What has that to do with you? It's your business to stay here."

He looked at me in amazement, then coolly turned round, put on his cap, and went to his place.

The result of the action had been fortunate. The Cossacks, it was reported, had made a brilliant attack, and had captured three bodies of the Tatars; the infantry had laid in a store of firewood, and had suffered in all a loss of six men wounded. In the artillery, from the whole array only Velenchúk and two horses were put *hors du combat.* Moreover, they had cut the forest for three *versts*, and cleared a place, so that it was impossible to recognize it; now, instead of a seemingly impenetrable forest girdle, a great field was opened up, covered with heaps of smoking bonfires, and lines of infantry and cavalry on their way to camp. Notwithstanding the fact that the enemy incessantly harassed us with cannonade and musketry, and followed us down to the very river where the cemetery was, that we had crossed in the morning, the retreat was successfully managed.

I was already beginning to dream of the cabbage-soup and rib of mutton with *kasha* gruel that were awaiting me at the camp, when the word came, that the general had commanded a redoubt to be thrown up on the riverbank, and that the third battalion of regiment K, and a division of the fourth battery, should stay behind till the next day for that purpose. The wagons with the firewood and the wounded, the Cossacks, the artillery, the infantry with muskets and fagots on their shoulders—all with noise and songs passed by us. On the faces of all shone enthusiasm and content, caused by the return from peril, and hope of rest; only we and the men of the third battalion were obliged to postpone these joyful feelings till the morrow.

X

While we of the artillery were busy about the guns, disposing the limbers and caissons, and picketing the horses, the foot-soldiers had stacked their arms, piled up bonfires, made shelters of boughs and cornstalks, and were cooking their grits.

It began to grow dark. Across the sky swept bluish-white clouds. The mist, changing into fine drizzling fog, began to wet the ground and the soldiers' cloaks. The horizon became contracted, and all our surroundings took on gloomy shadows. The dampness which I felt through my boots and on my neck, the incessant motion and chatter in which I took no part, the sticky mud with which my legs were covered, and my empty stomach, all combined to arouse in me a most uncomfortable and disagreeable frame of mind after a day of physical and moral fatigue. Velenchúk did not go out of my mind. The whole simple story of his soldier's life kept repeating itself before my imagination.

His last moments were as unclouded and peaceful as all the rest of his life. He had lived too honestly and simply for his artless faith in the heavenly life to come, to be shaken at the decisive moment.

"Your Honour," said Nikoláief, coming to me. "The captain begs you to be so kind as to come and drink tea with him."

Somehow making my way between stacks of arms and the campfires, I followed Nikoláief to where Captain Bolkhof was, and felt a glow of satisfaction in dreaming about the glass of hot tea and the gay converse which should drive away my gloomy thoughts.

"Well, has he come?" said Bolkhof's voice from his cornstalk wigwam, in which the light was gleaming.

"He is here, your honour,"* replied Nikoláief in his deep bass.

In the hut, on a dry *burka*, or Cossack mantle, sat the captain in *negligée*, and without his cap. Near him the samovar was singing, and a drum was standing, loaded with lunch. A bayonet stuck into the ground held a candle.

"How is this?" he said with some pride, glancing around his comfortable habitation. In fact, it was so pleasant in his wigwam, that, while we were at tea I absolutely forgot about the dampness, the gloom, and Velenchúk's wound. We talked about Moscow and subjects that had no relation to the war or the Caucasus.

---

* *váshie blagoródié.*

After one of the moments of silence which sometimes interrupt the most lively conversations, Bolkhof looked at me with a smile.

"Well, I suppose our talk this morning must have seemed very strange to you?" said he.

"No. Why should it? It only seemed to me that you were very frank; but there are things which we all know, but which it is not necessary to speak about."

"Oh, you are mistaken! If there were only some possibility of exchanging this life for any sort of life, no matter how tame and mean, but free from danger and service, I would not hesitate a minute."

"Why, then, don't you go back to Russia?" I asked.

"Why?" he repeated. "Oh, I have been thinking about that for a long time. I can't return to Russia until I have won the Anna and Vladimir, wear the Anna ribbon around my neck, and am major, as I expected when I came here."

"Why not, pray, if you feel that you are so unfitted as you say for service here?"

"Simply because I feel still more unfitted to return to Russia the same as I came. That also is one of the traditions existing in Russia which were handed down by Passek, Sleptsof, and others—that you must go to the Caucasus, so as to come home loaded with rewards. And all of us are expecting and working for this; but I have been here two years, have taken part in two expeditions, and haven't won anything. But still, I have so much vanity that I shall not go away from here until I am major, and have the Vladimir and Anna around my neck. I am already accustomed to having everything avoid me, when even Gnilokishkin gets promoted, and I don't. And so how could I show myself in Russia before the eyes of my elder, the merchant Kotelnikof, to whom I sell wheat, or to my aunty in Moscow, and all those people, if I had served two years in the Caucasus without getting promoted? It is true that I don't wish to know these people, and, of course, they don't care very much about me; but a man is so constituted, that though I don't wish to know them, yet on account of them I am wasting my best years, and destroying all the happiness of my life, and all my future."

XI

At this moment the voice of the battalion commander was heard on the outside, saying, "Who is it with you, Nikoláï Feódorovitch?" Bolkhof mentioned my name, and in a moment three officers came into the wigwam—Major Kirsánof, the adjutant of his battalion, and Company Commander Trosenko.

Kirsánof was a short, thick-set fellow, with black moustaches, ruddy cheeks, and little oily eyes. His little eyes were the most noticeable features of his physiognomy. When he laughed, there remained of them only two moist little stars; and these little stars, together with his pursed-up lips and long neck, sometimes gave him a peculiar expression of insipidity. Kirsánof considered himself better than anyone else in the regiment. The under officers did not dispute this; and the chiefs esteemed him, although the general impression about him was that he was very dull-witted. He knew his duties, was accurate and zealous, kept a carriage and a cook, and, naturally enough, managed to pass himself off as arrogant.

"What are you gossiping about, captain?" he asked as he came in.

"Oh, about the delights of the service here."

But at this instant Kirsánof caught sight of me, a mere yunker; and in order to make me gather a high impression of his knowledge, as though he had not heard Bolkhof's answer, and glancing at the drum, he asked—

"What, were you tired, captain?"

"No. You see, we . . ." began Bolkhof.

But once more, and it must have been the battalion commander's dignity that caused him to interrupt the answer, he put a new question:—

"Well, we had a splendid action today, didn't we?"

The adjutant of the battalion was a young fellow who belonged to the fourteenth army-rank, and had only lately been promoted from the yunker service. He was a modest and gentle young fellow, with a sensitive and good-natured face. I had met him before at Bolkhof's. The young man would come to see him often, make him a bow, sit down in a corner, and for hours at a time say nothing, and only make cigarettes and smoke them; and then he would get up, make another bow, and go away. He was the type of the poor son of the Russian noble family, who has chosen the profession of arms as the only one open to him in his circumstances, and who values above everything else in the world his official calling—an ingenuous and lovable type, notwithstanding his absurd, indefeasible peculiarities: his tobacco-pouch, his dressing-gown, his guitar, and his moustache brush, with which we used to picture him to ourselves. In the regiment they used to say of him that he boasted of being just but stern with his servant, and quoted him as saying, "I rarely punish; but when I am driven to it, then let 'em beware:" and once, when his servant got drunk, and plundered him, and began to rail at his master, they say he took him to the guard-house, and commanded them to have everything ready for the chastisement; but when he saw the preparations, he was so confused, that he could only stammer a few meaningless words: "Well, now you see—I might . . ." and, thoroughly upset, he set off home, and from that time never dared to look into the eyes of his man. His comrades gave him no peace, but were always nagging him about this; and I often heard how the ingenuous lad tried to defend himself, and, blushing to the roots of his hair, avowed that it was not true, but absolutely false.

The third character, Captain Trosenko, was an old Caucasian* in the full acceptation of the word: that is, he was a man for whom the company under his command stood for his family; the fortress where the staff was, his home; and the song-singers his only pleasure in life—a man for whom everything that was not

* *Kavkázets*

41

Caucasus was worthy of scorn, yes, was almost unworthy of belief; everything that was Caucasus was divided into two halves, ours and not ours. He loved the first, the second he hated with all the strength of his soul. And, above all, he was a man of iron nerve, of serene bravery, of rare goodness and devotion to his comrades and subordinates, and of desperate frankness, and even insolence in his bearing, toward those who did not please him; that is, adjutants and *bon jourists*. As he came into the wigwam, he almost bumped his head on the roof, then suddenly sank down and sat on the ground.

"Well, how is it?"[*] said he; and suddenly becoming cognizant of my presence, and recognizing me, he got up, turning upon me a troubled, serious gaze.

"Well, why were you talking about that?" asked the major, taking out his watch and consulting it, though I verily believe there was not the slightest necessity of his doing so.

"Well,[†] he asked me why I served here."

"Of course, Nikoláï Feódorovitch wants to win distinction here, and then go home."

"Well, now, you tell us, Abram Ilyitch, why you serve in the Caucasus."

"I? Because, as you know, in the first place we are all in duty bound to serve. What?" he added, though no one spoke. "Yesterday evening I received a letter from Russia, Nikoláï Feódorovitch," he continued, eager to change the conversation. "They write me that . . . what strange questions are asked!"

"What sort of questions?" asked Bolkhof.

He blushed.

"Really, now, strange questions . . . they write me, asking, 'Can there be jealousy without love?' . . . What?" he asked, looking at us all.

"How so?" said Bolkhof, smiling.

"Well, you know, in Russia it's a good thing," he continued, as though his phrases followed each other in perfectly logical

* *nu chto?*
† *da voi*

sequence. "When I was at Tambof in '52 I was invited everywhere, as though I were on the emperor's suite. Would you believe me, at a ball at the governor's, when I got there . . . well, don't you know, I was received very cordially. The governor's wife[*] herself, you know, talked with me, and asked me about the Caucasus; and so did all the rest . . . why, I don't know . . . they looked at my gold cap as though it were some sort of curiosity, and they asked me how I had won it, and how about the Anna and the Vladimir; and I told them all about it . . . What? That's why the Caucasus is good, Nikoláï Feódorovitch," he continued, not waiting for a response. "There they look on us Caucasians very kindly. A young man, you know, a staff-officer with the Anna and Vladimir—that means a great deal in Russia. What?"

"You boasted a little, I imagine, Abram Ilyitch," said Bolkhof.

"He-he," came his silly little laugh in reply. "You know, you have to. Yes, and didn't I feed royally those two months!"

"So it is fine in Russia, is it?" asked Trosenko, asking about Russia as though it were China or Japan.

"Yes, indeed![†] We drank so much champagne there in those two months, that it was a terror!"

"The idea! you?[‡] You drank lemonade probably. I should have died to show them how the *Kavkázets* drinks. The glory has not been won for nothing. I would show them how we drink . . . Hey, Bolkhof?" he added.

"Yes, you see, you have been already ten years in the Caucasus, uncle," said Bolkhof, "and you remember what Yermolof said; but Abram Ilyitch has been here only six . . ."

"Ten years, indeed! Almost sixteen."

"Let us have some *salvia,* Bolkhof: it's raw, b-rr! What?" he added, smiling, "Shall we drink, major?"

But the major was out of sorts, on account of the old captain's behaviour to him at first; and now he evidently retired into himself,

---

[*] *gubernátorsha*

[†] *da s*

[‡] *da chto vui*

and took refuge in his own greatness. He began to hum some song, and again looked at his watch.

"Well, I shall never go there again," continued Trosenko, paying no heed to the peevish major. "I have got out of the habit of going about and speaking Russian. They'd ask, 'What is this wonderful creature?' and the answer'd be, 'Asia.' Isn't that so, Nikoláï Feódorovitch? And so what is there for me in Russia? It's all the same, you'll get shot here sooner or later. They ask, 'Where is Trosenko?' And down you go! What will you do then in the eighth company—heh?" he added, continuing to address the major.

"Send the officer of the day to the battalion," shouted Kirsánof, not answering the captain, though I was again compelled to believe that there was no necessity upon him of giving any orders.

"But, young man, I think that you are glad now that you are having double pay?" said the major after a few moments' silence, addressing the adjutant of the battalion.

"Why, yes, very."

"I think that our salary is now very large, Nikoláï Feódorovitch," he went on to say. "A young man can live very comfortably, and even allow himself some little luxury."

"No, truly, Abram Ilyitch," said the adjutant timidly: "even though we get double pay, it's only so much; and you see, one must keep a horse . . ."

"What is that you say, young man? I myself have been an ensign, and I know. Believe me, with care, one can live very well. But you must calculate," he added, tapping his left palm with his little finger.

"We pledge all our salary before it's due: this is the way you economize," said Trosenko, drinking down a glass of vodka.

"Well, now, you see that's the very thing . . . What?"

At this instant at the door of the wigwam appeared a white head with a flattened nose; and a sharp voice with a German accent said—

"You there, Abram Ilyitch? The officer of the day is hunting for you."

"Come in, Kraft," said Bolkhof.

A tall form in the coat of the general's staff entered the door, and with remarkable zeal endeavoured to shake hands with everyone.

"Ah, my dear captain, you here too?" said he, addressing Trosenko.

The new guest, notwithstanding the darkness, rushed up to the captain and kissed him on the lips, to his extreme astonishment, and displeasure as it seemed to me.

"This is a German who wishes to be a hail fellow well met," I said to myself.

XII

My presumption was immediately confirmed. Captain Kraft called for some vodka, which he called corn-brandy,* and threw back his head, and made a terrible noise like a duck, in draining the glass.

"Well, gentlemen, we rolled about well today on the plains of the Chechnya," he began; but, catching sight of the officer of the day, he immediately stopped, to allow the major to give his directions.

"Well, you have made the tour of the lines?"

"I have."

"Are the pickets posted?"

"They are."

"Then you may order the captain of the guard to be as alert as possible."

---

* *gorílka* in the Malo-Russian dialect.

"I will."

The major blinked his eyes, and went into a brown study.

"Well, tell the boys to get their supper."

"That's what they're doing now."

"Good! Then you may go. Well,"* continued the major with a conciliating smile, and taking up the thread of the conversation that we had dropped, "we were reckoning what an officer needed: let us finish the calculation."

"We need one uniform and trousers, don't we?"†

"Yes. That, let us suppose would amount to fifty roubles every two years; say, twenty-five roubles a year for dress. Then for eating we need every day at least forty kopeks, don't we?‡"

"Yes, certainly as much as that."

"Well, I'll call it so. Now, for a horse and saddle for remount, thirty roubles; that's all. Twenty-five and a hundred and twenty and thirty make a hundred and seventy-five roubles. All the rest stands for luxuries—for tea and for sugar and for tobacco—twenty roubles. Will you look it over? It's right, isn't it, Nikoláï Feódorovitch?"

"Not quite. Excuse me, Abram Ilyitch," said the adjutant timidly, "nothing is left for tea and sugar. You reckon one suit for every two years, but here in field-service you can't get along with one pair of pantaloons and boots. Why, I wear out a new pair almost every month. And then linen, shirts, handkerchiefs, and leg-wrappers: all that sort of thing one has to buy. And when you have accounted for it, there isn't anything left at all. That's true, by God!§ Abram Ilyitch."

"Yes, it's splendid to wear leg-wrappers," said Kraft suddenly, after a moment's silence, with a loving emphasis on the word "leg-wrappers;"¶ "you know it's simply Russian fashion."

---

* *nu-s*
† *tak-s*
‡ *tak-s*
§ *Yéï Bogu*
¶ *podviortki*

"I will tell you," remarked Trosenko, "it all amounts to this, that our brother imagines that we have nothing to eat; but the fact is, that we all live, and have tea to drink, and tobacco to smoke, and our vodka to drink. If *you* served with me," he added, turning to the ensign, "you would soon learn how to live. I suppose you gentlemen know how he treated his *denshchik*."*

And Trosenko, dying with laughter, told us the whole story of the ensign and his man, though we had all heard it a thousand times.

"What makes you look so rosy, brother?" he continued, pointing to the ensign, who turned red, broke into a perspiration, and smiled with such constraint that it was painful to look at him.

"It's all right, brother. I used to be just like you; but now, you see, I have become hardened. Just let any young fellow come here from Russia—we have seen 'em—and here they would get all sorts of rheumatism and spasms; but look at me sitting here: it's my home, and bed, and all. You see . . ." Here he drank still another glass of vodka. "Hah?" he continued, looking straight into Kraft's eyes.

"That's what I like in you. He's a genuine old *Kavkázets*. Give us your hand."

And Kraft pushed through our midst, rushed up to Trosenko, and, grasping his hand, shook it with remarkable feeling.

"Yes, we can say that we have had all sorts of experiences here," he continued. "In '45 you must have been there, captain? Do you remember the night of the 24th and 25th, when we camped in mud up to our knees, and the next day went against the intrenchments? I was then with the commander-in-chief, and in one day we captured fifteen intrenchments. Do you remember, captain?"

Trosenko nodded assent, and, pushing out his lower lip, closed his eyes.

"You ought to have seen," Kraft began with extraordinary animation, making awkward gestures with his arms, and addressing the major.

---

* batman

But the major, who must have more than once heard this tale, suddenly threw such an expression of muddy stupidity into his eyes, as he looked at his comrade, that Kraft turned from him, and addressed Bolkhof and me, alternately looking at each of us. But he did not once look at Trosenko, from one end of his story to the other.

"You ought to have seen how in the morning the commander-in-chief came to me, and says, 'Kraft, take those intrenchments.' You know our military duty—no arguing, hand to visor. 'It shall be done, your Excellency,'* and I started. As soon as we came to the first intrenchment, I turn round, and shout to the soldiers, 'Boys, show your mettle! Be on your guard. The one who stops I shall cut down with my own hand.' With Russian soldiers you know you have to be plain-spoken. Then suddenly comes a shell—I look—one soldier, two soldiers, three soldiers, then the bullets—vz-zhin! vz-zhin! vz-zhin! I shout, 'Forward, boys; follow me!' As soon as we reach it, you know, I look and see—how it—you know: what do you call it?" and the narrator waved his hands in his search for the word.

"Rampart," suggested Bolkhof.

"No . . . *Ach!* What is it? My God, now, what is it? Yes, rampart," said he quickly. "Then clubbing their guns . . . hurrah! ta-ra-ta-ta-ta! The enemy—not a soul was left. Do you know, they were amazed. All right. We rush on—the second intrenchment. This was quite a different affair. Our hearts boiled within us, you know. As soon as we got there, I look and I see the second intrenchment—impossible to mount it. There—what was it—what was it we just called it? *Ach*, what was it?"

"Rampart," again I suggested.

"Not at all," said he with some heat. "Not rampart. Ah, now, what is it called?" and he made a sort of despairing gesture with his hand. "*Ach*, my God! What is it?"

He was evidently so cut up, that one could not help offering suggestions.

"Moat, perhaps," said Bolkhof.

* *slushäïu, váshe Siyátelstvo.*

"No; simply rampart. As soon as we reached it, if you will believe me, there was a fire poured in upon us—it was hell."

At the crisis, someone behind the wigwam inquired for me. It was Maksímof. As there still remained thirteen of the intrenchments to be taken in the same monotonous detail, I was glad to have an excuse to go to my division. Trosenko went with me.

"It's all a pack of lies," he said to me when we had gone a few steps from the wigwam. "He wasn't at the intrenchments at all;" and Trosenko laughed so good-naturedly, that I could not help joining him.

XIII

It was already dark night, and the camp was lighted only by the flickering bonfires, when I rejoined my soldiers, after giving my orders. A great smouldering log was lying on the coals. Around it were sitting only three of the men—Antónof, who had set his kettle on the fire to boil his *ryábko*, or hard-tack and tallow; Zhdánof, thoughtfully poking the ashes with a stick; and Chikin, with his pipe, which was forever in his mouth. The rest had already turned in, some under gun carriages, others in the hay, some around the fires. By the faint light of the coals I recognized the backs, the legs, and the heads of those whom I knew. Among the latter was the recruit, who, curling up close to the fire, was already fast asleep. Antónof made room for me. I sat down by him, and began to smoke a cigarette. The odour of the mist and of the smoke from the wet branches spreading through the air made one's eyes smart, and the same penetrating drizzle fell from the gloomy sky.

Behind us could be heard regular snoring, the crackling of wood in the fire, muffled conversation, and occasionally the clank of muskets among the infantry. Everywhere about us the watch-fires were glowing, throwing their red reflections within narrow circles on the dark forms of the soldiers. Around the nearer fires I distinguished, in places where it was light, the figures of naked soldiers waving their shirts in the very flames. Many of the men had not yet gone to bed, but were wandering round, and talking over a space of fifteen square *sazhens;* but the thick, gloomy night imparted a peculiarly mysterious tone to all this movement, as though each felt this gloomy silence, and feared to disturb its peaceful harmony. When I spoke, it seemed to me that my voice sounded strange. On the faces of all the soldiers sitting by the fire I read the same mood. I thought, that, when I joined them, they were talking about their wounded comrade; but it was nothing of the sort. Chikin was telling about the condition of things at Tiflis, and about school-children there.

Always and everywhere, especially in the Caucasus, I have remarked in our soldiery at the time of danger peculiar tact in ignoring or avoiding those things that might have a depressing effect upon their comrades' spirits. The spirit of the Russian soldier is not constituted, like the courage of the Southern nations, for quickly kindled and quickly cooling enthusiasm; it is as hard to set him on fire as it is to cause him to lose courage. For him it is not necessary to have accessories, speeches, martial shouts, songs, and drums; on the contrary, he wants calmness, order, and avoidance of everything unnatural. In the Russian, the genuine Russian soldier, you never find braggadocio, bravado, or the tendency to get demoralized or excited in time of danger; on the contrary, discretion, simplicity, and the faculty of seeing in peril something quite distinct from the peril, constitute the chief traits of his character. I have seen a soldier wounded in the leg, at the first moment mourning only over the hole in his new jacket; a messenger thrown from his horse, which was killed under him, unbuckling the girth so as to save the saddle. Who does not recollect the incident at the siege of Gergebil when the fuse of a loaded bomb was on fire in the powder-room, and the artillerist ordered two soldiers to take the bomb and fling it over the wall, and how the soldiers did not take it to the most convenient place, which was near the colonel's tent on the rampart, but carried it farther, lest it should wake the gentlemen who were asleep in the tent, and both of them were blown to pieces?

I remember, that, during this same expedition of 1852, one of the young soldiers, during action, said to someone that it was not proper for the division to go into danger, and how the whole division in scorn went for him for saying such shameful words that they would not even repeat them. And here now the thought of Velenchúk must have been in the mind of each; and when any second might bring upon us the broadside of the stealthy Tatars, all were listening to Chikin's lively story, and no one mentioned the events of the day, nor the present danger, nor their wounded friend, as though it had happened God knows how long ago, or had never been at all. But still, it seemed to me that their faces were more serious than usual; they listened with too little attention to Chikin's tale, and even Chikin himself felt that they were not listening to him, but let him talk to himself.

Maksímof came to the bonfire, and sat down by me. Chikin made room for him, stopped talking, and again began to suck at his pipe.

"The infantry have sent to camp for some vodka," said Maksímof after a considerably long silence. "They'll be back with it very soon." He spat into the fire. "A subaltern was saying that he had seen our comrade."

"Was he still alive?" asked Antónof, turning his kettle round.

"No, he is dead."

The recruit suddenly raised above the fire his graceful head within his red cap, for an instant gazed intently at Maksímof and me, then quickly dropped it, and rolled himself up in his cloak.

"You see, it was death that was coming upon him this morning when I woke him in the gun-park," said Antónof.

"Nonsense!" said Zhdánof, turning over the smouldering log; and all were silent.

Amid the general silence a shot was heard behind us in the camp. Our drummers took it up immediately, and beat the tattoo. When the last roll had ceased, Zhdánof was already up, and the first to take off his cap. The rest of us followed his example.

Amid the deep silence of the night a choir of harmonious male voices resounded:—

"Our Father who art in heaven, hallowed be thy name. Thy kingdom come; thy will be done, as on earth, so in heaven. Give us this day our daily bread, and forgive us our debts as we forgive our debtors. And lead us not into temptation, but deliver us from the evil one."

"It was just so with us in '45: one man was contused in this place," said Antónof when we had put on our hats and were sitting around the fire, "and so we carried him two days on the gun. Do you remember Shevchenko, Zhdánof? We left him there under a tree."

At this time a foot-soldier with tremendous whiskers and moustaches, carrying a gun and a knapsack, came to our fire.

"Please give a fellow-countryman a coal for his pipe," said he.

"Of course,* smoke away; there is plenty of fire," remarked Chikin.

"You were talking about Dargi, weren't you, friend?" asked the soldier, addressing Antónof.

The soldier shook his head, frowned, and squatted down near us on his heels.

"There were all sorts of things there," he remarked.

"Why did you leave him?" I asked of Antónof.

"He had awful cramps in his belly. When we stood still, he did not feel it; but when we moved, he screeched and screeched. He besought us by all that was holy to leave him: it was pitiful. Well, and when *he* began to vex us solely, and had killed three of our men at the guns and one officer, then our batteries opened on him, and did some execution too. We weren't able to drag out the guns, there was such mud."

---

* *chïo-sh*

"It was muddier under the Indian mountains than anywhere else," remarked the strange soldier.

"Well, but indeed it kept growing worse and worse for him; and we decided, Anóshenka—he was an old artillerist—and the rest of us, that indeed there was no chance for him but to say a prayer, and so we left him there. And so we decided. A tree grew there, welcome enough. We left some hard-tack for him—Zhdánof had some—we put him against the tree, put a clean shirt on him, said goodbye to him, and so we left him."

"Was he a man of importance?"

"Not at all: he was a soldier," remarked Zhdánof.

"And what became of him, God knows," added Antónof. "Many of our brothers were left there."

"At Dargi?" asked the infantry man, standing up and picking up his pipe, and again frowning and shaking his head. "There were all sorts of things there."

And he left us.

"Say, are there many of the soldiers in our battery who were at Dargi?" I asked.

"Let us see;* here is Zhdánof, myself, Patsan—who is now on furlough—and some six men more. There wouldn't be any others."

"Why has our Patsan gone off on leave of absence?" asked Chikin, shaking out his legs, and laying his head on a log. "It's almost a year since he went."

"Well, are you going to take your furlough?" I asked of Zhdánof.

"No, I'm not," he replied reluctantly.

"I tell you it's a good thing to go," said Antónof, "when you come from a rich home, or when you are able to work; and it's rather flattering to go and have the folks glad to see you."

"But how about going when you have a brother," asked Zhdánof, "and would have to be supported by him? They have enough for themselves, but there's nothing for a brother who's a soldier. Poor kind of help after serving twenty-five years. Besides, whether they are alive or no, who knows?"

---

* *da chio*

"But why haven't you written?" I asked.

"Written? I did send two letters, but they don't reply. Either they are dead, or they don't reply because, of course, they are poor. It's so everywhere."

"Have you written lately?"

"When we left Dargi I wrote my last letter."

"You had better sing that song about the birch," said Zhdánof to Antónof, who at this moment was on his knees, and was purring some song.

Antónof sang his "Song of the White Birch."

"That's Uncle Zhdánof's very most favourite song," said Chikin to me in a whisper, as he helped me on with my cloak. "The other day, as Filipp Antónuitch was singing it, he actually cried."

Zhdánof at first sat absolutely motionless, with his eyes fastened on the smouldering embers, and his face, shining in the ruddy glow, seemed extraordinarily gloomy; then his cheek under his moustaches began to move quicker and quicker; and at last he got up, and, spreading out his cloak, he lay down in the shadow behind the fire. Either he tossed about and groaned as he got ready for bed, or the death of Velenchúk and this wretched weather had completely upset me; but it certainly seemed to me that he was weeping.

The bottom of the log which had been rolled on the fire, occasionally blazing up, threw its light on Antónof's form, with his grey moustache, his red face, and the ribbons on the cloak flung over his shoulders, and brought into relief the boots, heads, or backs of other sleeping soldiers.

From above the same wretched drizzle was falling; in the atmosphere was the same odour of dampness and smoke; around us could be seen the same bright dots of the dying fires, and amid the general silence the melancholy notes of Antónof's song rang out. And when this ceased for a moment, the faint nocturnal sounds of the camp, the snoring, the clank of a sentinel's musket, and quiet conversation, chimed in with it.

"Second watch! Makatiuk and Zhdánof," shouted Maksímof.

Antónof ceased to sing; Zhdánof arose, drew a deep sigh, stepped across the log, and went off quietly to the guns.

The Snowstorm

[Written in 1856, two years after Tolstoy was lost in a snowstorm. First published in *Sovremennik*, a Russian literary, social, and political magazine, in 1856. This version is taken from *More Tales From Tolstoi*, a collection translated by R. Nesbit Bain and published by Brentano's, New York, in 1903.]

I

At seven o'clock in the evening, after drinking tea I departed from a post-station, the name of which I don't remember, but I recollect it was somewhere in the military district of the Don, near Novochirkask. It was already dark when, wrapped up in my furs, I sat down with Alec in the sledge. In the shelter of the post-station it seemed warm and still. Although there was no snow above us, not a single tiny star was visible above our heads, and the sky appeared to be extraordinarily low and black in comparison with the pure snowy plain stretching out before us.

We had scarce passed the dark figures of the mills—one of which was clumsily waving one of its huge wings—and got clear of the station when I observed that the road was heavier and more obstructed, and the wind began to blow upon my left side more violently and beat upon the flank, tail, and mane of the horse and regularly raise and carry away the snow torn up by the curved shafts of the sledge and the hoofs of the horses. The little sledge-bell began to be silent, a current of cold air began to flow from some opening into my sleeve and down my back, and the advice of the inspector not to go at all, lest I should wander about the whole night and be frozen to death on the road, at once occurred to me.

"Haven't we lost our way?" I said to the driver; and receiving no answer, I repeated the question in a still plainer form: "Do you think we shall reach the post-station, driver, or shall we lose our way?"

"God knows!" he replied, without turning his head, "It's only human to go astray, and the road is nowhere visible, my little master!"

"Will you tell me whether you think we shall get to the post-station or not?" I continued to ask. "Shall we get there, I say?"

"We ought to get there," said the driver, and he murmured something else which I could not quite catch because of the wind.

I didn't want to turn back, but to wander about all night in the frost and snow in the absolutely barren steppe as this part of the military district of the Don really is, was also not a very pleasant prospect to contemplate. Moreover, although I was unable to examine him very well in the darkness, my driver, somehow or other, did not please me, nor did he inspire me with confidence. He sat squarely instead of sideways; his body was too big; his voice had too much of a drawl; his hat, somehow or other, was not a driver's hat—it was too big and bulgy; he did not urge on the horses as he should have done; he held the reins in both hands as a lacquey does who sits on the box behind the coachman and, above all, I did not believe in him because his ears were tied round with a cloth. In a word, I did not like the look of him, and that serious hunched back of his bobbing up and down before me boded no good.

"In my opinion it would be better to turn back," said Alec; "it is no joke to get lost."

"My little master, you see what sort of driving it is: no road to be seen, and your eyes all bunged up!" growled the driver.

We hadn't gone a quarter of an hour when the driver stopped the horses, gave the reins to Alec, clumsily disengaged his legs from their sitting position and, trampling over the snow in his big boots, went to try and find the road.

"I say, where are you?" I cried, "Have we gone astray, or what?"

But the driver did not answer, me and turning his face in the opposite direction to that in which the wind was blowing—it had cut him in the very eyes—went away from the sledge.

"Well, what is it?" I asked when he had turned back again.

"Nothing at all," said he with sudden impatience and anger, as if it was my fault that he had lost the road, and slowly thrusting his big boots into the front part of the sledge again, he slowly grasped the reins together with his frozen mittens.

"What shall we do?" I asked when we had again moved forward.

"Do? Why, go whither God allows us!" And on we went at the

same jig-trot, obviously across country, sometimes over snow piled up bushels high, sometimes over brittle, naked ice.

Notwithstanding the cold, the snow on our collars thawed very quickly; the snow drift below increased continually, and fine dry flakes began to fall from above.

It was plain we were going God only knew whither, for after going along for another quarter of an hour we did not see a single verst post.[*]

"What do you think, eh?" I said again to the driver; "Do you think we shall get to the station?"

"To which station? We may get back, if the horses take it into their heads to try, they'll take us right enough, but as to reaching the other station, scarcely, we might perish, that's all."

"Then turn back by all means," said I, "at any rate . . ."

"Turn the horses round, do you mean?"

"Yes, turn 'em round!"

The driver let go the reins. The horses began to run more quickly, and although I observed that we had turned round, yet the wind had changed too, and soon, through the snow the windmills were visible. The driver took heart again and began to be loquacious.

"The Anudiuses got into the drifts and turned back just in the same way when they came from this station," said he, "and passed the night by the haystacks; they only got in by morning. They were only too thankful for the shelter of the haystacks; they might have easily frozen to death. It was cold, and one of them did have his legs frostbitten, so that he died of it three weeks later."

"But now you see it is not so cold, and it has grown quieter; might not we drive on now, eh?"

"It's fairly warm, warm, oh yes! and the snow's coming down. Now we'll turn back, as it seems easier going and the snow comes down thicker. You might drive if you had a courier, but you'll do it at your own risk. Are you joking? Why, you'd be frozen! And what should I say who am responsible for your honour?"

---

[*] Corresponding to our milestone

II

Just then there was a sound of little bells behind us, the bells of some *troika,* a three-horse sledge, which was rapidly overtaking us.

"That is a courier's bell," said my driver; "there's one such courier at every post-station."

And, indeed, the little bell of the front *troika*, the sound of which was now plainly borne to us by the wind, was an extraordinarily welcome sound to hear: a pure, musical, sonorous, and slightly droning sound. As I afterwards ascertained, it was a hunter's arrangement of three little bells—one big one in the centre and two little ones adjusted to tierce. The sound of this tierce and the droning quinte, resounding through the air, was extraordinarily penetrating and strangely pleasant in that vast and voiceless steppe.

"The post is in haste," said my driver when the foremost of the three horses was level with us.

"What sort of a road, eh? Can one get through?" cried he to the hindmost driver; but the fellow only shouted to his horses and didn't answer him.

The sound of the little bells quickly died away on the wind as soon as the post-car had passed us.

My driver must now have felt a bit ashamed, I fancy.

"We'll go on, sir," said he; "these people have gone on before us and have left a fresh track, which we can now follow."

I agreed, and again we turned towards the wind and crawled along a bit through the deep snow. I kept a sidelong glance upon the road so as to see that we did not wander away from the track made by the sledge. For two versts the track was plainly visible, after that the only thing observable was a very slight unevenness under the curved sides of the sledge, and I began to look straight in front of me.

The third verst pole we could still make out, but the fourth we could not find at all. As before, we were driving both against and with the wind, both left and right, and at last it got to such a pass that the driver said we had deviated to the right. I said we had gone to the left, while Alec proved that we were absolutely going back again. Once more we stopped for a while, the driver extricated his big feet and crawled out to find the road; but it was all in vain. I also made up my mind to get out for once and see for myself whether that was not the road which I saw glimmering indistinctly; but scarcely had I taken six steps forward, with the utmost difficulty, against the wind and persuaded myself that everywhere were the self-same uniform white layers of snow and that the road existed only in my imagination—than I no longer saw the sledge.

"Driver! Alec!" I cried, but my voice!—well I felt that the wind snatched it right out of my mouth and carried it in the twinkling of an eye away from me. I have a very distinct recollection of the loud, penetrating, and even desperate voice with which I once more yelled: "Driver!" when he was only two good paces distant from me. His black figure, whip in hand, and with his large hat perched on one side, suddenly grew up in front of me. He led me to the sledge.

"Still warm, thank goodness!" said he, "but it's bad if the frost does catch you, my little master!" said he.

"Let the horses go; we must go back," said I, taking, my seat on the sledge. "I suppose you can guide them, driver?"

"I must guide them."

He threw aside the reins, struck the saddle of the thill horse thrice with his whip and again we went on some whither for a bit. We went along for about half an hour. Suddenly we again heard in front of us the, to me, familiar little hunting-bell and two more besides; but this time they were coming towards us. It was the same three *troikas* returning to the post-station after delivering the mails, with the fresh horses fastened on behind. The courier's *troika,* with its three powerful horses with the hunting bells came rapidly forward. A single driver sat on the box, shouting lustily. Behind, in the middle of the empty sledge, sat a couple of drivers.

I could hear their loud and merry discourse. One of them was smoking a pipe, and the sparks, kindled by the wind, lit up part of his face.

As I looked at them I began to be ashamed that I had been afraid to go on, and my driver must have experienced much the same sensation, for we said with one voice: "Let us go after them."

III

The hindmost *troikas* had not yet passed when my driver turned clumsily and struck the attached horses with the sledge shafts. One of the *troika* team thereupon fell heavily, tearing away the traces and plunging to one side.

"You cock-eyed devil, don't you see where you're going, driving over people like that? Devil take you!" began one of the drivers in a hoarse, quavering voice.

He was smallish and an old fellow, as far as I could judge from his voice and his position. He had been sitting in the hinder *troika,* but now leaped quickly out of the sledge and ran to the horses, never ceasing the whole time to curse my driver in the most coarse and cruel manner.

But the horses would not be pacified. The driver ran after them, and in a minute both horses and driver had vanished in the white mist of the snowstorm.

"Vas-il-y! bring the chestnut hither, we shall never get them else," his voice still resounded.

One of the drivers, a very tall man, got out of the sledge, silently detached his three horses," saddled and bridled one of them, and, crunching the snow beneath him, disappeared in the direction of his comrade. We, with the two other horses, went after the courier's *troika*, which, ringing its bell, set off in front at full gallop; we just let ourselves go without troubling any more about the road.

"A pretty way of catching them!" said my driver, alluding to the other driver, who had gone off after the horses; "he'll never catch 'em, and he's leading the spare horse to a place he'll never get him out of again."

Ever since my driver had begun to go back, he had become in better spirits and more inclined to be talkative, which I, of course, did not fail to take advantage of as, so far, I had no desire to sleep. I began to ask him all about himself and whence he came, and soon found out that he was a fellow countryman, hailing from Tula country, being a small proprietor in the village of Kirpechny; that their land was of very little good to them and had quite ceased to produce grain since the cholera visitation; that there were two brothers at home, while a third had enlisted as a soldier; that the supply of bread would not hold out till Christmas, and they had to hire themselves out to make more money; that the younger brother was master in the house because he was married, while my friend was a widower; that an *artel*, or society of drivers, went forth from their village every year; that though he was not a coachman by profession he served at the post-station in order to be of some help to his brother; that he lived here, thank God, on 120 paper roubles a year, of which he sent a hundred home to his family, and that he had a pretty good time of it, but that couriers were veritable beasts, and that the people he had to do with here were always cursing him.

"That driver, for instance, why should he curse me? my little master! Did I overturn his horses on purpose? Why, I wouldn't do any harm to anyone! And why should he go scurrying after them? They would be sure to come back of their own accord. And now, he'll only make the horses starve to death besides coming to grief himself," repeated the God-fearing little muzhik.

"But what is that black thing yonder?" said I, observing some black objects just in front of us.

"A train of wagons!—a nice way of going along, I must say," continued he when we had come abreast with the huge wagons covered with mats, going one after another on wheels. "Look! not a soul to be seen; they are all asleep. The horse is the wisest of them all. He knows very well what he is about. Nothing in the world will make him miss the road. We too will go alongside of them and then we shall be all right," added he, "and know where we are going."

It really was a curious sight. There were those huge wagons covered with snow from the matting atop to the wheels below, moving along absolutely alone. Only in the front corner the snow-covered mat was raised a couple of inches for a moment as our little bells resounded close to the wagons and a hat popped up. The big piebald horse, with outstretched neck and straining back, deliberately proceeded along the absolutely hidden road, monotonously shaking his shaggy head beneath the whitening shaft and pricking up one snow-covered ear as we came abreast of him.

After we had gone on for another half-hour the driver again turned to me.

"What do you think, sir; we are going nicely along now, eh?"

"I don't know," I replied.

"Before, the wind was anyhow, but now we are going right in the midst of the storm. No, we shall not get there; we too have lost our way," he concluded with the utmost calmness.

Evidently, although a great coward, and afraid of his own shadow, he had become quite tranquil as soon as there were a good many of us together and he was not obliged to be our guide and responsible for us. With the utmost *sangfroid* he criticised the mistakes of the driver in front of us as if it had anything whatever to do with him. I observed indeed that now and then the *troika* in front was sometimes in profile, from my point of view, to the left and sometimes to the right, and it also seemed to me as if we were encircling a very limited space. However, it might have been an optical delusion, as also the circumstance that, occasionally, it seemed to me as if the *troika* in front was climbing up a mountain, or going along a declivity, or under the brow of a hill, whereas the steppe was everywhere uniformly level.

After we had proceeded for some time longer I observed, or so it seemed to me, far away, on the very horizon, a long, black, moving strip of something; but in a moment it became quite plain to me that this was the very same train of wagons which we had overtaken and outstripped. Just the same creaking wheels, some of them no longer turning, enveloped in snow; just the same people asleep beneath their mats, and just the same leading piebald horse, with steaming, distended nostrils, smelling out the road and pricking up his ears.

"Look, we have gone round and round and are coming out by this train of wagons again!" said my driver in a sulky tone. "The courier's horses are good ones, though he drives them villainously, but ours are so-so and always stopping, just as if we had been driving all night long."

He coughed a bit.

"Shall we turn off somewhere, sir, for our sins?"

"Why? We are bound to arrive somewhere as it is."

"Arrive somewhere! We shall have to make a night of it in the steppe: that's what we shall do. How it is snowing, my little master!"

Although it did seem strange to me that the driver in front of us, who had obviously lost his road and had no idea of the direction in which he was going, took no trouble to find it again, but continued to drive at full tilt, cheerily shouting to his horses, I did not want to separate from him all the same.

"Follow after them!" I said.

The driver went on, but he drove along even more unwillingly than before and no longer conversed with me.

V

The snowstorm was growing more and more violent. The flakes descended fine and dry, apparently it was freezing hard. My nose and cheeks grew numb with cold, currents of cold air penetrated my furs more and more frequently and it was necessary to huddle up in them more closely. Occasionally the sledge bumped up against a bare, ice-clad hummock, from which it scattered the snow in every direction.

As I had travelled some score or so of versts without a night's rest, notwithstanding the fact that I was very much interested in the issue of our wanderings, I involuntarily shut my eyes and dozed off. All at once, when I opened my eyes again, I was struck by what seemed to me in the first moment a bright light illuminating the white plain; the horizon had considerably widened, the low, black sky had suddenly disappeared; in every direction were visible white oblique lines of falling snow; the figures of the *troika* people in front appeared more plainly, and when I looked upwards it seemed to me for the first moment as if the clouds had parted and that only the falling snow covered the sky. Whilst I had been slumbering the moon had arisen and threw her cold and clear light through the scattered clouds and falling snow. The one thing I saw clearly was my sledge, the horses, the driver, and the three *troikas* going on in front: the first *troika*, the courier's, on the box of which one of the drivers was still sitting urging his horses on at a good round pace; the second, in which sat the two other drivers, who had thrown the reins aside and made themselves a shelter against the wind out of their *armyaks** never ceasing to smoke their pipes the whole time, as was clear from the sparks proceeding from that quarter, and the

---

* A peasant's cloak of rough camel-hair

third *troika,* in which nobody was visible—presumably the driver was sleeping in the middle of it. Before I went to sleep, however, the leading driver had at rare intervals stopped his horses and tried to find the way. Then, every time we stopped, the howling of the wind became more audible and the enormous quantity of snow suspended in the air more strikingly visible. I now saw by the light of the moon, half obscured by the snowstorm, the small, squat figure of the driver, with the big whip in his hand, with which he flicked at the snow in front of him, moving backwards and forwards in the bright mist and coming back again to the sledge, leaping sideways on to the box seat, and amidst the monotonous whistling of the wind the alert, sonorous ringing and clanging of the little bells was audible once more. Every time the driver in front leaped out to look for the road or the verst posts one could hear the brisk, self-confident voice of one of the drivers shouting to the driver in front:

"Do you hear, Ignashka! take the road to the left! You'll find more shelter to the right!" Or, "Why are you going round and round like a fool? Go by the snow; take the lee of it, and you'll come out all right!" Or, "A little more to the right, a little more to the right, my brother! Don't you see there's something black yonder—some sign-post or other?" Or, "Where are you going? Where are you going? Loose the piebald nag and go on in front and he'll guide you to the road straight away. It'll be much better if you do that!"

This self-same person, who was so fond of giving advice, not only did not lose the side-horse and go over the snow to look for the road, but did not even so much as thrust his nose from out of his *arrnyak*, and when Ignashka, the driver in front, in reply to one of his counsels, shouted to him to go in front himself if he knew where to go so well, the counsellor replied that if he had been travelling with courier's horses he *would* have gone on and led them to the right road straight away, "but *our* horses cannot go on in front in snow-drifts, not such nags as these, anyway."

"Then you can hold your jaw!" replied Ignashka, cheerily whistling to his horses.

The other driver, sitting in the same sledge with the counsellor, said not a word to Ignashka, and in fact did not interfere at all, although he was not asleep either, at least I assumed as much from the fact that his pipe continued unextinguished, and also from the circumstance that whenever we stopped I heard his measured, uninterrupted narration. He was telling some tale or other. Only when Ignashka suddenly halted for the sixth or seventh time, this other driver plainly became very angry at being interrupted by such leisurely procedure, and he shouted at him:

"What! stopping again! You want to find the road, eh? It's a snowstorm we're in, and there's an end of it! Why, even a land-surveyor wouldn't be able to find the road now. Go on as long as the horses can drag us! Never fear; we shan't freeze to death! Go on, I say!"

"Never fear, indeed! Last year a postilion *was* frozen to death!" observed my driver.

The driver of the third *troika* did not wake the whole time, only once, during a stoppage, the counsellor shouted:

"Philip! I say, Philip!" and receiving no answer observed: "I wonder if he's frozen? You might go and see, Ignashka!"

Ignashka, who hastened to do everyone's bidding, went to the sledge and began to shake the sleeper.

"Why, he's drunk as drunk—like a log!" said he, "I say! you! are you frozen?" he said, shaking him violently.

The sleeper babbled something or the other and cursed him.

"He's alive, all right, my brother!" said Ignashka; and again he ran forward and again we went on, and so quickly indeed, this time, that the little brown side horse attached to my *troika*, constantly lashed up from behind, more than once broke into a clumsy gallop.

V

I think it must have been almost midnight when we were joined by the little old man and Vas-il-y, who had been in pursuit of the stampeded horses. They had found the horses and pursued and overtaken us; but how they had done so in the dark, blinding snowstorm, in the midst of the barren steppe, has always remained unintelligible to me. The little old man, moving his elbows and legs, rode up at a gallop on the brown horse. The two other horses were attached to the collar: in the snowstorm it was impossible to leave the horses to themselves. On coming up to his, the old fellow began attacking my driver again.

"Look here, you cock-eyed devil, really if . . ."

"Hie, Uncle Matvich!" shouted the tale-teller from the second sledge, "Alive, eh? Crawl in here!" But the old man did not answer him, but went on with his cursing. When it appeared to him that he had cursed enough, he did go to the second sledge.

"Caught 'em all?" they said to him from that quarter.

"Of course! Why not?"

And his diminutive figure, on the trot, with the upper part of his body bobbing up and down on the back of the horse, after leaping out on to the snow, ran forward without stopping behind the sledge, and scrambled in to where they were, with his legs sticking up in the air as he forced his way through the orifice. Tall Vas-il-y, as before, took his seat in silence on the box seat in the foremost sledge alongside Ignashka, whom he helped to look for the road.

"You see what a curser he is, my little master!" murmured my driver.

We went along for some time after this, without stopping, over the white wilderness, in the cold, transparent, and quivering light of the snowstorm. Every time I opened my eyes, there in front of me was the self-same clumsy hat and back, covered with snow; there, too, was the self-same low shaft-bow, beneath which, between the tightly drawn leather reins, and always the same distance off, the head of the brown horse with the black mane deliberately bending in the direction of the wind, moved slowly up and down. Behind its back one could also see, to the right, the bay side-horse, with its tail tied up into a bunch, occasionally bumping against the front board of the sledge. Look down—and there was the self-same snow thumping against the sides of the sledge, which the wind stubbornly lifted and carried off in one direction. In front, always at the same distance, the leading *troika* ran steadily along; on the right and on the left everything was white and twinkling. In vain the eye sought for some new object: not a post, not a rick, not a fence—nothing at all was visible. Everywhere everything was white, white and mobile; sometimes the horizon seemed incomprehensibly far off, sometimes compressed within two paces distance in every direction. Sometimes a high white wall would grow up suddenly on the right and run alongside the sledge, then it would as suddenly disappear and grow up in front only to run further and further off and again disappear. If you looked up it would appear quite light the first instant, and you would seem to see little stars through the mist; but the little stars vanished from your view ever higher and higher, and all you saw was the snow, which fell past your eyes on to your face and into the collar of your furs; the sky was identically bright everywhere, identically white, colourless, uniform, and constantly mobile. The wind seemed to be perpetually shifting. Now it blew right against you and blinded your eyes, now it blew teasingly sideways and flung the collar of your fur coat over your head and mockingly flapped it in your face, now it would howl from behind through some unprotected crevice. Audible throughout was the faint, miserable crunching of hoofs and sledge-boards over the snow and the expiring tinkle of the little bells when we passed over deep snow. Only very rarely, when we drove against the wind, and over naked, frozen, stony ground, did the energetic whistling of Ignaty and the thrilling sound of the little bell with the resonant, droning quinte come flying, plainly audible, towards us, and then these sounds would immediately and pleasantly disturb the melancholy character of the wilderness, subsequently falling into a monotonous melody persisting with intolerable fidelity always on one and the same motif, which I involuntarily imagined to myself as I listened to them. One of my feet presently began to grow numb, and when I turned about a bit in order the better to shelter it, the snow which had accumulated on my collar and hat plunged down my neck and made me shiver; but, on the whole, I was still warm enough in my well-warmed furs, and a feeling of drowsiness came over me.

VI

Recollections and ideas alternated with the most strenuous rapidity in my imagination.

The counsellor also kept on bawling out of the second sledge—I wondered what sort of a yokel he might be. No doubt a rufus, well set up, with short legs, I thought to myself, something in the style of Theodor Filipovich, our old waiter. And then I saw before me the staircase of our big house, and four of the men-servants in linen suits, walking heavily and dragging the pianoforte out of one of the wings. Theodor Filipovich, with the sleeves of his nankeen surtout turned up, and carrying a pedal, was running on in front, unloosening the bars and bolts, and there he stood, tugging away at a napkin, bustling about, insinuating himself between their legs and making a mess of everything, never ceasing all the time to screech with a funny voice:

"This way, this way, you fellows in front! Like this, tail up, up, up, up, I say, carry it through the door! Like this!"

"We can manage it; leave us alone, Theodor Filipovich!" timidly observed the gardener, clinging to the balustrade, all red with the exertion and supporting one corner of the grand piano with all his remaining strength.

But Theodor Filipovich would not be quiet.

"What an idea?" I thought as I deliberated about it. "Does he fancy he is useful, indispensable, or is he simply glad because God has given him the self-confident, convincing eloquence which he dispenses with such sweet satisfaction? It must be so." And then I saw somewhere or other a pond, a lot of tired men-servants up to their knees in water dragging a fishing-net, and there again was Theodor Filipovich with a watering-can, running along the bank and shouting at them, but only very rarely approaching the water's edge in order to touch with his hands some golden carp and pour away the dirty water and fill his can with fresh. And then it was midday in the month of July. I was walking along somewhere, over some quite newly mown garden grass, beneath the burning, perpendicular rays of the sun; I was still very young; there was something I lacked, something I very much wanted. I was going to a pond, to my favourite spot, between beds of wild eglantine and an avenue of birch trees, and I lay down to sleep. I remember the feeling with which I lay down: I looked through the pretty, prickly branches of the eglantine at the black, dry hummocks of earth and at the translucent, bright-blue mirror of the pond. It was a sort of feeling of naïve self-satisfaction and melancholy. Everything around me was so exceedingly beautiful, and this beauty had such a strong effect upon me that it seemed to me as if I also were good; and the only vexatious thing was that nobody admired me. It was hot; I tried to sleep in order to get some rest, but the flies, the intolerable flies, gave me no respite even here, and they began to collect around me, and doggedly, thickly, like so many little pebbles, they darted about from my temples to my arms. The bees were humming not far from me, in the sun-burnt patches of the grass, and yellow-winged butterflies, as if wearied by the sultriness, were flitting from blade to blade of grass. I looked up: it pained my eyes—the sun shone too strongly through the bright leaves of the thick-foliaged birch tree loftily, but very gently, rocking its branches above my head, and it seemed hotter than ever. I covered my face with a pocket handkerchief. I felt oppressed, and the flies regularly stuck to my arms, on which a light sweat burst forth. The sparrows were busy in the dog-rose hedges. One of them hopped along the ground a few yards from me, pretended once or twice to be pecking the ground energetically, and making the tiny twigs crackle beneath his feet and chirping merrily, flew out of the bosque; another sparrow also perched upon the ground, trimmed his tail, glanced around him, and then, like a dart, flew chirping after the first sparrow. The blows of the mangling stick on the wet linen were audible from the pond, and the sound of these blows was borne downwards and carried along the surface of the pond. Audible also were the laughter, talking, and splashing of the bathers. The breeze shook noisily the summits of those birches that were further from me; nearer at hand I heard it begin to flutter the grass, and now the leaves of the dog-rose bosque fell a-quivering and rustled upon their branches, and now, raising the corner of the handkerchief and tickling my perspiring face, the fresh current of air careered right up to me. Through the opening made by the lifted 'kerchief flew a fly and buzzed terror-stricken round my moist mouth. An odd piece of dried twig insinuated itself under my back. No, lying down was impossible. Suppose I went and had a refreshing bath. But at that very moment I hear quite close to the bosque hastening footsteps and a terrified female voice saying:

"Alas Batyushka! What is to be done? There's not a man in sight!"

"What is it? What is it?" I ask, running out into the sun to the maid-servant who ran past me crying and wailing. She only looked round at me, waved her hands and ran on further. And now there appears old Martha, who is seventy years of age, holding a handkerchief in her hand which she had torn from her head, bounding along and dragging one leg after her in a woollen stocking and hastening to the pond. Two little girls were also running, holding each other by the hand, and a boy of ten, in his father's surtout, holding on to the skirt of one of them, hastened on behind.

"What's the matter?" I asked them.

"A muzhik has been drowned."

"Where?"

"In the pond."

"One of our people, eh?"

"No, a vagabond."

Ivan, the coachman, shuffling with his big slippers over the mown grass, and the fat messenger Yakov, breathing with difficulty, were also running to the pool, and I ran after them.

I remember the feeling within me, which said to me: "Go ahead! throw yourself into the pond and drag out the muzhik; save him and they'll all admire you so," which was what I desired above all.

"Where is he? Where is he?" I inquired of the crowd of house-servants collected round the shores of the pond.

"There he is, right at the bottom, over yonder, near to the bathing-place," said a washerwoman, placing her wet linen on a drying pole. "I saw him go under, and then he appeared somewhere else, and then he disappeared, and then he came up again once more; and how he shrieked, 'I'm sinking, Batyushka!' and down below he went again, and only bubbles came up after him; and as soon as I saw that a muzhik was drowning I cried out, 'Batyushka, there's a muzhik drowning!'"

And the washerwoman, throwing the yoke-beam over her shoulder, waddled along the narrow path away from the pond.

"It is a sin and a shame!" said Yakov Ivanov, the steward, with a despairing voice; "what a to-do the County Court will make about it! There will be no end to it!"

At last a muzhik, with a scythe in his hand, forced his way through the crowd of women, children and old men, elbowing each other on the shore, and hanging his scythe on the branch of a cytisus, very deliberately began to pull off his boots.

"Where was it? Where was he drowned?" I kept on asking,

wishing to pitch myself in there and do something or other out of the way.

But they only pointed out to me the smooth surface of the pond, which was rarely ruffled by a passing breeze. It was incomprehensible to me how he could have got drowned; the water, as smooth, beautiful, and indifferent as ever, stood above him, glistening like gold in the midday sun, and it seemed to me as if I could do nothing and astonish nobody, especially as I swam but awkwardly; but the muzhik had already drawn his shirt over his head and flung himself into the water straight away. They all kept looking at him with confidence and intense expectation; but when he had got up to his shoulders in the water the muzhik deliberately turned back again and put on his shirt: he did not know how to swim.

People came running together; the crowd grew denser and denser; the old women held on to each other, but none rendered the slightest assistance. Those who had only just arrived at once began to give advice, made a fuss, and their faces wore an expression of fear and despair; of those who had been there sometime already, some becoming tired of standing, sat down on the grass, and others turned back and went away. Old Matrena inquired of her daughter whether she had closed the door of the stove; the little boy in his father's surtout violently flung stones into the water.

But now, barking loudly and looking back doubtfully, Trezerka, the dog of Theodor Filipovich, came running down the hill, and presently the form of Theodor himself, also running down the hill and bawling something or the other, emerged from behind the dog-rose hedge.

"What's up?" he cried, taking off his surtout as he came along, "A man drowned and all of you stand gaping here! Give me a rope!"

They all gazed upon Theodor Filipovich with hope and terror, while he, resting one hand on the shoulder of one of the house-servants, worked off the boot on his right leg with the toe of his left foot.

"Over yonder, where the crowd is, on the right side of the willow, that's the spot, Theodor Filipovich, just there," someone said to him.

"I know," he answered, and frowning, no doubt in response to the indications of shamefacedness visible in the mob of women, he took off his shirt and little cross, which later he gave to the gardener's little boy, who stood before him in a cringing attitude, and energetically strutting over the mown grass, drew near to the pond.

Trezerka, who, in doubt as to the meaning of the rapid movements of his master, had stopped close to the crowd and, sitting down on the bank, snapped off several blades of grass, now looked inquiringly at him, and suddenly, with a joyful yelp, plunged into the water with his master. During the first moment nothing was visible except foam and water drops, which flew right over to where we stood; but presently Theodor Filipovich, gracefully waving his arms and rhythmically raising and lowering his back, was seen swimming briskly towards the shore. Trezerka too, snorting and choking, was also coming rapidly back, shaking himself in the midst of the crowd and rolling on his back on the shore to dry himself. At the self-same moment when Theodor Filipovich swam up to the shore, two coachmen came running up to the willow with a net wound round a pole. Theodor Filipovich, for some reason or other, lifted up his hands, sneezed once, twice, thrice, each time spurting a jet of water out of his mouth, shaking his hair neatly and making no answer to the questions which showered down upon him from all sides. At last he emerged on to the bank and, as far as I could make out, he was occupying himself solely with the proper adjustment of the net. They drew out the net, but at the bottom of it there was nothing but mud and a few little carp swimming about in it. Just as the net was being dragged in a second time I arrived on that side of the pond.

The only sounds audible were the voice of Theodor Filipovich distributing commands, the splashing in the water of the net-rope, and groans of horror.

"Now, then, put some heart into it and pull all together!" cried the voice of Theodor Filipovich.

"There's something this time! It drags heavily, my brethren!" cried a voice.

But now the net, in which two or three carp were floundering, all wet, and crushing the grass beneath it, was dragged ashore. And then dimly seen through the thin agitated layer of turbid water, something white was apparent in the extended net. A groan of horror, not loud but penetratingly audible in the death-like silence, ran through the crowd.

"Put a little more heart into it; drag it on to the dry ground!" sounded the authoritative voice of Theodor Filipovich; and the doomed man was dragged by main force over the cropped stalks of the burdocks and thistles right up to the willow tree.

And now I see before me my dear old aunt in her white dress; I see her fringed lilac sunshade so utterly out of place in this picture of death so horrible from its very simplicity, and I see her face ready at that very instant to burst into tears. I remember the expression of disenchantment in her face at the idea that these drag-nets were altogether useless, and I remember the sick, sorrowing feeling I experienced when she said to me with the naïve egoism of love: "Let us go, my friend! Ah! how horrible it is! And you to go and bathe and swim all alone as you do, too!"

I remember how bright and sultry the sun was; how it burnt up the dry, crumbling earth beneath our feet; how it played on the surface of the pond; how gigantic carp were hurrying and scurrying near the banks; how the smoothness of the centre of the pond was disturbed by shoals of fishes; how high in the sky a vulture was wheeling right above some ducks, who, quacking and splashing, were making for the middle of the pond through the reeds; how threatening, white, curly clouds were collecting on the horizon; how the mud, dragged ashore by the net, was gradually being trampled into the ground; and how, walking along the dyke, I again heard the stroke of a paddle resounding over the pond.

But this paddle was now ringing just as if the sound of the paddles was blending together into a tierce; and this sound tormented and wearied me all the more because I knew that this paddle was a bell and Theodor Filipovich could not make it keep quiet. And this paddle, like an instrument of torture, was pressing my leg, which was freezing, and I awoke.

It seemed to me as if I had been awakened by a sudden jolt and by two voices speaking close beside me.

"Hillo! Ignat! Ignat, I say!" cried the voice of my driver, "take a passenger! It's all one to you, and it's no use my trying to keep up. Take one, I say!"

The voice of Ignat answered close beside me:

"Why should I be responsible for a passenger? You've got half a stoop yet, haven't you?"

"Half a stoop, indeed! There's a quarter of a stoop, already!"

"A quarter of a stoop! What an idea!" screeched the other voice. "Fancy plaguing a horse for the sake of a quarter of a stoop!"

I opened my eyes. Always the same unendurable, quivering snow blizzard in one's eyes, and the self-same drivers and horses, but close beside me I saw a sledge. My driver had caught up Ignat, and we had been going on side by side for some time. Notwithstanding that the voice from the other sledges had advised my driver not to take in less weight than a half stoop, Ignat had suddenly stopped the *troika*.

"Let us change about then! A good job for you! Put in a quarter stoop, as we shall arrive tomorrow. How much do you make it, eh?"

My driver, with unusual vivacity, leaped out into the snow, bowed down before me, and begged me to transfer myself to Ignat. I was quite willing to do so, but it was clear that the God-fearing little muzhik was so satisfied with the new arrangement that he must needs pour forth his joy and gratitude on someone or other; he bowed down before me and thanked me and Alec and Ignashka.

"Well, there you are now, thank God. And I tell you what it is, my little master, we have been wandering about half the night, without knowing whither. That chap there will bring us in all right, my little master, and my horses are done up already."

And he transferred my things with energetic officiousness.

While they were transferring the things I, following the direction of the wind, which carried me along, as it were, went to the second sledge. The sledge, especially on that side on which the *armyak* was hung up over the heads of the two drivers, was a quarter covered with snow, but behind the *armyak* it was quiet and comfortable. The little old man was lying there with his legs stretched wide apart, and the tale-teller was going on with his tale: "At the very time when the general, in the King's name, you know, came, you know, to Mary in the dungeon, at that very time Mary said to him: General, I have no need of you and I cannot love you and, you know, you cannot be my lover, but my lover is the Prince himself.

"At that very time," he was going on, but perceiving me, he was silent for a moment and began to puff away at his pipe.

"What, sir, come to listen to the tale too?" said the other, whom I have called the Counsellor.

"You are having a rare fine time of it," said I. "It passes the time anyhow and prevents one from brooding."

"But tell me, do you know where we are now?"

This question did not appear to please the drivers.

"Where? Who can make that out? We may be going right away to the Calmucks," answered the Counsellor.

"But what shall we do then?"

"Do? We must go on, and perhaps we shall get through," said he surlily.

"And what if we don't get through, and the horses stop in the snow? What then?"

"What then? Why, nothing."

"We might be frozen."

"It's possible, certainly, for we cannot see any ricks, which means that we're going right into the Calmuck country. The first thing to do is to look at the snow."

"And aren't you at all afraid of being frozen?" asked the old man, with a tremulous voice.

Notwithstanding that he was making merry with me, it was plain that he was all of a tremble to the very last bone.

"Well, it's pretty cold," I said.

"Alas, for you, sir! If you were only like me; no, no, run along, that will make you warm."

"First of all, we ought to show him how to run after the sledge," said the Counsellor.

VII

"Ready if you please," bawled Alec to me from the sledge in front.

The snowstorm was so violent that only with the utmost exertion, bending right forward and grasping with both hands the folds of my mantle, was I able to traverse the few yards which separated me from the sledge, through the shifting snow, which the wind carried away from under my very feet. My former driver was already on his knees in the midst of the empty sledge, but seeing me, he took off his large hat, whereupon the wind furiously lifted his long locks on high, and he began asking me for vodka. He evidently didn't expect to get it, for he was not a bit offended at my refusal. He even thanked me, put on his hat, and said to me: "Well, God be with you, sir, and seizing the reins and smacking his lips, he departed from us immediately afterwards, Ignashka meanwhile waving his arms with all his might and shouting at his horses. Again the crunching of hoofs and the jangling of the little sledge bells superseded the whining of the wind, which was particularly audible whenever we stopped short.

For a quarter of an hour after the transfer I did not sleep, and amused myself by studying the figures of the new driver and the horses. Ignashka had all the ways of a young man; he was perpetually springing up, waving his arms, with his whip dangling over the horses, shouting at them, shifting from one foot to the other, bending forward from time to time, and readjusting the reins of the thill horse, which had a tendency perpetually to shift to the right. He was not big, but well put together apparently. Above his short pelisse he wore an ungirded *artnyak*, the collar of which was almost entirely thrown back, leaving the neck quite bare; his boots were not of felt but of leather, and his hat, which he was incessantly doffing and setting right, was a smallish one.

In all his movements was observable not merely energy, but, as it seemed to me, the longing to stimulate this energy. But the further we went and the more frequently he pulled himself together, and bounded on to the box-seat and fidgeted about with his feet and conversed with me and Alec, the more it seemed to me that at the bottom of his soul he was sore afraid. And the reason was this: his horses were good, but at every step the road became more and more difficult, and it was obvious that the horses were running unwillingly; already it was necessary to whip them up a bit, and the thill horse, a good, big, shaggy beast, had stumbled once or twice, although, immediately afterwards, terror-stricken, it tore on ahead again, bowing its shaggy head almost lower than the very sledge bell. The right-hand-side horse, which I watched involuntarily, together with the long leather cluster of the reins, jolting and plunging on the field-side, was visibly breaking away from the traces and required a touch of the whip, but, as is the way with good horses, even when excited, as if sorry for his weakness, he angrily lowered and raised his head, again readjusting the bridle. It was really terrible to see how the snowstorm and the cold were increasing; how the horses were getting weaker. The road was become worse and worse, and we absolutely did not know where we were or whither we were going. We were no longer sure of reaching, I will not say a posting station, but even a place of refuge—and it was ridiculous and terrible to hear how the sledge-bell kept on tinkling so unconcernedly and merrily, and how Ignashka boisterously and bravely shouted at the horses as if we were rolling away to church on a hard-frozen, sunny, rustic road at midday on the "Feast of the Epiphany," and especially terrible it was to think that we were driving continually and driving rapidly nobody knew whither, right away from the place where we were. Ignashka began to sing some song or other, in a villainous falsetto indeed, but so sonorously and with such long pauses, during which he fell a-whistling, that it was strange to feel timid while you listened to him.

"Hie, hie! What a throat you've got, Ignat!" sounded the voice of the Counsellor; "do stop for a bit."

"What?"

"Sto-o-o-op!"

Ignat stopped. Again all was silent, and the wind howled and whined, and the whirling snow began to fall more thickly into the sledge. The Counsellor came to us.

"Well, what is it?"

"What, indeed! Whither are we going?"

"Who knows!"

"Our feet are frozen, eh! Why are you clapping your hands?"

"We are quite benumbed."

"And as for you," this to Ignat, "just turn out and stir your stumps and see if there isn't a Calmuck encampment about here: it will warm up your feet a bit!"

"All right! hold the horses. Now for it."

And Ignat ran off in the direction indicated.

"One always ought to look out and pick one's way, you'll find it's all right; and, besides, there's such a thing as foolish driving," said the Counsellor to me. "Just see how the horses are steaming."

All this time Ignat was gone, and this lasted so long that I was beginning to be afraid that he would lose himself altogether. The Counsellor, in the calmest, most self-confident tone of voice, explained to me how people ought to act in a snowstorm; he said that the best thing of all was to outspan the horse and let her go right on, God only knows where, or sometimes it was possible to see and go by the stars, and he added that if he had gone on before as a pioneer, we should long ago have reached the station.

"Well, how is it?" he asked Ignat, who could now be seen returning, walking with the utmost difficulty, being up to his knees in snow.

"Yes, it's there right enough. I can make out a Calmuck encampment," answered Ignat, puffing and blowing, "but which it is I don't know. We ought, my brother, to be going straight towards the Prolgovsky Manor House. We ought to go more to the left"

"But why this delay? It must be those encampments of ours which are behind the post-station!" exclaimed the Counsellor. "But I say it is not!"

"What I've seen I know: it'll be what I say and not the Tomushenko lot. We must keep going more to the right all along. We shall be out on the great bridge presently; it is only eight versts off."

"But I say it is not I tell you I've just seen it," answered Ignat angrily.

"Ah, my brother, and you a driver too!"

"Driver be hanged! Go yourself!"

"Why should I go when I know already?"

It was plain that Ignat was very angry. Without answering, he leaped upon the box-seat and drove on further.

"You see how your feet grow numb if you don't warm them a bit," he said to Alec, continuing to hug his arms more and more frequently and wipe and shake off the snow which kept pouring into the leg of his boot.

I had a frightful desire to go to sleep.

VIII

"Can it be possible that I am already freezing to death?" I thought in the midst of my slumbers. Freezing to death always begins during slumber, they say. Why, it would be better to be drowned than to freeze and let myself be drawn out in a net, yet 'tis all one whether I drown or freeze if only this stick—it seems to be a stick—were not beating against my back and I could lose consciousness.

And for a second or so I did lose consciousness.

"Yet, how will all this end?" I suddenly said within my mind, opening my eyes for a moment and glancing at the white expanse;

"how will all this end if we do not find the ricks and the horses stop, which will happen pretty soon? We shall all be frozen." I confess that although a little afraid, the wish that something extraordinary, something tragical, might happen to us was stronger within me than my tiny bit of fear. It seemed to me that it would not be half bad if, by the morning, the horses were to drag us into some distant, unknown village half frozen; or, better still, some of us perhaps might be frozen to death outright. And in this mood a vision presented itself before me, with extraordinary rapidity and vividness. The horses stopped; the snow heaps grew bigger, and bigger, and now only the shaft-bow and the ears of the horses were visible; but suddenly Ignashka appeared on the surface with his *troika* and drove past us. We implored him with shrieks and yells to take us, but our cries were carried away by the wind, and there were no voices at all. Ignashka smoked slightly; shouted at his horses; whistled a bit, and vanished from our eyes into some deep abyss of drifted snow. Then the little old man leaped to the surface and began waving his arms, and wanted to spring off, but could not move from the spot; my old driver, with the large hat, flung himself upon him, dragged him to the ground, and trampled him in the snow. "You old sorcerer," he shrieked, "you curser; we'll sink or swim together." But the little old man burrowed in the snow drift with his head; he was not so much a little old man as a hare, and he slipped away from us. All the dogs came leaping after him. The counsellor, who was Theodor Filipovich, said that we should all sit round in a circle, and that it didn't matter a bit if the snow covered us, it would make us warm. And, indeed, we were very warm and comfortable, only we wanted something to drink. I got a case bottle, served out rum and sugar to them all, and drank myself with great satisfaction. The tale-teller was telling some tale about the rainbow—and above us, indeed, was a ceiling of snow and rainbow. "And now let each of us take his apartment in the snow and go to sleep," said I. The snow was warm and soft like fur. I made a room for myself, and was about to go into it, but Theodor Filipovich, who saw some money in my case bottle, said: "Stop, give me the money; it's all one if we die!" and caught me by the leg. I gave him the money, merely asking them to let me out; but they would not believe it was all the money I had, and wanted to kill me. I caught the arm of the old man and, with unspeakable delight, began to kiss it. The arm of the little old man was fresh and smooth. At first he tore it away from me, but afterwards he let me have it, and even began caressing me with the other arm. But Theodor Filipovich drew near and threatened me. I ran into my room, but it was not a room, but a long white corridor, and something held me by the leg. I tore myself away, but in the hands of him who held me remained my clothing and part of my skin; but I only felt cold and bashful, and all the more bashful because my aunt, with her sunshade, and with her homoeopathic pharmacopoeia under her arm, was coming towards me with the drowned man. They were laughing, and did not understand the signs I was making to them. I threw myself into the sledge, and my feet were dragging along the snow; but the little old man pursued me, waving his arms. The little old man was already close to me when I heard two little bells, and knew that I was safe if I could get to them. The little bells sounded more and more violently, but the little old man caught me up, and fell like a beast on my face, so that the bells were scarce audible. I again seized his arm and began to kiss it, but the little old man was not the little, old man, but the man who had been drowned, and he cried out: "Stop, Ignashka, these are the Akhmetkin ricks, I think; go and see!"

This was too terrible; far better to wake up! I opened my eyes. The wind had flapped my face with the corner of Alec's mantle; my knee was uncovered; we were going over a bare, frozen crest of snow, and the *tierce* of the little bells was very faintly audible in the air, along with the jangling quinte.

I looked to see where the rick was, but instead of the ricks, I saw with my wide-open eyes a house with a balcony and the crenelated wall of a fortress. It interested me very little to look at this house and fortress; my chief desire was to see again the white corridor along which I had run to hear the sound of the church bell, and to kiss the hand of the old man. I again closed my eyes and went to sleep.

IX

I slept deeply; but the *tierce* of the bell was audible the whole time, and there appeared to me in my dreams, sometimes in the shape of a dog, which barked and fell upon me; and sometimes as an organ, in which I was one of the pipes; sometimes the shape of French verses which I was composing. Sometimes it seemed to me as if this *tierce* was some instrument of torture continually squeezing my right heel. This was so violent that I woke, and opened my eyes, rubbing my foot. It was beginning to be frost-bitten. The night was just the same as before—bright. The self-same sort of movement was jolting me and the sledge; the self-same Ignashka was sitting on the box-seat and shuffling about with his feet; the self-same side horse, distending its neck and scarce lifting its feet, was trotting along over the deep snow; the little tassel of the harness was jumping up and down, and lashing the belly of the horse. The head of the thill horse, with dishevelled mane, the distended and loosening harness attached to the shaft-bow, was gently rocking up and down. But all this, far more than before, was covered, was loaded with snow. The snow came whirling down from in front, and sideways, was beginning to cover up the sledge-boards; the legs of the horses were up to their knees in snow, and the snow was pouring down from above upon our collars and hats. The wind was now from the right, and now from the left, and played with our collars, with the flap of Ignashka's *armyak*, and with the mane of the thill horse, and howled above the shaft-bow and in the shafts.

It had become frightfully cold; and scarcely had I wriggled myself free of my collar, than the frozen, dry snow, whirling along, fell full upon my eyelashes, nose, mouth, and flopped down my neck. All round about everything was white, bright, and snowy; there was nothing to be seen anywhere but turbid light and snow. I became seriously alarmed. Aleshka was asleep at my feet in the very bottom of the sledge, the whole of his back was covered by a thick layer of snow. Ignashka I did not see; he was tugging at the reins, shouting to the horses, and shuffling with his feet perpetually. The little bell sounded as strangely as ever. The horses kept snorting, yet on they ran, stumbling more and more frequently, and somewhat more softly. Ignashka again leaped up, waved his sleeves, and began singing his song in a thin, tense voice. Without finishing it he stopped the *troika*, threw the reins on to the upper part of the sledge, and dismounted. The wind was howling furiously, the snow, pouring down as if from a sieve, covered the skirt of his pelisse. I looked around, the third *troika* was no longer behind us, it had stopped somewhere. Round the second *troika*, which was visible through a snowy mist, I could see how the little old man was hopping about from foot to foot. Ignashka took three steps away from the sledge, sat down in the snow, ungirded himself, and set about taking off his shoes.

"What are you doing?" I asked.

"I must change my boots, my feet are quite frozen," he answered, continuing what he was doing.

It had made me cold merely to wriggle my neck free of my collar. I could not bear to look on and see him do this. I sat stiff and upright, looking at the side horse which, drawing back its feet, began wearily, like a sick thing, twitching its tucked-up tail all covered with snow. The jolt which Ignat had given to the sledge, when he leaped upon the sledge-ledge, had awakened me.

"I say, where are we now?" I asked; "shall we ever get anywhere?"

"Be easy, we shall manage it," he answered; "the great thing is to keep the feet warm. That's why I've changed my boots."

And off he started. The little bell sounded, the sledge again began to swing along, and the wind whistled beneath the curved sides of the sledge. And once more we set off swimming in a limitless sea of snow.

X

I slept soundly. When Alec, knocking me with his foot, awoke me, and I opened my eyes, it was already morning. It appeared to me to be colder than in the night. No snow was coming down from above; but a strong, dry wind continued to carry the snow-dust across the plain and especially beneath the hoofs of the horses and the sledge-curves. The sky, to the right, in the east, was heavy and of a dark bluish colour; but bright, orange-red, strips were becoming more and more plainly distinguishable in it. Above our heads, from behind the fugitive, white, faintly tinted clouds, a pale blue was revealing itself; to the left, the masses of cloud were bright, light, and mobile. All around, as far as the eye could reach, lay white, deep snow, distributed in heaps and layers. In one direction could be seen a greyish heap, over which a fine, dry, snowy dust was doggedly flying. Not a single trace of a sledge, or a human being, or an animal was anywhere visible. The outlines and colours of the back of the driver and the horses showed out clearly, and even sharply, against the white background. The rim of Ignashka's dark blue hat, his collar, his hair, and even his boots were white. The sledges were completely covered. The whole right part of the head of the dark grey thill horse and his forelock were covered with snow; my side horse was enwrapped in it up to the knees, and his sweating body was all plastered with snowy festoons on the right side. The tassel was still bobbing up and down as before, beating time to some unimaginable motifs and the side horse was running along just as before, only she had sunk lower in the snow, from which she raised and disengaged her body from time to time. It was plain from her dejected ears what she must be suffering. Only a single new object riveted our attention, and this was a verst post, from which the snow was being strewn on the ground, around which the wind had piled a whole hillock of snow to the right, and was still tearing up and casting the scattering snow from one side to the other. I was amazed that we had been driving along the whole night with single horses for twenty hours, not knowing whither, and without stopping, and yet had managed somehow to arrive. Our little bell was sounding more merrily than ever. Ignat wrapped himself up tighter, and kept shouting at the horses; behind us neighed the horses and jingled the bells of the *troika* of the little old man and the counsellor; but the sleeper must have parted from us in the steppe. After going along for another half verst we came upon the recent track of a sledge and *troika*, lightly powdered with snow, and, at rare intervals, pink patches of the blood of a horse which, as we could see, had been cruelly whipped.

"That is Philip. It is plain that he has got in before us!" said Ignashka.

But there stood a little house with a signboard alone on the road, in the midst of the snow, which reached almost up to the roof and windows. Near the inn stood a *troika* of three grey horses, crisp with sweat, with disengaged feet and dejected heads. Around the door the snow had been cleared away, and there stood a shovel, but from the roof the howling wind was still sweeping and whirling the snow.

From out of the door, at the sound of our bells, emerged a big, good-looking, rod-faced driver with a glass of wine in his hand, shouting something. Ignashka turned to me and asked permission to stop. Then for the first time I saw his face.

XI

His face was not darkish, dry, and straight-nosed, as I had expected, judging from his hair and physique. It was a round, merry, absolutely sun-burnt face, with a large mouth and brightly shining, round blue eyes. His cheeks and neck were as red as rubbed rags; his eyebrows, long eyelashes, and the hair symmetrically covering the lower part of his face, were clotted with snow and quite white. It was only half a verst to the station, and we stopped.

"Only be as quick as you can," I said.

"In one moment," answered Ignashka, and leaping from the box-seat, he ran to Philip.

"Give it here, my brother," taking off his glove and pitching it in the snow along with his whip, and, throwing back his head, he swallowed the proffered dram of vodka at a single gulp.

The innkeeper, most probably a discharged Cossack, came out of the door with a demi-stoop in his hand.

"Who's to have it?" said he.

Tall Vas-il-y, a leanish, red-bearded muzhik, with a goatee beard, and the counsellor, a stout, white eyebrowed fellow, with a thick white beard framing his red face, both came up and had a glass or two. The little old man would also have liked to have joined the group of drinkers, but he was not invited to have a dram, and he went to his horses, which were tied up behind the *troika*, and began to stroke them on the back and buttocks. The little old man was just as I had imagined him, a thin, little fellow with a wrinkled, bluish face, a sparse beard, a sharp nose, and stumpy yellow teeth. He wore a driver's hat, which was quite new, but his meagre litttle demi-pelisse, threadbare, stained with tar and torn at the shoulder and sides, did not cover his knees, and his hempen lower garment was stuffed into his huge felt boots. He was all bent and wrinkled, and his face and knees were quivering; he was busying himself about the sledge, with the obvious endeavour of getting warm.

"Hillo, Matvich! Why don't you have a half pint? Fine thing for making you warm!" said the counsellor.

Matvich persisted in what he was doing. He put the harness of his horses to rights, put the low shaft right also and came to me.

"Look here, sir!" said he, taking his hat from off his grey hair and bowing low, "all night long we've been wandering about with you, seeking the road; if only now you would stand a half pint. Yes, indeed, little father, your excellency! And there's nothing like that for warming one," he added with an obsequious smile.

I gave him a quarter-rouble. The innkeeper brought out a half-pint and handed it to the little old man. He drew off the whip-glove and extended a small, dark, crooked and slightly bluish hand towards the glass; but his thumb, which looked like someone else's, refused to obey him; he could not hold the glass, and, spilling the vodka, cast it upon the snow.

All the drivers began to laugh.

"Just look, Matvich is so frost-bitten that he cannot hold his wine."

But Matvich was very angry that the wine was spilled. However, they filled him another glass and poured it into his mouth. Immediately he became very lively and merry, ran into the inn, lighted his pipe, began to simper, and show his worn, yellow teeth, and uttered an oath at every word. After drinking a final dram, the drivers dispersed to their various *troikas* and we proceeded. The snow was just as white and glaring as ever, so that it stung the eye that gazed at it. The orange and reddish strips of cloud, mounting higher and higher, and growing ever brighter and brighter, spread over the sky; even the red sphere of the sun appeared on the horizon in the midst of dove-coloured clouds, the azure of the sky grew ever more dazzling and deeper. On the road, near the posting station, the track was clear, precise, and yellowish; here and there were holes; in the frozen, compressed air there was a sensation of pleasant lightness and freshness. My *troika* ran very swiftly. The head of the thill horse and her neck, with the mane spread widely over the shaft-bow, bobbed rapidly up and down, almost in one place; beneath sounded the pleasant bells whose tongues no longer beat, but rubbed against their sides. The good side horses, tugging together at the congealed and crooked reins, energetically bounded forward; the tassels kept bumping away beneath their very bellies and hindmost harness. Occasionally the side horse would stumble into one of the holes in the dilapidated road, and, with its eyes full of snow-dust, would struggle briskly out of it again. Ignashka now shouted to his horses in a merry tenor; the dry frost crackled beneath the sides of the sledges; from behind us came the solemnly sonorous sounds of two sledge-bells and the drunken shouting of the drivers. I glanced back, the grey, shaggy side horses, extending their necks, and breathing methodically, with curving bits, were bounding over the snow. Philip shaking his whip, was adjusting his hat; the little old man, with drawn up legs, was lying at full length, just as before, in the middle sledge.

In two minutes the sledge began to grate upon the well-swept boards of the approach to the posting-station, and Ignashka turned towards me his snow-covered, merry, weather-beaten face.

"We've arrived, you see, sir!" said he.

Three Deaths

[Written in 1858. First published in 1859. This version is a translation by Nathan Haskell Dole published in 1887.]

I

It was autumn.

Along the highway came two equipages at a brisk pace. In the first carriage sat two women. One was a lady, thin and pale; the other, her maid, with a brilliant red complexion, and plump. Her short, dry locks escaped from under a faded cap; her red hand, in a torn glove, put them back with a jerk. Her full bosom, incased in a tapestry shawl, breathed of health; her keen black eyes now gazed through the window at the fields hurrying by them, now rested on her mistress, now peered solicitously into the corners of the coach. Before the maid's face swung the lady's bonnet on the rack; on her knees lay a puppy; her feet were raised by packages lying on the floor, and could almost be heard drumming upon them above the noise of the creaking of the springs and the rattling of the windows.

The lady, with her hands resting in her lap and her eyes shut, feebly swayed on the cushions which supported her back, and, slightly frowning, tried to suppress her cough. She wore a white nightcap, and a blue neckerchief twisted around her delicate pale neck. A straight line, disappearing under the cap, parted her perfectly smooth blond hair, which was pomaded; and there was a dry deathly appearance about the whiteness of the skin, in this wide parting. The withered and rather sallow skin was loosely drawn over her delicate and pretty features, and there was a hectic flush on the cheeks and cheekbones. Her lips were dry and restless, her thin eyelashes had lost their curve, and a cloth travelling capote made straight folds over her sunken chest. Although her eyes were closed, her face gave the impression of weariness, irascibility, and habitual suffering.

The lackey, leaning back, was napping on the coachbox. The

yamshchik, or hired driver, shouting in a clear voice, urged on his four powerful and sweaty horses, occasionally looking back at the other driver, who was shouting just behind them in an open barouche. The tires of the wheels, in their even and rapid course, left wide parallel tracks on the limy mud of the highway. The sky was grey and cold, a moist mist was falling over the fields and the road. It was suffocating in the carriage, and smelt of eau de cologne and dust. The invalid leaned back her head, and slowly opened her eyes. Her great eyes were brilliant, and of a beautiful dark colour.

"Again!" said she, nervously, pushing away with her beautiful attenuated hand the end of her maid's cloak, which occasionally hit against her leg. Her mouth contracted painfully. Matriosha raised her cloak in both hands, lifting herself up on her strong legs, and then sat down again, farther away. Her fresh face was suffused with a brilliant scarlet. The invalid's beautiful dark eyes eagerly followed the maid's motions; and then with both hands she took hold of the seat, and did her best to raise herself a little higher, but her strength was not sufficient. Again her mouth became contracted, and her whole face took on an expression of unavailing, angry irony. "If you would only help me . . . ah! It's not necessary. I can do it myself. Only have the goodness not to put those pillows behind me . . . On the whole, you had better not touch them, if you don't understand!" The lady closed her eyes, and then again, quickly raising the lids, gazed at her maid. Matriosha looked at her, and gnawed her red lower lip. A heavy sigh escaped from the sick woman's breast; but the sigh was not ended, but was merged in a fit of coughing. She scowled, and turned her face away, clutching her chest with both hands. When the coughing fit was over, she once more shut her eyes, and continued to sit motionless. The coach and the barouche rolled into a village. Matriosha drew her fat hand from under her shawl, and made the sign of the cross.

"What is this?" demanded the lady.

"A post station, madam."

"Why did you cross yourself, I should like to know?"

"The church, madam."

The invalid lady looked out of the window, and began slowly to cross herself, gazing with all her eyes at the great village church, in front of which her carriage was now passing. The two vehicles came to a stop together at the post-house. The sick woman's husband and the doctor dismounted from the barouche, and came to the coach.

"How are you feeling?" asked the doctor, taking her pulse.

"Well, my dear, aren't you fatigued?" asked the husband in French. "Wouldn't you like to get out?"

Matriosha, gathering up the bundles, squeezed herself into the corner, so as not to interfere with the conversation.

"No matter, it's all the same thing," replied the invalid. "I will not get out."

The husband, after standing there a little, went into the post-house.

Matriosha, jumping from the coach, tiptoed across the muddy road into the enclosure.

"If I am miserable, there is no reason why the rest of you should not have breakfast," said the sick woman, smiling faintly to the doctor, who was standing by her window.

"It makes no difference to them how I am," she remarked to herself as the doctor, turning from her with slow step, started to run up the steps of the station house. "They are well, and it's all the same to them. O my God!"

"How now, Edward Ivanovitch?" said the husband, as he met the doctor, and rubbing his hands with a gay smile. "I have ordered my travelling-case brought; what do you say to that?"

"That's worthwhile," replied the doctor.

"Well, now, how about her?" asked the husband, with a sigh, lowering his voice and raising his brows.

"I have told you that she cannot reach Moscow, much less Italy, especially in such weather."

"What is to be done, then? Oh! My God! My God!" The husband covered his eyes with his hand. "Give it here," he added, addressing his man, who came bringing the travelling-case.

"You'll have to stop somewhere on the route," replied the doctor, shrugging his shoulders.

"But tell me, what can I do?" rejoined the husband. "I have employed every argument to keep her from going; I have spoken to her of our means, and of our children whom we should have to leave behind, and of my business. She would not hear a word. She has made her plans for living abroad, as if she were well. But if I should tell her what her real condition is, it would kill her."

"Well, she is a dead woman now; you may as well know it, Vasili Dmitrievitch. A person cannot live without lungs, and there is no way of making lungs grow again. It is melancholy, it is hard, but what is to be done about it? It is my business and yours to make her last days as easy as possible. The confessor is the person needed here."

"Oh, my God! Now just perceive how I am situated, in speaking to her of her last will. Let come whatever may, yet I cannot speak of that. And yet you know how good she is."

"Try at least to persuade her to wait until the roads are frozen," said the doctor, shaking his head significantly; "something might happen during the journey . . ."

"Aksiusha, oh, Aksiusha!" cried the superintendent's daughter, throwing a cloak over her head, and tiptoeing down the muddy back steps. "Come along. Let us have a look at the Shirkinskaya lady; the say she's got lung trouble, and they're taking her abroad. I never saw how any one looked in consumption."

Aksiusha jumped down from the door-sill; and the two girls, hand in hand, hurried out of the gates. Shortening their steps, they walked by the coach, and stared in at the lowered window. The invalid bent her head toward them; but, when she saw their inquisitiveness, she frowned and turned away. "Oh, de-e-ar!" said the superintendent's daughter, vigorously shaking her head. "How wonderfully pretty she used to be, and how she has changed! It is terrible! Did you see? Did you see, Aksiusha?"

"Yes, and how thin she is!" assented Aksiusha. "Let us go by and look again; we'll make believe we are going to the well. Did you see, she turned away from us; still I got a good view of her. Isn't it too bad, Masha?"

"Yes, but what terrible mud!" replied Masha, and both of them started to run back within the gates.

"It's evident that I have become a fright," thought the sick woman. "But we must hurry, hurry, and get abroad, and there shall soon get well."

"Well, and how are you, my dear?" inquired the husband coming to the coach with still a morsel of something in his mouth

"Always one and the same question," thought the sick woman, "and he's even eating!"

"It's no consequence," she murmured, between her teeth.

"Do you know, my dear, I am afraid that this journey in such weather will only make you worse. Edward Ivanovitch says the same thing. Hadn't we better turn back?"

She maintained an angry silence.

"Maybe the weather will improve, the roads will become good, and that would be better for you; then at least we could start all together."

"Pardon me. If I had not listened to you so long, I should at this moment be at Berlin and have entirely recovered."

"What's to be done, my angel? It was impossible, as you know. But now if you would wait a month, you would be ever so much better; I could finish up my business, and we could take the children with us . . ."

"The children are well, and I am not."

"But just see here, my love, if in this weather you should grow worse on the road . . . At least we should be at home."

"What is the use of being at home? . . . Die at home?" replied the invalid, peevishly. But the word die evidently startled her and she turned on her husband a supplicating and inquiring look. He dropped his eyes, and said nothing. The sick woman's mouth suddenly contracted in a childish fashion, and the tears sprang to her eyes. Her husband covered his face with his handkerchief, and silently turned from the coach.

"No, I will go," cried the invalid; and, lifting her eyes to the sky, she clasped her hands, and began to whisper incoherent words. "My God! Why must it be?" she said, and the tears flowed more violently. She prayed long and fervently, but still there was just the same sense of constriction and pain in her chest, just the me grey melancholy in the sky and the fields and the road; just the same autumnal mist, neither thicker nor more tenuous, but ver the same it in its monotony, falling on the muddy highway, n the roofs, on the carriage, and on the sheepskin coats of the rivers, who were talking in strong, gay voices, as they were oiling nd adjusting the carriage.

II

he coach was ready, but the driver loitered. He had gone into ne drivers' room*. In the *izba* it was warm, close, dark, and uffocating, smelling of human occupation, of cooking bread, of abbage, and of sheepskin garments. Several drivers were in the oom; the cook was engaged near the oven, on top of which lay a ck man wrapped up in his sheepskins.

"Uncle Khveódor! Hey, Uncle Khveódor," called a young nan, the driver, in a tulup, and with his knout in his belt, coming nto the room, and addressing the sick man.

"What do you want, rattlepate? What are you calling to Fyédka or?" asked one of the drivers. "There's your carriage waiting or you."

"I want to borrow his boots. Mine are worn out," replied the oung fellow, tossing back his curls and straightening his mittens n his belt. "Why? Is he asleep? Say, Uncle Khveódor!" he insisted, oing to the oven.

"What is it?" a weak voice was heard saying, and an emaciated

---

izba

face was lifted up from the oven. A broad, gaunt hand, bloodless and covered with hair, pulled up his overcoat over the dirty shirt that covered his bony shoulder. "Give me something to drink, brother; what is it you want?

The young fellow handed him a small dish of water.

"I say, Fyédka," said he, hesitating, "I reckon you won't want your new boots now; let me have them? Probably you won't need them anymore."

The sick man, dropping his weary head down to the lacquered bowl, and dipping his thin, hanging moustache into the brown water, drank feebly and eagerly. His tangled beard was unclean, his sunken, clouded eyes were with difficulty raised to the young man's face. When he had finished drinking, he tried to raise his hand to wipe his wet lips, but his strength failed him, and he wiped them on the sleeve of his overcoat. Silently, and breathing with difficulty through his nose, he looked straight into the young man's eyes, and tried to collect his strength.

"Maybe you have promised them to someone else?" said the young driver. "If that's so, all right. The worst of it is, it is wet outside, and I have to go out to my work, and so I said to myself, 'I reckon I'll ask Fyédka for his boots; I reckon he won't be needing them.' But may you will need them—just say."

Something began to bubble up and rumble in the sick man's chest; he bent over, and began to strangle, with a cough that rattled in his throat.

"Now I should like to know where he would need them?" unexpectedly snapped out the cook, angrily addressing the whole hovel. "This is the second month that he has not crept down from the oven. Just see how he is all broken up! And you can hear how it must hurt him inside. Where would he need boots? They would not think of burying him in new ones! And it was time long ago, God pardon me the sin of saying so. Just see how he chokes! He ought to be taken from this room to another, or somewhere. They say there's hospitals in the city; but what's you going to do? He takes up the whole room, and that's too much. There isn't any room at all. And yet you are expected to keep neat."

"Hey, Seryóha! Come along, take your place, the people are waiting," cried the head man of the station, coming to the door.

Seryóha started to go without waiting for his reply, but the sick man during his cough intimated by his eyes that he was going to speak.

"You take the boots, Seryóha," said he, conquering the cough, and getting his breath a little. "Only, do you hear, buy me a stone when I am dead," he added hoarsely.

"Thank you, uncle; then I will take them, and as for the stone—yei-yei!—I will buy you one."

"There, children, you are witnesses," the sick man was able to articulate, and then once more he bent over and began to choke.

"All right, we have heard," said one of the drivers. "But run, Seryóha, or else the starosta will be after you again. You know Lady Shirkinskaya is sick."

Seryóha quickly pulled off his ragged, unwieldy boots, and flung them under the bench. Uncle Feodor's new ones fitted his feet exactly, and the young driver could not keep his eyes off them as he went to the carriage.

"Ek! What splendid boots! Here's some grease," called another driver with the grease-pot in his hand, as Seryóha mounted to his box and gathered up the reins. "Get them for nothing?"

"So you're jealous, are you?" cried Seryóha, lifting up and tucking around his legs the tails of his overcoat. "Of with you, my darlings," he cried to the horses, cracking his knout; and the coach and barouche, with their occupants, trunks, and other belongings, were hidden in the thick autumnal mist, and rapidly whirled away over the wet road.

The sick driver remained on the oven in the stifling hovel, and, not being able to throw off the phlegm, by a supreme effort turned over on the other side, and stopped coughing.

Till evening there was a continual coming and going, and eating of meals in the room, and the sick man was not noticed. Before night came on, the cook climbed up on the oven, and got the sheepskin coat from the farther side of his legs.

"Don't be angry with me, Nastasya," exclaimed the sick man. "I shall soon leave your room."

"All right, all right, it's of no consequence," muttered the woman. "But what is the matter with you, uncle? Tell me."

"All my inwards are gnawed out. God knows what it is!"

"And I don't doubt your gullet hurts you when you cough so!"

"It hurts me all over. My death is at hand, that's what it is. Okh! Okh! Okh!" groaned the sick man.

"Mow cover up your legs this way," said Nastasya, comfortably arranging the overcoat so that it would cover him, and then getting down from the oven.

During the night the room was faintly lighted by a single taper. Nastasya and a dozen drivers were sleeping, snoring loudly, on the floor and the benches. Only the sick man feebly hawked and coughed, and tossed on the oven. In the morning, no sound was heard from him.

"I saw something wonderful in my sleep," said the cook, as she stretched herself in the early twilight the next morning. "I seemed to see Uncle Khveódor get down from the oven and go out to cut wood. 'Look here,' says he, 'I'm going to help you, Nastasya.' And I says to him, 'How can you split wood?' but he seizes the hatchet, and begins to cut so fast, so fast that nothing but chips fly. 'Why,' says I, 'haven't you been sick?' 'No,' says he, 'I am well,' and he kind of lifted up the axe, and I was scared; and I screamed and woke up. He can't be dead, can he? Uncle Khveódor! Hey, uncle!"

Feodor did not move.

"Now he can't be dead, can he? Go and see," said one of the drivers, who had just woken up.

The emaciated hand, covered with reddish hair, that hung down from the oven, was cold and pale.

"Go tell the superintendent; it seems he is dead," said the driver. Feodor had no relatives. He was a stranger. On the next day they buried him in the new burying-ground behind the grove; and Nastasya for many days had to tell everybody of the vision which she had seen, and how she had been the first to discover that Uncle Feodor was dead.

III

Spring had come.

Along the wet streets of the city swift streamlets ran purling between heaps of dung-covered ice; bright were the colours of people's dresses and the tones of their voices, as they hurried along. In the walled gardens, the buds on the trees were burgeoning, and the fresh breeze swayed their branches with a soft gentle murmur. Everywhere transparent drops were forming and falling . . . The sparrows chattered incoherently, and fluttered about on their little wings. On the sunny side, on the walls, houses, and trees, all was full of life and brilliancy. The sky, and the earth, and the heart of man overflowed with youth and joy.

In front of a great seigniorial mansion, in one of the principal streets, fresh straw had been laid down; in the house lay that same moribund invalid whom we saw hastening abroad. Near the closed doors of her room stood the sick lady's husband, and a lady well along in years. On a divan sat the confessor, with cast-down eyes, holding something wrapped up under his stole. In one corner, in a Voltaire easy-chair, reclined an old lady, the sick woman's mother, weeping violently. Near her stood the maid, holding a clean handkerchief, ready for the old lady's use when she should ask for it. Another maid was rubbing the old lady's temples, and blowing on her grey head underneath her cap.

"Well, Christ be with you, my dear," said the husband to the elderly lady who was standing with him near the door: "she has such confidence in you; you know how to talk with her; go and speak with her a little while, my darling, please go!"

He was about to open the door for her; but his cousin held him back, putting her handkerchief several times to her eyes, and shaking her head.

"There, now she will not see that I have been weeping," said she, and, opening the door herself, went to the invalid.

The husband was in the greatest excitement, and seemed quite beside himself. He started to go over to the old mother, but, after taking a few steps, he turned around, walked the length of the room, and approached the priest. The priest looked at him, raised his brows toward heaven, and sighed. The thick grey beard also was lifted and fell again.

"My God! My God!" said the husband.

"What can you do?" exclaimed the confessor, sighing and again lifting up his brows and beard, and letting them drop.

"And the old mother there!" exclaimed the husband almost in despair. "She will not be able to endure it. You see, she loved her so, she loved her so, that she . . . I don't know. You might try, father, to calm her a little, and persuade her to go away."

The confessor arose and went over to the old lady.

"It is true, no one can appreciate a mother's heart," said he, "but God is compassionate."

The old lady's face was suddenly convulsed, and a hysterical sob shook her frame.

"God is compassionate," repeated the priest, when she had grown a little calmer. "I will tell you, in my parish there was a sick man, and much worse than Marya Dmitrievna, and he, though he was only a shopkeeper, was cured in a very short time, by means of herbs. And this very same shopkeeper is now in Moscow. I have told Vasili Dmitrievitch about him; it might be tried, you know. At all events, it would satisfy the invalid. With God, all things are possible."

"No, she won't get well," persisted the old lady. "Why should God have taken her, and not me?" And again the hysterical sobbing overcame her, so violently that she fainted away.

The invalid's husband hid his face in his hands, and rushed from the room.

In the corridor the first person whom he met was a six-year-old boy, who was chasing his little sister with all his might and main.

"Do you bid me take the children to their *mamasha?*" inquired the nurse.

"No, she does not like to see them. They distract her."

The lad stopped for a moment, and, after looking eagerly into his father's face, he cut a dido with his leg, and with merry shouts ran on.

"I'm playing, she's a horse, papasha," cried the little fellow, pointing to his sister.

Meantime, in the next room, the cousin had taken her seat near the sick woman, and was skilfully bringing the conversation by degrees round so as to prepare her for the thought of death. The doctor stood by the window, mixing some draught.

The invalid, in a white capote, all surrounded by cushions, was sitting up in bed, and gazed silently at her cousin.

"Ah, my dear!" she exclaimed, unexpectedly interrupting her, "don't try to prepare me; don't treat me like a little child! I am a Christian woman. I know all about it. I know that I have not long to live; I know that if my husband had heeded me sooner, I should have been in Italy, and possibly, yes probably, should have been well by this time. They all told him so. But what is to be done? It's as God saw fit. We all of us have sinned, I know that; but I hope in the mercy of God, that all will be pardoned, ought to be pardoned. I am trying to sound my own heart. I also have committed many sins, my love. But how much I have suffered in atonement! I have tried to bear my sufferings patiently . . ."

"Then shall I have the confessor come in, my love? It will be all the easier for you, after you have been absolved," said the cousin.

The sick woman dropped her head in token of assent.

"O God! Pardon me, a sinner," she whispered.

The cousin went out, and beckoned to the confessor.

"She is an angel," she said to the husband, with tears in her eyes.

The husband wept. The priest went into the sick room; the old lady still remained unconscious, and in the room beyond all was perfectly quiet. At the end of five minutes the confessor came out, and, taking off his stole, arranged his hair.

"Thanks be to the Lord, she is calmer now," said he. "She wishes to see you."

The cousin and the husband went to the sick room. The invalid, gently weeping, was gazing at the images.

"I congratulate you, my love," said the husband.

"Thank you. How well I feel now! What ineffable joy I experience!" said the sick woman, and a faint smile played over her thin lips. "How merciful God is! Is He not? He is merciful and omnipotent!" And again with an eager prayer she turned her tearful eyes toward the holy images.

Then suddenly something seemed to occur to her mind. She beckoned to her husband. "You are never willing to do what I desire," said she, in a weak and querulous voice.

The husband, stretching his neck, listened to her submissively. "What is it, my love?"

"How many times I have told you that these doctors don't know anything! There are simple women doctors; they make cures. That's what the good father said . . . A shopkeeper . . . Send for him."

"For whom, my love?"

"Good heavens! You can never understand me." And the dying woman frowned, and closed her eyes.

The doctor came to her, and took her hand. Her pulse was evidently growing feebler and feebler. He made a sign to the husband. The sick woman remarked this gesture, and looked around in fright.

The cousin turned away to hide her tears. "Don't weep, don't torment yourselves on my account," said the invalid. "That takes away from me my last comfort."

"You are an angel!" exclaimed the cousin, kissing her hand.

"No, kiss me here. They only kiss the hands of those who are dead. My God! My God!"

That same evening the sick woman was a corpse, and the corpse in the coffin lay in the parlour of the great mansion. In the immense room, the doors of which were closed, sat the clerk, and with a monstrous voice read the Psalms of David through his nose.

The bright glare from the wax candles in the lofty silver candelabra fell on the white brow of the dead, on the heavy waxen hands, on the stiff folds of the cerement which brought out into awful relief the knees and the feet. The clerk, not varying his tones, continued to read on steadily, and in the silence of the chamber of death his words rang out and died away. Occasionally from distant rooms came the voice of children and their romping.

"Thou hidest thy face, they are troubled; thou takest away their breath, they die and return to their dust. Thou sendest forth thy Spirit, they are created; and thou renewest the fact of the earth. The glory of the Lord shall endure forever."

The face of the dead was stern and majestic. But there was no motion either on the pure cold brow, or the firmly closed lips. She was all attention! But did she perhaps now understand these majestic words?

IV

At the end of a month, over the grave of the dead a stone chapel was erected. Over the driver's there was as yet no stone, and only the fresh green grass sprouted over the mound which served as the sole record of the past existence of a man.

"It will be a sin and a shame, Seryóha," said the cook at the station-house one day, "if you don't buy a gravestone for Khveódor. You kept saying, 'it's winter, winter,' but now why don't you keep your word? I heard it all. He has already come back once to ask why you don't do it; if you don't buy him one, he will come again, he will choke you."

"Well, now, have I denied it?" urged Seryóha. "I am going to buy him a stone, as I said I would. I can get one for a rouble and a half. I have not forgotten about it; I'll have to get it. As soon as I happen to be in town, then I'll buy him one."

"You ought at least to put up a cross, that's what you ought to do," said an old driver. It isn't right at all. You're wearing those boots now."

"Yes. But where could I get him a cross? You wouldn't want to make one out of an old piece of stick, would you?"

"What is that you say? Make one out of an old piece of stick? No; take your axe, go out to the wood a little earlier than usual, and you can hew him out one. Take a little ash tree, and you can make one. You can have a covered cross. If you go then, you won't have to give the watchman a little drink of vodka. One doesn't want to give vodka for every trifle. Now, yesterday I broke my axletree, and I go and hew out a new one of green wood. No one said a word."

Early the next morning, almost before dawn, Seryóha took his axe, and went to the wood.

Over all things hung a cold, dead veil of falling mist, as yet untouched by the rays of the sun. The east gradually grew brighter, reflecting its pale light over the vault of heaven still covered by light clouds. Not a single grass-blade below, now a single leaf on the topmost branches of the tree-top, waved. Only from time to time could be heard the sound of fluttering wings in the thicket, or a rustling on the ground broke in on the silence of the forest. Suddenly a strange sound, foreign to this nature, resounded and died away at the edge of the forest. Again the noise sounded, and was monotonously repeated again and again, at the foot of one of the ancient, immovable trees. A tree-top began to shake in an extraordinary manner; the juicy leaves whispered something; and the warbler, sitting on one of the branches, flew off a couple of times with a shrill cry, and wagging its tail, finally perched on another tree.

The axe rang more and more frequently; the white chips, full of sap, were scattered upon the dewy grass, and a slight cracking was heard beneath the blows. The tree trembled with all its body, leaned over, and quickly straightened itself, shuddering with fear on its base. For an instant all was still, then once more the tree bent over; a crash was heard in its trunk; and, tearing the thicket, and dragging down the branches, it plunged toward the damp earth. The noise of the axe and of footsteps ceased. The warbler uttered a cry, and flew higher. The branch which she grazed with her wings shook for an instant, and then came to rest like all the others their foliage. The trees, more joyously than ever, extended their motionless branches over the new space that had been made in their midst.

The first sunbeams, breaking through the cloud, gleamed in the sky, and shone along the earth and heavens. The mist, in billows, began to float along the hollows; the dew, gleaming, played on the green foliage; translucent white clouds hurried along their azure path. The birds hopped about in the thicket, and, as if beside themselves, voiced their happiness; the juicy leaves joyfully and contentedly whispered on the tree-tops; and the branches of the living trees slowly and majestically waved over the dead and fallen tree.

Polikushka

[Tolstoy began writing this in March 1861. First published in 1863. The story, written in a sympathetic tone, realistically depicts the dark lives of the peasants. This version is a translation by Adolphus Norraikow taken from the collection *Ivan The Fool or The Old Devil and the Three Small Devils* published by Chas. L. Webster & Co. in 1891.]

Polikey was a court man—one of the staff of servants belonging to the court household of a *boyarinia* (lady of the nobility).

He held a very insignificant position on the estate, and lived in a rather poor, small house with his wife and children.

The house was built by the deceased nobleman whose widow he still continued to serve, and may be described as follows: The four walls surrounding the one *izba* (room) were built of stone, and the interior was ten yards square. A Russian stove stood in the centre, around which was a free passage. Each corner was fenced off as a separate inclosure to the extent of several feet, and the one nearest to the door (the smallest of all) was known as 'Polikey's corner.' Elsewhere in the room stood the bed (with quilt, sheet, and cotton pillows), the cradle (with a baby lying therein), and the three-legged table, on which the meals were prepared and the family washing was done. At the latter also Polikey was at work on the preparation of some materials for use in his profession—that of an amateur veterinary surgeon. A calf, some hens, the family clothes and household utensils, together with seven persons, filled the little home to the utmost of its capacity. It would indeed have been almost impossible for them to move around had it not been for the convenience of the stove, on which some of them slept at night, and which served as a table in the daytime.

It seemed hard to realize how so many persons managed to live in such close quarters.

Polikey's wife, Akulina, did the washing, spun and wove, bleached her linen, cooked and baked, and found time also to quarrel and gossip with her neighbours.

The monthly allowance of food which they received from the noblewoman's house was amply sufficient for the whole family, and there was always enough meal left to make mash for the cow. Their fuel they got free, and likewise the food for the cattle. In addition they were given a small piece of land on which to raise vegetables. They had a cow, a calf, and a number of chickens to care for.

Polikey was employed in the stables to take care of two stallions, and, when necessary, to bleed the horses and cattle and clean their hoofs.

In his treatment of the animals he used syringes, plasters, and various other remedies and appliances of his own invention. For these services he received whatever provisions were required by his family, and a certain sum of money—all of which would have been sufficient to enable them to live comfortably and even happily, if their hearts had not been filled with the shadow of a great sorrow.

This shadow darkened the lives of the entire family.

Polikey, while young, was employed in a horse-breeding establishment in a neighbouring village. The head stableman was a notorious horse-thief, known far and wide as a great rogue, who, for his many misdeeds, was finally exiled to Siberia. Under his instruction Polikey underwent a course of training, and, being but a boy, was easily induced to perform many evil deeds. He became so expert in the various kinds of wickedness practised by his teacher that, though he many times would gladly have abandoned his evil ways, he could not, owing to the great hold these early-formed habits had upon him. His father and mother died when he was but a child, and he had no one to point out to him the paths of virtue.

In addition to his other numerous shortcomings, Polikey was fond of strong drink. He also had a habit of appropriating other people's property, when the opportunity offered of his doing so without being seen. Collar-straps, padlocks, perch-bolts, and things even of greater value belonging to others found their way with remarkable rapidity and in great quantities to Polikey's home. He did not, however, keep such things for his own use, but sold them whenever he could find a purchaser. His payment consisted chiefly of whiskey, though sometimes he received cash.

This sort of employment, as his neighbours said, was both light and profitable; it required neither education nor labour. It had one drawback, however, which was calculated to reconcile his victims to their losses: Though he could for a time have all his needs supplied without expending either labour or money, there was always the possibility of his methods being discovered; and this result was sure to be followed by a long term of imprisonment. This impending danger made life a burden for Polikey and his family.

Such a setback indeed very nearly happened to Polikey early in his career. He married while still young, and God gave him much happiness. His wife, who was a shepherd's daughter, was a strong, intelligent, hard-working woman. She bore him many children, each of whom was said to be better than the preceding one.

Polikey still continued to steal, but once was caught with some small articles belonging to others in his possession. Among them was a pair of leather reins, the property of another peasant, who beat him severely and reported him to his mistress.

From that time on Polikey was an object of suspicion, and he was twice again detected in similar escapades. By this time the people began to abuse him, and the clerk of the court threatened to recruit him into the army as a soldier (which is regarded by the peasants as a great punishment and disgrace). His noble mistress severely reprimanded him; his wife wept from grief for his downfall, and everything went from bad to worse.

Polikey, notwithstanding his weakness, was a good-natured sort of man, but his love of strong drink had so overcome every moral instinct that at times he was scarcely responsible for his actions. This habit he vainly endeavoured to overcome. It often happened that when he returned home intoxicated, his wife, losing all patience, roundly cursed him and cruelly beat him. At times he would cry like a child, and bemoan his fate, saying: "Unfortunate man that I am, what shall I do? Let my eyes burst into pieces if I do not forever give up the vile habit! I will not again touch *vódka*."

In spite of all his promises of reform, but a short period (perhaps a month) would elapse when Polikey would again mysteriously disappear from his home and be lost for several days on a spree.

"From what source does he get the money he spends so freely?" the neighbours inquired of each other, as they sadly shook their heads.

One of his most unfortunate exploits in the matter of stealing was in connection with a clock which belonged to the estate of his mistress. The clock stood in the private office of the noblewoman, and was so old as to have outlived its usefulness, and was simply kept as an heirloom. It so happened that Polikey went into the office one day when no one was present but himself, and, seeing the old clock, it seemed to possess a peculiar fascination for him, and he speedily transferred it to his person. He carried it to a town not far from the village, where he very readily found a purchaser.

As if purposely to secure his punishment, it happened that the storekeeper to whom he sold it proved to be a relative of one of the court servants, and who, when he visited his friend on the next holiday, related all about his purchase of the clock.

An investigation was immediately instituted, and all the details of Polikey's transaction were brought to light and reported to his noble mistress. He was called into her presence, and, when confronted with the story of the theft, broke down and confessed all. He fell on his knees before the noblewoman and plead with her for mercy. The kind-hearted lady lectured him about God, the salvation of his soul, and his future life. She talked to him also about the misery and disgrace he brought upon his family, and altogether so worked upon his feelings that he cried like a child. In conclusion his kind mistress said: "I will forgive you this time on the condition that you promise faithfully to reform, and never again to take what does not belong to you."

Polikey, still weeping, replied: "I will never steal again in all my life, and if I break my promise may the earth open and swallow me up, and let my body be burned with red-hot irons!"

Polikey returned to his home, and throwing himself on the oven spent the entire day weeping and repeating the promise made to his mistress.

From that time on he was not again caught stealing, but his life became extremely sad, for he was regarded with suspicion by everyone and pointed to as a thief.

When the time came around for securing recruits for the army, all the peasants singled out Polikey as the first to be taken. The superintendent was especially anxious to get rid of him, and went to his mistress to induce her to have him sent away. The kind-hearted and merciful woman, remembering the peasant's repentance, refused to grant the superintendent's request, and told him he must take some other man in his stead.

II

One evening Polikey was sitting on his bed beside the table, preparing some medicine for the cattle, when suddenly the door was thrown wide open, and Aksiutka, a young girl from the court, rushed in. Almost out of breath, she said: "My mistress has ordered you, Polikey Illitch [son of Ilia], to come up to the court at once!"

The girl was standing and still breathing heavily from her late exertion as she continued: "Egor Mikhailovich, the superintendent, has been to see our lady about having you drafted into the army, and, Polikey Illitch, your name was mentioned among others. Our lady has sent me to tell you to come up to the court immediately."

As soon as Aksiutka had delivered her message she left the room in the same abrupt manner in which she had entered.

Akulina, without saying a word, got up and brought her husband's boots to him. They were poor, worn-out things which some soldier had given him, and his wife did not glance at him as she handed them to him.

"Are you going to change your shirt, Illitch?" she asked, at last.

"No," replied Polikey.

Akulina did not once look at him all the time he was putting on his boots and preparing to go to the court. Perhaps, after all, it was better that she did not do so. His face was very pale and his lips trembled. He slowly combed his hair and was about to depart without saying a word, when his wife stopped him to arrange the ribbon on his shirt, and, after toying a little with his coat, she put his hat on for him and he left the little home.

Polikey's next-door neighbours were a joiner and his wife. A thin partition only separated the two families, and each could hear what the other said and did. Soon after Polikey's departure a woman was heard to say: "Well, Polikey Illitch, so your mistress has sent for you!"

The voice was that of the joiner's wife on the other side of the partition. Akulina and the woman had quarrelled that morning about some trifling thing done by one of Polikey's children, and it afforded her the greatest pleasure to learn that her neighbour had been summoned into the presence of his noble mistress. She looked upon such a circumstance as a bad omen. She continued talking to herself and said: "Perhaps she wants to send him to the town to make some purchases for her household. I did not suppose she would select such a faithful man as you are to perform such a service for her. If it should prove that she *does* want to send you to the next town, just buy me a quarter-pound of tea. Will you, Polikey Illitch?"

Poor Akulina, on hearing the joiner's wife talking so unkindly of her husband, could hardly suppress the tears, and, the tirade continuing, she at last became angry, and wished she could in some way punish her.

Forgetting her neighbour's unkindness, her thoughts soon turned in another direction, and glancing at her sleeping children she said to herself that they might soon be orphans and she herself a soldier's widow. This thought greatly distressed her, and burying her face in her hands she seated herself on the bed, where several of her progeny were fast asleep. Presently a little voice interrupted her meditations by crying out, "*Mamushka* [little mother], you are crushing me," and the child pulled her nightdress from under her mother's arms.

Akulina, with her head still resting on her hands, said: "Perhaps it would be better if we all should die. I only seem to have brought you into the world to suffer sorrow and misery."

Unable longer to control her grief, she burst into violent weeping, which served to increase the amusement of the joiner's wife, who had not forgotten the morning's squabble, and she laughed loudly at her neighbour's woe.

III

About half an hour had passed when the youngest child began to cry and Akulina arose to feed it. She had by this time ceased to weep, and after feeding the infant she again fell into her old position, with her face buried in her hands. She was very pale, but this only increased her beauty. After a time she raised her head, and staring at the burning candle she began to question herself as to why she had married, and as to the reason that the Tsar required so many soldiers.

Presently she heard steps outside, and knew that her husband was returning. She hurriedly wiped away the last traces of her tears as she arose to let him pass into the centre of the room.

Polikey made his appearance with a look of triumph on his

face, threw his hat on the bed, and hastily removed his coat; but not a word did he utter.

Akulina, unable to restrain her impatience, asked, "Well, what did she want with you?"

"Pshaw!" he replied, "it is very well known that Polikushka is considered the worst man in the village; but when it comes to business of importance, who is selected then? Why, Polikushka, of course."

"What kind of business?" Akulina timidly inquired.

But Polikey was in no hurry to answer her question. He lighted his pipe with a very imposing air, and spit several times on the floor before he replied.

Still retaining his pompous manner, he said, "She has ordered me to go to a certain merchant in the town and collect a considerable sum of money."

"You to collect money?" questioned Akulina.

Polikey only shook his head and smiled significantly, saying:

"'You,' the mistress said to me, 'are a man resting under a grave suspicion—a man who is considered unsafe to trust in any capacity; but I have faith in you, and will intrust you with this important business of mine in preference to anyone else.'"

Polikey related all this in a loud voice, so that his neighbour might hear what he had to say.

"'You promised me to reform,' my noble mistress said to me, 'and I will be the first to show you how much faith I have in your promise. I want you to ride into town, and, going to the principal merchant there, collect a sum of money from him and bring it to me.' I said to my mistress: 'Everything you order shall be done. I will only too gladly obey your slightest wish.' Then my mistress said: 'Do you understand, Polikey, that your future lot depends upon the faithful performance of this duty I impose upon you?' I replied: 'Yes, I understand everything, and feel that I will succeed in performing acceptably any task which you may impose upon me. I have been accused of every kind of evil deed that it is possible to charge a man with, but I have never done anything seriously wrong against you, your honour.' In this way I talked to our mistress until

I succeeded in convincing her that my repentance was sincere, and she became greatly softened toward me, saying, 'If you are successful I will give you the first place at the court.'"

"And how much money are you to collect?" inquired Akulina.

"Fifteen hundred roubles," carelessly answered Polikey.

Akulina sadly shook her head as she asked, "When are you to start?"

"She ordered me to leave here tomorrow," Polikey replied. 'Take any horse you please,' she said. 'Come to the office, and I will see you there and wish you God-speed on your journey.'"

"Glory to Thee, O Lord!" said Akulina, as she arose and made the sign of the cross. "God, I am sure, will bless you, Illitch," she added, in a whisper, so that the people on the other side of the partition could not hear what she said, all the while holding on to his sleeve. "Illitch," she cried at last, excitedly, "for God's sake promise me that you will not touch a drop of *vódka*. Take an oath before God, and kiss the cross, so that I may be sure that you will not break your promise!"

Polikey replied in most contemptuous tones: "Do you think I will dare to touch *vódka* when I shall have such a large sum of money in my care?"

"Akulina, have a clean shirt ready for the morning," were his parting words for the night.

So Polikey and his wife went to sleep in a happy frame of mind and full of bright dreams for the future.

IV

Very early the next morning, almost before the stars had hidden themselves from view, there was seen standing before Polikey's home a low wagon, the same in which the superintendent himself used to ride; and harnessed to it was a large-boned, dark-brown mare, called for some unknown reason by the name of *Baraban* (drum). Aniutka, Polikey's eldest daughter, in spite of the heavy rain and the cold wind which was blowing, stood outside barefooted and held (not without some fear) the reins in one hand, while with the other she endeavoured to keep her green and yellow overcoat wound around her body, and also to hold Polikey's sheepskin coat.

In the house there were the greatest noise and confusion. The morning was still so dark that the little daylight there was failed to penetrate through the broken panes of glass, the window being stuffed in many places with rags and paper to exclude the cold air.

Akulina ceased from her cooking for a while and helped to get Polikey ready for the journey. Most of the children were still in bed, very likely as a protection against the cold, for Akulina had taken away the big overcoat which usually covered them and had substituted a shawl of her own. Polikey's shirt was all ready, nice and clean, but his shoes badly needed repairing, and this fact caused his devoted wife much anxiety. She took from her own feet the thick woollen stockings she was wearing, and gave them to Polikey. She then began to repair his shoes, patching up the holes so as to protect his feet from dampness.

While this was going on he was sitting on the side of the bed with his feet dangling over the edge, and trying to turn the sash which confined his coat at the waist. He was anxious to look as clean as possible, and he declared his sash looked like a dirty rope.

One of his daughters, enveloped in a sheepskin coat, was sent to a neighbour's house to borrow a hat.

Within Polikey's home the greatest confusion reigned, for the court servants were constantly arriving with innumerable small orders which they wished Polikey to execute for them in town. One wanted needles, another tea, another tobacco, and last came the joiner's wife, who by this time had prepared her samovar, and, anxious to make up the quarrel of the previous day, brought the traveller a cup of tea.

Neighbour Nikita refused the loan of the hat, so the old one had to be patched up for the occasion. This occupied some time, as there were many holes in it.

Finally Polikey was all ready, and jumping on the wagon started on his journey, after first making the sign of the cross.

At the last moment his little boy, Mishka, ran to the door, begging to be given a short ride; and then his little daughter, Mashka, appeared on the scene and pleaded that she, too, might have a ride, declaring that she would be quite warm enough without furs.

Polikey stopped the horse on hearing the children, and Akulina placed them in the wagon, together with two others belonging to a neighbour—all anxious to have a short ride.

As Akulina helped the little ones into the wagon she took occasion to remind Polikey of the solemn promise he had made her not to touch a drop of *vódka* during the journey.

Polikey drove the children as far as the blacksmith's place, where he let them out of the wagon, telling them they must return home. He then arranged his clothing, and, setting his hat firmly on his head, started his horse on a trot.

The two children, Mishka and Mashka, both barefooted, started running at such a rapid pace that a strange dog from another village, seeing them flying over the road, dropped his tail between his legs and ran home squealing.

The weather was very cold, a sharp cutting wind blowing continuously; but this did not disturb Polikey, whose mind was engrossed with pleasant thoughts. As he rode through the wintry blasts he kept repeating to himself: "So I am the man they wanted to send to Siberia, and whom they threatened to enrol as a soldier—the same man whom every one abused, and said he was lazy, and who was pointed out as a thief and given the meanest work on the estate to do! Now I am going to receive a large sum of money, for which my mistress is sending me because she trusts me. I am also riding in the same wagon that the superintendent himself uses when he is riding as a representative of the court. I have the same harness, leather horse-collar, reins, and all the other gear."

Polikey, filled with pride at thought of the mission with which he had been intrusted, drew himself up with an air of pride, and, fixing his old hat more firmly on his head, buttoned his coat tightly about him and urged his horse to greater speed.

"Just to think," he continued; "I shall have in my possession three thousand half-roubles [the peasant manner of speaking of money so as to make it appear a larger sum than it really is], and will carry them in my bosom. If I wished to I might run away to Odessa instead of taking the money to my mistress. But no; I will not do that. I will surely carry the money straight to the one who has been kind enough to trust me."

When Polikey reached the first *kabak* (tavern) he found that from long habit the mare was naturally turning her head toward it; but he would not allow her to stop, though money had been given him to purchase both food and drink. Striking the animal a sharp blow with the whip, he passed by the tavern. The performance was repeated when he reached the next *kabak*, which looked very inviting; but he resolutely set his face against entering, and passed on.

About noon he arrived at his destination, and getting down from the wagon approached the gate of the merchant's house where the servants of the court always stopped. Opening it he led the mare through, and (after unharnessing her) fed her. This done, he next entered the house and had dinner with the merchant's workingmen, and to them he related what an important mission he had been sent on, making himself very amusing by the pompous air which he assumed. Dinner over, he carried a letter to the merchant which the noblewoman had given him to deliver.

The merchant, knowing thoroughly the reputation which Polikey bore, felt doubtful of trusting him with so much money, and somewhat anxiously inquired if he really had received orders to carry so many roubles.

Polikey tried to appear offended at this question, but did not succeed, and he only smiled.

The merchant, after reading the letter a second time and being convinced that all was right, gave Polikey the money, which he put in his bosom for safe-keeping.

On his way to the house he did not once stop at any of the shops he passed. The clothing establishments possessed no attractions for him, and after he had safely passed them all he stood for a moment, feeling very pleased that he had been able to withstand temptation, and then went on his way.

"I have money enough to buy up everything," he said; "but I will not do so."

The numerous commissions which he had received compelled him to go to the bazaar. There he bought only what had been ordered, but he could not resist the temptation to ask the price of a very handsome sheepskin coat which attracted his attention. The merchant to whom he spoke looked at Polikey and smiled, not believing that he had sufficient money to purchase such an expensive coat. But Polikey, pointing to his breast, said that he could buy out the whole shop if he wished to. He thereupon ordered the shopkeeper to take his measure. He tried the coat on and looked himself over carefully, testing the quality and blowing upon the hair to see that none of it came out. Finally, heaving a deep sigh, he took it off.

"The price is too high," he said. "If you could let me have it for fifteen roubles—"

But the merchant cut him short by snatching the coat from him and throwing it angrily to one side.

Polikey left the bazaar and returned to the merchant's house in high spirits.

After supper he went out and fed the mare, and prepared everything for the night. Returning to the house he got up on the stove to rest, and while there he took out the envelope which contained the money and looked long and earnestly at it. He could not read, but asked one of those present to tell him what the writing on the envelope meant. It was simply the address and the announcement that it contained fifteen hundred roubles.

The envelope was made of common paper and was sealed with dark-brown sealing wax. There was one large seal in the centre and four smaller ones at the corners. Polikey continued to examine it carefully, even inserting his finger till he touched the crisp notes. He appeared to take a childish delight in having so much money in his possession.

Having finished his examination, he put the envelope inside the lining of his old battered hat, and placing both under his head he went to sleep; but during the night he frequently awoke and always felt to know if the money was safe. Each time that he found that it was safe he rejoiced at the thought that he, Polikey, abused and regarded by everyone as a thief, was intrusted with the care of such a large sum of money, and also that he was about to return with it quite as safely as the superintendent himself could have done.

V

Before dawn the next morning Polikey was up, and after harnessing the mare and looking in his hat to see that the money was all right, he started on his return journey.

Many times on the way Polikey took off his hat to see that the money was safe. Once he said to himself, "I think that perhaps it would be better if I should put it in my bosom." This would necessitate the untying of his sash, so he decided to keep it still in his hat, or until he should have made half the journey, when he would be compelled to stop to feed his horse and to rest.

He said to himself: "The lining is not sewn in very strongly and the envelope might fall out, so I think I had better not take off my hat until I reach home."

The money was safe—at least, so it seemed to him—and he began to think how grateful his mistress would be to him, and in his excited imagination he saw the five roubles he was so sure of receiving.

Once more he examined the hat to see that the money was safe, and finding everything all right he put on his hat and pulled it well down over his ears, smiling all the while at his own thoughts.

Akulina had carefully sewed all the holes in the hat, but it burst out in other places owing to Polikey's removing it so often.

In the darkness he did not notice the new rents, and tried to push the envelope further under the lining, and in doing so pushed one corner of it through the plush.

The sun was getting high in the heavens, and Polikey having slept but little the previous night and feeling its warm rays fell fast asleep, after first pressing his hat more firmly on his head. By this action he forced the envelope still further through the plush, and as he rode along his head bobbed up and down.

Polikey did not awake till he arrived near his own house, and his first act was to put his hand to his head to learn if his hat was all right. Finding that it was in its place, he did not think it necessary to examine it and see that the money was safe. Touching the mare gently with the whip she started into a trot, and as he rode along he arranged in his own mind how much he was to receive. With the air of a man already holding a high position at the court, he looked around him with an expression of lofty scorn on his face.

As he neared his house he could see before him the one room which constituted their humble home, and the joiner's wife next door carrying her rolls of linen. He saw also the office of the court and his mistress's house, where he hoped he would be able presently to prove that he was an honest, trustworthy man.

He reasoned with himself that any person can be abused by lying tongues, but when his mistress would see him she would say: "Well done, Polikey; you have shown that you can be honest. Here are three—it may be five—perhaps ten—roubles for you;" and also she would order tea for him, and might treat him to vódka—who knows? The latter thought gave him great pleasure, as he was feeling very cold.

Speaking aloud he said: "What a happy holy-day we can have with ten roubles! Having so much money, I could pay Nikita the four roubles fifty kopecks which I owe him, and yet have some left to buy shoes for the children."

When near the house Polikey began to arrange his clothes, smoothing down his fur collar, re-tying his sash, and stroking his hair. To do the latter he had to take off his hat, and when doing so felt in the lining for the envelope. Quicker and quicker he ran his hand around the lining, and not finding the money used both hands, first one and then the other. But the envelope was not to be found.

Polikey was by this time greatly distressed, and his face was white with fear as he passed his hand through the crown of his old hat. Polikey stopped the mare and began a diligent search through the wagon and its contents. Not finding the precious envelope, he felt in all his pockets—*but the money could not be found!*

Wildly clutching at his hair, he exclaimed: "*Batiushka!* What will I do now? What will become of me?" At the same time he realized that he was near his neighbours' house and could be seen by them; so he turned the mare around, and, pulling his hat down securely upon his head, he rode quickly back in search of his lost treasure.

VI

The whole day passed without anyone in the village of Pokrovski having seen anything of Polikey. During the afternoon his mistress inquired many times as to his whereabouts, and sent Aksiutka frequently to Akulina, who each time sent back word that Polikey had not yet returned, saying also that perhaps the merchant had kept him, or that something had happened the mare.

His poor wife felt a heavy load upon her heart, and was scarcely able to do her housework and put everything in order for the next day (which was to be a holy-day). The children also anxiously awaited their father's appearance, and, though for different reasons, could hardly restrain their impatience. The noblewoman and Akulina were concerned only in regard to Polikey himself, while the children were interested most in what he would bring them from the town.

The only news received by the villagers during the day concerning Polikey was to the effect that neighbouring peasants had seen him running up and down the road and asking everyone he met if he or she had found an envelope.

One of them had seen him also walking by the side of his tired-out horse. "I thought," said he, "that the man was drunk, and had not fed his horse for two days—the animal looked so exhausted."

Unable to sleep, and with her heart palpitating at every sound, Akulina lay awake all night vainly awaiting Polikey's return. When the cock crowed the third time she was obliged to get up to attend to the fire. Day was just dawning and the church bells had begun to ring. Soon all the children were also up, but there was still no tidings of the missing husband and father.

In the morning the chill blasts of winter entered their humble home, and on looking out they saw that the houses, fields, and roads were thickly covered with snow. The day was clear and cold, as if befitting the holy-day they were about to celebrate. They were able to see a long distance from the house, but no one was in sight.

Akulina was busy baking cakes, and had it not been for the joyous shouts of the children she would not have known that Polikey was coming up the road, for a few minutes later he came in with a bundle in his hand and walked quietly to his corner. Akulina noticed that he was very pale and that his face bore an expression of suffering—as if he would like to have cried but could not do so. But she did not stop to study it, but excitedly inquired: "What! Illitch, is everything all right with you?"

He slowly muttered something, but his wife could not understand what he said.

"What!" she cried out, "have you been to see our mistress?"

Polikey still sat on the bed in his corner, glaring wildly about him, and smiling bitterly. He did not reply for a long time, and Akulina again cried:

"Eh? Illitch! Why don't you answer me? Why don't you speak?"

Finally he said: "Akulina, I delivered the money to our mistress; and oh, how she thanked me!" Then he suddenly looked about him, with an anxious, startled air, and with a sad smile on his lips. Two things in the room seemed to engross the most of his attention: the baby in the cradle, and the rope which was attached to the ladder. Approaching the cradle, he began with his thin fingers quickly to untie the knot in the rope by which the two were connected. After untying it he stood for a few moments looking silently at the baby.

Akulina did not notice this proceeding, and with her cakes on the board went to place them in a corner.

Polikey quickly hid the rope beneath his coat, and again seated himself on the bed.

"What is it that troubles you, Illitch?" inquired Akulina. "You are not yourself."

"I have not slept," he answered.

Suddenly a dark shadow crossed the window, and a minute later the girl Aksiutka quickly entered the room, exclaiming:

"The *boyarinia* commands you, Polikey Illitch, to come to her this moment!"

Polikey looked first at Akulina and then at the girl.

"This moment!" he cried. "What more is wanted?"

He spoke the last sentence so softly that Akulina became quieted in her mind, thinking that perhaps their mistress intended to reward her husband.

"Say that I will come immediately," he said. But Polikey failed to follow the girl, and went instead to another place.

From the porch of his house there was a ladder reaching to the attic. Arriving at the foot of the ladder Polikey looked around him, and seeing no one about, he quickly ascended to the garret.

***

Meanwhile the girl had reached her mistress's house.

"What does it mean that Polikey does not come?" said the noblewoman impatiently. "Where can he be? Why does he not come at once?"

Aksiutka flew again to his house and demanded to see Polikey.

"He went a long time ago," answered Akulina, and looking around with an expression of fear on her face, she added, "He may have fallen asleep somewhere on the way."

About this time the joiner's wife, with hair unkempt and clothes bedraggled, went up to the loft to gather the linen which she had previously put there to dry. Suddenly a cry of horror was heard, and the woman, with her eyes closed, and crazed by fear, ran down the ladder like a cat.

"Illitch," she cried, "has hanged himself!"

Poor Akulina ran up the ladder before any of the people, who had gathered from the surrounding houses, could prevent her. With a loud shriek she fell back as if dead, and would surely have been killed had not one of the spectators succeeded in catching her in his arms.

Before dark the same day a peasant of the village, while returning from the town, found the envelope containing Polikey's money on the roadside, and soon after delivered it to the *boyarinia*.

My Dream

[Tolstoy completed this story in 1863. The version reproduced here is taken from the collection *The Forged Coupon and Other Stories* (1911) translated by Charles Theodore Hagberg Wright.]

I

"As a daughter she no longer exists for me. Can't you understand? She simply doesn't exist. Still, I cannot possibly leave her to the charity of strangers. I will arrange things so that she can live as she pleases, but I do not wish to hear of her. Who would ever have thought . . . the horror of it, the horror of it."

He shrugged his shoulders, shook his head, and raised his eyes. These words were spoken by Prince Michael Ivanovich to his brother Peter, who was governor of a province in Central Russia. Prince Peter was a man of fifty, Michael's junior by ten years.

On discovering that his daughter, who had left his house a year before, had settled here with her child, the elder brother had come from St. Petersburg to the provincial town, where the above conversation took place.

Prince Michael Ivanovich was a tall, handsome, white-haired, fresh coloured man, proud and attractive in appearance and bearing. His family consisted of a vulgar, irritable wife, who wrangled with him continually over every petty detail, a son, a ne'er-do-well, spendthrift and roue—yet a 'gentleman,' according to his father's code, two daughters, of whom the elder had married well, and was living in St. Petersburg; and the younger, Lisa—his favourite, who had disappeared from home a year before. Only a short while ago he had found her with her child in this provincial town.

Prince Peter wanted to ask his brother how, and under what circumstances, Lisa had left home, and who could possibly be the father of her child. But he could not make up his mind to inquire.

That very morning, when his wife had attempted to condole with her brother-in-law, Prince Peter had observed a look of pain on his brother's face. The look had at once been masked by an expression of unapproachable pride, and he had begun to question her about their flat, and the price she paid. At luncheon, before the family and guests, he had been witty and sarcastic as usual. Towards every one, excepting the children, whom he treated with almost reverent tenderness, he adopted an attitude of distant *hauteur*. And yet it was so natural to him that everyone somehow acknowledged his right to be haughty.

In the evening his brother arranged a game of whist. When he retired to the room which had been made ready for him, and was just beginning to take out his artificial teeth, someone tapped lightly on the door with two fingers.

"Who is that?"

"*C'est moi*, Michael."

Prince Michael Ivanovich recognized the voice of his sister-in-law, frowned, replaced his teeth, and said to himself, "What does she want?" Aloud he said, "*Entrez.*"

His sister-in-law was a quiet, gentle creature, who bowed in submission to her husband's will. But to many she seemed a crank, and some did not hesitate to call her a fool. She was pretty, but her hair was always carelessly dressed, and she herself was untidy and absent-minded. She had, also, the strangest, most unaristocratic ideas, by no means fitting in the wife of a high official. These ideas she would express most unexpectedly, to everybody's astonishment, her husband's no less than her friends'.

"*Vous pouvez me renvoyer, mais je ne m'en irai pas, je vous le dis d'avance,*" she began, in her characteristic, indifferent way.

"*Dieu preserve,*" answered her brother-in-law, with his usual somewhat exaggerated politeness, and brought forward a chair for her.

"*Ça ne vous dérange pas?*" she asked, taking out a cigarette. "I'm not going to say anything unpleasant, Michael. I only wanted to say something about Lisochka."

Michael Ivanovich sighed—the word pained him; but mastering himself at once, he answered with a tired smile. "Our conversation can only be on one subject, and that is the subject you wish to discuss." He spoke without looking at her, and avoided even naming the subject. But his plump, pretty little sister-in-law was unabashed. She continued to regard him with the same gentle, imploring look in her blue eyes, sighing even more deeply.

"Michael, *mon bon ami*, have pity on her. She is only human."

"I never doubted that," said Michael Ivanovich with a bitter smile.

"She is your daughter."

"She was—but my dear Aline, why talk about this?"

"Michael, dear, won't you see her? I only wanted to say, that the one who is to blame—"

Prince Michael Ivanovich flushed; his face became cruel.

"For heaven's sake, let us stop. I have suffered enough. I have now but one desire, and that is to put her in such a position that she will be independent of others, and that she shall have no further need of communicating with me. Then she can live her own life, and my family and I need know nothing more about her. That is all I can do."

"Michael, you say nothing but 'I'! She, too, is 'I.'"

"No doubt; but, dear Aline, please let us drop the matter. I feel it too deeply."

Alexandra Dmitrievna remained silent for a few moments, shaking her head. "And Masha, your wife, thinks as you do?"

"Yes, quite."

Alexandra Dmitrievna made an inarticulate sound.

"*Brisons la dessus et bonne nuit*," said he. But she did not go. She stood silent a moment. Then—

"Peter tells me you intend to leave the money with the woman where she lives. Have you the address?"

"I have."

"Don't leave it with the woman, Michael! Go yourself. Just see how she lives. If you don't want to see her, you need not. HE isn't there; there is no one there."

Michael Ivanovich shuddered violently.

"Why do you torture me so? It's a sin against hospitality!"

Alexandra Dmitrievna rose, and almost in tears, being touched by her own pleading, said, "She is so miserable, but she is such a dear."

He got up, and stood waiting for her to finish. She held out her hand.

"Michael, you do wrong," said she, and left him.

For a long while after she had gone Michael Ivanovich walked to and fro on the square of carpet. He frowned and shivered, and exclaimed, "Oh, oh!" And then the sound of his own voice frightened him, and he was silent.

His wounded pride tortured him. His daughter—his—brought up in the house of her mother, the famous Avdotia Borisovna, whom the Empress honoured with her visits, and acquaintance with whom was an honour for all the world! His daughter—; and he had lived his life as a knight of old, knowing neither fear nor blame. The fact that he had a natural son born of a Frenchwoman, whom he had settled abroad, did not lower his own self-esteem. And now this daughter, for whom he had not only done everything that a father could and should do; this daughter to whom he had given a splendid education and every opportunity to make a match in the best Russian society—this daughter to whom he had not only given all that a girl could desire, but whom he had really *loved*; whom he had admired, been proud of—this daughter had repaid him with such disgrace, that he was ashamed and could not face the eyes of men!

He recalled the time when she was not merely his child, and a member of his family, but his darling, his joy and his pride. He saw her again, a little thing of eight or nine, bright, intelligent, lively, impetuous, graceful, with brilliant black eyes and flowing auburn hair. He remembered how she used to jump up on his knees and hug him, and tickle his neck; and how she would laugh, regardless of his protests, and continue to tickle him, and kiss his lips, his eyes, and his cheeks. He was naturally opposed to all demonstration, but this impetuous love moved him, and he often submitted to her petting. He remembered also how sweet it was to caress her. To remember all this, when that sweet child had become what she now was, a creature of whom he could not think without loathing.

He also recalled the time when she was growing into

135

womanhood, and the curious feeling of fear and anger that he experienced when he became aware that men regarded her as a woman. He thought of his jealous love when she came coquettishly to him dressed for a ball, and knowing that she was pretty. He dreaded the passionate glances which fell upon her that she not only did not understand but rejoiced in. "Yes," thought he, "that superstition of woman's purity! Quite the contrary, they do not know shame—they lack this sense." He remembered how, quite inexplicably to him, she had refused two very good suitors. She had become more and more fascinated by her own success in the round of gaieties she lived in.

But this success could not last long. A year passed, then two, then three. She was a familiar figure, beautiful—but her first youth had passed, and she had become somehow part of the ball-room furniture. Michael Ivanovich remembered how he had realised that she was on the road to spinsterhood, and desired but one thing for her. He must get her married off as quickly as possible, perhaps not quite so well as might have been arranged earlier, but still a respectable match.

But it seemed to him she had behaved with a pride that bordered on insolence. Remembering this, his anger rose more and more fiercely against her. To think of her refusing so many decent men, only to end in this disgrace. "Oh, oh!" he groaned again.

Then stopping, he lit a cigarette, and tried to think of other things. He would send her money, without ever letting her see him. But memories came again. He remembered—it was not so very long ago, for she was more than twenty then—her beginning a flirtation with a boy of fourteen, a cadet of the Corps of Pages who had been staying with them in the country. She had driven the boy half crazy; he had wept in his distraction. Then how she had rebuked her father severely, coldly, and even rudely, when, to put an end to this stupid affair, he had sent the boy away. She seemed somehow to consider herself insulted. Since then father and daughter had drifted into undisguised hostility.

"I was right," he said to himself. "She is a wicked and shameless woman."

And then, as a last ghastly memory, there was the letter from Moscow, in which she wrote that she could not return home; that she was a miserable, abandoned woman, asking only to be forgiven and forgotten. Then the horrid recollection of the scene with his wife came to him; their surmises and their suspicions, which became a certainty. The calamity had happened in Finland, where they had let her visit her aunt; and the culprit was an insignificant Swede, a student, an empty-headed, worthless creature—and married.

All this came back to him now as he paced backwards and forwards on the bedroom carpet, recollecting his former love for her, his pride in her. He recoiled with terror before the incomprehensible fact of her downfall, and he hated her for the agony she was causing him. He remembered the conversation with his sister-in-law, and tried to imagine how he might forgive her. But as soon as the thought of 'him' arose, there surged up in his heart horror, disgust, and wounded pride. He groaned aloud, and tried to think of something else.

"No, it is impossible; I will hand over the money to Peter to give her monthly. And as for me, I have no longer a daughter."

And again a curious feeling overpowered him: a mixture of self-pity at the recollection of his love for her, and of fury against her for causing him this anguish.

II

During the last year Lisa had without doubt lived through more than in all the preceding twenty-five. Suddenly she had realised the emptiness of her whole life. It rose before her, base and sordid—this life at home and among the rich set in St. Petersburg—this animal existence that never sounded the depths, but only touched the shallows of life.

It was well enough for a year or two, or perhaps even three. But when it went on for seven or eight years, with its parties, balls, concerts, and suppers; with its costumes and coiffures to display the charms of the body; with its adorers old and young, all alike seemingly possessed of some unaccountable right to have everything, to laugh at everything; and with its summer months spent in the same way, everything yielding but a superficial pleasure, even music and reading merely touching upon life's problems, but never solving them—all this holding out no promise of change, and losing its charm more and more—she began to despair. She had desperate moods when she longed to die.

Her friends directed her thoughts to charity. On the one hand, she saw poverty which was real and repulsive, and a sham poverty even more repulsive and pitiable; on the other, she saw the terrible indifference of the lady patronesses who came in carriages and gowns worth thousands. Life became to her more and more unbearable. She yearned for something real, for life itself—not this playing at living, not this skimming life of its cream. Of real life there was none. The best of her memories was her love for the little cadet Koko. That had been a good, honest, straight-forward impulse, and now there was nothing like it. There could not be. She grew more and more depressed, and in this gloomy mood she went to visit an aunt in Finland. The fresh scenery and surroundings, the people strangely different to her own, appealed to her at any rate as a new experience.

How and when it all began she could not clearly remember. Her aunt had another guest, a Swede. He talked of his work, his people, the latest Swedish novel. Somehow, she herself did not know how that terrible fascination of glances and smiles began, the meaning of which cannot be put into words.

These smiles and glances seemed to reveal to each, not only the soul of the other, but some vital and universal mystery. Every word they spoke was invested by these smiles with a profound and wonderful significance. Music, too, when they were listening together, or when they sang duets, became full of the same deep meaning. So, also, the words in the books they read aloud. Sometimes they would argue, but the moment their eyes met, or a smile flashed between them, the discussion remained far behind. They soared beyond it to some higher plane consecrated to themselves.

How it had come about, how and when the devil, who had seized hold of them both, first appeared behind these smiles and glances, she could not say. But, when terror first seized her, the invisible threads that bound them were already so interwoven that she had no power to tear herself free. She could only count on him and on his honour. She hoped that he would not make use of his power; yet all the while she vaguely desired it.

Her weakness was the greater, because she had nothing to support her in the struggle. She was weary of society life and she had no affection for her mother. Her father, so she thought, had cast her away from him, and she longed passionately to live and to have done with play. Love, the perfect love of a woman for a man, held the promise of life for her. Her strong, passionate nature, too, was dragging her thither. In the tall, strong figure of this man, with his fair hair and light upturned moustache, under which shone a smile attractive and compelling, she saw the promise of that life for which she longed. And then the smiles and glances, the hope of something so incredibly beautiful, led, as they were bound to lead, to that which she feared but unconsciously awaited.

Suddenly all that was beautiful, joyous, spiritual, and full of promise for the future, became animal and sordid, sad and despairing.

She looked into his eyes and tried to smile, pretending that she feared nothing, that everything was as it should be; but deep down in her soul she knew it was all over. She understood that she had not found in him what she had sought; that which she had once known in herself and in Koko. She told him that he must write to her father asking her hand in marriage. This he promised to do; but when she met him next he said it was impossible for him to write just then. She saw something vague and furtive in his eyes, and her distrust of him grew. The following day he wrote to her, telling her that he was already married, though his wife had left him long since; that he knew she would despise him for the wrong he had done her, and implored her forgiveness. She made him come to see her. She said she loved him; that she felt herself bound to him for ever whether he was married or not, and would never leave him. The next time they met he told her that he and his parents were so poor that he could only offer her the meanest existence. She answered that she needed nothing, and was ready to go with him at once wherever he wished. He endeavoured to dissuade her, advising her to wait; and so she waited. But to live on with this secret, with occasional meetings, and merely corresponding with him, all hidden from her family, was agonising, and she insisted again that he must take her away. At first, when she returned to St. Petersburg, be wrote promising to come, and then letters ceased and she knew no more of him.

She tried to lead her old life, but it was impossible. She fell ill, and the efforts of the doctors were unavailing; in her hopelessness she resolved to kill herself. But how was she to do this, so that her death might seem natural? She really desired to take her life, and imagined that she had irrevocably decided on the step. So, obtaining some poison, she poured it into a glass, and in another instant would have drunk it, had not her sister's little son of five at that very moment run in to show her a toy his grandmother had given him. She caressed the child, and, suddenly stopping short, burst into tears.

The thought overpowered her that she, too, might have been a mother had he not been married, and this vision of motherhood made her look into her own soul for the first time. She began to think not of what others would say of her, but of her own life. To kill oneself because of what the world might say was easy; but the moment she saw her own life dissociated from the world, to take that life was out of the question. She threw away the poison, and ceased to think of suicide.

Then her life within began. It was real life, and despite the torture of it, had the possibility been given her, she would not have turned back from it. She began to pray, but there was no comfort in prayer; and her suffering was less for herself than for her father, whose grief she foresaw and understood.

Thus months dragged along, and then something happened which entirely transformed her life. One day, when she was at work upon a quilt, she suddenly experienced a strange sensation. No—it seemed impossible. Motionless she sat with her work in hand. Was it possible that this was *It*. Forgetting everything, his baseness and deceit, her mother's querulousness, and her father's sorrow, she smiled. She shuddered at the recollection that she was on the point of killing it, together with herself.

She now directed all her thoughts to getting away—somewhere where she could bear her child—and become a miserable, pitiful mother, but a mother withal. Somehow she planned and arranged it all, leaving her home and settling in a distant provincial town, where no one could find her, and where she thought she would be far from her people. But, unfortunately, her father's brother received an appointment there, a thing she could not possibly foresee. For four months she had been living in the house of a midwife—one Maria Ivanovna; and, on learning that her uncle had come to the town, she was preparing to fly to a still remoter hiding-place.

III

Michael Ivanovich awoke early next morning. He entered his brother's study, and handed him the cheque, filled in for a sum which he asked him to pay in monthly instalments to his daughter. He inquired when the express left for St. Petersburg. The train left at seven in the evening, giving him time for an early dinner before leaving. He breakfasted with his sister-in-law, who refrained from mentioning the subject which was so painful to him, but only looked at him timidly; and after breakfast he went out for his regular morning walk.

Alexandra Dmitrievna followed him into the hall.

"Go into the public gardens, Michael—it is very charming there, and quite near to Everything," said she, meeting his sombre looks with a pathetic glance.

Michael Ivanovich followed her advice and went to the public gardens, which were so near to Everything, and meditated with annoyance on the stupidity, the obstinacy, and heartlessness of women.

"She is not in the very least sorry for me," he thought of his sister-in-law. "She cannot even understand my sorrow. And what of her?" He was thinking of his daughter. "She knows what all this means to me—the torture. What a blow in one's old age! My days will be shortened by it! But I'd rather have it over than endure this agony. And all that '*pour les beaux yeux d'un chenapan*'—oh!" he moaned; and a wave of hatred and fury arose in him as he thought of what would be said in the town when everyone knew. (And no doubt everyone knew already.) Such a feeling of rage possessed him that he would have liked to beat it into her head, and make her understand what she had done. These women never understand. "It is quite near Everything," suddenly came to his mind, and getting out his notebook, he found her address. Vera Ivanovna Silvestrova, Kukonskaya Street, Abromov's house. She was living under this name. He left the gardens and called a cab.

"Whom do you wish to see, sir?" asked the midwife, Maria Ivanovna, when he stepped on the narrow landing of the steep, stuffy staircase.

"Does Madame Silvestrova live here?"

"Vera Ivanovna? Yes; please come in. She has gone out; she's gone to the shop round the corner. But she'll be back in a minute."

Michael Ivanovich followed the stout figure of Maria Ivanovna into a tiny parlour, and from the next room came the screams of a baby, sounding cross and peevish, which filled him with disgust. They cut him like a knife.

Maria Ivanovna apologised, and went into the room, and he could hear her soothing the child. The child became quiet, and she returned.

"That is her baby; she'll be back in a minute. You are a friend of hers, I suppose?"

"Yes—a friend—but I think I had better come back later on," said Michael Ivanovich, preparing to go. It was too unbearable, this preparation to meet her, and any explanation seemed impossible.

He had just turned to leave, when he heard quick, light steps on the stairs, and he recognized Lisa's voice.

"Maria Ivanovna—has he been crying while I've been gone—I was—"

Then she saw her father. The parcel she was carrying fell from her hands.

"Father!" she cried, and stopped in the doorway, white and trembling.

He remained motionless, staring at her. She had grown so thin. Her eyes were larger, her nose sharper, her hands worn and bony. He neither knew what to do, nor what to say. He forgot all his grief about his dishonour. He only felt sorrow, infinite sorrow for her; sorrow for her thinness, and for her miserable rough clothing; and most of all, for her pitiful face and imploring eyes.

"Father—forgive," she said, moving towards him.

"Forgive—forgive me," he murmured; and he began to sob like a child, kissing her face and hands, and wetting them with his tears.

In his pity for her he understood himself. And when he saw himself as he was, he realised how he had wronged her, how guilty he had been in his pride, in his coldness, even in his anger towards her. He was glad that it was he who was guilty, and that he had nothing to forgive, but that he himself needed forgiveness. She took him to her tiny room, and told him how she lived; but she did not show him the child, nor did she mention the past, knowing how painful it would be to him.

He told her that she must live differently.

"Yes; if I could only live in the country," said she.

"We will talk it over," he said. Suddenly the child began to wail and to scream. She opened her eyes very wide; and, not taking them from her father's face, remained hesitating and motionless.

"Well—I suppose you must feed him," said Michael Ivanovich, and frowned with the obvious effort.

She got up, and suddenly the wild idea seized her to show him whom she loved so deeply the thing she now loved best of all in the world. But first she looked at her father's face. Would he be angry or not? His face revealed no anger, only suffering.

"Yes, go, go," said he; "God bless you. Yes. I'll come again tomorrow, and we will decide. Goodbye, my darling—goodbye." Again he found it hard to swallow the lump in his throat.

When Michael Ivanovich returned to his brother's house, Alexandra Dmitrievna immediately rushed to him.

"Well?"

"Well? Nothing."

"Have you seen?" she asked, guessing from his expression that something had happened.

"Yes," he answered shortly, and began to cry. "I'm getting old and stupid," said he, mastering his emotion.

"No; you are growing wise—very wise."

144

The Prisoner of the Caucasus

[Written in 1870. First published in 1872. Republished in 1885. The story is drawn from a real incident that took place during Tolstoy's service in the Russian military. This version has been taken from *Twenty-three Tales* (1906), a collection translated by Louise and Aylmer Maude.]

I

An officer named Zhílin was serving in the army in the Caucasus.

One day he received a letter from home. It was from his mother, who wrote: "I am getting old, and should like to see my dear son once more before I die. Come and say goodbye to me and bury me, and then, if God pleases, return to service again with my blessing. But I have found a girl for you, who is sensible and good and has some property. If you can love her, you might marry her and remain at home."

Zhílin thought it over. It was quite true, the old lady was failing fast and he might not have another chance to see her alive. He had better go, and, if the girl was nice, why not marry her?

So he went to his Colonel, obtained leave of absence, said goodbye to his comrades, stood the soldiers four pailfuls of vódka* as a farewell treat, and got ready to go.

It was a time of war in the Caucasus. The roads were not safe by night or day. If ever a Russian ventured to ride or walk any distance away from his fort, the Tartars killed him or carried him off to the hills. So it had been arranged that twice every week a body of soldiers should march from one fortress to the next to convoy travellers from point to point.

It was summer. At daybreak the baggage-train got ready under shelter of the fortress; the soldiers marched out; and all started along the road. Zhílin was on horseback, and a cart with his things went with the baggage-train. They had sixteen miles to go. The baggage-train moved slowly; sometimes the soldiers stopped, or perhaps a wheel would come off one of the carts, or a horse refuse to go on, and then everybody had to wait.

---

* *Vódka* is a spirit distilled from rye. It is the commonest form of strong drink in Russia.

When by the sun it was already past noon, they had not gone half the way. It was dusty and hot, the sun was scorching and there was no shelter anywhere: a bare plain all round—not a tree, not a bush, by the road.

Zhílin rode on in front, and stopped, waiting for the baggage to overtake him. Then he heard the signal-horn sounded behind him: the company had again stopped. So he began to think: "Hadn't I better ride on by myself? My horse is a good one: if the Tartars do attack me, I can gallop away. Perhaps, however, it would be wiser to wait."

As he sat considering, Kostílin, an officer carrying a gun, rode up to him and said:

"Come along, Zhílin, let's go on by ourselves. It's dreadful; I am famished, and the heat is terrible. My shirt is wringing wet."

Kostílin was a stout, heavy man, and the perspiration was running down his red face. Zhílin thought awhile, and then asked: "Is your gun loaded?"

"Yes it is."

"Well, then, let's go, but on condition that we keep together."

So they rode forward along the road across the plain, talking, but keeping a look-out on both sides. They could see afar all round. But after crossing the plain the road ran through a valley between two hills, and Zhílin said: "We had better climb that hill and have a look round, or the Tartars may be on us before we know it."

But Kostílin answered: "What's the use? Let us go on."

Zhílin, however, would not agree.

"No," he said; "you can wait here if you like, but I'll go and look round." And he turned his horse to the left, up the hill. Zhílin's horse was a hunter, and carried him up the hillside as if it had wings. (He had bought it for a hundred roubles as a colt out of a herd, and had broken it in himself.) Hardly had he reached the top of the hill, when he saw some thirty Tartars not much more than a hundred yards ahead of him. As soon as he caught sight of them he turned round, but the Tartars had also seen him, and rushed after him at full gallop, getting their guns out as they went.

Down galloped Zhílin as fast as the horse's legs could go, shouting to Kostílin: "Get your gun ready!"

And, in thought, he said to his horse: "Get me well out of this, my pet; don't stumble, for if you do it's all up. Once I reach the gun, they shan't take me prisoner."

But, instead of waiting, Kostílin, as soon as he caught sight of the Tartars, turned back towards the fortress at full speed, whipping his horse now on one side now on the other, and its switching tail was all that could be seen of him in the dust.

Zhílin saw it was a bad look-out; the gun was gone, and what could he do with nothing but his sword? He turned his horse towards the escort, thinking to escape, but there were six Tartars rushing to cut him off. His horse was a good one, but theirs were still better; and besides, they were across his path. He tried to rein in his horse and to turn another way, but it was going so fast it could not stop, and dashed on straight towards the Tartars. He saw a red-bearded Tartar on a grey horse, with his gun raised, come at him, yelling and showing his teeth.

"Ah," thought Zhílin, "I know you, devils that you are. If you take me alive, you'll put me in a pit and flog me. I will not be taken alive!"

Zhílin, though not a big fellow, was brave. He drew his sword and dashed at the red-bearded Tartar, thinking: "Either I'll ride him down, or disable him with my sword."

He was still a horse's length away from him, when he was fired at from behind, and his horse was hit. It fell to the ground with all its weight, pinning Zhílin to the earth.

He tried to rise, but two ill-savoured Tartars were already sitting on him and binding his hands behind his back. He made an effort and flung them off, but three others jumped from their horses and began beating his head with the butts of their guns. His eyes grew dim, and he fell back. The Tartars seized him, and, taking spare girths from their saddles, twisted his hands behind him and tied them with a Tartar knot. They knocked his cap off, pulled off his boots, searched him all over, tore his clothes, and took his money and his watch.

Zhílin looked round at his horse. There it lay on its side, poor thing, just as it had fallen; struggling, its legs in the air, unable to touch the ground. There was a hole in its head, and black blood was pouring out, turning the dust to mud for a couple of feet around.

One of the Tartars went up to the horse and began taking the saddle off, it still kicked, so he drew a dagger and cut its windpipe. A whistling sound came from its throat, the horse gave one plunge, and all was over.

The Tartars took the saddle and trappings. The red-bearded Tartar mounted his horse, and the others lifted Zhílin into the saddle behind him. To prevent his falling off, they strapped him to the Tartar's girdle; and then they all rode away to the hills.

So there sat Zhílin, swaying from side to side, his head striking against the Tartar's stinking back. He could see nothing but that muscular back and sinewy neck, with its closely shaven, bluish nape. Zhílin's head was wounded: the blood had dried over his eyes, and he could neither shift his position on the saddle nor wipe the blood off. His arms were bound so tightly that his collarbones ached.

They rode up and down hills for a long way. Then they reached a river which they forded, and came to a hard road leading across a valley.

Zhílin tried to see where they were going, but his eyelids were stuck together with blood, and he could not turn.

Twilight began to fall; they crossed another river, and rode up a stony hillside. There was a smell of smoke here, and dogs were barking. They had reached an Aoul (a Tartar village). The Tartars got off their horses; Tartar children came and stood round Zhílin, shrieking with pleasure and throwing stones at him.

The Tartar drove the children away, took Zhílin off the horse, and called his man. A Nogáy* with high cheekbones, and nothing on but a shirt (and that so torn that his breast was all bare), answered the call. The Tartar gave him an order. He went and

---

* One of a certain Tartar tribe.

fetched shackles: two blocks of oak with iron rings attached, and a clasp and lock fixed to one of the rings.

They untied Zhílin's arms, fastened the shackles on his leg and dragged him to a barn, where they pushed him in and locked the door.

Zhílin fell on a heap of manure. He lay still awhile then groped about to find a soft place, and settled down.

That night Zhílin hardly slept at all. It was the time of year when the nights are short, and daylight soon showed itself through a chink in the wall. He rose, scratched to make the chink bigger, and peeped out.

Through the hole he saw a road leading downhill; to the right was a Tartar hut with two trees near it, a black dog lay on the threshold, and a goat and kids were moving about wagging their tails. Then he saw a young Tartar woman in a long, loose, bright-coloured gown, with trousers and high boots showing from under it. She had a coat thrown over her head, on which she carried a large metal jug filled with water. She was leading by the hand a small, closely-shaven Tartar boy, who wore nothing but a shirt; and as she went along balancing herself, the muscles of her back quivered. This woman carried the water into the hut, and, soon after, the red-bearded Tartar of yesterday came out dressed in a silk tunic, with a silver-hilted dagger hanging by his side, shoes on his bare feet, and a tall black sheepskin cap set far back on his head. He came out, stretched himself, and stroked his red beard. He stood awhile, gave an order to his servant, and went away.

Then two lads rode past from watering their horses. The horses' noses were wet. Some other closely-shaven boys ran out, without any trousers, and wearing nothing but their shirts. They crowded together, came to the barn, picked up a twig, and began pushing it in at the chink. Zhílin gave a shout, and the boys shrieked and scampered off, their little bare knees gleaming as they ran.

Zhílin was very thirsty: his throat was parched, and he thought: "If only they would come and so much as look at me!"

Then he heard someone unlocking the barn. The red-bearded Tartar entered, and with him was another, a smaller man, dark, with bright black eyes, red cheeks, and a short beard. He had a merry face, and was always laughing. This man was even more richly dressed than the other. He wore a blue silk tunic trimmed with gold, a large silver dagger in his belt, red morocco slippers worked with silver, and over these a pair of thick shoes, and he had a white sheepskin cap on his head.

The red-bearded Tartar entered, muttered something as if he were annoyed, and stood leaning against the doorpost, playing with his dagger, and glaring askance at Zhílin, like a wolf. The dark one, quick and lively, and moving as if on springs, came straight up to Zhílin, squatted down in front of him, slapped him on the shoulder, and began to talk very fast in his own language. His teeth showed, and he kept winking, clicking his tongue, and repeating, "Good Russ, good Russ."

Zhílin could not understand a word, but said, "Drink! Give me water to drink!"

The dark man only laughed. "Good Russ," he said, and went on talking in his own tongue.

Zhílin made signs with lips and hands that he wanted something to drink.

The dark man understood, and laughed. Then he looked out of the door, and called to someone: "Dina!"

A little girl came running in: she was about thirteen, slight, thin, and like the dark Tartar in face. Evidently she was his daughter.

She, too, had clear black eyes, and her face was good-looking. She had on a long blue gown with wide sleeves, and no girdle. The hem of her gown, the front, and the sleeves, were trimmed with red. She wore trousers and slippers, and over the slippers stouter shoes with high heels. Round her neck she had a necklace made of Russian silver coins. She was bareheaded, and her black hair was plaited with a ribbon and ornamented with gilt braid and silver coins.

Her father gave an order, and she ran away and returned with a metal jug. She handed the water to Zhílin and sat down, crouching so that her knees were as high as her head; and there she sat with wide open eyes watching Zhílin drink, as though he were a wild animal.

When Zhílin handed the empty jug back to her, she gave such a sudden jump back, like a wild goat, that it made her father laugh. He sent her away for something else. She took the jug, ran out, and brought back some unleavened bread on a round board, and once more sat down, crouching, and looking on with staring eyes.

Then the Tartars went away and again locked the door.

After a while the Nogáy came and said: "*Ayda*, the master, *Ayda!*"

He, too, knew no Russian. All Zhílin could make out was that he was told to go somewhere.

Zhílin followed the Nogáy, but limped, for the shackles dragged his feet so that he could hardly step at all. On getting out of the barn he saw a Tartar village of about ten houses, and a Tartar church with a small tower. Three horses stood saddled before one of the houses; little boys were holding them by the reins. The dark Tartar came out of this house, beckoning with his hand for Zhílin to follow him. Then he laughed, said something in his own language, and returned into the house.

Zhílin entered. The room was a good one: the walls smoothly plastered with clay. Near the front wall lay a pile of bright-coloured feather beds; the side walls were covered with rich carpets used as hangings, and on these were fastened guns, pistols and swords, all inlaid with silver. Close to one of the walls was a small stove on a level with the earthen floor. The floor itself was as clean as a thrashing-ground. A large space in one corner was spread over with felt, on which were rugs, and on these rugs were cushions stuffed with down. And on these cushions sat five Tartars, the dark one, the red-haired one, and three guests. They were wearing their indoor slippers, and each had a cushion behind his back. Before them were standing millet cakes on a round board, melted butter in a bowl, and a jug of *buza*, or Tartar beer. They ate both cakes and butter with their hands.

The dark man jumped up and ordered Zhílin to be placed on one side, not on the carpet but on the bare ground, then he sat down on the carpet again, and offered millet cakes and *buza* to his guests. The servant made Zhílin sit down, after which he took off his own overshoes, put them by the door where the other shoes were standing, and sat down nearer to his masters on the felt, watching them as they ate, and licking his lips.

The Tartars ate as much as they wanted, and a woman dressed in the same way as the girl—in a long gown and trousers, with a kerchief on her head—came and took away what was left, and brought a handsome basin, and an ewer with a narrow spout. The Tartars washed their hands, folded them, went down on their knees, blew to the four quarters, and said their prayers. After they had talked for a while, one of the guests turned to Zhílin and began to speak in Russian.

"You were captured by Kazi-Mohammed," he said, and pointed at the red-bearded Tartar. "And Kazi-Mohammed has given you to Abdul Murat," pointing at the dark one. "Abdul Murat is now your master."

Zhílin was silent. Then Abdul Murat began to talk, laughing, pointing to Zhílin, and repeating, "Soldier Russ, good Russ."

The interpreter said, "He orders you to write home and tell them to send a ransom, and as soon as the money comes he will set you free."

Zhílin thought for a moment, and said, "How much ransom does he want?"

The Tartars talked awhile, and then the interpreter said, "Three thousand roubles."

"No," said Zhílin, "I can't pay so much."

Abdul jumped up and, waving his arms, talked to Zhílin thinking, as before, that he would understand. The interpreter translated: "How much will you give?"

Zhílin considered, and said, "Five hundred roubles." At this the Tartars began speaking very quickly, all together. Abdul began to shout at the red-bearded one, and jabbered so fast that the spittle spurted out of his mouth. The red-bearded one only screwed up his eyes and clicked his tongue.

They quietened down after a while, and the interpreter said: "Five hundred roubles is not enough for the master. He paid two hundred for you himself. Kazi-Mohammed was in debt to him, and he took you in payment. Three thousand roubles! Less than that won't do. If you refuse to write, you will be put into a pit and flogged with a whip!"

"Eh!" thought Zhílin, "the more one fears them the worse it will be."

So he sprang to his feet, and said, "You tell that dog that if he tries to frighten me I will not write at all, and he will get nothing. I never was afraid of you dogs, and never will be!"

The interpreter translated, and again they all began to talk at once.

They jabbered for a long time, and then the dark man jumped up, came to Zhílin, and said: "*Dzhigit Russ, dzhigit Russ!*" (*Dzhigit* in their language means 'brave.') And he laughed, and said something to the interpreter, who translated: "One thousand roubles will satisfy him."

Zhílin stuck to it: "I will not give more than five hundred. And if you kill me you'll get nothing at all."

The Tartars talked awhile, then sent the servant out to fetch something, and kept looking, now at Zhílin, now at the door. The servant returned, followed by a stout, bare-footed, tattered man, who also had his leg shackled.

Zhílin gasped with surprise: it was Kostílin. He, too, had been taken. They were put side by side, and began to tell each other what had occurred. While they talked, the Tartars looked on in

ilence. Zhílin related what had happened to him; and Kostílin
old how his horse had stopped, his gun missed fire, and this same
Abdul had overtaken and captured him.

Abdul jumped up, pointed to Kostílin, and said something. The
interpreter translated that they both now belonged to one master,
and the one who first paid the ransom would be set free first.

"There now," he said to Zhílin, "you get angry, but your
comrade here is gentle; he has written home, and they will send
five thousand roubles. So he will be well fed and well treated."

Zhílin replied: "My comrade can do as he likes; maybe he is
rich, I am not. It must be as I said. Kill me, if you like—you will
gain nothing by it; but I will not write for more than five hundred
roubles."

They were silent. Suddenly up sprang Abdul, brought a little
box, took out a pen, ink, and a bit of paper, gave them to Zhílin,
slapped him on the shoulder, and made a sign that he should write.
He had agreed to take five hundred roubles.

"Wait a bit!" said Zhílin to the interpreter; "tell him that
he must feed us properly, give us proper clothes and boots, and
let us be together. It will be more cheerful for us. And he must
have these shackles taken off our feet," and Zhílin looked at his
master and laughed.

The master also laughed, heard the interpreter, and said: "I
will give them the best of clothes: a cloak and boots fit to be
married in. I will feed them like princes; and if they like they can
live together in the barn. But I can't take off the shackles, or they
will run away. They shall be taken off, however, at night." And he
jumped up and slapped Zhílin on the shoulder, exclaiming: "You
good, I good!"

Zhílin wrote the letter, but addressed it wrongly, so that it
should not reach its destination, thinking to himself: "I'll run away!"

Zhílin and Kostílin were taken back to the barn and given
some maize straw, a jug of water, some bread, two old cloaks, and
some worn-out military boots—evidently taken from the corpses
of Russian soldiers. At night their shackles were taken off their
feet, and they were locked up in the barn.

III

Zhílin and his friend lived in this way for a whole month. The master always laughed and said: "You, Iván, good! I, Abdul, good!" But he fed them badly, giving them nothing but unleavened bread of millet-flour baked into flat cakes, or sometimes only unbaked dough.

Kostílin wrote home a second time, and did nothing but mope and wait for the money to arrive. He would sit for days together in the barn sleeping, or counting the days till a letter could come.

Zhílin knew his letter would reach no one, and he did not write another. He thought: "Where could my mother get enough money to ransom me? As it is she lived chiefly on what I sent her. If she had to raise five hundred roubles, she would be quite ruined. With God's help I'll manage to escape!"

So he kept on the look-out, planning how to run away.

He would walk about the Aoul whistling; or would sit working, modelling dolls of clay, or weaving baskets out of twigs: for Zhílin was clever with his hands.

Once he modelled a doll with a nose and hands and feet and with a Tartar gown on, and put it up on the roof. When the Tartar women came out to fetch water, the master's daughter, Dina, saw the doll and called the women, who put down their jugs and stood looking and laughing. Zhílin took down the doll and held it out to them. They laughed, but dared not take it. He put down the doll and went into the barn, waiting to see what would happen.

Dina ran up to the doll, looked round, seized it, and ran away.

In the morning, at daybreak, he looked out. Dina came out of the house and sat down on the threshold with the doll, which she had dressed up in bits of red stuff, and she rocked it like a baby, singing a Tartar lullaby. An old woman came out and scolded her, and snatching the doll away she broke it to bits, and sent Dina about her business.

But Zhílin made another doll, better than the first, and gave it to Dina. Once Dina brought a little jug, put it on the ground, sat down gazing at him, and laughed, pointing to the jug.

"What pleases her so?" wondered Zhílin. He took the jug thinking it was water, but it turned out to be milk. He drank the milk and said: "That's good!"

How pleased Dina was! "Good, Iván, good!" said she, and she jumped up and clapped her hands. Then, seizing the jug, she ran away. After that, she stealthily brought him some milk every day.

The Tartars make a kind of cheese out of goat's milk, which they dry on the roofs of their houses; and sometimes, on the sly, she brought him some of this cheese. And once, when Abdul had killed a sheep, she brought Zhílin a bit of mutton in her sleeve. She would just throw the things down and run away.

One day there was a heavy storm, and the rain fell in torrents for a whole hour. All the streams became turbid. At the ford, the water rose till it was seven feet high, and the current was so strong that it rolled the stones about. Rivulets flowed everywhere, and the rumbling in the hills never ceased. When the storm was over, the water ran in streams down the village street. Zhílin got his master to lend him a knife, and with it he shaped a small cylinder, and cutting some little boards, he made a wheel to which he fixed two dolls, one on each side. The little girls brought him some bits of stuff, and he dressed the dolls, one as a peasant, the other as a peasant woman. Then he fastened them in their places, and set the wheel so that the stream should work it. The wheel began to turn and the dolls danced.

The whole village collected round. Little boys and girls, Tartar men and women, all came and clicked their tongues.

"Ah, Russ! Ah, Iván!"

Abdul had a Russian clock, which was broken. He called Zhílin and showed it to him, clicking his tongue.

"Give it to me, I'll mend it for you," said Zhílin.

He took it to pieces with the knife, sorted the pieces, and put them together again, so that the clock went all right.

The master was delighted, and made him a present of one of his old tunics which was all in holes. Zhílin had to accept it. He could, at any rate, use it as a coverlet at night.

After that Zhílin's fame spread; and Tartars came from distant villages, bringing him now the lock of a gun or of a pistol, now a watch, to mend. His master gave him some tools—pincers, gimlets, and a file.

One day a Tartar fell ill, and they came to Zhílin saying, "Come and heal him!" Zhílin knew nothing about doctoring, but he went to look, and thought to himself, "Perhaps he will get well anyway."

He returned to the barn, mixed some water with sand, and then in the presence of the Tartars whispered some words over it and gave it to the sick man to drink. Luckily for him, the Tartar recovered.

Zhílin began to pick up their language a little, and some of the Tartars grew familiar with him. When they wanted him, they would call: "Iván! Iván!" Others, however, still looked at him askance, as at a wild beast.

The red-bearded Tartar disliked Zhílin. Whenever he saw him he frowned and turned away, or swore at him. There was also an old man there who did not live in the Aoul, but used to come up from the foot of the hill. Zhílin only saw him when he passed on his way to the Mosque. He was short, and had a white cloth wound round his hat. His beard and moustaches were clipped, and white as snow; and his face was wrinkled and brick-red. His nose was hooked like a hawk's, his grey eyes looked cruel, and he had no teeth except two tusks. He would pass, with his turban on his head, leaning on his staff, and glaring round him like a wolf. If he saw Zhílin he would snort with anger and turn away.

Once Zhílin descended the hill to see where the old man lived. He went down along the pathway and came to a little garden surrounded by a stone wall; and behind the wall he saw cherry and apricot trees, and a hut with a flat roof. He came closer, and saw hives made of plaited straw, and bees flying about and humming. The old man was kneeling, busy doing something with a hive.

Zhílin stretched to look, and his shackles rattled. The old man turned round, and, giving a yell, snatched a pistol from his belt and shot at Zhílin, who just managed to shelter himself behind the stone wall.

The old man went to Zhílin's master to complain. The master called Zhílin, and said with a laugh, "Why did you go to the old man's house?"

"I did him no harm," replied Zhílin. "I only wanted to see how he lived."

The master repeated what Zhílin said.

But the old man was in a rage; he hissed and jabbered, showing his tusks, and shaking his fists at Zhílin.

Zhílin could not understand all, but he gathered that the old man was telling Abdul he ought not to keep Russians in the Aoul, but ought to kill them. At last the old man went away.

Zhílin asked the master who the old man was.

"He is a great man!" said the master. "He was the bravest of our fellows; he killed many Russians, and was at one time very rich. He had three wives and eight sons, and they all lived in one village. Then the Russians came and destroyed the village, and killed seven of his sons. Only one son was left, and he gave himself up to the Russians. The old man also went and gave himself up, and lived among the Russians for three months. At the end of that time he found his son, killed him with his own hands, and then escaped. After that he left off fighting, and went to Mecca to pray to God; that is why he wears a turban. One who has been to Mecca is called "Hadji," and wears a turban. He does not like you fellows. He tells me to kill you. But I can't kill you. I have paid money for you and, besides, I have grown fond of you, Iván. Far from killing you, I would not even let you go if I had not promised." And he laughed, saying in Russian, "You, Iván, good; I, Abdul, good!"

IV

Zhílin lived in this way for a month. During the day he sauntered about the Aoul or busied himself with some handicraft, but at night, when all was silent in the Aoul, he dug at the floor of the barn. It was no easy task digging, because of the stones; but he worked away at them with his file, and at last had made a hole under the wall large enough to get through.

"If only I could get to know the lay of the land," thought he, "and which way to go! But none of the Tartars will tell me."

So he chose a day when the master was away from home, and set off after dinner to climb the hill beyond the village, and to look around. But before leaving home the master always gave orders to his son to watch Zhílin, and not to lose sight of him. So the lad ran after Zhílin, shouting: "Don't go! Father does not allow it. I'll call the neighbours if you won't come back."

Zhílin tried to persuade him, and said: "I'm not going far; I only want to climb that hill. I want to find a herb—to cure sick people with. You come with me if you like. How can I run away with these shackles on? Tomorrow I'll make a bow and arrows for you."

So he persuaded the lad, and they went. To look at the hill, it did not seem far to the top; but it was hard walking with shackles on his leg. Zhílin went on and on, but it was all he could do to reach the top. There he sat down and noted how the land lay. To the south, beyond the barn, was a valley in which a herd of horses was pasturing and at the bottom of the valley one could see another Aoul. Beyond that was a still steeper hill, and another hill beyond that. Between the hills, in the blue distance, were forests, and still further off were mountains, rising higher and higher. The highest of them were covered with snow, white as sugar; and one snowy peak towered above all the rest. To the east and to the west were other such hills, and here and there smoke rose from Aouls in the ravines. "Ah," thought he, "all that is Tartar country." And he turned towards the Russian side. At his feet he saw a river, and the Aoul he lived in, surrounded by little gardens. He could see women, like tiny dolls, sitting by the river rinsing clothes. Beyond the Aoul was a hill, lower than the one to the south, and beyond it two other hills well wooded; and between these, a smooth bluish plain, and far, far across the plain something that looked like a cloud of smoke. Zhílin tried to remember where the sun used to rise and set when he was living in the fort, and he saw that there was no mistake: the Russian fort must be in that plain. Between those two hills he would have to make his way when he escaped.

The sun was beginning to set. The white, snowy mountains turned red, and the dark hills turned darker; mists rose from the ravine, and the valley, where he supposed the Russian fort to be, seemed on fire with the sunset glow. Zhílin looked carefully. Something seemed to be quivering in the valley like smoke from a chimney, and he felt sure the Russian fortress was there.

It had grown late. The Mullah's cry was heard. The herds were being driven home, the cows were lowing, and the lad kept saying, "Come home!" But Zhílin did not feel inclined to go away.

At last, however, they went back. "Well," thought Zhílin, "now that I know the way, it is time to escape." He thought of running away that night. The nights were dark—the moon had waned. But as ill-luck would have it, the Tartars returned home that evening. They generally came back driving cattle before them and in good spirits. But this time they had no cattle. All they brought home was the dead body of a Tartar—the red one's brother—who had been killed. They came back looking sullen, and they all gathered together for the burial. Zhílin also came out to see it.

They wrapped the body in a piece of linen, without any coffin, and carried it out of the village, and laid it on the grass under some plane-trees. The Mullah and the old men came. They wound clothes round their caps, took off their shoes, and squatted on their heels, side by side, near the corpse.

The Mullah was in front: behind him in a row were three old men in turbans, and behind them again the other Tartars. All cast down their eyes and sat in silence. This continued a long time, until the Mullah raised his head and said: "Allah!" (which means God). He said that one word, and they all cast down their eyes again, and were again silent for a long time. They sat quite still, not moving or making any sound.

Again the Mullah lifted his head and said, "Allah!" and they all repeated: "Allah! Allah!" and were again silent.

The dead body lay immovable on the grass, and they sat as still as if they too were dead. Not one of them moved. There was no sound but that of the leaves of the plane-trees stirring in the breeze. Then the Mullah repeated a prayer, and they all rose. They lifted the body and carried it in their arms to a hole in the ground. It was not an ordinary hole, but was hollowed out under the ground like a vault. They took the body under the arms and by the legs, bent it, and let it gently down, pushing it under the earth in a sitting posture, with the hands folded in front.

The Nogáy brought some green rushes, which they stuffed into the hole, and, quickly covering it with earth, they smoothed the ground, and set an upright stone at the head of the grave. Then they trod the earth down, and again sat in a row before the grave, keeping silence for a long time.

At last they rose, said "Allah! Allah! Allah!" and sighed.

The red-bearded Tartar gave money to the old men; then he too rose, took a whip, struck himself with it three times on the forehead, and went home.

The next morning Zhílin saw the red Tartar, followed by three others, leading a mare out of the village. When they were beyond the village, the red-bearded Tartar took off his tunic and turned up his sleeves, showing his stout arms. Then he drew a dagger and sharpened it on a whetstone. The other Tartars raised the mare's head, and he cut her throat, threw her down, and began skinning her, loosening the hide with his big hands. Women and girls came and began to wash the entrails and the inwards. The mare was cut up, the pieces taken into the hut,

162

and the whole village collected at the red Tartar's hut for a funeral feast.

For three days they went on eating the flesh of the mare, drinking *buza*, and praying for the dead man. All the Tartars were at home. On the fourth day at dinner-time Zhílin saw them preparing to go away. Horses were brought out, they got ready, and some ten of them (the red one among them) rode away; but Abdul stayed at home. It was new moon, and the nights were still dark.

"Ah!" thought Zhílin, "tonight is the time to escape." And he told Kostílin; but Kostílin's heart failed him.

"How can we escape?" he said. "We don't even know the way."

"I know the way," said Zhílin.

"Even if you do," said Kostílin, "we can't reach the fort in one night."

"If we can't," said Zhílin, "we'll sleep in the forest. See here, I have saved some cheeses. What's the good of sitting and moping here? If they send your ransom—well and good; but suppose they don't manage to collect it? The Tartars are angry now, because the Russians have killed one of their men. They are talking of killing us."

Kostílin thought it over.

"Well, let's go," said he.

V

Zhílin crept into the hole, widened it so that Kostílin might also get through, and then they both sat waiting till all should be quiet in the Aoul.

As soon as all was quiet, Zhílin crept under the wall, got out, and whispered to Kostílin, "Come!" Kostílin crept out, but in so doing he caught a stone with his foot and made a noise. The master had a very vicious watchdog, a spotted one called Oulyashin. Zhílin had been careful to feed him for some time before. Oulyashin heard the noise and began to bark and jump, and the other dogs did the same. Zhílin gave a slight whistle, and threw him a bit of cheese. Oulyashin knew Zhílin, wagged his tail, and stopped barking.

But the master had heard the dog, and shouted to him from his hut, "Hayt, hayt, Oulyashin!"

Zhílin, however, scratched Oulyashin behind the ears, and the dog was quiet, and rubbed against his legs, wagging his tail.

They sat hidden behind a corner for a while. All became silent again, only a sheep coughed inside a shed, and the water rippled over the stones in the hollow. It was dark, the stars were high overhead, and the new moon showed red as it set, horns upward, behind the hill. In the valleys the fog was white as milk.

Zhílin rose and said to his companion, "Well, friend, come along!"

They started; but they had only gone a few steps when they heard the Mullah crying from the roof, "Allah, Bismillah! Ilrahman!" That meant that the people would be going to the Mosque. So they sat down again, hiding behind a wall, and waited a long time till the people had passed. At last all was quiet again.

"Now then! May God be with us!" They crossed themselves,

and started once more. They passed through a yard and went down the hillside to the river, crossed the river, and went along the valley.

The mist was thick, but only near the ground; overhead the stars shone quite brightly. Zhílin directed their course by the stars. It was cool in the mist, and easy walking, only their boots were uncomfortable, being worn out and trodden down. Zhílin took his off, threw them away, and went barefoot, jumping from stone to stone, and guiding his course by the stars. Kostílin began to lag behind.

"Walk slower," he said, "these confounded boots have quite blistered my feet."

"Take them off!" said Zhílin. "It will be easier walking without them."

Kostílin went barefoot, but got on still worse. The stones cut his feet, and he kept lagging behind. Zhílin said: "If your feet get cut, they'll heal again; but if the Tartars catch us and kill us, it will be worse!"

Kostílin did not reply, but went on, groaning all the time.

Their way lay through the valley for a long time. Then, to the right, they heard dogs barking. Zhílin stopped, looked about, and began climbing the hill, feeling with his hands.

"Ah!" said he, "we have gone wrong, and have come too far to the right. Here is another Aoul, one I saw from the hill. We must turn back and go up that hill to the left. There must be a wood there."

But Kostílin said: "Wait a minute! Let me get breath. My feet are all cut and bleeding."

"Never mind, friend! They'll heal again. You should spring more lightly. Like this!"

And Zhílin ran back and turned to the left up the hill towards the wood.

Kostílin still lagged behind, and groaned. Zhílin only said "Hush!" and went on and on.

They went up the hill and found a wood as Zhílin had said. They entered the wood and forced their way through the brambles, which tore their clothes. At last they came to a path and followed it.

"Stop!" They heard the tramp of hoofs on the path, and waited, listening. It sounded like the tramping of a horse's feet, but then ceased. They moved on, and again they heard the tramping. When they paused, it also stopped. Zhílin crept nearer to it, and saw something standing on the path where it was not quite so dark. It looked like a horse, and yet not quite like one, and on it was something queer, not like a man. He heard it snorting. "What can it be?" Zhílin gave a low whistle, and off it dashed from the path into the thicket, and the woods were filled with the noise of crackling, as if a hurricane were sweeping through, breaking the branches.

Kostílin was so frightened that he sank to the ground. But Zhílin laughed and said: "It's a stag. Don't you hear him breaking the branches with his antlers? We were afraid of him, and he is afraid of us."

They went on. The Great Bear was already setting. It was near morning, and they did not know whether they were going the right way or not. Zhílin thought it was the way he had been brought by the Tartars, and that they were still some seven miles from the Russian fort; but he had nothing certain to go by, and at night one easily mistakes the way. After a time they came to a clearing. Kostílin sat down and said: "Do as you like, I can go no farther! My feet won't carry me."

Zhílin tried to persuade him.

"No, I shall never get there; I can't!"

Zhílin grew angry, and spoke roughly to him.

"Well, then, I shall go on alone. Goodbye!"

Kostílin jumped up and followed. They went another three miles. The mist in the wood had settled down still more densely; they could not see a yard before them, and the stars had grown dim.

Suddenly they heard the sound of a horse's hoofs in front of them. They heard its shoes strike the stones. Zhílin lay down flat, and listened with his ear to the ground.

"Yes, so it is! A horseman is coming towards us."

They ran off the path, crouched among the bushes, and waited. Zhílin crept to the road, looked, and saw a Tartar on horseback driving a cow and humming to himself. The Tartar rode past. Zhílin returned to Kostílin.

"God has led him past us; get up and let's go on!"

Kostílin tried to rise, but fell back again.

"I can't; on my word I can't! I have no strength left."

He was heavy and stout, and had been perspiring freely. Chilled by the mist, and with his feet all bleeding, he had grown quite limp.

Zhílin tried to lift him, when suddenly Kostílin screamed out: "Oh, how it hurts!"

Zhílin's heart sank.

"What are you shouting for? The Tartar is still near; he'll have heard you!" And he thought to himself, "He is really quite done up. What am I to do with him? It won't do to desert a comrade."

"Well, then, get up, and climb up on my back. I'll carry you if you really can't walk."

He helped Kostílin up, and put his arms under his thighs. Then he went out on to the path, carrying him.

"Only, for the love of heaven," said Zhílin, "don't throttle me with your hands! Hold on to my shoulders."

Zhílin found his load heavy; his feet, too, were bleeding, and he was tired out. Now and then he stooped to balance Kostílin better, jerking him up so that he should sit higher, and then went on again.

The Tartar must, however, really have heard Kostílin scream. Zhílin suddenly heard someone galloping behind and shouting in the Tartar tongue. He darted in among the bushes. The Tartar seized his gun and fired, but did not hit them, shouted in his own language, and galloped off along the road.

"Well, now we are lost, friend!" said Zhílin. "That dog will gather the Tartars together to hunt us down. Unless we can get a couple of miles away from here we are lost!" And he thought to himself, "Why the devil did I saddle myself with this block? I should have got away long ago had I been alone."

"Go on alone," said Kostílin. "Why should you perish because of me?"

"No I won't go. It won't do to desert a comrade."

Again he took Kostílin on his shoulders and staggered on. They went on in that way for another half-mile or more. They were still in the forest, and could not see the end of it. But the mist was already dispersing, and clouds seemed to be gathering; the stars were no longer to be seen. Zhílin was quite done up. They came to a spring walled in with stones by the side of the path. Zhílin stopped and set Kostílin down.

"Let me have a rest and a drink," said he, "and let us eat some of the cheese. It can't be much farther now."

But hardly had he lain down to get a drink, when he heard the sound of horses' feet behind him. Again they darted to the right among the bushes, and lay down under a steep slope.

They heard Tartar voices. The Tartars stopped at the very spot where they had turned off the path. The Tartars talked a bit, and then seemed to be setting a dog on the scent. There was a sound of crackling twigs, and a strange dog appeared from behind the bushes. It stopped, and began to bark.

Then the Tartars, also strangers, came climbing down, seized Zhílin and Kostílin, bound them, put them on horses, and rode away with them.

When they had ridden about two miles, they met Abdul, their owner, with two other Tartars following him. After talking with the strangers, he put Zhílin and Kostílin on two of his own horses and took them back to the Aoul.

Abdul did not laugh now, and did not say a word to them.

They were back at the Aoul by daybreak, and were set down in the street. The children came crowding round, throwing stones, shrieking, and beating them with whips.

The Tartars gathered together in a circle, and the old man from the foot of the hill was also there. They began discussing; and Zhílin heard them considering what should be done with him and Kostílin. Some said they ought to be sent farther into the mountains; but the old man said: "They must be killed!"

Abdul disputed with him, saying: "I gave money for them, and I must get ransom for them." But the old man said: "They will pay you nothing, but will only bring misfortune. It is a sin to feed Russians. Kill them, and have done with it!"

They dispersed. When they had gone, the master came up to Zhílin and said: "If the money for your ransom is not sent within a fortnight, I will flog you; and if you try to run away again, I'll kill you like a dog! Write a letter, and write properly!"

Paper was brought to them, and they wrote the letters. Shackles were put on their feet, and they were taken behind the Mosque to a deep pit about twelve feet square, into which they were let down.

VI

Life was now very hard for them. Their shackles were never taken off, and they were not let out into the fresh air. Unbaked dough was thrown to them as if they were dogs, and water was let down in a can.

It was wet and close in the pit, and there was a horrible stench. Kostílin grew quite ill, his body became swollen and he ached all over, and moaned or slept all the time. Zhílin, too, grew downcast; he saw it was a bad look-out, and could think of no way of escape.

He tried to make a tunnel, but there was nowhere to put the earth. His master noticed it, and threatened to kill him.

He was sitting on the floor of the pit one day, thinking of freedom and feeling very downhearted, when suddenly a cake fell into his lap, then another, and then a shower of cherries. He looked up, and there was Dina. She looked at him, laughed, and ran away. And Zhílin thought: "Might not Dina help me?"

He cleared out a little place in the pit, scraped up some clay, and began modelling toys. He made men, horses, and dogs, thinking, "When Dina comes I'll throw them up to her."

But Dina did not come next day. Zhílin heard the tramp of horses; some men rode past, and the Tartars gathered in council near the Mosque. They shouted and argued; the word 'Russians' was repeated several times. He could hear the voice of the old man. Though he could not distinguish what was said, he guessed that Russian troops were somewhere near, and that the Tartars, afraid they might come into the Aoul, did not know what to do with their prisoners.

After talking awhile, they went away. Suddenly he heard a rustling overhead, and saw Dina crouching at the edge of the pit, her knees higher than her head, and bending over so that the coins of her plait dangled above the pit. Her eyes gleamed like stars. She drew two cheeses out of her sleeve and threw them to him. Zhílin took them and said, "Why did you not come before? I have made some toys for you. Here, catch!" And he began throwing the toys up, one by one.

But she shook her head and would not look at them.

"I don't want any," she said. She sat silent for a while, and then went on, "Iván, they want to kill you!" And she pointed to her own throat.

"Who wants to kill me?"

"Father; the old men say he must. But I am sorry for you!"

Zhílin answered: "Well, if you are sorry for me, bring me a long pole."

She shook her head, as much as to say, "I can't!"

He clasped his hands and prayed her: "Dina, please do! Dear Dina, I beg of you!"

"I can't!" she said, "They would see me bringing it. They're all at home." And she went away.

So when evening came Zhílin still sat looking up now and then, and wondering what would happen. The stars were there, but the moon had not yet risen. The Mullah's voice was heard; then all was silent. Zhílin was beginning to doze, thinking: "The girl will be afraid to do it!"

Suddenly he felt clay falling on his head. He looked up, and saw a long pole poking into the opposite wall of the pit. It kept poking about for a time, and then it came down, sliding into the pit. Zhílin was glad indeed. He took hold of it and lowered it. It was a strong pole, one that he had seen before on the roof of his master's hut.

He looked up. The stars were shining high in the sky, and just above the pit Dina's eyes gleamed in the dark like a cat's. She stooped with her face close to the edge of the pit, and whispered, "Iván! Iván!" waving her hand in front of her face to show that he should speak low.

"What?" said Zhílin.

"All but two have gone away."

Then Zhílin said, "Well, Kostílin, come; let us have one last try; I'll help you up."

But Kostílin would not hear of it.

"No," said he, "It's clear I can't get away from here. How can I go, when I have hardly strength to turn round?"

"Well, goodbye, then! Don't think ill of me!" and they kissed each other. Zhílin seized the pole, told Dina to hold on, and began to climb. He slipped once or twice; the shackles hindered him. Kostílin helped him, and he managed to get to the top. Dina, with her little hands, pulled with all her might at his shirt, laughing.

Zhílin drew out the pole and said, "Put it back in its place, Dina, or they'll notice, and you will be beaten."

She dragged the pole away, and Zhílin went down the hill. When he had gone down the steep incline, he took a sharp stone and tried to wrench the lock off the shackles. But it was a strong lock and he could not manage to break it, and besides, it was difficult to get at. Then he heard someone running down the hill, springing lightly. He thought: "Surely, that's Dina again."

Dina came, took a stone, and said, "Let me try."

She knelt down and tried to wrench the lock off, but her little hands were as slender as little twigs, and she had not the strength. She threw the stone away and began to cry. Then Zhílin set to work again at the lock, and Dina squatted beside him with her hand on his shoulder.

Zhílin looked round and saw a red light to the left behind the hill. The moon was just rising. "Ah!" he thought, "before the moon has risen I must have passed the valley and be in the forest." So he rose and threw away the stone. Shackles or no, he must go on.

"Goodbye, Dina dear!" he said. "I shall never forget you!"

Dina seized hold of him and felt about with her hands for a place to put some cheeses she had brought. He took them from her.

"Thank you, my little one. Who will make dolls for you when I am gone?" And he stroked her head.

Dina burst into tears, hiding her face in her hands. Then she ran up the hill like a young goat, the coins in her plait clinking against her back.

Zhílin crossed himself, took the lock of his shackles in his hand to prevent its clattering, and went along the road, dragging his shackled leg, and looking towards the place where the moon was about to rise. He now knew the way. If he went straight he would have to walk nearly six miles. If only he could reach the wood before the moon had quite risen! He crossed the river; the light behind the hill was growing whiter. Still looking at it, he went along the valley. The moon was not yet visible. The light became brighter, and one side of the valley was growing lighter and lighter, and shadows were drawing in towards the foot of the hill, creeping nearer and nearer to him.

Zhílin went on, keeping in the shade. He was hurrying, but the moon was moving still faster; the tops of the hills on the right were already lit up. As he got near the wood the white moon appeared from behind the hills, and it became light as day. One could see all the leaves on the trees. It was light on the hill, but silent, as if nothing were alive; no sound could be heard but the gurgling of the river below.

Zhílin reached the wood without meeting any one, chose a dark spot, and sat down to rest.

He rested, and ate one of the cheeses. Then he found a stone and set to work again to knock off the shackles. He knocked his hands sore, but could not break the lock. He rose and went along the road. After walking the greater part of a mile he was quite done up, and his feet were aching. He had to stop every ten steps. "There is nothing else for it," thought he. "I must drag on as long as I have any strength left. If I sit down, I shan't be able to rise again. I can't reach the fortress; but when day breaks I'll lie down in the forest, remain there all day, and go on again at night."

He went on all night. Two Tartars on horseback passed him; but he heard them a long way off, and hid behind a tree.

The moon began to grow paler, the dew to fall. It was getting near dawn, and Zhílin had not reached the end of the forest. "Well," thought he, "I'll walk another thirty steps, and then turn in among the trees and sit down."

He walked another thirty steps, and saw that he was at the end of the forest. He went to the edge; it was now quite light, and straight before him was the plain and the fortress. To the left, quite close at the foot of the slope, a fire was dying out, and the smoke from it spread round. There were men gathered about the fire.

He looked intently, and saw guns glistening. They were soldiers—Cossacks!

Zhílin was filled with joy. He collected his remaining strength and set off down the hill, saying to himself: "God forbid that any mounted Tartar should see me now, in the open field! Near as I am, I could not get there in time."

Hardly had he said this when, a couple of hundred yards off, on a hillock to the left, he saw three Tartars.

They saw him also and made a rush. His heart sank. He waved his hands, and shouted with all his might, "Brothers, brothers! Help!"

The Cossacks heard him, and a party of them on horseback darted to cut across the Tartars' path. The Cossacks were far and the Tartars were near; but Zhílin, too, made a last effort. Lifting the shackles with his hand, he ran towards the Cossacks, hardly knowing what he was doing, crossing himself and shouting, "Brothers! Brothers! Brothers!"

There were some fifteen Cossacks. The Tartars were frightened, and stopped before reaching him. Zhílin staggered up to the Cossacks.

They surrounded him and began questioning him. "Who are you? What are you? Where from?"

But Zhílin was quite beside himself, and could only weep and repeat, "Brothers! Brothers!"

Then the soldiers came running up and crowded round Zhílin—one giving him bread, another buckwheat, a third vódka: one wrapping a cloak round him, another breaking his shackles.

The officers recognized him, and rode with him to the fortress. The soldiers were glad to see him back, and his comrades all gathered round him.

Zhílin told them all that had happened to him.

"That's the way I went home and got married!" said he. "No. It seems plain that fate was against it!"

So he went on serving in the Caucasus. A month passed before Kostílin was released, after paying five thousand roubles ransom. He was almost dead when they brought him back.

God Sees the Truth, But Waits

[Written and first published in 1872. Also translated as 'Exiled to Siberia' (1887). The version here is taken from the collection *Twenty-three Tales* (1906) translated by Louise and Aylmer Maude.

The story was adapted into *Katha Sagar* (1896), an Indian television series directed by Shyam Benegal.]

In the town of Vladímir lived a young merchant named Iván Dmitritch Aksyónof. He had two shops and a house of his own.

Aksyónof was a handsome, fair-haired, curly-headed fellow, full of fun, and very fond of singing. When quite a young man he had been given to drink, and was riotous when he had had too much; but after he married he gave up drinking, except now and then.

One summer Aksyónof was going to the Nízhny Fair, and as he bade goodbye to his family his wife said to him, "Iván Dmitritch, do not start today; I have had a bad dream about you."

Aksyónof laughed, and said, "You are afraid that when I get to the fair I shall go on the spree."

His wife replied: "I do not know what I am afraid of; all I know is that I had a bad dream. I dreamt you returned from the town, and when you took off your cap I saw that your hair was quite grey."

Aksyónof laughed. "That's a lucky sign," said he. "See if I don't sell out all my goods, and bring you some presents from the fair."

So he said goodbye to his family, and drove away.

When he had travelled half-way, he met a merchant whom he knew, and they put up at the same inn for the night. They had some tea together, and then went to bed in adjoining rooms.

It was not Aksyónof's habit to sleep late, and, wishing to travel while it was still cool, he aroused his driver before dawn, and told him to put in the horses.

Then he made his way across to the landlord of the inn (who lived in a cottage at the back), paid his bill, and continued his journey.

When he had gone about twenty-five miles, he stopped for the horses to be fed. Aksyónof rested awhile in the passage of the inn, then he stepped out into the porch, and, ordering a *samovár** to be heated, got out his guitar and began to play.

---

* The *samovár* ('self-boiler') is an urn in which water can be heated and kept on the boil.

Suddenly a *troika* drove up with tinkling bells, and an official alighted, followed by two soldiers. He came to Aksyónof and began to question him, asking him who he was and whence he came. Aksyónof answered him fully, and said, "Won't you have some tea with me?" But the official went on cross-questioning him and asking him, "Where did you spend last night? Were you alone, or with a fellow-merchant? Did you see the other merchant this morning? Why did you leave the inn before dawn?"

Aksyónof wondered why he was asked all these questions, but he described all that had happened, and then added, "Why do you cross-question me as if I were a thief or a robber? I am travelling on business of my own, and there is no need to question me."

Then the official, calling the soldiers, said, "I am the police officer of this district, and I question you because the merchant with whom you spent last night has been found with his throat cut. We must search your things."

They entered the house. The soldiers and the police officer unstrapped Aksyónof's luggage and searched it. Suddenly the officer drew a knife out of a bag, crying, "Whose knife is this?"

Aksyónof looked, and seeing a blood-stained knife taken from his bag, he was frightened.

"How is it there is blood on this knife?"

Aksyónof tried to answer, but could hardly utter a word, and only stammered: "I—I don't know—not mine."

Then the police officer said, "This morning the merchant was found in bed with his throat cut. You are the only person who could have done it. The house was locked from inside, and no one else was there. Here is this blood-stained knife in your bag, and your face and manner betray you! Tell me how you killed him, and how much money you stole?"

Aksyónof swore he had not done it; that he had not seen the merchant after they had had tea together; that he had no money except eight thousand roubles* of his own, and that the knife was

---

* The value of the rouble has varied at different times from more than three shillings to less than two shillings. For the purposes of ready calculation it

not his. But his voice was broken, his face pale, and he trembled with fear as though he were guilty.

The police officer ordered the soldiers to bind Aksyónof and to put him in the cart. As they tied his feet together and flung him into the cart, Aksyónof crossed himself and wept. His money and goods were taken from him, and he was sent to the nearest town and imprisoned there. Enquiries as to his character were made in Vladímir. The merchants and other inhabitants of that town said that in former days he used to drink and waste his time, but that he was a good man. Then the trial came on: he was charged with murdering a merchant from Ryazan, and robbing him of twenty thousand roubles.

His wife was in despair, and did not know what to believe. Her children were all quite small; one was a baby at her breast. Taking them all with her, she went to the town where her husband was in gaol. At first she was not allowed to see him; but, after much begging, she obtained permission from the officials, and was taken to him. When she saw her husband in prison dress and in chains, shut up with thieves and criminals, she fell down, and did not come to her senses for a long time. Then she drew her children to her, and sat down near him. She told him of things at home, and asked about what had happened to him. He told her all, and she asked, "What can we do now?"

"We must petition the Tsar not to let an innocent man perish."

His wife told him that she had sent a petition to the Tsar, but that it had not been accepted.

Aksyónof did not reply, but only looked downcast.

Then his wife said, "It was not for nothing I dreamt your hair had turned grey. You remember? You should not have started that day." And passing her fingers through his hair, she said: "Ványa dearest, tell your wife the truth; was it not you who did it?"

"So you, too, suspect me!" said Aksyónof, and, hiding his face in his hands, he began to weep. Then a soldier came to say that the

---

may be taken as two shillings. In reading these stories to children, the word 'florin' can be substituted for 'rouble' if preferred.

wife and children must go away; and Aksyónof said goodbye to his family for the last time.

When they were gone, Aksyónof recalled what had been said, and when he remembered that his wife also had suspected him, he said to himself, "It seems that only God can know the truth; it is to Him alone we must appeal, and from Him alone expect mercy."

And Aksyónof wrote no more petitions; gave up all hope, and only prayed to God.

Aksyónof was condemned to be flogged and sent to the mines. So he was flogged with a knout, and when the wounds made by the knout were healed, he was driven to Siberia with other convicts.

For twenty-six years Aksyónof lived as a convict in Siberia. His hair turned white as snow, and his beard grew long, thin, and grey. All his mirth went; he stooped; he walked slowly, spoke little, and never laughed, but he often prayed.

In prison Aksyónof learnt to make boots, and earned a little money, with which he bought *The Lives of the Saints*. He read this book when there was light enough in the prison; and on Sundays in the prison-church he read the lessons and sang in the choir; for his voice was still good.

The prison authorities liked Aksyónof for his meekness, and his fellow-prisoners respected him: they called him 'Grandfather,' and 'The Saint.' When they wanted to petition the prison authorities about anything, they always made Aksyónof their spokesman, and when there were quarrels among the prisoners they came to him to put things right, and to judge the matter.

No news reached Aksyónof from his home, and he did not even know if his wife and children were still alive.

One day a fresh gang of convicts came to the prison. In the evening the old prisoners collected round the new ones and asked them what towns or villages they came from, and what they were sentenced for. Among the rest Aksyónof sat down near the newcomers, and listened with downcast air to what was said.

One of the new convicts, a tall, strong man of sixty, with a closely-cropped grey beard, was telling the others what he had been arrested for.

"Well, friends," he said, "I only took a horse that was tied to a sledge, and I was arrested and accused of stealing. I said I had only taken it to get home quicker, and had then let it go; besides, the driver was a personal friend of mine. So I said, 'It's all right.' 'No,' said they, 'you stole it.' But how or where I stole it they could not say. I once really did something wrong, and ought by rights to have come here long ago, but that time I was not found out. Now I have been sent here for nothing at all . . . Eh, but it's lies I'm telling you; I've been to Siberia before, but I did not stay long."

"Where are you from?" asked someone.

"From Vladímir. My family are of that town. My name is Makár, and they also call me Semyónitch."

Aksyónof raised his head and said: "Tell me, Semyónitch, do you know anything of the merchants Aksyónof of Vladímir? Are they still alive?"

"Know them? Of course I do. The Aksyónofs are rich, though their father is in Siberia: a sinner like ourselves, it seems! As for you, Gran'dad, how did you come here?"

Aksyónof did not like to speak of his misfortune. He only sighed, and said, "For my sins I have been in prison these twenty-six years."

"What sins?" asked Makár Semyónitch.

But Aksyónof only said, "Well, well—I must have deserved it!" He would have said no more, but his companions told the newcomer how Aksyónof came to be in Siberia: how someone had killed a merchant, and had put a knife among Aksyónof's things, and Aksyónof had been unjustly condemned.

When Makár Semyónitch heard this, he looked at Aksyónof, slapped his own knee, and exclaimed, "Well, this is wonderful! Really wonderful! But how old you've grown, Gran'dad!"

The others asked him why he was so surprised, and where he had seen Aksyónof before; but Makár Semyónitch did not reply. He only said: "It's wonderful that we should meet here, lads!"

These words made Aksyónof wonder whether this man knew who had killed the merchant; so he said, "Perhaps, Semyónitch, you have heard of that affair, or maybe you've seen me before?"

"How could I help hearing? The world's full of rumours. But it's long ago, and I've forgotten what I heard."

"Perhaps you heard who killed the merchant?" asked Aksyónof.

Makár Semyónitch laughed, and replied, "It must have been him in whose bag the knife was found! If someone else hid the knife there, 'He's not a thief till he's caught,' as the saying is. How could anyone put a knife into your bag while it was under your head? It would surely have woken you up?"

When Aksyónof heard these words, he felt sure this was the man who had killed the merchant. He rose and went away. All that night Aksyónof lay awake. He felt terribly unhappy, and all sorts of images rose in his mind. There was the image of his wife as she was when he parted from her to go to the fair. He saw her as if she were present; her face and her eyes rose before him; he heard her speak and laugh. Then he saw his children, quite little, as they were at that time: one with a little cloak on, another at his mother's breast. And then he remembered himself as he used to be—young and merry. He remembered how he sat playing the guitar in the porch of the inn where he was arrested, and how free from care he had been. He saw, in his mind, the place where he was flogged, the executioner, and the people standing around; the chains, the convicts, all the twenty-six years of his prison life, and his premature old age. The thought of it all made him so wretched that he was ready to kill himself.

"And it's all that villain's doing!" thought Aksyónof. And his anger was so great against Makár Semyónitch that he longed for vengeance, even if he himself should perish for it. He kept repeating prayers all night, but could get no peace. During the day he did not go near Makár Semyónitch, nor even look at him.

A fortnight passed in this way. Aksyónof could not sleep at nights, and was so miserable that he did not know what to do.

One night as he was walking about the prison he noticed some earth that came rolling out from under one of the shelves on which the prisoners slept. He stopped to see what it was. Suddenly Makár Semyónitch crept out from under the shelf, and looked up at Aksyónof with frightened face. Aksyónof tried to pass without looking at him, but Makár seized his hand and told him that he had dug a hole under the wall, getting rid of the earth by putting it into his high-boots, and emptying it out every day on the road when the prisoners were driven to their work.

"Just you keep quiet, old man, and you shall get out too. If you blab they'll flog the life out of me, but I will kill you first."

Aksyónof trembled with anger as he looked at his enemy. He drew his hand away, saying, "I have no wish to escape, and you have no need to kill me; you killed me long ago! As to telling of you—I may do so or not, as God shall direct."

Next day, when the convicts were led out to work, the convoy soldiers noticed that one or other of the prisoners emptied some earth out of his boots. The prison was searched, and the tunnel found. The Governor came and questioned all the prisoners to find out who had dug the hole. They all denied any knowledge of it. Those who knew, would not betray Makár Semyónitch, knowing he would be flogged almost to death. At last the Governor turned to Aksyónof, whom he knew to be a just man, and said:

"You are a truthful old man; tell me, before God, who dug the hole?"

Makár Semyónitch stood as if he were quite unconcerned, looking at the Governor and not so much as glancing at Aksyónof. Aksyónof's lips and hands trembled, and for a long time he could not utter a word. He thought, "Why should I screen him who ruined my life? Let him pay for what I have suffered. But if I tell, they will probably flog the life out of him, and maybe I suspect him wrongly. And, after all, what good would it be to me?"

"Well, old man," repeated the Governor, "tell us the truth: who has been digging under the wall?"

Aksyónof glanced at Makár Semyónitch, and said, "I cannot say, your honour. It is not God's will that I should tell! Do what you like with me; I am in your hands."

However much the Governor tried, Aksyónof would say no more, and so the matter had to be left.

That night, when Aksyónof was lying on his bed and just beginning to doze, someone came quietly and sat down on his bed. He peered through the darkness and recognized Makár.

"What more do you want of me?" asked Aksyónof. "Why have you come here?"

Makár Semyónitch was silent. So Aksyónof sat up and said, "What do you want? Go away, or I will call the guard!"

Makár Semyónitch bent close over Aksyónof, and whispered, "Iván Dmitritch, forgive me!"

"What for?" asked Aksyónof.

"It was I who killed the merchant and hid the knife among your things. I meant to kill you too, but I heard a noise outside; so I hid the knife in your bag and escaped out of the window."

Aksyónof was silent, and did not know what to say. Makár Semyónitch slid off the bed-shelf and knelt upon the ground. "Iván Dmitritch," said he, "forgive me! For the love of God, forgive me! I will confess that it was I who killed the merchant, and you will be released and can go to your home."

"It is easy for you to talk," said Aksyónof, "but I have suffered for you these twenty-six years. Where could I go to now? . . . My wife is dead, and my children have forgotten me. I have nowhere to go . . ."

Makár Semyónitch did not rise, but beat his head on the floor. "Iván Dmitritch, forgive me!" he cried. "When they flogged me with the knout it was not so hard to bear as it is to see you now . . . yet you had pity on me, and did not tell. For Christ's sake forgive me, wretch that I am!" And he began to sob.

When Aksyónof heard him sobbing he, too, began to weep.

"God will forgive you!" said he. "Maybe I am a hundred times worse than you." And at these words his heart grew light, and the longing for home left him. He no longer had any desire to leave the prison, but only hoped for his last hour to come.

In spite of what Aksyónof had said, Makár Semyónitch confessed his guilt. But when the order for his release came, Aksyónof was already dead.

The Bear-Hunt

[Written around 1872. Also translated as 'Desire Stronger than Necessity'. This version has been taken from *Twenty-three Tales* (1906), a collection translated by Louise and Aylmer Maude.]

(The adventure here narrated is one that happened to Tolstoy himself in 1858. More than twenty years later he gave up hunting, on humanitarian grounds.)

We were out on a bear-hunting expedition. My comrade had shot at a bear, but only gave him a flesh-wound. There were traces of blood on the snow, but the bear had got away.

We all collected in a group in the forest, to decide whether we ought to go after the bear at once, or wait two or three days till he should settle down again. We asked the peasant bear-drivers whether it would be possible to get round the bear that day.

"No. It's impossible," said an old bear-driver. "You must let the bear quiet down. In five days' time it will be possible to surround him; but if you followed him now, you would only frighten him away, and he would not settle down."

But a young bear-driver began disputing with the old man, saying that it was quite possible to get round the bear now.

"On such snow as this," said he, "he won't go far, for he is a fat bear. He will settle down before evening; or, if not, I can overtake him on snowshoes."

The comrade I was with was against following up the bear, and advised waiting. But I said:

"We need not argue. You do as you like, but I will follow up the track with Damian. If we get round the bear, all right. If not, we lose nothing. It is still early, and there is nothing else for us to do today."

So it was arranged.

The others went back to the sledges, and returned to the village. Damian and I took some bread, and remained behind in the forest.

When they had all left us, Damian and I examined our guns, and after tucking the skirts of our warm coats into our belts, we started off, following the bear's tracks.

The weather was fine, frosty and calm; but it was hard work snow-shoeing. The snow was deep and soft: it had not caked together at all in the forest, and fresh snow had fallen the day before, so that our snowshoes sank six inches deep in the snow, and sometimes more.

The bear's tracks were visible from a distance, and we could see how he had been going; sometimes sinking in up to his belly and ploughing up the snow as he went. At first, while under large trees, we kept in sight of his track; but when it turned into a thicket of small firs, Damian stopped.

"We must leave the trail now," said he. "He has probably settled somewhere here. You can see by the snow that he has been squatting down. Let us leave the track and go round; but we must go quietly. Don't shout or cough, or we shall frighten him away."

Leaving the track, therefore, we turned off to the left. But when we had gone about five hundred yards, there were the bear's traces again right before us. We followed them, and they brought us out on to the road. There we stopped, examining the road to see which way the bear had gone. Here and there in the snow were prints of the bear's paw, claws and all, and here and there the marks of a peasant's bark shoes. The bear had evidently gone towards the village.

As we followed the road, Damian said:

"It's no use watching the road now. We shall see where he has turned off, to right or left, by the marks in the soft snow at the side. He must have turned off somewhere; for he won't have gone on to the village."

We went along the road for nearly a mile, and then saw, ahead of us, the bear's track turning off the road. We examined it. How strange! It was a bear's track right enough, only not going from the road into the forest, but from the forest on to the road! The toes were pointing towards the road.

"This must be another bear," I said.

Damian looked at it, and considered a while.

"No," said he. "It's the same one. He's been playing tricks, and walked backwards when he left the road."

We followed the track, and found it really was so! The bear had gone some ten steps backwards, and then, behind a fir tree, had turned round and gone straight ahead. Damian stopped and said:

"Now, we are sure to get round him. There is a marsh ahead of us, and he must have settled down there. Let us go round it."

We began to make our way round, through a fir thicket. I was tired out by this time, and it had become still more difficult to get along. Now I glided on to juniper bushes and caught my snowshoes in them, now a tiny fir tree appeared between my feet, or, from want of practise, my snowshoes slipped off; and now I came upon a stump or a log hidden by the snow. I was getting very tired, and was drenched with perspiration; and I took off my fur cloak. And there was Damian all the time, gliding along as if in a boat, his snowshoes moving as if of their own accord, never catching against anything, nor slipping off. He even took my fur and slung it over his shoulder, and still kept urging me on.

We went on for two more miles, and came out on the other side of the marsh. I was lagging behind. My snowshoes kept slipping off, and my feet stumbled. Suddenly Damian, who was ahead of me, stopped and waved his arm. When I came up to him, he bent down, pointing with his hand, and whispered:

"Do you see the magpie chattering above that undergrowth? It scents the bear from afar. That is where he must be."

We turned off and went on for more than another half-mile, and presently we came on to the old track again. We had, therefore, been right round the bear, who was now within the track we had left. We stopped, and I took off my cap and loosened all my clothes. I was as hot as in a steam bath, and as wet as a drowned rat. Damian too was flushed, and wiped his face with his sleeve.

"Well, sir," he said, "we have done our job, and now we must have a rest."

The evening glow already showed red through the forest. We took off our snowshoes and sat down on them, and got some bread and salt out of our bags. First I ate some snow, and then some bread; and the bread tasted so good, that I thought I had never in my life had any like it before. We sat there resting until it began to grow dusk, and then I asked Damian if it was far to the village.

"Yes," he said. "It must be about eight miles. We will go on there tonight, but now we must rest. Put on your fur coat, sir, or you'll be catching cold."

Damian flattened down the snow, and breaking off some fir branches made a bed of them. We lay down side by side, resting our heads on our arms. I do not remember how I fell asleep. Two hours later I woke up, hearing something crack.

I had slept so soundly that I did not know where I was. I looked around me. How wonderful! I was in some sort of a hall, all glittering and white with gleaming pillars, and when I looked up I saw, through delicate white tracery, a vault, raven black and studded with coloured lights. After a good look, I remembered that we were in the forest, and that what I took for a hall and pillars, were trees covered with snow and hoar-frost, and the coloured lights were stars twinkling between the branches.

Hoar-frost had settled in the night; all the twigs were thick with it, Damian was covered with it, it was on my fur coat, and it dropped down from the trees. I woke Damian; and we put on our snowshoes and started. It was very quiet in the forest. No sound was heard but that of our snowshoes pushing through the soft snow; except when now and then a tree, cracked by the frost, made the forest resound. Only once we heard the sound of a living creature. Something rustled close to us, and then rushed away. I felt sure it was the bear, but when we went to the spot whence the sound had come, we found the footmarks of hares, and saw several young aspen trees with their bark gnawed. We had startled some hares while they were feeding.

We came out on the road, and followed it, dragging our snowshoes behind us. It was easy walking now. Our snowshoes clattered as they slid behind us from side to side of the hard-trodden road. The snow creaked under our boots, and the cold hoar-frost settled on our faces like down. Seen through the branches, the stars seemed to be running to meet us, now twinkling, now vanishing, as if the whole sky were on the move.

I found my comrade sleeping, but woke him up, and related how we had got round the bear. After telling our peasant host to collect beaters for the morning, we had supper and lay down to sleep.

I was so tired that I could have slept on till midday, if my comrade had not roused me. I jumped up, and saw that he was already dressed, and busy doing something to his gun.

"Where is Damian?" said I.

"In the forest, long ago. He has already been over the tracks you made, and been back here, and now he has gone to look after the beaters."

I washed and dressed, and loaded my guns; and then we got into a sledge, and started.

The sharp frost still continued. It was quiet, and the sun could not be seen. There was a thick mist above us, and hoar-frost still covered everything.

After driving about two miles along the road, as we came near the forest, we saw a cloud of smoke rising from a hollow, and presently reached a group of peasants, both men and women, armed with cudgels.

We got out and went up to them. The men sat roasting potatoes, and laughing and talking with the women.

Damian was there too; and when we arrived the people got up, and Damian led them away to place them in the circle we had made the day before. They went along in single file, men and women, thirty in all. The snow was so deep that we could only see them from their waists upwards. They turned into the forest, and my friend and I followed in their track.

Though they had trodden a path, walking was difficult; but, on the other hand, it was impossible to fall: it was like walking between two walls of snow.

We went on in this way for nearly half a mile, when all at once we saw Damian coming from another direction—running towards us on his snowshoes, and beckoning us to join him. We went towards him, and he showed us where to stand. I took my place, and looked round me.

To my left were tall fir trees, between the trunks of which I could see a good way, and, like a black patch just visible behind the trees, I could see a beater. In front of me was a thicket of young firs, about as high as a man, their branches weighed down and stuck together with snow. Through this copse ran a path thickly covered with snow, and leading straight up to where I stood. The thicket stretched away to the right of me, and ended in a small glade, where I could see Damian placing my comrade.

I examined both my guns, and considered where I had better stand. Three steps behind me was a tall fir.

"That's where I'll stand," thought I, "and then I can lean my second gun against the tree"; and I moved towards the tree, sinking up to my knees in the snow at each step. I trod the snow down, and made a clearance about a yard square, to stand on. One gun I kept in my hand; the other, ready cocked, I placed leaning up against the tree. Then I unsheathed and replaced my dagger, to make sure that I could draw it easily in case of need.

Just as I had finished these preparations, I heard Damian shouting in the forest:

"He's up! He's up!"

And as soon as Damian shouted, the peasants round the circle all replied in their different voices.

"Up, up, up! Ou! Ou! Ou!" shouted the men.

"Ay! Ay! Ay!" screamed the women in high-pitched tones.

The bear was inside the circle, and as Damian drove him on, the people all round kept shouting. Only my friend and I stood silent and motionless, waiting for the bear to come towards us. As I stood gazing and listening, my heart beat violently. I trembled, holding my gun fast.

"Now now," I thought. "He will come suddenly. I shall aim, fire, and he will drop——"

Suddenly, to my left, but at a distance, I heard something falling on the snow. I looked between the tall fir trees, and, some fifty paces off, behind the trunks, saw something big and black. I took aim and waited, thinking:

"Won't he come any nearer?"

As I waited I saw him move his ears, turn, and go back; and then I caught a glimpse of the whole of him in profile. He was an immense brute. In my excitement, I fired, and heard my bullet go 'flop' against a tree. Peering through the smoke, I saw my bear scampering back into the circle, and disappearing among the trees.

"Well," thought I. "My chance is lost. He won't come back to me. Either my comrade will shoot him, or he will escape through the line of beaters. In any case he won't give me another chance."

I reloaded my gun, however, and again stood listening. The peasants were shouting all round, but to the right, not far from where my comrade stood, I heard a woman screaming in a frenzied voice:

"Here he is! Here he is! Come here, come here! Oh! Oh! Ay! Ay!"

Evidently she could see the bear. I had given up expecting him, and was looking to the right at my comrade. All at once I saw Damian with a stick in his hand, and without his snowshoes, running along a footpath towards my friend. He crouched down beside him, pointing his stick as if aiming at something, and then I saw my friend raise his gun and aim in the same direction. Crack! He fired.

"There," thought I. "He has killed him."

But I saw that my comrade did not run towards the bear. Evidently he had missed him, or the shot had not taken full effect.

"The bear will get away," I thought. "He will go back, but he won't come a second time towards me. But what is that?"

Something was coming towards me like a whirlwind, snorting as it came; and I saw the snow flying up quite near me. I glanced straight before me, and there was the bear, rushing along the path through the thicket right at me, evidently beside himself with fear. He was hardly half a dozen paces off, and I could see the whole of him—his black chest and enormous head with a reddish patch. There he was, blundering straight at me, and scattering the snow about as he came. I could see by his eyes that he did not see me, but, mad with fear, was rushing blindly along; and his path led him straight at the tree under which I was standing. I raised my gun and fired. He was almost upon me now, and I saw that I had missed. My bullet had gone past him, and he did not even hear me fire, but still came headlong towards me. I lowered my gun, and fired again, almost touching his head. Crack! I had hit, but not killed him!

He raised his head, and laying his ears back, came at me, showing his teeth.

I snatched at my other gun, but almost before I had touched it, he had flown at me and, knocking me over into the snow, had passed right over me.

"Thank goodness, he has left me," thought I.

I tried to rise, but something pressed me down, and prevented my getting up. The bear's rush had carried him past me, but he had turned back, and had fallen on me with the whole weight of his body. I felt something heavy weighing me down, and something warm above my face, and I realized that he was drawing my whole face into his mouth. My nose was already in it, and I felt the heat of it, and smelt his blood. He was pressing my shoulders down with his paws so that I could not move: all I could do was to draw my head down towards my chest away from his mouth, trying to free my nose and eyes, while he tried to get his teeth into them. Then I felt that he had seized my forehead just under the hair with the teeth of his lower jaw, and the flesh below my eyes with his upper jaw, and was closing his teeth. It was as if my face were being cut with knives. I struggled to get away, while he made haste to close his jaws like a dog gnawing. I managed to twist my face away, but he began drawing it again into his mouth.

"Now," thought I, "my end has come!"

Then I felt the weight lifted, and looking up, I saw that he was no longer there. He had jumped off me and run away.

When my comrade and Damian had seen the bear knock me down and begin worrying me, they rushed to the rescue. My comrade, in his haste, blundered, and instead of following the trodden path, ran into the deep snow and fell down. While he was struggling out of the snow, the bear was gnawing at me. But Damian just as he was, without a gun, and with only a stick in his hand, rushed along the path shouting:

"He's eating the master! He's eating the master!"

And as he ran, he called to the bear:

"Oh you idiot! What are you doing? Leave off! Leave off!"

The bear obeyed him, and leaving me ran away. When I rose, there was as much blood on the snow as if a sheep had been killed, and the flesh hung in rags above my eyes, though in my excitement I felt no pain.

My comrade had come up by this time, and the other people collected round: they looked at my wound, and put snow on it. But I, forgetting about my wounds, only asked:

"Where's the bear? Which way has he gone?"

Suddenly I heard:

"Here he is! Here he is!"

And we saw the bear again running at us. We seized our guns, but before anyone had time to fire he had run past. He had grown ferocious, and wanted to gnaw me again, but seeing so many people he took fright. We saw by his track that his head was bleeding, and we wanted to follow him up; but, as my wounds had become very painful, we went, instead, to the town to find a doctor.

The doctor stitched up my wounds with silk, and they soon began to heal.

A month later we went to hunt that bear again, but I did not get a chance of finishing him. He would not come out of the circle, but went round and round, growling in a terrible voice.

Damian killed him. The bear's lower jaw had been broken, and one of his teeth knocked out by my bullet.

He was a huge creature, and had splendid black fur.

I had him stuffed, and he now lies in my room. The wounds on my forehead healed up so that the scars can scarcely be seen.

Where Love is, There God is Also

[Written and first published in 1885. This story is one of Tolstoy's best-known stories for the people. It is also translated as 'Martin the Cobbler'. The translation reproduced here is by Nathan Haskell Dole published in 1887 by Thomas Y. Crowell & Co.]

In the city lived the shoemaker, Martuin Avdyeitch. He lived in a basement, in a little room with one window. The window looked out on the street. Through the window he used to watch the people passing by; although only their feet could be seen, yet by the boots, Martuin Avdyeitch recognized the people. Martuin Avdyeitch had lived long in one place, and had many acquaintances. Few pairs of boots in his district had not been in his hands once and again. Some he would half-sole, some he would patch, some he would stitch around, and occasionally he would also put on new uppers. And through the window he often recognized his work.

Avdyeitch had plenty to do, because he was a faithful workman, used good material, did not make exorbitant charges, and kept his word. If it was possible for him to finish an order by a certain time, he would accept it; otherwise, he would not deceive you—he would tell you so beforehand. And all knew Avdyeitch, and he was never out of work.

Avdyeitch had always been a good man; but as he grew old, he began to think more about his soul, and get nearer to God. Martuin's wife had died when he was still living with his master. His wife left him a boy three years old. None of their other children had lived. All the eldest had died in childhood. Martuin at first intended to send his little son to his sister in the village, but afterward he felt sorry for him; he thought to himself:—

"It will be hard for my Kapitoshka to live in a strange family. I shall keep him with me."

And Avdyeitch left his master, and went into lodgings with his little son. But God gave Avdyeitch no luck with his children. As Kapitoshka grew older, he began to help his father, and would have been a delight to him, but a sickness fell on him, he went to bed, suffered a week, and died. Martuin buried his son, and fell into despair. So deep was this despair that he began to complain of God. Martuin fell into such a melancholy state, that more than once he prayed to God for death, and reproached God because He had not taken him who was an old man, instead of his beloved only son. Avdyeitch also ceased to go to church.

And once a little old man from the same district came from Troïtsa* to see Avdyeitch; for seven years he had been wandering about. Avdyeitch talked with him, and began to complain about his sorrows.

"I have no desire to live any longer," he said, "I only wish I was dead. That is all I pray God for. I am a man without anything to hope for now."

And the little old man said to him:—

"You don't talk right, Martuin, we must not judge God's doings. The world moves, not by our skill, but by God's will. God decreed for your son to die—for you—to live. So it is for the best. And you are in despair, because you wish to live for your own happiness."

"But what shall one live for?" asked Martuin.

And the little old man said:—

"We must live for God, Martuin. He gives you life, and for His sake you must live. When you begin to live for Him, you will not grieve over anything, and all will seem easy to you."

Martuin kept silent for a moment, and then said, "But how can one live for God?"

And the little old man said:—

"Christ has taught us how to live for God. You know how to read? Buy a Testament, and read it; there you will learn how to live for God. Everything is explained there."

And these words kindled a fire in Avdyeitch's heart. And he went that very same day, bought a New Testament in large print, and began to read.

At first Avdyeitch intended to read only on holidays; but as he began to read, it so cheered his soul that he used to read every

---

* Trinity, a famous monastery, pilgrimage to which is reckoned a virtue. Avdyeitch calls this *zemlyak-starichok*, *Bozhi chelovyek*, God's man.

day. At times he would become so absorbed in reading that all the kerosene in the lamp would burn out, and still he could not tear himself away. And so Avdyeitch used to read every evening.

And the more he read, the clearer he understood what God wanted of him, and how one should live for God; and his heart kept growing easier and easier. Formerly, when he lay down to sleep, he used to sigh and groan, and always thought of his Kapitoshka; and now his only exclamation was:—

"Glory to Thee! Glory to Thee, Lord! Thy will be done."

And from that time Avdyeitch's whole life was changed. In other days he, too, used to drop into a public-house* as a holiday amusement, to drink a cup of tea; and he was not averse to a little brandy, either. He would take a drink with some acquaintance, and leave the saloon, not intoxicated, exactly, yet in a happy frame of mind, and inclined to talk nonsense, and shout, and use abusive language at a person. Now he left off that sort of thing. His life became quiet and joyful. In the morning he would sit down to work, finish his allotted task, then take the little lamp from the hook, put it on the table, get his book from the shelf, open it, and sit down to read. And the more he read, the more he understood, and the brighter and happier it grew in his heart.

Once it happened that Martuin read till late into the night. He was reading the Gospel of Luke. He was reading over the sixth chapter; and he was reading the verses:—

> "And unto him that smiteth thee on the one cheek offer also the other; and him that taketh away thy cloak forbid not to take thy coat also. Give to every man that asketh of thee; and of him that taketh away thy goods ask them not again. And as ye would that men should do to you, do ye also to them likewise."

He read farther also those verses, where God speaks:

---

* *Traktir.*

"And why call ye me, Lord, Lord, and do not the things which I say? Whosoever cometh to me, and heareth my sayings, and doeth them, I will shew you to whom he is like: he is like a man which built an house, and digged deep, and laid the foundation on a rock: and when the flood arose, the stream beat vehemently upon that house, and could not shake it; for it was founded upon a rock. But he that heareth, and doeth not, is like a man that without a foundation built an house upon the earth; against which the stream did beat vehemently, and immediately it fell; and the ruin of that house was great."

Avdyeitch read these words, and joy filled his soul. He took off his spectacles, put them down on the book, leaned his elbows on the table, and became lost in thought. And he began to measure his life by these words. And he thought to himself:—

"Is my house built on the rock, or on the sand? 'Tis well if on the rock. It is so easy when you are alone by yourself; it seems as if you had done everything as God commands; but when you forget yourself, you sin again. Yet I shall still struggle on. It is very good. Help me, Lord!"

Thus ran his thoughts; he wanted to go to bed, but he felt loath to tear himself away from the book. And he began to read farther in the seventh chapter. He read about the centurion, he read about the widow's son, he read about the answer given to John's disciples, and finally he came to that place where the rich Pharisee desired the Lord to sit at meat with him; and he read how the woman that was a sinner anointed His feet, and washed them with her tears, and how He forgave her. He reached the forty-fourth verse, and began to read:—

"And he turned to the woman, and said unto Simon, Seest thou this woman? I entered into thine house, thou gavest me no water for my feet: but she hath washed my feet with tears, and wiped them with the hair of her head. Thou gavest me no kiss: but this woman since the time I came in hath not ceased to kiss my feet. My head with oil thou didst not anoint: but this woman hath anointed my feet with ointment."

He finished reading these verses, and thought to himself:—

"Thou gavest me no water for my feet, thou gavest me no kiss. My head with oil thou didst not anoint."

And again Avdyeitch took off his spectacles, put them down on the book, and again he became lost in thought.

"It seems that Pharisee must have been such a man as I am. I, too, apparently have thought only of myself—how I might have my tea, be warm and comfortable, but never to think about my guest. He thought about himself, but there was not the least care taken of the guest. And who was his guest? The Lord Himself. If He had come to me, should I have done the same way?"

Avdyeitch rested his head upon both his arms, and did not notice that he fell asleep.

"Martuin!" suddenly seemed to sound in his ears.

Martuin started from his sleep:—

"Who is here?"

He turned around, glanced toward the door—no one.

Again he fell into a doze. Suddenly, he plainly heard:—

"Martuin! Ah, Martuin! Look tomorrow on the street. I am coming."

Martuin awoke, rose from the chair, and began to rub his eyes. He himself could not tell whether he heard those words in his dream, or in reality. He turned down his lamp, and went to bed.

At daybreak next morning, Avdyeitch rose, made his prayer to God, lighted the stove, put on the *shchi** and the *kasha*,† put

---

* Cabbage-soup.
† Gruel.

the water in the samovar, put on his apron, and sat down by the window to work.

And while he was working, he kept thinking about all that had happened the day before. It seemed to him at one moment that it was a dream, and now he had really heard a voice.

"Well," he said to himself, "such things have been."

Martuin was sitting by the window, and looking out more than he was working. When anyone passed by in boots which he did not know, he would bend down, look out of the window, in order to see, not only the feet, but also the face.

The *dvornik*[*] passed by in new felt boots,[†] the water-carrier passed by; then there came up to the window an old soldier of Nicholas's time, in an old pair of laced felt boots, with a shovel in his hands. Avdyeitch recognized him by his felt boots. The old man's name was Stepanuitch; and a neighbouring merchant, out of charity, gave him a home with him. He was required to assist the dvornik. Stepanuitch began to shovel away the snow from in front of Avdyeitch's window. Avdyeitch glanced at him, and took up his work again.

"Pshaw! I must be getting crazy in my old age," said Avdyeitch, and laughed at himself. "Stepanuitch is clearing away the snow, and I imagine that Christ is coming to see me. I was entirely out of my mind, old dotard that I am!"

Avdyeitch sewed about a dozen stitches, and then felt impelled to look through the window again. He looked out again through the window, and saw that Stepanuitch had leaned his shovel against the wall, and was warming himself, and resting. He was an old, broken-down man; evidently he had not strength enough even to shovel the snow. Avdyeitch said to himself:—

"I will give him some tea; by the way, the samovar has only just gone out." Avdyeitch laid down his awl, rose from his seat, put the samovar on the table, poured out the tea, and tapped with his finger at the glass. Stepanuitch turned around, and came

---

[*] House-porter.
[†] *Valenki.*

to the window. Avdyeitch beckoned to him, and went to open the door.

"Come in, warm yourself a little," he said. "You must be cold."

"May Christ reward you for this! My bones ache," said Stepanuitch.

Stepanuitch came in, and shook off the snow, tried to wipe his feet, so as not to soil the floor, but staggered.

"Don't trouble to wipe your feet. I will clean it up myself; we are used to such things. Come in and sit down," said Avdyeitch. "Here, drink a cup of tea."

And Avdyeitch lifted two glasses, and handed one to his guest; while he himself poured his tea into a saucer, and began to blow it.

Stepanuitch finished drinking his glass of tea, turned the glass upside down,* put the half-eaten lump of sugar on it, and began to express his thanks. But it was evident he wanted some more.

"Have some more," said Avdyeitch, filling both his own glass and his guest's. Avdyeitch drank his tea, but from time to time glanced out into the street.

"Are you expecting anyone?" asked his guest.

"Am I expecting anyone? I am ashamed even to tell whom I expect. I am, and I am not, expecting someone; but one word has kindled a fire in my heart. Whether it is a dream, or something else, I do not know. Don't you see, brother, I was reading yesterday the Gospel about Christ the Batyushka; how He suffered, how He walked on the earth. I suppose you have heard about it?"

"Indeed I have," replied Stepanuitch; "but we are people in darkness, we can't read."

"Well, now, I was reading about that very thing—how He walked on the earth; I read, you know, how He came to the Pharisee, and the Pharisee did not treat Him hospitably. Well, and so, my brother, I was reading yesterday, about this very thing, and was thinking to myself how he did not receive Christ, the Batyushka, with honour. Suppose, for example, He should come to me, or anyone else, I said to myself, I should not even know how

---

* To signify he was satisfied; a custom among the Russians.

to receive Him. And he gave Him no reception at all. Well! While I was thus thinking, I fell asleep, brother, and I heard someone call me by name. I got up; the voice, just as if someone whispered, said, 'Be on the watch; I shall come tomorrow.' And this happened twice. Well! Would you believe it, it got into my head? I scolded myself—and yet I am expecting Him, the Batyushka."

Stepanuitch shook his head, and said nothing; he finished drinking his glass of tea, and put it on the side; but Avdyeitch picked up the glass again, and filled it once more.

"Drink some more for your good health. You see, I have an idea that, when the Batyushka went about on this earth, He disdained no one, and had more to do with the simple people. He always went to see the simple people. He picked out His disciples more from among folk like such sinners as we are, from the working class. Said He, whoever exalts himself, shall be humbled, and he who is humbled shall become exalted. Said He, you call me Lord, and, said He, I wash your feet. Whoever wishes, said He, to be the first, the same shall be a servant to all. Because, said He, blessed are the poor, the humble, the kind, the generous."

And Stepanuitch forgot about his tea; he was an old man, and easily moved to tears. He was listening, and the tears rolled down his face.

"Come, now, have some more tea," said Avdyeitch; but Stepanuitch made the sign of the cross, thanked him, turned down his glass, and arose.

"Thanks to you," he says, "Martuin Avdyeitch, for treating me kindly, and satisfying me, soul and body."

"You are welcome; come in again; always glad to see a friend," said Avdyeitch.

Stepanuitch departed; and Martuin poured out the rest of the tea, drank it up, put away the dishes, and sat down again by the window to work, to stitch on a patch. He kept stitching away, and at the same time looking through the window. He was expecting Christ, and was all the while thinking of Him and His deeds, and his head was filled with the different speeches of Christ.

Two soldiers passed by: one wore boots furnished by the

crown, and the other one, boots that he had made; then the master[*] of the next house passed by in shining galoshes; then a baker with a basket passed by. All passed by; and now there came also by the window a woman in woollen stockings and rustic bashmaks on her feet. She passed by the window, and stood still near the window-case.

Avdyeitch looked up at her from the window, and saw it was a stranger, a woman poorly clad, and with a child; she was standing by the wall with her back to the wind, trying to wrap up the child, and she had nothing to wrap it up in. The woman was dressed in shabby summer clothes; and from behind the frame, Avdyeitch could hear the child crying, and the woman trying to pacify it; but she was not able to pacify it.

Avdyeitch got up, went to the door, ascended the steps, and cried:—

"My good woman. Hey! My good woman!"[†]

The woman heard him and turned around.

"Why are you standing in the cold with the child? Come into my room, where it is warm; you can manage it better. Here, this way!"

The woman was astonished. She saw an old, old man in an apron, with spectacles on his nose, calling her to him. She followed him. They descended the steps and entered the room; the old man led the woman to his bed.

"There," says he, "sit down, my good woman, nearer to the stove; you can get warm, and nurse the little one."

"I have no milk for him. I myself have not eaten anything since morning," said the woman; but, nevertheless, she took the baby to her breast.

Avdyeitch shook his head, went to the table, brought out the bread and a dish, opened the oven door, poured into the dish some cabbage soup, took out the pot with the gruel, but it was not cooked as yet; so he filled the dish with shchi only, and put it on

---

* *Khozyaïn.*

† *Umnitsa aumnitsa!* literally, clever one.

the table. He got the bread, took the towel down from the hook, and spread it upon the table.

"Sit down," he said, "and eat, my good woman; and I will mind the little one. You see, I once had children of my own; I know how to handle them."

The woman crossed herself, sat down at the table, and began to eat; while Avdyeitch took a seat on the bed near the infant. Avdyeitch kept smacking and smacking to it with his lips; but it was a poor kind of smacking, for he had no teeth. The little one kept on crying. And it occurred to Avdyeitch to threaten the little one with his finger; he waved, waved his finger right before the child's mouth, and hastily withdrew it. He did not put it to its mouth, because his finger was black, and soiled with wax. And the little one looked at his finger, and became quiet; then it began to smile, and Avdyeitch also was glad. While the woman was eating, she told who she was, and whither she was going.

Said she:—

"I am a soldier's wife. It is now seven months since they sent my husband away off, and no tidings. I lived out as cook; the baby was born; no one cared to keep me with a child. This is the third month that I have been struggling along without a place. I ate up all I had. I wanted to engage as a wet-nurse—no one would take me—I am too thin, they say. I have just been to the merchant's wife, where lives a young woman I know, and so they promised to take us in. I thought that was the end of it. But she told me to come next week. And she lives a long way off. I got tired out; and it tired him, too, my heart's darling. Fortunately, our landlady takes pity on us for the sake of Christ, and gives us a room, else I don't know how I should manage to get along."

Avdyeitch sighed, and said:

"Haven't you any warm clothes?"

"Now is the time, friend, to wear warm clothes; but yesterday I pawned my last shawl for a twenty-kopek piece."*

The woman came to the bed, and took the child; and Avdyeitch

---

* *Dvagrivennui*, silver, worth sixteen cents.

rose, went to the partition, rummaged round, and succeeded in finding an old coat.

"Na!" says he; "It is a poor thing, yet you may turn it to some use."

The woman looked at the coat and looked at the old man; she took the coat, and burst into tears; and Avdyeitch turned away his head; crawling under the bed, he pushed out a little trunk, rummaged in it, and sat down again opposite the woman.

And the woman said:—

"May Christ bless you, little grandfather!* He must have sent me to your window. My little baby would have frozen to death. When I started out it was warm, but now it has grown cold. And He, the Batyushka, led you to look through the window and take pity on me, an unfortunate."

Avdyeitch smiled, and said:—

"Indeed, He did that! I have been looking through the window, my good woman, for some wise reason."

And Martuin told the soldier's wife his dream, and how he heard the voice—how the Lord promised to come and see him that day.

"All things are possible," said the woman. She rose, put on the coat, wrapped up her little child in it; and, as she started to take leave, she thanked Avdyeitch again.

"Take this, for Christ's sake," said Avdyeitch, giving her a twenty-kopek piece; "redeem your shawl."

She made the sign of the cross, and Avdyeitch made the sign of the cross and went with her to the door.

The woman went away. Avdyeitch ate some shchi, washed the dishes, and sat down again to work. While he was working he still remembered the window; when the window grew darker he immediately looked out to see who was passing by. Acquaintances passed by and strangers passed by, and there was nothing out of the ordinary.

But here Avdyeitch saw that an old apple woman had stopped

---

* *Diedushka.*

206

in front of his window. She carried a basket with apples. Only a few were left, as she had evidently sold them nearly all out; and over her shoulder she had a bag full of chips. She must have gathered them up in some new building, and was on her way home. One could see that the bag was heavy on her shoulder; she tried to shift it to the other shoulder. So she lowered the bag on the sidewalk, stood the basket with the apples on a little post, and began to shake down the splinters in the bag. And while she was shaking her bag, a little boy in a torn cap came along, picked up an apple from the basket, and was about to make his escape; but the old woman noticed it, turned around, and caught the youngster by his sleeve. The little boy began to struggle, tried to tear himself away; but the old woman grasped him with both hands, knocked off his cap, and caught him by the hair.

The little boy was screaming, the old woman was scolding. Avdyeitch lost no time in putting away his awl; he threw it upon the floor, sprang to the door—he even stumbled on the stairs, and dropped his spectacles—and rushed out into the street.

The old woman was pulling the youngster by his hair, and was scolding and threatening to take him to the policeman; the youngster was defending himself, and denying the charge.

"I did not take it," he said; "What are you licking me for? Let me go!"

Avdyeitch tried to separate them. He took the boy by his arm, and said:—

"Let him go, babushka; forgive him, for Christ's sake."

"I will forgive him so that he won't forget it till the new broom grows. I am going to take the little villain to the police."

Avdyeitch began to entreat the old woman:—

"Let him go, babushka," he said, "he will never do it again. Let him go, for Christ's sake."

The old woman let him loose; the boy started to run, but Avdyeitch kept him back.

"Ask the babushka's forgiveness," he said, "and don't you ever do it again; I saw you take the apple."

The boy burst into tears, and began to ask forgiveness.

"There now! That's right; and here's an apple for you."

And Avdyeitch took an apple from the basket, and gave it to the boy.

"I will pay you for it, babushka," he said to the old woman.

"You ruin them that way, the good-for-nothings," said the old woman. "He ought to be treated so that he would remember it for a whole week."

"Eh, babushka, babushka," said Avdyeitch, "that is right according to our judgment, but not according to God's. If he is to be whipped for an apple, then what ought to be done to us for our sins?"

The old woman was silent.

And Avdyeitch told her the parable of the master who forgave a debtor all that he owed him, and how the debtor went and began to choke one who owed him.

The old woman listened, and the boy stood listening.

"God has commanded us to forgive," said Avdyeitch, "else we, too, may not be forgiven. All should be forgiven, and the thoughtless especially."

The old woman shook her head, and sighed.

"That's so," said she; "but the trouble is that they are very much spoiled."

"Then we who are older must teach them," said Avdyeitch.

"That's just what I say," remarked the old woman. "I myself have had seven of them—only one daughter is left."

And the old woman began to relate where and how she lived with her daughter, and how many grandchildren she had. "Here," she says, "my strength is only so-so, and yet I have to work. I pity the youngsters—my grandchildren—but what nice children they are! No one gives me such a welcome as they do. Aksintka won't go to anyone but me. 'Babushka, dear babushka, loveliest.'"

And the old woman grew quite sentimental.

"Of course, it is a childish trick. God be with him," said she, pointing to the boy.

The woman was just about to lift the bag up on her shoulder, when the boy ran up, and said:—

"Let me carry it, babushka; it is on my way."

The old woman nodded her head, and put the bag on the boy's back.

And side by side they passed along the street.

And the old woman even forgot to ask Avdyeitch to pay for the apple. Avdyeitch stood motionless, and kept gazing after them; and he heard them talking all the time as they walked away. After Avdyeitch saw them disappear, he returned to his room; he found his eye-glasses on the stairs—they were not broken; he picked up his awl, and sat down to work again.

After working a little while, it grew darker, so that he could not see to sew; he saw the lamplighter passing by to light the street lamps.

"It must be time to make a light," he said to himself; so he got his little lamp ready, hung it up, and he took himself again to his work. He had one boot already finished; he turned it around, looked at it: "Well done." He put away his tools, swept off the cuttings, cleared off the bristles and ends, took the lamp, set it on the table, and took down the Gospels from the shelf. He intended to open the book at the very place where he had yesterday put a piece of leather as a mark, but it happened to open at another place; and the moment Avdyeitch opened the Testament, he recollected his last night's dream. And as soon as he remembered it, it seemed as if he heard someone stepping about behind him. Avdyeitch looked around, and saw—there, in the dark corner, it seemed as if people were standing; he was at a loss to know who they were. And a voice whispered in his ear:—

"Martuin—ah, Martuin! Did you not recognize me?"

"Who?" exclaimed Avdyeitch.

"Me," repeated the voice. "It was I;" and Stepanuitch stepped forth from the dark corner; he smiled, and like a little cloud faded away, and soon vanished.

"And it was I," said the voice.

From the dark corner stepped forth the woman with her child; the woman smiled, the child laughed, and they also vanished,

"And it was I," continued the voice; both the old woman and the boy with the apple stepped forward; both smiled and vanished.

Avdyeitch's soul rejoiced; he crossed himself, put on his spectacles, and began to read the Evangelists where it happened to open. On the upper part of the page he read:—

"For I was an hungered, and ye gave me meat; I was thirsty, and ye gave me drink; I was a stranger, and ye took me in."

And on the lower part of the page he read this:—

"Inasmuch as ye have done it unto one of the least of these my brethren, ye have done it unto me."—St. Matthew, Chap. xxv.

And Avdyeitch understood that his dream had not deceived him; that the Saviour really called on him that day, and that he really received Him.

A Spark Neglected Burns the House

[Written and first published in 1885. The story is based on the
Christian commandment to not be angry. It is also translated as
'A Lost Opportunity' or 'Quench the Spark'. This version has been
taken from *Twenty-three Tales* (1906), a collection translated by
Louise and Aylmer Maude.]

'Then came Peter, and said to him, Lord, how oft shall my brother sin against me, and I forgive him? Until seven times? Jesus saith unto him, I say not unto thee, Until seven times; but, Until seventy times seven. Therefore is the kingdom of heaven likened unto a certain king, which would make a reckoning with his servants. And when he had begun to reckon, one was brought unto him, which owed him ten thousand talents. But forasmuch as he had not wherewith to pay, his lord commanded him to be sold, and his wife, and children, and all that he had, and payment to be made. The servant therefore fell down and worshipped him, saying, Lord, have patience with me, and I will pay thee all. And the lord of that servant, being moved with compassion, released him, and forgave him the debt. But that servant went out, and found one of his fellow-servants, which owed him a hundred pence: and he laid hold on him, and took him by the throat saying, Pay what thou owest. So his fellow-servant fell down and besought him, saying, Have patience with me, and I will pay thee. And he would not: but went and cast him into prison, till he should pay that which was due. So when his fellow-servants saw what was done, they were exceeding sorry, and came and told unto their lord all that was done. Then his lord called him unto him, and saith to him, Thou wicked servant, I forgave thee all that debt, because thou besoughtest me: shouldest not thou also have had mercy on thy fellow-servant, even as I had mercy on thee? And his lord was wroth, and delivered him to the tormentors, till he should pay all that was due. So shall also my heavenly Father do unto you, if ye forgive not every one his brother from your hearts.'

—Matt. xviii. 21-35

There once lived in a village a peasant named Iván Stcherbakóf. He was comfortably off, in the prime of life, the best worker in the village, and had three sons all able to work. The eldest was married, the second about to marry, and the third was a big lad who could mind the horses and was already beginning to plough. Iván's wife was an able and thrifty woman, and they were fortunate in having a quiet, hard-working daughter-in-law. There was nothing to prevent Iván and his family from living happily. They had only one idle mouth to feed; that was Iván's old father, who suffered from asthma and had been lying ill on the top of the brick oven for seven years. Iván had all he needed: three horses and a colt, a cow with a calf, and fifteen sheep. The women made all the clothing for the family, besides helping in the fields, and the men tilled the land. They always had grain enough of their own to last over beyond the next harvest and sold enough oats to pay the taxes and meet their other needs. So Iván and his children might have lived quite comfortably had it not been for a feud between him and his next-door neighbour, Limping Gabriel, the son of Gordéy Ivánof.

As long as old Gordéy was alive and Iván's father was still able to manage the household, the peasants lived as neighbours should. If the women of either house happened to want a sieve or a tub, or the men required a sack, or if a cart-wheel got broken and could not be mended at once, they used to send to the other house, and helped each other in neighbourly fashion. When a calf strayed into the neighbour's thrashing-ground they would just drive it out, and only say, "Don't let it get in again; our grain is lying there." And such things as locking up the barns and outhouses, hiding things from one another, or backbiting were never thought of in those days.

That was in the fathers' time. When the sons came to be at the head of the families, everything changed.

It all began about a trifle.

Iván's daughter-in-law had a hen that began laying rather early in the season, and she started collecting its eggs for Easter. Every day she went to the cart-shed, and found an egg in the cart; but one day the hen, probably frightened by the children, flew across the fence into the neighbour's yard and laid its egg there. The woman heard the cackling, but said to herself: "I have no time now; I must tidy up for Sunday. I'll fetch the egg later on." In the evening she went to the cart, but found no egg there. She went and asked her mother-in-law and brother-in-law whether they had taken the egg. "No," they had not; but her youngest brother-in-law, Tarás, said: "Your Biddy laid its egg in the neighbour's yard. It was there she was cackling, and she flew back across the fence from there."

The woman went and looked at the hen. There she was on the perch with the other birds, her eyes just closing ready to go to sleep. The woman wished she could have asked the hen and got an answer from her.

Then she went to the neighbour's, and Gabriel's mother came out to meet her.

"What do you want, young woman?"

"Why, Granny, you see, my hen flew across this morning. Did she not lay an egg here?"

"We never saw anything of it. The Lord be thanked, our own hens started laying long ago. We collect our own eggs and have no need of other people's! And we don't go looking for eggs in other people's yards, lass!"

The young woman was offended, and said more than she should have done. Her neighbour answered back with interest, and the women began abusing each other. Iván's wife, who had been to fetch water, happening to pass just then, joined in too. Gabriel's wife rushed out, and began reproaching the young woman with things that had really happened and with other things that never had happened at all. Then a general uproar commenced, all shouting at once, trying to get out two words at a time, and not choice words either.

"You're this!" and "You're that!" "You're a thief!" and "You're a slut!" and "You're starving your old father-in-law to death!" and "You're a good-for-nothing!" and so on.

"And you've made a hole in the sieve I lent you, you jade! And it's our yoke you're carrying your pails on—you just give back our yoke!"

Then they caught hold of the yoke, and spilt the water, snatched off one another's shawls, and began fighting. Gabriel, returning from the fields, stopped to take his wife's part. Out rushed Iván and his son and joined in with the rest. Iván was a strong fellow, he scattered the whole lot of them, and pulled a handful of hair out of Gabriel's beard. People came to see what the matter was, and the fighters were separated with difficulty.

That was how it all began.

Gabriel wrapped the hair torn from his beard in a paper, and went to the District Court to have the law of Iván. "I didn't grow my beard," said he, "for pockmarked Iván to pull it out!" And his wife went bragging to the neighbours, saying they'd have Iván condemned and sent to Siberia. And so the feud grew.

The old man, from where he lay on the top of the oven, tried from the very first to persuade them to make peace, but they would not listen. He told them, "It's a stupid thing you are after, children, picking quarrels about such a paltry matter. Just think! The whole thing began about an egg. The children may have taken it—well, what matter? What's the value of one egg? God sends enough for all! And suppose your neighbour did say an unkind word—put it right; show her how to say a better one! If there has been a fight—well, such things will happen; we're all sinners, but make it up, and let there be an end of it! If you nurse your anger it will be worse for you yourselves."

But the younger folk would not listen to the old man. They thought his words were mere senseless dotage. Iván would not humble himself before his neighbour.

"I never pulled his beard," he said, "he pulled the hair out himself. But his son has burst all the fastenings on my shirt, and torn it. . . . Look at it!"

And Iván also went to law. They were tried by the Justice of the Peace and by the District Court. While all this was going on, the coupling-pin of Gabriel's cart disappeared. Gabriel's womenfolk accused Iván's son of having taken it. They said: "We saw him in the night go past our window, towards the cart; and a neighbour says he saw him at the pub, offering the pin to the landlord."

So they went to law about that. And at home not a day passed without a quarrel or even a fight. The children, too, abused one another, having learnt to do so from their elders; and when the women happened to meet by the river-side, where they went to rinse the clothes, their arms did not do as much wringing as their tongues did nagging, and every word was a bad one.

At first the peasants only slandered one another; but afterwards they began in real earnest to snatch anything that lay handy, and the children followed their example. Life became harder and harder for them. Iván Stcherbakóf and Limping Gabriel kept suing one another at the Village Assembly, and at the District Court, and before the Justice of the Peace until all the judges were tired of them. Now Gabriel got Iván fined or imprisoned; then Iván did as much to Gabriel; and the more they spited each other the angrier they grew—like dogs that attack one another and get more and more furious the longer they fight. You strike one dog from behind, and it thinks it's the other dog biting him, and gets still fiercer. So these peasants: they went to law, and one or other of them was fined or locked up, but that only made them more and more angry with each other. "Wait a bit," they said, "and I'll make you pay for it." And so it went on for six years. Only the old man lying on the top of the oven kept telling them again and again: "Children, what are you doing? Stop all this paying back; keep to your work, and don't bear malice—it will be better for you. The more you bear malice, the worse it will be."

But they would not listen to him.

In the seventh year, at a wedding, Iván's daughter-in-law held Gabriel up to shame, accusing him of having been caught horse-stealing. Gabriel was tipsy, and unable to contain his anger, gave the woman such a blow that she was laid up for a week; and she was pregnant at the time. Iván was delighted. He went to the magistrate to lodge a complaint. "Now I'll get rid of my neighbour! He won't escape imprisonment, or exile to Siberia." But Iván's wish was not fulfilled. The magistrate dismissed the case. The woman was examined, but she was up and about and showed no sign of any injury. Then Iván went to the Justice of the Peace, but he referred the business to the District Court. Iván bestirred himself: treated the clerk and the Elder of the District Court to a gallon of liquor and got Gabriel condemned to be flogged. The sentence was read out to Gabriel by the clerk: "The Court decrees that the peasant Gabriel Gordéyef shall receive twenty lashes with a birch rod at the District Court."

Iván too heard the sentence read, and looked at Gabriel to see how he would take it. Gabriel grew as pale as a sheet, and turned

216

round and went out into the passage. Iván followed him, meaning to see to the horse, and he overheard Gabriel say, "Very well! He will have my back flogged: that will make it burn; but something of his may burn worse than that!"

Hearing these words, Iván at once went back into the Court, and said: "Upright judges! He threatens to set my house on fire! Listen: he said it in the presence of witnesses!"

Gabriel was recalled. "Is it true that you said this?"

"I haven't said anything. Flog me, since you have the power. It seems that I alone am to suffer, and all for being in the right, while he is allowed to do as he likes."

Gabriel wished to say something more, but his lips and his cheeks quivered, and he turned towards the wall. Even the officials were frightened by his looks. "He may do some mischief to himself or to his neighbour," thought they.

Then the old Judge said: "Look here, my men; you'd better be reasonable and make it up. Was it right of you, friend Gabriel, to strike a pregnant woman? It was lucky it passed off so well, but think what might have happened! Was it right? You had better confess and beg his pardon, and he will forgive you, and we will alter the sentence."

The clerk heard these words, and remarked: "That's impossible under Statute 117. An agreement between the parties not having been arrived at, a decision of the Court has been pronounced and must be executed."

But the Judge would not listen to the clerk.

"Keep your tongue still, my friend," said he. "The first of all laws is to obey God, Who loves peace." And the Judge began again to persuade the peasants, but could not succeed. Gabriel would not listen to him.

"I shall be fifty next year," said he, "and have a married son, and have never been flogged in my life, and now that pockmarked Iván has had me condemned to be flogged, and am I to go and ask his forgiveness? No; I've borne enough. . . . Iván shall have cause to remember me!"

Again Gabriel's voice quivered, and he could say no more, but turned round and went out.

It was seven miles from the Court to the village, and it was getting late when Iván reached home. He unharnessed his horse, put it up for the night, and entered the cottage. No one was there. The women had already gone to drive the cattle in, and the young fellows were not yet back from the fields. Iván went in, and sat down, thinking. He remembered how Gabriel had listened to the sentence, and how pale he had become, and how he had turned to the wall; and Iván's heart grew heavy. He thought how he himself would feel if he were sentenced, and he pitied Gabriel. Then he heard his old father up on the oven cough, and saw him sit up, lower his legs, and scramble down. The old man dragged himself slowly to a seat, and sat down. He was quite tired out with the exertion, and coughed a long time till he had cleared his throat. Then, leaning against the table, he said: "Well, has he been condemned?"

"Yes, to twenty strokes with the rods," answered Iván.

The old man shook his head.

"A bad business," said he. "You are doing wrong, Iván! Ah! It's very bad—not for him so much as for yourself! . . . Well, they'll flog him: but will that do you any good?"

"He'll not do it again," said Iván.

"What is it he'll not do again? What has he done worse than you?"

"Why, think of the harm he has done me!" said Iván. "He nearly killed my wife, and now he's threatening to burn us up. Am I to thank him for it?"

The old man sighed, and said: "You go about the wide world, Iván, while I am lying on the oven all these years, so you think you see everything, and that I see nothing. . . . Ah, lad! It's you that don't see; malice blinds you. Others' sins are before your eyes, but your own are behind your back. 'He's acted badly!' What a thing to say! If he were the only one to act badly, how could strife exist? Is strife among men ever bred by one alone? Strife is always between two. His badness you see, but your own you don't. If he were bad, but you were good, there would be no strife. Who pulled the hair out of his beard? Who spoilt his haystack? Who dragged him to the law court? Yet you put it all on him! You live a bad life yourself, that's what is wrong! It's not the way I used to live, lad, and it's not the way I taught you. Is that the way his old father and I used to live? How did we live? Why, as neighbours should! If he happened to run out of flour, one of the women would come across: 'Uncle Trol, we want some flour.' 'Go to the barn, dear,' I'd say: 'take what you need.' If he'd no one to take his horses to pasture, 'Go, Iván,' I'd say, 'and look after his horses.' And if I was short of anything, I'd go to him. 'Uncle Gordéy,' I'd say, 'I want so-and-so!' 'Take it, Uncle Troll!' That's how it was between us, and we had an easy time of it. But now? . . . That soldier the other day was telling us about the fight at Plevna*. Why, there's war between you worse than at Plevna! Is that living? . . . What a sin it is! You are a man and master of the house; it's you who will have to answer. What are you teaching the women and the children? To snarl and snap? Why, the other day your Taráska—that greenhorn—was swearing at neighbour Irena, calling her names; and his mother listened and laughed. Is that right? It is you will have to answer. Think of your soul. Is this all as it should be? You throw a word at me, and I give you two in return; you give me a blow, and I give you two. No, lad! Christ, when He walked on earth, taught us fools something very different . . . If you get a hard word from any one, keep silent, and his own conscience will accuse him. That is what our Lord taught. If you get a slap, turn the other cheek. 'Here, beat me, if that's what I deserve!' And his own conscience will rebuke him. He will soften, and will listen to you. That's the way He taught us, not to be proud! . . . Why don't you speak? Isn't it as I say?"

Iván sat silent and listened.

The old man coughed, and having with difficulty cleared his throat, began again: "You think Christ taught us wrong? Why, it's all for our own good. Just think of your earthly life; are you better off, or worse, since this Plevna began among you? Just reckon up what you've spent on all this law business—what the driving backwards and forwards and your food on the way have cost you!

---

* A town in Bulgaria, the scene of fierce and prolonged fighting between the Turks and the Russians in the war of 1877.

What fine fellows your sons have grown; you might live and get or well; but now your means are lessening. And why? All because of this folly; because of your pride. You ought to be ploughing with your lads, and do the sowing yourself; but the fiend carries you off to the judge, or to some pettifogger or other. The ploughing is not done in time, nor the sowing, and mother earth can't bear properly Why did the oats fail this year? When did you sow them? When you came back from town! And what did you gain? A burden for your own shoulders. . . . Eh, lad, think of your own business! Work with your boys in the field and at home, and if someone offends you, forgive him, as God wished you to. Then life will be easy, and your heart will always be light."

Iván remained silent.

"Iván, my boy, hear your old father! Go and harness the roan, and go at once to the Government office; put an end to all this affair there; and in the morning go and make it up with Gabriel in God's name, and invite him to your house for tomorrow's holiday" (it was the eve of the Virgin's Nativity). "Have tea ready, and get a bottle of vódka and put an end to this wicked business, so that there should not be any more of it in future, and tell the women and children to do the same."

Iván sighed, and thought, "What he says is true," and his heart grew lighter. Only he did not know how, now, to begin to put matters right.

But again the old man began, as if he had guessed what was in Iván's mind.

"Go, Iván, don't put it off! Put out the fire before it spreads, or it will be too late."

The old man was going to say more, but before he could do so the women came in, chattering like magpies. The news that Gabriel was sentenced to be flogged, and of his threat to set fire to the house, had already reached them. They had heard all about it and added to it something of their own, and had again had a row, in the pasture, with the women of Gabriel's household. They began telling how Gabriel's daughter-in-law threatened a fresh action: Gabriel had got the right side of the examining magistrate, who would now turn the whole affair upside down; and the schoolmaster was writing out another petition, to the Tsar himself this time, about Iván; and everything was in the petition—all about the coupling-pin and the kitchen-garden—so that half of Iván's homestead would be theirs soon. Iván heard what they were saying, and his heart grew cold again, and he gave up the thought of making peace with Gabriel.

In a farmstead there is always plenty for the master to do. Iván did not stop to talk to the women, but went out to the threshing-floor and to the barn. By the time he had tidied up there, the sun had set and the young fellows had returned from the field. They had been ploughing the field for the winter crops with two horses. Iván met them, questioned them about their work, helped to put everything in its place, set a torn horse-collar aside to be mended, and was going to put away some stakes under the barn, but it had grown quite dusk, so he decided to leave them where they were till next day. Then he gave the cattle their food, opened the gate, let out the horses Tarás was to take to pasture for the night, and again closed the gate and barred it. "Now," thought he, "I'll have my supper, and then to bed." He took the horse-collar and entered the hut. By this time he had forgotten about Gabriel and about what his old father had been saying to him. But, just as he took hold of the door-handle to enter the passage, he heard his neighbour on the other side of the fence cursing somebody in a hoarse voice: "What the devil is he good for?" Gabriel was saying. "He's only fit to be killed!" At these words all Iván's former bitterness towards his neighbour re-awoke. He stood listening while Gabriel scolded, and, when he stopped, Iván went into the hut.

There was a light inside; his daughter-in-law sat spinning, his wife was getting supper ready, his eldest son was making straps for bark shoes, his second sat near the table with a book, and Tarás was getting ready to go out to pasture the horses for the night. Everything in the hut would have been pleasant and bright, but for that plague—a bad neighbour!

Iván entered, sullen and cross; threw the cat down from the bench, and scolded the women for putting the slop-pail in the wrong place. He felt despondent, and sat down, frowning, to mend the horse-collar. Gabriel's words kept ringing in his ears: his threat at the law court, and what he had just been shouting in a hoarse voice about someone who was 'only fit to be killed.'

His wife gave Tarás his supper, and, having eaten it, Tarás put on an old sheepskin and another coat, tied a sash round his waist, took some bread with him, and went out to the horses. His eldest brother was going to see him off, but Iván himself rose instead, and went out into the porch. It had grown quite dark outside, clouds had gathered, and the wind had risen. Iván went down the steps, helped his boy to mount, started the foal after him, and stood listening while Tarás rode down the village and was there joined by other lads with their horses. Iván waited until they were all out of hearing. As he stood there by the gate he could not get Gabriel's words out of his head: "Mind that something of yours does not burn worse!"

"He is desperate," thought Iván. "Everything is dry, and it's windy weather besides. He'll come up at the back somewhere, set fire to something, and be off. He'll burn the place and escape scot free, the villain! . . . There now, if one could but catch him in the act, he'd not get off then!" And the thought fixed itself so firmly in his mind that he did not go up the steps but went out into the street and round the corner. "I'll just walk round the buildings; who can tell what he's after?" And Iván, stepping softly, passed out of the gate. As soon as he reached the corner, he looked round along the fence, and seemed to see something suddenly move at the opposite corner, as if someone had come out and disappeared again. Iván stopped, and stood quietly, listening and looking. Everything was still; only the leaves of the willows fluttered in the wind, and the straws of the thatch rustled. At first it seemed pitch dark, but, when his eyes had grown used to the darkness, he could see the far corner, and a plough that lay there, and the eaves. He looked a while, but saw no one.

"I suppose it was a mistake," thought Iván; "but still I will go round," and Iván went stealthily along by the shed. Iván stepped so softly in his bark shoes that he did not hear his own footsteps. As he reached the far corner, something seemed to flare up for a moment near the plough and to vanish again. Iván felt as if struck to the heart; and he stopped. Hardly had he stopped, when something flared up more brightly in the same place, and he clearly saw a man with a cap on his head, crouching down, with his back towards him, lighting a bunch of straw he held in his hand. Iván's heart fluttered within him like a bird. Straining every nerve, he approached with great strides, hardly feeling his legs under him. "Ah," thought Iván, "now he won't escape! I'll catch him in the act!"

Iván was still some distance off, when suddenly he saw a bright light, but not in the same place as before, and not a small flame. The thatch had flared up at the eaves, the flames were reaching up to the roof, and, standing beneath it, Gabriel's whole figure was clearly visible.

Like a hawk swooping down on a lark, Iván rushed at Limping Gabriel. "Now I'll have him; he shan't escape me!" thought Iván. But Gabriel must have heard his steps, and (however he managed it) glancing round, he scuttled away past the barn like a hare.

"You shan't escape!" shouted Iván, darting after him.

Just as he was going to seize Gabriel, the latter dodged him; but Iván managed to catch the skirt of Gabriel's coat. It tore right off, and Iván fell down. He recovered his feet, and shouting, "Help! Seize him! Thieves! Murder!" ran on again. But meanwhile Gabriel had reached his own gate. There Iván overtook him and was about to seize him, when something struck Iván a stunning blow, as though a stone had hit his temple, quite deafening him. It was Gabriel who, seizing an oak wedge that lay near the gate, had struck out with all his might.

Iván was stunned; sparks flew before his eyes, then all grew dark and he staggered. When he came to his senses Gabriel was no longer there: it was as light as day, and from the side where his homestead was, something roared and crackled like an engine at work. Iván turned round and saw that his back shed was all ablaze, and the side shed had also caught fire, and flames and smoke and bits of burning straw mixed with the smoke, were being driven towards his hut.

"What is this, friends? . . ." cried Iván, lifting his arms and striking his thighs. "Why, all I had to do was just to snatch it out from under the eaves and trample on it! What is this, friends? . . ." he kept repeating. He wished to shout, but his breath failed him; his voice was gone. He wanted to run, but his legs would not obey him, and got in each other's way. He moved slowly, but again staggered and again his breath failed. He stood still till he had regained breath, and then went on. Before he had got round the back shed to reach the fire, the side shed was also all ablaze; and the corner of the hut and the covered gateway had caught fire as well. The flames were leaping out of the hut, and it was impossible to get into the yard. A large crowd had collected, but nothing could be done. The neighbours were carrying their belongings out of their own houses, and driving the cattle out of their own sheds. After Iván's house, Gabriel's also caught fire, then, the wind rising, the flames spread to the other side of the street and half the village was burnt down.

At Iván's house they barely managed to save his old father; and the family escaped in what they had on; everything else, except the horses that had been driven out to pasture for the night, was lost; all the cattle, the fowls on their perches, the carts, ploughs, and harrows, the women's trunks with their clothes, and the grain in the granaries—all were burnt up!

At Gabriel's, the cattle were driven out, and a few things saved from his house.

The fire lasted all night. Iván stood in front of his homestead and kept repeating, "What is this? . . . Friends! . . . One need only have pulled it out and trampled on it!" But when the roof fell in, Iván rushed into the burning place, and seizing a charred beam, tried to drag it out. The women saw him, and called him back; but he pulled out the beam, and was going in again for another when he lost his footing and fell among the flames. Then his son made his way in after him and dragged him out. Iván had singed his hair and beard and burnt his clothes and scorched his hands, but he felt nothing. "His grief has stupefied him," said the people. The fire was burning itself out, but Iván still stood repeating: "Friends! . . . What is this? . . . One need only have pulled it out!"

In the morning the village Elder's son came to fetch Iván.

"Daddy Iván, your father is dying! He has sent for you to say goodbye."

Iván had forgotten about his father, and did not understand what was being said to him.

"What father?" he said. "Whom has he sent for?"

"He sent for you, to say goodbye; he is dying in our cottage! Come along, daddy Iván," said the Elder's son, pulling him by the arm; and Iván followed the lad.

When he was being carried out of the hut, some burning straw had fallen on to the old man and burnt him, and he had been taken to the village Elder's in the farther part of the village, which the fire did not reach.

When Iván came to his father, there was only the Elder's wife in the hut, besides some little children on the top of the oven. All the rest were still at the fire. The old man, who was lying on a bench holding a wax candle* in his hand, kept turning his eyes towards the door. When his son entered, he moved a little. The old woman went up to him and told him that his son had come. He asked to have him brought nearer. Iván came closer.

"What did I tell you, Iván?" began the old man. "Who has burnt down the village?"

"It was he, father!" Iván answered. "I caught him in the act. I saw him shove the firebrand into the thatch. I might have pulled away the burning straw and stamped it out, and then nothing would have happened."

"Iván," said the old man, "I am dying, and you in your turn will have to face death. Whose is the sin?"

Iván gazed at his father in silence, unable to utter a word.

"Now, before God, say whose is the sin? What did I tell you?"

Only then Iván came to his senses and understood it all. He sniffed and said, "Mine, father!" And he fell on his knees before

---

* Wax candles are much used in the services of the Russian Church, and it is usual to place one in the hand of a dying man, especially when he receives unction.

his father, saying, "Forgive me, father; I am guilty before you and before God."

The old man moved his hands, changed the candle from his right hand to his left, and tried to lift his right hand to his forehead to cross himself, but could not do it, and stopped.

"Praise the Lord! Praise the Lord!" said he, and again he turned his eyes towards his son.

"Iván! I say, Iván!"

"What, father?"

"What must you do now?"

Iván was weeping.

"I don't know how we are to live now, father!" he said.

The old man closed his eyes, moved his lips as if to gather strength, and opening his eyes again, said: "You'll manage. If you obey God's will, you'll manage!" He paused, then smiled, and said: "Mind, Iván! Don't tell who started the fire! Hide another man's sin, and God will forgive two of yours!" And the old man took the candle in both hands and, folding them on his breast, sighed, stretched out, and died.

Iván did not say anything against Gabriel, and no one knew what had caused the fire.

And Iván's anger against Gabriel passed away, and Gabriel wondered that Iván did not tell anybody. At first Gabriel felt afraid, but after a while he got used to it. The men left off quarrelling, and then their families left off also. While rebuilding their huts, both families lived in one house; and when the village was rebuilt and they might have moved farther apart, Iván and Gabriel built next to each other, and remained neighbours as before.

They lived as good neighbours should. Iván Stcherbakóf remembered his old father's command to obey God's law, and quench a fire at the first spark; and if any one does him an injury he now tries not to revenge himself, but rather to set matters right again; and if any one gives him a bad word, instead of giving a worse in return, he tries to teach the other not to use evil words; and so he teaches his womenfolk and children. And Iván Stcherbakóf has got on his feet again, and now lives better even than he did before.

What Men Live By

[Written in 1885. Published in his collection *What Men Live By,
and Other Tales* (1885). Based on the Christian commandment of
loving all people equally, it is among Tolstoy's best-known stories
for the people. This is a translation by Louise and Aylmer Maude.]

A shoemaker named Simon, who had neither house nor land of his own, lived with his wife and children in a peasant's hut, and earned his living by his work. Work was cheap, but bread was dear, and what he earned he spent for food. The man and his wife had but one sheepskin coat between them for winter wear, and even that was torn to tatters, and this was the second year he had been wanting to buy sheepskins for a new coat. Before winter Simon saved up a little money: a three-rouble note lay hidden in his wife's box, and five roubles and twenty kopeks were owed him by customers in the village.

So one morning he prepared to go to the village to buy the sheepskins. He put on over his shirt his wife's wadded nankeen jacket, and over that he put his own cloth coat. He took the three-rouble note in his pocket, cut himself a stick to serve as a staff, and started off after breakfast. "I'll collect the five roubles that are due to me," thought he, "add the three I have got, and that will be enough to buy sheepskins for the winter coat."

He came to the village and called at a peasant's hut, but the man was not at home. The peasant's wife promised that the money should be paid next week, but she would not pay it herself. Then Simon called on another peasant, but this one swore he had no money, and would only pay twenty kopeks which he owed for a pair of boots Simon had mended. Simon then tried to buy the sheepskins on credit, but the dealer would not trust him.

"Bring your money," said he, "then you may have your pick of the skins. We know what debt-collecting is like." So all the business the shoemaker did was to get the twenty kopeks for boots he had mended, and to take a pair of felt boots a peasant gave him to sole with leather.

Simon felt downhearted. He spent the twenty kopeks on vodka, and started homewards without having bought any skins. In the morning he had felt the frost; but now, after drinking the vodka, he felt warm, even without a sheepskin coat. He trudged along, striking his stick on the frozen earth with one hand, swinging the felt boots with the other, and talking to himself.

"I'm quite warm," said he, "though I have no sheepskin coat. I've had a drop, and it runs through all my veins. I need no sheepskins. I go along and don't worry about anything. That's the sort of man I am! What do I care? I can live without sheepskins. I don't need them. My wife will fret, to be sure. And, true enough, it is a shame; one works all day long, and then does not get paid. Stop a bit! If you don't bring that money along, sure enough I'll skin you, blessed if I don't. How's that? He pays twenty kopeks at a time! What can I do with twenty kopeks? Drink it—that's all one can do! Hard up, he says he is! So he may be—but what about me? You have a house, and cattle, and everything; I've only what I stand up in! You have corn of your own growing; I have to buy every grain. Do what I will, I must spend three roubles every week for bread alone. I come home and find the bread all used up, and I have to fork out another rouble and a half. So just pay up what you owe, and no nonsense about it!"

By this time he had nearly reached the shrine at the bend of the road. Looking up, he saw something whitish behind the shrine. The daylight was fading, and the shoemaker peered at the thing without being able to make out what it was. "There was no white stone here before. Can it be an ox? It's not like an ox. It has a head like a man, but it's too white; and what could a man be doing there?"

He came closer, so that it was clearly visible. To his surprise it really was a man, alive or dead, sitting naked, leaning motionless against the shrine. Terror seized the shoemaker, and he thought, "Someone has killed him, stripped him, and left him there. If I meddle I shall surely get into trouble."

So the shoemaker went on. He passed in front of the shrine so that he could not see the man. When he had gone some way, he looked back, and saw that the man was no longer leaning against the shrine, but was moving as if looking towards him. The shoemaker felt more frightened than before, and thought, "Shall I go back to him, or shall I go on? If I go near him something dreadful may happen. Who knows who the fellow is? He has not come here for any good. If I go near him he may jump up and throttle me, and there will be no getting away. Or if not, he'd still be a burden on one's hands. What could I do with a naked man? I couldn't give him my last clothes. Heaven only help me to get away!"

So the shoemaker hurried on, leaving the shrine behind him—when suddenly his conscience smote him, and he stopped in the road.

"What are you doing, Simon?" said he to himself. "The man may be dying of want, and you slip past afraid. Have you grown so rich as to be afraid of robbers? Ah, Simon, shame on you!"

So he turned back and went up to the man.

II

Simon approached the stranger, looked at him, and saw that he was a young man, fit, with no bruises on his body, only evidently freezing and frightened, and he sat there leaning back without looking up at Simon, as if too faint to lift his eyes. Simon went close to him, and then the man seemed to wake up. Turning his head, he opened his eyes and looked into Simon's face. That one look was enough to make Simon fond of the man. He threw the felt boots on the ground, undid his sash, laid it on the boots, and took off his cloth coat.

"It's not a time for talking," said he. "Come, put this coat on at once!" And Simon took the man by the elbows and helped him to rise. As he stood there, Simon saw that his body was clean and in good condition, his hands and feet shapely, and his face good and kind. He threw his coat over the man's shoulders, but the latter could not find the sleeves. Simon guided his arms into them, and drawing the coat well on, wrapped it closely about him, tying the sash round the man's waist.

Simon even took off his torn cap to put it on the man's head, but then his own head felt cold, and he thought: "I'm quite bald, while he has long curly hair." So he put his cap on his own head again. "It will be better to give him something for his feet," thought he; and he made the man sit down, and helped him to put on the felt boots, saying, "There, friend, now move about and warm yourself. Other matters can be settled later on. Can you walk?"

The man stood up and looked kindly at Simon, but could not say a word.

"Why don't you speak?" said Simon. "It's too cold to stay here, we must be getting home. There now, take my stick, and if you're feeling weak, lean on that. Now step out!"

The man started walking, and moved easily, not lagging behind.

As they went along, Simon asked him, "And where do you belong to?"

"I'm not from these parts."

"I thought as much. I know the folks hereabouts. But, how did you come to be there by the shrine?"

"I cannot tell."

"Has someone been ill-treating you?"

"No one has ill-treated me. God has punished me."

"Of course God rules all. Still, you'll have to find food and shelter somewhere. Where do you want to go to?"

"It is all the same to me."

Simon was amazed. The man did not look like a rogue, and he spoke gently, but yet he gave no account of himself. Still Simon thought, "Who knows what may have happened?" And he said to the stranger: "Well then, come home with me, and at least warm yourself awhile."

So Simon walked towards his home, and the stranger kept up with him, walking at his side. The wind had risen and Simon felt it cold under his shirt. He was getting over his tipsiness by now, and began to feel the frost. He went along sniffling and wrapping his wife's coat round him, and he thought to himself: "There now—talk about sheepskins! I went out for sheepskins and come home without even a coat to my back, and what is more, I'm bringing a naked man along with me. Matryona won't be pleased!" And when he thought of his wife he felt sad; but when he looked at the stranger and remembered how he had looked up at him at the shrine, his heart was glad.

III

Simon's wife had everything ready early that day. She had cut wood, brought water, fed the children, eaten her own meal, and now she sat thinking. She wondered when she ought to make bread: now or tomorrow? There was still a large piece left.

"If Simon has had some dinner in town," thought she, "and does not eat much for supper, the bread will last out another day."

She weighed the piece of bread in her hand again and again, and thought: "I won't make any more today. We have only enough flour left to bake one batch; We can manage to make this last out till Friday."

So Matryona put away the bread, and sat down at the table to patch her husband's shirt. While she worked she thought how her husband was buying skins for a winter coat.

"If only the dealer does not cheat him. My good man is much too simple; he cheats nobody, but any child can take him in. Eight roubles is a lot of money—he should get a good coat at that price. Not tanned skins, but still a proper winter coat. How difficult it was last winter to get on without a warm coat. I could neither get down to the river, nor go out anywhere. When he went out he put on all we had, and there was nothing left for me. He did not start very early today, but still it's time he was back. I only hope he has not gone on the spree!"

Hardly had Matryona thought this, when steps were heard on the threshold, and someone entered. Matryona stuck her needle into her work and went out into the passage. There she saw two men: Simon, and with him a man without a hat, and wearing felt boots.

Matryona noticed at once that her husband smelt of spirits. "There now, he has been drinking," thought she. And when she saw that he was coatless, had only her jacket on, brought no parcel, stood there silent, and seemed ashamed, her heart was ready to break with disappointment. "He has drunk the money," thought she, "and has been on the spree with some good-for-nothing fellow whom he has brought home with him."

Matryona let them pass into the hut, followed them in, and saw that the stranger was a young, slight man, wearing her husband's coat. There was no shirt to be seen under it, and he had no hat. Having entered, he stood, neither moving, nor raising his eyes, and Matryona thought: "He must be a bad man—he's afraid."

Matryona frowned, and stood beside the oven looking to see what they would do.

Simon took off his cap and sat down on the bench as if things were all right.

"Come, Matryona; if supper is ready, let us have some."

Matryona muttered something to herself and did not move, but stayed where she was, by the oven. She looked first at the one and then at the other of them, and only shook her head. Simon saw that his wife was annoyed, but tried to pass it off. Pretending not to notice anything, he took the stranger by the arm.

"Sit down, friend," said he, "and let us have some supper."

The stranger sat down on the bench.

"Haven't you cooked anything for us?" said Simon.

Matryona's anger boiled over. "I've cooked, but not for you. It seems to me you have drunk your wits away. You went to buy a sheepskin coat, but come home without so much as the coat you had on, and bring a naked vagabond home with you. I have no supper for drunkards like you."

"That's enough, Matryona. Don't wag your tongue without reason. You had better ask what sort of man—"

"And you tell me what you've done with the money?"

Simon found the pocket of the jacket, drew out the three-rouble note, and unfolded it.

"Here is the money. Trifonof did not pay, but promises to pay soon."

Matryona got still more angry; he had bought no sheepskins,

but had put his only coat on some naked fellow and had even brought him to their house.

She snatched up the note from the table, took it to put away in safety, and said: "I have no supper for you. We can't feed all the naked drunkards in the world."

"There now, Matryona, hold your tongue a bit. First hear what a man has to say—"

"Much wisdom I shall hear from a drunken fool. I was right in not wanting to marry you—a drunkard. The linen my mother gave me you drank; and now you've been to buy a coat—and have drunk it, too!"

Simon tried to explain to his wife that he had only spent twenty kopeks; tried to tell how he had found the man—but Matryona would not let him get a word in. She talked nineteen to the dozen, and dragged in things that had happened ten years before.

Matryona talked and talked, and at last she flew at Simon and seized him by the sleeve.

"Give me my jacket. It is the only one I have, and you must needs take it from me and wear it yourself. Give it here, you mangy dog, and may the devil take you."

Simon began to pull off the jacket, and turned a sleeve of it inside out; Matryona seized the jacket and it burst its seams. She snatched it up, threw it over her head, and went to the door. She meant to go out, but stopped undecided—she wanted to work off her anger, but she also wanted to learn what sort of a man the stranger was.

IV

Matryona stopped and said: "If he were a good man he would not be naked. Why, he hasn't even a shirt on him. If he were all right, you would say where you came across the fellow."

"That's just what I am trying to tell you," said Simon. "As I came to the shrine I saw him sitting all naked and frozen. It isn't quite the weather to sit about naked! God sent me to him, or he would have perished. What was I to do? How do we know what may have happened to him? So I took him, clothed him, and brought him along. Don't be so angry, Matryona. It is a sin. Remember, we all must die one day."

Angry words rose to Matryona's lips, but she looked at the stranger and was silent. He sat on the edge of the bench, motionless, his hands folded on his knees, his head drooping on his breast, his eyes closed, and his brows knit as if in pain. Matryona was silent: and Simon said: "Matryona, have you no love of God?"

Matryona heard these words, and as she looked at the stranger, suddenly her heart softened towards him. She came back from the door, and going to the oven she got out the supper. Setting a cup on the table, she poured out some kvas. Then she brought out the last piece of bread, and set out a knife and spoons.

"Eat, if you want to," said she.

Simon drew the stranger to the table.

"Take your place, young man," said he.

Simon cut the bread, crumbled it into the broth, and they began to eat. Matryona sat at the corner of the table resting her head on her hand and looking at the stranger.

And Matryona was touched with pity for the stranger, and began to feel fond of him. And at once the stranger's face lit up;

his brows were no longer bent, he raised his eyes and smiled at Matryona.

When they had finished supper, the woman cleared away the things and began questioning the stranger. "Where are you from?" said she.

"I am not from these parts."

"But how did you come to be on the road?"

"I may not tell."

"Did someone rob you?"

"God punished me."

"And you were lying there naked?"

"Yes, naked and freezing. Simon saw me and had pity on me. He took off his coat, put it on me and brought me here. And you have fed me, given me drink, and shown pity on me. God will reward you!"

Matryona rose, took from the window Simon's old shirt she had been patching, and gave it to the stranger. She also brought out a pair of trousers for him.

"There," said she, "I see you have no shirt. Put this on, and lie down where you please, in the loft or on the oven."

The stranger took off the coat, put on the shirt, and lay down in the loft. Matryona put out the candle, took the coat, and climbed to where her husband lay.

Matryona drew the skirts of the coat over her and lay down, but could not sleep; she could not get the stranger out of her mind.

When she remembered that he had eaten their last piece of bread and that there was none for tomorrow, and thought of the shirt and trousers she had given away, she felt grieved; but when she remembered how he had smiled, her heart was glad.

Long did Matryona lie awake, and she noticed that Simon also was awake—he drew the coat towards him.

"Simon!"

"Well?"

"You have had the last of the bread, and I have not put any to rise. I don't know what we shall do tomorrow. Perhaps I can borrow some of neighbour Martha."

"If we're alive we shall find something to eat."

The woman lay still awhile, and then said, "He seems a good man, but why does he not tell us who he is?"

"I suppose he has his reasons."

"Simon!"

"Well?"

"We give; but why does nobody give us anything?"

Simon did not know what to say; so he only said, "Let us stop talking," and turned over and went to sleep.

In the morning Simon awoke. The children were still asleep; his wife had gone to the neighbour's to borrow some bread. The stranger alone was sitting on the bench, dressed in the old shirt and trousers, and looking upwards. His face was brighter than it had been the day before.

Simon said to him, "Well, friend; the belly wants bread, and the naked body clothes. One has to work for a living. What work do you know?"

"I do not know any."

This surprised Simon, but he said, "Men who want to learn can learn anything."

"Men work, and I will work also."

"What is your name?"

"Michael."

"Well, Michael, if you don't wish to talk about yourself, that is your own affair; but you'll have to earn a living for yourself. If you will work as I tell you, I will give you food and shelter."

"May God reward you! I will learn. Show me what to do."

Simon took yarn, put it round his thumb and began to twist it.

"It is easy enough—see!"

Michael watched him, put some yarn round his own thumb in the same way, caught the knack, and twisted the yarn also.

Then Simon showed him how to wax the thread. This also Michael mastered. Next Simon showed him how to twist the bristle in, and how to sew, and this, too, Michael learned at once.

Whatever Simon showed him he understood at once, and after three days he worked as if he had sewn boots all his life. He worked without stopping, and ate little. When work was over he sat silently, looking upwards. He hardly went into the street, spoke only when necessary, and neither joked nor laughed. They never saw him smile, except that first evening when Matryona gave them supper.

VI

Day by day and week by week the year went round. Michael lived and worked with Simon. His fame spread till people said that no one sewed boots so neatly and strongly as Simon's workman, Michael; and from all the district round people came to Simon for their boots, and he began to be well off.

One winter day, as Simon and Michael sat working, a carriage on sledge-runners, with three horses and with bells, drove up to the hut. They looked out of the window; the carriage stopped at their door, a fine servant jumped down from the box and opened the door. A gentleman in a fur coat got out and walked up to Simon's hut. Up jumped Matryona and opened the door wide. The gentleman stooped to enter the hut, and when he drew himself up again his head nearly reached the ceiling, and he seemed quite to fill his end of the room.

Simon rose, bowed, and looked at the gentleman with astonishment. He had never seen anyone like him. Simon himself was lean, Michael was thin, and Matryona was dry as a bone, but this man was like someone from another world: red-faced, burly, with a neck like a bull's, and looking altogether as if he were cast in iron.

The gentleman puffed, threw off his fur coat, sat down on the bench, and said, "Which of you is the master bootmaker?"

"I am, your Excellency," said Simon, coming forward.

Then the gentleman shouted to his lad, "Hey, Fedka, bring the leather!"

The servant ran in, bringing a parcel. The gentleman took the parcel and put it on the table.

"Untie it," said he. The lad untied it.

The gentleman pointed to the leather.

"Look here, shoemaker," said he, "do you see this leather?"

"Yes, your honour."

"But do you know what sort of leather it is?"

Simon felt the leather and said, "It is good leather."

"Good, indeed! Why, you fool, you never saw such leather before in your life. It's German, and cost twenty roubles."

Simon was frightened, and said, "Where should I ever see leather like that?"

"Just so! Now, can you make it into boots for me?"

"Yes, your Excellency, I can."

Then the gentleman shouted at him: "You can, can you? Well, remember whom you are to make them for, and what the leather is. You must make me boots that will wear for a year, neither losing shape nor coming unsown. If you can do it, take the leather and

240

cut it up; but if you can't, say so. I warn you now if your boots become unsewn or lose shape within a year, I will have you put in prison. If they don't burst or lose shape for a year I will pay you ten roubles for your work."

Simon was frightened, and did not know what to say. He glanced at Michael and nudging him with his elbow, whispered: "Shall I take the work?"

Michael nodded his head as if to say, "Yes, take it."

Simon did as Michael advised, and undertook to make boots that would not lose shape or split for a whole year.

Calling his servant, the gentleman told him to pull the boot off his left leg, which he stretched out.

"Take my measure!" said he.

Simon stitched a paper measure seventeen inches long, smoothed it out, knelt down, wiped his hand well on his apron so as not to soil the gentleman's sock, and began to measure. He measured the sole, and round the instep, and began to measure the calf of the leg, but the paper was too short. The calf of the leg was as thick as a beam.

"Mind you don't make it too tight in the leg."

Simon stitched on another strip of paper. The gentleman twitched his toes about in his sock, looking round at those in the hut, and as he did so he noticed Michael.

"Whom have you there?" asked he.

"That is my workman. He will sew the boots."

"Mind," said the gentleman to Michael, "remember to make them so that they will last me a year."

Simon also looked at Michael, and saw that Michael was not looking at the gentleman, but was gazing into the corner behind the gentleman, as if he saw someone there. Michael looked and looked, and suddenly he smiled, and his face became brighter.

"What are you grinning at, you fool?" thundered the gentleman. "You had better look to it that the boots are ready in time."

"They shall be ready in good time," said Michael.

"Mind it is so," said the gentleman, and he put on his boots and his fur coat, wrapped the latter round him, and went to the door. But he forgot to stoop, and struck his head against the lintel.

He swore and rubbed his head. Then he took his seat in the carriage and drove away.

When he had gone, Simon said: "There's a figure of a man for you! You could not kill him with a mallet. He almost knocked out the lintel, but little harm it did him."

And Matryona said: "Living as he does, how should he not grow strong? Death itself can't touch such a rock as that."

VII

Then Simon said to Michael: "Well, we have taken the work, but we must see we don't get into trouble over it. The leather is dear, and the gentleman hot-tempered. We must make no mistakes. Come, your eye is truer and your hands have become nimbler than mine, so you take this measure and cut out the boots. I will finish off the sewing of the vamps."

Michael did as he was told. He took the leather, spread it out on the table, folded it in two, took a knife and began to cut out.

Matryona came and watched him cutting, and was surprised to see how he was doing it. Matryona was accustomed to seeing boots made, and she looked and saw that Michael was not cutting the leather for boots, but was cutting it round.

She wished to say something, but she thought to herself: "Perhaps I do not understand how gentleman's boots should be made. I suppose Michael knows more about it—and I won't interfere."

When Michael had cut up the leather, he took a thread and began to sew not with two ends, as boots are sewn, but with a single end, as for soft slippers.

Again Matryona wondered, but again she did not interfere. Michael sewed on steadily till noon. Then Simon rose for dinner, looked around, and saw that Michael had made slippers out of the gentleman's leather.

"Ah," groaned Simon, and he thought, "How is it that Michael, who has been with me a whole year and never made a mistake before, should do such a dreadful thing? The gentleman ordered high boots, welted, with whole fronts, and Michael has made soft slippers with single soles, and has wasted the leather. What am I to say to the gentleman? I can never replace leather such as this."

And he said to Michael, "What are you doing, friend? You have ruined me! You know the gentleman ordered high boots, but see what you have made!"

Hardly had he begun to rebuke Michael, when "rat-tat" went the iron ring that hung at the door. Someone was knocking. They looked out of the window; a man had come on horseback, and was fastening his horse. They opened the door, and the servant who had been with the gentleman came in.

"Good day," said he.

"Good day," replied Simon. "What can we do for you?"

"My mistress has sent me about the boots."

"What about the boots?"

"Why, my master no longer needs them. He is dead."

"Is it possible?"

"He did not live to get home after leaving you, but died in the carriage. When we reached home and the servants came to help him alight, he rolled over like a sack. He was dead already, and so stiff that he could hardly be got out of the carriage. My mistress sent me here, saying: 'Tell the bootmaker that the gentleman who ordered boots of him and left the leather for them no longer needs the boots, but that he must quickly make soft slippers for the corpse. Wait till they are ready, and bring them back with you.' That is why I have come."

Michael gathered up the remnants of the leather; rolled them up, took the soft slippers he had made, slapped them together, wiped them down with his apron, and handed them and the roll of leather to the servant, who took them and said: "Goodbye, masters, and good day to you!"

VIII

Another year passed, and another, and Michael was now living his sixth year with Simon. He lived as before. He went nowhere, only spoke when necessary, and had only smiled twice in all those years—once when Matryona gave him food, and a second time when the gentleman was in their hut. Simon was more than pleased with his workman. He never now asked him where he came from, and only feared lest Michael should go away.

They were all at home one day. Matryona was putting iron pots in the oven; the children were running along the benches and looking out of the window; Simon was sewing at one window, and Michael was fastening on a heel at the other.

One of the boys ran along the bench to Michael, leant on his shoulder, and looked out of the window.

"Look, Uncle Michael! There is a lady with little girls! She seems to be coming here. And one of the girls is lame."

When the boy said that, Michael dropped his work, turned to the window, and looked out into the street.

Simon was surprised. Michael never used to look out into the street, but now he pressed against the window, staring at something. Simon also looked out, and saw that a well-dressed woman was really coming to his hut, leading by the hand two little girls in fur coats and woollen shawls. The girls could hardly be told one from the other, except that one of them was crippled in her left leg and walked with a limp.

The woman stepped into the porch and entered the passage. Feeling about for the entrance she found the latch, which she lifted, and opened the door. She let the two girls go in first, and followed them into the hut.

"Good day, good folk!"

"Pray come in," said Simon. "What can we do for you?"

The woman sat down by the table. The two little girls pressed close to her knees, afraid of the people in the hut.

"I want leather shoes made for these two little girls for spring."

"We can do that. We never have made such small shoes, but we can make them; either welted or turnover shoes, linen lined. My man, Michael, is a master at the work."

Simon glanced at Michael and saw that he had left his work and was sitting with his eyes fixed on the little girls. Simon was surprised. It was true the girls were pretty, with black eyes, plump, and rosy-cheeked, and they wore nice kerchiefs and fur coats, but still Simon could not understand why Michael should look at them like that—just as if he had known them before. He was puzzled, but went on talking with the woman, and arranging the price. Having fixed it, he prepared the measure. The woman lifted the lame girl on to her lap and said: "Take two measures from this little girl. Make one shoe for the lame foot and three for the sound one. They both have the same size feet. They are twins."

Simon took the measure and, speaking of the lame girl, said: "How did it happen to her? She is such a pretty girl. Was she born so?"

"No, her mother crushed her leg."

Then Matryona joined in. She wondered who this woman was, and whose the children were, so she said: "Are not you their mother then?"

"No, my good woman; I am neither their mother nor

any relation to them. They were quite strangers to me, but I adopted them."

"They are not your children and yet you are so fond of them?"

"How can I help being fond of them? I fed them both at my own breasts. I had a child of my own, but God took him. I was not so fond of him as I now am of them."

"Then whose children are they?"

IX

The woman, having begun talking, told them the whole story.

"It is about six years since their parents died, both in one week: their father was buried on the Tuesday, and their mother died on the Friday. These orphans were born three days after their father's death, and their mother did not live another day. My husband and I were then living as peasants in the village. We were neighbours of theirs, our yard being next to theirs. Their father was a lonely man; a wood-cutter in the forest. When felling trees one day, they let one fall on him. It fell across his body and crushed his bowels out. They hardly got him home before his soul went to God; and that same week his wife gave birth to twins—these little girls. She was poor and alone; she had no one, young or old, with her. Alone she gave them birth, and alone she met her death."

"The next morning I went to see her, but when I entered the hut, she, poor thing, was already stark and cold. In dying she had rolled on to this child and crushed her leg. The village folk came to the hut, washed the body, laid her out, made a coffin, and buried her. They were good folk. The babies were left alone. What was to be done with them? I was the only woman there who had a baby at the time. I was nursing my first-born—eight weeks old. So I took them for a time. The peasants came together, and thought and thought what to do with them; and at last they said to me: 'For the present, Mary, you had better keep the girls, and later on we will arrange what to do for them.' So I nursed the sound one at my breast, but at first I did not feed this crippled one. I did not suppose she would live. But then I thought to myself, why should the poor innocent suffer? I pitied her, and began to feed her. And so I fed my own boy and these two—the three of them—at my own breast. I was young and strong, and had good food, and God gave me so much milk that at times it even overflowed. I used sometimes to feed two at a time, while the third was waiting. When one had enough I nursed the third. And God so ordered it that these grew up, while my own was buried before he was two years old. And I had no more children, though we prospered. Now my husband is working for the corn merchant at the mill. The pay is good, and we are well off. But I have no children of my own, and how lonely I should be without these little girls! How can I help loving them! They are the joy of my life!"

She pressed the lame little girl to her with one hand, while with the other she wiped the tears from her cheeks.

And Matryona sighed, and said: "The proverb is true that says, 'One may live without father or mother, but one cannot live without God.'"

So they talked together, when suddenly the whole hut was lighted up as though by summer lightning from the corner where Michael sat. They all looked towards him and saw him sitting, his hands folded on his knees, gazing upwards and smiling.

X

The woman went away with the girls. Michael rose from the bench, put down his work, and took off his apron. Then, bowing low to Simon and his wife, he said: "Farewell, masters. God has forgiven me. I ask your forgiveness, too, for anything done amiss."

And they saw that a light shone from Michael. And Simon rose, bowed down to Michael, and said: "I see, Michael, that you are no common man, and I can neither keep you nor question you. Only tell me this: how is it that when I found you and brought you home, you were gloomy, and when my wife gave you food you smiled at her and became brighter? Then when the gentleman came to order the boots, you smiled again and became brighter still? And now, when this woman brought the little girls, you smiled a third time, and have become as bright as day? Tell me, Michael, why does your face shine so, and why did you smile those three times?"

And Michael answered: "Light shines from me because I have been punished, but now God has pardoned me. And I smiled three times, because God sent me to learn three truths, and I have learnt them. One I learnt when your wife pitied me, and that is why I smiled the first time. The second I learnt when the rich man ordered the boots, and then I smiled again. And now, when I saw those little girls, I learn the third and last truth, and I smiled the third time."

And Simon said, "Tell me, Michael, what did God punish you for? And what were the three truths? That I, too, may know them."

And Michael answered: "God punished me for disobeying Him. I was an angel in heaven and disobeyed God. God sent me to fetch a woman's soul. I flew to earth, and saw a sick woman lying alone, who had just given birth to twin girls. They moved feebly at their mother's side, but she could not lift them to her breast. When she saw me, she understood that God had sent me for her soul, and she wept and said: 'Angel of God! My husband has just been buried, killed by a falling tree. I have neither sister, nor aunt, nor mother: no one to care for my orphans. Do not take my soul! Let me nurse my babes, feed them, and set them on their feet before I die. Children cannot live without father or mother.' And I hearkened to her. I placed one child at her breast and gave the other into her arms, and returned to the Lord in heaven. I flew to the Lord, and said: 'I could not take the soul of the mother. Her husband was killed by a tree; the woman has twins, and prays that her soul may not be taken. She says: "Let me nurse and feed my children, and set them on their feet. Children cannot live without father or mother." I have not taken her soul.' And God said: 'Go—take the mother's soul, and learn three truths: Learn What dwells in man, What is not given to man, and What men live by. When thou has learnt these things, thou shalt return to heaven.' So I flew again to earth and took the mother's soul. The babies dropped from her breasts. Her body rolled over on the bed and crushed one baby, twisting its leg. I rose above the village, wishing to take her soul to God; but a wind seized me, and my wings drooped and dropped off. Her soul rose alone to God, while I fell to earth by the roadside."

XI

And Simon and Matryona understood who it was that had lived with them, and whom they had clothed and fed. And they wept with awe and with joy. And the angel said: "I was alone in the field, naked. I had never known human needs, cold and hunger, till I became a man. I was famished, frozen, and did not know what to do. I saw, near the field I was in, a shrine built for God, and I went to it hoping to find shelter. But the shrine was locked, and I could not enter. So I sat down behind the shrine to shelter myself at least from the wind. Evening drew on. I was hungry, frozen, and in pain. Suddenly I heard a man coming along the road. He carried a pair of boots, and was talking to himself. For the first time since I became a man I saw the mortal face of a man, and his face seemed terrible to me and I turned from it. And I heard the man talking to himself of how to cover his body from the cold in winter, and how to feed wife and children. And I thought: 'I am perishing of cold and hunger, and here is a man thinking only of how to clothe himself and his wife, and how to get bread for themselves. He cannot help me.' When the man saw me he frowned and became still more terrible, and passed me by on the other side. I despaired; but suddenly I heard him coming back. I looked up, and did not recognize the same man; before, I had seen death in his face; but now he was alive, and I recognized in him the presence of God. He came up to me, clothed me, took me with him, and brought me to his home. I entered the house; a woman came to meet us and began to speak. The woman was still more terrible than the man had been; the spirit of death came from her mouth; I could not breathe for the stench of death that spread around her. She wished to drive me out into the cold, and I knew that if she did so she would die. Suddenly her husband spoke to her of God, and the woman changed at once. And when she brought me food and looked at me, I glanced at her and saw that death no longer dwelt in her; she had become alive, and in her, too, I saw God.

"Then I remembered the first lesson God had set me: 'Learn what dwells in man.' And I understood that in man dwells Love! I was glad that God had already begun to show me what He had promised, and I smiled for the first time. But I had not yet learnt all. I did not yet know What is not given to man, and What men live by.

"I lived with you, and a year passed. A man came to order boots that should wear for a year without losing shape or cracking. I looked at him, and suddenly, behind his shoulder, I saw my comrade—the angel of death. None but me saw that angel; but

I knew him, and knew that before the sun set he would take that rich man's soul. And I thought to myself, 'The man is making preparations for a year, and does not know that he will die before evening.' And I remembered God's second saying, 'Learn what is not given to man.'

"What dwells in man I already knew. Now I learnt what is not given him. It is not given to man to know his own needs. And I smiled for the second time. I was glad to have seen my comrade angel—glad also that God had revealed to me the second saying.

"But I still did not know all. I did not know What men live by. And I lived on, waiting till God should reveal to me the last lesson. In the sixth year came the girl-twins with the woman; and I recognized the girls, and heard how they had been kept alive. Having heard the story, I thought, 'Their mother besought me for the children's sake, and I believed her when she said that children cannot live without father or mother; but a stranger has nursed them, and has brought them up.' And when the woman showed her love for the children that were not her own, and wept over them, I saw in her the living God and understood What men live by. And I knew that God had revealed to me the last lesson, and had forgiven my sin. And then I smiled for the third time."

XII

And the angel's body was bared, and he was clothed in light so that eye could not look on him; and his voice grew louder, as though it came not from him but from heaven above. And the angel said:

"I have learnt that all men live not by care for themselves but by love.

"It was not given to the mother to know what her children needed for their life. Nor was it given to the rich man to know what he himself needed. Nor is it given to any man to know whether, when evening comes, he will need boots for his body or slippers for his corpse.

"I remained alive when I was a man, not by care of myself, but because love was present in a passer-by, and because he and his wife pitied and loved me. The orphans remained alive not because of their mother's care, but because there was love in the heart of a woman, a stranger to them, who pitied and loved them. And all men live not by the thought they spend on their own welfare, but because love exists in man.

"I knew before that God gave life to men and desires that they should live; now I understood more than that.

"I understood that God does not wish men to live apart, and therefore he does not reveal to them what each one needs for himself; but he wishes them to live united, and therefore reveals to each of them what is necessary for all.

"I have now understood that though it seems to men that they live by care for themselves, in truth it is love alone by which they live. He who has love, is in God, and God is in him, for God is love."

And the angel sang praise to God, so that the hut trembled at his voice. The roof opened, and a column of fire rose from earth to heaven. Simon and his wife and children fell to the ground. Wings appeared upon the angel's shoulders, and he rose into the heavens.

And when Simon came to himself the hut stood as before, and there was no one in it but his own family.

Evil Allures,
But Good Endures

[Written and first published in 1885. This story reflects the
Christian commandment to avoid anger. It is also translated as
'Hatred is Sweet, but God is Strong' by R. Nesbit Bain. The version
here is taken from the collection *Twenty-three Tales* (1906)
translated by Louise and Aylmer Maude.]

There lived in olden times a good and kindly man. He had this world's goods in abundance, and many slaves to serve him. And the slaves prided themselves on their master, saying:

"There is no better lord than ours under the sun. He feeds and clothes us well, and gives us work suited to our strength. He bears no malice, and never speaks a harsh word to anyone. He is not like other masters, who treat their slaves worse than cattle, punishing them whether they deserve it or not, and never giving them a friendly word. He wishes us well, does good, and speaks kindly to us. We do not wish for a better life."

Thus the slaves praised their lord, and the Devil, seeing it, was vexed that slaves should live in such love and harmony with their master. So getting one of them, whose name was Aleb, into his power, the Devil ordered him to tempt the other slaves. And one day, when they were all sitting together resting and talking of their master's goodness, Aleb raised his voice, and said:

"It is stupid to make so much of our master's goodness. The Devil himself would be kind to you, if you did what he wanted. We serve our master well, and humour him in all things. As soon as he thinks of anything, we do it: foreseeing all his wishes. What can he do but be kind to us? Just try how it will be if, instead of humouring him, we do him some harm instead. He will act like anyone else, and will repay evil for evil, as the worst of masters do.

The other slaves began denying what Aleb had said, and at last bet with him. Aleb undertook to make their master angry. If he failed, he was to lose his holiday garment; but if he succeeded, the other slaves were to give him theirs. Moreover, they promised to defend him against the master, and to set him free if he should be put in chains or imprisoned. Having arranged this bet, Aleb agreed to make his master angry next morning.

Aleb was a shepherd, and had in his charge a number of valuable, pure-bred sheep, of which his master was very fond.

Next morning, when the master brought some visitors into the inclosure to show them the valuable sheep, Aleb winked at his companions, as if to say:

"See, now, how angry I will make him."

All the other slaves assembled, looking in at the gates or over the fence, and the Devil climbed a tree near by to see how his servant would do his work. The master walked about the inclosure, showing his guests the ewes and lambs, and presently he wished to show them his finest ram.

"All the rams are valuable," said he, "but I have one with closely twisted horns, which is priceless. I prize him as the apple of my eye."

Startled by the strangers, the sheep rushed about the inclosure, so that the visitors could not get a good look at the ram. As soon as it stood still, Aleb startled the sheep as if by accident, and they all got mixed up again. The visitors could not make out which was the priceless ram. At last the master got tired of it.

"Aleb, dear friend," he said, "pray catch our best ram for me, the one with the tightly twisted horns. Catch him very carefully, and hold him still for a moment."

Scarcely had the master said this, when Aleb rushed in among the sheep like a lion, and clutched the priceless ram. Holding him fast by the wool, he seized the left hind leg with one hand, and, before his master's eyes, lifted it and jerked it so that it snapped like a dry branch. He had broken the ram's leg, and it fell bleating on to its knees. Then Aleb seized the right hind leg, while the left twisted round and hung quite limp. The visitors and the slaves exclaimed in dismay, and the Devil, sitting up in the tree, rejoiced that Aleb had done his task so cleverly. The master looked as black as thunder, frowned, bent his head, and did not say a word. The visitors and the slaves were silent, too, waiting to see what would follow. After remaining silent for a while, the master shook himself as if to throw off some burden. Then he lifted his head, and raising his eyes heavenward, remained so for a short time. Presently the wrinkles passed from his face, and he looked down at Aleb with a smile, saying:

"Oh, Aleb, Aleb! Your master bade you anger me; but my master is stronger than yours. I am not angry with you, but I will make your master angry. You are afraid that I shall punish you, and you have been wishing for your freedom. Know, then, Aleb, that I shall not punish you; but, as you wish to be free, here, before my guests, I set you free. Go where you like, and take your holiday garment with you!"

And the kind master returned with his guests to the house; but the Devil, grinding his teeth, fell down from the tree, and sank through the ground.

Two Old Men

[Written and first published in 1885. The Christian commandment to love all people alike is evident in this tale. The version here is taken from *Twenty-three Tales* (1906) translated by Louise and Aylmer Maude.]

I

'The woman saith unto him, Sir, I perceive that thou art a prophet. Our fathers worshipped in this mountain; and ye say, that in Jerusalem is the place where men ought to worship. Jesus saith unto her, Woman, believe me, the hour cometh when neither in this mountain, nor in Jerusalem, shall ye worship the Father . . . But the hour cometh, and now is, when the true worshippers shall worship the Father in spirit and truth: for such doth the Father seek to be his worshippers.'

—John iv. 19-21, 23.

There were once two old men who decided to go on a pilgrimage to worship God at Jerusalem. One of them was a well-to-do peasant named Efím Tarásitch Shevélef. The other, Elisha Bódrof, was not so well off.

Efím was a staid man, serious and firm. He neither drank nor smoked nor took snuff, and had never used bad language in his life. He had twice served as village Elder, and when he left office his accounts were in good order. He had a large family: two sons and a married grandson, all living with him. He was hale, long-bearded and erect, and it was only when he was past sixty that a little grey began to show itself in his beard.

Elisha was neither rich nor poor. He had formerly gone out carpentering, but now that he was growing old he stayed at home and kept bees. One of his sons had gone away to find work, the other was living at home. Elisha was a kindly and cheerful old man. It is true he drank sometimes, and he took snuff, and was fond of singing; but he was a peaceable man, and lived on good terms with his family and with his neighbours. He was short and dark, with a curly beard, and, like his patron saint Elisha, he was quite bald-headed.

The two old men had taken a vow long since and had arranged to go on a pilgrimage to Jerusalem together: but Efím could never spare the time; he always had so much business on hand; as soon as one thing was finished he started another. First he had to arrange his grandson's marriage; then to wait for his youngest son's return from the army, and after that he began building a new hut.

One holiday the two old men met outside the hut and, sitting down on some timber, began to talk.

"Well," asked Elisha, "when are we to fulfil our vow?"

Efím made a wry face.

"We must wait," he said. "This year has turned out a hard one for me. I started building this hut thinking it would cost me something over a hundred roubles, but now it's getting on for three hundred and it's still not finished. We shall have to wait till the summer. In summer, God willing, we will go without fail."

"It seems to me we ought not to put it off, but should go at once," said Elisha. "Spring is the best time."

"The time's right enough, but what about my building? How can I leave that?"

"As if you had no one to leave in charge! Your son can look after it."

"But how? My eldest son is not trustworthy—he sometimes takes a glass too much."

"Ah, neighbour, when we die they'll get on without us. Let your son begin now to get some experience."

"That's true enough; but somehow when one begins a thing one likes to see it done."

"Eh, friend, we can never get through all we have to do. The other day the women-folk at home were washing and house-cleaning for Easter. Here something needed doing, there something else, and they could not get everything done. So my eldest daughter-in-law, who's a sensible woman, says: 'We may be thankful the holiday comes without waiting for us, or however hard we worked we should never be ready for it.'"

Efím became thoughtful.

"I've spent a lot of money on this building," he said, "and one can't start on the journey with empty pockets. We shall want a hundred roubles apiece—and it's no small sum."

Elisha laughed.

"Now, come, come, old friend!" he said, "you have ten times as much as I, and yet you talk about money. Only say when we are to start, and though I have nothing now I shall have enough by then."

Efím also smiled.

"Dear me, I did not know you were so rich!" said he. "Why, where will you get it from?"

"I can scrape some together at home, and if that's not enough, I'll sell half a score of hives to my neighbour. He's long been wanting to buy them."

"If they swarm well this year, you'll regret it."

"Regret it! Not I, neighbour! I never regretted anything in my life, except my sins. There's nothing more precious than the soul."

"That's so; still it's not right to neglect things at home."

"But what if our souls are neglected? That's worse. We took the vow, so let us go! Now, seriously, let us go!"

Elisha succeeded in persuading his comrade. In the morning, after thinking it well over, Efím came to Elisha.

"You are right," said he, "let us go. Life and death are in God's hands. We must go now, while we are still alive and have the strength."

A week later the old men were ready to start. Efím had money enough at hand. He took a hundred roubles himself, and left two hundred with his wife.

Elisha, too, got ready. He sold ten hives to his neighbour, with any new swarms that might come from them before the summer. He took seventy roubles for the lot. The rest of the hundred roubles he scraped together from the other members of his household, fairly clearing them all out. His wife gave him all she had been saving up for her funeral; and his daughter-in-law also gave him what she had.

Efím gave his eldest son definite orders about everything: when and how much grass to mow, where to cart the manure, and how to finish off and roof the cottage. He thought out everything, and gave his orders accordingly. Elisha, on the other hand, only explained to his wife that she was to keep separate the swarms from the hives he had sold, and to be sure to let the neighbour have them all, without any tricks. As to household affairs, he did not even mention them.

"You will see what to do and how to do it, as the needs arise," he said. "You are the masters, and will know how to do what's best for yourselves."

So the old men got ready. Their people baked them cakes, and made bags for them, and cut them linen for leg-bands.* They put on new leather shoes, and took with them spare shoes of platted bark. Their families went with them to the end of the village and there took leave of them, and the old men started on their pilgrimage.

Elisha left home in a cheerful mood, and as soon as he was out of the village forgot all his home affairs. His only care was how to please his comrade, how to avoid saying a rude word to any one, how to get to his destination and home again in peace and love. Walking along the road, Elisha would either whisper some prayer to himself or go over in his mind such of the lives of the saints as he was able to remember. When he came across any one on the road, or turned in anywhere for the night, he

---

* Worn by Russian peasants instead of stockings.

tried to behave as gently as possible and to say a godly word. So he journeyed on, rejoicing. One thing only he could not do, he could not give up taking snuff. Though he had left his snuff-box behind, he hankered after it. Then a man he met on the road gave him some snuff; and every now and then he would lag behind (not to lead his comrade into temptation) and would take a pinch of snuff.

Efím too walked well and firmly; doing no wrong and speaking no vain words, but his heart was not so light. Household cares weighed on his mind. He kept worrying about what was going on at home. Had he not forgotten to give his son this or that order? Would his son do things properly? If he happened to see potatoes being planted or manure carted, as he went along, he wondered if his son was doing as he had been told. And he almost wanted to turn back and show him how to do things, or even do them himself.

III

The old men had been walking for five weeks, they had worn out their home-made bark shoes, and had to begin buying new ones when they reached Little Russia.* From the time they left home they had had to pay for their food and for their night's lodging, but when they reached Little Russia the people vied with one another in asking them into their huts. They took them in and fed them,

---

* Little Russia is situated in the south-western part of Russia, and consists of the Governments of Kief, Poltava, Tchernigof, and part of Kharkof and Kherson.

and would accept no payment; and more than that, they put bread or even cakes into their bags for them to eat on the road.

The old men travelled some five hundred miles in this manner free of expense, but after they had crossed the next province, they came to a district where the harvest had failed. The peasants still gave them free lodging at night, but no longer fed them for nothing. Sometimes, even, they could get no bread: they offered to pay for it, but there was none to be had. The people said the harvest had completely failed the year before. Those who had been rich were ruined and had had to sell all they possessed; those of moderate means were left destitute, and those of the poor who had not left those parts, wandered about begging, or starved at home in utter want. In the winter they had had to eat husks and goosefoot.

One night the old men stopped in a small village; they bought fifteen pounds of bread, slept there, and started before sunrise, to get well on their way before the heat of the day. When they had gone some eight miles, on coming to a stream they sat down, and, filling a bowl with water, they steeped some bread in it, and ate it. Then they changed their leg-bands, and rested for a while. Elisha took out his snuff-box. Efím shook his head at him.

"How is it you don't give up that nasty habit?" said he.

Elisha waved his hand. "The evil habit is stronger than I," he said.

Presently they got up and went on. After walking for nearly another eight miles, they came to a large village and passed right through it. It had now grown hot. Elisha was tired out and wanted to rest and have a drink, but Efím did not stop. Efím was the better walker of the two, and Elisha found it hard to keep up with him.

"If I could only have a drink," said he.

"Well, have a drink," said Efím. "I don't want any."

Elisha stopped.

"You go on," he said, "but I'll just run in to the little hut there. I will catch you up in a moment."

"All right," said Efím, and he went on along the high road alone, while Elisha turned back to the hut.

It was a small hut plastered with clay, the bottom a dark colour, the top whitewashed; but the clay had crumbled away. Evidently it was long since it had been re-plastered, and the thatch was off the roof on one side. The entrance to the hut was through the yard. Elisha entered the yard, and saw, lying close to a bank of earth that ran round the hut, a gaunt, beardless man with his shirt tucked into his trousers, as is the custom in Little Russia.[*] The man must have lain down in the shade, but the sun had come round and now shone full on him. Though not asleep, he still lay there. Elisha called to him, and asked for a drink, but the man gave no answer.

"He is either ill or unfriendly," thought Elisha; and going to the door he heard a child crying in the hut. He took hold of the ring that served as a door-handle, and knocked with it.

"Hey, masters!" he called. No answer. He knocked again with his staff.

"Hey, Christians!" Nothing stirred.

"Hey, servants of God!" Still no reply.

Elisha was about to turn away, when he thought he heard a groan the other side of the door.

"Dear me, some misfortune must have happened to the people? I had better have a look."

And Elisha entered the hut.

---

[*] In Great Russia the peasants let their shirt hang outside their trousers.

IV

Elisha turned the ring; the door was not fastened. He opened it and went along up the narrow passage. The door into the dwelling-room was open. To the left was a brick oven; in front against the wall was an icon-stand* and a table before it; by the table was a bench on which sat an old woman, bareheaded and wearing only a single garment. There she sat with her head resting on the table, and near her was a thin, wax-coloured boy, with a protruding stomach. He was asking for something, pulling at her sleeve, and crying bitterly. Elisha entered. The air in the hut was very foul. He looked round, and saw a woman lying on the floor behind the oven: she lay flat on the ground with her eyes closed and her throat rattling, now stretching out a leg, now dragging it in, tossing from side to side; and the foul smell came from her. Evidently she could do nothing for herself and no one had been attending to her needs. The old woman lifted her head, and saw the stranger.

"What do you want?" said she. "What do you want man? We have nothing."

Elisha understood her, though she spoke in the Little-Russian dialect.

"I came in for a drink of water, servant of God," he said.

"There's no one—no one—we have nothing to fetch it in. Go your way."

Then Elisha asked:

"Is there no one among you, then, well enough to attend to that woman?"

---

* An icon (properly ikón) is a representation of God, Christ, an angel, or a saint, usually painted, enamelled, or embossed.

"No, we have no one. My son is dying outside, and we are dying in here."

The little boy had ceased crying when he saw the stranger, but when the old woman began to speak, he began again, and clutching hold of her sleeve cried:

"Bread, Granny, bread."

Elisha was about to question the old woman, when the man staggered into the hut. He came along the passage, clinging to the wall, but as he was entering the dwelling-room he fell in the corner near the threshold, and without trying to get up again to reach the bench, he began to speak in broken words. He brought out a word at a time, stopping to draw breath, and gasping.

"Illness has seized us . . ." said he, "and famine. He is dying . . . of hunger."

And he motioned towards the boy, and began to sob.

Elisha jerked up the sack behind his shoulder and, pulling the straps off his arms, put it on the floor. Then he lifted it on to the bench, and untied the strings. Having opened the sack, he took out a loaf of bread, and, cutting off a piece with his knife, handed it to the man. The man would not take it, but pointed to the little boy and to a little girl crouching behind the oven, as if to say:

"Give it to them."

Elisha held it out to the boy. When the boy smelt bread, he stretched out his arms, and seizing the slice with both his little hands, bit into it so that his nose disappeared in the chunk. The little girl came out from behind the oven and fixed her eyes on the bread. Elisha gave her also a slice. Then he cut off another piece and gave it to the old woman, and she too began munching it.

"If only some water could be brought," she said, "their mouths are parched. I tried to fetch some water yesterday—or was it today—I can't remember, but I fell down and could go no further, and the pail has remained there, unless someone has taken it."

Elisha asked where the well was. The old woman told him. Elisha went out, found the pail, brought some water, and gave the people a drink. The children and the old woman ate some more bread with the water, but the man would not eat.

"I cannot eat," he said.

All this time the younger woman did not show any consciousness, but continued to toss from side to side. Presently Elisha went to the village shop and bought some millet, salt, flour, and oil. He found an axe, chopped some wood, and made a fire. The little girl came and helped him. Then he boiled some soup, and gave the starving people a meal.

The man ate a little, the old woman had some too, and the little girl and boy licked the bowl clean, and then curled up and fell fast asleep in one another's arms.

The man and the old woman then began telling Elisha how they had sunk to their present state.

"We were poor enough before," said they, "but when the crops failed, what we gathered hardly lasted us through the autumn. We had nothing left by the time winter came, and had to beg from the neighbours and from any one we could. At first they gave, then they began to refuse. Some would have been glad enough to help us, but had nothing to give. And we were ashamed of asking: we were in debt all round, and owed money, and flour, and bread."

"I went to look for work," the man said, "but could find none. Everywhere people were offering to work merely for their own keep. One day you'd get a short job, and then you might spend two days looking for work. Then the old woman and the girl went begging, further away. But they got very little; bread was so scarce. Still we scraped food together somehow, and hoped to struggle through till next harvest, but towards spring people ceased to give anything. And then this illness seized us. Things became worse and worse. One day we might have something to eat, and then nothing for two days. We began eating grass. Whether it was the grass, or what, made my wife ill, I don't know. She could not keep on her legs, and I had no strength left, and there was nothing to help us to recovery."

"I struggled on alone for a while," said the old woman, "but at last I broke down too for want of food, and grew quite weak. The girl also grew weak and timid. I told her to go to the neighbours— she would not leave the hut, but crept into a corner and sat there. The day before yesterday a neighbour looked in, but seeing that we were ill and hungry she turned away and left us. Her husband has had to go away, and she has nothing for her own little ones to eat. And so we lay, waiting for death."

Having heard their story, Elisha gave up the thought of overtaking his comrade that day, and remained with them all night. In the morning he got up and began doing the housework, just as if it were his own home. He kneaded the bread with the old woman's help, and lit the fire. Then he went with the little girl to the neighbours to get the most necessary things; for there was nothing in the hut: everything had been sold for bread—cooking utensils, clothing, and all. So Elisha began replacing what was necessary, making some things himself, and buying some. He remained there one day, then another, and then a third. The little boy picked up strength and, whenever Elisha sat down, crept along the bench and nestled up to him. The little girl brightened up and helped in all the work, running after Elisha and calling, "Daddy, daddy."

The old woman grew stronger, and managed to go out to see a neighbour. The man too improved, and was able to get about, holding on to the wall. Only the wife could not get up, but even she regained consciousness on the third day, and asked for food.

"Well," thought Elisha, "I never expected to waste so much time on the way. Now I must be getting on."

VI

The fourth day was the feast day after the summer fast, and Elisha thought:

"I will stay and break the fast with these people. I'll go and buy them something, and keep the feast with them, and tomorrow evening I will start."

So Elisha went into the village, bought milk, wheat-flour and dripping, and helped the old woman to boil and bake for the morrow. On the feast day Elisha went to church, and then broke the fast with his friends at the hut. That day the wife got up, and managed to move about a bit. The husband had shaved and put on a clean shirt, which the old woman had washed for him; and he went to beg for mercy of a rich peasant in the village to whom his ploughland and meadow were mortgaged. He went to beg the rich peasant to grant him the use of the meadow and field till after the harvest; but in the evening he came back very sad, and began to weep. The rich peasant had shown no mercy, but had said: "Bring me the money."

Elisha again grew thoughtful. "How are they to live now?" thought he to himself. "Other people will go haymaking, but there will be nothing for these to mow, their grass land is mortgaged. The rye will ripen. Others will reap (and what a fine crop mother-earth is giving this year), but they have nothing to look forward to. Their three acres are pledged to the rich peasant. When I am gone, they'll drift back into the state I found them in."

Elisha was in two minds, but finally decided not to leave that evening, but to wait until the morrow. He went out into the yard to sleep. He said his prayers, and lay down; but he could not sleep. On the one hand he felt he ought to be going, for he had spent too much time and money as it was; on the other hand he felt sorry for the people.

"There seems to be no end to it," he said. "First I only meant to bring them a little water and give them each a slice of bread: and just see where it has landed me. It's a case of redeeming the meadow and the cornfield. And when I have done that, I shall have to buy a cow for them, and a horse for the man to cart his sheaves. A nice coil you've got yourself into, brother Elisha! You've slipped your cables and lost your reckoning!"

Elisha got up, lifted his coat which he had been using for a pillow, unfolded it, got out his snuff-box and took a pinch, thinking that it might perhaps clear his thoughts.

But no! He thought and thought, and came to no conclusion. He ought to be going; and yet pity held him back. He did not know what to do. He refolded his coat and put it under his head again. He lay thus for a long time, till the cocks had already crowed once: then he was quite drowsy. And suddenly it seemed as if someone had roused him. He saw that he was dressed for the journey, with the sack on his back and the staff in his hand, and the gate stood ajar so that he could just squeeze through. He was about to pass out, when his sack caught against the fence on one side: he tried to free it, but then his leg-band caught on the other side and came undone. He pulled at the sack, and saw that it had not caught on the fence, but that the little girl was holding it and crying.

"Bread, daddy, bread!"

He looked at his foot, and there was the tiny boy holding him by the leg-band, while the master of the hut and the old woman were looking at him through the window.

Elisha awoke, and said to himself in an audible voice:

"Tomorrow I will redeem their cornfield, and will buy them a horse, and flour to last till the harvest, and a cow for the little ones; or else while I go to seek the Lord beyond the sea, I may lose Him in myself."

Then Elisha fell asleep, and slept till morning. He awoke early, and going to the rich peasant, redeemed both the cornfield and the meadow land. He bought a scythe (for that also had been sold) and brought it back with him. Then he sent the man to mow, and himself went into the village. He heard that there was a horse and cart for sale at the public-house, and he struck a bargain with the owner, and bought them. Then he bought a sack of flour, put it in the cart, and went to see about a cow. As he was going along he overtook two women talking as they went. Though they spoke the Little-Russian dialect, he understood what they were saying.

"At first, it seems, they did not know him; they thought he was just an ordinary man. He came in to ask for a drink of water, and then he remained. Just think of the things he has bought for them! Why they say he bought a horse and cart for them at the publican's, only this morning! There are not many such men in the world. It's worthwhile going to have a look at him."

Elisha heard and understood that he was being praised, and he did not go to buy the cow, but returned to the inn, paid for the horse, harnessed it, drove up to the hut, and got out. The people in the hut were astonished when they saw the horse. They thought it might be for them, but dared not ask. The man came out to open the gate.

"Where did you get a horse from, grandfather," he asked.

"Why, I bought it," said Elisha. "It was going cheap. Go and cut some grass and put it in the manger for it to eat during the night. And take in the sack."

The man unharnessed the horse, and carried the sack into the barn. Then he mowed some grass and put it in the manger. Everybody lay down to sleep. Elisha went outside and lay by the roadside. That evening he took his bag out with him. When everyone was asleep, he got up, packed and fastened his bag, wrapped the linen bands round his legs, put on his shoes and coat, and set off to follow Efím.

VII

When Elisha had walked rather more than three miles it began to grow light. He sat down under a tree, opened his bag, counted his money, and found he had only seventeen roubles and twenty kopeks left.

"Well," thought he, "it is no use trying to cross the sea with this. If I beg my way it may be worse than not going at all. Friend Efím will get to Jerusalem without me, and will place a candle at the shrines in my name. As for me, I'm afraid I shall never fulfil my vow in this life. I must be thankful it was made to a merciful Master, and to one who pardons sinners."

Elisha rose, jerked his bag well up on his shoulders, and turned back. Not wishing to be recognized by any one, he made a circuit to avoid the village, and walked briskly homeward. Coming from home the way had seemed difficult to him, and he had found it hard to keep up with Efím, but now on his return journey, God helped him to get over the ground so that he hardly felt fatigue. Walking seemed like child's play. He went along swinging his staff, and did his forty to fifty miles a day.

When Elisha reached home the harvest was over. His family were delighted to see him again, and all wanted to know what had happened: Why and how he had been left behind? And why he had returned without reaching Jerusalem? But Elisha did not tell them.

"It was not God's will that I should get there," said he. "I lost my money on the way, and lagged behind my companion. Forgive me, for the Lord's sake!"

Elisha gave his old wife what money he had left. Then he questioned them about home affairs. Everything was going on well; all the work had been done, nothing neglected, and all were living in peace and concord.

Efím's family heard of his return the same day, and came for news of their old man; and to them Elisha gave the same answers.

"Efím is a fast walker. We parted three days before St. Peter's day, and I meant to catch him up again, but all sorts of things happened. I lost my money, and had no means to get any further, so I turned back."

The folks were astonished that so sensible a man should have acted so foolishly: should have started and not got to his destination, and should have squandered all his money. They wondered at it for a while, and then forgot all about it; and Elisha forgot it too. He set to work again on his homestead. With his son's help he cut wood for fuel for the winter. He and the women threshed the corn. Then he mended the thatch on the outhouses, put the bees under cover, and handed over to his neighbour the ten hives he had sold him in spring, and all the swarms that had come from them. His wife tried not to tell how many swarms there had been from these hives, but Elisha knew well enough from which there had been swarms and from which not. And instead of ten, he handed over seventeen swarms to his neighbour. Having got everything ready for the winter, Elisha sent his son away to find work, while he himself took to platting shoes of bark, and hollowing out logs for hives.

VIII

All that day while Elisha stopped behind in the hut with the sick people, Efím waited for him. He only went on a little way before he sat down. He waited and waited, had a nap, woke up again, and again sat waiting; but his comrade did not come. He gazed till his eyes ached. The sun was already sinking behind a tree, and still no Elisha was to be seen.

"Perhaps he has passed me," thought Efím, "or perhaps someone gave him a lift and he drove by while I slept, and did not see me. But how could he help seeing me? One can see so far here in the steppe. Shall I go back? Suppose he is on in front, we shall then miss each other completely and it will be still worse. I had better go on, and we shall be sure to meet where we put up for the night."

He came to a village, and told the watchman, if an old man of a certain description came along, to bring him to the hut where Efím stopped. But Elisha did not turn up that night. Efím went on, asking all he met whether they had not seen a little, bald-headed, old man? No one had seen such a traveller. Efím wondered, but went on alone, saying:

"We shall be sure to meet in Odessa, or on board the ship," and he did not trouble more about it.

On the way, he came across a pilgrim wearing a priest's coat, with long hair and a skull-cap such as priests wear. This pilgrim had been to Mount Athos, and was now going to Jerusalem for the second time. They both stopped at the same place one night, and, having met, they travelled on together.

They got safely to Odessa, and there had to wait three days for a ship. Many pilgrims from many different parts were in the same case. Again Efím asked about Elisha, but no one had seen him.

Efím got himself a foreign passport, which cost him five roubles. He paid forty roubles for a return ticket to Jerusalem, and bought a supply of bread and herrings for the voyage.

The pilgrim began explaining to Efím how he might get on to the ship without paying his fare; but Efím would not listen. "No, I came prepared to pay, and I shall pay," said he.

The ship was freighted, and the pilgrims went on board, Efím and his new comrade among them. The anchors were weighed, and the ship put out to sea.

All day they sailed smoothly, but towards night a wind arose, rain came on, and the vessel tossed about and shipped water. The people were frightened: the women wailed and screamed, and some of the weaker men ran about the ship looking for shelter. Efím too was frightened, but he would not show it, and remained at the place on deck where he had settled down when first he came on board, beside some old men from Tambóf. There they sat silent, all night and all next day, holding on to their sacks. On the third day it grew calm, and on the fifth day they anchored at Constantinople. Some of the pilgrims went on shore to visit the Church of St. Sophia, now held by the Turks. Efím remained on the ship, and only bought some white bread. They lay there for twenty-four hours, and then put to sea again. At Smyrna they stopped again; and at Alexandria; but at last they arrived safely at Jaffa, where all the pilgrims had to disembark. From there still it was more than forty miles by road to Jerusalem. When disembarking the people were again much frightened. The ship was high, and the people were dropped into boats, which rocked so much that it was easy to miss them and fall into the water. A couple of men did get a wetting, but at last all were safely landed.

They went on foot, and at noon on the third day reached Jerusalem. They stopped outside the town, at the Russian inn, where their passports were indorsed. Then, after dinner, Efím visited the Holy Places with his companion, the pilgrim. It was not the time when they could be admitted to the Holy Sepulchre, but they went to the Patriarchate. All the pilgrims assembled there. The women were separated from the men, who were all told to sit in a circle, barefoot. Then a monk came in with a towel to wash their feet. He washed, wiped, and then kissed their feet, and did this to everyone in the circle. Efím's feet were washed and kissed, with the rest. He stood through vespers and matins, prayed, placed candles at the shrines, handed in booklets inscribed with his parents' names, that they might be mentioned in the church prayers. Here at the Patriarchate food and wine were given them. Next morning they went to the cell of Mary of Egypt, where she had lived doing penance. Here too they placed candles and had prayers read. From there they went to Abraham's Monastery, and saw the place where Abraham intended to slay his son as an offering to God. Then they visited the spot where Christ appeared to Mary Magdalene, and the Church of James, the Lord's brother. The pilgrim showed Efím all these places, and told him how much money to give at each place. At mid-day they returned to the inn and had dinner. As they were preparing to lie down and rest, the pilgrim cried out, and began to search his clothes, feeling them all over.

"My purse has been stolen, there were twenty-three roubles in it," said he, "two ten-rouble notes and the rest in change."

He sighed and lamented a great deal, but as there was no help for it, they lay down to sleep.

IX

As Efím lay there, he was assailed by temptation.

"No one has stolen any money from this pilgrim," thought he, "I do not believe he had any. He gave none away anywhere, though he made me give, and even borrowed a rouble from me."

This thought had no sooner crossed his mind, than Efím rebuked himself, saying: "What right have I to judge a man? It is a sin. I will think no more about it." But as soon as his thoughts began to wander, they turned again to the pilgrim: how interested he seemed to be in money, and how unlikely it sounded when he declared that his purse had been stolen.

"He never had any money," thought Efím. "It's all an invention."

Towards evening they got up, and went to midnight Mass at the great Church of the Resurrection, where the Lord's Sepulchre

s. The pilgrim kept close to Efím and went with him everywhere.
They came to the Church; a great many pilgrims were there; some
Russians and some of other nationalities: Greeks, Armenians,
Turks, and Syrians. Efím entered the Holy Gates with the crowd.
A monk led them past the Turkish sentinels, to the place where
the Saviour was taken down from the cross and anointed, and
where candles were burning in nine great candlesticks. The monk
showed and explained everything. Efím offered a candle there.
Then the monk led Efím to the right, up the steps to Golgotha,
to the place where the cross had stood. Efím prayed there. Then
they showed him the cleft where the ground had been rent asunder
to its nethermost depths; then the place where Christ's hands and
feet were nailed to the cross; then Adam's tomb, where the blood
of Christ had dripped on to Adam's bones. Then they showed him
the stone on which Christ sat when the crown of thorns was placed
on His head; then the post to which Christ was bound when He
was scourged. Then Efím saw the stone with two holes for Christ's
feet. They were going to show him something else, but there was
a stir in the crowd, and the people all hurried to the church of the
Lord's Sepulchre itself. The Latin Mass had just finished there, and
the Russian Mass was beginning. And Efím went with the crowd
to the tomb cut in the rock.

He tried to get rid of the pilgrim, against whom he was still
sinning in his mind, but the pilgrim would not leave him, but went
with him to the Mass at the Holy Sepulchre. They tried to get
to the front, but were too late. There was such a crowd that it
was impossible to move either backwards or forwards. Efím stood
looking in front of him, praying, and every now and then feeling
for his purse. He was in two minds: sometimes he thought that the
pilgrim was deceiving him, and then again he thought that if the
pilgrim spoke the truth and his purse had really been stolen, the
same thing might happen to him.

X

Efím stood there gazing into the little chapel in which was the Holy Sepulchre itself with thirty-six lamps burning above it. As he stood looking over the people's heads, he saw something that surprised him. Just beneath the lamps in which the sacred fire burns, and in front of every one, Efím saw an old man in a grey coat, whose bald, shining head was just like Elisha Bódrof.

"It is like him," thought Efím, "but it cannot be Elisha. He could not have got ahead of me. The ship before ours started a week sooner. He could not have caught that; and he was not on ours, for I saw every pilgrim on board."

Hardly had Efím thought this, when the little old man began to pray, and bowed three times: once forwards to God, then once on each side—to the brethren. And as he turned his head to the right, Efím recognized him. It was Elisha Bódrof himself, with his dark, curly beard turning grey at the cheeks, with his brows, his eyes and nose, and his expression of face. Yes, it was he!

Efím was very pleased to have found his comrade again, and wondered how Elisha had got ahead of him.

"Well done, Elisha!" thought he. "See how he has pushed ahead. He must have come across someone who showed him the way. When we get out, I will find him, get rid of this fellow in the skull-cap, and keep to Elisha. Perhaps he will show me how to get to the front also."

Efím kept looking out, so as not to lose sight of Elisha. But when the Mass was over, the crowd began to sway, pushing forward to kiss the tomb, and pushed Efím aside. He was again seized with fear lest his purse should be stolen. Pressing it with his hand, he began elbowing through the crowd, anxious only to get out. When he reached the open, he went about for a long time searching for Elisha both outside and in the Church itself. In the cells of the Church he saw many people of all kinds, eating, and drinking wine, and reading and sleeping there. But Elisha was nowhere to be seen. So Efím returned to the inn without having found his comrade. That evening the pilgrim in the skull-cap did not turn up. He had gone off without repaying the rouble, and Efím was left alone.

The next day Efím went to the Holy Sepulchre again, with an old man from Tambóf, whom he had met on the ship. He tried to get to the front, but was again pressed back; so he stood by a pillar and prayed. He looked before him, and there in the foremost place under the lamps, close to the very Sepulchre of the Lord, stood Elisha, with his arms spread out like a priest at the altar, and with his bald head all shining.

"Well, now," thought Efím, "I won't lose him!"

He pushed forward to the front, but when he got there, there was no Elisha: he had evidently gone away.

Again on the third day Efím looked, and saw at the Sepulchre, in the holiest place, Elisha standing in the sight of all men, his arms outspread, and his eyes gazing upwards as if he saw something above. And his bald head was all shining.

"Well, this time," thought Efím, "he shall not escape me! I will go and stand at the door, then we can't miss one another!"

Efím went out and stood by the door till past noon. Everyone had passed out, but still Elisha did not appear.

Efím remained six weeks in Jerusalem, and went everywhere: to Bethlehem, and to Bethany, and to the Jordan. He had a new shirt sealed at the Holy Sepulchre for his burial, and he took a bottle of water from the Jordan, and some holy earth, and bought candles that had been lit at the sacred flame. In eight places he inscribed names to be prayed for, and he spent all his money, except just enough to get home with. Then he started homeward. He walked to Jaffa, sailed thence to Odessa, and walked home from there on foot.

XI

Efím travelled the same road he had come by; and as he drew nearer home his former anxiety returned as to how affairs were getting on in his absence. 'Much water flows away in a year,' the proverb says. It takes a lifetime to build up a homestead, but not long to ruin it, thought he. And he wondered how his son had managed without him, what sort of spring they were having, how the cattle had wintered, and whether the cottage was well finished. When Efím came to the district where he had parted from Elisha the summer before, he could hardly believe that the people living there were the same. The year before they had been starving, but now they were living in comfort. The harvest had been good, and the people had recovered, and had forgotten their former misery.

One evening Efím reached the very place where Elisha had remained behind; and as he entered the village, a little girl in a white smock ran out of a hut.

"Daddy, daddy, come to our house!"

Efím meant to pass on, but the little girl would not let him. She took hold of his coat, laughing, and pulled him towards the hut, where a woman with a small boy came out into the porch and beckoned to him.

"Come in, grandfather," she said. "Have supper and spend the night with us."

So Efím went in.

"I may as well ask about Elisha," he thought. "I fancy this is the very hut he went to for a drink of water."

The woman helped him off with the bag he carried, and gave him water to wash his face. Then she made him sit down to table, and set milk, curd-cakes and porridge before him. Efím thanked her, and praised her for her kindness to a pilgrim. The woman shook her head.

"We have good reason to welcome pilgrims," she said. "It was a pilgrim who showed us what life is. We were living forgetful of God, and God punished us almost to death. We reached such a pass last summer, that we all lay ill and helpless with nothing to eat. And we should have died, but that God sent an old man to help us—just such a one as you. He came in one day to ask for a drink of water, saw the state we were in, took pity on us, and remained with us. He gave us food and drink, and set us on our feet again; and he redeemed our land, and bought a cart and horse and gave them to us."

Here the old woman entering the hut, interrupted the younger one and said:

"We don't know whether it was a man, or an angel from God. He loved us all, pitied us all, and went away without telling us his name, so that we don't even know whom to pray for. I can see it all before me now! There I lay waiting for death, when in comes a bald-headed old man. He was not anything much to look at, and he asked for a drink of water. I, sinner that I am, thought to myself: "What does he come prowling about here for?" And just think what he did! As soon as he saw us, he let down his bag, on this very spot, and untied it."

Here the little girl joined in.

"No, Granny," said she, "first he put it down here in the middle of the hut, and then he lifted it on to the bench."

And they began discussing and recalling all he had said and done, where he sat and slept, and what he had said to each of them.

At night the peasant himself came home on his horse, and he too began to tell about Elisha and how he had lived with them.

"Had he not come we should all have died in our sins. We were dying in despair, murmuring against God and man. But he set us on our feet again; and through him we learned to know God, and to believe that there is good in man. May the Lord bless him! We used to live like animals; he made human beings of us."

After giving Efím food and drink, they showed him where he was to sleep; and lay down to sleep themselves.

But though Efím lay down, he could not sleep. He could not get Elisha out of his mind, but remembered how he had seen him three times at Jerusalem, standing in the foremost place.

"So that is how he got ahead of me," thought Efím. "God may or may not have accepted my pilgrimage, but He has certainly accepted his!"

Next morning Efím bade farewell to the people, who put some patties in his sack before they went to their work, and he continued his journey.

XII

Efím had been away just a year, and it was spring again when he reached home one evening. His son was not at home, but had gone to the public-house, and when he came back, he had had a drop too much. Efím began questioning him. Everything showed that the young fellow had been unsteady during his father's absence. The money had all been wrongly spent, and the work had been neglected. The father began to upbraid the son; and the son answered rudely.

"Why didn't you stay and look after it yourself?" he said. "You go off, taking the money with you, and now you demand it of me!"

The old man grew angry, and struck his son.

In the morning Efím went to the village Elder to complain of his son's conduct. As he was passing Elisha's house, his friend's wife greeted him from the porch.

"How do you do, neighbour?" she said. "How do you do, dear friend? Did you get to Jerusalem safely?"

Efím stopped.

"Yes, thank God," he said. "I have been there. I lost sight of your old man, but I hear he got home safely."

The old woman was fond of talking:

"Yes, neighbour, he has come back," said she. "He's been back a long time. Soon after Assumption, I think it was, he returned. And we were glad the Lord had sent him back to us! We were dull without him. We can't expect much work from him anymore, his years for work are past; but still he is the head of the household and it's more cheerful when he's at home. And how glad our lad was! He said, 'It's like being without sunlight, when father's away!' It was dull without him, dear friend. We're fond of him, and take good care of him."

"Is he at home now?"

"He is, dear friend. He is with his bees. He is hiving the swarms. He says they are swarming well this year. The Lord has given such strength to the bees that my husband doesn't remember the like. 'The Lord is not rewarding us according to our sins,' he says. Come in, dear neighbour, he will be so glad to see you again."

Efím passed through the passage into the yard and to the apiary, to see Elisha. There was Elisha in his grey coat, without any face-net or gloves, standing, under the birch trees, looking upwards, his arms stretched out and his bald head shining, as Efím had seen him at the Holy Sepulchre in Jerusalem: and above him the sunlight shone through the birches as the flames of fire had done in the holy place, and the golden bees flew round his head like a halo, and did not sting him.

Efím stopped. The old woman called to her husband.

"Here's your friend come," she cried.

Elisha looked round with a pleased face, and came towards Efím, gently picking bees out of his own beard.

"Good day, neighbour, good day, dear friend. Did you get there safely?"

"My feet walked there, and I have brought you some water

from the river Jordan. You must come to my house for it. Bu
whether the Lord accepted my efforts . . ."

"Well the Lord be thanked! May Christ bless you!" said Elisha

Efím was silent for a while, and then added:

"My feet have been there, but whether my soul, or another's
has been there more truly . . ."

"That's God's business, neighbour, God's business,'
interrupted Elisha.

"On my return journey I stopped at the hut where you
remained behind . . ."

Elisha was alarmed, and said hurriedly:

"God's business, neighbour, God's business! Come into the
cottage, I'll give you some of our honey." And Elisha changed the
conversation, and talked of home affairs.

Efím sighed, and did not speak to Elisha of the people in
the hut, nor of how he had seen him in Jerusalem. But he now
understood that the best way to keep one's vows to God and to do
His will, is for each man while he lives to show love and do good
to others.

Little Girls
Wiser than Men

[Written and first published in 1885. This version is taken from
Twenty-three Tales (1906) translated by Louise and Aylmer
Maude.]

It was an early Easter. Sledging was only just over; snow still lay in the yards; and water ran in streams down the village street.

Two little girls from different houses happened to meet in a lane between two homesteads, where the dirty water after running through the farm-yards had formed a large puddle. One girl was very small, the other a little bigger. Their mothers had dressed them both in new frocks. The little one wore a blue frock, the other a yellow print, and both had red kerchiefs on their heads. They had just come from church when they met, and first they showed each other their finery, and then they began to play. Soon the fancy took them to splash about in the water, and the smaller one was going to step into the puddle, shoes and all, when the elder checked her:

"Don't go in so, Malásha," said she, "your mother will scold you. I will take off my shoes and stockings, and you take off yours."

They did so; and then, picking up their skirts, began walking towards each other through the puddle. The water came up to Malásha's ankles, and she said:

"It is deep, Akoúlya, I'm afraid!"

"Come on," replied the other. "Don't be frightened. It won't get any deeper."

When they got near one another, Akoúlya said:

"Mind, Malásha, don't splash. Walk carefully!"

She had hardly said this, when Malásha plumped down her foot so that the water splashed right on to Akoúlya's frock. The frock was splashed, and so were Akoúlya's eyes and nose. When she saw the stains on her frock, she was angry and ran after Malásha to strike her. Malásha was frightened, and seeing that she had got herself into trouble, she scrambled out of the puddle, and prepared to run home. Just then Akoúlya's mother happened to be passing, and seeing that her daughter's skirt was splashed, and her sleeves dirty, she said:

"You naughty, dirty girl, what have you been doing?"

"Malásha did it on purpose," replied the girl.

At this Akoúlya's mother seized Malásha, and struck her on the back of her neck. Malásha began to howl so that she could be heard all down the street. Her mother came out.

"What are you beating my girl for?" said she; and began scolding her neighbour. One word led to another and they had an angry quarrel. The men came out, and a crowd collected in the street, every one shouting and no one listening. They all went on quarrelling, till one gave another a push, and the affair had very nearly come to blows, when Akoúlya's old grandmother, stepping in among them, tried to calm them.

"What are you thinking of, friends? Is it right to behave so? On a day like this, too! It is a time for rejoicing, and not for such folly as this."

They would not listen to the old woman, and nearly knocked her off her feet. And she would not have been able to quiet the crowd, if it had not been for Akoúlya and Malásha themselves. While the women were abusing each other, Akoúlya had wiped the mud off her frock, and gone back to the puddle. She took a stone and began scraping away the earth in front of the puddle to make a channel through which the water could run out into the street. Presently Malásha joined her, and with a chip of wood helped her dig the channel. Just as the men were beginning to fight, the water from the little girls' channel ran streaming into the street towards the very place where the old woman was trying to pacify the men. The girls followed it; one running each side of the little stream.

"Catch it, Malásha! Catch it!" shouted Akoúlya; while Malásha could not speak for laughing.

Highly delighted, and watching the chip float along on their stream, the little girls ran straight into the group of men; and the old woman, seeing them, said to the men:

"Are you not ashamed of yourselves? To go fighting on account of these lassies, when they themselves have forgotten all about it, and are playing happily together. Dear little souls! They are wiser than you!"

The men looked at the little girls, and were ashamed, and, laughing at themselves, went back each to his own home.

"Except ye turn, and become as little children, ye shall in no wise enter into the kingdom of heaven."

Ilyás

[Written and first published in 1885. It is one of the five stories for the people which depict the evil resulting when one does not follow by design or by chance the Christian religious teachings. The story is also translated as 'Elias' by R. Nesbit Bain. This version is taken from *Twenty-three Tales* (1906) translated by Louise and Aylmer Maude.]

There once lived, in the Government of Oufá, a Bashkír named Ilyás. His father, who died a year after he had found his son a wife, did not leave him much property. Ilyás then had only seven mares, two cows, and about a score of sheep. He was a good manager, however, and soon began to acquire more. He and his wife worked from morn till night; rising earlier than others and going later to bed; and his possessions increased year by year. Living in this way, Ilyás little by little acquired great wealth. At the end of thirty-five years he had 200 horses, 150 head of cattle, and 1,200 sheep. Hired labourers tended his flocks and herds, and hired women milked his mares and cows, and made kumiss*, butter and cheese. Ilyás had abundance of everything, and everyone in the district envied him. They said of him:

"Ilyás is a fortunate man: he has plenty of everything. This world must be a pleasant place for him."

People of position heard of Ilyás and sought his acquaintance. Visitors came to him from afar; and he welcomed every one, and gave them food and drink. Whoever might come, there was always kumiss, tea, sherbet, and mutton to set before them. Whenever visitors arrived a sheep would be killed, or sometimes two; and if many guests came he would even slaughter a mare for them.

Ilyás had three children: two sons and a daughter; and he married them all off. While he was poor, his sons worked with him, and looked after the flocks and herds themselves; but when he grew rich they got spoiled, and one of them took to drink. The eldest was killed in a brawl; and the younger, who had married a self-willed woman, ceased to obey his father, and they could not live together any more.

So they parted, and Ilyás gave his son a house and some of the

---

* *Kumiss* (or more properly *koumýs*) is a fermented drink prepared from mare's milk.

cattle; and this diminished his wealth. Soon after that, a disease broke out among Ilyás's sheep, and many died. Then followed a bad harvest, and the hay crop failed; and many cattle died that winter. Then the Kirghíz captured his best herd of horses; and Ilyás's property dwindled away. It became smaller and smaller, while at the same time his strength grew less; till, by the time he was seventy years old, he had begun to sell his furs, carpets, saddles, and tents. At last he had to part with his remaining cattle, and found himself face to face with want. Before he knew how it had happened, he had lost everything, and in their old age he and his wife had to go into service. Ilyás had nothing left, except the clothes on his back, a fur cloak, a cup, his indoor shoes and overshoes, and his wife, Sham-Shemagi, who also was old by this time. The son who had parted from him had gone into a far country, and his daughter was dead, so that there was no one to help the old couple.

Their neighbour, Muhammad-Shah, took pity on them. Muhammad-Shah was neither rich nor poor, but lived comfortably, and was a good man. He remembered Ilyás's hospitality, and pitying him, said:

"Come and live with me, Ilyás, you and your old woman. In summer you can work in my melon-garden as much as your strength allows, and in winter feed my cattle; and Sham-Shemagi shall milk my mares and make kumiss. I will feed and clothe you both. When you need anything, tell me, and you shall have it."

Ilyás thanked his neighbour, and he and his wife took service with Muhammad-Shah as labourers. At first the position seemed hard to them, but they got used to it, and lived on, working as much as their strength allowed.

Muhammad-Shah found it was to his advantage to keep such people, because, having been masters themselves, they knew how to manage and were not lazy, but did all the work they could. Yet it grieved Muhammad-Shah to see people brought so low who had been of such high standing.

It happened once that some of Muhammad-Shah's relatives came from a great distance to visit him, and a Mullah came too.

Muhammad-Shah told Ilyás to catch a sheep and kill it. Ilyás skinned the sheep, and boiled it, and sent it in to the guests. The guests ate the mutton, had some tea, and then began drinking kumiss. As they were sitting with their host on down cushions on a carpet, conversing and sipping kumiss from their cups, Ilyás, having finished his work, passed by the open door. Muhammad-Shah, seeing him pass, said to one of the guests:

"Did you notice that old man who passed just now?"

"Yes," said the visitor, "what is there remarkable about him?"

"Only this—that he was once the richest man among us," replied the host. "His name is Ilyás. You may have heard of him."

"Of course I have heard of him," the guest answered, "I never saw him before, but his fame has spread far and wide."

"Yes, and now he has nothing left," said Muhammad-Shah, "and he lives with me as my labourer, and his old woman is here too—she milks the mares."

The guest was astonished: he clicked with his tongue, shook his head, and said:

"Fortune turns like a wheel. One man it lifts, another it sets down! Does not the old man grieve over all he has lost?"

"Who can tell. He lives quietly and peacefully, and works well."

"May I speak to him?" asked the guest. "I should like to ask him about his life."

"Why not?" replied the master, and he called from the *kibítka**
in which they were sitting:

"Babay;" (which in the Bashkir tongue means 'Grandfather') "come in and have a cup of kumiss with us, and call your wife here also."

Ilyás entered with his wife; and after exchanging greetings with his master and the guests, he repeated a prayer, and seated himself near the door. His wife passed in behind the curtain and sat down with her mistress.

---

* A *kibítka* is a movable dwelling, made up of detachable wooden frames, forming a round, and covered over with felt.

A cup of kumiss was handed to Ilyás; he wished the guests and his master good health, bowed, drank a little, and put down the cup.

"Well, Daddy," said the guest who had wished to speak to him, "I suppose you feel rather sad at the sight of us. It must remind you of your former prosperity, and of your present sorrows."

Ilyás smiled, and said:

"If I were to tell you what is happiness and what is misfortune, you would not believe me. You had better ask my wife. She is a woman, and what is in her heart is on her tongue. She will tell you the whole truth."

The guest turned towards the curtain.

"Well, Granny," he cried, "tell me how your former happiness compares with your present misfortune."

And Sham-Shemagi answered from behind the curtain:

"This is what I think about it: My old man and I lived for fifty years seeking happiness and not finding it; and it is only now, these last two years, since we had nothing left and have lived as labourers, that we have found real happiness, and we wish for nothing better than our present lot."

The guests were astonished, and so was the master; he even rose and drew the curtain back, so as to see the old woman's face. There she stood with her arms folded, looking at her old husband, and smiling; and he smiled back at her. The old woman went on:

"I speak the truth and do not jest. For half a century we sought for happiness, and as long as we were rich we never found it. Now that we have nothing left, and have taken service as labourers, we have found such happiness that we want nothing better."

"But in what does your happiness consist?" asked the guest.

"Why, in this," she replied, "when we were rich, my husband and I had so many cares that we had no time to talk to one another, or to think of our souls, or to pray to God. Now we had visitors, and had to consider what food to set before them, and what presents to give them, lest they should speak ill of us. When they left, we had to look after our labourers, who were always trying to shirk work and get the best food, while we wanted to get all we could out of them. So we sinned. Then we were in fear lest a wolf should kill a foal or a calf, or thieves steal our horses. We lay awake at night, worrying lest the ewes should overlie their lambs, and we got up again and again to see that all was well. One thing attended to, another care would spring up: how, for instance, to get enough fodder for the winter. And besides that, my old man and I used to disagree. He would say we must do so and so, and I would differ from him; and then we disputed—sinning again. So we passed from one trouble to another, from one sin to another, and found no happiness."

"Well, and now?"

"Now, when my husband and I wake in the morning, we always have a loving word for one another, and we live peacefully, having nothing to quarrel about. We have no care but how best to serve our master. We work as much as our strength allows, and do it with a will, that our master may not lose, but profit by us. When we come in, dinner or supper is ready and there is kumiss to drink. We have fuel to burn when it is cold, and we have our fur cloak. And we have time to talk, time to think of our souls, and time to pray. For fifty years we sought happiness, but only now at last have we found it."

The guests laughed.

But Ilyás said:

"Do not laugh, friends. It is not a matter for jesting—it is the truth of life. We also were foolish at first, and wept at the loss of our wealth; but now God has shown us the truth, and we tell it, not for our own consolation, but for your good."

And the Mullah said:

"That is a wise speech. Ilyás has spoken the exact truth. The same is said in Holy Writ."

And the guests ceased laughing and became thoughtful.

The Three Hermits

AN OLD LEGEND CURRENT IN THE VÓLGA DISTRICT

[Written and first published in 1885. This version is a translation
by Louise and Aylmer Maude collected in *Twenty-three Tales*
(1906).]

'And in praying use not vain repetitions, as the Gentiles do: for they think that they shall be heard for their much speaking. Be not therefore like unto them: for your Father knoweth what things ye have need of, before ye ask Him.'

—Matt. vi. 7, 8.

A Bishop was sailing from Archangel to the Solovétsk Monastery; and on the same vessel were a number of pilgrims on their way to visit the shrines at that place. The voyage was a smooth one. The wind favourable, and the weather fair. The pilgrims lay on deck, eating, or sat in groups talking to one another. The Bishop, too, came on deck, and as he was pacing up and down, he noticed a group of men standing near the prow and listening to a fisherman, who was pointing to the sea and telling them something. The Bishop stopped, and looked in the direction in which the man was pointing. He could see nothing, however, but the sea glistening in the sunshine. He drew nearer to listen, but when the man saw him, he took off his cap and was silent. The rest of the people also took off their caps, and bowed.

"Do not let me disturb you, friends," said the Bishop. "I came to hear what this good man was saying."

"The fisherman was telling us about the hermits," replied one, a tradesman, rather bolder than the rest.

"What hermits?" asked the Bishop, going to the side of the vessel and seating himself on a box. "Tell me about them. I should like to hear. What were you pointing at?"

"Why, that little island you can just see over there," answered the man, pointing to a spot ahead and a little to the right. "That is the island where the hermits live for the salvation of their souls."

"Where is the island?" asked the Bishop. "I see nothing."

"There, in the distance, if you will please look along my hand. Do you see that little cloud? Below it, and a bit to the left, there is just a faint streak. That is the island."

The Bishop looked carefully, but his unaccustomed eyes could make out nothing but the water shimmering in the sun.

"I cannot see it," he said. "But who are the hermits that live there?"

"They are holy men," answered the fisherman. "I had long heard tell of them, but never chanced to see them myself till the year before last."

And the fisherman related how once, when he was out fishing, he had been stranded at night upon that island, not knowing where he was. In the morning, as he wandered about the island, he came across an earth hut, and met an old man standing near it. Presently two others came out, and after having fed him, and dried his things, they helped him mend his boat.

"And what are they like?" asked the Bishop.

"One is a small man and his back is bent. He wears a priest's cassock and is very old; he must be more than a hundred, I should say. He is so old that the white of his beard is taking a greenish tinge, but he is always smiling, and his face is as bright as an angel's from heaven. The second is taller, but he also is very old. He wears tattered, peasant coat. His beard is broad, and of a yellowish grey colour. He is a strong man. Before I had time to help him, he turned my boat over as if it were only a pail. He too, is kindly and cheerful. The third is tall, and has a beard as white as snow and reaching to his knees. He is stern, with overhanging eyebrows; and he wears nothing but a mat tied round his waist."

"And did they speak to you?" asked the Bishop.

"For the most part they did everything in silence, and spoke but little even to one another. One of them would just give a glance, and the others would understand him. I asked the tallest whether they had lived there long. He frowned, and muttered something as if he were angry; but the oldest one took his hand and smiled, and then the tall one was quiet. The oldest one only said: 'Have mercy upon us,' and smiled."

While the fisherman was talking, the ship had drawn nearer to the island.

"There, now you can see it plainly, if your Grace will please to look," said the tradesman, pointing with his hand.

The Bishop looked, and now he really saw a dark streak—which was the island. Having looked at it a while, he left the prow of the vessel, and going to the stern, asked the helmsman:

"What island is that?"

"That one," replied the man, "has no name. There are many such in this sea."

"Is it true that there are hermits who live there for the salvation of their souls?"

"So it is said, your Grace, but I don't know if it's true. Fishermen say they have seen them; but of course they may only be spinning yarns."

"I should like to land on the island and see these men," said the Bishop. "How could I manage it?"

"The ship cannot get close to the island," replied the helmsman, "but you might be rowed there in a boat. You had better speak to the captain."

The captain was sent for and came.

"I should like to see these hermits," said the Bishop. "Could I not be rowed ashore?"

The captain tried to dissuade him.

"Of course it could be done," said he, "but we should lose much time. And if I might venture to say so to your Grace, the old men are not worth your pains. I have heard say that they are foolish old fellows, who understand nothing, and never speak a word, any more than the fish in the sea."

"I wish to see them," said the Bishop, "and I will pay you for your trouble and loss of time. Please let me have a boat."

There was no help for it; so the order was given. The sailors trimmed the sails, the steersman put up the helm, and the ship's course was set for the island. A chair was placed at the prow for the Bishop, and he sat there, looking ahead. The passengers all collected at the prow, and gazed at the island. Those who had the sharpest eyes could presently make out the rocks on it, and then a mud hut was seen. At last one man saw the hermits themselves.

The captain brought a telescope and, after looking through it, handed it to the Bishop.

"It's right enough. There are three men standing on the shore. There, a little to the right of that big rock."

The Bishop took the telescope, got it into position, and he saw the three men: a tall one, a shorter one, and one very small and bent, standing on the shore and holding each other by the hand.

The captain turned to the Bishop.

"The vessel can get no nearer in than this, your Grace. If you wish to go ashore, we must ask you to go in the boat, while we anchor here."

The cable was quickly let out, the anchor cast, and the sails furled. There was a jerk, and the vessel shook. Then a boat having been lowered, the oarsmen jumped in, and the Bishop descended the ladder and took his seat. The men pulled at their oars, and the boat moved rapidly towards the island. When they came within a stone's throw, they saw three old men: a tall one with only a mat tied round his waist: a shorter one in a tattered peasant coat, and a very old one bent with age and wearing an old cassock—all three standing hand in hand.

The oarsmen pulled in to the shore, and held on with the boathook while the Bishop got out.

The old men bowed to him, and he gave them his benediction, at which they bowed still lower. Then the Bishop began to speak to them.

"I have heard," he said, "that you, godly men, live here saving your own souls, and praying to our Lord Christ for your fellow men. I, an unworthy servant of Christ, am called, by God's mercy, to keep and teach His flock. I wished to see you, servants of God, and to do what I can to teach you, also."

The old men looked at each other smiling, but remained silent.

"Tell me," said the Bishop, "what you are doing to save your souls, and how you serve God on this island."

The second hermit sighed, and looked at the oldest, the very ancient one. The latter smiled, and said:

"We do not know how to serve God. We only serve and support ourselves, servant of God."

"But how do you pray to God?" asked the Bishop.

"We pray in this way," replied the hermit. "Three are ye, three are we, have mercy upon us."

And when the old man said this, all three raised their eyes to heaven, and repeated:

"Three are ye, three are we, have mercy upon us!"

The Bishop smiled.

"You have evidently heard something about the Holy Trinity," said he. "But you do not pray aright. You have won my affection, godly men. I see you wish to please the Lord, but you do not know how to serve Him. That is not the way to pray; but listen to me, and I will teach you. I will teach you, not a way of my own, but the way in which God in the Holy Scriptures has commanded all men to pray to Him."

And the Bishop began explaining to the hermits how God had revealed Himself to men; telling them of God the Father, and God the Son, and God the Holy Ghost.

"God the Son came down on earth," said he, "to save men, and this is how He taught us all to pray. Listen, and repeat after me: 'Our Father.'"

And the first old man repeated after him, "Our Father," and the second said, "Our Father," and the third said, "Our Father."

"Which art in heaven," continued the Bishop.

The first hermit repeated, "Which art in heaven," but the second blundered over the words, and the tall hermit could not say them properly. His hair had grown over his mouth so that he could not speak plainly. The very old hermit, having no teeth, also mumbled indistinctly.

The Bishop repeated the words again, and the old men repeated them after him. The Bishop sat down on a stone, and the old men stood before him, watching his mouth, and repeating the words as he uttered them. And all day long the Bishop laboured, saying a word twenty, thirty, a hundred times over, and the old men repeated it after him. They blundered, and he corrected them, and made them begin again.

The Bishop did not leave off till he had taught them the whole of the Lord's prayer so that they could not only repeat it after him, but could say it by themselves. The middle one was the first to know it, and to repeat the whole of it alone. The Bishop made him say it again and again, and at last the others could say it too.

It was getting dark, and the moon was appearing over the water, before the Bishop rose to return to the vessel. When he took leave of the old men, they all bowed down to the ground before him. He raised them, and kissed each of them, telling them to pray as he had taught them. Then he got into the boat and returned to the ship.

And as he sat in the boat and was rowed to the ship he could hear the three voices of the hermits loudly repeating the Lord's prayer. As the boat drew near the vessel their voices could no longer be heard, but they could still be seen in the moonlight, standing as he had left them on the shore, the shortest in the middle, the tallest on the right, the middle one on the left. As soon as the Bishop had reached the vessel and got on board, the anchor was weighed and the sails unfurled. The wind filled them, and the ship sailed away, and the Bishop took a seat in the stern and watched the island they had left. For a time he could still see the hermits, but presently they disappeared from sight, though the island was still visible. At last it too vanished, and only the sea was to be seen, rippling in the moonlight.

The pilgrims lay down to sleep, and all was quiet on deck. The Bishop did not wish to sleep, but sat alone at the stern, gazing at the sea where the island was no longer visible, and thinking of the good old men. He thought how pleased they had been to learn the Lord's prayer; and he thanked God for having sent him to teach and help such godly men.

So the Bishop sat, thinking, and gazing at the sea where the island had disappeared. And the moonlight flickered before his eyes, sparkling, now here, now there, upon the waves. Suddenly he saw something white and shining, on the bright path which the moon cast across the sea. Was it a seagull, or the little gleaming sail of some small boat? The Bishop fixed his eyes on it, wondering.

"It must be a boat sailing after us," thought he, "but it is overtaking us very rapidly. It was far, far away a minute ago, but now it is much nearer. It cannot be a boat, for I can see no sail; but whatever it may be, it is following us, and catching us up."

And he could not make out what it was. Not a boat, nor a bird, nor a fish! It was too large for a man, and besides a man could not be out there in the midst of the sea. The Bishop rose, and said to the helmsman:

"Look there, what is that, my friend? What is it?" the Bishop repeated, though he could now see plainly what it was—the three hermits running upon the water, all gleaming white, their grey beards shining, and approaching the ship as quickly as though it were not moving.

The steersman looked and let go the helm in terror.

"Oh Lord! The hermits are running after us on the water as though it were dry land!"

The passengers hearing him, jumped up, and crowded to the stern. They saw the hermits coming along hand in hand, and the two outer ones beckoning the ship to stop. All three were gliding along upon the water without moving their feet. Before the ship could be stopped, the hermits had reached it, and raising their heads, all three as with one voice, began to say:

"We have forgotten your teaching, servant of God. As long as we kept repeating it we remembered, but when we stopped saying it for a time, a word dropped out, and now it has all gone to pieces. We can remember nothing of it. Teach us again."

The Bishop crossed himself, and leaning over the ship's side, said:

"Your own prayer will reach the Lord, men of God. It is not for me to teach you. Pray for us sinners."

And the Bishop bowed low before the old men; and they turned and went back across the sea. And a light shone until daybreak on the spot where they were lost to sight.

Ivan the Fool

[A fairy tale written and first published in 1885. This version is a
translation by Adolphus Norraikow taken from the collection
Ivan The Fool, or The Old Devil and the Three Small Devils
published by Chas. L. Webster & Co. in 1891.]

I

In a certain kingdom there lived a rich peasant, who had three sons—Simeon (a soldier), Tarras-Briukhan (a fat man), and Ivan (a fool)—and one daughter, Milania, born dumb. Simeon went to war, to serve the Tsar; Tarras went to a city and became a merchant; and Ivan, with his sister, remained at home to work on the farm.

For his valiant service in the army, Simeon received an estate with high rank, and married a noble's daughter. Besides his large pay, he was in receipt of a handsome income from his estate; yet he was unable to make ends meet. What the husband saved, the wife wasted in extravagance. One day Simeon went to the estate to collect his income, when the steward informed him that there was no income, saying:

"We have neither horses, cows, fishing-nets, nor implements; it is necessary first to buy everything, and then to look for income."

Simeon thereupon went to his father and said:

"You are rich, *batiushka* [little father], but you have given nothing to me. Give me one-third of what you possess as my share, and I will transfer it to my estate."

The old man replied: "You did not help to bring prosperity to our household. For what reason, then, should you now demand the third part of everything? It would be unjust to Ivan and his sister."

"Yes," said Simeon; "but he is a fool, and she was born dumb. What need have they of anything?"

"See what Ivan will say."

Ivan's reply was: "Well, let him take his share."

Simeon took the portion allotted to him, and went again to serve in the army.

Tarras also met with success. He became rich and married a merchant's daughter, but even this failed to satisfy his desires, and he also went to his father and said, "Give me my share."

The old man, however, refused to comply with his request, saying: "You had no hand in the accumulation of our property, and what our household contains is the result of Ivan's hard work. It would be unjust," he repeated, "to Ivan and his sister."

Tarras replied: "But he does not need it. He is a fool, and cannot marry, for no one will have him; and sister does not require anything, for she was born dumb." Turning then to Ivan he continued: "Give me half the grain you have, and I will not touch the implements or fishing-nets; and from the cattle I will take only the dark mare, as she is not fit to plough."

Ivan laughed and said: "Well, I will go and arrange matters so that Tarras may have his share," whereupon Tarras took the brown mare with the grain to town, leaving Ivan with one old horse to work on as before and support his father, mother, and sister.

II

It was disappointing to the *Stary Tchert* (Old Devil) that the brothers did not quarrel over the division of the property, and that they separated peacefully; and he cried out, calling his three small devils (*Tchertionki*).

"See here," said he, "there are living three brothers—Simeon the soldier, Tarras-Briukhan, and Ivan the Fool. It is necessary that they should quarrel. Now they live peacefully, and enjoy each other's hospitality. The Fool spoiled all my plans. Now you three go and work with them in such a manner that they will be ready to tear each other's eyes out. Can you do this?"

"We can," they replied.

"How will you accomplish it?"

"In this way: We will first ruin them to such an extent that they will have nothing to eat, and we will then gather them together in one place where we are sure that they will fight."

"Very well; I see you understand your business. Go, and do not return to me until you have created a feud between the three brothers—or I will skin you alive."

The three small devils went to a swamp to consult as to the best means of accomplishing their mission. They disputed for a long time—each one wanting the easiest part of the work—and not being able to agree, concluded to draw lots; by which it was decided that the one who was first finished had to come and help the others. This agreement being entered into, they appointed a time when they were again to meet in the swamp—to find out who was through and who needed assistance.

The time having arrived, the young devils met in the swamp as agreed, when each related his experience. The first, who went to Simeon, said: "I have succeeded in my undertaking, and tomorrow Simeon returns to his father."

His comrades, eager for particulars, inquired how he had done it.

"Well," he began, "the first thing I did was to blow some courage into his veins, and, on the strength of it, Simeon went to the Tsar and offered to conquer the whole world for him. The Emperor made him commander-in-chief of the forces, and sent him with an army to fight the Viceroy of India. Having started on their mission of conquest, they were unaware that I, following in their wake, had wet all their powder. I also went to the Indian ruler and showed him how I could create numberless soldiers from straw. Simeon's army, seeing that they were surrounded by such a vast number of Indian warriors of my creation, became frightened, and Simeon commanded to fire from cannons and rifles, which of course they were unable to do. The soldiers, discouraged, retreated n great disorder. Thus Simeon brought upon himself the terrible disgrace of defeat. His estate was confiscated, and tomorrow he is to be executed. All that remains for me to do, therefore," concluded the young devil, "is to release him tomorrow morning. Now, then, who wants my assistance?"

The second small devil (from Tarras) then related his story.

"I do not need any help," he began. "My business is also all right. My work with Tarras will be finished in one week. In the first place I made him grow thin. He afterward became so covetous that he wanted to possess everything he saw, and he spent all the money he had in the purchase of immense quantities of goods. When his capital was gone he still continued to buy with borrowed money, and has become involved in such difficulties that he cannot free himself. At the end of one week the date for the payment of his notes will have expired, and, his goods being seized upon, he will become a bankrupt; and he also will return to his father."

At the conclusion of this narrative they inquired of the third devil how things had fared between him and Ivan.

"Well," said he, "my report is not so encouraging. The first thing I did was to spit into his jug of *quass* [a sour drink made from rye], which made him sick at his stomach. He afterward went to plough his summer-fallow, but I made the soil so hard that the plough could scarcely penetrate it. I thought the Fool would not succeed, but he started to work nevertheless. Moaning with pain, he still continued to labour. I broke one plough, but he replaced it with another, fixing it securely, and resumed work. Going beneath the surface of the ground I took hold of the ploughshares, but did not succeed in stopping Ivan. He pressed so hard, and the colter was so sharp, that my hands were cut; and despite my utmost efforts, he went over all but a small portion of the field."

He concluded with: "Come, brothers, and help me, for if we do not conquer him our whole enterprise will be a failure. If the Fool is permitted successfully to conduct his farming, they will have no need, for he will support his brothers."

III

Ivan having succeeded in ploughing all but a small portion of his land, he returned the next day to finish it. The pain in his stomach continued, but he felt that he must go on with his work. He tried to start his plough, but it would not move; it seemed to have struck a hard root. It was the small devil in the ground who had wound his feet around the ploughshares and held them.

"This is strange," thought Ivan. "There were never any roots here before, and this is surely one."

Ivan put his hand in the ground, and, feeling something soft, grasped and pulled it out. It was like a root in appearance, but seemed to possess life. Holding it up he saw that it was a little devil. Disgusted, he exclaimed, "See the nasty thing," and he proceeded to strike it a blow, intending to kill it, when the young devil cried out:

"Do not kill me, and I will grant your every wish."

"What can you do for me?"

"Tell me what it is you most wish for," the little devil replied.

Ivan, peasant-fashion, scratched the back of his head as he thought, and finally he said:

"I am dreadfully sick at my stomach. Can you cure me?"

"I can," the little devil said.

"Then do so."

The little devil bent toward the earth and began searching for roots, and when he found them he gave them to Ivan, saying: "If you will swallow some of these you will be immediately cured of whatsoever disease you are afflicted with."

Ivan did as directed, and obtained instant relief.

"I beg of you to let me go now," the little devil pleaded; "I will pass into the earth, never to return."

"Very well; you may go, and God bless you;" and as Ivan pronounced the name of God—the small devil disappeared into the earth like a flash, and only a slight opening in the ground remained.

Ivan placed in his hat what roots he had left, and proceeded to plough. Soon finishing his work, he turned his plough over and returned home.

When he reached the house he found his brother Simeon and his wife seated at the supper-table. His estate had been confiscated, and he himself had barely escaped execution by making his way out of prison, and having nothing to live upon had come back to his father for support.

Turning to Ivan he said: "I came to ask you to care for us until I can find something to do."

"Very well," Ivan replied; "you may remain with us."

Just as Ivan was about to sit down to the table Simeon's wife made a wry face, indicating that she did not like the smell of Ivan's sheepskin coat; and turning to her husband she said, "I shall not sit at the table with a *moujik* [peasant] who smells like that."

Simeon the soldier turned to his brother and said: "My lady objects to the smell of your clothes. You may eat in the porch."

Ivan said: "Very well, it is all the same to me. I will soon have to go and feed my horse any way."

Ivan took some bread in one hand, and his *kaftan* (coat) in the other, and left the room.

IV

The small devil finished with Simeon that night, and according to agreement went to the assistance of his comrade who had charge of Ivan, that he might help to conquer the Fool. He went to the field and searched everywhere, but could find nothing but the hole through which the small devil had disappeared.

"Well, this is strange," he said; "something must have happened to my companion, and I will have to take his place and continue the work he began. The Fool is through with his ploughing, so I must look about me for some other means of compassing his destruction. I must overflow his meadow and prevent him from cutting the grass."

The little devil accordingly overflowed the meadow with muddy water, and, when Ivan went at dawn next morning with his scythe set and sharpened and tried to mow the grass, he found that it resisted all his efforts and would not yield to the implement as usual.

Many times Ivan tried to cut the grass, but always without success. At last, becoming weary of the effort, he decided to return home and have his scythe again sharpened, and also to procure a quantity of bread, saying: "I will come back here and will not leave until I have mown all the meadow, even if it should take a whole week."

Hearing this, the little devil became thoughtful, saying: "That Ivan is a *koolak* [hard case], and I must think of some other way of conquering him."

Ivan soon returned with his sharpened scythe and started to mow.

The small devil hid himself in the grass, and as the point of the scythe came down he buried it in the earth and made it almost impossible for Ivan to move the implement. He, however, succeeded in mowing all but one small spot in the swamp, where again the small devil hid himself, saying: "Even if he should cut my hands I will prevent him from accomplishing his work."

When Ivan came to the swamp he found that the grass was not very thick. Still, the scythe would not work, which made him so angry that he worked with all his might, and one blow more powerful than the others cut off a portion of the small devil's tail, who had hidden himself there.

Despite the little devil's efforts he succeeded in finishing his work, when he returned home and ordered his sister to gather up the grass while he went to another field to cut rye. But the devil preceded him there, and fixed the rye in such a manner that it was almost impossible for Ivan to cut it; however, after continuous hard labour he succeeded, and when he was through with the rye he said to himself: "Now I will start to mow oats."

On hearing this, the little devil thought to himself: "I could not prevent him from mowing the rye, but I will surely stop him from mowing the oats when the morning comes."

Early next day, when the devil came to the field, he found that the oats had been already mowed. Ivan did it during the night, so as to avoid the loss that might have resulted from the grain being too ripe and dry. Seeing that Ivan again had escaped him, the little devil became greatly enraged, saying:

"He cut me all over and made me tired, that fool. I did not meet such misfortune even on the battle-field. He does not even sleep;" and the devil began to swear. "I cannot follow him," he continued. "I will go now to the heaps and make everything rotten."

Accordingly he went to a heap of the new-mown grain and began his fiendish work. After wetting it he built a fire and warmed himself, and soon was fast asleep.

Ivan harnessed his horse, and, with his sister, went to bring the rye home from the field. After lifting a couple of sheaves from the first heap his pitchfork came into contact with the little devil's back, which caused the latter to howl with pain and to jump around in every direction. Ivan exclaimed:

"See here! What nastiness! You again here?"

"I am another one!" said the little devil. "That was my brother. I am the one who was sent to your brother Simeon."

"Well," said Ivan, "it matters not who you are. I will fix you all the same."

As Ivan was about to strike the first blow the devil pleaded: "Let me go and I will do you no more harm. I will do whatever you wish."

"What can you do for me?" asked Ivan.

"I can make soldiers from almost anything."

"And what will they be good for?"

"Oh, they will do everything for you!"

"Can they sing?"

"They can."

"Well, make them."

"Take a bunch of straw and scatter it on the ground, and see if each straw will not turn into a soldier."

Ivan shook the straws on the ground, and, as he expected, each straw turned into a soldier, and they began marching with a band at their head.

"*Ishty* [look you], that was well done! How it will delight the village maidens!" he exclaimed.

The small devil now said: "Let me go; you do not need me any longer."

But Ivan said: "No, I will not let you go just yet. You have converted the straw into soldiers, and now I want you to turn them again into straw, as I cannot afford to lose it, but I want it with the grain on."

The devil replied: "Say: 'So many soldiers, so much straw.'"

Ivan did as directed, and got back his rye with the straw.

The small devil again begged for his release.

Ivan, taking him from the pitchfork, said: "With God's blessing you may depart"; and, as before at the mention of God's name, the little devil was hurled into the earth like a flash, and nothing was left but the hole to show where he had gone.

Soon afterward Ivan returned home, to find his brother Tarras and his wife there. Tarras-Briukhan could not pay his debts, and was forced to flee from his creditors and seek refuge under his father's roof. Seeing Ivan, he said: "Well, Ivan, may we remain here until I start in some new business?"

Ivan replied as he had before to Simeon: "Yes, you are perfectly welcome to remain here as long as it suits you."

With that announcement he removed his coat and seated himself at the supper-table with the others. But Tarras-Briukhan's wife objected to the smell of his clothes, saying: "I cannot eat with a fool; neither can I stand the smell."

Then Tarras-Briukhan said: "Ivan, from your clothes there comes a bad smell; go and eat by yourself in the porch."

"Very well," said Ivan; and he took some bread and went out as ordered, saying, "It is time for me to feed my mare."

V

The small devil who had charge of Tarras finished with him that night, and according to agreement proceeded to the assistance of the other two to help them conquer Ivan. Arriving at the ploughed field he looked around for his comrades, but found only the hole through which one had disappeared; and on going to the meadow he discovered the severed tail of the other, and in the rye-field he found yet another hole.

"Well," he thought, "it is quite clear that my comrades have met with some great misfortune, and that I will have to take their places and arrange the feud between the brothers."

The small devil then went in search of Ivan. But he, having

finished with the field, was nowhere to be found. He had gone to the forest to cut logs to build homes for his brothers, as they found it inconvenient for so many to live under the same roof.

The small devil at last discovered his whereabouts, and going to the forest climbed into the branches of the trees and began to interfere with Ivan's work. Ivan cut down a tree, which failed, however, to fall to the ground, becoming entangled in the branches of other trees; yet he succeeded in getting it down after a hard struggle. In chopping down the next tree he met with the same difficulties, and also with the third. Ivan had supposed he could cut down fifty trees in a day, but he succeeded in chopping but ten before darkness put an end to his labours for a time. He was now exhausted, and, perspiring profusely, he sat down alone in the woods to rest. He soon after resumed his work, cutting down one more tree; but the effort gave him a pain in his back, and he was obliged to rest again. Seeing this, the small devil was full of joy.

"Well," he thought, "now he is exhausted and will stop work, and I will rest also." He then seated himself on some branches and rejoiced.

Ivan again arose, however, and, taking his axe, gave the tree a terrific blow from the opposite side, which felled it instantly to the ground, carrying the little devil with it; and Ivan, proceeding to cut the branches, found the devil alive. Very much astonished, Ivan exclaimed:

"Look you! Such nastiness! Are you again here?"

"I am another one," replied the devil. "I was with your brother Tarras."

"Well," said Ivan, "that makes no difference; I will fix you." And he was about to strike him a blow with the axe when the devil pleaded:

"Do not kill me, and whatever you wish you shall have."

Ivan asked, "What can you do?"

"I can make for you all the money you wish."

Ivan then told the devil he might proceed, whereupon the latter began to explain to him how he might become rich.

"Take," said he to Ivan, "the leaves of this oak tree and rub them in your hands, and the gold will fall to the ground."

Ivan did as he was directed, and immediately the gold began to drop about his feet; and he remarked:

"This will be a fine trick to amuse the village boys with."

"Can I now take my departure?" asked the devil, to which Ivan replied, "With God's blessing you may go."

At the mention of the name of God, the devil disappeared into the earth.

VI

The brothers, having finished their houses, moved into them and lived apart from their father and brother. Ivan, when he had completed his ploughing, made a great feast, to which he invited his brothers, telling them that he had plenty of beer for them to drink. The brothers, however, declined Ivan's hospitality, saying, "We have seen the beer *moujiks* drink, and want none of it."

Ivan then gathered around him all the peasants in the village and with them drank beer until he became intoxicated, when he joined the *Khorovody* (a street gathering of the village boys and girls, who sing songs), and told them they must sing his praises, saying that in return he would show them such sights as they had never before seen in their lives. The little girls laughed and began to sing songs praising Ivan, and when they had finished they said: "Very well; now give us what you said you would."

Ivan replied, "I will soon show you," and, taking an empty bag in his hand, he started for the woods. The little girls laughed as they said, "What a fool he is!" and resuming their play they forgot all about him.

Sometime after Ivan suddenly appeared among them carrying in his hand the bag, which was now filled.

"Shall I divide this with you?" he said.

"Yes; divide!" they sang in chorus.

So Ivan put his hand into the bag and drew it out full of gold coins, which he scattered among them.

"*Batiushka*," they cried as they ran to gather up the precious pieces.

The *moujiks* then appeared on the scene and began to fight among themselves for the possession of the yellow objects. In the melee one old woman was nearly crushed to death.

Ivan laughed and was greatly amused at the sight of so many persons quarrelling over a few pieces of gold.

"Oh! you duratchki" (little fools), he said, "why did you almost crush the life out of the old grandmother? Be more gentle. I have plenty more, and I will give them to you;" whereupon he began throwing about more of the coins.

The people gathered around him, and Ivan continued throwing until he emptied his bag. They clamoured for more, but Ivan replied: "The gold is all gone. Another time I will give you more. Now we will resume our singing and dancing."

The little children sang, but Ivan said to them, "Your songs are no good."

The children said, "Then show us how to sing better."

To this Ivan replied, "I will show you people who can sing better than you." With that remark Ivan went to the barn and, securing a bundle of straw, did as the little devil had directed him; and presently a regiment of soldiers appeared in the village street, and he ordered them to sing and dance.

The people were astonished and could not understand how Ivan had produced the strangers.

The soldiers sang for some time, to the great delight of the villagers; and when Ivan commanded them to stop they instantly ceased.

Ivan then ordered them off to the barn, telling the astonished and mystified *moujiks* that they must not follow him. Reaching the barn, he turned the soldiers again into straw and went home to sleep off the effects of his debauch.

VII

The next morning Ivan's exploits were the talk of the village, and news of the wonderful things he had done reached the ears of his brother Simeon, who immediately went to Ivan to learn all about it.

"Explain to me," he said; "from whence did you bring the soldiers, and where did you take them?"

"And what do you wish to know for?" asked Ivan.

"Why, with soldiers we can do almost anything we wish— whole kingdoms can be conquered," replied Simeon.

This information greatly surprised Ivan, who said: "Well, why did you not tell me about this before? I can make as many as you want."

Ivan then took his brother to the barn, but he said: "While I am willing to create the soldiers, you must take them away from here; for if it should become necessary to feed them, all the food in the village would last them only one day."

Simeon promised to do as Ivan wished, whereupon Ivan proceeded to convert the straw into soldiers. Out of one bundle of straw he made an entire regiment; in fact, so many soldiers appeared as if by magic that there was not a vacant spot in the field.

Turning to Simeon Ivan said, "Well, is there a sufficient number?"

Beaming with joy, Simeon replied: "Enough! enough! Thank you, Ivan!"

"Glad you are satisfied," said Ivan, "and if you wish more I will make them for you. I have plenty of straw now."

Simeon divided his soldiers into battalions and regiments, and after having drilled them he went forth to fight and to conquer.

Simeon had just gotten safely out of the village with his soldiers when Tarras, the other brother, appeared before Ivan—he also having heard of the previous day's performance and wanting to learn the secret of his power. He sought Ivan, saying: "Tell me the secret of your supply of gold, for if I had plenty of money I could with its assistance gather in all the wealth in the world."

Ivan was greatly surprised on hearing this statement, and said: "You might have told me this before, for I can obtain for you as much money as you wish."

Tarras was delighted, and he said, "You might get me about three bushels."

"Well," said Ivan, "we will go to the woods, or, better still, we will harness the horse, as we could not possibly carry so much money ourselves."

The brothers went to the woods and Ivan proceeded to gather the oak leaves, which he rubbed between his hands, the dust falling to the ground and turning into gold pieces as quickly as it fell.

When quite a pile had accumulated Ivan turned to Tarras and asked if he had rubbed enough leaves into money, whereupon Tarras replied: "Thank you, Ivan; that will be sufficient for this time."

Ivan then said: "If you wish more, come to me and I will rub as much as you want, for there are plenty of leaves."

Tarras, with his *tarantas* (wagon) filled with gold, rode away to the city to engage in trade and increase his wealth; and thus both brothers went their way, Simeon to fight and Tarras to trade.

Simeon's soldiers conquered a kingdom for him and Tarras-Briukhan made plenty of money.

Some time afterward the two brothers met and confessed to each other the source from whence sprang their prosperity, but they were not yet satisfied.

Simeon said: "I have conquered a kingdom and enjoy a very pleasant life, but I have not sufficient money to procure food for my soldiers;" while Tarras confessed that he was the possessor of enormous wealth, but the care of it caused him much uneasiness.

"Let us go again to our brother," said Simeon; "I will order him to make more soldiers and will give them to you, and you may then tell him that he must make more money so that we can buy food for them."

They went again to Ivan, and Simeon said: "I have not sufficient soldiers; I want you to make me at least two divisions more." But Ivan shook his head as he said: "I will not create soldiers for nothing; you must pay me for doing it."

"Well, but you promised," said Simeon.

"I know I did," replied Ivan; "but I have changed my mind since that time."

"But, fool, why will you not do as you promised?"

"For the reason that your soldiers kill men, and I will not make any more for such a cruel purpose." With this reply Ivan remained stubborn and would not create any more soldiers.

Tarras-Briukhan next approached Ivan and ordered him to make more money; but, as in the case of Tarras, Ivan only shook his head, as he said: "I will not make you any money unless you pay me for doing it. I cannot work without pay."

Tarras then reminded him of his promise.

"I know I promised," replied Ivan; "but still I must refuse to do as you wish."

"But why, fool, will you not fulfil your promise?" asked Tarras.

"For the reason that your gold was the means of depriving Mikhailovna of her cow."

"But how did that happen?" inquired Tarras.

"It happened in this way," said Ivan. "Mikhailovna always kept a cow, and her children had plenty of milk to drink; but some time ago one of her boys came to me to beg for some milk, and I asked, 'Where is your cow?' when he replied, 'A clerk of Tarras-Briukhan came to our home and offered three gold pieces for her. Our mother could not resist the temptation, and now we have no

319

milk to drink. I gave you the gold pieces for your pleasure, and you put them to such poor use that I will not give you any more.'"

The brothers, on hearing this, took their departure to discuss as to the best plan to pursue in regard to a settlement of their troubles.

Simeon said: "Let us arrange it in this way: I will give you the half of my kingdom, and soldiers to keep guard over your wealth; and you give me money to feed the soldiers in my half of the kingdom."

To this arrangement Tarras agreed, and both the brothers became rulers and very happy.

VIII

Ivan remained on the farm and worked to support his father, mother, and dumb sister. Once it happened that the old dog, which had grown up on the farm, was taken sick, when Ivan thought he was dying, and, taking pity on the animal, placed some bread in his hat and carried it to him. It happened that when he turned out the bread the root which the little devil had given him fell out also. The old dog swallowed it with the bread and was almost instantly cured, when he jumped up and began to wag his tail as an expression of joy. Ivan's father and mother, seeing the dog cured so quickly, asked by what means he had performed such a miracle.

Ivan replied: "I had some roots which would cure any disease, and the dog swallowed one of them."

It happened about that time that the Tsar's daughter became ill, and her father had it announced in every city, town, and village that whosoever would cure her would be richly rewarded; and if the lucky person should prove to be a single man he would give her in marriage to him.

This announcement, of course, appeared in Ivan's village.

Ivan's father and mother called him and said: "If you have any of those wonderful roots, go and cure the Tsar's daughter. You will be much happier for having performed such a kind act—indeed, you will be made happy for all your after life."

"Very well," said Ivan; and he immediately made ready for the journey. As he reached the porch on his way out he saw a poor woman standing directly in his path and holding a broken arm. The woman accosted him, saying: "I was told that you could cure me, and will you not please do so, as I am powerless to do anything for myself?"

Ivan replied: "Very well, my poor woman; I will relieve you if I can."

He produced a root which he handed to the poor woman and told her to swallow it.

She did as Ivan told her and was instantly cured, and went away rejoicing that she had recovered the use of her arm.

Ivan's father and mother came out to wish him good luck on his journey, and to them he told the story of the poor woman, saying that he had given her his last root. On hearing this his parents were much distressed, as they now believed him to be without the means of curing the Tsar's daughter, and began to scold him.

"You had pity for a beggar and gave no thought to the Tsar's daughter," they said.

"I have pity for the Tsar's daughter also," replied Ivan, after which he harnessed his horse to his wagon and took his seat ready for his departure; whereupon his parents said: "Where are you going, you fool—to cure the Tsar's daughter, and without anything to do it with?"

"Very well," replied Ivan, as he drove away.

In due time he arrived at the palace, and the moment he appeared on the balcony the Tsar's daughter was cured. The Tsar was overjoyed and ordered Ivan to be brought into his presence.

He dressed him in the richest robes and addressed him as his son-in-law. Ivan was married to the Czarevna, and, the Tsar dying soon after, Ivan became ruler. Thus the three brothers became rulers in different kingdoms.

IX

The brothers lived and reigned. Simeon, the eldest brother, with his straw soldiers took captive the genuine soldiers and trained all alike. He was feared by everyone.

Tarras-Briukhan, the other brother, did not squander the gold he obtained from Ivan, but instead greatly increased his wealth, and at the same time lived well. He kept his money in large trunks, and, while having more than he knew what to do with, still continued to collect money from his subjects. The people had to work for the money to pay the taxes which Tarras levied on them, and life was made burdensome to them.

Ivan the Fool did not enjoy his wealth and power to the same extent as did his brothers. As soon as his father-in-law, the late Tsar, was buried, he discarded the Imperial robes which had fallen to him and told his wife to put them away, as he had no further use for them. Having cast aside the insignia of his rank, he once more donned his peasant garb and started to work as of old.

"I felt lonesome," he said, "and began to grow enormously stout, and yet I had no appetite, and neither could I sleep."

Ivan sent for his father, mother, and dumb sister, and brought them to live with him, and they worked with him at whatever he chose to do.

The people soon learned that Ivan was a fool. His wife one day said to him, "The people say you are a fool, Ivan."

"Well, let them think so if they wish," he replied.

His wife pondered this reply for some time, and at last decided that if Ivan was a fool she also was one, and that it would be useless to go contrary to her husband, thinking in her mind of the old proverb that "where the needle goes there goes the thread also." She therefore cast aside her magnificent robes, and, putting them into the trunk with Ivan's, dressed herself in cheap clothing and joined her dumb sister-in-law, with the intention of learning to work. She succeeded so well that she soon became a great help to Ivan.

Seeing that Ivan was a fool, all the wise men left the kingdom and only the fools remained. They had no money, their wealth consisting only of the products of their labour. But they lived peacefully together, supported themselves in comfort, and had plenty to spare for the needy and afflicted.

X

The old devil grew tired of waiting for the good news which he expected the little devils to bring him. He waited in vain to hear of the ruin of the brothers, so he went in search of the emissaries which he had sent to perform that work for him. After looking around for some time, and seeing nothing but the three holes in the ground, he decided that they had not succeeded in their work and that he would have to do it himself.

The old devil next went in search of the brothers, but he could learn nothing of their whereabouts. After some time he found them in their different kingdoms, contented and happy. This greatly incensed the old devil, and he said, "I will now have to accomplish their mission myself."

He first visited Simeon the soldier, and appeared before him as a *voyevoda* (general), saying: "You, Simeon, are a great warrior, and I also have had considerable experience in warfare, and am desirous of serving you."

Simeon questioned the disguised devil, and seeing that he was an intelligent man took him into his service.

The new General taught Simeon how to strengthen his army until it became very powerful. New implements of warfare were introduced.

Cannons capable of throwing one hundred balls a minute were also constructed, and these, it was expected, would be of deadly effect in battle.

Simeon, on the advice of his new General, ordered all young men above a certain age to report for drill. On the same advice Simeon established gun-shops, where immense numbers of cannons and rifles were made.

The next move of the new General was to have Simeon declare war against the neighbouring kingdom. This he did, and with his immense army marched into the adjoining territory, which he pillaged and burned, destroying more than half the enemy's soldiers. This so frightened the ruler of that country that he willingly gave up half of his kingdom to save the other half.

Simeon, overjoyed at his success, declared his intention of marching into Indian territory and subduing the Viceroy of that country.

But Simeon's intentions reached the ears of the Indian ruler, who prepared to do battle with him. In addition to having secured all the latest implements of warfare, he added still others of his own invention. He ordered all boys over fourteen and all single women to be drafted into the army, until its proportions became much larger than Simeon's. His cannons and rifles were of the same pattern as Simeon's, and he invented a flying-machine from which bombs could be thrown into the enemy's camp.

Simeon went forth to conquer the Viceroy with full confidence in his own powers to succeed. This time luck forsook him, and instead of being the conqueror he was himself conquered.

The Indian ruler had so arranged his army that Simeon could not even get within shooting distance, while the bombs from the flying-machine carried destruction and terror in their path, completely routing his army, so that Simeon was left alone.

The Viceroy took possession of his kingdom and Simeon had to fly for his life.

Having finished with Simeon, the old devil next approached Tarras. He appeared before him disguised as one of the merchants of his kingdom, and established factories and began to make money. The 'merchant' paid the highest price for everything he purchased, and the people ran after him to sell their goods. Through this 'merchant' they were enabled to make plenty of money, paying up all their arrears of taxes as well as the others when they came due.

Tarras was overjoyed at this condition of affairs and said: "Thanks to this merchant, now I will have more money than before, and life will be much pleasanter for me."

He wished to erect new buildings, and advertised for workmen, offering the highest prices for all kinds of labour. Tarras thought the people would be as anxious to work as formerly, but instead he was much surprised to learn that they were working for the 'merchant.' Thinking to induce them to leave the 'merchant,' he increased his offers, but the former, equal to the emergency, also raised the wages of his workmen. Tarras, having plenty of money, increased the offers still more; but the 'merchant' raised them still higher and got the better of him. Thus, defeated at every point, Tarras was compelled to abandon the idea of building.

Tarras next announced that he intended laying out gardens and erecting fountains, and the work was to be commenced in the fall, but no one came to offer his services, and again he was obliged to forego his intentions. Winter set in, and Tarras wanted some sable fur with which to line his great-coat, and he sent his man to procure it for him; but the servant returned without it, saying: "There are no sables to be had. The 'merchant' has bought them all, paying a very high price for them."

Tarras needed horses and sent a messenger to purchase them, but he returned with the same story as on former occasions—that none were to be found, the 'merchant' having bought them all to carry water for an artificial pond he was constructing. Tarras was at last compelled to suspend business, as he could not find anyone willing to work for him. They had all gone over to the 'merchant's' side. The only dealings the people had with Tarras were when they went to pay their taxes. His money accumulated so fast that he could not find a place to put it, and his life became miserable. He abandoned all idea of entering upon the new venture, and only thought of how to exist peaceably. This he found it difficult to do, for, turn which way he would, fresh obstacles confronted him. Even his cooks, coachmen, and all his other servants forsook him and joined the 'merchant.' With all his wealth he had nothing to eat, and when he went to market he found the 'merchant' had been there before him and had bought up all the provisions. Still, the people continued to bring him money.

Tarras at last became so indignant that he ordered the 'merchant' out of his kingdom. He left, but settled just outside the boundary line, and continued his business with the same result as before, and Tarras was frequently forced to go without food for days. It was rumoured that the 'merchant' wanted to buy even Tarras himself. On hearing this the latter became very much alarmed and could not decide as to the best course to pursue.

About this time his brother Simeon arrived in the kingdom, and said: "Help me, for I have been defeated and ruined by the Indian Viceroy."

Tarras replied: "How can I help you, when I have had no food myself for two days?"

XI

The old devil, having finished with the second brother, went to Ivan the Fool. This time he disguised himself as a General, the same as in the case of Simeon, and, appearing before Ivan, said: "Get an army together. It is disgraceful for the ruler of a kingdom to be without an army. You call your people to assemble, and I will form them into a fine large army."

Ivan took the supposed General's advice, and said: "Well, you may form my people into an army, but you must also teach them to sing the songs I like."

The old devil then went through Ivan's kingdom to secure recruits for the army, saying: "Come, shave your heads [the heads of recruits are always shaved in Russia] and I will give each of you a red hat and plenty of vódka" (whiskey).

At this the fools only laughed, and said: "We can have all the vódka we want, for we distil it ourselves; and of hats, our little girls make all we want, of any colour we please, and with handsome fringes."

Thus was the devil foiled in securing recruits for his army; so he returned to Ivan and said: "Your fools will not volunteer to be soldiers. It will therefore be necessary to force them."

"Very well," replied Ivan, "you may use force if you want to."

The old devil then announced that all the fools must become soldiers, and those who refused, Ivan would punish with death.

The fools went to the General; and said: "You tell us that Ivan will punish with death all those who refuse to become soldiers, but you have omitted to state what will be done with us soldiers. We have been told that we are only to be killed."

"Yes, that is true," was the reply.

The fools on hearing this became stubborn and refused to go.

"Better kill us now if we cannot avoid death, but we will not become soldiers," they declared.

"Oh! you fools," said the old devil, "soldiers may and may not be killed; but if you disobey Ivan's orders you will find certain death at his hands."

The fools remained absorbed in thought for some time and finally went to Ivan to question him in regard to the matter.

On arriving at his house they said: "A General came to us with an order from you that we were all to become soldiers, and if we refused you were to punish us with death. Is it true?"

Ivan began to laugh heartily on hearing this, and said: "Well, how I alone can punish you with death is something I cannot understand. If I was not a fool myself, I would be able to explain it to you, but as it is I cannot."

"Well, then, we will not go," they said.

"Very well," replied Ivan, "you need not become soldiers unless you wish to."

The old devil, seeing his schemes about to prove failures, went to the ruler of Tarakania and became his friend, saying: "Let us go and conquer Ivan's kingdom. He has no money, but he has plenty of cattle, provisions, and various other things that would be useful to us."

The Tarakanian ruler gathered his large army together, and equipping it with cannons and rifles, crossed the boundary line into Ivan's kingdom. The people went to Ivan and said: "The ruler of Tarakania is here with a large army to fight us."

"Let them come," replied Ivan.

The Tarakanian ruler, after crossing the line into Ivan's kingdom, looked in vain for soldiers to fight against; and waiting some time and none appearing, he sent his own warriors to attack the villages.

They soon reached the first village, which they began to plunder. The fools of both sexes looked calmly on, offering not the least resistance when their cattle and provisions were being taken from them. On the contrary, they invited the soldiers to come and live with them, saying: "If you, dear friends, find it is difficult to earn a living in your own land, come and live with us, where everything is plentiful."

The soldiers decided to remain, finding the people happy and prosperous, with enough surplus food to supply many of their neighbours. They were surprised at the cordial greetings which they everywhere received, and, returning to the ruler of Tarakania, they said: "We cannot fight with these people—take us to another place. We would much prefer the dangers of actual warfare to this unsoldierly method of subduing the village."

The Tarakanian ruler, becoming enraged, ordered the soldiers to destroy the whole kingdom, plunder the villages, burn the houses and provisions, and slaughter the cattle.

"Should you disobey my orders," said he, "I will have every one of you executed."

The soldiers, becoming frightened, started to do as they were ordered, but the fools wept bitterly, offering no resistance, men, women, and children all joining in the general lamentation.

"Why do you treat us so cruelly?" they cried to the invading soldiers. "Why do you wish to destroy everything we have? If you have more need of these things than we have, why not take them with you and leave us in peace?"

The soldiers, becoming saddened with remorse, refused further to pursue their path of destruction—the entire army scattering in many directions.

XII

The old devil, failing to ruin Ivan's kingdom with soldiers, transformed himself into a nobleman, dressed exquisitely, and became one of Ivan's subjects, with the intention of compassing the downfall of his kingdom—as he had done with that of Tarras.

The 'nobleman' said to Ivan: "I desire to teach you wisdom and to render you other service. I will build you a palace and factories."

"Very well," said Ivan; "you may live with us."

The next day the 'nobleman' appeared on the Square with a sack of gold in his hand and a plan for building a house, saying to the people: "You are living like pigs, and I am going to teach you how to live decently. You are to build a house for me according to this plan. I will superintend the work myself, and will pay you for your services in gold," showing them at the same time the contents of his sack.

The fools were amused. They had never before seen any money. Their business was conducted entirely by exchange of farm products or by hiring themselves out to work by the day in return for whatever they most needed. They therefore glanced at the gold pieces with amazement, and said, "What nice toys they would be to play with!" In return for the gold they gave their services and brought the 'nobleman' the produce of their farms.

The old devil was overjoyed as he thought, "Now my enterprise is on a fair road and I will be able to ruin the Fool—as I did his brothers."

The fools obtained sufficient gold to distribute among the entire community, the women and young girls of the village wearing much of it as ornaments, while to the children they gave some pieces to play with on the streets. When they had secured all they wanted they stopped working and the 'noblemen' did not get his house more than half finished. He had neither provisions nor cattle for the year, and ordered the people to bring him both. He directed them also to go on with the building of the palace and factories. He promised to pay them liberally in gold for everything they did. No one responded to his call—only once in a while a little boy or girl would call to exchange eggs for his gold.

Thus was the 'nobleman' deserted, and, having nothing to eat, he went to the village to procure some provisions for his dinner. He went to one house and offered gold in return for a chicken, but was refused, the owner saying: "We have enough of that already and do not want any more."

He next went to a fish-woman to buy some herring, when she, too, refused to accept his gold in return for fish, saying: "I do not wish it, my dear man; I have no children to whom I can give it to play with. I have three pieces which I keep as curiosities only."

He then went to a peasant to buy bread, but he also refused to accept the gold. "I have no use for it," said he, "unless you wish to give it for Christ's sake; then it will be a different matter, and I will tell my *baba* [old woman] to cut a piece of bread for you."

The old devil was so angry that he ran away from the peasant, spitting and cursing as he went.

Not only did the offer to accept in the name of Christ anger him, but the very mention of the name was like the thrust of a knife in his throat.

The old devil did not succeed in getting any bread, and in his efforts to secure other articles of food he met with the same failure. The people had all the gold they wanted and what pieces they had they regarded as curiosities. They said to the old devil: "If you bring us something else in exchange for food, or come to ask for Christ's sake, we will give you all you want."

But the old devil had nothing but gold, and was too lazy to work; and being unable to accept anything for Christ's sake, he was greatly enraged.

"What else do you want?" he said. "I will give you gold with which you can buy everything you want, and you need labour no longer."

But the fools would not accept his gold, nor listen to him. Thus the old devil was obliged to go to sleep hungry.

Tidings of this condition of affairs soon reached the ears of Ivan. The people went to him and said: "What shell we do? This nobleman appeared among us; he is well dressed; he wishes to eat and drink of the best, but is unwilling to work, and does not beg for food for Christ's sake. He only offers every one gold pieces. At first we gave him everything he wanted, taking the gold pieces in exchange just as curiosities; but now we have enough of them and refuse to accept any more from him. What shall we do with him? He may die of hunger!"

Ivan heard all they had to say, and told them to employ him as a shepherd, taking turns in doing so.

The old devil saw no other way out of the difficulty and was obliged to submit.

It soon came the old devil's turn to go to Ivan's house. He went there to dinner and found Ivan's dumb sister preparing the meal. She was often cheated by the lazy people, who while they did not work, yet ate up all the gruel. But she learned to know the lazy people from the condition of their hands. Those with great welts on their hands she invited first to the table, and those having smooth white hands had to take what was left.

The old devil took a seat at the table, but the dumb girl, taking his hands, looked at them, and seeing them white and clean, and with long nails, swore at him and put him from the table.

Ivan's wife said to the old devil: "You must excuse my sister-in-law; she will not allow anyone to sit at the table whose hands have not been hardened by toil, so you will have to wait until the dinner is over and then you can have what is left. With it you must be satisfied."

The old devil was very much offended that he was made to eat with "pigs," as he expressed it, and complained to Ivan, saying: "The foolish law you have in your kingdom, that all persons must work, is surely the invention of fools. People who work for a living are not always forced to labour with their hands. Do you think wise men labour so?"

Ivan replied: "Well, what do fools know about it? We all work with our hands."

"And for that reason you are fools," replied the devil. "I can teach you how to use your brains, and you will find such labour more beneficial."

Ivan was surprised at hearing this, and said: "Well, it is perhaps not without good reason that we are called fools."

"It is not so easy to work with the brain," the old devil said. "You will not give me anything to eat because my hands have not the appearance of being toil-hardened, but you must understand that it is much harder to do brain-work, and sometimes the head feels like bursting with the effort it is forced to make."

"Then why do you not select some light work that you can perform with your hands?" Ivan asked.

The devil said: "I torment myself with brain-work because I have pity for you fools, for, if I did not torture myself, people like you would remain fools for all eternity. I have exercised my brain a great deal during my life, and now I am able to teach you."

Ivan was greatly surprised and said: "Very well; teach us, so that when our hands are tired we can use our heads to replace them."

The devil promised to instruct the people, and Ivan announced the fact throughout his kingdom.

The devil was willing to teach all those who came to him how to use the head instead of the hands, so as to produce more with the former than with the latter.

In Ivan's kingdom there was a high tower, which was reached by a long, narrow ladder leading up to the balcony, and Ivan told the old devil that from the top of the tower every one could see him.

So the old devil went up to the balcony and addressed the people.

The fools came in great crowds to hear what the old devil

had to say, thinking that he really meant to tell them how to work with the head. But the old devil only told them in words what to do, and did not give them any practical instruction. He said that men working only with their hands could not make a living. The fools did not understand what he said to them and looked at him in amazement, and then departed for their daily work.

The old devil addressed them for two days from the balcony, and at the end of that time, feeling hungry, he asked the people to bring him some bread. But they only laughed at him and told him if he could work better with his head than with his hands he could also find bread for himself. He addressed the people for yet another day, and they went to hear him from curiosity, but soon left him to return to their work.

Ivan asked, "Well, did the nobleman work with his head?"

"Not yet," they said; "so far he has only talked."

One day, while the old devil was standing on the balcony, he became weak, and, falling down, hurt his head against a pole.

Seeing this, one of the fools ran to Ivan's wife and said, "The gentleman has at last commenced to work with his head."

She ran to the field to tell Ivan, who was much surprised, and said, "Let us go and see him."

He turned his horses' heads in the direction of the tower, where the old devil remained weak from hunger and was still suspended from the pole, with his body swaying back and forth and his head striking the lower part of the pole each time it came in contact with it. While Ivan was looking, the old devil started down the steps head-first—as they supposed, to count them.

"Well," said Ivan, "he told the truth after all—that sometimes from this kind of work the head bursts. This is far worse than welts on the hands."

The old devil fell to the ground head-foremost. Ivan approached him, but at that instant the ground opened and the devil disappeared, leaving only a hole to show where he had gone.

Ivan scratched his head and said: "See here; such nastiness! This is yet another devil. He looks like the father of the little ones."

Ivan still lives, and people flock to his kingdom. His brothers come to him and he feeds them.

To everyone who comes to him and says, "Give us food," he replies: "Very well; you are welcome. We have plenty of everything."

There is only one unchangeable custom observed in Ivan's kingdom: The man with toil-hardened hands is always given a seat at the table, while the possessor of soft white hands must be contented with what is left.

Kholstomír

THE HISTORY OF A HORSE[*]

[Tolstoy began writing this story in 1863. It was completed and published in 1885. One of the most significant stories in Russian literature, it is known for the prominent use of 'defamiliarization'—an artistic technique of making common and familiar elements appear strange and unfamiliar.

This version is a translation by Nathan Haskell Dole taken from the collection *The Invaders and Other Stories* published in 1887 by Thomas Y. Crowell & Co. It has also been translated as *Strider: the Story of a Horse* by Louise and Aylmer Maude.]

[*] Dedicated to the memory of M. A. Stakhovitch, the originator of the subject, which was given by his brother to Count Tolstoy.

I

Constantly higher and higher the sky lifted itself, wider and wider spread the dawn, whiter and whiter grew the unpolished silver of the dew, more and more lifeless the sickle of the moon, more vocal the forest. The men began to arise; and at the stables belonging to the bárin were heard with increasing frequency the whinnying of the horses, the stamping of hoofs on the straw, and also the angry, shrill neighing of the animals collecting together, and even disputing with each other over something.

"Noo! you got time enough; mighty hungry, ain't you?" said the old drover, quickly opening the creaking gates. "Where you going?" he shouted, waving his hands at a mare which tried to run through the gate.

Nester, the drover, was dressed in a Cossack coat,* with a decorated leather belt around his waist; his knout was slung over his shoulder, and a handkerchief, containing some bread, was tied into his belt. In his arms he carried a saddle and halter.

The horses were not in the least startled, nor did they show any resentment, at the drover's sarcastic tone: they made believe that it was all the same to them, and leisurely moved back from the gate— all except one old dark-bay mare, with a long flowing mane, who laid back her ears and quickly turned around. At this opportunity a young mare, who was standing behind, and had nothing at all to do with this, whinnied, and began to kick at the first horse that she fell in with.

"No!" shouted the drover still more loudly and angrily, and turned to the corner of the yard.†

---

* *kasakín.*

† *dvor.*

Out of all the horses—there must have been nearly a hundred—that were moving off toward their breakfast, none manifested so little impatience as a piebald gelding, which stood alone in one corner under the shed, and gazed with half-shut eyes, and bit on the oaken lining of the shed.

It is hard to say what enjoyment the piebald gelding got from this, but his expression while doing so was solemn and thoughtful.

"Nonsense!" again cried the drover in the same tone, turning to him; and going up to him he laid the saddle and shiny blanket on a pile of manure near him.

The piebald gelding ceased biting, and looked long at Nester without moving. He did not manifest any sign of mirth or anger or sullenness, but only drew in his whole belly and sighed heavily, heavily, and then turned away. The drover took him by the neck, and gave him his breakfast.

"What are you sighing for?" asked Nester.

The horse switched his tail as though to say, "Well, it's nothing, Nester." Nester put on the blanket and saddle, whereupon the horse pricked up his ears, expressing as plainly as could be his disgust; but he received nothing but execrations for this 'rot,' and then the saddle-girth was pulled tight.

At this the gelding tried to swell out; but his mouth was thrust open, and a knee was pressed into his side, so that he was forced to let out his breath. Notwithstanding this, when they got the bit between his teeth, he still pricked back his ears, and even turned round. Though he knew that this was of no avail, yet he seemed to reckon it essential to express his displeasure, and always showed it. When he was saddled, he pawed with his swollen right leg, and began to champ the bit—here also for some special reason, because it was full time for him to know that there could be no taste in bits.

Nester mounted the gelding by the short stirrups, unwound his knout, freed his Cossack coat from under his knee, settled down in the saddle in that position peculiar to coachmen, hunters, and drivers, and twitched on the reins. The gelding lifted his head, showing a disposition to go where he should be directed, but he stirred not from the spot. He knew that before he went there would be much shouting on the part of him who sat on his back, and many orders to be given to Vaska, the other drover, and to the horses. In fact Nester began to shout, "Vaska! ha, Vaska! have you let out any of the mares—hey? Where are you, you old devil? No-o! Are you asleep? Open the gate. Let the mares go first," and so on.

The gates creaked. Vaska, morose, and still full of sleep, holding a horse by the bridle, stood at the gate-post and let the horses out. The horses, one after the other, gingerly stepping over the straw and sniffing it, began to pass out—the young fillies, the yearlings, the little colts; while the mares with young stepped along needfully, one at a time, avoiding all contact. The young fillies sometimes crowded in two at once, three at once, throwing their heads across each other's backs, and hitting their hoofs against the gates, each time receiving a volley of abuse from the drovers. The colts sometimes kicked the mares whom they did not know, and whinnied loudly in answer to the short neighing of their mothers.

A young filly, full of wantonness, as soon as she got outside the gate, tossed her head up and around, began to back, and whinnied, but nevertheless did not venture to dash ahead of the old grey, grain-bestrewed Zhuldiba, who, with a gentle but solid step, swinging her belly from side to side, was always the dignified leader of the other horses.

After a few moments the lively yard was left in melancholy loneliness; the posts stood out in sadness under the empty sheds, and only the sodden straw, soiled with dung, was to be seen.

Familiar as this picture of emptiness was to the piebald gelding, it seemed to have a melancholy effect upon him. He slowly, as though making a bow, lowered and lifted his head, sighed as deeply as the tightly drawn girth permitted, and dragging his somewhat bent and decrepit legs, he started off after the herd, carrying the old Nester on his bony back.

"I know now. As soon as we get out on the road, he will go to work to make a light, and smoke his wooden pipe with its copper mounting and chain," thought the gelding. "I am glad of this, because it is early in the morning and the dew is on the grass, and this odour is agreeable to me, and brings up many pleasant recollections. I am sorry only that when the old man has his pipe in his mouth he always becomes excited, gets to imagining things, and sits on one side, far over on one side, and on that side it always hurts. However, God be with him. It's no new thing for me to suffer for the sake of others. I have even come to find some equine satisfaction in this. Let him play that he's cock of the walk, poor fellow; but it's for his own pleasure that he looks so big, since no one sees him at all. Let him ride sidewise," said the horse to himself; and, stepping gingerly on his crooked legs, he walked along the middle of the road.

II

After driving the herd down to the river, near which the horses were to graze, Nester dismounted and took off the saddle. Meantime the herd began slowly to scatter over the as yet untrodden field, covered with dew and with vapour rising alike from the damp meadow and the river that encircled it.

Taking off the blanket from the piebald gelding, Nester scratched him on his neck; and the horse in reply expressed his happiness and satisfaction by shutting his eyes.

"The old dog likes it," said Nester.

The gelding really did not like this scratching very much, and only out of delicacy intimated that it was agreeable to him. He shook his head as a sign of assent. But suddenly, unexpectedly, and without any reason, Nester, imagining perhaps that too great familiarity might give the horse false ideas about what he meant— Nester, without any warning, pushed away his head, and, lifting up the bridle, struck the horse very severely with the buckle on his bare leg, and, without saying anything, went up the hillock to a stump, near which he sat down as though nothing had happened.

Though this proceeding incensed the gelding, he did not manifest it; and leisurely switching his thin tail, and sniffing at something, and merely for recreation cropping at the grass, he wandered down toward the river.

Not paying any heed to the antics played around him by the young fillies, the colts, and the yearlings, and knowing that the health of everybody, and especially one who had attained his years, was subserved by getting a good drink of water on an empty stomach, and then eating, he turned his steps to where the bank was less steep and slippery; and wetting his hoofs and gambrels, he thrust his snout into the river, and began to suck the water through his lips drawn back, to puff with his distending sides, and out of pure satisfaction to switch his thin, piebald tail with its leathery stump.

A chestnut filly, always mischievous, always nagging the old horse, and causing him manifold unpleasantnesses, came down to the water as though for her own necessities, but really merely for the sake of roiling the water in front of his nose.

But the gelding had already drunk enough, and apparently giving no thought to the impudent mare, calmly put one miry leg before the other, shook his head, and, turning aside from the wanton youngster, began to eat. Dragging his legs in a peculiar manner, and not tramping down the abundant grass, the horse grazed for nearly three hours, scarcely stirring from the spot. Having eaten so much that his belly hung down like a bag from his thin, sharp ribs, he stood solidly on his four weak legs, so that as little strain as possible might come on any one of them—at least on the right foreleg, which was weaker than all—and went to sleep.

There is an honourable old age, there is a miserable old age, there is a pitiable old age; there is also an old age that is both honourable and miserable. The old age which the piebald gelding had reached was of this latter sort.

The old horse was of a great size—more than seventeen hands

high.* His colour was white, spotted with black; at least, it used to be so, but now the black spots had changed to a dirty brown. The regions of black spots were three in number: one on the head, including the mane, and side of the nose, the star on the forehead, and half of the neck; the long mane, tangled with burrs, was striped white and brownish; the second spotted place ran along the right side, and covered half the belly; the third was on the flank, including the upper part of the tail and half of the loins; the rest of the tail was whitish, variegated.

The huge, corrugated head, with deep hollows under the eyes, and with pendent black lips, somewhat lacerated, sat heavily and draggingly on the neck, which bent under its leanness, and seemed to be made of wood. From under the pendent lip could be seen the dark-red tongue protruding on one side, and the yellow, worn tusks of his lower teeth. His ears, one of which was slit, fell over sidewise, and only occasionally he twitched them a little to scare away the sticky flies. One long tuft still remaining of the forelock hung behind the ears; the broad forehead was hollowed and rough; the skin hung loose on the big cheekbones. On the neck and head the veins stood out in knots, trembling and twitching whenever a fly touched them. The expression of his face was sternly patient, deeply thoughtful, and expressive of pain.

His forelegs were crooked at the knees. On both hoofs were swellings; and on the one which was half covered by the marking, there was near the knee at the back a sore boil. The hind legs were in better condition, but there had been severe bruises long before on the haunches, and the hair did not grow on those places. His legs seemed disproportionately long, because his body was so emaciated. His ribs, though also thick, were so exposed and drawn that the hide seemed dried in the hollows between them.

The back and withers were variated with old scars, and behind was still a freshly galled and purulent slough. The black stump of the tail, where the vertebra could be counted, stood out long and almost bare. On the brown flank near the tail, where it was overgrown with

---

* Two *arshin*, three *vershoks* = 6.65 feet.

white hair, was a scar as big as one's hand, which must have been from a bite. Another cicatrice was to be seen on the off shoulder. The houghs of the hind legs and the tail were foul with excrement. The hair all over the body, though short, stood out straight.

But in spite of the filthy old age to which this horse had come, anyone looking at him would have involuntarily thought, and a *connoisseur* would have said immediately, that he must have been in his day a remarkably fine horse. The *connoisseur* would have said also that there was only one breed in Russia that could give such broad bones, such huge joints, such hoofs, such slender leg-bones, such an arched neck, and, most of all, such a skull—eyes large, black, and brilliant, and such a thoroughbred network of nerves over his head and neck, and such delicate skin and hair.

In reality there was something noble in the form of this horse, and in the terrible union in him of the repulsive signs of decrepitude, the increased variegatedness of his hide, and his actions, and the expression of self-dependence, and the calm consciousness of beauty and strength.

Like a living ruin he stood in the middle of the dewy field, alone; while not far away from him were heard the galloping, the neighing, the lively whinnying, the snorting, of the scattered herd.

III

The sun was now risen above the forest, and shone brightly on the grass and the winding river. The dew dried away and fell off in drops. Like smoke the last of the morning mist rolled up. Curly clouds made their appearance, but as yet there was no wind. On the other side of the gleaming river stood the rye, bending on its stalks, and the air was fragrant with bright verdure and the flowers. The cuckoo cooed from the forest with echoing voice; and Nester, lying flat on his back, was reckoning up how many years of life lay before him. The larks arose from the rye and the field. The belated hare stood up among the horses and leaped without restraint, and sat down by the copse and pricked up his ears to listen.

Vaska went to sleep, burying his head in the grass; the mares, making wide circuits around him, scattered themselves on the field below. The older ones, neighing, picked out a shining track across the dewy grass, and constantly tried to find some place where they might be undisturbed. They no longer grazed, but only nibbled on the sweet grass-blades. The whole herd was imperceptibly moving in one direction.

And again the old Zhuldiba, stately stepping before the others, showed how far it was possible to go. The young Mushka, who had cast her first foal, constantly hinnying, and lifting her tail, was scolding her violet-coloured colt. The young Atlásnaya, with smooth and shining skin, dropping her head so that her black and silken forelock hid her forehead and eyes, was gambolling in the grass, nipping and tossing and stamping her leg, with its hairy fetlock. One of the older little colts—he must have been imagining, some kind of game—lifting, for the twenty-sixth time, his rather short and tangled tail, like a plume, gambolled around his dam, who calmly picked at the herbage, having evidently had time to sum up her son's character, and only occasionally stopping to look askance at him out of her big black eye.

One of these same young colts—black as a coal, with a large head with a marvellous top-knot rising above his ears, and his tail still inclining to the side on which he had laid in his mother's belly—pricking up his ears, and opening his stupid eyes, as he stood motionless in his place, looked steadily at the colt jumping and dancing, not at all understanding why he did it, whether out of jealousy or indignation.

Some suckle, butting with their noses; others, for some unknown reason, notwithstanding their mothers' invitation,

345

move along in a short, awkward trot, in a diametrically opposite direction, as though seeking something, and then, no one knows why, stop short and hinny in a desperately penetrating voice. Some lie on their sides in a row; some take lessons in grazing; some try to scratch themselves with their hind legs behind the ear.

Two mares, still with young, go off by themselves, and slowly moving their legs continue to graze. Evidently their condition is respected by the others, and none of the young colts ventures to go near or disturb them. If any saucy young steed takes it into his head to approach too near to them, then merely a motion of an ear or tail is sufficient to show him all the impropriety of his behaviour.

The yearlings and the young fillies pretend to be full-grown and dignified, and rarely indulge in pranks, or join their gay companions. They ceremoniously nibble at the blades of grass, bending their swan-like, short-shorn necks, and, as though they also were blessed with tails, switch their little brushes. Just like the big horses, some of them lie down, roll over, and scratch each others' backs.

A very jolly band consists of the two-year-old and the three-year-old mares who have never foaled. They almost all wander off by themselves, and make a specially jolly virgin throng. Among them is heard a great tramping and stamping, hinnying and whinnying. They gather together, lay their heads over each others' shoulders, snuff the air, leap; and sometimes, lifting the tail like an oriflamme, proudly and coquettishly, in a half-trot, half-gallop, caracole in front of their companions.

Conspicuous for beauty and sprightly dashing ways, among all this young throng, was the wanton bay mare. Whatever she set on foot, the others also did; wherever she went, there in her track followed also the whole throng of beauties.

The wanton was in a specially playful frame of mind this morning. The spirit of mischief was in her, just as it sometimes comes upon men. Even at the riverside, playing her pranks upon the old gelding, she had galloped along in the water, pretending that something had scared her, snorting, and then dashed off at full speed across the field; so that Vaska was constrained to gallop after her, and after the others who were at her heels. Then, after grazing a little while, she began to roll, then to tease the old mares, by dashing in front of them. Then she separated a suckling colt from its dam, and began to chase after it, pretending that she wanted to bite it. The mother was frightened, and ceased to graze; the little colt squealed in piteous tones. But the wanton young mare did not touch it, but only scared it, and made a spectacle for her comrades, who looked with sympathy on her antics.

Then she set out to turn the head of the roan horse, which a muzhík, far away on the other side of the river, was driving with a plough in the rye-field. She stood proudly, somewhat on one side, lifting her head high, shook herself, and neighed in a sweet, significant, and alluring voice.

"'Tis the time when the rail-bird, running from place to place among the thick reeds, passionately calls his mate; when also the cuckoo and the quail sing of love; and the flowers send to each other, on the breeze, their aromatic dust.

"And I am young and kind and strong," said the jolly wanton's neighing, "and till now it has not been given to me to experience the sweetness of this feeling, never yet to feel it; and no lover, no, not one, has yet come to woo me."

And the significant neighing rang with youthful melancholy over lowland and field, and it came to the ears of the roan horse far away. He pricked up his ears, and stopped. The muzhík kicked him with his wooden shoe; but the roan was bewitched by the silver sound of the distant neighing, and whinnied in reply. The muzhík grew angry, twitched him with the reins, and again kicked him in the belly with his bast shoe, so that he did not have a chance to complete all that he had to say in his neighing, but was forced to go on his way. And the roan horse felt a sweet sadness in his heart; and the sounds from the far-off rye-field, of that unfinished and passionate neigh, and the angry voice of the muzhík, long echoed in the ears of the herd.

If through one sound of her voice the roan horse could become so captivated as to forget his duty, what would have become of him if he had had full view of the beautiful wanton, as she stood pricking up her ears, inflating her nostrils, breathing in the air, and filled with longing, while her young and beauteous body trembled as she called to him?

But the wanton did not long ponder over her novel sensations. When the voice of the roan was still, she whinnied scornfully, and, sinking her head, began to paw the ground; and then she trotted off to wake up and tease the piebald gelding. The piebald gelding was a long-suffering butt for the amusement of this happy young wanton. She made him suffer more than men did. But in neither case did he give way to wrath. He was indispensable to men, but why should these young horses torment him?

IV

He was old, they were young; he was lean, they were fat; he was sad, they were happy. So he was thoroughly strange, alien, an absolutely different creature; and it was impossible for them to have compassion on him. Horses have pity only on themselves, and rarely on those whose places they may easily come themselves to fill. But, indeed, was not the piebald gelding himself to blame, that he was old and gaunt and crippled? . . .

One would think that he was not to blame. But in equine ethics he was, and only those were right who were strong, young, and happy; those who had all life before them; those whose every muscle was tense with superfluous energy, and curled their tails into a wheel.

Maybe the piebald gelding himself understood this, and in

tranquil moments was agreed that he was to blame because he had lived out all his life, that he must pay for his life; but he was after all only a horse, and he could not restrain himself often from feeling hurt, melancholy, and discontented, when he looked on all these young horses who tormented him for the very thing to which they would be subjected when they came to the end of their lives.

The reason for the heartlessness of these horses was a peculiarly aristocratic feeling. Every one of them was related, either on the side of father or mother, to the celebrated Smetanka; but it was not known from what stock the piebald gelding sprang. The gelding was a chance comer, bought at market three years before for eighty paper roubles.

The young chestnut mare, as though accidentally wandering about, came up to the piebald gelding's very nose, and brushed against him. He knew beforehand what it meant, and did not open his eyes, but laid back his ears and showed his teeth. The mare wheeled around, and made believe that she was going to let fly at him with her heels. He opened his eyes, and wandered off to another part. He had no desire to sleep, and began to crop the grass. Again the wanton young mare, accompanied by her confederates, went to the gelding. A two-year-old mare with a star on her forehead, very stupid, always in mischief, and always ready to imitate the chestnut mare, trotted along with her, and, as imitators always do, began to play the same trick that the instigator had done.

The brown mare marched along at an ordinary gait, as though bent on her own affairs, and passed by the gelding's very nose, not looking at him, so that he really did not know whether to be angry or not; and this was the very fun of the thing.

This was what she did; but the starred mare following in her steps, and feeling very gay, hit the gelding on the chest. He showed his teeth once more, whinnied, and, with a quickness of motion unexpected on his part, sprang at the mare, and bit her on the flank. The young mare with the star flew out with her bind legs, and kicked the old horse heavily on his thin bare ribs. The old horse uttered a hoarse noise, and was about to make another lunge, but thought better of it, and sighing deeply turned away.

It must have been that all the young horses of the drove regarded as a personal insult the boldness which the piebald gelding permitted himself to show toward the starred mare; for all the rest of the day they gave him no chance to graze, and left him not a moment of peace, so that the drover several times rebuked them, and could not comprehend what they were doing.

The gelding was so abused that he himself walked up to Nester when it was time for the old man to drive back the drove, and he showed greater happiness and content when Nester saddled him and mounted him.

God knows what the old gelding's thoughts were as he bore on his back the old man Nester. Did he think with bitterness of these importunate and merciless youngsters? Or, with a scornful and silent pride peculiar to old age, did he pardon his persecutors? At all events, he did not make manifest any of his thoughts till he reached home.

That evening some cronies had come to see Nester; and as the horses were driven by the huts of the domestics, he noticed a horse and telyéga standing at his doorstep. After he had driven in the horses, he was in such a hurry that he did not take the saddle off: he left the gelding at the yard,* and shouted to Vaska to unsaddle the animal, then shut the gate, and hurried to his friends.

Perhaps owing to the affront put upon the starred mare, the descendant of Smetanka, by that 'low trash' bought for a horse, and not knowing father or mother, and therefore offending the aristocratic sentiment of the whole community; or because the gelding with the high saddle without a rider presented a strangely fantastic spectacle for the horses—at all events, that night something extraordinary took place in the paddock. All the horses, young and old, showing their teeth, tagged after the gelding, and drove him from one part of the yard to the other; the trampling of their hoofs echoed around him as he sighed and drew in his thin sides.

The gelding could no longer endure this, could no longer avoid their kicks. He halted in the middle of the field: his face expressed

* *dvor.*

the repulsive, weak anger of helpless old age, and despair besides. He laid back his ears, and suddenly[*] something happened that caused all the horses suddenly to become quiet. A very old mare, Viazopúrikha, came up and sniffed the gelding, and sighed. The gelding also sighed. . . .

In the middle of the yard, flooded with the moonlight, stood the tall, gaunt figure of the gelding, still wearing the high saddle with its prominent pommel. The horses, motionless and in deep silence, stood around him, as though they were learning something new and extraordinary from him. And, indeed, something new and extraordinary they learned from him.

This is what they learned from him:—

FIRST NIGHT

"Yes, I was sired by Liubeznuï I. Baba was my dam. According to the genealogy my name is Muzhík I. Muzhík I, I am according to my pedigree; but generally I am known as Kholstomír, on account of a long and glorious gallop, the like of which never took place in Russia. In lineage no horse in the world stands higher than I, for good blood. I would never have told you this. Why should I? You would never have known me as Viazopúrikha knew me when we used to be together at Khrénova, and who only just now recognized me. You would not have believed me had it not been for

---

* So in the original.

Viazopúrikha's witness, and I would never have told you this. I do not need the pity of my kind. But you insisted upon it. Well, I am that Kholstomír whom the amateurs are seeking for and cannot find, that Kholstomír whom the count himself named, and whom he let go from his stud because I outran his favourite 'Lebedi.'

"When I was born I did not know what they meant when they called me a piebald;* I thought that I was a horse. The first remark made about my hide, I remember, deeply surprised me and my dam.

"I must have been foaled in the night. In the morning, licked clean by my dam's tongue, I stood on my legs. I remember all my sensations, and that everything seemed to me perfectly wonderful, and, at the same time, perfectly simple. Our stalls were in a long, warm corridor, with latticed gates, through which nothing could be seen.

"My dam tempted me to suckle; but I was so innocent as yet that I bunted her with my nose, now under her fore-legs, now in other places. Suddenly my dam gazed at the latticed gate, and, throwing her leg over me, stepped to one side. One of the grooms was looking in at us through the lattice.

"'See, Baba has foaled!' he exclaimed, and began to draw the bolt. He came in over the straw bed, and took me up in his arms. 'Come and look, Taras!' he cried; 'see what a piebald colt, a perfect magpie!'

"I tore myself away from him, and fell on my knees.

"'See, a perfect little devil!' he said.

"My dam became disquieted; but she did not take my part, and merely drew a long, long breath, and stepped to one side. The grooms came, and began to look at me. One ran to tell the equerry.

"All laughed as they looked at my spotting, and gave me various odd names. I did not understand these names, nor did my dam either. Up to that time in all my family there had never been a single piebald known. We had no idea that there was anything disgraceful in it. And then all examined my structure and strength.

* *pyégi.*

"'See what a lively one!' said the hostler. 'You can't hold him.'

"In a little while came the equerry, and began to marvel at my colouring. He also seemed disgusted.

"'What a nasty beast!' he cried. 'The general will not keep him in the stud. Ekh! Baba, you have caused me much trouble,' he said, turning to my dam. 'You ought to have foaled a colt with a star, but this is completely piebald.'

"My dam vouchsafed no answer, and, as always in such circumstances, merely sighed again.

"'What kind of a devil was his sire? A regular muzhík!' he went on to say. 'It is impossible to keep him in the stud; it's a shame! But we'll see, we'll see,' said he; and all said the same as they looked at me.

"After a few days the general himself came. He took a look at me, and again all seemed horror-struck, and scolded me and my mother also on account of my hide. 'But we'll see, we'll see,' said every one, as soon as they caught sight of me.

"Until spring we young colts lived in separate cells with our dams; only occasionally, when the snow on the roof of the sheds began to melt in the sun, they would let us out into the wide yard, spread with fresh straw. There for the first time I became acquainted with all my kin, near and remote. There I saw how from different doors issued all the famous mares of that time with their colts. There was the old Holland mare, Mushka, sired by Smetankin, Krasnukha, the saddle-horse Dobrokhotíkha, all celebrities at that time. All gathered together there with their colts, walked up and down in the sunshine, rolled over on the fresh straw, and sniffed of each other like ordinary horses.

"I cannot even now forget the sight of that paddock, full of the beauties of that day. It may seem strange to you to think of me as ever having been young and frisky, but I used to be. This very same Viazopúrikha was there then, a yearling, whose mane had just been cut,*—a kind, jolly, frolicsome little horse. But let it not be taken as unkindly meant when I say, that, though she is

---

* All expressed in the word *strigúnchik*.

now considered a rarity among you on account of her pedigree then she was only one of the meanest horses of that stud. She herself will corroborate this.

"Though my coat of many colours had been displeasing to the men, it was exceedingly attractive to all the horses. They all stood round me, expressing their delight, and frisking with me. I even began to forget the words of the men about my hide, and felt happy. But I soon experienced the first sorrow of my life, and the cause of it was my dam. As soon as it began to thaw, and the swallow chirped on the roof, and the spring made itself felt more and more in the air, my dam began to change in her behaviour toward me.

"Her whole character was transformed. Suddenly, without any reason, she began to frisk, galloping around the yard, which certainly did not accord with her dignified growth; then she would pause and consider, and begin to whinny; then she would bite and kick her sister mares; then she began to smell of me, and neigh with dissatisfaction; then trotting out into the sun she would lay her head across the shoulder of my two-year-old sister Kúpchika, and long and earnestly scratch her back, and push me away from nursing her. One time the equerry came, commanded the halter to be put on her, and they led her out of the paddock. She whinnied, I replied to her, and darted after her, but she would not even look at me. The groom Taras seized me in both arms, just as they shut the door on my mother's retreating form.

"I struggled, threw the groom on the straw; but the door was closed, and I only heard my mother's whinnying growing fainter and fainter. And in this whinnying I perceived that she called not for me, but I perceived a very different expression. In reply to her voice, there was heard in the distance a mighty voice.

"I don't remember how Taras got out of my stall; it was too grievous for me. I felt that I had forever lost my mother's love; and wholly because I was a piebald, I said to myself, remembering what the people said of my hide; and such passionate anger came over me, that I began to pound the sides of the stall with my head and feet, and I pounded them until the sweat poured from me, and I could not stand up from exhaustion.

"After some time my dam returned to me. I heard her as she came along the corridor in a prancing trot, wholly unusual to her, and entered our stall. The door was opened for her. I did not recognize her, so much younger and handsomer had she grown. She snuffed at me, neighed, and began to snort. But in her whole expression I could see that she did not love me.

"Soon they led us to pasture. I now began to experience new pleasures which consoled me for the loss of my mother's love. I had friends and companions. We learned together to eat grass, to neigh like the old horses, and to lift our tails and gallop in wide circles around our dams. This was a happy time. Everything was forgiven to me; all loved me, and were loved by me, and looked indulgently on all that I did. This did not last long.

"Here something terrible happened to me."

The gelding sighed deeply, deeply, and moved aside from the horses.

The dawn was already far advanced. The gates creaked. Nester came. The horses scattered. The drover straightened the saddle on the gelding's back, and drove away the horses.

VI

SECOND NIGHT

As soon as the horses were driven in, they once more gathered around the piebald.

"In the month of August," continued the horse, "I was separated from my mother, and I did not experience any unusual grief. I saw that she was already suckling a small brother—the famous Usan—and I was not what I had been before. I was no jealous, but I felt that I had become more than ever cool toward her Besides, I knew that in leaving my mother I should be transferred to the general division of young horses, where we were stalled in twos and threes, and every day all went out to exercise.

"I was in one stall with Milui. Milui was a saddle-horse, and afterwards belonged to the emperor himself, and was put into pictures and statuary. At that time he was a mere colt, with a shiny soft coat, a swan-like neck, and slender straight legs. He was always lively, good-natured, and lovable; was always ready to frisk, and be caressed, and sport with either horse or man. He and I could not help being good friends, living together as we did; and our friendship lasted till we grew up. He was gay, and inclined to be wanton. Even then he began to feel the tender passion to disport with the fillies, and he used to make sport of my guilelessness To my unhappiness I myself, out of egotism, tried to follow his example, and very soon was in love. And this early inclination of mine was the cause, in great measure, of my fate.

"But I am not going to relate all the story of my unhappy first love; she herself remembers my stupid passion, which ended for me in the most important change in my life.

"The drovers came along, drove her away, and pounded me. In the evening they led me into a special stall. I whinnied the whole night long, as though with a presentiment of what was coming on the morrow.

"In the morning the general, the equerry, the under grooms, and the hostlers came into the corridor where my stall was, and set up a terrible screaming. The general screamed to the head groom; the groom justified himself, saying that he had not given orders to send me away, but that the under grooms had done it of their own free will. The general said that it had spoiled everything, but that it was impossible to keep young stallions. The head groom replied that he would have it attended to. They calmed down and went out, I did not understand it at all—except that something concerning me was under consideration.

"On the next day I had ceased forever to whinny; I became what I am now. All the light of my eyes was quenched. Nothing seemed sweet to me; I became self-absorbed, and began to be pensive. At first I felt indifferent to everything. I ceased even to eat, to drink, and to run; and all thought of sprightly sport was gone. Then it nevermore came into my mind to kick up my heels, to roll over, to whinny, without bringing up the terrible question—'Why? For what purpose?' And my vigour died away.

"Once they led me out at eventide, at the time when they were driving the stud home from the field. From afar I saw already the cloud of dust in which could be barely distinguished the familiar lineaments of all of our mothers. I heard the cheerful snorting, and the trampling of hoofs. I stopped short, though the halter-rope by which the groom held me cut my neck; and I gazed at the approaching drove as one gazes at happiness that is lost forever and will ne'er return again. They drew near, and my eyes fell upon forms so well known to me—beautiful, grand, plump, full of life every one. Who among them all deigned to glance at me? I did not feel the pain that the groom in pulling the rope inflicted. I forgot myself, and involuntarily tried to whinny as of yore, and to gallop off; but my whinnying sounded melancholy, ridiculous, and unbecoming. There was no ribaldry among the stud, but I noticed that many of them from politeness turned away from me.

"It was evident that in their eyes I was despicable and pitiable, and worst of all ridiculous. My slender, weakly neck, my big head (I had become thin), my long, thick legs, and the awkward gait that I struck up, in my old fashion, around the groom, all must have seemed absurd to them. No one heeded my whinnying, all turned away from me.

"Suddenly I comprehended it all, comprehended how I was forever sundered from them, every one; and I know not how I stumbled home behind the groom.

"I had already shown a tendency toward gravity and thoughtfulness; but now a decided change came over me. My variegated coat, which occasioned such a strange prejudice in men, my terrible and unexpected unhappiness, and, moreover, my peculiarly isolated position in the stud—which I felt, but could never explain to myself—compelled me to turn my thoughts inward upon myself. I pondered on the disgust that people showed when they berated me for being a piebald; I pondered on the inconstancy of maternal and especially of female affection, and its dependence upon physical conditions; and, above all, I pondered on the characteristics of that strange race of mortals with whom we are so closely bound, and whom we call men— those characteristics which were the source of the peculiarity of my position in the stud, felt by me but incomprehensible.

"The significance of this, peculiarity, and of the human characteristics on which it was based, was discovered to me by the following incident:—

"It was winter, at Christmas-tide. All day long no fodder had been given to me, nor had I been led out to water. I afterwards learned that this arose from our groom being drunk. On this day the equerry came to me, saw that I had no food, and began to use hard language about the missing groom, and went away.

"On the next day, the groom with his mates came out to our stalls to give us some hay. I noticed that he was especially pale and glum, and in the expression of his long back there was a something significant and demanding sympathy.

"He austerely flung the hay behind the grating. I laid my head over his shoulder; but he struck me such a hard blow with his fist on the nose, that I started back. Then he kicked me in the belly with his boot.

"'If it hadn't been for this scurvy beast,' said he, 'there wouldn't have been any trouble.'

"'Why?' asked another groom.

"'He doesn't come to inquire about the count's you bet! But twice a day he comes out to look after his own.'

"'Have they given him the piebald?' inquired another.

"'Whether they've given it to him or sold it to him, the dog only knows! The count's might die o' starvation—it wouldn't make any difference; but see how it upset him when I didn't give *his* horse his fodder! 'Go to bed,' says he, 'and then you'll get a basting.' No Christianity in it. More pity on the cattle than on a man. I don't believe he's ever been christened, he himself counted the blows, the barbarian! The general did not use the whip so. He made my back all welts. There's no soul of a Christian in him!'

"Now, what they said about whips and Christianity, I understood well enough; but it was perfectly dark to me as to the meaning of the words, *my horse, his horse*, by which I perceived that men understood some sort of bond between me and the groom. Wherein consisted this bond, I could not then understand at all. Only long after, when I was separated from the other horses, I came to learn what it meant. At that time I could not understand at all that it meant that they considered *me* the property of a man. To say *my horse* in reference to me, a live horse, seemed to me as strange as to say, *my earth, my atmosphere, my water.*

"But these words had a monstrous influence upon me. I pondered upon them ceaselessly; and only after long and varied relations with men did I come at last to comprehend the meaning that men find in these strange words.

"The meaning is this: Men rule in life, not by deeds, but by words. They love not so much the possibility of doing or not doing anything, as the possibility of talking about different objects in words agreed upon between them. Such words, considered very important among them, are the words, *my, mine, ours,* which they employ for various things, beings, and objects; even for the earth, people, and horses. In regard to any particular thing, they agree that only one person shall say 'It is *mine.*' And he who in this play, which they engage in, can say *mine* in regard to the greatest number of things, is considered the most fortunate among them. Why this is so, I know not; but it is so. Long before, I had tried to explain this to my satisfaction, by some direct advantage; but it seemed that I was wrong.

"Many of the men who, for instance, called me their horse, did not ride on me, but entirely different men rode on me. They themselves did not feed me, but entirely different people fed me. Again, it was not those who called me their horse who treated me kindly, but the coachman, the veterinary, and, as a general thing, outside men.

"Afterwards, as I widened the sphere of my experiences, I became convinced that the concept *my*, as applied not only to us horses, but to other things, has no other foundation than a low and animal, a human instinct, which they call the sentiment or right of property. Man says, *my house,* and never lives in it, but is only cumbered with the building and maintenance of it. The merchant says, *my shop*—my clothing shop, for example—and he does not even wear clothes made of the best cloth in the shop.

"There are people who call land theirs, and have never seen their land, and have never been on it. There are men who call other people theirs, but have never seen these people; and the whole relationship of these owners, to these people, consists in doing them harm.

"There are men who call women theirs—their wives or mistresses; but these women live with other men. And men struggle in life not to do what they consider good, but to be possessors of what they call their own.

"I am convinced now that herein lies the substantial difference between men and us. And, therefore, not speaking of other things, where we are superior to men, we are able boldly to say that in this one respect at least, we stand, in the scale of living beings, higher than men. The activity of men—at all events, of those with whom I have had to do—is guided by words; ours, by deeds.

"And here the head groom obtained this right to say about me, *my horse;* and hence he lashed the hostler. This discovery deeply disturbed me; and those thoughts and opinions which my variegated coat aroused in men, and the thoughtfulness aroused in me by the change in my mother, together subserved to make me into that solemn and contemplative gelding that I am.

"I was threefold unhappy: I was piebald; I was a gelding; and men imagined that I did not belong to God and myself, as is the prerogative of every living thing, but that I belonged to the equerry.

"The consequences of their imagining this about me were many. The first was, that they kept me apart from the others, fed me better, led me more often, and harnessed me up earlier. They harnessed me first when I was in my third year. I remember the first time, the equerry himself, who imagined that I was his, began, with a crowd of grooms, to harness me, expecting from me some ebullition of temper or contrariness. They put leather straps on me, and conducted me into the stalls. They laid on my back a wide leather cross, and attached it to the thills, so that I should not kick; but I was only waiting an opportunity to show my gait, and my love for work.

"They marvelled because I went like an old horse. They began to drive me, and I began to practise trotting. Every day I made greater and greater improvement, so that in three months the general himself, and many others, praised my gait. But this was a strange thing: for the very reason that they imagined that I was the equerry's, and not theirs, my gait had for them an entirely different significance.

"The stallions, my brothers, were put through their paces; their time was reckoned; people came to see them; they were driven in gilded drozhkies. Costly saddles were put upon them. But I was driven in the equerry's simple drozhkies, when he had business at Chesmenka and other manor-houses. All this resulted from the fact that I was piebald, but more than all from the fact that I was, according to their idea, not the property of the count, but of the equerry.

"Tomorrow, if we are alive, I will tell you what a serious influence upon me was exercised by this right of proprietorship which the equerry arrogated to himself."

All that day the horses treated Kholstomír with great consideration; but Nester, from old custom, rode him into the field. But Nester's ways were so rough! The muzhík's grey stallion, coming toward the drove, whinnied: and again the chestnut filly coquettishly replied to him.

VII

THIRD NIGHT

The moon had quartered; and her narrow band poured a mild light
on Kholstomír, standing in the middle of the yard, with the horses
clustered around him.

"The principal and most surprising consequence to me of the
fact that I was not the property of the count nor of God, but of the
equerry," continued the piebald, "was that what constitutes our chief
activity—the eager race—was made the cause of my banishment.
They were driving Lebedi around the ring; and a jockey from
Chesmenka was riding me, and entered the course. Lebedi dashed
past us. He trotted well, but he seemed to want to show off. He had
not that skill which I had cultivated in myself; that is, of compelling
one leg instantly to follow on the motion of the other, and not to
waste the least degree of energy, but use it all in pressing forward.
Lebedi dashed by us. I entered the ring: the jockey did not hold
me back.

"'Say, will you time my piebald?' he cried; and when Lebedi
came abreast of us a second time, he let me out. He had the
advantage of his momentum, and so I was left behind in the first
heat; but in the second I began to gain on him; came up to him in
the drozhsky, caught up with him, passed beyond him, and won
the race. They tried it a second time—the same thing. I was the
swifter. And this filled them all with dismay. The general begged
them to send me away as soon as possible, so that I might not be
heard of again. 'Otherwise the count will know about it, and there
will be trouble,' said he. And they sent me to the horse-dealer. I did
not remain there long. A hussar, who came along to get a remount,
bought me. All this had been so disagreeable, so cruel, that I was

glad when they took me from Khrénova, and forever separated me from all that had been near and dear to me. It was too hard for me among them. Before *them* stood love, honour, freedom; before me labour, humiliation—humiliation, labour, to the end of my days. Why? Because I was piebald, and because I was compelled to be somebody's horse."

VIII

FOURTH NIGHT

The next evening when the gates were closed, and all was still, the piebald continued thus:—

"I had many experiences, both among men and among my own kind, while changing about from hand to hand. I staid with two masters the longest: with the prince, the officer of the hussars, and then with an old man who lived at Nikola Yavleonoï Church.

"I spent the happiest days of my life with the hussar.

"Though he was the cause of my destruction, though he loved nothing and nobody, yet I loved him, and still love him, for this very reason.

"He pleased me precisely, because he was handsome, fortunate, rich, and therefore loved no one.

"You are familiar with this lofty equine sentiment of ours. His coldness, and my dependence upon him, added greatly to the strength of my affection for him. Because he beat me, and drove me to death, I used to think in those happy days, for that very reason I was all the happier.

"He bought me of the horse-dealer to whom the equerry had sold me, for eight hundred roubles. He bought me because there was no demand for piebald horses. Those were my happiest days.

"He had a mistress. I knew it because every day I took him to her; and I took her out driving, and sometimes took them together.

"His mistress was a handsome woman, and he was handsome, and his coachman was handsome; and I loved them all because they were. And life was worth living then.

"This is the way that my life was spent: In the morning the man came to groom me—not the coachman, but the groom. The groom was a young lad, taken from among the muzhíks. He would open the door, let the wind drive out the steam from the horses, shovel out the manure, take off the blanket, begin to flourish the brush over my body, and with the curry-comb to brush out the scruff on the floor of the stall, marked by the stamping of hoofs. I would make believe bite his sleeves, would push him with my leg.

"Then we were led out, one after the other, to drink from a tub of cold water; and the youngster admired my sleek spotted coat, my legs straight as an arrow, my broad hoofs, my polished flank, and back wide enough to sleep on. Then he would throw the hay behind the broad rack, and pour the oats into the oaken cribs. Then Feofán and the old coachman would come.

"The master and the coachman were alike. Neither the one nor the other feared any one or loved anyone except themselves, and therefore everybody loved them. Feofán came in a red shirt, plush breeches, and coat. I used to like to hear him when, all pomaded for a holiday, he would come to the stable in his coat, and cry—

"'Well, cattle, are you asleep?' and poke me in the loin with the handle of his fork; but never so as to hurt, only in fun. I could instantly take a joke, and I would lay back my ears and show my teeth.

"We had a chestnut stallion that belonged to a pair. Sometimes they would harness us together. This Polkan could not understand a joke, and was simply ugly as the devil. I used to stand in the next stall to him, and feel seriously pained. Feofán was not afraid of him. He used to go straight up to him, shout to him—it seemed as though he were going to kick him—but no, straight by, and put on the halter.

"Once we ran away together, in a pair, over the Kuznetskoë. Neither the master nor the coachman was frightened; they laughed, they shouted to the people, and they sawed on the reins and pulled up, and so I did not run over anybody.

"In their service I expended my best qualities, and half of my life. Then I was given too much water to drink, and my legs gave out . . . But in spite of everything, that was the best part of my life. At twelve they would come, harness us, oil my hoofs, moisten my forelock and mane, and put us between the thills.

"The sledge was of cane, plaited, upholstered in velvet. The harness had little silver buckles, the reins of silk, and once I wore a fly-net. The whole harness was such, that, when all the straps and belts were put on and drawn, it was impossible to make out where the harness ended and the horse began. They would finish harnessing in the shed. Feofán would come out, his middle wider than his shoulders, with his red girdle under his arms. He would inspect the harness, take his seat, straighten his kaftan, put his foot in the stirrup, get off some joke, always crack his whip, though he scarcely ever touched me with it—merely for form's sake—and cry, 'Now off with you!'* And frisking at every step, I would prance out of the gate; and the cook, coming out to empty her slops, would pause in the road; and the muzhík, bringing in his firewood, would open his eyes. We would drive up and down, occasionally stopping. The lackeys come out, the coachmen drive up. There is constant conversation. Always kept waiting. Sometimes for three hours we were kept at the door; occasionally we take a turn around, and talk a while, and again we halt.

"At last there would be a tumult in the hallway; the grey-haired Tikhon, fat in paunch, comes out in his dress-coat. 'Drive on;' then there was none of that use of superfluous words that obtains now. Feofán clucks as if I did not know what 'forward' meant; comes

---

* *pushchaï.*

up to the door, and drives away quickly, unconcernedly, as though there was nothing wonderful either in the sledge or the horses, or Feofán himself, as he bends his back and holds out his hands in such a way that it would seem impossible to keep it up long.

"The prince comes out in his shako and cloak, with a grey beaver collar concealing his handsome, ruddy, black-browed face, which ought never to be covered. He would come out with clanking sabre, jingling spurs, and copper-heeled boots; stepping over the carpet as though in a hurry, and not paying any heed to me or to Feofán, whom everybody except himself looked at and admired.

"Feofán clucks. I pull at the reins, and with a respectable rapid trot we are off and away. I glance round at the prince, and toss my aristocratic head and delicate topknot. The prince is in good spirits; he sometimes jests with Feofán. Feofán replies, half turning round to the prince his handsome face, and, not dropping his hands, makes some ridiculous motion with the reins which I understand; and on, on, on, with ever wider and wider strides, straining every muscle, and sending the muddy snow over the dasher, off I go! Then there was none of the absurd way that obtains today of crying, O! as though the coachman were in pain, and couldn't speak. 'G'long! Look out there!* G'long! Look out there,' shouts Feofán; and the people clear the way, and stand craning their necks to see the handsome gelding, the handsome coachman, and the handsome harm . . .

"I loved especially to outstrip some racer. When Feofán and I would see in the distance some team worthy of our mettle, flying like a whirlwind, we would gradually come nearer and nearer to him. And soon tossing the mud over the dasher, I would be even with the passenger, and would snort over his head, then even with the saddle, with the bell-bow;† then I would already see him and hear him behind me, gradually getting farther and farther away. But the prince and Feofán and I, we all kept silent, and made believe that we were merely out for a drive, and by our actions that

---

* *podi! belegis.*
† *dugá.*

we did not notice those with slow horses whom we overtook on our way. I loved to race, but I loved also to meet a good racer. One wink, sound, glance, and we would be off, and would fly along, each on his own side of the road. . . ."

Here the gates creaked, and the voices of Nester and Vaska were heard.

IX

FIFTH NIGHT

The weather began to change. The sky was overcast; and in the morning there was no dew, but it was warm, and the flies were sticky. As soon as the herd was driven in, the horses gathered around the piebald, and thus he finished his story:—

"The happy days of my life were soon over. I lived so only two years. At the end of the second winter, there happened an event which was most delightful to me, and immediately after came my deepest sorrow. It was at Shrove-tide. I took the prince to the races. Atlásnui and Buichók also ran in the race.

"I don't know what they were doing in the summer-house; but I know that he came, and ordered Feofán to enter the ring. I remember they drove me into the ring, stationed me and stationed Atlásnui. Atlásnui was in racing gear, but I was harnessed in a city sleigh. At the turning stake I left him behind. A laugh and a cry of victory greeted my achievement. When they began to lead me round, a crowd followed after, and a man offered the prince five thousand. He only laughed, showing his white teeth.

"'No,' said he, 'this isn't a horse, it's a friend. I wouldn't sell him for a mountain of gold. Good-day, gentlemen!'*

"He threw open the fur robes, and got in.

"'To Ostozhenka.'

"That was where his mistress lived. And we flew . . .

"It was our last happy day. We reached her home. He called her *his*. But she loved someone else, and had gone off with him. The prince ascertained this at her room. It was five o'clock; and, not letting me be unharnessed, he started in pursuit of her, though she had never really been his. They applied the knout to me, and made me gallop. For the first time, I began to flag, and I am ashamed to say, I wanted to rest.

"But suddenly I heard the prince himself shouting in an unnatural voice, 'Hurry up!'† And the knout whistled and cut me; and I dashed ahead again, my leg hitting against the iron of the dasher. We overtook her, after going twenty-five versts. I got him there; but I trembled all night, and could not eat anything. In the morning they gave me water. I drank it, and forever ceased to be the horse that I was. I was sick. They tortured me and maimed me—treated me as men are accustomed to do. My hoofs came off. I had abscesses, and my legs grew bent. I had no strength in my chest. Laziness and weakness were everywhere apparent. I was sent to the horse-dealer. He fed me on carrots and other things, and made me something quite unlike my old self, but yet capable of deceiving one who did not know. But there was no strength and no swiftness in me.

"Moreover, the horse-dealer tormented me, by coming to my stall when customers were on hand, and beginning to stir me up, and torture me with the knout, so that it drove me to madness. Then he would wipe the bloody foam off the whip, and lead me out.

"An old lady bought me of the dealer. She used to keep coming to Nikola Yavlennoï, and she used to whip the coachman. The coachman would come and weep in my stall. And I knew that his

---

* *do svidánya = au revoir.*

† *valyaï.*

368

tears had an agreeable salt taste. Then the old woman chid her overseer,[*] took me into the country, and sold me to a peddler; then I was fed on wheat, and grew sicker still. I was sold to a muzhík. There I had to plough, had almost nothing to eat, and I cut my leg with a ploughshare. I became sick again. A gypsy got possession of me. He tortured me horribly, and at last I was sold to the overseer here. And here I am. . . ." All were silent. The rain began to fall.

X

As the herd returned home the following evening, they met the master[†] and a guest. Zhulduiba, leading the way, cast her eyes on two men's figures: one was the young master in a straw hat; the other, a tall, stout, military man, with wrinkled face. The old mare gazed at the man, and swerving went near to him; the rest, the younger ones, were thrown into some confusion, huddled together, especially when the master and his guest came directly into the midst of the horses, making gestures to each other, and talking.

"Here's this one. I bought it of Voyéïkof—the dapple-grey horse," said the master.

"And that young black mare, with the white legs—where did you get her? Fine one," said the guest. They examined many of the horses as they walked around, or stood on the field. They remarked also the chestnut mare.

"That's one of the saddle-horses—the breed of Khrenovsky."

---

* *priskashchik.*
† *khozhyáïn.*

They quietly gazed at all the horses as they went by. The master shouted to Nester; and the old man, hastily digging his heels into the sides of the piebald, trotted out. The piebald horse hobbled along, limping on one leg; but his gait was such that it was evident that in other circumstances he would not have complained, even if he had been compelled to go in this way, as long as his strength held out, to the world's end. He was ready even to go at full gallop, and at first even broke into one.

"I have no hesitation in saying that there isn't a better horse in Russia than that one," said the master, pointing to one of the mares. The guest corroborated this praise. The master, full of satisfaction, walked up and down, made observations, and told the story and pedigree of each of the horses.

It was apparently somewhat of a bore to the guest to listen to the master; but he devised questions, to make it seem as if he were interested in it.

"Yes, yes," said he in some confusion.

"Look," said the host, not replying to the questions, "look at those legs, look at the . . . She cost me dear, but I shall have a three-year-old from her that'll go!"

"Does she trot well?" asked the guest.

Thus they scrutinized almost all the horses, and there was nothing more to show. And they were silent.

"Well, shall we go?"

"Yes, let us go."

They went out through the gate. The guest was glad that the exhibition was over, and that he was going home where he would eat, drink, smoke, and have a good time. As they went by Nester, who was sitting on the piebald and waiting for further orders, the guest struck his big fat hand on the horse's side.

"Here's good blood," said he. "He's like the piebald horse, if you remember, that I told you about."

The master perceived that it was not of his horses that the guest was speaking; and he did not listen, but, looking around, continued to gaze at his stud.

Suddenly, at his very ear, was heard a dull, weak, senile neigh.

It was the piebald horse that began to neigh, but could not finish it. Becoming, as it were, confused, he broke short off.

Neither the guest nor the master paid any attention to this neigh, but went home. Kholstomír had recognized in the wrinkled old man his beloved former master, the once brilliant, handsome, and wealthy Sierpukhovskoï.

XI

The rain continued to fall. In the paddock it was gloomy, but at the manor-house* it was quite the reverse. The luxurious evening meal was spread in the luxurious dining-room. At the table sat master, mistress, and the guest who had just arrived.

The master held in his hand a box of specially fine ten-year-old cigars, such as no one else had, according to his story, and proceeded to offer them to the guest. The master was a handsome young man of twenty-five, fresh, neatly dressed, smoothly brushed. He was dressed in a fresh, loosely-fitting suit of clothes, made in London. On his watch-chain were big expensive charms. His cuff-buttons were of gold, large, even massive, set with turquoises. His beard was *à la Napoleon III*; and his moustaches were waxed, and stood out as though he had got them nowhere else than in Paris.

The lady wore a silk-muslin dress, brocaded with large variegated flowers; on her head, large gold hair-pins in her thick auburn hair, which was beautiful, though not entirely her own. Her hands were adorned with bracelets and rings, all expensive.

* *barski dom.*

371

The samovar was silver, the service exquisite. The lackey, magnificent in his dress-coat and white vest and necktie, stood like a statue at the door, awaiting orders. The furniture was of bent wood, and bright; the wall-papers dark, with large flowers. Around the table tinkled a cunning little dog, with a silver collar bearing an extremely hard English name, which neither of them could pronounce because they knew not English.

In the corner, among the flowers, stood the pianoforte, inlaid with mother-of-pearl.* Everything breathed of newness, luxury, and rareness. Everything was extremely good; but it all bore a peculiar impress of profusion, wealth, and an absence of intellectual interests.

The master was a great lover of racing, strong and hot-headed; one of those whom one meets everywhere, who drive out in sable furs, send costly bouquets to actresses, drink the most expensive wine, of the very latest brand, at the most expensive restaurant, offer prizes in their own names, and entertain the most expensive. . . .

The new-comer, Nikíta Sierpukhovskoï, was a man of forty years, tall, stout, bald, with huge moustaches and side-whiskers. He ought to have been very handsome; but it was evident that he had wasted his forces—physical and moral and pecuniary.

He was so deeply in debt that he was obliged to go into the service so as to escape the sponging-house. He had now come to the government city as chief of the imperial stud. His influential relations had obtained this for him.

He was dressed in an army kittel and blue trousers. His kittel and trousers were such as only those who are rich can afford to wear; so with his linen also. His watch was English. His boots had peculiar soles, as thick as a finger.

Nikíta Sierpukhovskoï had squandered a fortune of two millions, and was still in debt to the amount of one hundred and twenty thousand roubles. From such a course there always remains a certain momentum of life, giving credit, and the possibility of living almost luxuriously for another ten years.

---

* *incrusté.*

The ten years had already passed, and the momentum was finished; and it had become hard for him to live. He had already begun to drink too much; that is, to get fuddled with wine, which had never been the case with him before. Properly speaking, he had never begun and never finished drinking.

More noticeable in him than all else was the restlessness of his eyes (they had begun to wander), and the uncertainty of his intonations and motions. This restlessness was surprising, from the fact that it was evidently a new thing in him, because it could be seen that he had been accustomed, all his life long, to fear nothing and nobody, and that now he endured severe sufferings from some dread that was thoroughly alien to his nature.

The host and hostess* remarked this, exchanged glances, showing that they understood each other, postponed until they should get to bed the consideration of this subject; and, evidently, merely endured poor Sierpukhovskoï.

The sight of the young master's happiness humiliated Nikíta, and compelled him to painful envy, as he remembered his own irrevocable past.

"You don't object to cigars, Marie?" he asked, addressing the lady in that peculiar tone, acquired only by practice, full of urbanity and friendliness, but not wholly satisfactory—such as men use who are familiar with the society of women not enjoying the dignity of wifehood. Not that he could have wished to insult her: on the contrary, he was much more anxious to gain her good-will and that of the host, though he would not for anything have acknowledged it to himself. But he was already used to talking thus with such women. He knew that she would have been astonished, even affronted, if he had behaved to her as toward a lady. Moreover, it was necessary for him to preserve that peculiar shade of deference for the acknowledged wife of his friend. He treated such women always with consideration, not because he shared those so-called convictions that are promulgated in newspapers (he never read such trash), about esteem as the

---

* *khozyáïn* and *khozyáïka*.

prerogative of every man, about the absurdity of marriage, etc., because all well-bred men act thus, and he was a well-bred man, though inclined to drink.

He took a cigar. But his host awkwardly seized a handful of cigars, and placed them before the guest.

"No, just see how good these are! Try them."

Nikíta pushed away the cigars with his hand, and in his eyes flashed something like injury and shame.

"Thanks,"—he took out his cigar-case—"try mine."

The lady was on the watch. She perceived how it affected him. She began hastily to talk with him.

"I am very fond of cigars. I should smoke myself if everybody about did not smoke."

And she gave him one of her bright, kindly smiles. He half-smiled in reply. Two of his teeth were gone.

"No, take this," continued the host, not heeding. "Those others are not so strong. *Fritz, bringen Sie noch eine Kasten,*" he said, "*dort zwei.*"

The German lackey brought another box.

"Do you like these larger ones? They are stronger. This is a very good kind. Take them all," he added, continuing to force them upon his guest.

He was evidently glad that there was someone on whom he could lavish his rarities, and he saw nothing out of the way in it. Sierpukhovskoï began to smoke, and hastened to take up the subject that had been dropped.

"How much did you have to go on Atlásnui?" he asked.

"He cost me dear—not less than five thousand, but at all events I am secured. Plenty of colts, I tell you!"

"Do they trot?" inquired Sierpukhovskoï.

"First-rate. Today Atlásnui's colt took three prizes: one at Tula, one at Moscow, and one at Petersburg. He raced with Voyéïkof's Vorónui. The rascally jockey made four abatements, and almost put him out of the race."

"He was rather raw; too much Dutch stock in him, I should say," said Sierpukhovskoï.

"Well, but the mares are finer ones. I will show you tomorrow. I paid three thousand for Dobruina, two thousand for Laskovaya."

And again the host began to enumerate his wealth. The mistress saw that this was hard for Sierpukhovskoï, and that he only pretended to listen.

"Won't you have some more tea?" asked the hostess.

"I don't care for any more," said the host, and he went on with his story. She got up; the host detained her, took her in his arms, and kissed her.

Sierpukhovskoï smiled at first, as he looked at them; but his smile seemed to them unnatural. When his host got up, and took her in his arms, and went out with her as far as the *portière,* his face suddenly changed; he sighed deeply, and an expression of despair took possession of his wrinkled face. There was also wrath in it.

"Yes, you said that you bought him of Voyéïkof," said Sierpukhovskoï, with assumed indifference.

XII

The host returned, and smiled as he sat down opposite his guest. Neither of them spoke.

"Oh, yes! I was speaking of Atlásnui. I had a great mind to buy the mares of Dubovitsky. Nothing but rubbish was left."

"He was *burned* out," said Sierpukhovskoï, and suddenly stood up and looked around. He remembered that he owed this ruined man twenty thousand roubles; and that, if *burned* out were said of any one, it might by good rights be said about himself. He began to laugh.

Both kept silence long. The master was revolving in his mind how he might boast a little before his guest. Sierpukhovskoï was cogitating how he might show that he did not consider himself burned out. But the thoughts of both moved with difficulty, in spite of the fact that they tried to enliven themselves with cigars.

"Well, when shall we have something to drink?" asked the guest of himself.

"At all events, we must have something to drink, else we shall die of the blues," said the host to himself.

"How is it? Are you going to stay here long?" asked Sierpukhovskoï.

"About a month yet. Shall we have a little lunch? What say you? Fritz, is everything ready?"

They went back to the dining-room. There, under a hanging lamp, stood the table loaded with candles and very extraordinary things: siphons, and bottles with fancy stoppers, extraordinary wine in decanters, extraordinary liqueurs and vodka. They drank, sat down, drank again, sat down, and tried to talk. Sierpukhovskoï grew flushed, and began to speak unreservedly.

They talked about women: who kept such and such and one; the gypsy, the ballet-girl, the *soubrette*.[*]

"Why, you left Mathieu, didn't you?" asked the host.

This was the mistress who had caused Sierpukhovskoï such pain.

"No, she left me. O my friend,[†] how one remembers what one has squandered in life! Now I am glad, fact, when I get a thousand roubles; glad, fact, when I get out of everybody's way. I cannot in Moscow. Ah! what's to be said!"

The host was bored to listen to Sierpukhovskoï. He wanted to talk about himself—to brag. But Sierpukhovskoï also wanted to talk about himself—about his glittering past. The host poured out some more wine, and waited till he had finished, so as to tell him about his affairs—how he was going to arrange his stud as no one

---

[*] *Frantsuzhenka.*

[†] *akh, brat* brother.

ever had before; and how Marie loved him, not for his money, but for himself.

"I was going to tell you that in my stud . . ." he began. But Sierpukhovskoï interrupted him.

"There was a time, I may say," he began, "when I loved, and knew how to live. You were talking just now about racing; please tell me what is your best racer."

The host was glad of the chance to tell some more about his stud, but Sierpukhovskoï again interrupted him.

"Yes, yes," said he. "But the trouble with you breeders is, that you do it only for ostentation, and not for pleasure, for life. It wasn't so with me. I was telling you this very day that I used to have a piebald racer, with just such spots as I saw among your colts. *Okh!* what a horse he was! You can't imagine it: this was in '42. I had just come to Moscow. I went to a dealer, and saw a piebald gelding. All in best form. He pleased me. Price? Thousand roubles. He pleased me. I took him, and began to ride him. I never had, and you never had and never will have, such a horse. I never knew a better horse, either for gait, or strength, or beauty. You were a lad then. You could not have known, but you may have heard, I suppose. All Moscow knew him."

"Yes, I heard about him," said the host reluctantly; "but I was going to tell you about my . . ."

"So you heard about him. I bought him just as he was, without pedigree, without proof; but then I knew Voyéïkof, and I traced him. He was sired by Liubeznuï I. He was called Kholstomír.* He'd measure linen for you! On account of his spotting, he was given to the equerry at the Khrenovsky stud; and he had him gelded, and sold him to the dealer. Aren't any horses like him anymore, friend! *Akh!* "What a time that was! *Akh!* vanished youth!" he said, quoting the words of a gypsy song. He began to get wild. "*Ekh!* that was a golden time! I was twenty-five. I had eighty thousand a

---

* *Kholstomír* means a cloth measurer: suggesting the greatest distance from linger to linger of the outstretched arms, and rapidity in accomplishing the motion.

year income; then I hadn't a grey hair; all my teeth like pearls . . . Whatever I undertook prospered. And yet all came to an end. . . ."

"Well, you didn't have such lively times then," said the host, taking advantage of the interruption. "I tell you that my first horses began to run without . . ."

"Your horses! Horses were more mettlesome then . . ."

"How more mettlesome?"

"Yes, more mettlesome. I remember how one time I was at Moscow at the races. None of my horses were in it. I did not care for racing; but I had blooded horses, General Chaulet, Mahomet. I had my piebald with me. My coachman was a splendid young fellow. I liked him. But he was rather given to drink, so I drove.— 'Sierpukhovskoï,' said they, 'when are you going to get some trotters?'—'I don't care for your low-bred beasts,* the devil take 'em! I have a hackdriver's piebald that's worth all of yours.'— 'Yes, but he doesn't race.'—'Bet you a thousand roubles.' They took me up. He went round in five seconds, won the wager of a thousand roubles. But that was nothing. With my blooded horses I went in a troïka a hundred versts in three hours. All Moscow knew about it."

And Sierpukhovskoï began to brag so fluently and steadily that the host could not get in a word, and sat facing him with dejected countenance. Only, by way of diversion, he would fill up his glass and that of his companion.

It began already to grow light, but still they sat there. It became painfully tiresome to the host. He got up.

"Sleep—let's go to sleep, then," said Sierpukhovskoï, as he got up, and went staggering and puffing to the room that had been assigned to him.

The master of the house rejoined his mistress.

"Oh, he's unendurable. He got drunk, and lied faster than he could talk."

"And he made love to me too."

"I fear that he's going to borrow of me."

---

* *literally, muzhíks.*

Sierpukhovskoï threw himself on the bed without undressing, and drew a long breath.

"I must have talked a good deal of nonsense," he thought. "Well, it's all the same. Good wine, but he's a big hog. Something cheap about him.* And I am a hog myself," he remarked, and laughed aloud. "Well, I used to support others: now it's my turn. I guess the Winkler girl will help me. I'll borrow some money of her. He may come to it. Suppose I've got to undress. Can't get my boot off. Hey, hey!" he cried; but the man who had been ordered to wait on him had long before gone to bed.

He sat up, took off his kittel and his vest, and somehow managed to crawl out of his trousers; but it was long before his boots would stir: with his stout belly it was hard work to stoop over. He got one off; he struggled and struggled with the other, got out of breath, and gave it up. And so with one leg in the boot he threw himself down, and began to snore, filling the whole room with the odour of wine, tobacco, and vile old age.

XIII

If Kholstomír remembered anything that night, it was the frolic that Vaska gave him. He threw over him a blanket, and galloped off. He was left till morning at the door of a tavern, with a muzhík's horse. They licked each other. When it became light he went back to the herd, and itched all over.

"Something makes me itch fearfully," he thought.

---

* *kupésheskoe*, merchant-like.

Five days passed. They brought a veterinary. He said cheerfully—

"The mange. You'll have to dispose of him to the gypsies."

"Better have his throat cut; only have it done today."

The morning was calm and clear. The herd had gone to pasture. Kholstomír remained behind. A strange man came along; thin, dark, dirty, in a kaftan spotted with something black. This was the scavenger. He took Kholstomír by the halter, and without looking at him started off. The horse followed quietly, not looking round, and, as always, dragging his legs and kicking up the straw with his hind-legs.

As he went out of the gate, he turned his head toward the well; but the scavenger twitched the halter, and said—

"It's not worth while."

The scavenger, and Vaska who followed, proceeded to a depression behind the brick barn, and stopped, as though there were something peculiar in this most ordinary place; and the scavenger, handing the halter to Vaska, took off his kaftan, rolled up his sleeves, and produced a knife and whetstone from his boot-leg.

The piebald pulled at the halter, and out of sheer *ennui* tried to bite it, but it was too far off. He sighed, and closed his eyes. He hung down his lip, showing his worn yellow teeth, and began to drowse, lulled by the sound of the knife on the stone. Only his sick and swollen leg trembled a little.

Suddenly he perceived that he was grasped by the lower jaw, and that his head was lifted up. He opened his eyes. Two dogs were in front of him. One was snuffing in the direction of the scavenger, the other sat looking at the gelding as though expecting something especially from him. The gelding looked at them, and began to rub his jaw against the hand that held him.

"Of course they want to cure me," he said: "let it come!"

And the thought had hardly passed through his mind, before they did something to his throat. It hurt him; he started back, stamped his foot, but restrained himself, and waited for what was to follow . . . What followed, was some liquid pouring in a stream down his neck and breast. He drew a deep breath, lifting his sides. And it seemed easier, much easier, to him.

The whole burden of his life was taken from him.

He closed his eyes, and began to droop his head—no one held it. Then his legs quivered, his whole body swayed. He was not so much terrified as he was astonished. . . .

Everything was so new. He was astonished; he tried to run ahead, up the hill . . . but instead of this, his legs, moving where he stood, interfered. He began to roll over on his side, and while expecting to make a step he fell forward, and on his left side.

The scavenger waited till the death-struggle was over, drove away the dogs that were creeping nearer, and then seized the horse by the legs, turned him over on the back, and, telling Vaska to hold his leg, began to take off the hide.

"That was a horse indeed!" said Vaska.

"If he'd been fatter, it would have been a fine hide," said the scavenger.

That evening the herd passed by the hill; and those who were on the left wing saw a red object below them, and around it some dogs busily romping, and crows and hawks flying over it. One dog, with his paws on the carcass, and shaking his head, was growling over what he was tearing with his teeth. The brown filly stopped, lifted her head and neck, and long sniffed the air. It took force to drive her away.

At sunrise, in a ravine of the ancient forest, in the bottom of an overgrown glade, some wolf-whelps were beside themselves with joy. There were five of them—four about of a size, and one little one with a head bigger than his body. A lean, hairless she-wolf, her belly with hanging dugs almost touching the ground, crept out of the bushes, and sat down in front of the wolves. The wolves sat in a semi-circle in front of her. She went to the smallest, and lowering her stumpy tail, and bending her nose to the ground, made a few convulsive motions, and opening her jaws filled with teeth she struggled, and disgorged a great piece of horse-flesh.

The larger whelps made a movement to seize it; but she restrained them with a threatening growl, and let the little one have it all. The little one, as though in anger, seized the morsel, hiding it under him, and began to devour it. Then the she-wolf disgorged for the second, and the third, and in the same way for all five, and finally lay down in front of them to rest.

At the end of a week there lay behind the brick barn only the great skull, and two shoulder-blades; all the rest had disappeared. In the summer a muzhík who gathered up the bones carried off also the skull and shoulder-blades, and put them to use.

The dead body of Sierpukhovskoï who had been about in the world, and had eaten and drunken, was buried long after. Neither his skin nor his flesh nor his bones were of any use.

And just as his dead body, which had been about in the world, had been a great burden to others for twenty years, so the disposal of this body became only an additional charge upon men. Long it had been useless to everyone, long it had been only a burden. But still the dead who bury their dead found it expedient to dress this soon-to-be-decaying, swollen body, in a fine uniform, in fine boots; to place it in a fine new coffin, with new tassels on the four corners; then to place this new coffin in another, made of lead, and carry it to Moscow; and there to dig up the bones of people long buried, and then to lay away this mal-odorous body devoured by worms, in its new uniform and polished boots, and to cover the whole with earth.

A Grain as Big as
a Hen's Egg

[Written and first published in 1886. This version is a
translation by Louise and Aylmer Maude collected in
Twenty-three Tales (1906).]

One day some children found, in a ravine, a thing shaped like a grain of corn, with a groove down the middle, but as large as a hen's egg. A traveller passing by saw the thing, bought it from the children for a penny, and taking it to town sold it to the King as a curiosity.

The King called together his wise men, and told them to find out what the thing was. The wise men pondered and pondered and could not make head or tail of it, till one day, when the thing was lying on a window-sill, a hen flew in and pecked at it till she made a hole in it, and then everyone saw that it was a grain of corn. The wise men went to the King, and said:

"It is a grain of corn."

At this the King was much surprised; and he ordered the learned men to find out when and where such corn had grown. The learned men pondered again, and searched in their books, but could find nothing about it. So they returned to the King and said:

"We can give you no answer. There is nothing about it in our books. You will have to ask the peasants; perhaps some of them may have heard from their fathers when and where grain grew to such a size."

So the King gave orders that some very old peasant should be brought before him; and his servants found such a man and brought him to the King. Old and bent, ashy pale and toothless, he just managed with the help of two crutches to totter into the King's presence.

The King showed him the grain, but the old man could hardly see it; he took it, however, and felt it with his hands. The King questioned him, saying:

"Can you tell us, old man, where such grain as this grew? Have you ever bought such corn, or sown such in your fields?"

The old man was so deaf that he could hardly hear what the King said, and only understood with great difficulty.

"No!" he answered at last, "I never sowed nor reaped any like it in my fields, nor did I ever buy any such. When we bought corn, the grains were always as small as they are now. But you might ask my father. He may have heard where such grain grew."

So the King sent for the old man's father, and he was found and brought before the King. He came walking with one crutch. The King showed him the grain, and the old peasant, who was still able to see, took a good look at it. And the King asked him:

"Can you not tell us, old man, where corn like this used to grow? Have you ever bought any like it, or sown any in your fields?"

Though the old man was rather hard of hearing, he still heard better than his son had done.

"No," he said, "I never sowed nor reaped any grain like this in my field. As to buying, I never bought any, for in my time money was not yet in use. Every one grew his own corn, and when there was any need we shared with one another. I do not know where corn like this grew. Ours was larger and yielded more flour than present-day grain, but I never saw any like this. I have, however, heard my father say that in his time the grain grew larger and yielded more flour than ours. You had better ask him."

So the King sent for this old man's father, and they found him too, and brought him before the King. He entered walking easily and without crutches: his eye was clear, his hearing good, and he spoke distinctly. The King showed him the grain, and the old grandfather looked at it, and turned it about in his hand.

"It is long since I saw such a fine grain," said he, and he bit a piece off and tasted it.

"It's the very same kind," he added.

"Tell me, grandfather," said the King, "when and where was such corn grown? Have you ever bought any like it, or sown any in your fields?"

And the old man replied:

"Corn like this used to grow everywhere in my time. I lived on corn like this in my young days, and fed others on it. It was grain like this that we used to sow and reap and thrash."

And the King asked:

"Tell me, grandfather, did you buy it anywhere, or did you grow it all yourself?"

The old man smiled.

"In my time," he answered, "no one ever thought of such a sin as buying or selling bread; and we knew nothing of money. Each man had corn enough of his own."

"Then tell me, grandfather," asked the King, "where was your field, where did you grow corn like this?"

And the grandfather answered:

"My field was God's earth. Wherever I ploughed, there was my field. Land was free. It was a thing no man called his own. Labour was the only thing men called their own."

"Answer me two more questions," said the King. "The first is, Why did the earth bear such grain then, and has ceased to do so now? And the second is, Why your grandson walks with two crutches, your son with one, and you yourself with none? Your eyes are bright, your teeth sound, and your speech clear and pleasant to the ear. How have these things come about?"

And the old man answered:

"These things are so, because men have ceased to live by their own labour, and have taken to depending on the labour of others. In the old time, men lived according to God's law. They had what was their own, and coveted not what others had produced."

How Much Land does a Man Need?

[Written and first published in 1886. Regarded by James Joyce as
'the greatest story that the literature of the world knows',
this tale is one of the most celebrated stories of Tolstoy.
This version has been taken from *Twenty-three Tales* (1906),
a collection translated by Louise and Aylmer Maude.]

I

An elder sister came to visit her younger sister in the country. The elder was married to a tradesman in town, the younger to a peasant in the village. As the sisters sat over their tea talking, the elder began to boast of the advantages of town life: saying how comfortably they lived there, how well they dressed, what fine clothes her children wore, what good things they ate and drank, and how she went to the theatre, promenades, and entertainments.

The younger sister was piqued, and in turn disparaged the life of a tradesman, and stood up for that of a peasant.

"I would not change my way of life for yours," said she. "We may live roughly, but at least we are free from anxiety. You live in better style than we do, but though you often earn more than you need, you are very likely to lose all you have. You know the proverb, "Loss and gain are brothers twain." It often happens that people who are wealthy one day are begging their bread the next. Our way is safer. Though a peasant's life is not a fat one, it is a long one. We shall never grow rich, but we shall always have enough to eat."

The elder sister said sneeringly:

"Enough? Yes, if you like to share with the pigs and the calves! What do you know of elegance or manners! However much your good man may slave, you will die as you are living—on a dung heap—and your children the same."

"Well, what of that?" replied the younger. "Of course our work is rough and coarse. But, on the other hand, it is sure; and we need not bow to anyone. But you, in your towns, are surrounded by temptations; today all may be right, but tomorrow the Evil One may tempt your husband with cards, wine, or women, and all will go to ruin. Don't such things happen often enough?"

Pahóm, the master of the house, was lying on the top of the oven, and he listened to the women's chatter.

"It is perfectly true," thought he. "Busy as we are from childhood tilling mother earth, we peasants have no time to let any nonsense settle in our heads. Our only trouble is that we haven't land enough. If I had plenty of land, I shouldn't fear the Devil himself!"

The women finished their tea, chatted a while about dress, and then cleared away the tea-things and lay down to sleep.

But the Devil had been sitting behind the oven, and had heard all that was said. He was pleased that the peasant's wife had led her husband into boasting, and that he had said that if he had plenty of land he would not fear the Devil himself.

"All right," thought the Devil. "We will have a tussle. I'll give you land enough; and by means of that land I will get you into my power."

II

Close to the village there lived a lady, a small landowner, who had an estate of about three hundred acres*. She had always lived on good terms with the peasants, until she engaged as her steward an old soldier, who took to burdening the people with fines. However careful Pahóm tried to be, it happened again and again that now a horse of his got among the lady's oats, now a cow strayed into her

---

* 120 desyatins. The desyatina is properly 2.7 acres; but in this story round numbers are used.

garden, now his calves found their way into her meadows—and he always had to pay a fine.

Pahóm paid, but grumbled, and, going home in a temper, was rough with his family. All through that summer, Pahóm had much trouble because of this steward; and he was even glad when winter came and the cattle had to be stabled. Though he grudged the fodder when they could no longer graze on the pasture-land, at least he was free from anxiety about them.

In the winter the news got about that the lady was going to sell her land, and that the keeper of the inn on the high road was bargaining for it. When the peasants heard this they were very much alarmed.

"Well," thought they, "if the innkeeper gets the land, he will worry us with fines worse than the lady's steward. We all depend on that estate."

So the peasants went on behalf of their Commune, and asked the lady not to sell the land to the innkeeper; offering her a better price for it themselves. The lady agreed to let them have it. Then the peasants tried to arrange for the Commune to buy the whole estate, so that it might be held by all in common. They met twice to discuss it, but could not settle the matter; the Evil One sowed discord among them, and they could not agree. So they decided to buy the land individually, each according to his means; and the lady agreed to this plan as she had to the other.

Presently Pahóm heard that a neighbour of his was buying fifty acres, and that the lady had consented to accept one half in cash and to wait a year for the other half. Pahóm felt envious.

"Look at that," thought he, "the land is all being sold, and I shall get none of it." So he spoke to his wife.

"Other people are buying," said he, "and we must also buy twenty acres or so. Life is becoming impossible. That steward is simply crushing us with his fines."

So they put their heads together and considered how they could manage to buy it. They had one hundred roubles laid by. They sold a colt, and one half of their bees; hired out one of their sons as a labourer, and took his wages in advance; borrowed the rest from a brother-in-law, and so scraped together half the purchase money.

Having done this, Pahóm chose out a farm of forty acres, some of it wooded, and went to the lady to bargain for it. They came to an agreement, and he shook hands with her upon it, and paid her a deposit in advance. Then they went to town and signed the deeds; he paying half the price down, and undertaking to pay the remainder within two years.

So now Pahóm had land of his own. He borrowed seed, and sowed it on the land he had bought. The harvest was a good one, and within a year he had managed to pay off his debts both to the lady and to his brother-in-law. So he became a landowner, ploughing and sowing his own land, making hay on his own land, cutting his own trees, and feeding his cattle on his own pasture. When he went out to plough his fields, or to look at his growing corn, or at his grass-meadows, his heart would fill with joy. The grass that grew and the flowers that bloomed there, seemed to him unlike any that grew elsewhere. Formerly, when he had passed by that land, it had appeared the same as any other land, but now it seemed quite different.

III

So Pahóm was well-contented, and everything would have been right if the neighbouring peasants would only not have trespassed on his corn-fields and meadows. He appealed to them most civilly, but they still went on: now the Communal herdsmen would let the village cows stray into his meadows; then horses from the night pasture would get among his corn. Pahóm turned them out again and again, and forgave their owners, and for a long time he forbore from prosecuting any one. But at last he lost patience and complained to the District Court. He knew it was the peasants' want of land, and no evil intent on their part, that caused the trouble; but he thought:

"I cannot go on overlooking it, or they will destroy all I have. They must be taught a lesson."

So he had them up, gave them one lesson, and then another, and two or three of the peasants were fined. After a time Pahóm's neighbours began to bear him a grudge for this, and would now and then let their cattle on to his land on purpose. One peasant even got into Pahóm's wood at night and cut down five young lime trees for their bark. Pahóm passing through the wood one day noticed something white. He came nearer, and saw the stripped trunks lying on the ground, and close by stood the stumps, where the tree had been. Pahóm was furious.

"If he had only cut one here and there it would have been bad enough," thought Pahóm, "but the rascal has actually cut down a whole clump. If I could only find out who did this, I would pay him out."

He racked his brains as to who it could be. Finally he decided: "It must be Simon—no one else could have done it." So he went to Simon's homestead to have a look round, but he found nothing, and only had an angry scene. However, he now felt more certain than ever that Simon had done it, and he lodged a complaint. Simon was summoned. The case was tried, and retried, and at the end of it all Simon was acquitted, there being no evidence against him. Pahóm felt still more aggrieved, and let his anger loose upon the Elder and the Judges.

"You let thieves grease your palms," said he. "If you were honest folk yourselves, you would not let a thief go free."

So Pahóm quarrelled with the Judges and with his neighbours. Threats to burn his building began to be uttered. So though Pahóm had more land, his place in the Commune was much worse than before.

About this time a rumour got about that many people were moving to new parts.

"There's no need for me to leave my land," thought Pahóm. "But some of the others might leave our village, and then there would be more room for us. I would take over their land myself, and make my estate a bit bigger. I could then live more at ease. As it is, I am still too cramped to be comfortable."

One day Pahóm was sitting at home, when a peasant passing through the village, happened to call in. He was allowed to stay the night, and supper was given him. Pahóm had a talk with this peasant and asked him where he came from. The stranger answered that he came from beyond the Vólga, where he had been working. One word led to another, and the man went on to say that many people were settling in those parts. He told how some people from his village had settled there. They had joined the Commune, and had had twenty-five acres per man granted them. The land was so good, he said, that the rye sown on it grew as high as a horse, and so thick that five cuts of a sickle made a sheaf. One peasant, he said, had brought nothing with him but his bare hands, and now he had six horses and two cows of his own.

Pahóm's heart kindled with desire. He thought:

"Why should I suffer in this narrow hole, if one can live so well elsewhere? I will sell my land and my homestead here, and with the money I will start afresh over there and get everything new. In this crowded place one is always having trouble. But I must first go and find out all about it myself."

Towards summer he got ready and started. He went down the Vólga on a steamer to Samára, then walked another three hundred miles on foot, and at last reached the place. It was just as the stranger had said. The peasants had plenty of land: every man had twenty-five acres of Communal land given him for his use, and anyone who had money could buy, besides, at two shillings an acre* as much good freehold land as he wanted.

Having found out all he wished to know, Pahóm returned

---

* Three roubles per *desyatina*.

home as autumn came on, and began selling off his belongings. He sold his land at a profit, sold his homestead and all his cattle, and withdrew from membership of the Commune. He only waited till the spring, and then started with his family for the new settlement.

IV

As soon as Pahóm and his family arrived at their new abode, he applied for admission into the Commune of a large village. He stood treat to the Elders, and obtained the necessary documents. Five shares of Communal land were given him for his own and his sons' use: that is to say—125 acres (not all together, but in different fields) besides the use of the Communal pasture. Pahóm put up the buildings he needed, and bought cattle. Of the Communal land alone he had three times as much as at his former home, and the land was good corn land. He was ten times better off than he had been. He had plenty of arable land and pasturage, and could keep as many head of cattle as he liked.

At first, in the bustle of building and settling down, Pahóm was pleased with it all, but when he got used to it he began to think that even here he had not enough land. The first year, he sowed wheat on his share of the Communal land, and had a good crop. He wanted to go on sowing wheat, but had not enough Communal land for the purpose, and what he had already used was not available; for in those parts wheat is only sown on virgin soil or on fallow land. It is sown for one or two years, and then the land lies fallow till it is again overgrown with prairie grass. There were many who wanted such land, and there was not enough for all; so that people quarrelled about it. Those who were better off, wanted it for growing wheat, and those who were poor, wanted it to let to dealers, so that they might raise money to pay their taxes. Pahóm wanted to sow more wheat; so he rented land from a dealer for a year. He sowed much wheat and had a fine crop, but the land was too far from the village—the wheat had to be carted more than ten miles. After a time Pahóm noticed that some peasant-dealers were living on separate farms, and were growing wealthy; and he thought:

"If I were to buy some freehold land, and have a homestead on it, it would be a different thing, altogether. Then it would all be nice and compact."

The question of buying freehold land recurred to him again and again.

He went on in the same way for three years; renting land and sowing wheat. The seasons turned out well and the crops were good, so that he began to lay money by. He might have gone on living contentedly, but he grew tired of having to rent other people's land every year, and having to scramble for it. Wherever there was good land to be had, the peasants would rush for it and it was taken up at once, so that unless you were sharp about it you got none. It happened in the third year that he and a dealer together rented a piece of pasture land from some peasants; and they had already ploughed it up, when there was some dispute, and the peasants went to law about it, and things fell out so that the labour was all lost.

"If it were my own land," thought Pahóm, "I should be independent, and there would not be all this unpleasantness."

So Pahóm began looking out for land which he could buy; and he came across a peasant who had bought thirteen hundred acres, but having got into difficulties was willing to sell again cheap. Pahóm bargained and haggled with him, and at last they settled the price at 1,500 roubles, part in cash and part to be paid later. They had all but clinched the matter, when a passing dealer happened to stop at Pahóm's one day to get a feed for his horse. He drank tea with Pahóm, and they had a talk. The dealer said that he was just returning from the land of the Bashkírs, far away, where he had bought thirteen thousand acres of land all for 1,000 roubles. Pahóm questioned him further, and the tradesman said:

"All one need do is to make friends with the chiefs. I gave away about one hundred roubles' worth of dressing-gowns and carpets, besides a case of tea, and I gave wine to those who would drink it; and I got the land for less than twopence an acre*. And he showed Pahóm the title-deeds, saying:

"The land lies near a river, and the whole prairie is virgin soil."

Pahóm plied him with questions, and the tradesman said:

"There is more land there than you could cover if you walked a year, and it all belongs to the Bashkírs. They are as simple as sheep, and land can be got almost for nothing."

"There now," thought Pahóm, "with my one thousand roubles, why should I get only thirteen hundred acres, and saddle myself with a debt besides? If I take it out there, I can get more than ten times as much for the money."

V

Pahóm inquired how to get to the place, and as soon as the tradesman had left him, he prepared to go there himself. He left his wife to look after the homestead, and started on his journey taking his man with him. They stopped at a town on their way, and bought

---

* Five kopeks for a *desyatina*.

a case of tea, some wine, and other presents, as the tradesman had advised. On and on they went until they had gone more than three hundred miles, and on the seventh day they came to a place where the Bashkírs had pitched their tents. It was all just as the tradesman had said. The people lived on the steppes, by a river, in felt-covered tents[*]. They neither tilled the ground, nor ate bread. Their cattle and horses grazed in herds on the steppe. The colts were tethered behind the tents, and the mares were driven to them twice a day. The mares were milked, and from the milk kumiss was made. It was the women who prepared kumiss, and they also made cheese. As far as the men were concerned, drinking kumiss and tea, eating mutton, and playing on their pipes, was all they cared about. They were all stout and merry, and all the summer long they never thought of doing any work. They were quite ignorant, and knew no Russian, but were good-natured enough.

As soon as they saw Pahóm, they came out of their tents and gathered round their visitor. An interpreter was found, and Pahóm told them he had come about some land. The Bashkírs seemed very glad; they took Pahóm and led him into one of the best tents, where they made him sit on some down cushions placed on a carpet, while they sat round him. They gave him tea and kumiss, and had a sheep killed, and gave him mutton to eat. Pahóm took presents out of his cart and distributed them among the Bashkírs, and divided amongst them the tea. The Bashkírs were delighted. They talked a great deal among themselves, and then told the interpreter to translate.

"They wish to tell you," said the interpreter, "that they like you, and that it is our custom to do all we can to please a guest and to repay him for his gifts. You have given us presents, now tell us which of the things we possess please you best, that we may present them to you."

"What pleases me best here," answered Pahóm, "is your land. Our land is crowded, and the soil is exhausted; but you have plenty of land and it is good land. I never saw the like of it."

---

[*] *Kibítkas*, as described in footnote on p. 286.

The interpreter translated. The Bashkírs talked among themselves for a while. Pahóm could not understand what they were saying, but saw that they were much amused, and that they shouted and laughed. Then they were silent and looked at Pahóm while the interpreter said:

"They wish me to tell you that in return for your presents they will gladly give you as much land as you want. You have only to point it out with your hand and it is yours."

The Bashkírs talked again for a while and began to dispute. Pahóm asked what they were disputing about, and the interpreter told him that some of them thought they ought to ask their Chief about the land and not act in his absence, while others thought there was no need to wait for his return.

VI

While the Bashkírs were disputing, a man in a large fox-fur cap appeared on the scene. They all became silent and rose to their feet. The interpreter said, "This is our Chief himself."

Pahóm immediately fetched the best dressing-gown and five pounds of tea, and offered these to the Chief. The Chief accepted them, and seated himself in the place of honour. The Bashkírs at once began telling him something. The Chief listened for a while, then made a sign with his head for them to be silent, and addressing himself to Pahóm, said in Russian:

"Well, let it be so. Choose whatever piece of land you like; we have plenty of it."

"How can I take as much as I like?" thought Pahóm. "I must

get a deed to make it secure, or else they may say, "It is yours," and afterwards may take it away again."

"Thank you for your kind words," he said aloud. "You have much land, and I only want a little. But I should like to be sure which bit is mine. Could it not be measured and made over to me? Life and death are in God's hands. You good people give it to me, but your children might wish to take it away again."

"You are quite right," said the Chief. "We will make it over to you."

"I heard that a dealer had been here," continued Pahóm, "and that you gave him a little land, too, and signed title-deeds to that effect. I should like to have it done in the same way."

The Chief understood.

"Yes," replied he, "that can be done quite easily. We have a scribe, and we will go to town with you and have the deed properly sealed."

"And what will be the price?" asked Pahóm.

"Our price is always the same: one thousand roubles a day."

Pahóm did not understand.

"A day? What measure is that? How many acres would that be?"

"We do not know how to reckon it out," said the Chief. "We sell it by the day. As much as you can go round on your feet in a day is yours, and the price is one thousand roubles a day."

Pahóm was surprised.

"But in a day you can get round a large tract of land," he said.

The Chief laughed.

"It will all be yours!" said he. "But there is one condition: If you don't return on the same day to the spot whence you started, your money is lost."

"But how am I to mark the way that I have gone?"

"Why, we shall go to any spot you like, and stay there. You must start from that spot and make your round, taking a spade with you. Wherever you think necessary, make a mark. At every turning, dig a hole and pile up the turf; then afterwards we will go round with a plough from hole to hole. You may make as large a circuit as you please, but before the sun sets you must return to the place you started from. All the land you cover will be yours."

Pahóm was delighted. It was decided to start early next morning. They talked a while, and after drinking some more kumiss and eating some more mutton, they had tea again, and then the night came on. They gave Pahóm a feather-bed to sleep on, and the Bashkírs dispersed for the night, promising to assemble the next morning at daybreak and ride out before sunrise to the appointed spot.

VII

Pahóm lay on the feather-bed, but could not sleep. He kept thinking about the land.

"What a large tract I will mark off!" thought he. "I can easily do thirty-five miles in a day. The days are long now, and within a circuit of thirty-five miles what a lot of land there will be! I will sell the poorer land, or let it to peasants, but I'll pick out the best and farm it. I will buy two ox-teams, and hire two more labourers. About a hundred and fifty acres shall be plough-land, and I will pasture cattle on the rest."

Pahóm lay awake all night, and dozed off only just before dawn. Hardly were his eyes closed when he had a dream. He thought he was lying in that same tent, and heard somebody chuckling outside. He wondered who it could be, and rose and went out, and he saw the Bashkír Chief sitting in front of the tent holding his side and rolling about with laughter. Going nearer to the Chief, Pahóm asked: "What are you laughing at?" But he saw that it was no longer the Chief, but the dealer who had recently stopped at his house and had told him about the land. Just as Pahóm was going to ask, "Have you been here long?" he saw that it was not the dealer, but the peasant who had come up from the Vólga, long ago, to Pahóm's old home. Then he saw that it was not the peasant either, but the Devil himself with hoofs and horns, sitting there and chuckling, and before him lay a man barefoot, prostrate on the ground, with only trousers and a shirt on. And Pahóm dreamt that he looked more attentively to see what sort of a man it was lying there, and he saw that the man was dead, and that it was himself! He awoke horror-struck.

"What things one does dream," thought he.

Looking round he saw through the open door that the dawn was breaking.

"It's time to wake them up," thought he. "We ought to be starting."

He got up, roused his man (who was sleeping in his cart), bade him harness; and went to call the Bashkírs.

"It's time to go to the steppe to measure the land," he said.

The Bashkírs rose and assembled, and the Chief came, too. Then they began drinking kumiss again, and offered Pahóm some tea, but he would not wait.

"If we are to go, let us go. It is high time," said he.

VIII

The Bashkírs got ready and they all started: some mounted on horses, and some in carts. Pahóm drove in his own small cart with his servant, and took a spade with him. When they reached the steppe, the morning red was beginning to kindle. They ascended a hillock (called by the Bashkírs a *shikhan*) and dismounting from their carts and their horses, gathered in one spot. The Chief came up to Pahóm and stretched out his arm towards the plain:

"See," said he, "all this, as far as your eye can reach, is ours. You may have any part of it you like."

Pahóm's eyes glistened: it was all virgin soil, as flat as the palm of your hand, as black as the seed of a poppy, and in the hollows different kinds of grasses grew breast high.

The Chief took off his fox-fur cap, placed it on the ground and said:

"This will be the mark. Start from here, and return here again. All the land you go round shall be yours."

Pahóm took out his money and put it on the cap. Then he took off his outer coat, remaining in his sleeveless under coat. He unfastened his girdle and tied it tight below his stomach, put a little bag of bread into the breast of his coat, and tying a flask of water to his girdle, he drew up the tops of his boots, took the spade from his man, and stood ready to start. He considered for some moments which way he had better go—it was tempting everywhere.

"No matter," he concluded, "I will go towards the rising sun."

He turned his face to the east, stretched himself, and waited for the sun to appear above the rim.

"I must lose no time," he thought, "and it is easier walking while it is still cool."

The sun's rays had hardly flashed above the horizon, before Pahóm, carrying the spade over his shoulder, went down into the steppe.

Pahóm started walking neither slowly nor quickly. After having gone a thousand yards he stopped, dug a hole, and placed pieces of turf one on another to make it more visible. Then he went on; and now that he had walked off his stiffness he quickened his pace. After a while he dug another hole.

Pahóm looked back. The hillock could be distinctly seen in the sunlight, with the people on it, and the glittering tyres of the cartwheels. At a rough guess Pahóm concluded that he had walked three miles. It was growing warmer; he took off his under-coat, flung it across his shoulder, and went on again. It had grown quite warm now; he looked at the sun, it was time to think of breakfast.

"The first shift is done, but there are four in a day, and it is too soon yet to turn. But I will just take off my boots," said he to himself.

He sat down, took off his boots, stuck them into his girdle, and went on. It was easy walking now.

"I will go on for another three miles," thought he, "and then turn to the left. The spot is so fine, that it would be a pity to lose it. The further one goes, the better the land seems."

He went straight on for a while, and when he looked round, the hillock was scarcely visible and the people on it looked like black ants, and he could just see something glistening there in the sun.

"Ah," thought Pahóm, "I have gone far enough in this direction, it is time to turn. Besides I am in a regular sweat, and very thirsty."

He stopped, dug a large hole, and heaped up pieces of turf. Next he untied his flask, had a drink, and then turned sharply to the left. He went on and on; the grass was high, and it was very hot.

Pahóm began to grow tired: he looked at the sun and saw that it was noon.

"Well," he thought, "I must have a rest."

He sat down, and ate some bread and drank some water; but he did not lie down, thinking that if he did he might fall asleep. After sitting a little while, he went on again. At first he walked easily: the food had strengthened him; but it had become terribly hot, and he felt sleepy; still he went on, thinking: "An hour to suffer, a life-time to live."

He went a long way in this direction also, and was about to turn to the left again, when he perceived a damp hollow: "It would be a pity to leave that out," he thought. "Flax would do well there." So he went on past the hollow, and dug a hole on the other side of it before he turned the corner. Pahóm looked towards the hillock. The heat made the air hazy: it seemed to be quivering, and through the haze the people on the hillock could scarcely be seen.

"Ah!" thought Pahóm, "I have made the sides too long; I must make this one shorter." And he went along the third side, stepping faster. He looked at the sun: it was nearly half way to the horizon, and he had not yet done two miles of the third side of the square. He was still ten miles from the goal.

"No," he thought, "though it will make my land lop-sided, I must hurry back in a straight line now. I might go too far, and as it is I have a great deal of land."

So Pahóm hurriedly dug a hole, and turned straight towards the hillock.

IX

Pahóm went straight towards the hillock, but he now walked with difficulty. He was done up with the heat, his bare feet were cut and bruised, and his legs began to fail. He longed to rest, but it was impossible if he meant to get back before sunset. The sun waits for no man, and it was sinking lower and lower.

"Oh dear," he thought, "if only I have not blundered trying for too much! What if I am too late?"

He looked towards the hillock and at the sun. He was still far from his goal, and the sun was already near the rim.

Pahóm walked on and on; it was very hard walking, but he went quicker and quicker. He pressed on, but was still far from the place. He began running, threw away his coat, his boots, his flask, and his cap, and kept only the spade which he used as a support.

"What shall I do," he thought again, "I have grasped too much, and ruined the whole affair. I can't get there before the sun sets."

And this fear made him still more breathless. Pahóm went on running, his soaking shirt and trousers stuck to him, and his mouth was parched. His breast was working like a blacksmith's bellows, his heart was beating like a hammer, and his legs were giving way as if they did not belong to him. Pahóm was seized with terror lest he should die of the strain.

Though afraid of death, he could not stop. "After having run all that way they will call me a fool if I stop now," thought he. And he ran on and on, and drew near and heard the Bashkírs yelling and shouting to him, and their cries inflamed his heart still more. He gathered his last strength and ran on.

The sun was close to the rim, and cloaked in mist looked large, and red as blood. Now, yes now, it was about to set! The sun was quite low, but he was also quite near his aim. Pahóm could already see the people on the hillock waving their arms to hurry him up. He could see the fox-fur cap on the ground, and the money on it, and the Chief sitting on the ground holding his sides. And Pahóm remembered his dream.

"There is plenty of land," thought he, "but will God let me live on it? I have lost my life, I have lost my life! I shall never reach that spot!"

Pahóm looked at the sun, which had reached the earth: one side of it had already disappeared. With all his remaining strength he rushed on, bending his body forward so that his legs could hardly follow fast enough to keep him from falling. Just as he reached the hillock it suddenly grew dark. He looked up—the sun had already set. He gave a cry: "All my labour has been in vain," thought he, and was about to stop, but he heard the Bashkírs still shouting, and remembered that though to him, from below, the sun seemed to have set, they on the hillock could still see it. He took a long breath and ran up the hillock. It was still light there. He reached the top and saw the cap. Before it sat the Chief laughing and holding his sides. Again Pahóm remembered his dream, and he uttered a cry: his legs gave way beneath him, he fell forward and reached the cap with his hands.

"Ah, what a fine fellow!" exclaimed the Chief. "He has gained much land!"

Pahóm's servant came running up and tried to raise him, but he saw that blood was flowing from his mouth. Pahóm was dead!

The Bashkírs clicked their tongues to show their pity.

His servant picked up the spade and dug a grave long enough for Pahóm to lie in, and buried him in it. Six feet from his head to his heels was all he needed.

The Imp and The Crust

[Written and first published in 1886, this Russian folk tale explores how evil finds its way when one fails to obey the Christian teachings. The story has also been translated as 'Promoting a Devil'. This version is taken from *Twenty-three Tales* (1906) translated by Louise and Aylmer Maude.]

A poor peasant set out early one morning to plough, taking with him for his breakfast a crust of bread. He got his plough ready, wrapped the bread in his coat, put it under a bush, and set to work. After a while, when his horse was tired and he was hungry, the peasant fixed the plough, let the horse loose to graze, and went to get his coat and his breakfast.

He lifted the coat, but the bread was gone! He looked and looked, turned the coat over, shook it out—but the bread was gone. The peasant could not make this out at all.

"That's strange," thought he; "I saw no one, but all the same someone has been here and has taken the bread!"

It was an imp who had stolen the bread while the peasant was ploughing, and at that moment he was sitting behind the bush, waiting to hear the peasant swear and call on the Devil.

The peasant was sorry to lose his breakfast, but "It can't be helped," said he. "After all, I shan't die of hunger! No doubt whoever took the bread needed it. May it do him good!"

And he went to the well, had a drink of water, and rested a bit. Then he caught his horse, harnessed it, and began ploughing again.

The imp was crestfallen at not having made the peasant sin, and he went to report what had happened to the Devil, his master.

He came to the Devil and told how he had taken the peasant's bread, and how the peasant instead of cursing had said, "May it do him good!"

The Devil was angry, and replied: "If the man got the better of you, it was your own fault—you don't understand your business! If the peasants, and their wives after them, take to that sort of thing, it will be all up with us. The matter can't be left like that! Go back at once," said he, "and put things right. If in three years you don't get the better of that peasant, I'll have you ducked in holy water!"

The imp was frightened. He scampered back to earth, thinking how he could redeem his fault. He thought and thought, and at last hit upon a good plan.

He turned himself into a labouring man, and went and took service with the poor peasant. The first year he advised the peasant to sow corn in a marshy place. The peasant took his advice, and sowed in the marsh. The year turned out a very dry one, and the crops of the other peasants were all scorched by the sun, but the poor peasant's corn grew thick and tall and full-earned. Not only had he grain enough to last him for the whole year, but he had much left over besides.

The next year the imp advised the peasant to sow on the hill; and it turned out a wet summer. Other people's corn was beaten down and rotted and the ears did not fill; but the peasant's crop, up on the hill, was a fine one. He had more grain left over than before, so that he did not know what to do with it all.

Then the imp showed the peasant how he could mash the grain and distil spirit from it; and the peasant made strong drink, and began to drink it himself and to give it to his friends.

So the imp went to the Devil, his master, and boasted that he had made up for his failure. The Devil said that he would come and see for himself how the case stood.

He came to the peasant's house, and saw that the peasant had invited his well-to-do neighbours and was treating them to drink. His wife was offering the drink to the guests, and as she handed it round she tumbled against the table and spilt a glassful.

The peasant was angry, and scolded his wife: "What do you mean, you slut? Do you think it's ditchwater, you cripple, that you must go pouring good stuff like that over the floor?"

The imp nudged the Devil, his master, with his elbow: "See," said he, "that's the man who did not grudge his last crust!"

The peasant, still railing at his wife, began to carry the drink round himself. Just then a poor peasant returning from work came in uninvited. He greeted the company, sat down, and saw that they were drinking. Tired with his day's work, he felt that he too would like a drop. He sat and sat, and his mouth kept watering, but the host instead of offering him any only muttered: "I can't find drink for everyone who comes along."

This pleased the Devil; but the imp chuckled and said, "Wait a bit, there's more to come yet!"

The rich peasants drank, and their host drank too. And they began to make false, oily speeches to one another.

The Devil listened and listened, and praised the imp.

"If," said he, "the drink makes them so foxy that they begin to cheat each other, they will soon all be in our hands."

"Wait for what's coming," said the imp. "Let them have another glass all round. Now they are like foxes, wagging their tails and trying to get round one another; but presently you will see them like savage wolves."

The peasants had another glass each, and their talk became wilder and rougher. Instead of oily speeches, they began to abuse and snarl at one another. Soon they took to fighting, and punched one another's noses. And the host joined in the fight, and he too got well beaten.

The Devil looked on and was much pleased at all this.

"This is first-rate!" said he.

But the imp replied: "Wait a bit—the best is yet to come. Wait till they have had a third glass. Now they are raging like wolves, but let them have one more glass, and they will be like swine."

The peasants had their third glass, and became quite like brutes. They muttered and shouted, not knowing why, and not listening to one another.

Then the party began to break up. Some went alone, some in twos, and some in threes, all staggering down the street. The host went out to speed his guests, but he fell on his nose into a puddle, smeared himself from top to toe, and lay there grunting like a hog.

This pleased the Devil still more.

"Well," said he, "you have hit on a first-rate drink, and have quite made up for your blunder about the bread. But now tell me how this drink is made. You must first have put in fox's blood: that was what made the peasants sly as foxes. Then, I suppose, you added wolf's blood: that is what made them fierce like wolves. And you

410

must have finished off with swine's blood, to make them behave like swine."

"No," said the imp, "that was not the way I did it. All I did was to see that the peasant had more corn than he needed. The blood of the beasts is always in man; but as long as he has only enough corn for his needs, it is kept in bounds. While that was the case, the peasant did not grudge his last crust. But when he had corn left over, he looked for ways of getting pleasure out of it. And I showed him a pleasure—drinking! And when he began to turn God's good gifts into spirits for his own pleasure—the fox's, wolf's and swine's blood in him all came out. If only he goes on drinking, he will always be a beast!"

The Devil praised the imp, forgave him for his former blunder, and advanced him to a post of high honour.

The Repentant Sinner

[Written and first published in 1886. The theme of forgiveness is at the heart of this story. It has also been translated as 'The Penitent Sinner' by R. Nesbit Bain in 1903. The version here is a translation by Louise and Aylmer Maude collected in *Twenty-three Tales* (1906).]

'And he said unto Jesus, Lord, remember me when thou comest into thy Kingdom. And Jesus said unto him, Verily I say unto thee, Today shalt thou be with me in paradise.'

—Luke xxiii. 42, 43

There was once a man who lived for seventy years in the world, and lived in sin all that time. He fell ill, but even then did not repent. Only at the last moment, as he was dying, he wept and said:

"Lord! Forgive me, as Thou forgavest the thief upon the cross."

And as he said these words, his soul left his body. And the soul of the sinner, feeling love towards God and faith in His mercy, went to the gates of heaven, and knocked, praying to be let into the heavenly kingdom.

Then a voice spoke from within the gate:

"What man is it that knocks at the gates of Paradise, and what deeds did he do during his life?"

And the voice of the Accuser replied, recounting all the man's evil deeds, and not a single good one.

And the voice from within the gates answered:

"Sinners cannot enter into the kingdom of heaven. Go hence!"

Then the man said:

"Lord, I hear thy voice, but cannot see thy face, nor do I know thy name."

The voice answered:

"I am Peter, the Apostle."

And the sinner replied:

"Have pity on me, Apostle Peter! Remember man's weakness, and God's mercy. Wert not thou a disciple of Christ? Didst not thou hear his teaching from his own lips, and hadst thou not his example before thee? Remember then how, when he sorrowed and was grieved in spirit, and three times asked thee to keep awake and pray, thou didst sleep, because thine eyes were heavy, and three times he found thee sleeping. So it was with me. Remember, also, how thou didst promise to be faithful unto death, and yet didst thrice deny him, when he was taken before Caiaphas. So it was with me. And remember, too, how when the cock crowed thou didst go out and didst weep bitterly. So it is with me. Thou canst not refuse to let me in."

And the voice behind the gates was silent.

Then the sinner stood a little while, and again began to knock, and to ask to be let into the kingdom of heaven.

And he heard another voice behind the gates, which said:

"Who is this man, and how did he live on earth?"

And the voice of the Accuser again repeated all the sinner's evil deeds, and not a single good one.

And the voice from behind the gates replied:

"Go hence! Such sinners cannot live with us in Paradise." Then the sinner said:

"Lord, I hear thy voice, but I see thee not, nor do I know thy name."

And the voice answered:

"I am David; king and prophet."

The sinner did not despair, nor did he leave the gates of paradise, but said:

"Have pity on me, King David! Remember man's weakness, and God's mercy. God loved thee and exalted thee among men. Thou hadst all: a kingdom, and honour, and riches, and wives, and children; but thou sawest from thy house-top the wife of a poor man, and sin entered into thee, and thou tookest the wife of Uriah, and didst slay him with the sword of the Ammonites. Thou, a rich man, didst take from the poor man his one ewe lamb, and didst kill him. I have done likewise. Remember, then, how thou didst repent, and how thou saidst, "I acknowledge my transgressions: my sin is ever before me?" I have done the same. Thou canst not refuse to let me in."

And the voice from within the gates was silent.

The sinner having stood a little while, began knocking again, and asking to be let into the kingdom of heaven. And a third voice was heard within the gates, saying:

"Who is this man, and how has he spent his life on earth?"

And the voice of the Accuser replied for the third time, recounting the sinner's evil deeds, and not mentioning one good deed.

And the voice within the gates said:

"Depart hence! Sinners cannot enter into the kingdom of heaven."

And the sinner said:

"Thy voice I hear, but thy face I see not, neither do I know thy name."

Then the voice replied:

"I am John the Divine, the beloved disciple of Christ."

And the sinner rejoiced and said:

"Now surely I shall be allowed to enter. Peter and David must let me in, because they know man's weakness and God's mercy; and thou wilt let me in, because thou lovest much. Was it not thou, John the Divine, who wrote that God is Love, and that he who loves not, knows not God? And in thine old age didst thou not say unto men: "Brethren, love one another." How, then, canst thou look on me with hatred, and drive me away? Either thou must renounce what thou hast said, or loving me, must let me enter the kingdom of heaven."

And the gates of Paradise opened, and John embraced the repentant sinner and took him into the kingdom of heaven.

The Empty Drum

(A FOLK TALE LONG CURRENT IN THE REGION OF THE VÓLGA)

[This common Vólga folk tale based on religious legends was first published in the year 1891. The version here is taken from the collection *Twenty-three Tales* (1906) translated by Louise and Aylmer Maude.]

Emelyán was a labourer and worked for a master. Crossing the meadows one day on his way to work, he nearly trod on a frog that jumped right in front of him, but he just managed to avoid it. Suddenly he heard someone calling to him from behind.

Emelyán looked round and saw a lovely lassie, who said to him: "Why don't you get married, Emelyán?"

"How can I marry, my lass?" said he. "I have but the clothes I stand up in, nothing more, and no one would have me for a husband."

"Take me for a wife," said she.

Emelyán liked the maid. "I should be glad to," said he, "but where and how could we live?"

"Why trouble about that?" said the girl. "One only has to work more and sleep less, and one can clothe and feed oneself anywhere."

"Very well then, let us marry," said Emelyán. "Where shall we go to?"

"Let us go to town."

So Emelyán and the lass went to town, and she took him to a small hut on the very edge of the town, and they married and began housekeeping.

One day the King, driving through the town, passed by Emelyán's hut. Emelyán's wife came out to see the King. The King noticed her and was quite surprised.

"Where did such a beauty come from?" said he, and stopping his carriage he called Emelyán's wife and asked her: "Who are you?"

"The peasant Emelyán's wife," said she.

"Why did you, who are such a beauty, marry a peasant?" said the King. "You ought to be a queen!"

"Thank you for your kind words," said she, "but a peasant husband is good enough for me."

The King talked to her awhile and then drove on. He returned to the palace, but could not get Emelyán's wife out of his head. All night he did not sleep, but kept thinking how to get her for himself. He could think of no way of doing it, so he called his servants and told them they must find a way.

The King's servants said: "Command Emelyán to come to the palace to work, and we will work him so hard that he will die. His wife will be left a widow, and then you can take her for yourself."

The King followed their advice. He sent an order that Emelyán should come to the palace as a workman, and that he should live at the palace, and his wife with him.

The messengers came to Emelyán and gave him the King's message. His wife said, "Go, Emelyán; work all day, but come back home at night."

So Emelyán went, and when he got to the palace the King's steward asked him, "Why have you come alone, without your wife?"

"Why should I drag her about?" said Emelyán. "She has a house to live in."

At the King's palace they gave Emelyán work enough for two. He began the job not hoping to finish it; but when evening came, lo and behold! it was all done. The steward saw that it was finished, and set him four times as much for next day.

Emelyán went home. Everything there was swept and tidy; the oven was heated, his supper was cooked and ready, and his wife sat by the table sewing and waiting for his return. She greeted him, laid the table, gave him to eat and drink, and then began to ask him about his work.

"Ah!" said he, "it's a bad business: they give me tasks beyond my strength, and want to kill me with work."

"Don't fret about the work," said she, "don't look either before or behind to see how much you have done or how much there is left to do; only keep on working and all will be right."

So Emelyán lay down and slept. Next morning he went to work again and worked without once looking round. And, lo and behold! by the evening it was all done, and before dark he came home for the night.

Again and again they increased Emelyán's work, but he always got through it in good time and went back to his hut to sleep. A week passed, and the King's servants saw they could not crush him with rough work, so they tried giving him work that required skill. But this also was of no avail. Carpentering, and masonry, and roofing, whatever they set him to do, Emelyán had it ready in time, and went home to his wife at night. So a second week passed.

Then the King called his servants and said: "Am I to feed you for nothing? Two weeks have gone, and I don't see that you have done anything. You were going to tire Emelyán out with work, but I see from my windows how he goes home every evening— singing cheerfully! Do you mean to make a fool of me?"

The King's servants began to excuse themselves. "We tried our best to wear him out with rough work," they said, "but nothing was too hard for him; he cleared it all off as though he had swept it away with a broom. There was no tiring him out. Then we set him to tasks needing skill, which we did not think he was clever enough to do, but he managed them all. No matter what one sets him, he does it all, no one knows how. Either he or his wife must know some spell that helps them. We ourselves are sick of him, and wish to find a task he cannot master. We have now thought of setting him to build a cathedral in a single day. Send for Emelyán, and order him to build a cathedral in front of the palace in a single day. Then, if he does not do it, let his head be cut off for disobedience."

The King sent for Emelyán. "Listen to my command," said he: "build me a new cathedral on the square in front of my palace, and have it ready by tomorrow evening. If you have it ready I will reward you, but if not I will have your head cut off."

When Emelyán heard the King's command he turned away and went home. "My end is near," thought he. And coming to his wife, he said: "Get ready, wife, we must fly from here, or I shall be lost by no fault of my own."

"What has frightened you so?" said she, "and why should we run away?"

"How can I help being frightened? The King has ordered me, tomorrow, in a single day, to build him a cathedral. If I fail he will cut my head off. There is only one thing to be done: we must fly while there is yet time."

But his wife would not hear of it. "The King has many soldiers," said she. "They would catch us anywhere. We cannot escape from him, but must obey him as long as strength holds out."

"How can I obey him when the task is beyond my strength?"

"Eh, goodman, don't be downhearted. Eat your supper now, and go to sleep. Rise early in the morning and all will get done."

So Emelyán lay down and slept. His wife roused him early next day. "Go quickly," said she, "and finish the cathedral. Here are nails and a hammer; there is still enough work there for a day."

Emelyán went into the town, reached the palace square, and there stood a large cathedral not quite finished. Emelyán set to work to do what was needed, and by the evening all was ready.

When the King awoke he looked out from his palace, and saw the cathedral, and Emelyán going about driving in nails here and there. And the King was not pleased to have the cathedral—he was annoyed at not being able to condemn Emelyán and take his wife. Again he called his servants. "Emelyán has done this task also," said the King, "and there is no excuse for putting him to death. Even this work was not too hard for him. You must find a more cunning plan, or I will cut off your heads as well as his."

So his servants planned that Emelyán should be ordered to make a river round the palace, with ships sailing on it. And the King sent for Emelyán and set him this new task.

"If," said he, "you could build a cathedral in one night, you can also do this. Tomorrow all must be ready. If not, I will have your head off."

Emelyán was more downcast than before, and returned to his wife sad at heart.

"Why are you so sad?" said his wife. "Has the King set you a fresh task?"

Emelyán told her about it. "We must fly," said he.

But his wife replied: "There is no escaping the soldiers; they will catch us wherever we go. There is nothing for it but to obey."

"How can I do it?" groaned Emelyán.

"Eh! eh! Goodman," said she, "don't be downhearted. Eat your supper now, and go to sleep. Rise early, and all will get done in good time."

So Emelyán lay down and slept. In the morning his wife woke him. "Go," said she, "to the palace—all is ready. Only, near the wharf in front of the palace, there is a mound left; take a spade and level it."

When the King awoke he saw a river where there had not been one; ships were sailing up and down, and Emelyán was levelling a mound with a spade. The King wondered, but was pleased neither with the river nor with the ships, so vexed was he at not being able to condemn Emelyán. "There is no task," thought he, "that he cannot manage. What is to be done?" And he called his servants and again asked their advice.

"Find some task," said he, "which Emelyán cannot compass. For whatever we plan he fulfils, and I cannot take his wife from him."

The King's servants thought and thought, and at last devised a plan. They came to the King and said: "Send for Emelyán and say to him: 'Go to "there, don't know where," and bring back "that, don't know what." Then he will not be able to escape you. No matter where he goes, you can say that he has not gone to the right place, and no matter what he brings, you can say it is not the right thing. Then you can have him beheaded and can take his wife."

The King was pleased. "That is well thought of," said he. So the King sent for Emelyán and said to him: "Go to 'there, don't know where,' and bring back 'that, don't know what.' If you fail to bring it, I will have you beheaded."

Emelyán returned to his wife and told her what the King had said. His wife became thoughtful.

"Well," said she, "they have taught the King how to catch you. Now we must act warily." So she sat and thought, and at last said to her husband: "You must go far, to our Grandam—the old peasant woman, the mother of soldiers—and you must ask her aid. If she helps you to anything, go straight to the palace with it, I shall be there: I cannot escape them now. They will take me by force, but it will not be for long. If you do everything as Grandam directs, you will soon save me."

So the wife got her husband ready for the journey. She gave him a wallet, and also a spindle. "Give her this," said she. "By this token she will know that you are my husband." And his wife showed him his road.

Emelyán set off. He left the town behind, and came to where some soldiers were being drilled. Emelyán stood and watched them. After drill the soldiers sat down to rest. Then Emelyán went up to them and asked: "Do you know, brothers, the way to 'there, don't know where?' and how I can get 'that, don't know what?'"

The soldiers listened to him with surprise. "Who sent you on this errand?" said they.

"The King," said he.

"We ourselves," said they, "from the day we became soldiers, go we 'don't know where,' and never yet have we got there; and we seek we 'don't know what,' and cannot find it. We cannot help you."

Emelyán sat a while with the soldiers and then went on again. He trudged many a mile, and at last came to a wood. In the wood was a hut, and in the hut sat an old, old woman, the mother of peasant soldiers, spinning flax and weeping. And as she spun she did not put her fingers to her mouth to wet them with spittle, but to her eyes to wet them with tears. When the old woman saw Emelyán she cried out at him: "Why have you come here?" Then Emelyán gave her the spindle and said his wife had sent it.

The old woman softened at once and began to question him. And Emelyán told her his whole life: how he married the lass; how they went to live in the town; how he had worked, and what he had done at the palace; how he built the cathedral, and made a river with ships on it, and how the King had now told him to go to 'there, don't know where,' and bring back 'that, don't know what.'

The Grandam listened to the end, and ceased weeping. She muttered to herself: "The time has surely come," and said to him: "All right, my lad. Sit down now, and I will give you something to eat."

Emelyán ate, and then the Grandam told him what to do. "Here," said she, "is a ball of thread; roll it before you, and follow where it goes. You must go far till you come right to the sea. When you get there, you will see a great city. Enter the city and ask for a night's lodging at the furthest house. There look out for what you are seeking."

"How shall I know it when I see it, Granny?" said he.

"When you see something men obey more than father or mother, that is it. Seize that, and take it to the King. When you bring it to the King, he will say it is not right, and you must answer: "If it is not the right thing it must be smashed," and you must beat it, and carry it to the river, break it in pieces, and throw it into the water. Then you will get your wife back and my tears will be dried."

Emelyán bade farewell to the Grandam and began rolling his ball before him. It rolled and rolled until at last it reached the sea. By the sea stood a great city, and at the further end of the city was a big house. There Emelyán begged for a night's lodging, and was granted it. He lay down to sleep, and in the morning awoke and heard a father rousing his son to go and cut wood for the fire. But the son did not obey. "It is too early," said he, "there is time enough." Then Emelyán heard the mother say, "Go, my son, your father's bones ache; would you have him go himself? It is time to be up!"

But the son only murmured some words and fell asleep again. Hardly was he asleep when something thundered and rattled in the street. Up jumped the son and quickly putting on his clothes ran out into the street. Up jumped Emelyán, too, and ran after him to see what it was that a son obeys more than father or mother. What he saw was a man walking along the street carrying, tied to his stomach, a thing which he beat with sticks, and *that* it was that rattled and thundered so, and that the son had obeyed. Emelyán ran up and had a look at it. He saw it was round, like a small tub, with a skin stretched over both ends, and he asked what it was called.

He was told, "A drum."

"And is it empty?"

"Yes, it is empty."

Emelyán was surprised. He asked them to give the thing to him, but they would not. So Emelyán left off asking, and followed the drummer. All day he followed, and when the drummer at last lay down to sleep, Emelyán snatched the drum from him and ran away with it.

He ran and ran, till at last he got back to his own town. He went to see his wife, but she was not at home. The day after he went away, the King had taken her. So Emelyán went to the palace, and sent in a message to the King: "He has returned who went to 'there, don't know where,' and he has brought with him 'that, don't know what.'"

They told the King, and the King said he was to come again next day.

But Emelyán said, "Tell the King I am here today, and have brought what the King wanted. Let him come out to me, or I will go in to him!"

The King came out. "Where have you been?" said he.

Emelyán told him.

"That's not the right place," said the King. "What have you brought?"

Emelyán pointed to the drum, but the King did not look at it. "That is not it."

"If it is not the right thing," said Emelyán, "it must be smashed, and may the devil take it!"

And Emelyán left the palace, carrying the drum and beating it. And as he beat it all the King's army ran out to follow Emelyán, and they saluted him and waited his commands.

The King, from his window, began to shout at his army telling them not to follow Emelyán. They did not listen to what he said, but all followed Emelyán.

When the King saw that, he gave orders that Emelyán's wife should be taken back to him, and he sent to ask Emelyán to give him the drum.

"It can't be done," said Emelyán. "I was told to smash it and to throw the splinters into the river."

So Emelyán went down to the river carrying the drum, and the soldiers followed him. When he reached the river bank Emelyán smashed the drum to splinters, and threw the splinters into the stream. And then all the soldiers ran away.

Emelyán took his wife and went home with her. And after that the King ceased to trouble him; and so they lived happily ever after.

The Godson

[Written and first published in 1886. This story is based on the commandment of not resisting evil with force. Also translated as 'The Godfather'. The version reproduced here has been taken from the collection *Twenty-three Tales* (1906) translated by Louise and Aylmer Maude.]

'Ye have heard that it was said, An eye for an eye, and a tooth for a tooth, but I say unto you, Resist not him that is evil.'

—Matt. v. 38, 39

'Vengeance is mine; I will repay.'

—Rom. xii. 19

I

A son was born to a poor peasant. He was glad, and went to his neighbour to ask him to stand godfather to the boy. The neighbour refused—he did not like standing godfather to a poor man's child. The peasant asked another neighbour, but he too refused, and after that the poor father went to every house in the village, but found no one willing to be godfather to his son. So he set off to another village, and on the way he met a man who stopped and said:

"Good day, my good man; where are you off to?"

"God has given me a child," said the peasant, "to rejoice my eyes in youth, to comfort my old age, and to pray for my soul after death. But I am poor, and no one in our village will stand godfather to him, so I am now on my way to seek a godfather for him elsewhere."

"Let me be godfather," said the stranger.

The peasant was glad, and thanked him, but added:

"And whom shall I ask to be godmother?"

"Go to the town," replied the stranger, "and, in the square, you will see a stone house with shop-windows in the front. At the entrance you will find the tradesman to whom it belongs. Ask him to let his daughter stand godmother to your child."

The peasant hesitated.

"How can I ask a rich tradesman?" said he. "He will despise me, and will not let his daughter come."

"Don't trouble about that. Go and ask. Get everything ready by tomorrow morning, and I will come to the christening."

The poor peasant returned home, and then drove to the town to find the tradesman. He had hardly taken his horse into the yard, when the tradesman himself came out.

"What do you want?" said he.

"Why, sir," said the peasant, "you see God has given me a son to rejoice my eyes in youth, to comfort my old age, and to pray for my soul after death. Be so kind as to let your daughter stand godmother to him."

"And when is the christening?" said the tradesman.

"Tomorrow morning."

"Very well. Go in peace. She shall be with you at Mass tomorrow morning."

The next day the godmother came, and the godfather also, and the infant was baptized. Immediately after the christening the godfather went away. They did not know who he was, and never saw him again.

II

The child grew up to be a joy to his parents. He was strong, willing to work, clever and obedient. When he was ten years old his parents sent him to school to learn to read and write. What others learnt in five years, he learnt in one, and soon there was nothing more they could teach him.

Easter came round, and the boy went to see his godmother, to give her his Easter greeting.

"Father and mother," said he when he got home again, "where does my godfather live? I should like to give him my Easter greeting, too."

And his father answered:

"We know nothing about your godfather, dear son. We often regret it ourselves. Since the day you were christened we have never seen him, nor had any news of him. We do not know where he lives, or even whether he is still alive."

The son bowed to his parents.

"Father and mother," said he, "let me go and look for my godfather. I must find him and give him my Easter greeting.

So his father and mother let him go, and the boy set off to find his godfather.

III

The boy left the house and set out along the road. He had been walking for several hours when he met a stranger who stopped him and said:

"Good day to you, my boy. Where are you going?"

And the boy answered:

"I went to see my godmother and to give her my Easter greeting, and when I got home I asked my parents where my godfather lives, that I might go and greet him also. They told me they did not know. They said he went away as soon as I was christened, and they know nothing about him, not even if he be still alive. But I wished to see my godfather, and so I have set out to look for him."

Then the stranger said: "I am your godfather."

The boy was glad to hear this. After kissing his godfather three times for an Easter greeting, he asked him:

"Which way are you going now, godfather? If you are coming our way, please come to our house; but if you are going home, I will go with you."

"I have no time now," replied his godfather, "to come to your house. I have business in several villages; but I shall return home again tomorrow. Come and see me then."

"But how shall I find you, godfather?"

"When you leave home, go straight towards the rising sun, and you will come to a forest; going through the forest you will come to a glade. When you reach this glade sit down and rest awhile, and look around you and see what happens. On the further side of the forest you will find a garden, and in it a house with a golden roof. That is my home. Go up to the gate, and I will myself be there to meet you."

And having said this the godfather disappeared from his godson's sight.

IV

The boy did as his godfather had told him. He walked eastward until he reached a forest, and there he came to a glade, and in the midst of the glade he saw a pine tree to a branch of which was tied a rope supporting a heavy log of oak. Close under this log stood a wooden trough filled with honey. Hardly had the boy had time to wonder why the honey was placed there, and why the log hung above it, when he heard a crackling in the wood, and saw some bears approaching; a she-bear, followed by a yearling and three tiny cubs. The she-bear, sniffing the air, went straight to the trough, the cubs following her. She thrust her muzzle into the honey, and called the cubs to do the same. They scampered up and began to eat. As they did so, the log, which the she-bear had moved aside with her head, swung away a little and, returning, gave the cubs a push. Seeing this the she-bear shoved the log away with her paw. It swung further out and returned more forcibly, striking one cub on the back and another on the head. The cubs ran away howling with pain, and the mother, with a growl, caught the log in her fore paws and, raising it above her head, flung it away. The log flew high in the air, and the yearling, rushing to the trough, pushed his muzzle into the honey and began to suck noisily. The others also drew near, but they had not reached the trough when the log, flying back, struck the yearling on the head and killed him. The mother growled louder than before and, seizing the log, flung it from her with all her might. It flew higher than the branch it was tied to; so high that the rope slackened; and the she-bear returned to the trough, and the little cubs after her. The log flew higher and higher, then stopped, and began to fall. The nearer it came the faster it swung, and at last, at full speed, it crashed down on her head. The she-bear rolled over, her legs jerked, and she died! The cubs ran away into the forest.

V

The boy watched all this in surprise, and then continued his way. Leaving the forest, he came upon a large garden in the midst of which stood a lofty palace with a golden roof. At the gate stood his godfather, smiling. He welcomed his godson, and led him through the gateway into the garden. The boy had never dreamed of such beauty and delight as surrounded him in that place.

Then his godfather led him into the palace, which was even more beautiful inside than outside. The godfather showed the boy through all the rooms: each brighter and finer than the other, but at last they came to one door that was sealed up.

"You see this door," said he. "It is not locked, but only sealed. It can be opened, but I forbid you to open it. You may live here, and go where you please, and enjoy all the delights of the place. My only command is—do not open that door! But should you ever do so, remember what you saw in the forest."

Having said this the godfather went away. The godson remained in the palace, and life there was so bright and joyful that he thought he had only been there three hours, when he had really lived there thirty years. When thirty years had gone by, the godson happened to be passing the sealed door one day, and he wondered why his godfather had forbidden him to enter that room.

"I'll just look in and see what is there," thought he, and he gave the door a push. The seals gave way, the door opened, and the godson entering saw a hall more lofty and beautiful than all the others, and in the midst of it a throne. He wandered about the hall for a while, and then mounted the steps and seated himself upon the throne. As he sat there he noticed a sceptre leaning against the throne, and took it in his hand. Hardly had he done so when the four walls of the hall suddenly disappeared. The godson looked around, and saw the whole world, and all that men were doing in it. He looked in front, and saw the sea with ships sailing on it. He looked to the right, and saw where strange heathen people lived. He looked to the left, and saw where men who were Christians, but not Russians, lived. He looked round, and on the fourth side, he saw Russian people, like himself.

"I will look," said he, "and see what is happening at home, and whether the harvest is good."

He looked towards his father's fields and saw the sheaves standing in stooks. He began counting them to see whether there was much corn, when he noticed a peasant driving in a cart. It was night, and the godson thought it was his father coming to cart the corn by night. But as he looked he recognized Vasíly Koudryashóf, the thief, driving into the field and beginning to load the sheaves on to his cart. This made the godson angry, and he called out:

"Father, the sheaves are being stolen from our field!"

His father, who was out with the horses in the night-pasture, woke up.

"I dreamt the sheaves were being stolen," said he. "I will just ride down and see."

So he got on a horse and rode out to the field. Finding Vasíly there, he called together other peasants to help him, and Vasíly was beaten, bound, and taken to prison.

Then the godson looked at the town, where his godmother lived. He saw that she was now married to a tradesman. She lay asleep, and her husband rose and went to his mistress. The godson shouted to her:

"Get up, get up, your husband has taken to evil ways."

The godmother jumped up and dressed, and finding out where her husband was, she shamed and beat his mistress, and drove him away.

Then the godson looked for his mother, and saw her lying asleep in her cottage. And a thief crept into the cottage and began to break open the chest in which she kept her things. The mother awoke and screamed, and the robber seizing an axe, swung it over his head to kill her.

The godson could not refrain from hurling the sceptre at the robber. It struck him upon the temple, and killed him on the spot.

VI

As soon as the godson had killed the robber, the walls closed and the hall became just as it had been before.

Then the door opened and the godfather entered, and coming up to his godson he took him by the hand and led him down from the throne.

"You have not obeyed my command," said he. "You did one wrong thing, when you opened the forbidden door; another, when you mounted the throne and took my sceptre into your hands; and you have now done a third wrong, which has much increased the evil in the world. Had you sat here an hour longer, you would have ruined half mankind."

Then the godfather led his godson back to the throne, and took the sceptre in his hand; and again the walls fell asunder and all things became visible. And the godfather said:

"See what you have done to your father. Vasíly has now been a year in prison, and has come out having learnt every kind of wickedness, and has become quite incorrigible. See, he has stolen two of your father's horses, and he is now setting fire to his barn. All this you have brought upon your father."

The godson saw his father's barn breaking into flames, but

his godfather shut off the sight from him, and told him to look another way.

"Here is your godmother's husband," he said. "It is a year since he left his wife, and now he goes after other women. His former mistress has sunk to still lower depths. Sorrow has driven his wife to drink. That's what you have done to your godmother."

The godfather shut off this also, and showed the godson his father's house. There he saw his mother weeping for her sins, repenting, and saying:

"It would have been better had the robber killed me that night. I should not have sinned so heavily."

"That," said the godfather, "is what you have done to your mother."

He shut this off also, and pointed downwards; and the godson saw two warders holding the robber in front of a prison-house.

And the godfather said:

"This man had murdered ten men. He should have expiated his sins himself, but by killing him you have taken his sins on yourself. Now you must answer for all his sins. That is what you have done to yourself. The she-bear pushed the log aside once, and disturbed her cubs; she pushed it again, and killed her yearling; she pushed it a third time, and was killed herself. You have done the same. Now I give you thirty years to go into the world and atone for the robber's sins. If you do not atone for them, you will have to take his place."

"How am I to atone for his sins?" asked the godson.

And the godfather answered:

"When you have rid the world of as much evil as you have brought into it, you will have atoned both for your own sins and for those of the robber."

"How can I destroy evil in the world?" the godson asked.

"Go out," replied the godfather, "and walk straight towards the rising sun. After a time you will come to a field with some men in it. Notice what they are doing, and teach them what you know. Then go on and note what you see. On the fourth day you will come to a forest. In the midst of the forest is a cell, and in the cell lives a hermit. Tell him all that has happened. He will teach you what to do. When you have done all he tells you, you will have atoned for your own and the robber's sins."

And, having said this, the godfather led his godson out of the gate.

VII

The godson went his way, and as he went he thought: How am I to destroy evil in the world? Evil is destroyed by banishing evil men, keeping them in prison, or putting them to death. How then am I to destroy evil without taking the sins of others upon myself?"

The godson pondered over it for a long time, but could come to no conclusion. He went on until he came to a field where corn was growing thick and good and ready for the reapers. The godson saw that a little calf had got in among the corn. Some men who were at hand saw it, and mounting their horses they chased it backwards and forwards through the corn. Each time the calf was about to come out of the corn, someone rode up and the calf got frightened and turned back again, and they all galloped after it, trampling down the corn. On the road stood a woman crying.

"They will chase my calf to death," she said.

And the godson said to the peasants:

"What are you doing? Come out of the cornfield, all of you, and let the woman call her calf."

The men did so; and the woman came to the edge of the cornfield and called to the calf. "Come along, browney, come along," said she. The calf pricked up its ears, listened a while, and then ran towards the woman of its own accord, and hid its head in her skirts, almost knocking her over. The men were glad, the woman was glad, and so was the little calf.

The godson went on, and he thought:

"Now I see that evil spreads evil. The more people try to drive away evil, the more the evil grows. Evil, it seems, cannot be destroyed by evil; but in what way it can be destroyed, I do not know. The calf obeyed its mistress and so all went well; but if it had not obeyed her, how could we have got it out of the field?"

The godson pondered again, but came to no conclusion, and continued his way.

VIII

He went on until he came to a village. At the furthest end he stopped and asked leave to stay the night. The woman of the house was there alone, house-cleaning, and she let him in. The godson entered, and taking his seat upon the brick oven he watched what the woman was doing. He saw her finish scrubbing the room and begin scrubbing the table. Having done this, she began wiping the table with a dirty cloth. She wiped it from side to side—but it did not come clean. The soiled cloth left streaks of dirt. Then she wiped it the other way. The first streaks disappeared, but others came in their place. Then she wiped it from one end to the other, but again the same thing happened. The soiled cloth messed the table; when one streak was wiped off another was left on. The godson watched for awhile in silence, and then said:

"What are you doing, mistress?"

"Don't you see I'm cleaning up for the holiday. Only I can't manage this table, it won't come clean. I'm quite tired out."

"You should rinse your cloth," said the godson, "before you wipe the table with it."

The woman did so, and soon had the table clean.

"Thank you for telling me," said she.

In the morning he took leave of the woman and went on his way. After walking a good while, he came to the edge of a forest. There he saw some peasants who were making wheel-rims of bent wood. Coming nearer, the godson saw that the men were going round and round, but could not bend the wood.

He stood and looked on, and noticed that the block, to which the piece of wood was fastened, was not fixed, but as the men moved round it went round too. Then the godson said:

"What are you doing, friends?"

"Why, don't you see, we are making wheel-rims. We have twice steamed the wood, and are quite tired out, but the wood will not bend."

"You should fix the block, friends," said the godson, "or else it goes round when you do."

The peasants took his advice and fixed the block, and then the work went on merrily.

The godson spent the night with them, and then went on. He walked all day and all night, and just before dawn he came upon some drovers encamped for the night, and lay down beside them. He saw that they had got all their cattle settled, and were trying to light a fire. They had taken dry twigs and lighted them, but before the twigs had time to burn up, they smothered them with damp brushwood. The brushwood hissed, and the fire smouldered and went out. Then the drovers brought more dry wood, lit it, and again put on the brushwood—and again the fire went out. They struggled with it for a long time, but could not get the fire to burn. Then the godson said:

"Do not be in such a hurry to put on the brushwood. Let the dry wood burn up properly before you put any on. When the fire is well alight you can put on as much as you please."

The drovers followed his advice. They let the fire burn up fiercely before adding the brushwood, which then flared up so that they soon had a roaring fire.

The godson remained with them for a while, and then continued his way. He went on, wondering what the three things he had seen might mean; but he could not fathom them.

IX

The godson walked the whole of that day, and in the evening came to another forest. There he found a hermit's cell, at which he knocked.

"Who is there?" asked a voice from within.

"A great sinner," replied the godson. "I must atone for another's sins as well as for my own."

The hermit hearing this came out.

"What sins are those that you have to bear for another?"

The godson told him everything: about his godfather; about the she-bear with the cubs; about the throne in the sealed room; about the commands his godfather had given him, as well as about the peasants he had seen trampling down the corn, and the calf that ran out when its mistress called it.

"I have seen that one cannot destroy evil by evil," said he, "but I cannot understand how it is to be destroyed. Teach me how it can be done."

"Tell me," replied the hermit, "what else you have seen on your way."

The godson told him about the woman washing the table, and the men making cart-wheels, and the drovers fighting their fire.

The hermit listened to it all, and then went back to his cell and brought out an old jagged axe.

"Come with me," said he.

When they had gone some way, the hermit pointed to a tree.

"Cut it down," he said.

The godson felled the tree.

"Now chop it into three," said the hermit.

The godson chopped the tree into three pieces. Then the hermit went back to his cell, and brought out some blazing sticks.

"Burn those three logs," said he.

So the godson made a fire, and burnt the three logs till only three charred stumps remained.

"Now plant them half in the ground, like this."

The godson did so.

"You see that river at the foot of the hill. Bring water from there in your mouth, and water these stumps. Water this stump, as you taught the woman: this one, as you taught the wheel-wrights: and this one, as you taught the drovers. When all three have taken root and from these charred stumps apple trees have sprung, you will know how to destroy evil in men, and will have atoned for all your sins."

Having said this, the hermit returned to his cell. The godson pondered for a long time, but could not understand what the hermit meant. Nevertheless he set to work to do as he had been told.

X

The godson went down to the river, filled his mouth with water, and returning, emptied it on to one of the charred stumps. This he did again and again, and watered all three stumps. When he was hungry and quite tired out, he went to the cell to ask the old hermit for some food. He opened the door, and there upon a bench he saw the old man lying dead. The godson looked round for food, and he found some dried bread and ate a little of it. Then he took a spade and set to work to dig the hermit's grave. During the night he carried water and watered the stumps, and in the day he dug the grave. He had hardly finished the grave, and was about to bury the corpse, when some people from the village came, bringing food for the old man.

The people heard that the old hermit was dead, and that he had given the godson his blessing, and left him in his place. So they buried the old man, gave the bread they had brought to the godson, and promising to bring him some more, they went away.

The godson remained in the old man's place. There he lived, eating the food people brought him, and doing as he had been told: carrying water from the river in his mouth and watering the charred stumps.

He lived thus for a year, and many people visited him. His fame spread abroad, as a holy man who lived in the forest and brought water from the bottom of a hill in his mouth to water charred stumps for the salvation of his soul. People flocked to see him. Rich merchants drove up bringing him presents, but he kept only the barest necessaries for himself and gave the rest away to the poor.

And so the godson lived: carrying water in his mouth and

watering the stumps half the day, and resting and receiving people the other half. And he began to think that this was the way he had been told to live in order to destroy evil and atone for his sins.

He spent two years in this manner, not omitting for a single day to water the stumps. But still not one of them sprouted.

One day, as he sat in his cell, he heard a man ride past, singing as he went. The godson came out to see what sort of a man it was. He saw a strong young fellow, well dressed, and mounted on a handsome, well-saddled horse.

The godson stopped him, and asked him who he was, and where he was going.

"I am a robber," the man answered, drawing rein. "I ride about the highways killing people; and the more I kill, the merrier are the songs I sing."

The godson was horror-struck, and thought:

"How can the evil be destroyed in such a man as this? It is easy to speak to those who come to me of their own accord and confess their sins. But this one boasts of the evil he does."

So he said nothing, and turned away, thinking: "What am I to do now? This robber may take to riding about here, and he will frighten away the people. They will leave off coming to me. It will be a loss to them, and I shall not know how to live."

So the godson turned back, and said to the robber:

"People come to me here, not to boast of their sins, but to repent, and to pray for forgiveness. Repent of your sins, if you fear God; but if there is no repentance in your heart, then go away and never come here again. Do not trouble me, and do not frighten people away from me. If you do not hearken, God will punish you."

The robber laughed:

"I am not afraid of God, and I will not listen to you. You are not my master," said he. "You live by your piety, and I by my robbery. We all must live. You may teach the old women who come to you, but you have nothing to teach me. And because you have reminded me of God, I will kill two more men tomorrow. I would kill you, but I do not want to soil my hands just now. See that in future you keep out of my way!"

Having uttered this threat, the robber rode away. He did not come again, and the godson lived in peace, as before, for eight more years.

XI

One night the godson watered his stumps, and, after returning to his cell, he sat down to rest, and watched the footpath, wondering if someone would soon come. But no one came at all that day. He sat alone till evening, feeling lonely and dull, and he thought about his past life. He remembered how the robber had reproached him for living by his piety; and he reflected on his way of life. "I am not living as the hermit commanded me to," thought he. "The hermit laid a penance upon me, and I have made both a living and fame out of it; and have been so tempted by it, that now I feel dull when people do not come to me; and when they do come, I only rejoice because they praise my holiness. That is not how one should live. I have been led astray by love of praise. I have not atoned for my past sins, but have added fresh ones. I will go to another part of the forest where people will not find me; and I will live so as to atone for my old sins and commit no fresh ones."

Having come to this conclusion the godson filled a bag with dried bread and, taking a spade, left the cell and started for a ravine he knew of in a lonely spot, where he could dig himself a cave and hide from the people.

As he was going along with his bag and his spade he saw

the robber riding towards him. The godson was frightened, and started to run away, but the robber overtook him.

"Where are you going?" asked the robber.

The godson told him he wished to get away from the people and live somewhere where no one would come to him. This surprised the robber.

"What will you live on, if people do not come to see you?" asked he.

The godson had not even thought of this, but the robber's question reminded him that food would be necessary.

"On what God pleases to give me," he replied.

The robber said nothing, and rode away.

"Why did I not say anything to him about his way of life?" thought the godson. "He might repent now. Today he seems in a gentler mood, and has not threatened to kill me." And he shouted to the robber:

"You have still to repent of your sins. You cannot escape from God."

The robber turned his horse, and drawing a knife from his girdle threatened the hermit with it. The latter was alarmed, and ran away further into the forest.

The robber did not follow him, but only shouted:

"Twice I have let you off, old man, but next time you come in my way I will kill you!"

Having said this, he rode away. In the evening when the godson went to water his stumps—one of them was sprouting! A little apple tree was growing out of it.

XII

After hiding himself from everybody, the godson lived all alone. When his supply of bread was exhausted, he thought: "Now I must go and look for some roots to eat." He had not gone far, however, before he saw a bag of dried bread hanging on a branch. He took it down, and as long as it lasted he lived upon that.

When he had eaten it all, he found another bagful on the same branch. So he lived on, his only trouble being his fear of the robber. Whenever he heard the robber passing, he hid, thinking:

"He may kill me before I have had time to atone for my sins."

In this way he lived for ten more years. The one apple tree continued to grow, but the other two stumps remained exactly as they were.

One morning the godson rose early and went to his work. By the time he had thoroughly moistened the ground round the stumps, he was tired out and sat down to rest. As he sat there he thought to himself:

"I have sinned, and have become afraid of death. It may be God's will that I should redeem my sins by death."

Hardly had this thought crossed his mind when he heard the robber riding up, swearing at something. When the godson heard this, he thought:

"No evil and no good can befall me from anyone but from God."

And he went to meet the robber. He saw the robber was not alone, but behind him on the saddle sat another man, gagged, and bound hand and foot. The man was doing nothing, but the robber was abusing him violently. The godson went up and stood in front of the horse.

"Where are you taking this man?" he asked.

"Into the forest," replied the robber. "He is a merchant's son, and will not tell me where his father's money is hidden. I am going to flog him till he tells me."

And the robber spurred on his horse, but the godson caught hold of his bridle, and would not let him pass.

"Let this man go!" he said.

The robber grew angry, and raised his arm to strike.

"Would you like a taste of what I am going to give this man? Have I not promised to kill you? Let go!"

The godson was not afraid.

"You shall not go," said he. "I do not fear you. I fear no one but God, and He wills that I should not let you pass. Set this man free!"

The robber frowned, and snatching out his knife, cut the ropes with which the merchant's son was bound, and set him free.

"Get away both of you," he said, "and beware how you cross my path again."

The merchant's son jumped down and ran away. The robber was about to ride on, but the godson stopped him again, and again spoke to him about giving up his evil life. The robber heard him to the end in silence, and then rode away without a word.

The next morning the godson went to water his stumps and lo! The second stump was sprouting. A second young apple tree had begun to grow.

XIII

Another ten years had gone by. The godson was sitting quietly one day, desiring nothing, fearing nothing, and with a heart full of joy.

"What blessings God showers on men!" thought he. "Yet how needlessly they torment themselves. What prevents them from living happily?"

And remembering all the evil in men, and the troubles they bring upon themselves, his heart filled with pity.

"It is wrong of me to live as I do," he said to himself. "I must go and teach others what I have myself learnt."

Hardly had he thought this, when he heard the robber approaching. He let him pass, thinking:

"It is no good talking to him, he will not understand."

That was his first thought, but he changed his mind and went out into the road. He saw that the robber was gloomy, and was riding with downcast eyes. The godson looked at him, pitied him, and running up to him laid his hand upon his knee.

"Brother, dear," said he, "have some pity on your own soul! In you lives the spirit of God. You suffer, and torment others, and lay up more and more suffering for the future. Yet God loves you, and has prepared such blessings for you. Do not ruin yourself utterly. Change your life!"

The robber frowned and turned away.

"Leave me alone!" said he.

But the godson held the robber still faster, and began to weep.

Then the robber lifted his eyes and looked at the godson. He looked at him for a long time, and alighting from his horse, fell on his knees at the godson's feet.

"You have overcome me, old man," said he. "For twenty years I have resisted you, but now you have conquered me. Do what you will with me, for I have no more power over myself. When you first tried to persuade me, it only angered me more. Only when you hid yourself from men did I begin to consider your words: for I saw then that you asked nothing of them for yourself. Since that day I have brought food for you, hanging it upon the tree."

Then the godson remembered that the woman got her table clean only after she had rinsed her cloth. In the same way, it was only when he ceased caring about himself, and cleansed his own heart, that he was able to cleanse the hearts of others.

The robber went on.

"When I saw that you did not fear death, my heart turned."

Then the godson remembered that the wheel-wrights could not bend the rims until they had fixed their block. So, not till he had cast away the fear of death and made his life fast in God, could he subdue this man's unruly heart.

"But my heart did not quite melt," continued the robber, "until you pitied me and wept for me."

The godson, full of joy, led the robber to the place where the stumps were. And when they got there, they saw that from the third stump an apple tree had begun to sprout. And the godson remembered that the drovers had not been able to light the damp wood until the fire had burnt up well. So it was only when his own heart burnt warmly, that another's heart had been kindled by it.

And the godson was full of joy that he had at last atoned for his sins.

He told all this to the robber, and died. The robber buried him, and lived as the godson had commanded him, teaching to others what the godson had taught him.

The Coffee House of Surat

[Adapted by Tolstoy in 1887 from Bernardin de Saint-Pierre's French short story 'Le café de Surate' (1791). Published in 1893 in *Severny Vestnik*, a popular Russian literary magazine. The version reproduced below has been taken from *Twenty-three Tales* (1906) translated by Louise and Aylmer Maude.]

(AFTER BERNARDIN DE SAINT-PIERRE)

In the town of Surat, in India, was a coffee house where many travellers and foreigners from all parts of the world met and conversed.

One day a learned Persian theologian visited this coffee house. He was a man who had spent his life studying the nature of the Deity, and reading and writing books upon the subject. He had thought, read, and written so much about God, that eventually he lost his wits, became quite confused, and ceased even to believe in the existence of a God. The Shah, hearing of this, had banished him from Persia.

After having argued all his life about the First Cause, this unfortunate theologian had ended by quite perplexing himself, and instead of understanding that he had lost his own reason, he began to think that there was no higher Reason controlling the universe.

This man had an African slave who followed him everywhere. When the theologian entered the coffee house, the slave remained outside, near the door, sitting on a stone in the glare of the sun, and driving away the flies that buzzed around him. The Persian having settled down on a divan in the coffee house, ordered himself a cup of opium. When he had drunk it and the opium had begun to quicken the workings of his brain, he addressed his slave through the open door:

"Tell me, wretched slave," said he, "do you think there is a God, or not?"

"Of course there is," said the slave, and immediately drew from under his girdle a small idol of wood.

"There," said he, "that is the God who has guarded me from the day of my birth. Everyone in our country worships the fetish tree, from the wood of which this God was made."

This conversation between the theologian and his slave was listened to with surprise by the other guests in the coffee house. They were astonished at the master's question, and yet more so at the slave's reply.

One of them, a Brahmin, on hearing the words spoken by the slave, turned to him and said:

"Miserable fool! Is it possible you believe that God can be carried under a man's girdle? There is one God—Brahma, and he is greater than the whole world, for he created it. Brahma is the One, the mighty God, and in His honour are built the temples on the Ganges' banks, where his true priests, the Brahmins, worship him. They know the true God, and none but they. A thousand score of years have passed, and yet through revolution after revolution these priests have held their sway, because Brahma, the one true God, has protected them."

So spoke the Brahmin, thinking to convince everyone; but a Jewish broker who was present replied to him, and said:

"No! The temple of the true God is not in India. Neither does God protect the Brahmin caste. The true God is not the God of the Brahmins, but of Abraham, Isaac, and Jacob. None does He protect but His chosen people, the Israelites. From the commencement of the world, our nation has been beloved of Him, and ours alone. If we are now scattered over the whole earth, it is but to try us; for God has promised that He will one day gather His people together in Jerusalem. Then, with the Temple of Jerusalem—the wonder of the ancient world—restored to its splendour, shall Israel be established a ruler over all nations."

So spoke the Jew, and burst into tears. He wished to say more, but an Italian missionary who was there interrupted him.

"What you are saying is untrue," said he to the Jew. "You attribute injustice to God. He cannot love your nation above the rest. Nay rather, even if it be true that of old He favoured the Israelites, it is now nineteen hundred years since they angered Him, and caused Him to destroy their nation and scatter them over the earth, so that their faith makes no converts and has died out except here and there. God shows preference to no nation, but calls all who wish to be saved to the bosom of the Catholic Church of Rome, the one outside whose borders no salvation can be found."

So spoke the Italian. But a Protestant minister, who happened to be present, growing pale, turned to the Catholic missionary and exclaimed:

"How can you say that salvation belongs to your religion? Those only will be saved, who serve God according to the Gospel, in spirit and in truth, as bidden by the word of Christ."

Then a Turk, an office-holder in the custom-house at Surat, who was sitting in the coffee house smoking a pipe, turned with an air of superiority to both the Christians.

"Your belief in your Roman religion is vain," said he. "It was superseded twelve hundred years ago by the true faith: that of Mohammed! You cannot but observe how the true Mohammed faith continues to spread both in Europe and Asia, and even in the enlightened country of China. You say yourselves that God has rejected the Jews; and, as a proof, you quote the fact that the Jews are humiliated and their faith does not spread. Confess then the truth of Mohammedanism, for it is triumphant and spreads far and wide. None will be saved but the followers of Mohammed, God's latest prophet; and of them, only the followers of Omar, and not of Ali, for the latter are false to the faith."

To this the Persian theologian, who was of the sect of Ali, wished to reply; but by this time a great dispute had arisen among all the strangers of different faiths and creeds present. There were Abyssinian Christians, Llamas from Thibet, Ismailians and Fireworshippers. They all argued about the nature of God, and how He should be worshipped. Each of them asserted that in his country alone was the true God known and rightly worshipped.

Every one argued and shouted, except a Chinaman, a student of Confucius, who sat quietly in one corner of the coffee house, not joining in the dispute. He sat there drinking tea and listening to what the others said, but did not speak himself.

The Turk noticed him sitting there, and appealed to him, saying:

"You can confirm what I say, my good Chinaman. You hold your peace, but if you spoke I know you would uphold my opinion. Traders from your country, who come to me for assistance, tell me that though many religions have been introduced into China, you Chinese consider Mohammedanism the best of all, and adopt it willingly. Confirm, then, my words, and tell us your opinion of the true God and of His prophet."

"Yes, yes," said the rest, turning to the Chinaman, "let us hear what you think on the subject."

The Chinaman, the student of Confucius, closed his eyes, and thought a while. Then he opened them again, and drawing his hands out of the wide sleeves of his garment, and folding them on his breast, he spoke as follows, in a calm and quiet voice.

Sirs, it seems to me that it is chiefly pride that prevents men agreeing with one another on matters of faith. If you care to listen to me, I will tell you a story which will explain this by an example.

I came here from China on an English steamer which had been round the world. We stopped for fresh water, and landed on the east coast of the island of Sumatra. It was midday, and some of us, having landed, sat in the shade of some coconut palms by the seashore, not far from a native village. We were a party of men of different nationalities.

As we sat there, a blind man approached us. We learned afterwards that he had gone blind from gazing too long and too persistently at the sun, trying to find out what it is, in order to seize its light.

He strove a long time to accomplish this, constantly looking at the sun; but the only result was that his eyes were injured by its brightness, and he became blind.

Then he said to himself:

"The light of the sun is not a liquid; for if it were a liquid it would be possible to pour it from one vessel into another, and it would be moved, like water, by the wind. Neither is it fire; for if it were fire, water would extinguish it. Neither is light a spirit, for it is seen by the eye; nor is it matter, for it cannot be moved. Therefore, as the light of the sun is neither liquid, nor fire, nor spirit, nor matter, it is—nothing!"

So he argued, and, as a result of always looking at the sun and always thinking about it, he lost both his sight and his reason. And when he went quite blind, he became fully convinced that the sun did not exist.

With this blind man came a slave, who after placing his master in the shade of a cocoanut tree, picked up a cocoanut from the ground, and began making it into a night-light. He twisted a wick from the fibre of the coconut: squeezed oil from the nut in the shell, and soaked the wick in it.

As the slave sat doing this, the blind man sighed and said to him:

"Well, slave, was I not right when I told you there is no sun? Do you not see how dark it is? Yet people say there is a sun . . . But if so, what is it?"

"I do not know what the sun is," said the slave. "That is no business of mine. But I know what light is. Here I have made a night-light, by the help of which I can serve you and find anything I want in the hut."

And the slave picked up the coconut shell, saying:

"This is my sun."

A lame man with crutches, who was sitting near by, heard these words, and laughed:

"You have evidently been blind all your life," said he to the blind man, "not to know what the sun is. I will tell you what it is. The sun is a ball of fire, which rises every morning out of the sea and goes down again among the mountains of our island each evening. We have all seen this, and if you had had your eyesight you too would have seen it."

A fisherman, who had been listening to the conversation said:

"It is plain enough that you have never been beyond your own island. If you were not lame, and if you had been out as I have in a fishing-boat, you would know that the sun does not set among the mountains of our island, but as it rises from the ocean every morning so it sets again in the sea every night. What I am telling you is true, for I see it every day with my own eyes."

Then an Indian who was of our party, interrupted him by saying:

"I am astonished that a reasonable man should talk such nonsense. How can a ball of fire possibly descend into the water and not be extinguished? The sun is not a ball of fire at all, it is the Deity named Deva, who rides for ever in a chariot round the golden mountain, Meru. Sometimes the evil serpents Ragu and Ketu attack Deva and swallow him: and then the earth is dark. But our priests pray that the Deity may be released, and then he is set free. Only such ignorant men as you, who have never been beyond their own island, can imagine that the sun shines for their country alone."

Then the master of an Egyptian vessel, who was present, spoke in his turn.

"No," said he, "you also are wrong. The sun is not a Deity, and does not move only round India and its golden mountain. I have sailed much on the Black Sea, and along the coasts of Arabia, and have been to Madagascar and to the Philippines. The sun lights the whole earth, and not India alone. It does not circle round one mountain, but rises far in the East, beyond the Isles of Japan, and sets far, far away in the West, beyond the islands of England. That is why the Japanese call their country 'Nippon,' that is, 'the birth of the sun.' I know this well, for I have myself seen much, and heard more from my grandfather, who sailed to the very ends of the sea."

He would have gone on, but an English sailor from our ship interrupted him.

"There is no country," he said "where people know so much about the sun's movements as in England. The sun, as everyone in England knows, rises nowhere and sets nowhere. It is always moving round the earth. We can be sure of this for we have just been round the world ourselves, and nowhere knocked up against the sun. Wherever we went, the sun showed itself in the morning and hid itself at night, just as it does here."

And the Englishman took a stick and, drawing circles on the sand, tried to explain how the sun moves in the heavens and goes round the world. But he was unable to explain it clearly, and pointing to the ship's pilot said:

"This man knows more about it than I do. He can explain it properly."

The pilot, who was an intelligent man, had listened in silence to the talk till he was asked to speak. Now everyone turned to him, and he said:

"You are all misleading one another, and are yourselves deceived. The sun does not go round the earth, but the earth goes round the sun, revolving as it goes, and turning towards the sun in the course of each twenty-four hours, not only Japan, and the Philippines, and Sumatra where we now are, but Africa, and Europe, and America, and many lands besides. The sun does not shine for some one mountain, or for some one island, or for some one sea, nor even for one earth alone, but for other planets as well as our earth. If you would only look up at the heavens, instead of at the ground beneath your own feet, you might all understand this, and would then no longer suppose that the sun shines for you, or for your country alone."

Thus spoke the wise pilot, who had voyaged much about the world, and had gazed much upon the heavens above.

"So on matters of faith," continued the Chinaman, the student of Confucius, "it is pride that causes error and discord among men. As with the sun, so it is with God. Each man wants to have a special God of his own, or at least a special God for his native land. Each nation wishes to confine in its own temples Him, whom the world cannot contain.

"Can any temple compare with that which God Himself has built to unite all men in one faith and one religion?

"All human temples are built on the model of this temple, which is God's own world. Every temple has its fonts, its vaulted roof, its lamps, its pictures or sculptures, its inscriptions, its books of the law, its offerings, its altars and its priests. But in what temple is there such a font as the ocean; such a vault as that of the heavens; such lamps as the sun, moon, and stars; or any figures to be compared with living, loving, mutually helpful men? Where are there any records of God's goodness so easy to understand as the blessings which God has strewn abroad for man's happiness? Where is there any book of the law so clear to each man as that written in his heart? What sacrifices equal the self-denials which loving men and women make for one another? And what altar can be compared with the heart of a good man, on which God Himself accepts the sacrifice?

"The higher a man's conception of God, the better will he know Him. And the better he knows God, the nearer will he draw to Him, imitating His goodness, His mercy, and His love of man.

"Therefore, let him who sees the sun's whole light filling the world, refrain from blaming or despising the superstitious man, who in his own idol sees one ray of that same light. Let him not despise even the unbeliever who is blind and cannot see the sun at all."

So spoke the Chinaman, the student of Confucius; and all who were present in the coffee house were silent, and disputed no more as to whose faith was the best.

The Young Tsar

[Written in 1894. The version here is taken from the collection
The Forged Coupon and Other Stories (1911) translated by
Charles Theodore Hagberg Wright.]

The young Tsar had just ascended the throne. For five weeks he had worked without ceasing, in the way that Tsars are accustomed to work. He had been attending to reports, signing papers, receiving ambassadors and high officials who came to be presented to him, and reviewing troops. He was tired, and as a traveller exhausted by heat and thirst longs for a draught of water and for rest, so he longed for a respite of just one day at least from receptions, from speeches, from parades—a few free hours to spend like an ordinary human being with his young, clever, and beautiful wife, to whom he had been married only a month before.

It was Christmas Eve. The young Tsar had arranged to have a complete rest that evening. The night before he had worked till very late at documents which his ministers of state had left for him to examine. In the morning he was present at the *Te Deum*, and then at a military service. In the afternoon he received official visitors; and later he had been obliged to listen to the reports of three ministers of state, and had given his assent to many important matters. In his conference with the Minister of Finance he had agreed to an increase of duties on imported goods, which should in the future add many millions to the State revenues. Then he sanctioned the sale of brandy by the Crown in various parts of the country, and signed a decree permitting the sale of alcohol in villages having markets. This was also calculated to increase the principal revenue to the State, which was derived from the sale of spirits. He had also approved of the issuing of a new gold loan required for a financial negotiation. The Minister of justice having reported on the complicated case of the succession of the Baron Snyders, the young Tsar confirmed the decision by his signature; and also approved the new rules relating to the application of Article 1830 of the penal code, providing for the punishment of tramps. In his conference with the Minister of the Interior he ratified the order concerning the collection of taxes in arrears, signed the order settling what measures should be taken in regard to the persecution of religious dissenters, and also one providing for the continuance of martial law in those provinces where it had already been established. With the Minister of War he arranged for the nomination of a new Corps Commander for the raising of recruits, and for punishment of breach of discipline. These things kept him occupied till dinner-time, and even then his freedom was not complete. A number of high officials had been invited to dinner, and he was obliged to talk to them: not in the way he felt disposed to do, but according to what he was expected to say. At last the tiresome dinner was over, and the guests departed.

The young Tsar heaved a sigh of relief, stretched himself and retired to his apartments to take off his uniform with the decorations on it, and to don the jacket he used to wear before his accession to the throne. His young wife had also retired to take off her dinner-dress, remarking that she would join him presently.

When he had passed the row of footmen who were standing erect before him, and reached his room; when he had thrown off his heavy uniform and put on his jacket, the young Tsar felt glad to be free from work; and his heart was filled with a tender emotion which sprang from the consciousness of his freedom, of his joyous, robust young life, and of his love. He threw himself on the sofa, stretched out his legs upon it, leaned his head on his hand, fixed his gaze on the dull glass shade of the lamp, and then a sensation which he had not experienced since his childhood—the pleasure of going to sleep, and a drowsiness that was irresistible—suddenly came over him.

"My wife will be here presently and will find me asleep. No, I must not go to sleep," he thought. He let his elbow drop down, laid his cheek in the palm of his hand, made himself comfortable, and was so utterly happy that he only felt a desire not to be aroused from this delightful state.

And then what happens to all of us every day happened to him—he fell asleep without knowing himself when or how. He passed from one state into another without his will having any share in it, without even desiring it, and without regretting the state out of which he had passed. He fell into a heavy sleep which was like death. How long he had slept he did not know, but he was suddenly aroused by the soft touch of a hand upon his shoulder.

"It is my darling, it is she," he thought. "What a shame to have dozed off!"

But it was not she. Before his eyes, which were wide open and blinking at the light, she, that charming and beautiful creature whom he was expecting, did not stand, but he stood. Who he was the young Tsar did not know, but somehow it did not strike him that he was a stranger whom he had never seen before. It seemed as if he had known him for a long time and was fond of him, and as if he trusted him as he would trust himself. He had expected his beloved wife, but in her stead that man whom he had never seen before had come. Yet to the young Tsar, who was far from feeling regret or astonishment, it seemed not only a most natural, but also a necessary thing to happen.

"Come!" said the stranger.

"Yes, let us go," said the young Tsar, not knowing where he was to go, but quite aware that he could not help submitting to the command of the stranger. "But how shall we go?" he asked.

"In this way."

The stranger laid his hand on the Tsar's head, and the Tsar for a moment lost consciousness. He could not tell whether he had been unconscious a long or a short time, but when he recovered his senses he found himself in a strange place. The first thing he was aware of was a strong and stifling smell of sewage. The place in which he stood was a broad passage lit by the red glow of two dim lamps. Running along one side of the passage was a thick wall with windows protected by iron gratings. On the other side were doors secured with locks. In the passage stood a soldier, leaning up against the wall, asleep. Through the doors the young Tsar heard the muffled sound of living human beings: not of one alone, but of many. He was standing at the side of the young Tsar, and pressing his shoulder slightly with his soft hand, pushed him to the first door, unmindful of the sentry. The young Tsar felt he could not do otherwise than yield, and approached the door. To his amazement the sentry looked straight at him, evidently without seeing him, as he neither straightened himself up nor saluted, but yawned loudly and, lifting his hand, scratched the back of his neck. The door had a small hole, and in obedience to the pressure of the hand that pushed him, the young Tsar approached a step nearer and put his eye to the small opening. Close to the door, the foul smell that stifled him was stronger, and the young Tsar hesitated to go nearer, but the hand pushed him on. He leaned forward, put his eye close to the opening, and suddenly ceased to perceive the odour. The sight he saw deadened his sense of smell. In a large room, about ten yards long and six yards wide, there walked unceasingly from one end to the other, six men in long grey coats, some in felt boots, some barefoot. There were over twenty men in all in the room, but in that first moment the young Tsar only saw those who were walking with quick, even, silent steps. It was a horrid sight to watch the continual, quick, aimless movements of the men who passed and overtook each other, turning sharply when they reached the wall, never looking at one another, and evidently concentrated each on his own thoughts. The young Tsar had observed a similar sight one day when he was watching a tiger in a menagerie pacing rapidly with noiseless tread from one end of his cage to the other, waving its tail, silently turning when it reached the bars, and looking at nobody. Of these men one, apparently a young peasant, with curly hair, would have been handsome were it not for the unnatural pallor of his face, and the concentrated, wicked, scarcely human, look in his eyes. Another was a Jew, hairy and gloomy. The third was a lean old man, bald, with a beard that had been shaven and had since grown like bristles. The fourth was extraordinarily heavily built, with well-developed muscles, a low receding forehead and a flat nose. The fifth was hardly more than a boy, long, thin, obviously consumptive. The sixth was small and dark, with nervous, convulsive movements. He walked as if he were skipping, and muttered continuously to himself. They were all walking rapidly backwards and forwards past the hole through which the young Tsar was looking. He watched their faces and their gait with keen interest. Having examined them closely, he presently became aware of a number of other men at the back of the room, standing round, or lying on the shelf that served as a bed. Standing close to the door he also saw the pail which caused such an unbearable stench. On the shelf about ten men, entirely covered with their cloaks, were sleeping. A red-haired man with a huge beard was sitting sideways on the shelf, with his shirt off. He was examining it, lifting it up to the light, and evidently catching the vermin on it. Another man, aged and white as snow, stood with his profile turned towards the door. He was praying, crossing himself, and bowing low, apparently so absorbed in his devotions as to be oblivious of all around him.

"I see—this is a prison," thought the young Tsar. "They certainly deserve pity. It is a dreadful life. But it cannot be helped. It is their own fault."

But this thought had hardly come into his head before he, who was his guide, replied to it.

"They are all here under lock and key by your order. They have all been sentenced in your name. But far from meriting their present condition which is due to your human judgment, the greater part of them are far better than you or those who were their judges and who keep them here. This one"—he pointed to the handsome, curly-headed fellow—"is a murderer. I do not consider him more guilty than those who kill in war or in duelling, and are rewarded for their deeds. He had neither education nor moral guidance, and his life had been cast among thieves and drunkards. This lessens his guilt, but he has done wrong, nevertheless, in being a murderer. He killed a merchant, to rob him. The other man, the Jew, is a thief, one of a gang of thieves. That uncommonly strong fellow is a horse-stealer, and guilty also, but compared with others not as culpable. Look!"— and suddenly the young Tsar found himself in an open field on a vast frontier. On the right were potato fields; the plants had been rooted out, and were lying in heaps, blackened by the frost; in alternate streaks were rows of winter corn. In the distance a little village with its tiled roofs was visible; on the left were fields of winter corn, and fields of stubble. No one was to be seen on any side, save a black human figure in front at the border-line, a gun slung on his back, and at his feet a dog. On the spot where the young Tsar stood, sitting beside him, almost at his feet, was a young Russian soldier with a green band on his cap, and with his rifle slung over his shoulders, who was rolling up a paper to make a cigarette. The soldier was obviously unaware of the presence of the young Tsar and his companion, and had not heard them. He did now turn round when the Tsar, who was standing directly over the soldier, asked, "Where are we?" "On the Prussian frontier," his guide answered. Suddenly, far away in front of them, a shot was fired. The soldier jumped to his feet, and seeing two men running, bent low to the ground, hastily put his tobacco into his pocket, and ran after one of them. "Stop, or I'll shoot!" cried the soldier. The fugitive, without stopping, turned his head and called out something evidently abusive or blasphemous.

"Damn you!" shouted the soldier, who put one foot a little forward and stopped, after which, bending his head over his rifle, and raising his right hand, he rapidly adjusted something, took aim, and, pointing the gun in the direction of the fugitive, probably fired, although no sound was heard. "Smokeless powder, no doubt," thought the young Tsar, and looking after the fleeing man saw him take a few hurried steps, and bending lower and lower, fall to the ground and crawl on his hands and knees. At last he remained lying and did not move. The other fugitive, who was ahead of him, turned round and ran back to the man who was lying on the ground. He did something for him and then resumed his flight.

"What does all this mean?" asked the Tsar.

"These are the guards on the frontier, enforcing the revenue laws. That man was killed to protect the revenues of the State."

"Has he actually been killed?"

The guide again laid his hand upon the head of the young Tsar, and again the Tsar lost consciousness. When he had recovered his senses he found himself in a small room—the customs office. The dead body of a man, with a thin grizzled beard, an aquiline nose, and big eyes with the eyelids closed, was lying on the floor. His arms were thrown asunder, his feet bare, and his thick, dirty toes were turned up at right angles and stuck out straight. He had a wound in his side, and on his ragged cloth jacket, as well as on his blue shirt, were stains of clotted blood, which had turned black save for a few red spots here and there. A woman stood close to the wall, so wrapped up in shawls that her face could scarcely be seen. Motionless she gazed at the aquiline nose, the upturned feet, and the protruding eyeballs; sobbing and sighing, and drying her tears at long, regular intervals. A pretty girl of thirteen was standing at her mother's side, with her eyes and mouth wide open. A boy of eight clung to his mother's skirt, and looked intensely at his dead father without blinking.

From a door near them an official, an officer, a doctor, and a clerk with documents, entered. After them came a soldier, the one who had shot the man. He stepped briskly along behind his superiors, but the instant he saw the corpse he went suddenly pale, and quivered; and dropping his head stood still. When the official asked him whether that was the man who was escaping across the frontier, and at whom he had fired, he was unable to answer. His lips trembled, and his face twitched. "The s—s—s—" he began, but could not get out the words which he wanted to say. "The same, your excellency." The officials looked at each other and wrote something down.

"You see the beneficial results of that same system!"

In a room of sumptuous vulgarity two men sat drinking wine. One of them was old and grey, the other a young Jew. The young Jew was holding a roll of bank-notes in his hand, and was bargaining with the old man. He was buying smuggled goods.

"You've got 'em cheap," he said, smiling.

"Yes—but the risk—"

"This is indeed terrible," said the young Tsar; but it cannot be avoided. Such proceedings are necessary."

His companion made no response, saying merely, "Let us move on," and laid his hand again on the head of the Tsar. When the Tsar recovered consciousness, he was standing in a small room lit by a shaded lamp. A woman was sitting at the table sewing. A boy of eight was bending over the table, drawing, with his feet doubled up under him in the armchair. A student was reading aloud. The father and daughter of the family entered the room noisily.

"You signed the order concerning the sale of spirits," said the guide to the Tsar.

"Well?" said the woman.

"He's not likely to live."

"What's the matter with him?"

"They've kept him drunk all the time."

"It's not possible!" exclaimed the wife.

"It's true. And the boy's only nine years old, that Vania Moroshkine."

"What did you do to try to save him?" asked the wife.

"I tried everything that could be done. I gave him an emetic and put a mustard-plaster on him. He has every symptom of delirium tremens."

"It's no wonder—the whole family are drunkards. Annisia is only a little better than the rest, and even she is generally more or less drunk," said the daughter.

"And what about your temperance society?" the student asked his sister.

"What can we do when they are given every opportunity of drinking? Father tried to have the public-house shut up, but the law is against him. And, besides, when I was trying to convince Vasily Ermiline that it was disgraceful to keep a public-house and ruin the people with drink, he answered very haughtily, and indeed got the better of me before the crowd: 'But I have a license with the Imperial eagle on it. If there was anything wrong in my business, the Tsar wouldn't have issued a decree authorising it.' Isn't it terrible? The whole village has been drunk for the last three days. And as for feast days, it is simply horrible to think of! It has been proved conclusively that alcohol does no good in any case, but invariably does harm, and it has been demonstrated to be an absolute poison. Then, ninety-nine per cent of the crimes in the world are committed through its influence. We all know how the standard of morality and the general welfare improved at once in all the countries where drinking has been suppressed—like Sweden and Finland, and we know that it can be suppressed by exercising a moral influence over the masses. But in our country the class which could exert that influence—the Government, the Tsar and his officials—simply encourage drink. Their main revenues are drawn from the continual drunkenness of the people. They drink themselves—they are always drinking the health of somebody: 'Gentlemen, the Regiment!' The preachers drink, the bishops drink—"

Again the guide touched the head of the young Tsar, who again lost consciousness. This time he found himself in a peasant's cottage. The peasant—a man of forty, with red face and blood-shot eyes—was furiously striking the face of an old man, who tried in vain to protect himself from the blows. The younger peasant seized the beard of the old man and held it fast.

"For shame! To strike your father—!"

"I don't care, I'll kill him! Let them send me to Siberia, I don't care!"

The women were screaming. Drunken officials rushed into the cottage and separated father and son. The father had an arm broken and the son's beard was torn out. In the doorway a drunken girl was making violent love to an old besotted peasant.

"They are beasts!" said the young Tsar.

Another touch of his guide's hand and the young Tsar awoke in a new place. It was the office of the justice of the peace. A fat, bald-headed man, with a double chin and a chain round his neck, had just risen from his seat, and was reading the sentence in a loud voice, while a crowd of peasants stood behind the grating. There was a woman in rags in the crowd who did not rise. The guard gave her a push.

"Asleep! I tell you to stand up!" The woman rose.

"According to the decree of his Imperial Majesty—" the judge began reading the sentence. The case concerned that very woman. She had taken away half a bundle of oats as she was passing the thrashing-floor of a landowner. The justice of the peace sentenced her to two months' imprisonment. The landowner whose oats had been stolen was among the audience. When the judge adjourned the court the landowner approached, and shook hands, and the judge entered into conversation with him. The next case was about a stolen samovar. Then there was a trial about some timber which had been cut, to the detriment of the landowner. Some peasants were being tried for having assaulted the constable of the district.

When the young Tsar again lost consciousness, he awoke to find himself in the middle of a village, where he saw hungry, half-frozen children and the wife of the man who had assaulted the constable broken down from overwork.

Then came a new scene. In Siberia, a tramp is being flogged with the lash, the direct result of an order issued by the Minister of justice. Again oblivion, and another scene. The family of a Jewish watchmaker is evicted for being too poor. The children are crying, and the Jew, Isaaks, is greatly distressed. At last they come to an arrangement, and he is allowed to stay on in the lodgings.

The chief of police takes a bribe. The governor of the province also secretly accepts a bribe. Taxes are being collected. In the village, while a cow is sold for payment, the police inspector is bribed by a factory owner, who thus escapes taxes altogether. And again a village court scene, and a sentence carried into execution—the lash!

"Ilia Vasilievich, could you not spare me that?"

"No."

The peasant burst into tears. "Well, of course, Christ suffered, and He bids us suffer too."

Then other scenes. The Stundists—a sect—being broken up and dispersed; the clergy refusing first to marry, then to bury a Protestant. Orders given concerning the passage of the Imperial railway train. Soldiers kept sitting in the mud—cold, hungry, and cursing. Decrees issued relating to the educational institutions of the Empress Mary Department. Corruption rampant in the foundling homes. An undeserved monument. Thieving among the clergy. The reinforcement of the political police. A woman being searched. A prison for convicts who are sentenced to be deported. A man being hanged for murdering a shop assistant.

Then the result of military discipline: soldiers wearing uniform and scoffing at it. A gipsy encampment. The son of a millionaire exempted from military duty, while the only support of a large family is forced to serve. The university: a teacher relieved of military service, while the most gifted musicians are compelled to perform it. Soldiers and their debauchery—and the spreading of disease.

Then a soldier who has made an attempt to desert. He is being tried. Another is on trial for striking an officer who has insulted his mother. He is put to death. Others, again, are tried for having refused to shoot. The runaway soldier sent to a disciplinary battalion and flogged to death. Another, who is guiltless, flogged, and his wounds sprinkled with salt till he dies. One of the superior officers stealing money belonging to the soldiers. Nothing but drunkenness, debauchery, gambling, and arrogance on the part of the authorities.

What is the general condition of the people: the children are half-starving and degenerate; the houses are full of vermin; an everlasting dull round of labour, of submission, and of sadness. On the other hand: ministers, governors of provinces, covetous, ambitious, full of vanity, and anxious to inspire fear.

"But where are men with human feelings?"

"I will show you where they are."

Here is the cell of a woman in solitary confinement at Schlusselburg. She is going mad. Here is another woman—a girl—indisposed, violated by soldiers. A man in exile, alone, embittered, half-dead. A prison for convicts condemned to hard labour, and women flogged. They are many.

Tens of thousands of the best people. Some shut up in prisons, others ruined by false education, by the vain desire to bring them up as we wish. But not succeeding in this, whatever might have been is ruined as well, for it is made impossible. It is as if we were trying to make buckwheat out of corn sprouts by splitting the ears. One may spoil the corn, but one could never change it to buckwheat. Thus all the youth of the world, the entire younger generation, is being ruined.

But woe to those who destroy one of these little ones, woe to you if you destroy even one of them. On your soul, however, are hosts of them, who have been ruined in your name, all of those over whom your power extends.

"But what can I do?" exclaimed the Tsar in despair. "I do not wish to torture, to flog, to corrupt, to kill any one! I only want the welfare of all. Just as I yearn for happiness myself, so I want the world to be happy as well. Am I actually responsible for everything that is done in my name? What can I do? What am I to do to rid myself of such a responsibility? What can I do? I do not admit that the responsibility for all this is mine. If I felt myself responsible for one-hundredth part of it, I would shoot myself on the spot. It would not be possible to live if that were true. But how can I put an end, to all this evil? It is bound up with the very existence of the State. I am the head of the State! What am I to do? Kill myself? Or abdicate? But that would mean renouncing my duty. O God, O God, God, help me!" He burst into tears and awoke.

"How glad I am that it was only a dream," was his first thought. But when he began to recollect what he had seen in his dream, and to compare it with actuality, he realised that the problem propounded to him in dream remained just as important and as insoluble now that he was awake. For the first time the young Tsar became aware of the heavy responsibility weighing on him, and was aghast. His thoughts no longer turned to the young Queen and to the happiness he had anticipated for that evening, but became centred on the unanswerable question which hung over him: "What was to be done?"

In a state of great agitation he arose and went into the next room. An old courtier, a co-worker and friend of his father's, was standing there in the middle of the room in conversation with the young Queen, who was on her way to join her husband. The young Tsar approached them, and addressing his conversation principally to the old courtier, told him what he had seen in his dream and what doubts the dream had left in his mind.

"That is a noble idea. It proves the rare nobility of your spirit," said the old man. "But forgive me for speaking frankly—you are too kind to be an emperor, and you exaggerate your responsibility. In the first place, the state of things is not as you imagine it to be. The people are not poor. They are well-to-do. Those who are poor are poor through their own fault. Only the guilty are punished, and if an unavoidable mistake does sometimes occur, it is like a thunder-bolt—an accident, or the will of God. You have but one responsibility: to fulfil your task courageously and to retain the power that is given to you. You wish the best for your people and God sees that. As for the errors which you have committed unwittingly, you can pray for forgiveness, and God will guide you and pardon you. All the more because you have done nothing that demands forgiveness, and there never have been and never will be men possessed of such extraordinary qualities as you and your father. Therefore all we implore you to do is to live, and to reward our endless devotion and love with your favour, and every one, save scoundrels who deserve no happiness, will be happy."

"What do you think about that?" the young Tsar asked his wife.

"I have a different opinion," said the clever young woman, who had been brought up in a free country. "I am glad you had that dream, and I agree with you that there are grave responsibilities resting upon you. I have often thought about it with great anxiety, and I think there is a simple means of casting off a part of the responsibility you are unable to bear, if not all of it. A large proportion of the power which is too heavy for you, you should delegate to the people, to its representatives, reserving for yourself only the supreme control, that is, the general direction of the affairs of State."

The Queen had hardly ceased to expound her views, when the old courtier began eagerly to refute her arguments, and they started a polite but very heated discussion.

For a time the young Tsar followed their arguments, but presently he ceased to be aware of what they said, listening only to the voice of him who had been his guide in the dream, and who was now speaking audibly in his heart.

"You are not only the Tsar," said the voice, "but more. You are a human being, who only yesterday came into this world, and will perchance tomorrow depart out of it. Apart from your duties as a Tsar, of which that old man is now speaking, you have more immediate duties not by any means to be disregarded; human duties, not the duties of a Tsar towards his subjects, which are only accidental, but an eternal duty, the duty of a man in his relation to God, the duty toward your own soul, which is to save it, and also, to serve God in establishing his kingdom on earth. You are not to be guarded in your actions either by what has been or what will be, but only by what it is your own duty to do.

He opened his eyes—his wife was awakening him. Which of the three courses the young Tsar chose, will be told in fifty years.

Master and Man

[Tolstoy had come up with this short story in his dream in
September 1894. He began writing it soon after and completed
it the following year after much reworking. It was first published
in February 1895. The story has been considered Tolstoy's
masterpiece. The version here is a translation by
Louise and Aylmer Maude.]

I

It happened in the seventies in winter, on the day after St. Nicholas's Day. There was a fete in the parish and the innkeeper, Vasili Andreevich Brekhunov, a Second Guild merchant, being a church elder had to go to church, and had also to entertain his relatives and friends at home.

But when the last of them had gone he at once began to prepare to drive over to see a neighbouring proprietor about a grove which he had been bargaining over for a long time. He was now in a hurry to start, lest buyers from the town might forestall him in making a profitable purchase.

The youthful landowner was asking ten thousand roubles for the grove simply because Vasili Andreevich was offering seven thousand. Seven thousand was, however, only a third of its real value. Vasili Andreevich might perhaps have got it down to his own price, for the woods were in his district and he had a long-standing agreement with the other village dealers that no one should run up the price in another's district, but he had now learnt that some timber-dealers from town meant to bid for the Goryachkin grove, and he resolved to go at once and get the matter settled. So as soon as the feast was over, he took seven hundred roubles from his strong box, added to them two thousand three hundred roubles of church money he had in his keeping, so as to make up the sum to three thousand; carefully counted the notes, and having put them into his pocket-book made haste to start.

Nikita, the only one of Vasili Andreevich's labourers who was not drunk that day, ran to harness the horse. Nikita, though an habitual drunkard, was not drunk that day because since the last day before the fast, when he had drunk his coat and leather boots, he had sworn off drink and had kept his vow for two months, and was still keeping it despite the temptation of the vodka that had been drunk everywhere during the first two days of the feast.

Nikita was a peasant of about fifty from a neighbouring village, "not a manager" as the peasants said of him, meaning that he was not the thrifty head of a household but lived most of his time away from home as a labourer. He was valued everywhere for his industry, dexterity, and strength at work, and still more for his kindly and pleasant temper. But he never settled down anywhere for long because about twice a year, or even oftener, he had a drinking bout, and then besides spending all his clothes on drink he became turbulent and quarrelsome. Vasili Andreevich himself had turned him away several times, but had afterwards taken him back again—valuing his honesty, his kindness to animals, and especially his cheapness. Vasili Andreevich did not pay Nikita the eighty roubles a year such a man was worth, but only about forty, which he gave him haphazard, in small sums, and even that mostly not in cash but in goods from his own shop and at high prices.

Nikita's wife Martha, who had once been a handsome vigorous woman, managed the homestead with the help of her son and two daughters, and did not urge Nikita to live at home: first because she had been living for some twenty years already with a cooper, a peasant from another village who lodged in their house; and secondly because though she managed her husband as she pleased when he was sober, she feared him like fire when he was drunk. Once when he had got drunk at home, Nikita, probably to make up for his submissiveness when sober, broke open her box, took out her best clothes, snatched up an axe, and chopped all her undergarments and dresses to bits. All the wages Nikita earned went to his wife, and he raised no objection to that. So now, two days before the holiday, Martha had been twice to see Vasili Andreevich and had got from him wheat flour, tea, sugar, and a quart of vodka, the lot costing three roubles, and also five roubles in cash, for which she thanked him as for a special favour, though he owed Nikita at least twenty roubles.

"What agreement did we ever draw up with you?" said Vasili Andreevich to Nikita. "If you need anything, take it; you will work it off. I'm not like others to keep you waiting, and making up accounts and reckoning fines. We deal straight-forwardly. You serve me and I don't neglect you."

And when saying this Vasili Andreevich was honestly convinced that he was Nikita's benefactor, and he knew how to put it so plausibly that all those who depended on him for their money, beginning with Nikita, confirmed him in the conviction that he was their benefactor and did not overreach them.

"Yes, I understand, Vasili Andreevich. You know that I serve you and take as much pains as I would for my own father. I understand very well!" Nikita would reply. He was quite aware that Vasili Andreevich was cheating him, but at the same time he felt that it was useless to try to clear up his accounts with him or explain his side of the matter, and that as long as he had nowhere to go he must accept what he could get.

Now, having heard his master's order to harness, he went as usual cheerfully and willingly to the shed, stepping briskly and easily on his rather turned-in feet; took down from a nail the heavy tasselled leather bridle, and jingling the rings of the bit went to the closed stable where the horse he was to harness was standing by himself.

"What, feeling lonely, feeling lonely, little silly?" said Nikita in answer to the low whinny with which he was greeted by the good-tempered, medium-sized bay stallion, with a rather slanting crupper, who stood alone in the shed. "Now then, now then, there's time enough. Let me water you first," he went on, speaking to the horse just as to someone who understood the words he was using, and having whisked the dusty, grooved back of the well-fed young stallion with the skirt of his coat, he put a bridle on his handsome head, straightened his ears and forelock, and having taken off his halter led him out to water.

Picking his way out of the dung-strewn stable, Mukhorty frisked, and making play with his hind leg pretended that he meant to kick Nikita, who was running at a trot beside him to the pump.

"Now then, now then, you rascal!" Nikita called out, well knowing how carefully Mukhorty threw out his hind leg just to touch his greasy sheepskin coat but not to strike him—a trick Nikita much appreciated.

After a drink of the cold water the horse sighed, moving his strong wet lips, from the hairs of which transparent drops fell into the trough; then standing still as if in thought, he suddenly gave a loud snort.

"If you don't want any more, you needn't. But don't go asking for any later," said Nikita quite seriously and fully explaining his conduct to Mukhorty. Then he ran back to the shed pulling the playful young horse, who wanted to gambol all over the yard, by the rein.

There was no one else in the yard except a stranger, the cook's husband, who had come for the holiday.

"Go and ask which sledge is to be harnessed—the wide one or the small one—there's a good fellow!"

The cook's husband went into the house, which stood on an iron foundation and was iron-roofed, and soon returned saying that the little one was to be harnessed. By that time Nikita had put the collar and brass-studded belly-band on Mukhorty and, carrying a light, painted shaft-bow in one hand, was leading the horse with the other up to two sledges that stood in the shed.

"All right, let it be the little one!" he said, backing the intelligent horse, which all the time kept pretending to bite him, into the shafts, and with the aid of the cook's husband he proceeded to harness. When everything was nearly ready and only the reins had to be adjusted, Nikita sent the other man to the shed for some straw and to the barn for a drugget.

"There, that's all right! Now, now, don't bristle up!" said Nikita, pressing down into the sledge the freshly threshed oat straw the cook's husband had brought. "And now let's spread the sacking like this, and the drugget over it. There, like that it will be comfortable sitting," he went on, suiting the action to the words and tucking the drugget all round over the straw to make a seat.

"Thank you, dear man. Things always go quicker with two working at it!" he added. And gathering up the leather reins fastened together by a brass ring, Nikita took the driver's seat and started the impatient horse over the frozen manure which lay in the yard, towards the gate.

"Uncle Nikita! I say, Uncle, Uncle!" a high-pitched voice shouted, and a seven-year-old boy in a black sheepskin coat, new white felt boots, and a warm cap, ran hurriedly out of the house into the yard. "Take me with you!" he cried, fastening up his coat as he ran.

"All right, come along, darling!" said Nikita, and stopping the sledge he picked up the master's pale thin little son, radiant with joy, and drove out into the road.

It was past two o'clock and the day was windy, dull, and cold, with more than twenty degrees Fahrenheit of frost. Half the sky was hidden by a lowering dark cloud. In the yard it was quiet, but in the street the wind was felt more keenly. The snow swept down from a neighbouring shed and whirled about in the corner near the bath-house.

Hardly had Nikita driven out of the yard and turned the horse's head to the house, before Vasili Andreevich emerged from the high porch in front of the house with a cigarette in his mouth and wearing a cloth-covered sheepskin coat tightly girdled low at his waist, and stepped onto the hard-trodden snow which squeaked under the leather soles of his felt boots, and stopped. Taking a last whiff of his cigarette he threw it down, stepped on it, and letting the smoke escape through his moustache and looking askance at the horse that was coming up, began to tuck in his sheepskin collar on both sides of his ruddy face, clean-shaven except for the moustache, so that his breath should not moisten the collar.

"See now! The young scamp is there already!" he exclaimed when he saw his little son in the sledge. Vasili Andreevich was excited by the vodka he had drunk with his visitors, and so he was even more pleased than usual with everything that was his and all that he did. The sight of his son, whom he always thought of as his heir, now gave him great satisfaction. He looked at him, screwing up his eyes and showing his long teeth.

His wife—pregnant, thin and pale, with her head and

shoulders wrapped in a shawl so that nothing of her face could be seen but her eyes—stood behind him in the vestibule to see him off.

"Now really, you ought to take Nikita with you," she said timidly, stepping out from the doorway.

Vasili Andreevich did not answer. Her words evidently annoyed him and he frowned angrily and spat.

"You have money on you," she continued in the same plaintive voice. "What if the weather gets worse! Do take him, for goodness' sake!"

"Why? Don't I know the road that I must needs take a guide?" exclaimed Vasili Andreevich, uttering every word very distinctly and compressing his lips unnaturally, as he usually did when speaking to buyers and sellers.

"Really you ought to take him. I beg you in God's name!" his wife repeated, wrapping her shawl more closely round her head.

"There, she sticks to it like a leech! . . . Where am I to take him?"

"I'm quite ready to go with you, Vasili Andreevich," said Nikita cheerfully. "But they must feed the horses while I am away," he added, turning to his master's wife.

"I'll look after them, Nikita dear. I'll tell Simon," replied the mistress.

"Well, Vasili Andreevich, am I to come with you?" said Nikita, awaiting a decision.

"It seems I must humour my old woman. But if you're coming you'd better put on a warmer cloak," said Vasili Andreevich, smiling again as he winked at Nikita's short sheepskin coat, which was torn under the arms and at the back, was greasy and out of shape, frayed to a fringe round the skirt, and had endured many things in its lifetime.

"Hey, dear man, come and hold the horse!" shouted Nikita to the cook's husband, who was still in the yard.

"No, I will myself, I will myself!" shrieked the little boy, pulling his hands, red with cold, out of his pockets, and seizing the cold leather reins.

"Only don't be too long dressing yourself up. Look alive!" shouted Vasili Andreevich, grinning at Nikita.

"Only a moment, Father, Vasili Andreevich!" replied Nikita, and running quickly with his inturned toes in his felt boots with their soles patched with felt, he hurried across the yard and into the workmen's hut.

"Arinushka! Get my coat down from the stove. I'm going with the master," he said, as he ran into the hut and took down his girdle from the nail on which it hung.

The workmen's cook, who had had a sleep after dinner and was now getting the samovar ready for her husband, turned cheerfully to Nikita, and infected by his hurry began to move as quickly as he did, got down his miserable worn-out cloth coat from the stove where it was drying, and began hurriedly shaking it out and smoothing it down.

"There now, you'll have a chance of a holiday with your good man," said Nikita, who from kind-hearted politeness always said something to anyone he was alone with.

Then, drawing his worn narrow girdle round him, he drew in his breath, pulling in his lean stomach still more, and girdled himself as tightly as he could over his sheepskin.

"There now," he said addressing himself no longer to the cook but the girdle, as he tucked the ends in at the waist, "now you won't come undone!" And working his shoulders up and down to free his arms, he put the coat over his sheepskin, arched his back more strongly to ease his arms, poked himself under the armpits, and took down his leather-covered mittens from the shelf. "Now we're all right!"

"You ought to wrap your feet up, Nikita. Your boots are very bad."

Nikita stopped as if he had suddenly realized this.

"Yes, I ought to . . . But they'll do like this. It isn't far!" and he ran out into the yard.

"Won't you be cold, Nikita?" said the mistress as he came up to the sledge.

"Cold? No, I'm quite warm," answered Nikita as he pushed

some straw up to the forepart of the sledge so that it should cover his feet, and stowed away the whip, which the good horse would not need, at the bottom of the sledge.

Vasili Andreevich, who was wearing two fur-lined coats one over the other, was already in the sledge, his broad back filling nearly its whole rounded width, and taking the reins he immediately touched the horse. Nikita jumped in just as the sledge started, and seated himself in front on the left side, with one leg hanging over the edge.

II

The good stallion took the sledge along at a brisk pace over the smooth-frozen road through the village, the runners squeaking slightly as they went.

"Look at him hanging on there! Hand me the whip, Nikita!" shouted Vasili Andreevich, evidently enjoying the sight of his 'heir,' who standing on the runners was hanging on at the back of the sledge. "I'll give it you! Be off to mamma, you dog!"

The boy jumped down. The horse increased his amble and, suddenly changing foot, broke into a fast trot.

The Crosses, the village where Vasili Andreevich lived, consisted of six houses. As soon as they had passed the blacksmith's hut, the last in the village, they realized that the wind was much stronger than they had thought. The road could hardly be seen. The tracks left by the sledge-runners were immediately covered by snow and the road was only distinguished by the fact that it was higher than the rest of the ground. There was a swirl of snow over the fields and the line where sky and earth met could not be seen. The Telyatin forest, usually clearly visible, now only loomed up occasionally and dimly through the driving snowy dust. The wind came from the left, insistently blowing over to one side the mane on Mukhorty's sleek neck and carrying aside even his fluffy tail, which was tied in a simple knot. Nikita's wide coat-collar, as he sat on the windy side, pressed close to his cheek and nose.

"This road doesn't give him a chance—it's too snowy," said Vasili Andreevich, who prided himself on his good horse. "I once drove to Pashutino with him in half an hour."

"What?" asked Nikita, who could not hear on account of his collar.

"I say I once went to Pashutino in half an hour," shouted Vasili Andreevich.

"It goes without saying that he's a good horse," replied Nikita.

They were silent for a while. But Vasili Andreevich wished to talk.

"Well, did you tell your wife not to give the cooper any vodka?" he began in the same loud tone, quite convinced that Nikita must feel flattered to be talking with so clever and important a person as himself, and he was so pleased with his jest that it did not enter his head that the remark might be unpleasant to Nikita.

The wind again prevented Nikita's hearing his master's words.

Vasili Andreevich repeated the jest about the cooper in his loud, clear voice.

"That's their business, Vasili Andreevich. I don't pry into their affairs. As long as she doesn't ill-treat our boy—God be with them."

"That's so," said Vasili Andreevich. "Well, and will you be buying a horse in spring?" he went on, changing the subject.

"Yes, I can't avoid it," answered Nikita, turning down his collar and leaning back towards his master.

The conversation now became interesting to him and he did not wish to lose a word.

"The lad's growing up. He must begin to plough for himself, but till now we've always had to hire someone," he said.

"Well, why not have the lean-cruppered one. I won't charge much for it," shouted Vasili Andreevich, feeling animated, and consequently starting on his favourite occupation—that of horse-dealing—which absorbed all his mental powers.

"Or you might let me have fifteen roubles and I'll buy one at the horse-market," said Nikita, who knew that the horse Vasili Andreevich wanted to sell him would be dear at seven roubles, but that if he took it from him it would be charged at twenty-five, and then he would be unable to draw any money for half a year.

"It's a good horse. I think of your interest as of my own—according to conscience. Brekhunov isn't a man to wrong anyone. Let the loss be mine. I'm not like others. Honestly!" he shouted in the voice in which he hypnotized his customers and dealers. "It's a real good horse."

"Quite so!" said Nikita with a sigh, and convinced that there was nothing more to listen to, he again released his collar, which immediately covered his ear and face.

They drove on in silence for about half an hour. The wind blew sharply onto Nikita's side and arm where his sheepskin was torn.

He huddled up and breathed into the collar which covered his mouth, and was not wholly cold.

"What do you think—shall we go through Karamyshevo or by the straight road?" asked Vasili Andreevich.

The road through Karamyshevo was more frequented and was well marked with a double row of high stakes. The straight road was nearer but little used and had no stakes, or only poor ones covered with snow.

Nikita thought awhile.

"Though Karamyshevo is farther, it is better going," he said.

"But by the straight road, when once we get through the hollow by the forest, it's good going—sheltered," said Vasili Andreevich, who wished to go the nearest way.

"Just as you please," said Nikita, and again let go of his collar. Vasili Andreevich did as he had said, and having gone about half a verst came to a tall oak stake which had a few dry leaves still dangling on it, and there he turned to the left.

On turning they faced directly against the wind, and snow was beginning to fall. Vasili Andreevich, who was driving, inflated his cheeks, blowing the breath out through his moustache. Nikita dozed.

So they went on in silence for about ten minutes. Suddenly Vasili Andreevich began saying something.

"Eh, what?" asked Nikita, opening his eyes.

Vasili Andreevich did not answer, but bent over, looking behind them and then ahead of the horse. The sweat had curled Mukhorty's coat between his legs and on his neck. He went at a walk.

"What is it?" Nikita asked again.

"What is it? What is it?" Vasili Andreevich mimicked him angrily. "There are no stakes to be seen! We must have got off the road!"

"Well, pull up then, and I'll look for it," said Nikita, and jumping down lightly from the sledge and taking the whip from under the straw, he went off to the left from his own side of the sledge.

The snow was not deep that year, so that it was possible to walk anywhere, but still in places it was knee-deep and got into Nikita's boots. He went about feeling the ground with his feet and the whip, but could not find the road anywhere.

"Well, how is it?" asked Vasili Andreevich when Nikita came back to the sledge.

"There is no road this side. I must go to the other side and try there," said Nikita.

"There's something there in front. Go and have a look."

Nikita went to what had appeared dark, but found that it was earth which the wind had blown from the bare fields of winter oats and had strewn over the snow, colouring it. Having searched to the right also, he returned to the sledge, brushed the snow from his coat, shook it out of his boots, and seated himself once more.

"We must go to the right," he said decidedly. "The wind was

blowing on our left before, but now it is straight in my face. Drive to the right," he repeated with decision.

Vasili Andreevich took his advice and turned to the right, but still there was no road. They went on in that direction for some time. The wind was as fierce as ever and it was snowing lightly.

"It seems, Vasili Andreevich, that we have gone quite astray," Nikita suddenly remarked, as if it were a pleasant thing. "What is that?" he added, pointing to some potato vines that showed up from under the snow.

Vasili Andreevich stopped the perspiring horse, whose deep sides were heaving heavily.

"What is it?"

"Why, we are on the Zakharov lands. See where we've got to!"

"Nonsense!" retorted Vasili Andreevich.

"It's not nonsense, Vasili Andreevich. It's the truth," replied Nikita. "You can feel that the sledge is going over a potato-field, and there are the heaps of vines which have been carted here. It's the Zakharov factory land."

"Dear me, how we have gone astray!" said Vasili Andreevich. "What are we to do now?"

"We must go straight on, that's all. We shall come out somewhere—if not at Zakharov, then at the proprietor's farm," said Nikita.

Vasili Andreevich agreed, and drove as Nikita had indicated. So they went on for a considerable time. At times they came onto bare fields and the sledge-runners rattled over frozen lumps of earth. Sometimes they got onto a winter-rye field, or a fallow field on which they could see stalks of wormwood, and straws sticking up through the snow and swaying in the wind; sometimes they came onto deep and even white snow, above which nothing was to be seen.

The snow was falling from above and sometimes rose from below. The horse was evidently exhausted, his hair had all curled up from sweat and was covered with hoar-frost, and he went at a walk. Suddenly he stumbled and sat down in a ditch or water-course. Vasili Andreevich wanted to stop, but Nikita cried to him:

"Why stop? We've got in and must get out. Hey, pet! Hey, darling! Gee up, old fellow!" he shouted in a cheerful tone to the horse, jumping out of the sledge and himself getting stuck in the ditch.

The horse gave a start and quickly climbed out onto the frozen bank. It was evidently a ditch that had been dug there.

"Where are we now?" asked Vasili Andreevich.

"We'll soon find out!" Nikita replied. "Go on, we'll get somewhere."

"Why, this must be the Goryachkin forest!" said Vasili Andreevich, pointing to something dark that appeared amid the snow in front of them.

"We'll see what forest it is when we get there," said Nikita.

He saw that beside the black thing they had noticed, dry, oblong willow-leaves were fluttering, and so he knew it was not a forest but a settlement, but he did not wish to say so. And in fact they had not gone twenty-five yards beyond the ditch before something in front of them, evidently trees, showed up black, and they heard a new and melancholy sound. Nikita had guessed right: it was not a wood, but a row of tall willows with a few leaves still fluttering on them here and there. They had evidently been planted along the ditch round a threshing-floor. Coming up to the willows, which moaned sadly in the wind, the horse suddenly planted his forelegs above the height of the sledge, drew up his hind legs also, pulling the sledge onto higher ground, and turned to the left, no longer sinking up to his knees in snow. They were back on a road.

"Well, here we are, but heaven only knows where!" said Nikita.

The horse kept straight along the road through the drifted snow, and before they had gone another hundred yards the straight line of the dark wattle wall of a barn showed up black before them, its roof heavily covered with snow which poured down from it. After passing the barn the road turned to the wind and they drove into a snow-drift. But ahead of them was a lane with houses on either side, so evidently the snow had been blown across the road and they had to drive through the drift. And so in fact it was.

Having driven through the snow they came out into a street. At the end house of the village some frozen clothes hanging on a line—shirts, one red and one white, trousers, leg-bands, and a petticoat—fluttered wildly in the wind. The white shirt in particular struggled desperately, waving its sleeves about.

"There now, either a lazy woman or a dead one has not taken her clothes down before the holiday," remarked Nikita, looking at the fluttering shirts.

III

At the entrance to the street the wind still raged and the road was thickly covered with snow, but well within the village it was calm, warm, and cheerful. At one house a dog was barking, at another a woman, covering her head with her coat, came running from somewhere and entered the door of a hut, stopping on the threshold to have a look at the passing sledge. In the middle of the village girls could be heard singing.

Here in the village there seemed to be less wind and snow, and the frost was less keen.

"Why, this is Grishkino," said Vasili Andreevich.

"So it is," responded Nikita.

It really was Grishkino, which meant that they had gone too far to the left and had travelled some six miles, not quite in the direction they aimed at, but towards their destination for all that.

From Grishkino to Goryachkin was about another four miles.

In the middle of the village they almost ran into a tall man walking down the middle of the street.

491

"Who are you?" shouted the man, stopping the horse, and recognizing Vasili Andreevich he immediately took hold of the shaft, went along it hand over hand till he reached the sledge, and placed himself on the driver's seat.

He was Isay, a peasant of Vasili Andreevich's acquaintance, and well known as the principal horse-thief in the district.

"Ah, Vasili Andreevich! Where are you off to?" said Isay, enveloping Nikita in the odour of the vodka he had drunk.

"We were going to Goryachkin."

"And look where you've got to! You should have gone through Molchanovka."

"Should have, but didn't manage it," said Vasili Andreevich, holding in the horse.

"That's a good horse," said Isay, with a shrewd glance at Mukhorty, and with a practised hand he tightened the loosened knot high in the horse's bushy tail.

"Are you going to stay the night?"

"No, friend. I must get on."

"Your business must be pressing. And who is this? Ah, Nikita Stepanych!"

"Who else?" replied Nikita. "But I say, good friend, how are we to avoid going astray again?"

"Where can you go astray here? Turn back straight down the street and then when you come out keep straight on. Don't take to the left. You will come out onto the high road, and then turn to the right."

"And where do we turn off the high road? As in summer, or the winter way?" asked Nikita.

"The winter way. As soon as you turn off you'll see some bushes, and opposite them there is a way-mark—a large oak, one with branches—and that's the way."

Vasili Andreevich turned the horse back and drove through the outskirts of the village.

"Why not stay the night?" Isay shouted after them.

But Vasili Andreevich did not answer and touched up the horse. Four miles of good road, two of which lay through the forest, seemed easy to manage, especially as the wind was apparently quieter and the snow had stopped.

Having driven along the trodden village street, darkened here and there by fresh manure, past the yard where the clothes hung out and where the white shirt had broken loose and was now attached only by one frozen sleeve, they again came within sound of the weird moan of the willows, and again emerged on the open fields. The storm, far from ceasing, seemed to have grown yet stronger. The road was completely covered with drifting snow, and only the stakes showed that they had not lost their way. But even the stakes ahead of them were not easy to see, since the wind blew in their faces.

Vasili Andreevich screwed up his eyes, bent down his head, and looked out for the way-marks, but trusted mainly to the horse's sagacity, letting it take its own way. And the horse really did not lose the road but followed its windings, turning now to the right and now to the left and sensing it under his feet, so that though the snow fell thicker and the wind strengthened they still continued to see way-marks now to the left and now to the right of them.

So they travelled on for about ten minutes, when suddenly, through the slanting screen of wind-driven snow, something black showed up which moved in front of the horse.

This was another sledge with fellow-travellers. Mukhorty overtook them, and struck his hoofs against the back of the sledge in front of them.

"Pass on . . . hey there . . . get in front!" cried voices from the sledge.

Vasili Andreevich swerved aside to pass the other sledge.

In it sat three men and a woman, evidently visitors returning from a feast. One peasant was whacking the snow-covered croup of their little horse with a long switch, and the other two sitting in front waved their arms and shouted something. The woman, completely wrapped up and covered with snow, sat drowsing and bumping at the back.

"Who are you?" shouted Vasili Andreevich.

"From A-a-a . . ." was all that could be heard.

"I say, where are you from?"

"From A-a-a-a!" one of the peasants shouted with all his might, but still it was impossible to make out who they were.

"Get along! Keep up!" shouted another, ceaselessly beating his horse with the switch.

"So you're from a feast, it seems?"

"Go on, go on! Faster, Simon! Get in front! Faster!"

The wings of the sledges bumped against one another, almost got jammed but managed to separate, and the peasants' sledge began to fall behind.

Their shaggy, big-bellied horse, all covered with snow, breathed heavily under the low shaft-bow and, evidently using the last of its strength, vainly endeavoured to escape from the switch, hobbling with its short legs through the deep snow which it threw up under itself.

Its muzzle, young-looking, with the nether lip drawn up like that of a fish, nostrils distended and ears pressed back from fear, kept up for a few seconds near Nikita's shoulder and then began to fall behind.

"Just see what liquor does!" said Nikita. "They've tired that little horse to death. What pagans!"

For a few minutes they heard the panting of the tired little horse and the drunken shouting of the peasants. Then the panting and the shouts died away, and around them nothing could be heard but the whistling of the wind in their ears and now and then the squeak of their sledge-runners over a windswept part of the road.

This encounter cheered and enlivened Vasili Andreevich, and he drove on more boldly without examining the way-marks, urging on the horse and trusting to him.

Nikita had nothing to do, and as usual in such circumstances he drowsed, making up for much sleepless time. Suddenly the horse stopped and Nikita nearly fell forward onto his nose.

"You know we're off the track again!" said Vasili Andreevich.

"How's that?"

"Why, there are no way-marks to be seen. We must have got off the road again."

"Well, if we've lost the road we must find it," said Nikita curtly, and getting out and stepping lightly on his pigeon-toed feet he started once more going about on the snow.

He walked about for a long time, now disappearing and now reappearing, and finally he came back.

"There is no road here. There may be farther on," he said, getting into the sledge.

It was already growing dark. The snowstorm had not increased but had also not subsided.

"If we could only hear those peasants!" said Vasili Andreevich.

"Well they haven't caught us up. We must have gone far astray. Or maybe they have lost their way too."

"Where are we to go then?" asked Vasili Andreevich.

"Why, we must let the horse take its own way," said Nikita. "He will take us right. Let me have the reins."

Vasili Andreevich gave him the reins, the more willingly because his hands were beginning to feel frozen in his thick gloves.

Nikita took the reins, but only held them, trying not to shake them and rejoicing at his favourite's sagacity. And indeed the clever horse, turning first one ear and then the other now to one side and then to the other, began to wheel round.

"The one thing he can't do is to talk," Nikita kept saying. "See what he is doing! Go on, go on! You know best. That's it, that's it!"

The wind was now blowing from behind and it felt warmer.

"Yes, he's clever," Nikita continued, admiring the horse. "A Kirgiz horse is strong but stupid. But this one—just see what he's doing with his ears! He doesn't need any telegraph. He can scent a mile off."

Before another half-hour had passed they saw something dark ahead of them—a wood or a village—and stakes again appeared to the right. They had evidently come out onto the road.

"Why, that's Grishkino again!" Nikita suddenly exclaimed.

And indeed, there on their left was that same barn with the snow flying from it, and farther on the same line with the frozen washing, shirts and trousers, which still fluttered desperately in the wind.

Again they drove into the street and again it grew quiet, warm, and cheerful, and again they could see the manure-stained street and hear voices and songs and the barking of a dog. It was already so dark that there were lights in some of the windows.

Half-way through the village Vasili Andreevich turned the horse towards a large double-fronted brick house and stopped at the porch.

Nikita went to the lighted snow-covered window, in the rays of which flying snow-flakes glittered, and knocked at it with his whip.

"Who is there?" a voice replied to his knock.

"From Kresty, the Brekhunovs, dear fellow," answered Nikita. "Just come out for a minute."

Someone moved from the window, and a minute or two later there was the sound of the passage door as it came unstuck, then the latch of the outside door clicked and a tall white-bearded peasant, with a sheepskin coat thrown over his white holiday shirt, pushed his way out holding the door firmly against the wind, followed by a lad in a red shirt and high leather boots.

"Is that you, Andreevich?" asked the old man.

"Yes, friend, we've gone astray," said Vasili Andreevich. "We wanted to get to Goryachkin but found ourselves here. We went a second time but lost our way again."

"Just see how you have gone astray!" said the old man. "Petrushka, go and open the gate!" he added, turning to the lad in the red shirt.

"All right," said the lad in a cheerful voice, and ran back into the passage.

"But we're not staying the night," said Vasili Andreevich.

"Where will you go in the night? You'd better stay!"

"I'd be glad to, but I must go on. It's business, and it can't be helped."

"Well, warm yourself at least. The samovar is just ready."

"Warm myself? Yes, I'll do that," said Vasili Andreevich. "It won't get darker. The moon will rise and it will be lighter. Let's go in and warm ourselves, Nikita."

"Well, why not? Let us warm ourselves," replied Nikita, who was stiff with cold and anxious to warm his frozen limbs.

Vasili Andreevich went into the room with the old man, and Nikita drove through the gate opened for him by Petrushka, by whose advice he backed the horse under the penthouse. The ground was covered with manure and the tall bow over the horse's head caught against the beam. The hens and the cock had already settled to roost there, and clucked peevishly, clinging to the beam with their claws. The disturbed sheep shied and rushed aside trampling the frozen manure with their hooves. The dog yelped desperately with fright and anger and then burst out barking like a puppy at the stranger.

Nikita talked to them all, excused himself to the fowls and assured them that he would not disturb them again, rebuked the sheep for being frightened without knowing why, and kept soothing the dog, while he tied up the horse.

"Now that will be all right," he said, knocking the snow off his clothes. "Just hear how he barks!" he added, turning to the dog. "Be quiet, stupid! Be quiet. You are only troubling yourself for nothing. We're not thieves, we're friends . . ."

"And these are, it's said, the three domestic counsellors," remarked the lad, and with his strong arms he pushed under the pent-roof the sledge that had remained outside.

"Why counsellors?" asked Nikita.

"That's what is printed in Paulson. A thief creeps to a house—the dog barks, that means 'Be on your guard!' The cock crows, that means, 'Get up!' The cat licks herself—that means, 'A welcome guest is coming. Get ready to receive him!'" said the lad with a smile.

Petrushka could read and write and knew Paulson's primer, his only book, almost by heart, and he was fond of quoting sayings from it that he thought suited the occasion, especially when he had had something to drink, as today.

"That's so," said Nikita.

"You must be chilled through and through," said Petrushka.

"Yes, I am rather," said Nikita, and they went across the yard and the passage into the house.

IV

The household to which Vasili Andreevich had come was one of the richest in the village. The family had five allotments, besides renting other land. They had six horses, three cows, two calves, and some twenty sheep. There were twenty-two members belonging to the homestead: four married sons, six grandchildren (one of whom, Petrushka, was married), two great-grandchildren, three orphans, and four daughters-in-law with their babies. It was one of the few homesteads that remained still undivided, but even here the dull internal work of disintegration which would inevitably lead to separation had already begun, starting as usual among the women. Two sons were living in Moscow as water-carriers, and one was in the army. At home now were the old man and his wife, their second son who managed the homestead, the eldest who had come from Moscow for the holiday, and all the women and children. Besides these members of the family there was a visitor, a neighbour who was godfather to one of the children.

Over the table in the room hung a lamp with a shade, which brightly lit up the tea-things, a bottle of vodka, and some refreshments, besides illuminating the brick walls, which in the far corner were hung with icons on both sides of which were pictures. At the head of the table sat Vasili Andreevich in a black sheepskin coat, sucking his frozen moustache and observing the room and the people around him with his prominent hawk-like eyes. With him sat the old, bald, white-bearded master of the house in a white homespun shirt, and next him the son home from Moscow for the holiday—a man with a sturdy back and powerful shoulders and clad in a thin print shirt—then the second son, also broad-shouldered, who acted as head of the house, and then a lean red-haired peasant—the neighbour.

Having had a drink of vodka and something to eat, they were about to take tea, and the samovar standing on the floor beside the brick oven was already humming. The children could be seen in the top bunks and on the top of the oven. A woman sat on a lower bunk with a cradle beside her. The old housewife, her face covered with wrinkles which wrinkled even her lips, was waiting on Vasili Andreevich.

As Nikita entered the house she was offering her guest a small tumbler of thick glass which she had just filled with vodka.

"Don't refuse, Vasili Andreevich, you mustn't! Wish us a merry feast. Drink it, dear!" she said.

The sight and smell of vodka, especially now when he was chilled through and tired out, much disturbed Nikita's mind. He frowned, and having shaken the snow off his cap and coat, stopped in front of the icons as if not seeing anyone, crossed himself three times, and bowed to the icons. Then, turning to the old master of the house and bowing first to him, then to all those at table, then to the women who stood by the oven, and muttering: "A merry holiday!" he began taking off his outer things without looking at the table.

"Why, you're all covered with hoar-frost, old fellow!" said the eldest brother, looking at Nikita's snow-covered face, eyes, and beard.

Nikita took off his coat, shook it again, hung it up beside the oven, and came up to the table. He too was offered vodka. He went through a moment of painful hesitation and nearly took up the glass and emptied the clear fragrant liquid down his throat, but he glanced at Vasili Andreevich, remembered his oath and the boots that he had sold for drink, recalled the cooper, remembered his son for whom he had promised to buy a horse by spring, sighed, and declined it.

"I don't drink, thank you kindly," he said frowning, and sat down on a bench near the second window.

"How's that?" asked the eldest brother.

"I just don't drink," replied Nikita without lifting his eyes but looking askance at his scanty beard and moustache and getting the icicles out of them.

"It's not good for him," said Vasili Andreevich, munching a cracknel after emptying his glass.

"Well, then, have some tea," said the kindly old hostess. "You must be chilled through, good soul. Why are you women dawdling so with the samovar?"

"It is ready," said one of the young women, and after flicking with her apron the top of the samovar which was now boiling over, she carried it with an effort to the table, raised it, and set it down with a thud.

Meanwhile Vasili Andreevich was telling how he had lost his way, how they had come back twice to this same village, and how they had gone astray and had met some drunken peasants. Their hosts were surprised, explained where and why they had missed their way, said who the tipsy people they had met were, and told them how they ought to go.

"A little child could find the way to Molchanovka from here. All you have to do is to take the right turning from the high road. There's a bush you can see just there. But you didn't even get that far!" said the neighbour.

"You'd better stay the night. The women will make up beds for you," said the old woman persuasively.

"You could go on in the morning and it would be pleasanter," said the old man, confirming what his wife had said.

"I can't, friend. Business!" said Vasili Andreevich. "Lose an hour and you can't catch it up in a year," he added, remembering the grove and the dealers who might snatch that deal from him. "We shall get there, shan't we?" he said, turning to Nikita.

Nikita did not answer for some time, apparently still intent on thawing out his beard and moustache.

"If only we don't go astray again," he replied gloomily. He was gloomy because he passionately longed for some vodka, and the only thing that could assuage that longing was tea and he had not yet been offered any.

"But we have only to reach the turning and then we shan't go wrong. The road will be through the forest the whole way," said Vasili Andreevich.

"It's just as you please, Vasili Andreevich. If we're to go, let us go," said Nikita, taking the glass of tea he was offered.

"We'll drink our tea and be off."

Nikita said nothing but only shook his head, and carefully pouring some tea into his saucer began warming his hands, the fingers of which were always swollen with hard work, over the steam. Then, biting off a tiny bit of sugar, he bowed to his hosts, said, "Your health!" and drew in the steaming liquid.

"If somebody would see us as far as the turning," said Vasili Andreevich.

"Well, we can do that," said the eldest son. "Petrushka will harness and go that far with you."

"Well, then, put in the horse, lad, and I shall be thankful to you for it."

"Oh, what for, dear man?" said the kindly old woman. "We are heartily glad to do it."

"Petrushka, go and put in the mare," said the eldest brother.

"All right," replied Petrushka with a smile, and promptly snatching his cap down from a nail he ran away to harness.

While the horse was being harnessed the talk returned to the point at which it had stopped when Vasili Andreevich drove up to the window. The old man had been complaining to his neighbour, the village elder, about his third son who had not sent him anything for the holiday though he had sent a French shawl to his wife.

"The young people are getting out of hand," said the old man.

"And how they do!" said the neighbour. "There's no managing them! They know too much. There's Demochkin now, who broke his father's arm. It's all from being too clever, it seems."

Nikita listened, watched their faces, and evidently would have liked to share in the conversation, but he was too busy drinking his tea and only nodded his head approvingly. He emptied one tumbler after another and grew warmer and warmer and more and more comfortable. The talk continued on the same subject for a long time—the harmfulness of a household dividing up—and it was clearly not an abstract discussion but concerned the question of a separation in that house; a separation demanded by the second son who sat there morosely silent.

It was evidently a sore subject and absorbed them all, but out of propriety they did not discuss their private affairs before strangers. At last, however, the old man could not restrain himself, and with tears in his eyes declared that he would not consent to a break-up of the family during his lifetime, that his house was prospering, thank God, but that if they separated they would all have to go begging.

"Just like the Matveevs," said the neighbour. "They used to have a proper house, but now they've split up none of them has anything."

"And that is what you want to happen to us," said the old man, turning to his son.

The son made no reply and there was an awkward pause. The silence was broken by Petrushka, who having harnessed the horse had returned to the hut a few minutes before this and had been listening all the time with a smile.

"There's a fable about that in Paulson," he said. "A father gave his sons a broom to break. At first they could not break it, but when they took it twig by twig they broke it easily. And it's the same here," and he gave a broad smile. "I'm ready!" he added.

"If you're ready, let's go," said Vasili Andreevich. "And as to separating, don't you allow it, Grandfather. You got everything together and you're the master. Go to the Justice of the Peace. He'll say how things should be done."

"He carries on so, carries on so," the old man continued in a whining tone. "There's no doing anything with him. It's as if the devil possessed him."

Nikita having meanwhile finished his fifth tumbler of tea laid it on its side instead of turning it upside down, hoping to be offered a sixth glass. But there was no more water in the samovar, so the hostess did not fill it up for him. Besides, Vasili Andreevich was putting his things on, so there was nothing for it but for Nikita to get up too, put back into the sugar-basin the lump of sugar he had nibbled all round, wipe his perspiring face with the skirt of his sheepskin, and go to put on his overcoat.

Having put it on he sighed deeply, thanked his hosts, said goodbye, and went out of the warm bright room into the cold dark passage, through which the wind was howling and where snow was blowing through the cracks of the shaking door, and from there into the yard.

Petrushka stood in his sheepskin in the middle of the yard by his horse, repeating some lines from Paulson's primer. He said with a smile:

> *"Storms with mist the sky conceal,*
> *Snowy circles wheeling wild.*
> *Now like savage beast 'twill howl,*
> *And now 'tis wailing like a child."*

Nikita nodded approvingly as he arranged the reins.

The old man, seeing Vasili Andreevich off, brought a lantern into the passage to show him a light, but it was blown out at once. And even in the yard it was evident that the snowstorm had become more violent.

"Well, this is weather!" thought Vasili Andreevich. "Perhaps we may not get there after all. But there is nothing to be done. Business! Besides, we have got ready, our host's horse has been harnessed, and we'll get there with God's help!"

Their aged host also thought they ought not to go, but he had already tried to persuade them to stay and had not been listened to.

"It's no use asking them again. Maybe my age makes me timid. They'll get there all right, and at least we shall get to bed in good time and without any fuss," he thought.

Petrushka did not think of danger. He knew the road and the whole district so well, and the lines about "snowy circles wheeling wild" described what was happening outside so aptly that it cheered him up. Nikita did not wish to go at all, but he had been accustomed not to have his own way and to serve others for so long that there was no one to hinder the departing travellers.

V

Vasili Andreevich went over to his sledge, found it with difficulty in the darkness, climbed in and took the reins.

"Go on in front!" he cried.

Petrushka kneeling in his low sledge started his horse. Mukhorty, who had been neighing for some time past, now scenting a mare ahead of him started after her, and they drove out into the street. They drove again through the outskirts of the village and along the same road, past the yard where the frozen linen had hung (which, however, was no longer to be seen), past the same barn, which was now snowed up almost to the roof and from which the snow was still endlessly pouring past the same dismally moaning, whistling, and swaying willows, and again entered into the sea of blustering snow raging from above and below. The wind was so strong that when it blew from the side and the travellers steered against it, it tilted the sledges and turned the horses to one side. Petrushka drove his good mare in front at a brisk trot and kept shouting lustily. Mukhorty pressed after her.

After travelling so for about ten minutes, Petrushka turned round and shouted something. Neither Vasili Andreevich nor Nikita could hear anything because of the wind, but they guessed that they had arrived at the turning. In fact Petrushka had turned to the right, and now the wind that had blown from the side blew straight in their faces, and through the snow they saw something dark on their right. It was the bush at the turning.

"Well now, God speed you!"

"Thank you, Petrushka!"

"Storms with mist the sky conceal!" shouted Petrushka as he disappeared.

"There's a poet for you!" muttered Vasili Andreevich, pulling at the reins.

"Yes, a fine lad—a true peasant," said Nikita.

They drove on.

Nikita, wrapping his coat closely about him and pressing his head down so close to his shoulders that his short beard covered his throat, sat silently, trying not to lose the warmth he had obtained while drinking tea in the house. Before him he saw the straight lines of the shafts which constantly deceived him into thinking they were on a well-travelled road, and the horse's swaying crupper with his knotted tail blown to one side, and farther ahead the high shaft-bow and the swaying head and neck of the horse with its waving mane. Now and then he caught sight of a way-sign, so that he knew they were still on a road and that there was nothing for him to be concerned about.

Vasili Andreevich drove on, leaving it to the horse to keep to the road. But Mukhorty, though he had had a breathing-space in the village, ran reluctantly, and seemed now and then to get off the road, so that Vasili Andreevich had repeatedly to correct him.

"Here's a stake to the right, and another, and here's a third," Vasili Andreevich counted, "and here in front is the forest," thought he, as he looked at something dark in front of him. But what had seemed to him a forest was only a bush. They passed the bush and drove on for another hundred yards but there was no fourth way-mark nor any forest.

"We must reach the forest soon," thought Vasili Andreevich, and animated by the vodka and the tea he did not stop but shook the reins, and the good obedient horse responded, now ambling, now slowly trotting in the direction in which he was sent, though he knew that he was not going the right way. Ten minutes went by, but there was still no forest.

"There now, we must be astray again," said Vasili Andreevich, pulling up.

Nikita silently got out of the sledge and holding his coat, which the wind now wrapped closely about him and now almost tore off, started to feel about in the snow, going first to one side and then to the other. Three or four times he was completely lost to sight. At last he returned and took the reins from Vasili Andreevich's hand.

"We must go to the right," he said sternly and peremptorily, as he turned the horse.

"Well, if it's to the right, go to the right," said Vasili Andreevich, yielding up the reins to Nikita and thrusting his freezing hands into his sleeves.

Nikita did not reply.

"Now then, friend, stir yourself!" he shouted to the horse, but in spite of the shake of the reins Mukhorty moved only at a walk.

The snow in places was up to his knees, and the sledge moved by fits and starts with his every movement.

Nikita took the whip that hung over the front of the sledge and struck him once. The good horse, unused to the whip, sprang forward and moved at a trot, but immediately fell back into an amble and then to a walk. So they went on for five minutes. It was dark and the snow whirled from above and rose from below, so that sometimes the shaft-bow could not be seen. At times the sledge seemed to stand still and the field to run backwards. Suddenly the horse stopped abruptly, evidently aware of something close in front of him. Nikita again sprang lightly out, throwing down the reins, and went ahead to see what had brought him to a standstill, but hardly had he made a step in front of the horse before his feet slipped and he went rolling down an incline.

"Whoa, whoa, whoa!" he said to himself as he fell, and he tried to stop his fall but could not, and only stopped when his feet plunged into a thick layer of snow that had drifted to the bottom of the hollow.

The fringe of a drift of snow that hung on the edge of the hollow, disturbed by Nikita's fall, showered down on him and got inside his collar.

"What a thing to do!" said Nikita reproachfully, addressing the drift and the hollow and shaking the snow from under his collar.

"Nikita! Hey, Nikita!" shouted Vasili Andreevich from above. But Nikita did not reply. He was too occupied in shaking out the snow and searching for the whip he had dropped when rolling down the incline. Having found the whip he tried to climb straight up the bank where he had rolled down, but it was impossible to do so: he kept rolling down again, and so he had to go along at the foot of the hollow to find a way up. About seven yards farther on he managed with difficulty to crawl up the incline on all fours, then he followed the edge of the hollow back to the place where the horse should have been. He could not see either horse or sledge, but as he walked against the wind he heard Vasili Andreevich's shouts and Mukhorty's neighing, calling him.

"I'm coming! I'm coming! What are you cackling for?" he muttered.

Only when he had come up to the sledge could he make out the horse, and Vasili Andreevich standing beside it and looking gigantic.

"Where the devil did you vanish to? We must go back, if only to Grishkino," he began reproaching Nikita.

"I'd be glad to get back, Vasili Andreevich, but which way are we to go? There is such a ravine here that if we once get in it we shan't get out again. I got stuck so fast there myself that I could hardly get out."

"What shall we do, then? We can't stay here! We must go somewhere!" said Vasili Andreevich.

Nikita said nothing. He seated himself in the sledge with his back to the wind, took off his boots, shook out the snow that had got into them, and taking some straw from the bottom of the sledge, carefully plugged with it a hole in his left boot.

Vasili Andreevich remained silent, as though now leaving everything to Nikita. Having put his boots on again, Nikita drew his feet into the sledge, put on his mittens and took up the reins, and directed the horse along the side of the ravine. But they had not gone a hundred yards before the horse again stopped short. The ravine was in front of him again.

Nikita again climbed out and again trudged about in the snow. He did this for a considerable time and at last appeared from the opposite side to that from which he had started.

"Vasili Andreevich, are you alive?" he called out.

"Here!" replied Vasili Andreevich. "Well, what now?"

"I can't make anything out. It's too dark. There's nothing but ravines. We must drive against the wind again."

They set off once more. Again Nikita went stumbling through the snow, again he fell in, again climbed out and trudged about, and at last quite out of breath he sat down beside the sledge.

"Well, how now?" asked Vasili Andreevich.

"Why, I am quite worn out and the horse won't go."

"Then what's to be done?"

"Why, wait a minute."

Nikita went away again but soon returned.

"Follow me!" he said, going in front of the horse.

Vasili Andreevich no longer gave orders but implicitly did what Nikita told him.

"Here, follow me!" Nikita shouted, stepping quickly to the right, and seizing the rein he led Mukhorty down towards a snow-drift.

At first the horse held back, then he jerked forward, hoping to leap the drift, but he had not the strength and sank into it up to his collar.

"Get out!" Nikita called to Vasili Andreevich who still sat in the sledge, and taking hold of one shaft he moved the sledge closer to the horse. "It's hard, brother!" he said to Mukhorty, "but it can't be helped. Make an effort! Now, now, just a little one!" he shouted.

The horse gave a tug, then another, but failed to clear himself and settled down again as if considering something.

"Now, brother, this won't do!" Nikita admonished him. "Now once more!"

Again Nikita tugged at the shaft on his side, and Vasili Andreevich did the same on the other.

Mukhorty lifted his head and then gave a sudden jerk.

"That's it! That's it!" cried Nikita. "Don't be afraid—you won't sink!"

One plunge, another, and a third, and at last Mukhorty was out of the snow-drift, and stood still, breathing heavily and shaking the snow off himself. Nikita wished to lead him farther, but Vasili Andreevich, in his two fur coats, was so out of breath that he could not walk farther and dropped into the sledge.

"Let me get my breath!" he said, unfastening the kerchief with which he had tied the collar of his fur coat at the village.

"It's all right here. You lie there," said Nikita. "I will lead him along." And with Vasili Andreevich in the sledge he led the horse by the bridle about ten paces down and then up a slight rise, and stopped.

The place where Nikita had stopped was not completely in the hollow where the snow sweeping down from the hillocks might have buried them altogether, but still it was partly sheltered from the wind by the side of the ravine. There were moments when the wind seemed to abate a little, but that did not last long and as if to make up for that respite the storm swept down with tenfold vigour and tore and whirled the more fiercely. Such a gust struck them at the moment when Vasili Andreevich, having recovered his breath, got out of the sledge and went up to Nikita to consult him as to what they should do. They both bent down involuntarily and waited till the violence of the squall should have passed. Mukhorty too laid back his ears and shook his head discontentedly. As soon as the violence of the blast had abated a little, Nikita took off his mittens, stuck them into his belt, breathed onto his hands, and began to undo the straps of the shaft-bow.

"What's that you are doing there?" asked Vasili Andreevich.

"Unharnessing. What else is there to do? I have no strength left," said Nikita as though excusing himself.

"Can't we drive somewhere?"

"No, we can't. We shall only kill the horse. Why, the poor beast is not himself now," said Nikita, pointing to the horse, which was standing submissively waiting for what might come, with his steep wet sides heaving heavily. "We shall have to stay the night here," he said, as if preparing to spend the night at an inn, and he proceeded to unfasten the collar-straps. The buckles came undone.

"But shan't we be frozen?" remarked Vasili Andreevich.

"Well, if we are we can't help it," said Nikita.

VI

Although Vasili Andreevich felt quite warm in his two fur coats, especially after struggling in the snow-drift, a cold shiver ran down his back on realizing that he must really spend the night where they were. To calm himself he sat down in the sledge and got out his cigarettes and matches.

Nikita meanwhile unharnessed Mukhorty. He unstrapped the belly-band and the back-band, took away the reins, loosened the collar-strap, and removed the shaft-bow, talking to him all the time to encourage him.

"Now come out! come out!" he said, leading him clear of the shafts. "Now we'll tie you up here and I'll put down some straw and take off your bridle. When you've had a bite you'll feel more cheerful."

But Mukhorty was restless and evidently not comforted by Nikita's remarks. He stepped now on one foot and now on another, and pressed close against the sledge, turning his back to the wind and rubbing his head on Nikita's sleeve. Then, as if not to pain Nikita by refusing his offer of the straw he put before him, he hurriedly snatched a wisp out of the sledge, but immediately decided that it was now no time to think of straw and threw it down, and the wind instantly scattered it, carried it away, and covered it with snow.

"Now we will set up a signal," said Nikita, and turning the front of the sledge to the wind he tied the shafts together with a strap and set them up on end in front of the sledge. "There now, when the snow covers us up, good folk will see the shafts and dig us out," he said, slapping his mittens together and putting them on. "That's what the old folk taught us!"

Vasili Andreevich meanwhile had unfastened his coat, and holding its skirts up for shelter, struck one sulphur match after another on the steel box. But his hands trembled, and one match after another either did not kindle or was blown out by the wind just as he was lifting it to the cigarette. At last a match did burn up, and its flame lit up for a moment the fur of his coat, his hand with the gold ring on the bent forefinger, and the snow-sprinkled oat-straw that stuck out from under the drugget. The cigarette lighted, he eagerly took a whiff or two, inhaled the smoke, let it out through his moustache, and would have inhaled again, but the wind tore off the burning tobacco and whirled it away as it had done the straw.

But even these few puffs had cheered him.

"If we must spend the night here, we must!" he said with decision. "Wait a bit, I'll arrange a flag as well," he added, picking up the kerchief which he had thrown down in the sledge after taking it from round his collar, and drawing off his gloves and standing up on the front of the sledge and stretching himself to reach the strap, he tied the handkerchief to it with a tight knot.

The kerchief immediately began to flutter wildly, now clinging round the shaft, now suddenly streaming out, stretching and flapping.

"Just see what a fine flag!" said Vasili Andreevich, admiring his handiwork and letting himself down into the sledge. "We should be warmer together, but there's not room enough for two," he added.

"I'll find a place," said Nikita. "But I must cover up the horse first—he sweated so, poor thing. Let go!" he added, drawing the drugget from under Vasili Andreevich.

Having got the drugget he folded it in two, and after taking off the breechband and pad, covered Mukhorty with it.

"Anyhow it will be warmer, silly!" he said, putting back the breechband and the pad on the horse over the drugget. Then having finished that business he returned to the sledge, and addressing Vasili Andreevich, said: "You won't need the sackcloth, will you? And let me have some straw."

And having taken these things from under Vasili Andreevich, Nikita went behind the sledge, dug out a hole for himself in the snow, put straw into it, wrapped his coat well round him, covered himself with the sackcloth, and pulling his cap well down seated himself on the straw he had spread, and leant against the wooden back of the sledge to shelter himself from the wind and the snow.

Vasili Andreevich shook his head disapprovingly at what Nikita was doing, as in general he disapproved of the peasant's stupidity and lack of education, and he began to settle himself down for the night.

He smoothed the remaining straw over the bottom of the sledge, putting more of it under his side. Then he thrust his hands into his sleeves and settled down, sheltering his head in the corner of the sledge from the wind in front.

He did not wish to sleep. He lay and thought: thought ever of the one thing that constituted the sole aim, meaning, pleasure, and pride of his life—of how much money he had made and might still make, of how much other people he knew had made and possessed, and of how those others had made and were making it, and how he, like them, might still make much more. The purchase of the Goryachkin grove was a matter of immense importance to him. By that one deal he hoped to make perhaps ten thousand roubles. He began mentally to reckon the value of the wood he had inspected in autumn, and on five acres of which he had counted all the trees.

"The oaks will go for sledge-runners. The undergrowth will take care of itself, and there'll still be some thirty sazheens of fire-wood left on each desyatin," said he to himself. "That means there will be at least two hundred and twenty-five roubles' worth left on each desyatin. Fifty-six desyatins means fifty-six hundreds, and fifty-six hundreds, and fifty-six tens, and another fifty-six tens, and then fifty-six fives . . ." He saw that it came out to more than twelve thousand roubles, but could not reckon it up exactly without a counting-frame. "But I won't give ten thousand, anyhow. I'll give about eight thousand with a deduction on account of the glades. I'll grease the surveyor's palm—give him a hundred roubles, or a hundred and fifty, and he'll reckon that there are some five desyatins of glade to be deducted. And he'll let it go for eight thousand. Three thousand cash down. That'll move him, no fear!" he thought, and he pressed his pocket-book with his forearm.

"God only knows how we missed the turning. The forest ought to be there, and a watchman's hut, and dogs barking. But the damned things don't bark when they're wanted." He turned his collar down from his ear and listened, but as before only the whistling of the wind could be heard, the flapping and fluttering of the kerchief tied to the shafts, and the pelting of the snow against the woodwork of the sledge. He again covered up his ear.

"If I had known I would have stayed the night. Well, no matter, we'll get there tomorrow. It's only one day lost. And the others won't travel in such weather." Then he remembered that on the 9th he had to receive payment from the butcher for his oxen. "He meant to come himself, but he won't find me, and my wife won't know how to receive the money. She doesn't know the right way of doing things," he thought, recalling how at their party the day before she had not known how to treat the police-officer who was their guest. "Of course she's only a woman! Where could she have seen anything? In my father's time what was our house like? Just a rich peasant's house: just an oatmill and an inn—that was the whole property. But what have I done in these fifteen years? A shop, two taverns, a flour-mill, a grain-store, two farms leased out, and a house with an iron-roofed barn," he thought proudly. "Not as it was in Father's time! Who is talked of in the whole district now? Brekhunov! And why? Because I stick to business. I take trouble, not like others who lie abed or waste their time on foolishness while I don't sleep of nights. Blizzard or no blizzard I start out. So business gets done. They think money-making is a joke. No, take pains and rack your brains! You get overtaken out of doors at night, like this, or keep awake night after night till the thoughts whirling in your head make the pillow turn," he meditated with pride. "They think people get on through luck. After all, the Mironovs are now millionaires. And why? Take pains and God gives. If only He grants me health!"

The thought that he might himself be a millionaire like Mironov, who began with nothing, so excited Vasili Andreevich that he felt the need of talking to somebody. But there was no one to talk to . . . If only he could have reached Goryachkin he would have talked to the landlord and shown him a thing or two.

"Just see how it blows! It will snow us up so deep that we shan't be able to get out in the morning!" he thought, listening to a gust of wind that blew against the front of the sledge, bending it and lashing the snow against it. He raised himself and looked round. All he could see through the whirling darkness was Mukhorty's dark head, his back covered by the fluttering drugget, and his thick knotted tail; while all round, in front and behind, was the same fluctuating whity darkness, sometimes seeming to get a little lighter and sometimes growing denser still.

"A pity I listened to Nikita," he thought. "We ought to have driven on. We should have come out somewhere, if only back to Grishkino and stayed the night at Taras's. As it is we must sit here all night. But what was I thinking about? Yes, that God gives to those who take trouble, but not to loafers, lie-abeds, or fools. I must have a smoke!"

He sat down again, got out his cigarette-case, and stretched himself flat on his stomach, screening the matches with the skirt of his coat. But the wind found its way in and put out match after match. At last he got one to burn and lit a cigarette. He was very glad that he had managed to do what he wanted, and though the wind smoked more of the cigarette than he did, he still got two or three puffs and felt more cheerful. He again leant back, wrapped himself up, started reflecting and remembering, and suddenly and quite unexpectedly lost consciousness and fell asleep.

Suddenly something seemed to give him a push and awoke him. Whether it was Mukhorty who had pulled some straw from under him, or whether something within him had startled him, at all events it woke him, and his heart began to beat faster and faster so that the sledge seemed to tremble under him. He opened his eyes. Everything around him was just as before. "It looks lighter," he thought. "I expect it won't be long before dawn." But he at once remembered that it was lighter because the moon had risen. He sat up and looked first at the horse. Mukhorty still stood with his back to the wind, shivering all over. One side of the drugget, which was completely covered with snow, had been blown back, the breeching had slipped down and the snow-covered head with its waving forelock and mane were now more visible. Vasili Andreevich leant over the back of the sledge and looked behind. Nikita still sat in the same position in which he had settled himself. The sacking with which he was covered, and his legs, were thickly covered with snow.

"If only that peasant doesn't freeze to death! His clothes are so wretched. I may be held responsible for him. What shiftless people they are—such a want of education," thought Vasili Andreevich, and he felt like taking the drugget off the horse and putting it over Nikita, but it would be very cold to get out and move about and, moreover, the horse might freeze to death. "Why did I bring him with me? It was all her stupidity!" he thought, recalling his unloved wife, and he rolled over into his old place at the front part of the sledge. "My uncle once spent a whole night like this," he reflected, "and was all right." But another case came at once to his mind. "But when they dug Sebastian out he was dead—stiff like a frozen carcass. If I'd only stopped the night in Grishkino all this would not have happened!"

And wrapping his coat carefully round him so that none of the warmth of the fur should be wasted but should warm him all over, neck, knees, and feet, he shut his eyes and tried to sleep again. But try as he would he could not get drowsy, on the contrary he felt wide awake and animated. Again he began counting his gains and the debts due to him, again he began bragging to himself and feeling pleased with himself and his position, but all this was continually disturbed by a stealthily approaching fear and by the unpleasant regret that he had not remained in Grishkino.

"How different it would be to be lying warm on a bench!"

He turned over several times in his attempts to get into a more comfortable position more sheltered from the wind, he wrapped up his legs closer, shut his eyes, and lay still. But either his legs in their strong felt boots began to ache from being bent in one position, or the wind blew in somewhere, and after lying still for a short time he again began to recall the disturbing fact that he might now have been lying quietly in the warm hut at Grishkino. He again sat up, turned about, muffled himself up, and settled down once more.

Once he fancied that he heard a distant cock-crow. He felt glad, turned down his coat-collar and listened with strained attention, but in spite of all his efforts nothing could be heard but the wind whistling between the shafts, the flapping of the kerchief, and the snow pelting against the frame of the sledge.

Nikita sat just as he had done all the time, not moving and not even answering Vasili Andreevich who had addressed him a couple of times. "He doesn't care a bit—he's probably asleep!" thought Vasili Andreevich with vexation, looking behind the sledge at Nikita who was covered with a thick layer of snow.

Vasili Andreevich got up and lay down again some twenty times. It seemed to him that the night would never end. "It must be getting near morning," he thought, getting up and looking around. "Let's have a look at my watch. It will be cold to unbutton, but if I only know that it's getting near morning I shall at any rate feel more cheerful. We could begin harnessing."

In the depth of his heart Vasili Andreevich knew that it could not yet be near morning, but he was growing more and more afraid, and wished both to get to know and yet to deceive himself. He carefully undid the fastening of his sheepskin, pushed in his hand, and felt about for a long time before he got to his waistcoat. With great difficulty he managed to draw out his silver watch with its enamelled flower design, and tried to make out the time. He could not see anything without a light. Again he went down on his knees and elbows as he had done when he lighted a cigarette, got out his matches, and proceeded to strike one. This time he went to work more carefully, and feeling with his fingers for a match with the largest head and the greatest amount of phosphorus, lit it at the first try. Bringing the face of the watch under the light he could hardly believe his eyes . . . It was only ten minutes past twelve. Almost the whole night was still before him.

"Oh, how long the night is!" he thought, feeling a cold shudder run down his back, and having fastened his fur coats again and wrapped himself up, he snuggled into a corner of the sledge intending to wait patiently. Suddenly, above the monotonous roar of the wind, he clearly distinguished another new and living sound. It steadily strengthened, and having become quite clear diminished just as gradually. Beyond all doubt it was a wolf, and he was so near that the movement of his jaws as he changed his cry was brought down the wind. Vasili Andreevich turned back the collar of his coat and listened attentively. Mukhorty too strained to listen, moving his ears, and when the wolf had ceased its howling he shifted from foot to foot and gave a warning snort. After this Vasili Andreevich could not fall asleep again or even calm himself. The more he tried to think of his accounts, his business, his reputation, his worth and his wealth, the more and more was he mastered by fear, and regrets that he had not stayed the night at Grishkino dominated and mingled in all his thoughts.

"Devil take the forest! Things were all right without it, thank God. Ah, if we had only put up for the night!" he said to himself. "They say it's drunkards that freeze," he thought, "and I have had some drink." And observing his sensations he noticed that he was beginning to shiver, without knowing whether it was from cold or from fear. He tried to wrap himself up and lie down as before, but could no longer do so. He could not stay in one position. He wanted to get up, to do something to master the gathering fear that was rising in him and against which he felt himself powerless. He again got out his cigarettes and matches, but only three matches were left and they were bad ones. The phosphorus rubbed off them all without lighting.

"The devil take you! Damned thing! Curse you!" he muttered, not knowing whom or what he was cursing, and he flung away the crushed cigarette. He was about to throw away the matchbox too, but checked the movement of his hand and put the box in his pocket instead. He was seized with such unrest that he could no longer remain in one spot. He climbed out of the sledge and standing with his back to the wind began to shift his belt again, fastening it lower down in the waist and tightening it.

"What's the use of lying and waiting for death? Better mount the horse and get away!" The thought suddenly occurred to him. "The horse will move when he has someone on his back. As for him," he thought of Nikita—"it's all the same to him whether he lives or dies. What is his life worth? He won't grudge his life, but I have something to live for, thank God."

He untied the horse, threw the reins over his neck and tried to mount, but his coats and boots were so heavy that he failed. Then he clambered up in the sledge and tried to mount from there, but the sledge tilted under his weight, and he failed again. At last he drew Mukhorty nearer to the sledge, cautiously balanced on one side of it, and managed to lie on his stomach across the horse's back. After lying like that for a while he shifted forward once and again, threw a leg over, and finally seated himself, supporting his feet on the loose breeching-straps. The shaking of the sledge awoke Nikita. He raised himself, and it seemed to Vasili Andreevich that he said something.

"Listen to such fools as you! Am I to die like this for nothing?" exclaimed Vasili Andreevich. And tucking the loose skirts of his fur coat in under his knees, he turned the horse and rode away from the sledge in the direction in which he thought the forest and the forester's hut must be.

VII

From the time he had covered himself with the sackcloth and seated himself behind the sledge, Nikita had not stirred. Like all those who live in touch with nature and have known want, he was patient and could wait for hours, even days, without growing restless or irritable. He heard his master call him, but did not answer because he did not want to move or talk. Though he still felt some warmth from the tea he had drunk and from his energetic struggle when clambering about in the snowdrift, he knew that this warmth would not last long and that he had no strength left to warm himself again by moving about, for he felt as tired as a horse when it stops and refuses to go further in spite of the whip, and its master sees that it must be fed before it can work again. The foot in the boot with a hole in it had already grown numb, and he could no longer feel his big toe. Besides that, his whole body began to feel colder and colder.

The thought that he might, and very probably would, die that night occurred to him, but did not seem particularly unpleasant or dreadful. It did not seem particularly unpleasant, because his whole life had been not a continual holiday, but on the contrary an unceasing round of toil of which he was beginning to feel weary. And it did not seem particularly dreadful, because besides the masters he had served here, like Vasili Andreevich, he always felt himself dependent on the Chief Master, who had sent him into this life, and he knew that when dying he would still be in that Master's power and would not be ill-used by Him. "It seems a pity to give up what one is used to and accustomed to. But there's nothing to be done, I shall get used to the new things."

"Sins?" he thought, and remembered his drunkenness, the money that had gone on drink, how he had offended his wife, his cursing, his neglect of church and of the fasts, and all the things the priest blamed him for at the confession. "Of course they are sins. But then, did I take them on of myself? That's evidently how God made me. Well, and the sins? Where am I to escape to?"

So at first he thought of what might happen to him that night, and then did not return to such thoughts but gave himself up to whatever recollections came into his head of themselves. Now he thought of Martha's arrival, of the drunkenness among the workers and his own renunciation of drink, then of their present journey and of Taras's house and the talk about the breaking-up of the family, then of his own lad, and of Mukhorty now sheltered under the drugget, and then of his master who made the sledge creak as he tossed about in it. "I expect you're sorry yourself that you started out, dear man," he thought. "It would seem hard to leave a life such as his! It's not like the likes of us."

Then all these recollections began to grow confused and got mixed in his head, and he fell asleep.

But when Vasili Andreevich, getting on the horse, jerked the sledge, against the back of which Nikita was leaning, and it shifted away and hit him in the back with one of its runners, he awoke and had to change his position whether he liked it or not. Straightening his legs with difficulty and shaking the snow off them he got up, and an agonizing cold immediately penetrated his whole body. On making out what was happening he called to Vasili Andreevich to leave him the drugget which the horse no longer needed, so that he might wrap himself in it.

But Vasili Andreevich did not stop, but disappeared amid the powdery snow.

Left alone Nikita considered for a moment what he should do. He felt that he had not the strength to go off in search of a house. It was no longer possible to sit down in his old place—it was by now all filled with snow. He felt that he could not get warmer in the sledge either, for there was nothing to cover himself with, and his coat and sheepskin no longer warmed him at all. He felt as cold as though he had nothing on but a shirt. He became frightened. "Lord, heavenly Father!" he muttered, and was comforted by the consciousness that he was not alone but that there was One who heard him and would not abandon him. He gave a deep sigh, and keeping the sackcloth over his head he got inside the sledge and lay down in the place where his master had been.

But he could not get warm in the sledge either. At first he shivered all over, then the shivering ceased and little by little he began to lose consciousness. He did not know whether he was dying or falling asleep, but felt equally prepared for the one as for the other.

VIII

Meanwhile Vasili Andreevich, with his feet and the ends of the reins, urged the horse on in the direction in which for some reason he expected the forest and forester's hut to be. The snow covered his eyes and the wind seemed intent on stopping him, but bending forward and constantly lapping his coat over and pushing it between himself and the cold harness pad which prevented him from sitting properly, he kept urging the horse on. Mukhorty ambled on obediently though with difficulty, in the direction in which he was driven.

Vasili Andreevich rode for about five minutes straight ahead, as he thought, seeing nothing but the horse's head and the white waste, and hearing only the whistle of the wind about the horse's ears and his coat collar.

Suddenly a dark patch showed up in front of him. His heart beat with joy, and he rode towards the object, already seeing in imagination the walls of village houses. But the dark patch was not stationary, it kept moving; and it was not a village but some tall stalks of wormwood sticking up through the snow on the boundary between two fields, and desperately tossing about under the pressure of the wind which beat it all to one side and whistled through it. The sight of that wormwood tormented by the pitiless wind made Vasili Andreevich shudder, he knew not why, and he hurriedly began urging the horse on, not noticing that when riding up to the wormwood he had quite changed his direction and was now heading the opposite way, though still imagining that he was riding towards where the hut should be. But the horse kept making towards the right, and Vasili Andreevich kept guiding it to the left.

Again something dark appeared in front of him. Again he rejoiced, convinced that now it was certainly a village. But once more it was the same boundary line overgrown with wormwood, once more the same wormwood desperately tossed by the wind and carrying unreasoning terror to his heart. But its being the same wormwood was not all, for beside it there was a horse's track partly snowed over. Vasili Andreevich stopped, stooped down and looked carefully. It was a horse-track only partially covered with snow, and could be none but his own horse's hoof prints. He had evidently gone round in a small circle. "I shall perish like that!" he thought, and not to give way to his terror he urged on the horse still more, peering into the snowy darkness in which he saw only flitting and fitful points of light. Once he thought he heard the barking of dogs or the howling of wolves, but the sounds were so faint and indistinct that he did not know whether he heard them or merely imagined them, and he stopped and began to listen intently.

Suddenly some terrible, deafening cry resounded near his ears, and everything shivered and shook under him. He seized Mukhorty's neck, but that too was shaking all over and the terrible cry grew still more frightful. For some seconds Vasili Andreevich could not collect himself or understand what was happening. It was only that Mukhorty, whether to encourage himself or to call for help, had neighed loudly and resonantly. "Ugh, you wretch!

How you frightened me, damn you!" thought Vasili Andreevich. But even when he understood the cause of his terror he could not shake it off.

"I must calm myself and think things over," he said to himself, but yet he could not stop, and continued to urge the horse on, without noticing that he was now going with the wind instead of against it. His body, especially between his legs where it touched the pad of the harness and was not covered by his overcoats, was getting painfully cold, especially when the horse walked slowly. His legs and arms trembled and his breathing came fast. He saw himself perishing amid this dreadful snowy waste, and could see no means of escape.

Suddenly the horse under him tumbled into something and, sinking into a snow-drift, began to plunge and fell on his side. Vasili Andreevich jumped off, and in so doing dragged to one side the breechband on which his foot was resting, and twisted round the pad to which he held as he dismounted. As soon as he had jumped off, the horse struggled to his feet, plunged forward, gave one leap and another, neighed again, and dragging the drugget and the breechband after him, disappeared, leaving Vasili Andreevich alone on the snow-drift.

The latter pressed on after the horse, but the snow lay so deep and his coats were so heavy that, sinking above his knees at each step, he stopped breathless after taking not more than twenty steps. "The copse, the oxen, the lease-hold, the shop, the tavern, the house with the iron-roofed barn, and my heir," thought he. "How can I leave all that? What does this mean? It cannot be!" These thoughts flashed through his mind. Then he thought of the wormwood tossed by the wind, which he had twice ridden past, and he was seized with such terror that he did not believe in the reality of what was happening to him. "Can this be a dream?" he thought, and tried to wake up but could not. It was real snow that lashed his face and covered him and chilled his right hand from which he had lost the glove, and this was a real desert in which he was now left alone like that wormwood, awaiting an inevitable, speedy, and meaningless death.

"Queen of Heaven! Holy Father Nicholas, teacher of temperance!" he thought, recalling the service of the day before and the holy icon with its black face and gilt frame, and the tapers which he sold to be set before that icon and which were almost immediately brought back to him scarcely burnt at all, and which he put away in the store-chest. He began to pray to that same Nicholas the Wonder-Worker to save him, promising him a thanksgiving service and some candles. But he clearly and indubitably realized that the icon, its frame, the candles, the priest, and the thanksgiving service, though very important and necessary in church, could do nothing for him here, and that there was and could be no connexion between those candles and services and his present disastrous plight. "I must not despair," he thought. "I must follow the horse's track before it is snowed under. He will lead me out, or I may even catch him. Only I must not hurry, or I shall stick fast and be more lost than ever."

But in spite of his resolution to go quietly, he rushed forward and even ran, continually falling, getting up and falling again. The horse's track was already hardly visible in places where the snow did not lie deep. "I am lost!" thought Vasili Andreevich. "I shall lose the track and not catch the horse." But at that moment he saw something black. It was Mukhorty, and not only Mukhorty, but the sledge with the shafts and the kerchief. Mukhorty, with the sacking and the breechband twisted round to one side, was standing not in his former place but nearer to the shafts, shaking his head which the reins he was stepping on drew downwards. It turned out that Vasili Andreevich had sunk in the same ravine Nikita had previously fallen into, and that Mukhorty had been bringing him back to the sledge and he had got off his back no more than fifty paces from where the sledge was.

IX

Having stumbled back to the sledge Vasili Andreevich caught hold of it and for a long time stood motionless, trying to calm himself and recover his breath. Nikita was not in his former place, but something, already covered with snow, was lying in the sledge and Vasili Andreevich concluded that this was Nikita. His terror had now quite left him, and if he felt any fear it was lest the dreadful terror should return that he had experienced when on the horse and especially when he was left alone in the snow-drift. At any cost he had to avoid that terror, and to keep it away he must do something—occupy himself with something. And the first thing he did was to turn his back to the wind and open his fur coat. Then, as soon as he recovered his breath a little, he shook the snow out of his boots and out of his left-hand glove (the right-hand glove was hopelessly lost and by this time probably lying somewhere under a dozen inches of snow); then as was his custom when going out of his shop to buy grain from the peasants, he pulled his girdle low down and tightened it and prepared for action. The first thing that occurred to him was to free Mukhorty's leg from the rein. Having done that, and tethered him to the iron cramp at the front of the sledge where he had been before, he was going round the horse's quarters to put the breechband and pad straight and cover him with the cloth, but at that moment he noticed that something was moving in the sledge and Nikita's head rose up out of the snow that covered it. Nikita, who was half frozen, rose with great difficulty and sat up, moving his hand before his nose in a strange manner just as if he were driving away flies. He waved his hand and said something, and seemed to Vasili Andreevich to be calling him. Vasili Andreevich left the cloth unadjusted and went up to the sledge.

"What is it?" he asked. "What are you saying?"

"I'm dy . . . ing, that's what," said Nikita brokenly and with difficulty. "Give what is owing to me to my lad, or to my wife, no matter."

"Why, are you really frozen?" asked Vasili Andreevich.

"I feel it's my death. Forgive me for Christ's sake . . ." said Nikita in a tearful voice, continuing to wave his hand before his face as if driving away flies.

Vasili Andreevich stood silent and motionless for half a minute. Then suddenly, with the same resolution with which he used to strike hands when making a good purchase, he took a step back and turning up his sleeves began raking the snow off Nikita and out of the sledge. Having done this he hurriedly undid his girdle, opened out his fur coat, and having pushed Nikita down, lay down on top of him, covering him not only with his fur coat but with the whole of his body, which glowed with warmth. After pushing the skirts of his coat between Nikita and the sides of the sledge, and holding down its hem with his knees, Vasili Andreevich lay like that face down, with his head pressed against the front of the sledge. Here he no longer heard the horse's movements or the whistling of the wind, but only Nikita's breathing. At first and for a long time Nikita lay motionless, then he sighed deeply and moved.

"There, and you say you are dying! Lie still and get warm, that's our way . . ." began Vasili Andreevich.

But to his great surprise he could say no more, for tears came to his eyes and his lower jaw began to quiver rapidly. He stopped speaking and only gulped down the risings in his throat. "Seems I was badly frightened and have gone quite weak," he thought. But this weakness was not only unpleasant, but gave him a peculiar joy such as he had never felt before.

"That's our way!" he said to himself, experiencing a strange and solemn tenderness. He lay like that for a long time, wiping his eyes on the fur of his coat and tucking under his knee the right skirt, which the wind kept turning up.

But he longed so passionately to tell somebody of his joyful condition that he said: "Nikita!"

"It's comfortable, warm!" came a voice from beneath.

"There, you see, friend, I was going to perish. And you would have been frozen, and I should have . . ."

But again his jaws began to quiver and his eyes to fill with tears, and he could say no more.

"Well, never mind," he thought. "I know about myself what I know."

He remained silent and lay like that for a long time.

Nikita kept him warm from below and his fur coats from above. Only his hands, with which he kept his coat-skirts down round Nikita's sides, and his legs which the wind kept uncovering, began to freeze, especially his right hand which had no glove. But he did not think of his legs or of his hands but only of how to warm the peasant who was lying under him. He looked out several times at Mukhorty and could see that his back was uncovered and the drugget and breeching lying on the snow, and that he ought to get up and cover him, but he could not bring himself to leave Nikita and disturb even for a moment the joyous condition he was in. He no longer felt any kind of terror.

"No fear, we shan't lose him this time!" he said to himself, referring to his getting the peasant warm with the same boastfulness with which he spoke of his buying and selling.

Vasili Andreevich lay in that way for one hour, another, and a third, but he was unconscious of the passage of time. At first impressions of the snowstorm, the sledge-shafts, and the horse with the shaft-bow shaking before his eyes, kept passing through his mind, then he remembered Nikita lying under him, then recollections of the festival, his wife, the police-officer, and the box of candles, began to mingle with these; then again Nikita, this time lying under that box, then the peasants, customers and traders, and the white walls of his house with its iron roof with Nikita lying underneath, presented themselves to his imagination. Afterwards all these impressions blended into one nothingness. As the colours of the rainbow unite into one white light, so all these different impressions mingled into one, and he fell asleep.

For a long time he slept without dreaming, but just before dawn the visions recommenced. It seemed to him that he was standing by the box of tapers and that Tikhon's wife was asking for a five kopek taper for the Church fete. He wished to take one out and give it to her, but his hands would not life, being held tight in his pockets. He wanted to walk round the box but his feet would not move and his new clean goloshes had grown to the stone floor, and he could neither lift them nor get his feet out of the goloshes. Then the taper-box was no longer a box but a bed, and suddenly Vasili Andreevich saw himself lying in his bed at home. He was lying in his bed and could not get up. Yet it was necessary for him to get up because Ivan Matveich, the police-officer, would soon call for him and he had to go with him—either to bargain for the forest or to put Mukhorty's breeching straight.

He asked his wife: "Nikolaevna, hasn't he come yet?" "No, he hasn't," she replied. He heard someone drive up to the front steps. "It must be him." "No, he's gone past." "Nikolaevna! I say, Nikolaevna, isn't he here yet?" "No." He was still lying on his bed and could not get up, but was always waiting. And this waiting was uncanny and yet joyful. Then suddenly his joy was completed. He whom he was expecting came; not Ivan Matveich the police-officer, but someone else—yet it was he whom he had been waiting for. He came and called him; and it was he who had called him and told him to lie down on Nikita. And Vasili Andreevich was glad that that one had come for him.

"I'm coming!" he cried joyfully, and that cry awoke him, but woke him up not at all the same person he had been when he fell asleep. He tried to get up but could not, tried to move his arm and could not, to move his leg and also could not, to turn his head and could not. He was surprised but not at all disturbed by this. He understood that this was death, and was not at all disturbed by that either.

He remembered that Nikita was lying under him and that he had got warm and was alive, and it seemed to him that he was Nikita and Nikita was he, and that his life was not in himself but in Nikita. He strained his ears and heard Nikita breathing and even slightly snoring. "Nikita is alive, so I too am alive!" he said to himself triumphantly.

And he remembered his money, his shop, his house, the buying and selling, and Mironov's millions, and it was hard for him to understand why that man, called Vasili Brekhunov, had troubled himself with all those things with which he had been troubled.

"Well, it was because he did not know what the real thing was," he thought, concerning that Vasili Brekhunov. "He did not know, but now I know and know for sure. Now I know!" And again he heard the voice of the one who had called him before. "I'm coming! Coming!" he responded gladly, and his whole being was filled with joyful emotion. He felt himself free and that nothing could hold him back any longer.

After that Vasili Andreevich neither saw, heard, nor felt anything more in this world.

All around the snow still eddied. The same whirlwinds of snow circled about, covering the dead Vasili Andreevich's fur coat, the shivering Mukhorty, the sledge, now scarcely to be seen, and Nikita lying at the bottom of it, kept warm beneath his dead master.

X

Nikita awoke before daybreak. He was aroused by the cold that had begun to creep down his back. He had dreamt that he was coming from the mill with a load of his master's flour and when crossing the stream had missed the bridge and let the cart get stuck. And he saw that he had crawled under the cart and was trying to lift it by arching his back. But strange to say the cart did not move, it stuck to his back and he could neither lift it nor get out from under it. It was crushing the whole of his loins. And how cold it felt! Evidently he must crawl out. "Have done!" he exclaimed to whoever was pressing the cart down on him. "Take out the sacks!" But the cart pressed down colder and colder, and then he heard a strange knocking, awoke completely, and remembered everything. The cold cart was his dead and frozen master lying upon him. And the knock was produced by Mukhorty, who had twice struck the sledge with his hoof.

"Andreevich! Eh, Andreevich!" Nikita called cautiously, beginning to realize the truth, and straightening his back. But Vasili Andreevich did not answer and his stomach and legs were stiff and cold and heavy like iron weights.

"He must have died! May the Kingdom of Heaven be his!" thought Nikita.

He turned his head, dug with his hand through the snow about him and opened his eyes. It was daylight; the wind was whistling as before between the shafts, and the snow was falling in the same way, except that it was no longer driving against the frame of the sledge but silently covered both sledge and horse deeper and deeper, and neither the horse's movements nor his breathing were any longer to be heard.

"He must have frozen too," thought Nikita of Mukhorty, and indeed those hoof knocks against the sledge, which had awakened Nikita, were the last efforts the already numbed Mukhorty had made to keep on his feet before dying.

"O Lord God, it seems Thou art calling me too!" said Nikita. "Thy Holy Will be done. But it's uncanny . . . Still, a man can't die twice and must die once. If only it would come soon!"

And he again drew in his head, closed his eyes, and became unconscious, fully convinced that now he was certainly and finally dying.

It was not till noon that day that peasants dug Vasili Andreevich and Nikita out of the snow with their shovels, not more than seventy yards from the road and less than half a mile from the village.

The snow had hidden the sledge, but the shafts and the kerchief tied to them were still visible. Mukhorty, buried up to his belly in snow, with the breeching and drugget hanging down, stood all white, his dead head pressed against his frozen throat: icicles hung from his nostrils, his eyes were covered with hoar-frost as though filled with tears, and he had grown so thin in that one night that he was nothing but skin and bone.

Vasili Andreevich was stiff as a frozen carcass, and when they rolled him off Nikita his legs remained apart and his arms stretched out as they had been. His bulging hawk eyes were frozen, and his open mouth under his clipped moustache was full of snow. But Nikita though chilled through was still alive. When he had been brought to, he felt sure that he was already dead and that what was taking place with him was no longer happening in this world but in the next. When he heard the peasants shouting as they dug him out and rolled the frozen body of Vasili Andreevich from off him, he was at first surprised that in the other world peasants should be shouting in the same old way and had the same kind of body, and then when he realized that he was still in this world he was sorry rather than glad, especially when he found that the toes on both his feet were frozen.

Nikita lay in hospital for two months. They cut off three of his toes, but the others recovered so that he was still able to work and went on living for another twenty years, first as a farm-labourer, then in his old age as a watchman. He died at home as he had wished, only this year, under the icons with a lighted taper in his hands. Before he died he asked his wife's forgiveness and forgave her for the cooper. He also took leave of his son and grandchildren, and died sincerely glad that he was relieving his son and daughter-in-law of the burden of having to feed him, and that he was now really passing from this life of which he was weary into that other life which every year and every hour grew clearer and more desirable to him. Whether he is better or worse off there where he awoke after his death, whether he was disappointed or found there what he expected, we shall all soon learn.

Too Dear!

(TOLSTOY'S ADAPTATION OF A STORY BY GUY DE MAUPASSANT)

[First published in 1897. This version is taken from the collection *Twenty-three Tales* (1906) translated by Louise and Aylmer Maude.]

Near the borders of France and Italy, on the shore of the Mediterranean Sea, lies a tiny little kingdom called Monaco. Many a small country town can boast more inhabitants than this kingdom, for there are only about seven thousand of them all told, and if all the land in the kingdom were divided there would not be an acre for each inhabitant. But in this toy kingdom there is a real kinglet; and he has a palace, and courtiers, and ministers, and a bishop, and generals, and an army.

It is not a large army, only sixty men in all, but still it is an army. There were also taxes in this kingdom, as elsewhere: a tax on tobacco, and on wine and spirits, and a poll-tax. But though the people there drink and smoke as people do in other countries, there are so few of them that the King would have been hard put to it to feed his courtiers and officials and to keep himself, if he had not found a new and special source of revenue. This special revenue comes from a gaming house, where people play roulette. People play, and whether they win or lose the keeper always gets a percentage on the turnover; and out of his profits he pays a large sum to the King. The reason he pays so much is that it is the only such gambling establishment left in Europe. Some of the little German Sovereigns used to keep gaming houses of the same kind, but some years ago they were forbidden to do so. The reason they were stopped was because these gaming houses did so much harm. A man would come and try his luck, then he would risk all he had and lose it, then he would even risk money that did not belong to him and lose that too, and then, in despair, he would drown or shoot himself. So the Germans forbade their rulers to make money in this way; but there was no one to stop the King of Monaco, and he remained with a monopoly of the business.

So now every one who wants to gamble goes to Monaco. Whether they win or lose, the King gains by it. 'You can't earn stone palaces by honest labour,' as the proverb says; and the

Kinglet of Monaco knows it is a dirty business, but what is he to do? He has to live; and to draw a revenue from drink and from tobacco is also not a nice thing. So he lives and reigns, and rakes in the money, and holds his court with all the ceremony of a real king.

He has his coronation, his levees; he rewards, sentences, and pardons, and he also has his reviews, councils, laws, and courts of justice: just like other kings, only all on a smaller scale.

Now it happened a few years ago that a murder was committed in this toy King's domains. The people of that kingdom are peaceable, and such a thing had not happened before. The judges assembled with much ceremony and tried the case in the most judicial manner. There were judges, and prosecutors, and jurymen, and barristers. They argued and judged, and at last they condemned the criminal to have his head cut off as the law directs. So far so good. Next they submitted the sentence to the King. The King read the sentence and confirmed it. "If the fellow must be executed, execute him."

There was only one hitch in the matter; and that was that they had neither a guillotine for cutting heads off, nor an executioner. The Ministers considered the matter, and decided to address an inquiry to the French Government, asking whether the French could not lend them a machine and an expert to cut off the criminal's head; and if so, would the French kindly inform them what the cost would be. The letter was sent. A week later the reply came: a machine and an expert could be supplied, and the cost would be 16,000 francs. This was laid before the King. He thought it over. Sixteen thousand francs! "The wretch is not worth the money," said he. "Can't it be done, somehow, cheaper? Why 16,000 francs is more than two francs a head on the whole population. The people won't stand it, and it may cause a riot!"

So a Council was called to consider what could be done; and it was decided to send a similar inquiry to the King of Italy. The French Government is republican, and has no proper respect for kings; but the King of Italy was a brother monarch, and might be induced to do the thing cheaper. So the letter was written, and a prompt reply was received.

The Italian Government wrote that they would have pleasure in supplying both a machine and an expert; and the whole cost would be 12,000 francs, including travelling expenses. This was cheaper, but still it seemed too much. The rascal was really not worth the money. It would still mean nearly two francs more per head on the taxes. Another Council was called. They discussed and considered how it could be done with less expense. Could not one of the soldiers perhaps be got to do it in a rough and homely fashion? The General was called and was asked: "Can't you find us a soldier who would cut the man's head off? In war they don't mind killing people. In fact, that is what they are trained for." So the General talked it over with the soldiers to see whether one of them would not undertake the job. But none of the soldiers would do it. "No," they said, "we don't know how to do it; it is not a thing we have been taught."

What was to be done? Again the Ministers considered and reconsidered. They assembled a Commission, and a Committee, and a Sub-Committee, and at last they decided that the best thing would be to alter the death sentence to one of imprisonment for life. This would enable the King to show his mercy, and it would come cheaper.

The King agreed to this, and so the matter was arranged. The only hitch now was that there was no suitable prison for a man sentenced for life. There was a small lock-up where people were sometimes kept temporarily, but there was no strong prison fit for permanent use. However, they managed to find a place that would do, and they put the young fellow there and placed a guard over him. The guard had to watch the criminal, and had also to fetch his food from the palace kitchen.

The prisoner remained there month after month till a year had passed. But when a year had passed, the Kinglet, looking over the account of his income and expenditure one day, noticed a new item of expenditure. This was for the keep of the criminal; nor was it a small item either. There was a special guard, and there was also the man's food. It came to more than 600 francs a year. And the worst of it was that the fellow was still young and healthy, and might live for fifty years. When one came to reckon it up, the matter was serious. It would never do. So the King summoned his Ministers and said to them:

"You must find some cheaper way of dealing with this rascal. The present plan is too expensive." And the Ministers met and considered and reconsidered, till one of them said: "Gentlemen, in my opinion we must dismiss the guard." "But then," rejoined another Minister, "the fellow will run away." "Well," said the first speaker, "let him run away, and be hanged to him!" So they reported the result of their deliberations to the Kinglet, and he agreed with them. The guard was dismissed, and they waited to see what would happen. All that happened was that at dinner time the criminal came out, and, not finding his guard, he went to the King's kitchen to fetch his own dinner. He took what was given him, returned to the prison, shut the door on himself, and stayed inside. Next day the same thing occurred. He went for his food at the proper time; but as for running away, he did not show the least sign of it! What was to be done? They considered the matter again.

"We shall have to tell him straight out," said they, "that we do not want to keep him." So the Minister of Justice had him brought before him.

"Why do you not run away?" said the Minister. "There is no guard to keep you. You can go where you like, and the King will not mind."

"I daresay the King would not mind," replied the man, "but I have nowhere to go. What can I do? You have ruined my character by your sentence, and people will turn their backs on me. Besides, I have got out of the way of working. You have treated me badly. It is not fair. In the first place, when once you sentenced me to death you ought to have executed me; but you did not do it. That is one thing. I did not complain about that. Then you sentenced me to imprisonment for life and put a guard to bring me my food; but after a time you took him away again and I had to fetch my own food. Again I did not complain. But now you actually want me to go away! I can't agree to that. You may do as you like, but I won't go away!"

What was to be done? Once more the Council was summoned. What course could they adopt? The man would not go. They reflected and considered. The only way to get rid of him was to offer him a pension. And so they reported to the King. "There is nothing else for it," said they; "we must get rid of him somehow." The sum fixed was 600 francs, and this was announced to the prisoner.

"Well," said he, "I don't mind, so long as you undertake to pay it regularly. On that condition I am willing to go."

So the matter was settled. He received one-third of his annuity in advance, and left the King's dominions. It was only a quarter of an hour by rail; and he emigrated, and settled just across the frontier, where he bought a bit of land, started market-gardening, and now lives comfortably. He always goes at the proper time to draw his pension. Having received it, he goes to the gaming tables, stakes two or three francs, sometimes wins and sometimes loses, and then returns home. He lives peaceably and well.

It is a good thing that he did not commit his crime in a country where they do not grudge expense to cut a man's head off, or to keeping him in prison for life.

Father Sergius

[Tolstoy began writing this story in 1890 and finished it in 1898.
It reflects his own struggle between the desire to lead a spiritual
life and sexual temptations. It was published posthumously.
Reproduced here is a translation by Louise and Aylmer Maude.]

I

In Petersburg in the eighteen-forties a surprising event occurred. An officer of the Cuirassier Life Guards, a handsome prince who everyone predicted would become aide-de-camp to the Emperor Nicholas I and have a brilliant career, left the service, broke off his engagement to a beautiful maid of honour, a favourite of the Empress's, gave his small estate to his sister, and retired to a monastery to become a monk.

This event appeared extraordinary and inexplicable to those who did not know his inner motives, but for Prince Stepan Kasatsky himself it all occurred so naturally that he could not imagine how he could have acted otherwise.

His father, a retired colonel of the Guards, had died when Stepan was twelve, and sorry as his mother was to part from her son, she entered him at the Military College as her deceased husband had intended.

The widow herself, with her daughter, Varvara, moved to Petersburg to be near her son and have him with her for the holidays.

The boy was distinguished both by his brilliant ability and by his immense self-esteem. He was first both in his studies—especially in mathematics, of which he was particularly fond—and also in drill and in riding. Though of more than average height, he was handsome and agile, and he would have been an altogether exemplary cadet had it not been for his quick temper. He was remarkably truthful, and was neither dissipated nor addicted to drink. The only faults that marred his conduct were fits of fury to which he was subject and during which he lost control of himself and became like a wild animal. He once nearly threw out of the window another cadet who had begun to tease him about his collection of minerals. On another occasion he came almost completely to grief by flinging a whole dish of cutlets at an officer who was acting as steward, attacking him and, it was said, striking him for having broken his word and told a barefaced lie. He would certainly have been reduced to the ranks had not the Director of the College hushed up the whole matter and dismissed the steward.

By the time he was eighteen he had finished his College course and received a commission as lieutenant in an aristocratic regiment of the Guards.

The Emperor Nicholas Pavlovich (Nicholas I) had noticed him while he was still at the College, and continued to take notice of him in the regiment, and it was on this account that people predicted for him an appointment as aide-de-camp to the Emperor. Kasatsky himself strongly desired it, not from ambition only but chiefly because since his cadet days he had been passionately devoted to Nicholas Pavlovich. The Emperor had often visited the Military College and every time Kasatsky saw that tall erect figure, with breast expanded in its military overcoat, entering with brisk step, saw the cropped side-whiskers, the moustache, the aquiline nose, and heard the sonorous voice exchanging greetings with the cadets, he was seized by the same rapture that he experienced later on when he met the woman he loved. Indeed, his passionate adoration of the Emperor was even stronger: he wished to sacrifice something—everything, even himself—to prove his complete devotion. And the Emperor Nicholas was conscious of evoking this rapture and deliberately aroused it. He played with the cadets, surrounded himself with them, treating them sometimes with childish simplicity, sometimes as a friend, and then again with majestic solemnity. After that affair with the officer, Nicholas Pavlovich said nothing to Kasatsky, but when the latter approached he waved him away theatrically, frowned, shook his finger at him, and afterwards when leaving, said: "Remember that I know everything. There are some things I would rather not know, but they remain here," and he pointed to his heart.

When on leaving College the cadets were received by the Emperor, he did not again refer to Kasatsky's offence, but told them all, as was his custom, that they should serve him and the fatherland loyally, that he would always be their best friend, and that when necessary they might approach him direct. All the cadets were as usual greatly moved, and Kasatsky even shed tears, remembering the past, and vowed that he would serve his beloved Tsar with all his soul.

When Kasatsky took up his commission his mother moved with her daughter first to Moscow and then to their country estate. Kasatsky gave half his property to his sister and kept only enough to maintain himself in the expensive regiment he had joined.

To all appearance he was just an ordinary, brilliant young officer of the Guards making a career for himself; but intense and complex strivings went on within him. From early childhood his efforts had seemed to be very varied, but essentially they were all one and the same. He tried in everything he took up to attain such success and perfection as would evoke praise and surprise. Whether it was his studies or his military exercises, he took them up and worked at them till he was praised and held up as an example to others. Mastering one subject he took up another, and obtained first place in his studies. For example, while still at College he noticed in himself an awkwardness in French conversation, and contrived to master French till he spoke it as well as Russian, and then he took up chess and became an excellent player.

Apart from his main vocation, which was the service of his Tsar and the fatherland, he always set himself some particular aim, and however unimportant it was, devoted himself completely to it and lived for it until it was accomplished. And as soon as it was attained another aim would immediately present itself, replacing its predecessor. This passion for distinguishing himself, or for accomplishing something in order to distinguish himself, filled his life. On taking up his commission he set himself to acquire the utmost perfection in knowledge of the service, and very soon became a model officer, though still with the same fault of ungovernable irascibility, which here in the service again led him to commit actions inimical to his success. Then he took to reading, having once in conversation in society felt himself deficient in general education—and again achieved his purpose. Then, wishing to secure a brilliant position in high society, he learnt to dance excellently and very soon was invited to all the balls in the best circles, and to some of their evening gatherings. But this did not satisfy him: he was accustomed to being first, and in this society was far from being so.

The highest society then consisted, and I think always consist, of four sorts of people: rich people who are received at Court, people not wealthy but born and brought up in Court circles, rich people who ingratiate themselves into the Court set, and people neither rich nor belonging to the Court but who ingratiate themselves into the first and second sets.

Kasatsky did not belong to the first two sets, but was readily welcomed in the others. On entering society he determined to have relations with some society lady, and to his own surprise quickly accomplished this purpose. He soon realized, however, that the circles in which he moved were not the highest, and that though he was received in the highest spheres he did not belong to them. They were polite to him, but showed by their whole manner that they had their own set and that he was not of it. And Kasatsky wished to belong to that inner circle. To attain that end it would be necessary to be an aide-de-camp to the Emperor—which he expected to become—or to marry into that exclusive set, which he resolved to do. And his choice fell on a beauty belonging to the Court, who not merely belonged to the circle into which he wished to be accepted, but whose friendship was coveted by the very highest people and those most firmly established in that highest circle. This was Countess Korotkova. Kasatsky began to pay court to her, and not merely for the sake of his career. She was extremely attractive and he soon fell in love with her. At first she was noticeably cool towards him, but then suddenly changed and became gracious, and her mother gave him pressing invitations to visit them. Kasatsky proposed and was accepted. He was surprised at the facility with which he attained such happiness. But though he noticed something strange and unusual in the behaviour towards him of both mother and daughter, he was blinded by being so deeply in love, and did not realize what almost the whole town knew—namely, that his fiancée had been the Emperor Nicholas's mistress the previous year.

Two weeks before the day arranged for the wedding, Kasatsky was at Tsarskoe Selo at his fiancée's country place. It was a hot day in May. He and his betrothed had walked about the garden and were sitting on a bench in a shady linden alley. Mary's white muslin dress suited her particularly well, and she seemed the personification of innocence and love as she sat, now bending her head, now gazing up at the very tall and handsome man who was speaking to her with particular tenderness and self-restraint, as if he feared by word or gesture to offend or sully her angelic purity.

Kasatsky belonged to those men of the eighteen-forties (they are now no longer to be found) who while deliberately and without any conscientious scruples condoning impurity in themselves, required ideal and angelic purity in their women, regarded all unmarried women of their circle as possessed of such purity, and treated them accordingly. There was much that was false and harmful in this outlook, as concerning the laxity the men permitted themselves, but in regard to the women that old-fashioned view (sharply differing from that held by young people today who see in every girl merely a female seeking a mate) was, I think, of value. The girls, perceiving such adoration, endeavoured with more or less success to be goddesses.

Such was the view Kasatsky held of women, and that was how he regarded his fiancée. He was particularly in love that day, but did not experience any sensual desire for her. On the contrary he regarded her with tender adoration as something unattainable.

He rose to his full height, standing before her with both hands on his sabre.

"I have only now realized what happiness a man can experience! And it is you, my darling, who have given me this happiness," he said with a timid smile.

Endearments had not yet become usual between them, and feeling himself morally inferior he felt terrified at this stage to use them to such an angel.

"It is thanks to you that I have come to know myself. I have learnt that I am better than I thought."

"I have known that for a long time. That was why I began to love you."

Nightingales trilled near by and the fresh leafage rustled, moved by a passing breeze.

He took her hand and kissed it, and tears came into his eyes.

She understood that he was thanking her for having said she loved him. He silently took a few steps up and down, and then approached her again and sat down.

"You know . . . I have to tell you . . . I was not disinterested when I began to make love to you. I wanted to get into society; but later . . . how unimportant that became in comparison with you— when I got to know you. You are not angry with me for that?"

She did not reply but merely touched his hand. He understood that this meant: "No, I am not angry."

"You said . . ." He hesitated. It seemed too bold to say. "You said that you began to love me. I believe it—but there is something that troubles you and checks your feeling. What is it?"

"Yes—now or never!" thought she. "He is bound to know of it anyway. But now he will not forsake me. Ah, if he should, it would be terrible!" And she threw a loving glance at his tall, noble, powerful figure. She loved him now more than she had loved the Tsar, and apart from the Imperial dignity would not have preferred the Emperor to him.

"Listen! I cannot deceive you. I have to tell you. You ask what it is? It is that I have loved before."

She again laid her hand on his with an imploring gesture. He was silent.

"You want to know who it was? It was—the Emperor."

"We all love him. I can imagine you, a schoolgirl at the Institute . . ."

"No, it was later. I was infatuated, but it passed . . . I must tell you . . ."

"Well, what of it?"

"No, it was not simply—" She covered her face with her hands.

"What? You gave yourself to him?"

She was silent.

"His mistress?"

She did not answer.

He sprang up and stood before her with trembling jaws, pale as death. He now remembered how the Emperor, meeting him on the Nevsky, had amiably congratulated him.

"O God, what have I done! Stiva!"

"Don't touch me! Don't touch me! Oh, how it pains!"

He turned away and went to the house. There he met her mother.

"What is the matter, Prince? I . . ." She became silent on seeing his face. The blood had suddenly rushed to his head.

"You knew it, and used me to shield them! If you weren't a woman . . .!" he cried, lifting his enormous fist, and turning aside he ran away.

Had his fiancée's lover been a private person he would have killed him, but it was his beloved Tsar.

Next day he applied both for furlough and his discharge, and professing to be ill, so as to see no one, he went away to the country.

He spent the summer at his village arranging his affairs. When summer was over he did not return to Petersburg, but entered a monastery and there became a monk.

His mother wrote to try to dissuade him from this decisive step, but he replied that he felt God's call which transcended all other considerations. Only his sister, who was as proud and ambitious as he, understood him.

She understood that he had become a monk in order to be above those who considered themselves his superiors. And she understood him correctly. By becoming a monk he showed contempt for all that seemed most important to others and had seemed so to him while he was in the service, and he now ascended a height from which he could look down on those he had formerly envied . . . But it was not this alone, as his sister Varvara supposed, that influenced him. There was also in him something else—a sincere religious feeling which Varvara did not know, which intertwined itself with the feeling of pride and the desire for pre-eminence, and guided him. His disillusionment with Mary, whom he had thought of angelic purity, and his sense of injury, were so strong that they brought him to despair, and the despair led him—to what? To God, to his childhood's faith which had never been destroyed in him.

Kasatsky entered the monastery on the feast of the Intercession of the Blessed Virgin. The Abbot of that monastery was a gentleman by birth, a learned writer and a starets, that is, he belonged to that succession of monks originating in Walachia who each choose a director and teacher whom they implicitly obey. This Superior had been a disciple of the starets Ambrose, who was a disciple of Makarius, who was a disciple of the starets Leonid, who was a disciple of Paussy Velichkovsky.

To this Abbot Kasatsky submitted himself as to his chosen director. Here in the monastery, besides the feeling of ascendency over others that such a life gave him, he felt much as he had done in the world: he found satisfaction in attaining the greatest possible perfection outwardly as well as inwardly. As in the regiment he had been not merely an irreproachable officer but had even exceeded his duties and widened the borders of perfection, so also as a monk he tried to be perfect, and was always industrious, abstemious, submissive, and meek, as well as pure both in deed and in thought, and obedient. This last quality in particular made life far easier for him. If many of the demands of life in the monastery, which was near the capital and much frequented, did not please him and were temptations to him, they were all nullified by obedience: 'It is not for me to reason; my business is to do the task set me, whether it be standing beside the relics, singing in the choir, or making up accounts in the monastery guest-house.' All possibility of doubt about anything was silenced by obedience to the starets. Had it not been for this, he would have been oppressed by the length and monotony of the church services, the bustle of the many visitors, and the bad qualities of the other monks. As it was, he not only bore it all joyfully but found in it solace and support. "I don't know why it is necessary to hear the same prayers several times a day, but I know that it is necessary; and knowing this I find joy in them." His director told him that as material food is necessary for the maintenance of the life of the body, so spiritual food—the church prayers—is necessary for the maintenance of the spiritual life. He believed this, and though the church services, for which he had to get up early in the morning, were a difficulty, they certainly calmed him and gave him joy. This was the result of his consciousness of humility, and the certainty that whatever he had to do, being fixed by the starets, was right.

The interest of his life consisted not only in an ever greater and greater subjugation of his will, but in the attainment of all the Christian virtues, which at first seemed to him easily attainable. He had given his whole estate to his sister and did not regret it, he had no personal claims, humility towards his inferiors was not merely easy for him but afforded him pleasure. Even victory over the sins of the flesh, greed and lust, was easily attained. His director had specially warned him against the latter sin, but Kasatsky felt free from it and was glad.

One thing only tormented him—the remembrance of his fiancée; and not merely the remembrance but the vivid image of what might have been. Involuntarily he recalled a lady he knew who had been a favourite of the Emperor's, but had afterwards married and become an admirable wife and mother. The husband had a high position, influence and honour, and a good and penitent wife.

In his better hours Kasatsky was not disturbed by such thoughts, and when he recalled them at such times he was merely glad to feel that the temptation was past. But there were moments when all that made up his present life suddenly grew dim before him, moments when, if he did not cease to believe in the aims he had set himself, he ceased to see them and could evoke no confidence in them but was seized by a remembrance of, and—terrible to say—a regret for, the change of life he had made.

The only thing that saved him in that state of mind was obedience and work, and the fact that the whole day was occupied by prayer. He went through the usual forms of prayer, he bowed in prayer, he even prayed more than usual, but it was lip-service only and his soul was not in it. This condition would continue for a day, or sometimes for two days, and would then pass of itself. But those days were dreadful. Kasatsky felt that he was neither in his own hands nor in God's, but was subject to something else. All he could do then was to obey the starets, to restrain himself, to undertake nothing, and simply to wait. In general all this time he lived not by his own will but by that of the starets, and in this obedience he found a special tranquillity.

So he lived in his first monastery for seven years. At the end of the third year he received the tonsure and was ordained to the priesthood by the name of Sergius. The profession was an important event in his inner life. He had previously experienced a great consolation and spiritual exaltation when receiving communion, and now when he himself officiated, the performance of the preparation filled him with ecstatic and deep emotion. But subsequently that feeling became more and more deadened, and once when he was officiating in a depressed state of mind he felt that the influence produced on him by the service would not endure. And it did in fact weaken till only the habit remained.

In general in the seventh year of his life in the monastery Sergius grew weary. He had learnt all there was to learn and had attained all there was to attain, there was nothing more to do and his spiritual drowsiness increased. During this time he heard of his mother's death and his sister Varvara's marriage, but both events were matters of indifference to him. His whole attention and his whole interest were concentrated on his inner life.

In the fourth year of his priesthood, during which the Bishop had been particularly kind to him, the starets told him that he ought not to decline it if he were offered an appointment to higher duties. Then monastic ambition, the very thing he had found so repulsive in other monks, arose within him. He was assigned to a monastery near the metropolis. He wished to refuse but the starets ordered him to accept the appointment. He did so, and took leave of the starets and moved to the other monastery.

The exchange into the metropolitan monastery was an important event in Sergius's life. There he encountered many temptations, and his whole will-power was concentrated on meeting them.

In the first monastery, women had not been a temptation to him, but here that temptation arose with terrible strength and even took definite shape. There was a lady known for her frivolous behaviour who began to seek his favour. She talked to him and asked him to visit her. Sergius sternly declined, but was horrified by the definiteness of his desire. He was so alarmed that he wrote about it to the starets. And in addition, to keep himself in hand, he spoke to a young novice and, conquering his sense of shame, confessed his weakness to him, asking him to keep watch on him and not let him go anywhere except to service and to fulfil his duties.

Besides this, a great pitfall for Sergius lay in the fact of his extreme antipathy to his new Abbot, a cunning worldly man who was making a career for himself in the Church. Struggle with himself as he might, he could not master that feeling. He was submissive to the Abbot, but in the depths of his soul he never ceased to condemn him. And in the second year of his residence at the new monastery that ill-feeling broke out.

The Vigil service was being performed in the large church on the eve of the feast of the Intercession of the Blessed Virgin, and there were many visitors. The Abbot himself was conducting the service. Father Sergius was standing in his usual place and praying:

that is, he was in that condition of struggle which always occupied him during the service, especially in the large church when he was not himself conducting the service. This conflict was occasioned by his irritation at the presence of fine folk, especially ladies. He tried not to see them or to notice all that went on: how a soldier conducted them, pushing the common people aside, how the ladies pointed out the monks to one another—especially himself and a monk noted for his good looks. He tried as it were to keep his mind in blinkers, to see nothing but the light of the candles on the altar-screen, the icons, and those conducting the service. He tried to hear nothing but the prayers that were being chanted or read, to feel nothing but self-oblivion in consciousness of the fulfilment of duty—a feeling he always experienced when hearing or reciting in advance the prayers he had so often heard.

So he stood, crossing and prostrating himself when necessary, and struggled with himself, now giving way to cold condemnation and now to a consciously evoked obliteration of thought and feeling. Then the sacristan, Father Nicodemus—also a great stumbling-block to Sergius who involuntarily reproached him for flattering and fawning on the Abbot—approached him and, bowing low, requested his presence behind the holy gates. Father Sergius straightened his mantle, put on his biretta, and went circumspectly through the crowd.

"*Lise, regarde à droite, c'est lui!*" he heard a woman's voice say.

"*Où, où? Il n'est pas tellement beau.*"

He knew that they were speaking of him. He heard them and, as always at moments of temptation, he repeated the words, "Lead us not into temptation," and bowing his head and lowering his eyes went past the ambo and in by the north door, avoiding the canons in their cassocks who were just then passing the altar-screen. On entering the sanctuary he bowed, crossing himself as usual and bending double before the icons. Then, raising his head but without turning, he glanced out of the corner of his eye at the Abbot, whom he saw standing beside another glittering figure.

The Abbot was standing by the wall in his vestments. Having freed his short plump hands from beneath his chasuble he had folded them over his fat body and protruding stomach, and fingering the cords of his vestments was smilingly saying something to a military man in the uniform of a general of the Imperial suite, with its insignia and shoulder-knots which Father Sergius's experienced eye at once recognized. This general had been the commander of the regiment in which Sergius had served. He now evidently occupied an important position, and Father Sergius at once noticed that the Abbot was aware of this and that his red face and bald head beamed with satisfaction and pleasure. This vexed and disgusted Father Sergius, the more so when he heard that the Abbot had only sent for him to satisfy the general's curiosity to see a man who had formerly served with him, as he expressed it.

"Very pleased to see you in your angelic guise," said the general, holding out his hand. "I hope you have not forgotten an old comrade."

The whole thing—the Abbot's red, smiling face amid its fringe of grey, the general's words, his well-cared-for face with its self-satisfied smile and the smell of wine from his breath and of cigars from his whiskers—revolted Father Sergius. He bowed again to the Abbot and said:

"Your reverence deigned to send for me?"—and stopped, the whole expression of his face and eyes asking why.

"Yes, to meet the General," replied the Abbot.

"Your reverence, I left the world to save myself from temptation," said Father Sergius, turning pale and with quivering lips. "Why do you expose me to it during prayers and in God's house?"

"You may go! Go!" said the Abbot, flaring up and frowning.

Next day Father Sergius asked pardon of the Abbot and of the brethren for his pride, but at the same time, after a night spent in prayer, he decided that he must leave this monastery, and he wrote to the starets begging permission to return to him. He wrote that he felt his weakness and incapacity to struggle against temptation without his help and penitently confessed his sin of pride. By return of post came a letter from the starets, who wrote that Sergius's pride was the cause of all that had happened. The old man pointed out that his fits of anger were due to the fact that in refusing all clerical honours he humiliated himself not for the sake of God but for the sake of his pride. "There now, am I not a splendid man not to want anything?" That was why he could not tolerate the Abbot's action. "I have renounced everything for the glory of God, and here I am exhibited like a wild beast!" "Had you renounced vanity for God's sake you would have borne it. Worldly pride is not yet dead in you. I have thought about you, Sergius my son, and prayed also, and this is what God has suggested to me. At the Tambov hermitage the anchorite Hilary, a man of saintly life, has died. He had lived there eighteen years. The Tambov Abbot is asking whether there is not a brother who would take his place. And here comes your letter. Go to Father Paissy of the Tambov Monastery. I will write to him about you, and you must ask for Hilary's cell. Not that you can replace Hilary, but you need solitude to quell your pride. May God bless you!"

Sergius obeyed the starets, showed his letter to the Abbot, and having obtained his permission, gave up his cell, handed all his possessions over to the monastery, and set out for the Tambov hermitage.

There the Abbot, an excellent manager of merchant origin, received Sergius simply and quietly and placed him in Hilary's cell, at first assigning to him a lay brother but afterwards leaving him alone, at Sergius's own request. The cell was a dual cave, dug into the hillside, and in it Hilary had been buried. In the back part was Hilary's grave, while in the front was a niche for sleeping, with a straw mattress, a small table, and a shelf with icons and books. Outside the outer door, which fastened with a hook, was another shelf on which, once a day, a monk placed food from the monastery.

And so Sergius became a hermit.

III

At Carnival time, in the sixth year of Sergius's life at the hermitage, a merry company of rich people, men and women from a neighbouring town, made up a *troika*-party, after a meal of carnival-pancakes and wine. The company consisted of two lawyers, a wealthy landowner, an officer, and four ladies. One lady was the officer's wife, another the wife of the landowner, the third his sister—a young girl—and the fourth a divorcee, beautiful, rich, and eccentric, who amazed and shocked the town by her escapades.

The weather was excellent and the snow-covered road smooth as a floor. They drove some seven miles out of town, and then stopped and consulted as to whether they should turn back or drive farther.

"But where does this road lead to?" asked Makovkina, the beautiful divorcee.

"To Tambov, eight miles from here," replied one of the lawyers, who was having a flirtation with her.

"And then where?"

"Then on to L——, past the Monastery."

"Where that Father Sergius lives?"

"Yes."

"Kasatsky, the handsome hermit?"

"Yes."

"Mesdames et messieurs, let us drive on and see Kasatsky! We can stop at Tambov and have something to eat."

"But we shouldn't get home tonight!"

"Never mind, we will stay at Kasatsky's."

"Well, there is a very good hostelry at the Monastery. I stayed there when I was defending Makhin."

"No, I shall spend the night at Kasatsky's!"

"Impossible! Even your omnipotence could not accomplish that!"

"Impossible? Will you bet?"

"All right! If you spend the night with him, the stake shall be whatever you like."

"A DISCRETION!"

"But on your side too!"

"Yes, of course. Let us drive on."

Vodka was handed to the drivers, and the party got out a box of pies, wine, and sweets for themselves. The ladies wrapped up in their white dogskins. The drivers disputed as to whose *troika* should go ahead, and the youngest, seating himself sideways with a dashing air, swung his long knout and shouted to the horses. The *troika*-bells tinkled and the sledge-runners squeaked over the snow.

The sledge swayed hardly at all. The shaft-horse, with his tightly bound tail under his decorated breechband, galloped smoothly and briskly; the smooth road seemed to run rapidly backwards, while the driver dashingly shook the reins. One of the lawyers and the officer sitting opposite talked nonsense to Makovkina's neighbour, but Makovkina herself sat motionless and in thought, tightly wrapped in her fur. "Always the same and always nasty! The same red shiny faces smelling of wine and cigars! The same talk, the same thoughts, and always about the same things! And they are all satisfied and confident that it should be so, and will go on living like that till they die. But I can't. It bores me. I want something that would upset it all and turn it upside down. Suppose it happened to us as to those people—at Saratov was it?—who kept on driving and froze to death . . . What would our people do? How would they behave? Basely, for certain. Each for himself. And I too should act badly. But I at any rate have beauty. They all know it. And how about that monk? Is it possible that he has become indifferent to it? No! That is the one thing they all care for—like that cadet last autumn. What a fool he was!"

"Ivan Nikolaevich!" she said aloud.

"What are your commands?"

"How old is he?"

"Who?"

"Kasatsky."

"Over forty, I should think."

"And does he receive all visitors?"

"Yes, everybody, but not always."

"Cover up my feet. Not like that—how clumsy you are! No! More, more—like that! But you need not squeeze them!"

So they came to the forest where the cell was.

Makovkina got out of the sledge, and told them to drive on. They tried to dissuade her, but she grew irritable and ordered them to go on.

When the sledges had gone she went up the path in her white dogskin coat. The lawyer got out and stopped to watch her.

It was Father Sergius's sixth year as a recluse, and he was now forty-nine. His life in solitude was hard—not on account of the fasts and the prayers (they were no hardship to him) but on account of an inner conflict he had not at all anticipated. The sources of that conflict were two: doubts, and the lust of the flesh. And these two enemies always appeared together. It seemed to him that they were two foes, but in reality they were one and the same. As soon as doubt was gone so was the lustful desire. But thinking them to be two different fiends he fought them separately.

"O my God, my God!" thought he. "Why dost thou not grant me faith? There is lust, of course: even the saints had to fight that—Saint Anthony and others. But they had faith, while I have moments, hours, and days, when it is absent. Why does the whole world, with all its delights, exist if it is sinful and must be renounced? Why hast Thou created this temptation? Temptation? Is it not rather a temptation that I wish to abandon all the joys of earth and prepare something for myself there where perhaps there is nothing?" And he became horrified and filled with disgust at himself. "Vile creature! And it is you who wish to become a saint!" he upbraided himself, and he began to pray. But as soon as he started to pray he saw himself vividly as he had been at the

Monastery, in a majestic post in biretta and mantle, and he shook his head. "No, that is not right. It is deception. I may deceive others, but not myself or God. I am not a majestic man, but a pitiable and ridiculous one!" And he threw back the folds of his cassock and smiled as he looked at his thin legs in their underclothing.

Then he dropped the folds of the cassock again and began reading the prayers, making the sign of the cross and prostrating himself. "Can it be that this couch will be my bier?" he read. And it seemed as if a devil whispered to him: "A solitary couch is itself a bier. Falsehood!" And in imagination he saw the shoulders of a widow with whom he had lived. He shook himself, and went on reading. Having read the precepts he took up the Gospels, opened the book, and happened on a passage he often repeated and knew by heart: "Lord, I believe. Help thou my unbelief!"— and he put away all the doubts that had arisen. As one replaces an object of insecure equilibrium, so he carefully replaced his belief on its shaky pedestal and carefully stepped back from it so as not to shake or upset it. The blinkers were adjusted again and he felt tranquillized, and repeating his childhood's prayer: "Lord, receive me, receive me!" he felt not merely at ease, but thrilled and joyful. He crossed himself and lay down on the bedding on his narrow bench, tucking his summer cassock under his head. He fell asleep at once, and in his light slumber he seemed to hear the tinkling of sledge bells. He did not know whether he was dreaming or awake, but a knock at the door aroused him. He sat up, distrusting his senses, but the knock was repeated. Yes, it was a knock close at hand, at his door, and with it the sound of a woman's voice.

"My God! Can it be true, as I have read in *The Lives of the Saints*, that the devil takes on the form of a woman? Yes—it is a woman's voice. And a tender, timid, pleasant voice. Phui!" And he spat to exorcise the devil. "No, it was only my imagination," he assured himself, and he went to the corner where his lectern stood, falling on his knees in the regular and habitual manner which of itself gave him consolation and satisfaction. He sank down, his hair hanging over his face, and pressed his head, already going bald in front, to the cold damp strip of drugget on the draughty floor. He read the psalm old Father Pimon had told him warded off temptation. He easily raised his light and emaciated body on his strong sinewy legs and tried to continue saying his prayers, but instead of doing so he involuntarily strained his hearing. He wished to hear more. All was quiet. From the corner of the roof regular drops continued to fall into the tub below. Outside was a mist and fog eating into the snow that lay on the ground. It was still, very still. And suddenly there was a rustling at the window and a voice—that same tender, timid voice, which could only belong to an attractive woman—said:

"Let me in, for Christ's sake!"

It seemed as though his blood had all rushed to his heart and settled there. He could hardly breathe. "Let God arise and let his enemies be scattered . . ."

"But I am not a devil!" It was obvious that the lips that uttered this were smiling. "I am not a devil, but only a sinful woman who has lost her way, not figuratively but literally!" She laughed. "I am frozen and beg for shelter."

He pressed his face to the window, but the little icon-lamp was reflected by it and shone on the whole pane. He put his hands to both sides of his face and peered between them. Fog, mist, a tree, and—just opposite him—she herself. Yes, there, a few inches from him, was the sweet, kindly frightened face of a woman in a cap and a coat of long white fur, leaning towards him. Their eyes met with instant recognition: not that they had ever known one another, they had never met before, but by the look they exchanged they—and he particularly—felt that they knew and understood one another. After that glance to imagine her to be a devil and not a simple, kindly, sweet, timid woman, was impossible.

"Who are you? Why have you come?" he asked.

"Do please open the door!" she replied, with capricious authority. "I am frozen. I tell you I have lost my way."

"But I am a monk—a hermit."

"Oh, do please open the door—or do you wish me to freeze under your window while you say your prayers?"

"But how have you . . ."

"I shan't eat you. For God's sake let me in! I am quite frozen."

She really did feel afraid, and said this in an almost tearful voice.

He stepped back from the window and looked at an icon of the Saviour in His crown of thorns. "Lord, help me! Lord, help me!" he exclaimed, crossing himself and bowing low. Then he went to the door, and opening it into the tiny porch, felt for the hook that fastened the outer door and began to lift it. He heard steps outside. She was coming from the window to the door. "Ah!" she suddenly exclaimed, and he understood that she had stepped into the puddle that the dripping from the roof had formed at the threshold. His hands trembled, and he could not raise the hook of the tightly closed door.

"Oh, what are you doing? Let me in! I am all wet. I am frozen! You are thinking about saving your soul and are letting me freeze to death . . ."

He jerked the door towards him, raised the hook, and without considering what he was doing, pushed it open with such force that it struck her.

"Oh—PARDON!" he suddenly exclaimed, reverting completely to his old manner with ladies.

She smiled on hearing that PARDON. "He is not quite so terrible, after all," she thought. "It's all right. It is you who must pardon me," she said, stepping past him. "I should never have ventured, but such an extraordinary circumstance . . ."

"If you please!" he uttered, and stood aside to let her pass him. A strong smell of fine scent, which he had long not encountered, struck him. She went through the little porch into the cell where he lived. He closed the outer door without fastening the hook, and stepped in after her.

"Lord Jesus Christ, Son of God, have mercy on me a sinner! Lord, have mercy on me a sinner!" he prayed unceasingly, not merely to himself but involuntarily moving his lips. "If you please!" he said to her again. She stood in the middle of the room, moisture dripping from her to the floor as she looked him over. Her eyes were laughing.

"Forgive me for having disturbed your solitude. But you see what a position I am in. It all came about from our starting from town for a sledge-drive, and my making a bet that I would walk back by myself from the Vorobevka to the town. But then I lost my way, and if I had not happened to come upon your cell . . ." She began lying, but his face confused her so that she could not continue, but became silent. She had not expected him to be at all such as he was. He was not as handsome as she had imagined, but was nevertheless beautiful in her eyes: his greyish hair and beard, slightly curling, his fine, regular nose, and his eyes like glowing coal when he looked at her, made a strong impression on her.

He saw that she was lying.

"Yes . . . so," said he, looking at her and again lowering his eyes. "I will go in there, and this place is at your disposal."

And taking down the little lamp, he lit a candle, and bowing low to her went into the small cell beyond the partition, and she heard him begin to move something about there. "Probably he is barricading himself in from me!" she thought with a smile, and throwing off her white dogskin cloak she tried to take off her cap, which had become entangled in her hair and in the woven kerchief she was wearing under it. She had not got at all wet when standing under the window, and had said so only as a pretext to get him to let her in. But she really had stepped into the puddle at the door, and her left foot was wet up to the ankle and her overshoe full of water. She sat down on his bed—a bench only covered by a bit of carpet—and began to take off her boots. The little cell seemed to her charming. The narrow little room, some seven feet by nine, was as clean as glass. There was nothing in it but the bench on which she was sitting, the book-shelf above it, and a lectern in the corner. A sheepskin coat and a cassock hung on nails by the door. Above the lectern was the little lamp and an icon of Christ in His crown of thorns. The room smelt strangely of perspiration and of earth. It all pleased her—even that smell. Her wet feet, especially one of them, were uncomfortable, and she quickly began to take off her boots and stockings without ceasing to smile, pleased not so much at having achieved her object as because she perceived that she had abashed that charming, strange, striking, and attractive man. "He did not respond, but what of that?" she said to herself.

"Father Sergius! Father Sergius! Or how does one call you?"

"What do you want?" replied a quiet voice.

"Please forgive me for disturbing your solitude, but really I could not help it. I should simply have fallen ill. And I don't know that I shan't now. I am all wet and my feet are like ice."

"Pardon me," replied the quiet voice. "I cannot be of any assistance to you."

"I would not have disturbed you if I could have helped it. I am only here till daybreak."

He did not reply and she heard him muttering something, probably his prayers.

"You will not be coming in here?" she asked, smiling. "For I must undress to dry myself."

He did not reply, but continued to read his prayers.

"Yes, that is a man!" thought she, getting her dripping boot off with difficulty. She tugged at it, but could not get it off. The absurdity of it struck her and she began to laugh almost inaudibly. But knowing that he would hear her laughter and would be moved by it just as she wished him to be, she laughed louder, and her laughter—gay, natural, and kindly—really acted on him just in the way she wished.

"Yes, I could love a man like that—such eyes and such a simple noble face, and passionate too despite all the prayers he mutters!" thought she. "You can't deceive a woman in these things. As soon as he put his face to the window and saw me, he understood and knew. The glimmer of it was in his eyes and remained there. He began to love me and desired me. Yes—desired!" said she, getting her overshoe and her boot off at last and starting to take off her stockings. To remove those long stockings fastened with elastic it was necessary to raise her skirts. She felt embarrassed and said:

"Don't come in!"

But there was no reply from the other side of the wall. The steady muttering continued and also a sound of moving.

"He is prostrating himself to the ground, no doubt," thought she. "But he won't bow himself out of it. He is thinking of me just as I am thinking of him. He is thinking of these feet of mine with the same feeling that I have!" And she pulled off her wet stockings and put her feet up on the bench, pressing them under her. She sat a while like that with her arms round her knees and looking pensively before her. "But it is a desert, here in this silence. No one would ever know . . ."

She rose, took her stockings over to the stove, and hung them on the damper. It was a queer damper, and she turned it about, and then, stepping lightly on her bare feet, returned to the bench and sat down there again with her feet up.

There was complete silence on the other side of the partition. She looked at the tiny watch that hung round her neck. It was two o'clock. "Our party should return about three!" She had not more than an hour before her. "Well, am I to sit like this all alone? What nonsense! I don't want to. I will call him at once."

"Father Sergius, Father Sergius! Sergey Dmitritch! Prince Kasatsky!"

Beyond the partition all was silent.

"Listen! This is cruel. I would not call you if it were not necessary. I am ill. I don't know what is the matter with me!" she exclaimed in a tone of suffering. "Oh! Oh!" she groaned, falling back on the bench. And strange to say she really felt that her strength was failing, that she was becoming faint, that everything in her ached, and that she was shivering with fever.

"Listen! Help me! I don't know what is the matter with me. "Oh! Oh!" She unfastened her dress, exposing her breast, and lifted her arms, bare to the elbow. "Oh! Oh!"

All this time he stood on the other side of the partition and prayed. Having finished all the evening prayers, he now stood motionless, his eyes looking at the end of his nose, and mentally repeated with all his soul: "Lord Jesus Christ, Son of God, have mercy upon me!"

562

But he had heard everything. He had heard how the silk rustled when she took off her dress, how she stepped with bare feet on the floor, and had heard how she rubbed her feet with her hand. He felt his own weakness, and that he might be lost at any moment. That was why he prayed unceasingly. He felt rather as the hero in the fairy-tale must have felt when he had to go on and on without looking round. So Sergius heard and felt that danger and destruction were there, hovering above and around him, and that he could only save himself by not looking in that direction for an instant. But suddenly the desire to look seized him. At the same instant she said:

"This is inhuman. I may die . . ."

"Yes, I will go to her, but like the Saint who laid one hand on the adulteress and thrust his other into the brazier. But there is no brazier here." He looked round. The lamp! He put his finger over the flame and frowned, preparing himself to suffer. And for a rather long time, as it seemed to him, there was no sensation, but suddenly—he had not yet decided whether it was painful enough—he writhed all over, jerked his hand away, and waved it in the air. "No, I can't stand that!"

"For God's sake come to me! I am dying! Oh!"

"Well—shall I perish? No, not so!"

"I will come to you directly," he said, and having opened his door, he went without looking at her through the cell into the porch where he used to chop wood. There he felt for the block and for an axe which leant against the wall.

"Immediately!" he said, and taking up the axe with his right hand he laid the forefinger of his left hand on the block, swung the axe, and struck with it below the second joint. The finger flew off more lightly than a stick of similar thickness, and bounding up, turned over on the edge of the block and then fell to the floor.

He heard it fall before he felt any pain, but before he had time to be surprised he felt a burning pain and the warmth of flowing blood. He hastily wrapped the stump in the skirt of his cassock, and pressing it to his hip went back into the room, and standing in front of the woman, lowered his eyes and asked in a low voice: "What do you want?"

She looked at his pale face and his quivering left cheek, and suddenly felt ashamed. She jumped up, seized her fur cloak, and throwing it round her shoulders, wrapped herself up in it.

"I was in pain . . . I have caught cold . . . I . . . Father Sergius . . . I . . ."

He let his eyes, shining with a quiet light of joy, rest upon her, and said:

"Dear sister, why did you wish to ruin your immortal soul? Temptations must come into the world, but woe to him by whom temptation comes. Pray that God may forgive us!"

She listened and looked at him. Suddenly she heard the sound of something dripping. She looked down and saw that blood was flowing from his hand and down his cassock.

"What have you done to your hand?" She remembered the sound she had heard, and seizing the little lamp ran out into the porch. There on the floor she saw the bloody finger. She returned with her face paler than his and was about to speak to him, but he silently passed into the back cell and fastened the door.

"Forgive me!" she said. "How can I atone for my sin?"

"Go away."

"Let me tie up your hand."

"Go away from here."

She dressed hurriedly and silently, and when ready sat waiting in her furs. The sledge-bells were heard outside.

"Father Sergius, forgive me!"

"Go away. God will forgive."

"Father Sergius! I will change my life. Do not forsake me!"

"Go away."

"Forgive me—and give me your blessing!"

"In the name of the Father and of the Son and of the Holy Ghost!"—she heard his voice from behind the partition. "Go!"

She burst into sobs and left the cell. The lawyer came forward to meet her.

"Well, I see I have lost the bet. It can't be helped. Where will you sit?"

"It is all the same to me."

She took a seat in the sledge, and did not utter a word all the way home.

A year later she entered a convent as a novice, and lived a strict life under the direction of the hermit Arseny, who wrote letters to her at long intervals.

IV

Father Sergius lived as a recluse for another seven years.

At first he accepted much of what people brought him—tea, sugar, white bread, milk, clothing, and fire-wood. But as time went on he led a more and more austere life, refusing everything superfluous, and finally he accepted nothing but rye-bread once a week. Everything else that was brought to him he gave to the poor who came to him. He spent his entire time in his cell, in prayer or in conversation with callers, who became more and more numerous as time went on. Only three times a year did he go out to church, and when necessary he went out to fetch water and wood.

The episode with Makovkina had occurred after five years of his hermit life. That occurrence soon became generally known— her nocturnal visit, the change she underwent, and her entry into a convent. From that time Father Sergius's fame increased. More and more visitors came to see him, other monks settled down near his cell, and a church was erected there and also a hostelry. His fame, as usual exaggerating his feats, spread ever more and more widely. People began to come to him from a distance, and began bringing invalids to him whom they declared he cured.

His first cure occurred in the eighth year of his life as a hermit. It was the healing of a fourteen-year-old boy, whose mother brought him to Father Sergius insisting that he should lay his hand on the child's head. It had never occurred to Father Sergius that he could cure the sick. He would have regarded such a thought as a great sin of pride; but the mother who brought the boy implored him insistently, falling at his feet and saying: "Why do you, who heal others, refuse to help my son?" She besought him in Christ's name. When Father Sergius assured her that only God could heal the sick, she replied that she only wanted him to lay his hands on the boy and pray for him. Father Sergius refused and returned to his cell. But next day (it was in autumn and the nights were already cold) on going out for water he saw the same mother with her son, a pale boy of fourteen, and was met by the same petition.

He remembered the parable of the unjust judge, and though he had previously felt sure that he ought to refuse, he now began to hesitate and, having hesitated, took to prayer and prayed until a decision formed itself in his soul. This decision was, that he ought to accede to the woman's request and that her faith might save her son. As for himself, he would in this case be but an insignificant instrument chosen by God.

And going out to the mother he did what she asked—laid his hand on the boy's head and prayed.

The mother left with her son, and a month later the boy recovered, and the fame of the holy healing power of the starets Sergius (as they now called him) spread throughout the whole district. After that, not a week passed without sick people coming, riding or on foot, to Father Sergius; and having acceded to one petition he could not refuse others, and he laid his hands on many and prayed. Many recovered, and his fame spread more and more.

So seven years passed in the Monastery and thirteen in his hermit's cell. He now had the appearance of an old man: his beard was long and grey, but his hair, though thin, was still black and curly.

V

For some weeks Father Sergius had been living with one persistent thought: whether he was right in accepting the position in which he had not so much placed himself as been placed by the Archimandrite and the Abbot. That position had begun after the recovery of the fourteen-year-old boy. From that time, with each month, week, and day that passed, Sergius felt his own inner life wasting away and being replaced by external life. It was as if he had been turned inside out.

Sergius saw that he was a means of attracting visitors and contributions to the monastery, and that therefore the authorities arranged matters in such a way as to make as much use of him as possible. For instance, they rendered it impossible for him to do any manual work. He was supplied with everything he could want, and they only demanded of him that he should not refuse his blessing to those who came to seek it. For his convenience they appointed days when he would receive. They arranged a reception-room for men, and a place was railed in so that he should not be pushed over by the crowds of women visitors, and so that he could conveniently bless those who came.

They told him that people needed him, and that fulfilling Christ's law of love he could not refuse their demand to see him, and that to avoid them would be cruel. He could not but agree with this, but the more he gave himself up to such a life the more he felt that what was internal became external, and that the fount of living water within him dried up, and that what he did now was done more and more for men and less and less for God.

Whether he admonished people, or simply blessed them, or prayed for the sick, or advised people about their lives, or listened to expressions of gratitude from those he had helped by precepts, or alms, or healing (as they assured him)—he could not help being pleased at it, and could not be indifferent to the results of his activity and to the influence he exerted. He thought himself a shining light, and the more he felt this the more was he conscious of a weakening, a dying down of the divine light of truth that shone within him.

"In how far is what I do for God and in how far is it for men?" That was the question that insistently tormented him and to which he was not so much unable to give himself an answer as unable to face the answer.

In the depth of his soul he felt that the devil had substituted an activity for men in place of his former activity for God. He felt this because, just as it had formerly been hard for him to be torn from his solitude so now that solitude itself was hard for him. He was oppressed and wearied by visitors, but at the bottom of his heart he was glad of their presence and glad of the praise they heaped upon him.

There was a time when he decided to go away and hide. He even planned all that was necessary for that purpose. He prepared for himself a peasant's shirt, trousers, coat, and cap. He explained that he wanted these to give to those who asked. And he kept these clothes in his cell, planning how he would put them on, cut his hair short, and go away. First he would go some three hundred versts by train, then he would leave the train and walk from village to village. He asked an old man who had been a soldier how he tramped: what people gave him, and what shelter they allowed him. The soldier told him where people were most charitable, and where they would take a wanderer in for the night, and Father Sergius intended to avail himself of this information. He even put on those clothes one night in his desire to go, but he could not decide what was best—to remain or to escape. At first he was in doubt, but afterwards this indecision passed. He submitted to custom and yielded to the devil, and only the peasant garb reminded him of the thought and feeling he had had.

Every day more and more people flocked to him and less and less time was left him for prayer and for renewing his spiritual strength. Sometimes in lucid moments he thought he was like a place where there had once been a spring. "There used to be a feeble spring of living water which flowed quietly from me and through me. That was true life, the time when she tempted me!" (He always thought with ecstasy of that night and of her who was now Mother Agnes.) She had tasted of that pure water, but since then there had not been time for it to collect before thirsty people came crowding in and pushing one another aside. And they had trampled everything down and nothing was left but mud.

So he thought in rare moments of lucidity, but his usual state of mind was one of weariness and a tender pity for himself because of that weariness.

It was in spring, on the eve of the mid-Pentecostal feast. Father Sergius was officiating at the Vigil Service in his hermitage church, where the congregation was as large as the little church could hold—about twenty people. They were all well-to-do proprietors or merchants. Father Sergius admitted anyone, but a selection was made by the monk in attendance and by an assistant who was sent to the hermitage every day from the monastery. A crowd of some eighty people—pilgrims and peasants, and especially peasant-women—stood outside waiting for Father Sergius to come out and bless them. Meanwhile he conducted the service, but at the point at which he went out to the tomb of his predecessor, he staggered and would have fallen had he not been caught by a merchant standing behind him and by the monk acting as deacon.

"What is the matter, Father Sergius? Dear man! O Lord!" exclaimed the women. "He is as white as a sheet!"

But Father Sergius recovered immediately, and though very pale, he waved the merchant and the deacon aside and continued to chant the service.

Father Seraphim, the deacon, the acolytes, and Sofya Ivanovna, a lady who always lived near the hermitage and tended Father Sergius, begged him to bring the service to an end.

"No, there's nothing the matter," said Father Sergius, slightly smiling from beneath his moustache and continuing the service. "Yes, that is the way the Saints behave!" thought he.

"A holy man—an angel of God!" he heard just then the voice of Sofya Ivanovna behind him, and also of the merchant who had supported him. He did not heed their entreaties, but went on with the service. Again crowding together they all made their way by the narrow passages back into the little church, and there, though abbreviating it slightly, Father Sergius completed vespers.

Immediately after the service Father Sergius, having pronounced the benediction on those present, went over to the bench under the elm tree at the entrance to the cave. He wished to rest and breathe the fresh air—he felt in need of it. But as soon as he left the church the crowd of people rushed to him soliciting his blessing, his advice, and his help. There were pilgrims who constantly tramped from one holy place to another and from one starets to another, and were always entranced by every shrine and every starets. Father Sergius knew this common, cold, conventional, and most irreligious type. There were pilgrims, for the most part discharged soldiers, unaccustomed to a settled life, poverty-stricken, and many of them drunken old men, who tramped from monastery to monastery merely to be fed. And there were rough peasants and peasant-women who had come with their selfish requirements, seeking cures or to have doubts about quite practical affairs solved for them: about marrying off a daughter, or hiring a shop, or buying a bit of land, or how to atone for having overlaid a child or having an illegitimate one.

All this was an old story and not in the least interesting to him. He knew he would hear nothing new from these folk, that they would arouse no religious emotion in him; but he liked to see the crowd to which his blessing and advice was necessary and precious, so while that crowd oppressed him it also pleased him. Father Seraphim began to drive them away, saying that Father Sergius was tired.

But Father Sergius, remembering the words of the Gospel: "Forbid them" (children) "not to come unto me," and feeling tenderly towards himself at this recollection, said they should be allowed to approach.

He rose, went to the railing beyond which the crowd had

gathered, and began blessing them and answering their questions, but in a voice so weak that he was touched with pity for himself. Yet despite his wish to receive them all he could not do it. Things again grew dark before his eyes, and he staggered and grasped the railings. He felt a rush of blood to his head and first went pale and then suddenly flushed.

"I must leave the rest till tomorrow. I cannot do more today," and, pronouncing a general benediction, he returned to the bench. The merchant again supported him, and leading him by the arm helped him to be seated.

"Father!" came voices from the crowd. "Dear Father! Do not forsake us. Without you we are lost!"

The merchant, having seated Father Sergius on the bench under the elm, took on himself police duties and drove the people off very resolutely. It is true that he spoke in a low voice so that Father Sergius might not hear him, but his words were incisive and angry.

"Be off, be off! He has blessed you, and what more do you want? Get along with you, or I'll wring your necks! Move on there! Get along, you old woman with your dirty leg-bands! Go, go! Where are you shoving to? You've been told that it is finished. Tomorrow will be as God wills, but for today he has finished!"

"Father! Only let my eyes have a glimpse of his dear face!" said an old woman.

"I'll glimpse you! Where are you shoving to?"

Father Sergius noticed that the merchant seemed to be acting roughly, and in a feeble voice told the attendant that the people should not be driven away. He knew that they would be driven away all the same, and he much desired to be left alone and to rest, but he sent the attendant with that message to produce an impression.

"All right, all right! I am not driving them away. I am only remonstrating with them," replied the merchant. "You know they wouldn't hesitate to drive a man to death. They have no pity, they only consider themselves . . . You've been told you cannot see him. Go away! Tomorrow!" And he got rid of them all.

He took all these pains because he liked order and liked to domineer and drive the people away, but chiefly because he wanted to have Father Sergius to himself. He was a widower with an only daughter who was an invalid and unmarried, and whom he had brought fourteen hundred versts to Father Sergius to be healed. For two years past he had been taking her to different places to be cured: first to the university clinic in the chief town of the province, but that did no good; then to a peasant in the province of Samara, where she got a little better; then to a doctor in Moscow to whom he paid much money, but this did no good at all. Now he had been told that Father Sergius wrought cures, and had brought her to him. So when all the people had been driven away he approached Father Sergius, and suddenly falling on his knees loudly exclaimed:

"Holy Father! Bless my afflicted offspring that she may be healed of her malady. I venture to prostrate myself at your holy feet."

And he placed one hand on the other, cup-wise. He said and did all this as if he were doing something clearly and firmly appointed by law and usage—as if one must and should ask for a daughter to be cured in just this way and no other. He did it with such conviction that it seemed even to Father Sergius that it should be said and done in just that way, but nevertheless he bade him rise and tell him what the trouble was. The merchant said that his daughter, a girl of twenty-two, had fallen ill two years ago, after her mother's sudden death. She had moaned (as he expressed it) and since then had not been herself. And now he had brought her fourteen hundred versts and she was waiting in the hostelry till Father Sergius should give orders to bring her. She did not go out during the day, being afraid of the light, and could only come after sunset.

"Is she very weak?" asked Father Sergius.

"No, she has no particular weakness. She is quite plump, and is only 'nerastenic' the doctors say. If you will only let me bring her this evening, Father Sergius, I'll fly like a spirit to fetch her. Holy Father! Revive a parent's heart, restore his line, save his afflicted daughter by your prayers!" And the merchant again threw himself on his knees and bending sideways, with his head resting on his clenched fists, remained stock still. Father Sergius again told him to get up, and thinking how heavy his activities were and how he went through with them patiently notwithstanding, he sighed heavily and after a few seconds of silence, said:

"Well, bring her this evening. I will pray for her, but now I am tired . . ." and he closed his eyes. "I will send for you."

The merchant went away, stepping on tiptoe, which only made his boots creak the louder, and Father Sergius remained alone.

His whole life was filled by Church services and by people who came to see him, but today had been a particularly difficult one. In the morning an important official had arrived and had had a long conversation with him; after that a lady had come with her son. This son was a sceptical young professor whom the mother, an ardent believer and devoted to Father Sergius, had brought that he might talk to him. The conversation had been very trying. The young man, evidently not wishing to have a controversy with a monk, had agreed with him in everything as with someone who was mentally inferior. Father Sergius saw that the young man did not believe but yet was satisfied, tranquil, and at ease, and the memory of that conversation now disquieted him.

"Have something to eat, Father," said the attendant.

"All right, bring me something."

The attendant went to a hut that had been arranged some ten paces from the cave, and Father Sergius remained alone.

The time was long past when he had lived alone doing everything for himself and eating only rye-bread, or rolls prepared for the Church. He had been advised long since that he had no right to neglect his health, and he was given wholesome, though Lenten, food. He ate sparingly, though much more than he had done, and often he ate with much pleasure, and not as formerly with aversion and a sense of guilt. So it was now. He had some gruel, drank a cup of tea, and ate half a white roll.

The attendant went away, and Father Sergius remained alone under the elm tree.

It was a wonderful May evening, when the birches, aspens, elms, wild cherries, and oaks, had just burst into foliage.

The bush of wild cherries behind the elm tree was in full bloom and had not yet begun to shed its blossoms, and the nightingales— one quite near at hand and two or three others in the bushes down by the river—burst into full song after some preliminary twitters. From the river came the far-off songs of peasants returning, no doubt, from their work. The sun was setting behind the forest, its last rays glowing through the leaves. All that side was brilliant green, the other side with the elm tree was dark. The cockchafers flew clumsily about, falling to the ground when they collided with anything.

After supper Father Sergius began to repeat a silent prayer: "O Lord Jesus Christ, Son of God, have mercy upon us!" and then he read a psalm, and suddenly in the middle of the psalm a sparrow flew out from the bush, alighted on the ground, and hopped towards him chirping as it came, but then it took fright at something and flew away. He said a prayer which referred to his abandonment of the world, and hastened to finish it in order to send for the merchant with the sick daughter. She interested him in that she presented a distraction, and because both she and her father considered him a saint whose prayers were efficacious. Outwardly he disavowed that idea, but in the depths of his soul he considered it to be true.

He was often amazed that this had happened, that he, Stepan Kasatsky, had come to be such an extraordinary saint and even a worker of miracles, but of the fact that he was such there could not be the least doubt. He could not fail to believe in the miracles he himself witnessed, beginning with the sick boy and ending with the old woman who had recovered her sight when he had prayed for her.

Strange as it might be, it was so. Accordingly the merchant's daughter interested him as a new individual who had faith in him, and also as a fresh opportunity to confirm his healing powers and enhance his fame. "They bring people a thousand versts and write about it in the papers. The Emperor knows of it, and they know of it in Europe, in unbelieving Europe"—thought he. And suddenly he felt ashamed of his vanity and again began to pray. "Lord, King of Heaven, Comforter, Soul of Truth! Come and enter into me and cleanse me from all sin and save and bless my soul. Cleanse me from the sin of worldly vanity that troubles me!" he repeated, and he remembered how often he had prayed about this and how vain till now his prayers had been in that respect. His prayers worked miracles for others, but in his own case God had not granted him liberation from this petty passion.

He remembered his prayers at the commencement of his life at the hermitage, when he prayed for purity, humility, and love, and how it seemed to him then that God heard his prayers. He had retained his purity and had chopped off his finger. And he lifted the shrivelled stump of that finger to his lips and kissed it. It seemed to him now that he had been humble then when he had always seemed loathsome to himself on account of his sinfulness; and when he remembered the tender feelings with which he had then met an old man who was bringing a drunken soldier to him to ask alms; and how he had received HER, it seemed to him that he had then possessed love also. But now? And he asked himself whether he loved anyone, whether he loved Sofya Ivanovna, or Father Seraphim, whether he had any feeling of love for all who had come to him that day—for that learned young man with whom he had had that instructive discussion in which he was concerned only to show off his own intelligence and that he had not lagged behind the times in knowledge. He wanted and needed their love, but felt none towards them. He now had neither love nor humility nor purity.

He was pleased to know that the merchant's daughter was twenty-two, and he wondered whether she was good-looking. When he inquired whether she was weak, he really wanted to know if she had feminine charm.

"Can I have fallen so low?" he thought. "Lord, help me! Restore me, my Lord and God!" And he clasped his hands and began to pray.

The nightingales burst into song, a cockchafer knocked against him and crept up the back of his neck. He brushed it off. "But does

He exist? What if I am knocking at a door fastened from outside? The bar is on the door for all to see. Nature—the nightingales and the cockchafers—is that bar. Perhaps the young man was right." And he began to pray aloud. He prayed for a long time till these thoughts vanished and he again felt calm and confident. He rang the bell and told the attendant to say that the merchant might bring his daughter to him now.

The merchant came, leading his daughter by the arm. He led her into the cell and immediately left her.

She was a very fair girl, plump and very short, with a pale, frightened, childish face and a much developed feminine figure. Father Sergius remained seated on the bench at the entrance and when she was passing and stopped beside him for his blessing he was aghast at himself for the way he looked at her figure. As she passed by him he was acutely conscious of her femininity, though he saw by her face that she was sensual and feeble-minded. He rose and went into the cell. She was sitting on a stool waiting for him, and when he entered she rose.

"I want to go back to Papa," she said.

"Don't be afraid," he replied. "What are you suffering from?"

"I am in pain all over," she said, and suddenly her face lit up with a smile.

"You will be well," said he. "Pray!"

"What is the use of praying? I have prayed and it does no good"—and she continued to smile. "I want you to pray for me and lay your hands on me. I saw you in a dream."

"How did you see me?"

"I saw you put your hands on my breast like that." She took his hand and pressed it to her breast. "Just here."

He yielded his right hand to her.

"What is your name?" he asked, trembling all over and feeling that he was overcome and that his desire had already passed beyond control.

"Marie. Why?"

She took his hand and kissed it, and then put her arm round his waist and pressed him to herself.

"What are you doing?" he said. "Marie, you are a devil!"

"Oh, perhaps. What does it matter?"

And embracing him she sat down with him on the bed.

At dawn he went out into the porch.

"Can this all have happened? Her father will come and she will tell him everything. She is a devil! What am I to do? Here is the axe with which I chopped off my finger." He snatched up the axe and moved back towards the cell.

The attendant came up.

"Do you want some wood chopped? Let me have the axe."

Sergius yielded up the axe and entered the cell. She was lying there asleep. He looked at her with horror, and passed on beyond the partition, where he took down the peasant clothes and put them on. Then he seized a pair of scissors, cut off his long hair, and went out along the path down the hill to the river, where he had not been for more than three years.

A road ran beside the river and he went along it and walked till noon. Then he went into a field of rye and lay down there. Towards evening he approached a village, but without entering it went towards the cliff that overhung the river. There he again lay down to rest.

It was early morning, half an hour before sunrise. All was damp and gloomy and a cold early wind was blowing from the west. "Yes, I must end it all. There is no God. But how am I to end it? Throw myself into the river? I can swim and should not drown. Hang myself? Yes, just throw this sash over a branch." This seemed so feasible and so easy that he felt horrified. As usual at moments of despair he felt the need of prayer. But there was no one to pray to. There was no God. He lay down resting on his arm, and suddenly such a longing for sleep overcame him that he could no longer support his head on his hand, but stretched out his arm, laid his head upon it, and fell asleep. But that sleep lasted only for a moment. He woke up immediately and began not to dream but to remember.

He saw himself as a child in his mother's home in the country. A carriage drives up, and out of it steps Uncle Nicholas Sergeevich, with his long, spade-shaped, black beard, and with him Pashenka,

577

a thin little girl with large mild eyes and a timid pathetic face. And into their company of boys Pashenka is brought and they have to play with her, but it is dull. She is silly, and it ends by their making fun of her and forcing her to show how she can swim. She lies down on the floor and shows them, and they all laugh and make a fool of her. She sees this and blushes red in patches and becomes more pitiable than before, so pitiable that he feels ashamed and can never forget that crooked, kindly, submissive smile. And Sergius remembered having seen her since then. Long after, just before he became a monk, she had married a landowner who squandered all her fortune and was in the habit of beating her. She had had two children, a son and a daughter, but the son had died while still young. And Sergius remembered having seen her very wretched. Then again he had seen her in the monastery when she was a widow. She had been still the same, not exactly stupid, but insipid, insignificant, and pitiable. She had come with her daughter and her daughter's fiancé. They were already poor at that time and later on he had heard that she was living in a small provincial town and was very poor.

"Why am I thinking about her?" he asked himself, but he could not cease doing so. "Where is she? How is she getting on? Is she still as unhappy as she was then when she had to show us how to swim on the floor? But why should I think about her? What am I doing? I must put an end to myself."

And again he felt afraid, and again, to escape from that thought, he went on thinking about Pashenka.

So he lay for a long time, thinking now of his unavoidable end and now of Pashenka. She presented herself to him as a means of salvation. At last he fell asleep, and in his sleep he saw an angel who came to him and said: "Go to Pashenka and learn from her what you have to do, what your sin is, and wherein lies your salvation."

He awoke, and having decided that this was a vision sent by God, he felt glad, and resolved to do what had been told him in the vision. He knew the town where she lived. It was some three hundred versts (two hundred miles) away, and he set out to walk there.

VI

Pashenka had already long ceased to be Pashenka and had become old, withered, wrinkled Praskovya Mikhaylovna, mother-in-law of that failure, the drunken official Mavrikyev. She was living in the country town where he had had his last appointment, and there she was supporting the family: her daughter, her ailing neurasthenic son-in-law, and her five grandchildren. She did this by giving music lessons to tradesmen's daughters, giving four and sometimes five lessons a day of an hour each, and earning in this way some sixty roubles (six pounds) a month. So they lived for the present, in expectation of another appointment. She had sent letters to all her relations and acquaintances asking them to obtain a post for her son-in-law, and among the rest she had written to Sergius, but that letter had not reached him.

It was a Saturday, and Praskovya Mikhaylovna was herself mixing dough for currant bread such as the serf-cook on her father's estate used to make so well. She wished to give her grandchildren a treat on the Sunday.

Masha, her daughter, was nursing her youngest child, the eldest boy and girl were at school, and her son-in-law was asleep, not having slept during the night. Praskovya Mikhaylovna had remained awake too for a great part of the night, trying to soften her daughter's anger against her husband.

She saw that it was impossible for her son-in-law, a weak creature, to be other than he was, and realized that his wife's reproaches could do no good—so she used all her efforts to soften those reproaches and to avoid recrimination and anger. Unkindly relations between people caused her actual physical suffering. It was so clear to her that bitter feelings do not make anything better, but only make everything worse. She did not in fact think about this: she simply suffered at the sight of anger as she would from a bad smell, a harsh noise, or from blows on her body.

She had—with a feeling of self-satisfaction—just taught Lukerya how to mix the dough, when her six-year-old grandson Misha, wearing an apron and with darned stockings on his crooked little legs, ran into the kitchen with a frightened face.

"Grandma, a dreadful old man wants to see you."

Lukerya looked out at the door.

"There is a pilgrim of some kind, a man . . ."

Praskovya Mikhaylovna rubbed her thin elbows against one another, wiped her hands on her apron and went upstairs to get a five-kopek piece [about a penny] out of her purse for him, but remembering that she had nothing less than a ten-kopek piece she decided to give him some bread instead. She returned to the cupboard, but suddenly blushed at the thought of having grudged the ten-kopek piece, and telling Lukerya to cut a slice of bread, went upstairs again to fetch it. "It serves you right," she said to herself. "You must now give twice over."

She gave both the bread and the money to the pilgrim, and when doing so—far from being proud of her generosity—she excused herself for giving so little. The man had such an imposing appearance.

Though he had tramped two hundred versts as a beggar, though he was tattered and had grown thin and weather-beaten, though he had cropped his long hair and was wearing a peasant's cap and boots, and though he bowed very humbly, Sergius still had the impressive appearance that made him so attractive. But Praskovya Mikhaylovna did not recognize him. She could hardly do so, not having seen him for almost twenty years.

"Don't think ill of me, Father. Perhaps you want something to eat?"

He took the bread and the money, and Praskovya Mikhaylovna was surprised that he did not go, but stood looking at her.

"Pashenka, I have come to you! Take me in . . ."

His beautiful black eyes, shining with the tears that started in them, were fixed on her with imploring insistence. And under his greyish moustache his lips quivered piteously.

Praskovya Mikhaylovna pressed her hands to her withered breast, opened her mouth, and stood petrified, staring at the pilgrim with dilated eyes.

"It can't be! Stepa! Sergey! Father Sergius!"

"Yes, it is I," said Sergius in a low voice. "Only not Sergius, or Father Sergius, but a great sinner, Stepan Kasatsky—a great and lost sinner. Take me in and help me!"

"It's impossible! How have you so humbled yourself? But come in."

She reached out her hand, but he did not take it and only followed her in.

But where was she to take him? The lodging was a small one. Formerly she had had a tiny room, almost a closet, for herself, but later she had given it up to her daughter, and Masha was now sitting there rocking the baby.

"Sit here for the present," she said to Sergius, pointing to a bench in the kitchen.

He sat down at once, and with an evidently accustomed movement slipped the straps of his wallet first off one shoulder and then off the other.

"My God, my God! How you have humbled yourself, Father! Such great fame, and now like this . . ."

Sergius did not reply, but only smiled meekly, placing his wallet under the bench on which he sat.

"Masha, do you know who this is?"—And in a whisper Praskovya Mikhaylovna told her daughter who he was, and together they then carried the bed and the cradle out of the tiny room and cleared it for Sergius.

Praskovya Mikhaylovna led him into it.

"Here you can rest. Don't take offence . . . but I must go out."

"Where to?"

"I have to go to a lesson. I am ashamed to tell you, but I teach music!"

"Music? But that is good. Only just one thing, Praskovya Mikhaylovna, I have come to you with a definite object. When can I have a talk with you?"

"I shall be very glad. Will this evening do?"

"Yes. But one thing more. Don't speak about me, or say who I am. I have revealed myself only to you. No one knows where I have gone to. It must be so."

"Oh, but I have told my daughter."

"Well, ask her not to mention it."

And Sergius took off his boots, lay down, and at once fell asleep after a sleepless night and a walk of nearly thirty miles.

When Praskovya Mikhaylovna returned, Sergius was sitting in the little room waiting for her. He did not come out for dinner, but had some soup and gruel which Lukerya brought him.

"How is it that you have come back earlier than you said?" asked Sergius. "Can I speak to you now?"

"How is it that I have the happiness to receive such a guest? I have missed one of my lessons. That can wait . . . I had always been planning to go to see you. I wrote to you, and now this good fortune has come."

"Pashenka, please listen to what I am going to tell you as to a confession made to God at my last hour. Pashenka, I am not a holy man, I am not even as good as a simple ordinary man; I am a loathsome, vile, and proud sinner who has gone astray, and who, if not worse than everyone else, is at least worse than most very bad people."

Pashenka looked at him at first with staring eyes. But she believed what he said, and when she had quite grasped it she touched his hand, smiling pityingly, and said:

"Perhaps you exaggerate, Stiva?"

"No, Pashenka. I am an adulterer, a murderer, a blasphemer, and a deceiver."

"My God! How is that?" exclaimed Praskovya Mikhaylovna.

"But I must go on living. And I, who thought I knew everything, who taught others how to live—I know nothing and ask you to teach me."

"What are you saying, Stiva? You are laughing at me. Why do you always make fun of me?"

"Well, if you think I am jesting you must have it as you please.

But tell me all the same how you live, and how you have lived your life."

"I? I have lived a very nasty, horrible life, and now God is punishing me as I deserve. I live so wretchedly, so wretchedly . . ."

"How was it with your marriage? How did you live with your husband?"

"It was all bad. I married because I fell in love in the nastiest way. Papa did not approve. But I would not listen to anything and just got married. Then instead of helping my husband I tormented him by my jealousy, which I could not restrain."

"I heard that he drank . . ."

"Yes, but I did not give him any peace. I always reproached him, though you know it is a disease! He could not refrain from it. I now remember how I tried to prevent his having it, and the frightful scenes we had!"

And she looked at Kasatsky with beautiful eyes, suffering from the remembrance.

Kasatsky remembered how he had been told that Pashenka's husband used to beat her, and now, looking at her thin withered neck with prominent veins behind her ears, and her scanty coil of hair, half grey half auburn, he seemed to see just how it had occurred.

"Then I was left with two children and no means at all."

"But you had an estate!"

"Oh, we sold that while Vasya was still alive, and the money was all spent. We had to live, and like all our young ladies I did not know how to earn anything. I was particularly useless and helpless. So we spent all we had. I taught the children and improved my own education a little. And then Mitya fell ill when he was already in the fourth form, and God took him. Masha fell in love with Vanya, my son-in-law. And—well, he is well-meaning but unfortunate. He is ill."

"Mamma!"—her daughter's voice interrupted her—"Take Mitya! I can't be in two places at once."

Praskovya Mikhaylovna shuddered, but rose and went out of the room, stepping quickly in her patched shoes. She soon came back with a boy of two in her arms, who threw himself backwards and grabbed at her shawl with his little hands.

"Where was I? Oh yes, he had a good appointment here, and his chief was a kind man too. But Vanya could not go on, and had to give up his position."

"What is the matter with him?"

"Neurasthenia—it is a dreadful complaint. We consulted a doctor, who told us he ought to go away, but we had no means . . . I always hope it will pass of itself. He has no particular pain, but . . ."

"Lukerya!" cried an angry and feeble voice. "She is always sent away when I want her. Mamma . . . "

"I'm coming!" Praskovya Mikhaylovna again interrupted herself. "He has not had his dinner yet. He can't eat with us."

She went out and arranged something, and came back wiping her thin dark hands.

"So that is how I live. I always complain and am always dissatisfied, but thank God the grandchildren are all nice and healthy, and we can still live. But why talk about me?"

"But what do you live on?"

"Well, I earn a little. How I used to dislike music, but how useful it is to me now!" Her small hand lay on the chest of drawers beside which she was sitting, and she drummed an exercise with her thin fingers.

"How much do you get for a lesson?"

"Sometimes a rouble, sometimes fifty kopeks, or sometimes thirty. They are all so kind to me."

"And do your pupils get on well?" asked Kasatsky with a slight smile.

Praskovya Mikhaylovna did not at first believe that he was asking seriously, and looked inquiringly into his eyes.

"Some of them do. One of them is a splendid girl—the butcher's daughter—such a good kind girl! If I were a clever woman I ought, of course, with the connexions Papa had, to be able to get an appointment for my son-in-law. But as it is I have not been able to do anything, and have brought them all to this—as you see."

"Yes, yes," said Kasatsky, lowering his head. "And how is it, Pashenka—do you take part in Church life?"

"Oh, don't speak of it. I am so bad that way, and have neglected it so! I keep the fasts with the children and sometimes go to church, and then again sometimes I don't go for months. I only send the children."

"But why don't you go yourself?"

"To tell the truth" (she blushed) "I am ashamed, for my daughter's sake and the children's, to go there in tattered clothes, and I haven't anything else. Besides, I am just lazy."

"And do you pray at home?"

"I do. But what sort of prayer is it? Only mechanical. I know it should not be like that, but I lack real religious feeling. The only thing is that I know how bad I am . . ."

"Yes, yes, that's right!" said Kasatsky, as if approvingly.

"I'm coming! I'm coming!" she replied to a call from her son-in-law, and tidying her scanty plait she left the room.

But this time it was long before she returned. When she came back, Kasatsky was sitting in the same position, his elbows resting on his knees and his head bowed. But his wallet was strapped on his back.

When she came in, carrying a small tin lamp without a shade, he raised his fine weary eyes and sighed very deeply.

"I did not tell them who you are," she began timidly. "I only said that you are a pilgrim, a nobleman, and that I used to know you. Come into the dining-room for tea."

"No . . ."

"Well then, I'll bring some to you here."

"No, I don't want anything. God bless you, Pashenka! I am going now. If you pity me, don't tell anyone that you have seen me. For the love of God don't tell anyone. Thank you. I would bow to your feet but I know it would make you feel awkward. Thank you, and forgive me for Christ's sake!"

"Give me your blessing."

"God bless you! Forgive me for Christ's sake!"

He rose, but she would not let him go until she had given him bread and butter and rusks. He took it all and went away.

It was dark, and before he had passed the second house he was lost to sight. She only knew he was there because the dog at the priest's house was barking.

"So that is what my dream meant! Pashenka is what I ought to have been but failed to be. I lived for men on the pretext of living for God, while she lived for God imagining that she lives for men. Yes, one good deed—a cup of water given without thought of reward—is worth more than any benefit I imagined I was bestowing on people. But after all was there not some share of sincere desire to serve God?" he asked himself, and the answer was: "Yes, there was, but it was all soiled and overgrown by desire for human praise. Yes, there is no God for the man who lives, as I did, for human praise. I will now seek Him!"

And he walked from village to village as he had done on his way to Pashenka, meeting and parting from other pilgrims, men and women, and asking for bread and a night's rest in Christ's name. Occasionally some angry housewife scolded him, or a drunken peasant reviled him, but for the most part he was given food and drink and even something to take with him. His noble bearing disposed some people in his favour, while others on the contrary seemed pleased at the sight of a gentleman who had come to beggary.

But his gentleness prevailed with everyone.

Often, finding a copy of the Gospels in a hut he would read it aloud, and when they heard him the people were always touched and surprised, as at something new yet familiar.

When he succeeded in helping people, either by advice, or by his knowledge of reading and writing, or by settling some quarrel, he did not wait to see their gratitude but went away directly afterwards. And little by little God began to reveal Himself within him.

Once he was walking along with two old women and a soldier. They were stopped by a party consisting of a lady and gentleman in a gig and another lady and gentleman on horseback. The husband was on horseback with his daughter, while in the gig his wife was driving with a Frenchman, evidently a traveller.

The party stopped to let the Frenchman see the pilgrims who, in accord with a popular Russian superstition, tramped about from place to place instead of working.

They spoke French, thinking that the others would not understand them.

"*Demandez-leur,*" said the Frenchman, "*s'ils sont bien sur de ce que leur pelerinage est agreable a Dieu.*"

The question was asked, and one old woman replied:

"As God takes it. Our feet have reached the holy places, but our hearts may not have done so."

They asked the soldier. He said that he was alone in the world and had nowhere else to go.

They asked Kasatsky who he was.

"A servant of God."

"*Qu'est-ce qu'il dit? Il ne repond pas.*"

"*Il dit qu'il est un serviteur de Dieu. Cela doit etre un fils de preetre. Il a de la race. Avez-vous de la petite monnaie?*"

The Frenchman found some small change and gave twenty kopeks to each of the pilgrims.

"*Mais dites-leur que ce n'est pas pour les cierges que je leur donne, mais pour qu'ils se regalent de the. Chay, chay pour vous, mon vieux!*" he said with a smile. And he patted Kasatsky on the shoulder with his gloved hand.

"May Christ bless you," replied Kasatsky without replacing his cap and bowing his bald head.

He rejoiced particularly at this meeting, because he had disregarded the opinion of men and had done the simplest, easiest thing—humbly accepted twenty kopeks and given them to his comrade, a blind beggar. The less importance he attached to the opinion of men the more did he feel the presence of God within him.

For eight months Kasatsky tramped on in this manner, and in the ninth month he was arrested for not having a passport. This happened at a night-refuge in a provincial town where he had passed the night with some pilgrims. He was taken to the police-station, and when asked who he was and where was his passport, he replied that he had no passport and that he was a servant of God. He was classed as a tramp, sentenced, and sent to live in Siberia.

In Siberia he has settled down as the hired man of a well-to-do peasant, in which capacity he works in the kitchen-garden, teaches children, and attends to the sick.

Work, Death and Sickness

A LEGEND

[One of the three stories written in 1903 as a contribution to an anthology aiding the victims of the Jewish pogrom in Russia. Also translated as 'The Right Way'. This version is taken from *Twenty-three Tales* (1906) translated by Louise and Aylmer Maude.]

This is a legend current among the South American Indians.

God, say they, at first made men so that they had no need to work: they needed neither houses, nor clothes, nor food, and they all lived till they were a hundred, and did not know what illness was.

When, after some time, God looked to see how people were living, he saw that instead of being happy in their life, they had quarrelled with one another, and, each caring for himself, had brought matters to such a pass that far from enjoying life, they cursed it.

Then God said to himself: "This comes of their living separately, each for himself." And to change this state of things, God so arranged matters that it became impossible for people to live without working. To avoid suffering from cold and hunger, they were now obliged to build dwellings, and to dig the ground, and to grow and gather fruits and grain.

"Work will bring them together," thought God. "They cannot make their tools, prepare and transport their timber, build their houses, sow and gather their harvests, spin and weave, and make their clothes, each one alone by himself."

"It will make them understand that the more heartily they work together, the more they will have and the better they will live; and this will unite them."

Time passed on, and again God came to see how men were living, and whether they were now happy.

But he found them living worse than before. They worked together (that they could not help doing), but not all together, being broken up into little groups. And each group tried to snatch work from other groups, and they hindered one another, wasting time and strength in their struggles, so that things went ill with them all.

Having seen that this, too, was not well, God decided so as to arrange things that man should not know the time of his death, but might die at any moment; and he announced this to them.

"Knowing that each of them may die at any moment," thought God, "they will not, by grasping at gains that may last so short a time, spoil the hours of life allotted to them."

But it turned out otherwise. When God returned to see how people were living, he saw that their life was as bad as ever.

Those who were strongest, availing themselves of the fact that men might die at any time, subdued those who were weaker, killing some and threatening others with death. And it came about that the strongest and their descendants did no work, and suffered from the weariness of idleness, while those who were weaker had to work beyond their strength, and suffered from lack of rest. Each set of men feared and hated the other. And the life of man became yet more unhappy.

Having seen all this, God, to mend matters, decided to make use of one last means; he sent all kinds of sickness among men. God thought that when all men were exposed to sickness they would understand that those who are well should have pity on those who are sick, and should help them, that when they themselves fall ill, those who are well might in turn help them.

And again God went away; but when He came back to see how men lived now that they were subject to sicknesses, he saw that their life was worse even than before. The very sickness that in God's purpose should have united men, had divided them more than ever. Those men who were strong enough to make others work, forced them also to wait on them in times of sickness; but they did not, in their turn, look after others who were ill. And those who were forced to work for others and to look after them when sick, were so worn with work that they had no time to look after their own sick, but left them without attendance. That the sight of sick folk might not disturb the pleasures of the wealthy, houses were arranged in which these poor people suffered and died, far from those whose sympathy might have cheered them, and in the arms of hired people who nursed them without compassion, or even with disgust. Moreover, people considered many of the illnesses infectious, and, fearing to catch them, not only avoided the sick, but even separated themselves from those who attended the sick.

Then God said to Himself: "If even this means will not bring men to understand wherein their happiness lies, let them be taught by suffering." And God left men to themselves.

And, left to themselves, men lived long before they understood that they all ought to, and might be, happy. Only in the very latest times have a few of them begun to understand that work ought not to be a bugbear to some and like galley-slavery for others, but should be a common and happy occupation, uniting all men. They have begun to understand that with death constantly threatening each of us, the only reasonable business of every man is to spend the years, months, hours, and minutes, allotted him—in unity and love. They have begun to understand that sickness, far from dividing men, should, on the contrary, give opportunity for loving union with one another.

Esarhaddon, King of Assyria

[A modern parable, it was written in 1903 as a contribution to an anthology aiding the victims of the Jewish pogrom in Russia. This is the version translated by Louise and Aylmer Maude included in the collection *Twenty-three Tales* (1906).]

The Assyrian King, Esarhaddon, had conquered the kingdom of King Lailie, had destroyed and burnt the towns, taken all the inhabitants captive to his own country, slaughtered the warriors, beheaded some chieftains and impaled or flayed others, and had confined King Lailie himself in a cage.

As he lay on his bed one night, King Esarhaddon was thinking how he should execute Lailie, when suddenly he heard a rustling near his bed, and opening his eyes saw an old man with a long grey beard and mild eyes.

"You wish to execute Lailie?" asked the old man.

"Yes," answered the King. "But I cannot make up my mind how to do it."

"But you are Lailie," said the old man.

"That's not true," replied the King. "Lailie is Lailie, and I am I."

"You and Lailie are one," said the old man. "You only imagine you are not Lailie, and that Lailie is not you."

"What do you mean by that?" said the King. "Here am I, lying on a soft bed; around me are obedient men-slaves and women-slaves, and tomorrow I shall feast with my friends as I did today; whereas Lailie is sitting like a bird in a cage, and tomorrow he will be impaled, and with his tongue hanging out will struggle till he dies, and his body will be torn in pieces by dogs."

"You cannot destroy his life," said the old man.

"And how about the fourteen thousand warriors I killed, with whose bodies I built a mound?" said the King. "I am alive, but they no longer exist. Does not that prove that I can destroy life?"

"How do you know they no longer exist?"

"Because I no longer see them. And, above all, they were tormented, but I was not. It was ill for them, but well for me."

"That, also, only seems so to you. You tortured yourself, but not them."

"I do not understand," said the King.

"Do you wish to understand?"

"Yes, I do."

"Then come here," said the old man, pointing to a large font full of water.

The King rose and approached the font.

"Strip, and enter the font."

Esarhaddon did as the old man bade him.

"As soon as I begin to pour this water over you," said the old man, filling a pitcher with the water, "dip down your head."

The old man tilted the pitcher over the King's head, and the King bent his head till it was under water.

And as soon as King Esarhaddon was under the water, he felt that he was no longer Esarhaddon, but someone else. And, feeling himself to be that other man, he saw himself lying on a rich bed, beside a beautiful woman. He had never seen her before, but he knew she was his wife. The woman raised herself and said to him:

"Dear husband, Lailie! You were wearied by yesterday's work and have slept longer than usual, and I have guarded your rest, and have not roused you. But now the Princes await you in the Great Hall. Dress and go out to them."

And Esarhaddon—understanding from these words that he was Lailie, and not feeling at all surprised at this, but only wondering that he did not know it before—rose, dressed, and went into the Great Hall where the Princes awaited him.

The Princes greeted Lailie, their King, bowing to the ground, and then they rose, and at his word sat down before him; and the eldest of the Princes began to speak, saying that it was impossible longer to endure the insults of the wicked King Esarhaddon, and that they must make war on him. But Lailie disagreed, and gave orders that envoys shall be sent to remonstrate with King Esarhaddon; and he dismissed the Princes from the audience. Afterwards he appointed men of note to act as ambassadors, and impressed on them what they were to say to King Esarhaddon. Having finished this business, Esarhaddon—feeling himself to be

Lailie—rode out to hunt wild asses. The hunt was successful. He killed two wild asses himself, and, having returned home, feasted with his friends, and witnessed a dance of slave girls. The next day he went to the Court, where he was awaited by petitioners, suitors, and prisoners brought for trial; and there as usual he decided the cases submitted to him. Having finished this business, he again rode out to his favourite amusement: the hunt. And again he was successful: this time killing with his own hand an old lioness, and capturing her two cubs. After the hunt he again feasted with his friends, and was entertained with music and dances, and the night he spent with the wife whom he loved.

So, dividing his time between kingly duties and pleasures, he lived for days and weeks, awaiting the return of the ambassadors he had sent to that King Esarhaddon who used to be himself. Not till a month had passed did the ambassadors return, and they returned with their noses and ears cut off.

King Esarhaddon had ordered them to tell Lailie that what had been done to them—the ambassadors—would be done to King Lailie himself also, unless he sent immediately a tribute of silver, gold, and cypress-wood, and came himself to pay homage to King Esarhaddon.

Lailie, formerly Esarhaddon, again assembled the Princes, and took counsel with them as to what he should do. They all with one accord said that war must be made against Esarhaddon, without waiting for him to attack them. The King agreed; and taking his place at the head of the army, started on the campaign. The campaign lasts seven days. Each day the King rode round the army to rouse the courage of his warriors. On the eighth day his army met that of Esarhaddon in a broad valley through which a river flowed. Lailie's army fought bravely, but Lailie, formerly Esarhaddon, saw the enemy swarming down from the mountains like ants, over-running the valley and overwhelming his army; and, in his chariot, he flung himself into the midst of the battle, hewing and felling the enemy. But the warriors of Lailie were but as hundreds, while those of Esarhaddon were as thousands; and Lailie felt himself wounded and taken prisoner. Nine days he journeyed with other captives, bound, and guarded by the warriors of Esarhaddon.

On the tenth day he reached Nineveh, and was placed in a cage. Lailie suffered not so much from hunger and from his wound as from shame and impotent rage. He felt how powerless he was to avenge himself on his enemy for all he was suffering. All he could do was to deprive his enemies of the pleasure of seeing his sufferings; and he firmly resolved to endure courageously, without a murmur, all they could do to him. For twenty days he sat in his cage, awaiting execution. He saw his relatives and friends led out to death; he heard the groans of those who were executed: some had their hands and feet cut off, others were flayed alive, but he showed neither disquietude, nor pity, nor fear. He saw the wife he loved, bound, and led by two black eunuchs. He knew she was being taken as a slave to Esarhaddon. That, too, he bore without a murmur. But one of the guards placed to watch him said, "I pity you, Lailie; you were a king, but what are you now?" And hearing these words, Lailie remembered all he had lost. He clutched the bars of his cage, and, wishing to kill himself, beat his head against them. But he had not the strength to do so; and, groaning in despair, he fell upon the floor of his cage.

At last two executioners opened his cage door, and having strapped his arms tight behind him, led him to the place of execution, which was soaked with blood. Lailie saw a sharp stake dripping with blood, from which the corpse of one of his friends had just been torn, and he understood that this had been done that the stake might serve for his own execution. They stripped Lailie of his clothes. He was startled at the leanness of his once strong, handsome body. The two executioners seized that body by its lean thighs; they lifted him up and were about to let him fall upon the stake.

"This is death, destruction!" thought Lailie, and, forgetful of his resolve to remain bravely calm to the end, he sobbed and prayed for mercy. But no one listened to him.

"But this cannot be," thought he. "Surely I am asleep. It is a dream." And he made an effort to rouse himself, and did indeed awake, to find himself neither Esarhaddon nor Lailie—but some kind of an animal. He was astonished that he was an animal, and astonished, also, at not having known this before.

He was grazing in a valley, tearing the tender grass with his teeth, and brushing away flies with his long tail. Around him was frolicking a long-legged, dark-grey ass-colt, striped down its back. Kicking up its hind legs, the colt galloped full speed to Esarhaddon, and poking him under the stomach with its smooth little muzzle, searched for the teat, and, finding it, quieted down, swallowing regularly. Esarhaddon understood that he was a she-ass, the colt's mother, and this neither surprised nor grieved him, but rather gave him pleasure. He experienced a glad feeling of simultaneous life in himself and in his offspring.

But suddenly something flew near with a whistling sound and hit him in the side, and with its sharp point entered his skin and flesh. Feeling a burning pain, Esarhaddon—who was at the same time the ass—tore the udder from the colt's teeth, and laying back his ears galloped to the herd from which he had strayed. The colt kept up with him, galloping by his side. They had already nearly reached the herd, which had started off, when another arrow in full flight struck the colt's neck. It pierced the skin and quivered in its flesh. The colt sobbed piteously and fell upon its knees. Esarhaddon could not abandon it, and remained standing over it. The colt rose, tottered on its long, thin legs, and again fell. A fearful two-legged being—a man—ran up and cut its throat.

"This cannot be; it is still a dream!" thought Esarhaddon, and made a last effort to awake. "Surely I am not Lailie, nor the ass, but Esarhaddon!"

He cried out, and at the same instant lifted his head out of the font . . . The old man was standing by him, pouring over his head the last drops from the pitcher.

"Oh, how terribly I have suffered! And for how long!" said Esarhaddon.

"Long?" replied the old man, "you have only dipped your head under water and lifted it again; see, the water is not yet all out of the pitcher. Do you now understand?"

Esarhaddon did not reply, but only looked at the old man with terror.

"Do you now understand," continued the old man, "that Lailie is you, and the warriors you put to death were you also? And not the warriors only, but the animals which you slew when hunting and ate at your feasts, were also you. You thought life dwelt in you alone, but I have drawn aside the veil of delusion, and have let you see that by doing evil to others you have done it to yourself also. Life is one in them all, and yours is but a portion of this same common life. And only in that one part of life that is yours, can you make life better or worse—increasing or decreasing it. You can only improve life in yourself by destroying the barriers that divide your life from that of others, and by considering others as yourself, and loving them. By so doing you increase your share of life. You injure your life when you think of it as the only life, and try to add to its welfare at the expense of other lives. By so doing you only lessen it. To destroy the life that dwells in others is beyond your power. The life of those you have slain has vanished from your eyes, but is not destroyed. You thought to lengthen your own life and to shorten theirs, but you cannot do this. Life knows neither time nor space. The life of a moment, and the life of a thousand years: your life, and the life of all the visible and invisible beings in the world, are equal. To destroy life, or to alter it, is impossible; for life is the one thing that exists. All else, but seems to us to be."

Having said this the old man vanished.

Next morning King Esarhaddon gave orders that Lailie and all the prisoners should be set at liberty, and that the executions should cease.

On the third day he called his son Assur-bani-pal, and gave the kingdom over into his hands; and he himself went into the desert to think over all he had learnt. Afterwards he went about as a wanderer through the towns and villages, preaching to the people that all life is one, and that when men wish to harm others, they really do evil to themselves.

Three Questions

[One of the three stories written in 1903 as a contribution to an
anthology aiding the victims of the Jewish pogrom in Russia.
This version is a translation by Louise and Aylmer Maude
published in the collection *Twenty-three Tales* (1906).]

It once occurred to a certain king, that if he always knew the right time to begin everything; if he knew who were the right people to listen to, and whom to avoid; and, above all, if he always knew what was the most important thing to do, he would never fail in anything he might undertake.

And this thought having occurred to him, he had it proclaimed throughout his kingdom that he would give a great reward to anyone who would teach him what was the right time for every action, and who were the most necessary people, and how he might know what was the most important thing to do.

And learned men came to the King, but they all answered his questions differently.

In reply to the first question, some said that to know the right time for every action, one must draw up in advance, a table of days, months and years, and must live strictly according to it. Only thus, said they, could everything be done at its proper time. Others declared that it was impossible to decide beforehand the right time for every action; but that, not letting oneself be absorbed in idle pastimes, one should always attend to all that was going on, and then do what was most needful. Others, again, said that however attentive the King might be to what was going on, it was impossible for one man to decide correctly the right time for every action, but that he should have a Council of wise men, who would help him to fix the proper time for everything.

But then again others said there were some things which could not wait to be laid before a Council, but about which one had at once to decide whether to undertake them or not. But in order to decide that, one must know beforehand what was going to happen. It is only magicians who know that; and, therefore, in order to know the right time for every action, one must consult magicians.

Equally various were the answers to the second question. Some said, the people the King most needed were his councilors; others, the priests; others, the doctors; while some said the warriors were the most necessary.

To the third question, as to what was the most important occupation: some replied that the most important thing in the world was science. Others said it was skill in warfare; and others, again, that it was religious worship.

All the answers being different, the King agreed with none of them, and gave the reward to none. But still wishing to find the right answers to his questions, he decided to consult a hermit, widely renowned for his wisdom.

The hermit lived in a wood which he never quitted, and he received none but common folk. So the King put on simple clothes, and before reaching the hermit's cell dismounted from his horse, and, leaving his bodyguard behind, went on alone.

When the King approached, the hermit was digging the ground in front of his hut. Seeing the King, he greeted him and went on digging. The hermit was frail and weak, and each time he stuck his spade into the ground and turned a little earth, he breathed heavily.

The King went up to him and said: "I have come to you, wise hermit, to ask you to answer three questions: How can I learn to do the right thing at the right time? Who are the people I most need, and to whom should I, therefore, pay more attention than to the rest? And, what affairs are the most important, and need my first attention?"

The hermit listened to the King, but answered nothing. He just spat on his hand and recommenced digging.

"You are tired," said the King, "let me take the spade and work awhile for you."

"Thanks!" said the hermit, and, giving the spade to the King, he sat down on the ground.

When he had dug two beds, the King stopped and repeated his questions. The hermit again gave no answer, but rose, stretched out his hand for the spade, and said:

"Now rest awhile—and let me work a bit."

But the King did not give him the spade, and continued to dig. One hour passed, and another. The sun began to sink behind the trees, and the King at last stuck the spade into the ground, and said:

"I came to you, wise man, for an answer to my questions. If you can give me none, tell me so, and I will return home."

"Here comes someone running," said the hermit, "let us see who it is."

The King turned round, and saw a bearded man come running out of the wood. The man held his hands pressed against his stomach, and blood was flowing from under them. When he reached the King, he fell fainting on the ground moaning feebly. The King and the hermit unfastened the man's clothing. There was a large wound in his stomach. The King washed it as best he could, and bandaged it with his handkerchief and with a towel the hermit had. But the blood would not stop flowing, and the King again and again removed the bandage soaked with warm blood, and washed and rebandaged the wound. When at last the blood ceased flowing, the man revived and asked for something to drink. The King brought fresh water and gave it to him. Meanwhile the sun had set, and it had become cool. So the King, with the hermit's help, carried the wounded man into the hut and laid him on the bed. Lying on the bed the man closed his eyes and was quiet; but the King was so tired with his walk and with the work he had done, that he crouched down on the threshold, and also fell asleep—so soundly that he slept all through the short summer night. When he awoke in the morning, it was long before he could remember where he was, or who was the strange bearded man lying on the bed and gazing intently at him with shining eyes.

"Forgive me!" said the bearded man in a weak voice, when he saw that the King was awake and was looking at him.

"I do not know you, and have nothing to forgive you for," said the King.

"You do not know me, but I know you. I am that enemy of yours who swore to revenge himself on you, because you executed his brother and seized his property. I knew you had gone alone to see the hermit, and I resolved to kill you on your way back. But the day passed and you did not return. So I came out from my ambush to find you, and I came upon your bodyguard, and they recognized me, and wounded me. I escaped from them, but should have bled to death had you not dressed my wound. I wished to kill you, and you have saved my life. Now, if I live, and if you wish it, I will serve you as your most faithful slave, and will bid my sons do the same. Forgive me!"

The King was very glad to have made peace with his enemy so easily, and to have gained him for a friend, and he not only forgave him, but said he would send his servants and his own physician to attend him, and promised to restore his property.

Having taken leave of the wounded man, the King went out into the porch and looked around for the hermit. Before going away he wished once more to beg an answer to the questions he had put. The hermit was outside, on his knees, sowing seeds in the beds that had been dug the day before.

The King approached him, and said:

"For the last time, I pray you to answer my questions, wise man."

"You have already been answered!" said the hermit still crouching on his thin legs, and looking up at the King, who stood before him.

"How answered? What do you mean?" asked the King.

"Do you not see," replied the hermit. "If you had not pitied my weakness yesterday, and had not dug those beds for me, but had gone your way, that man would have attacked you, and you would have repented of not having stayed with me. So the most important time was when you were digging the beds; and I was the most important man; and to do me good was your most important business. Afterwards when that man ran to us, the most important time was when you were attending to him, for if you had not bound up his wounds he would have died without having made peace with you. So he was the most important man, and what you did for him was your most important business. Remember then: there is only one time that is important—Now! It is the most important time because it is the only time when we have any power. The most necessary man is he with whom you are, for no man knows whether he will ever have dealings with anyone else: and the most important affair is, to do him good, because for that purpose alone was man sent into this life!"

After the Dance

[Written in 1903. Published posthumously. This version is from the collection *The Forged Coupon and Other Stories* (1911) translated by Charles Theodore Hagberg Wright.]

"—And you say that a man cannot, of himself, understand what is good and evil; that it is all environment, that the environment swamps the man. But I believe it is all chance. Take my own case . . ."

Thus spoke our excellent friend, Ivan Vasilievich, after a conversation between us on the impossibility of improving individual character without a change of the conditions under which men live. Nobody had actually said that one could not of oneself understand good and evil; but it was a habit of Ivan Vasilievich to answer in this way the thoughts aroused in his own mind by conversation, and to illustrate those thoughts by relating incidents in his own life. He often quite forgot the reason for his story in telling it; but he always told it with great sincerity and feeling.

He did so now.

"Take my own case. My whole life was moulded, not by environment, but by something quite different."

"By what, then?" we asked.

"Oh, that is a long story. I should have to tell you about a great many things to make you understand."

"Well, tell us then."

Ivan Vasilievich thought a little, and shook his head.

"My whole life," he said, "was changed in one night, or, rather, morning."

"Why, what happened?" one of us asked.

"What happened was that I was very much in love. I have been in love many times, but this was the most serious of all. It is a thing of the past; she has married daughters now. It was Varinka B—." Ivan Vasilievich mentioned her surname. "Even at fifty she is remarkably handsome; but in her youth, at eighteen, she was exquisite—tall, slender, graceful, and stately. Yes, stately is the word; she held herself very erect, by instinct as it were; and carried her head high, and that together with her beauty and height gave her a queenly air in spite of being thin, even bony one might say. It might indeed have been deterring had it not been for her smile, which was always gay and cordial, and for the charming light in her eyes and for her youthful sweetness."

"What an entrancing description you give, Ivan Vasilievich!"

"Description, indeed! I could not possibly describe her so that you could appreciate her. But that does not matter; what I am going to tell you happened in the forties. I was at that time a student in a provincial university. I don't know whether it was a good thing or no, but we had no political clubs, no theories in our universities then. We were simply young and spent our time as young men do, studying and amusing ourselves. I was a very gay, lively, careless fellow, and had plenty of money too. I had a fine horse, and used to go tobogganing with the young ladies. Skating had not yet come into fashion. I went to drinking parties with my comrades—in those days we drank nothing but champagne—if we had no champagne we drank nothing at all. We never drank vodka, as they do now. Evening parties and balls were my favourite amusements. I danced well, and was not an ugly fellow."

"Come, there is no need to be modest," interrupted a lady near him. "We have seen your photograph. Not ugly, indeed! You were a handsome fellow."

"Handsome, if you like. That does not matter. When my love for her was at its strongest, on the last day of the carnival, I was at a ball at the provincial marshal's, a good-natured old man, rich and hospitable, and a court chamberlain. The guests were welcomed by his wife, who was as good-natured as himself. She was dressed in puce-coloured velvet, and had a diamond diadem on her forehead, and her plump, old white shoulders and bosom were bare like the portraits of Empress Elizabeth, the daughter of Peter the Great.

"It was a delightful ball. It was a splendid room, with a gallery for the orchestra, which was famous at the time, and consisted of serfs belonging to a musical landowner. The refreshments were magnificent, and the champagne flowed in rivers. Though I was fond of champagne I did not drink that night, because without it I was drunk with love. But I made up for it by dancing waltzes and polkas till I was ready to drop—of course, whenever possible, with Varinka. She wore a white dress with a pink sash, white shoes, and white kid gloves, which did not quite reach to her thin pointed elbows. A disgusting engineer named Anisimov robbed me of the mazurka with her—to this day I cannot forgive him. He asked her for the dance the minute she arrived, while I had driven to the hair-dresser's to get a pair of gloves, and was late. So I did not dance the mazurka with her, but with a German girl to whom I had previously paid a little attention; but I am afraid I did not behave very politely to her that evening. I hardly spoke or looked at her, and saw nothing but the tall, slender figure in a white dress, with a pink sash, a flushed, beaming, dimpled face, and sweet, kind eyes. I was not alone; they were all looking at her with admiration, the men and women alike, although she outshone all of them. They could not help admiring her.

"Although I was not nominally her partner for the mazurka, I did as a matter of fact dance nearly the whole time with her. She always came forward boldly the whole length of the room to pick me out. I flew to meet her without waiting to be chosen, and she thanked me with a smile for my intuition. When I was brought up to her with somebody else, and she guessed wrongly, she took the other man's hand with a shrug of her slim shoulders, and smiled at me regretfully.

"Whenever there was a waltz figure in the mazurka, I waltzed with her for a long time, and breathing fast and smiling, she would say, 'Encore'; and I went on waltzing and waltzing, as though unconscious of any bodily existence."

"Come now, how could you be unconscious of it with your arm round her waist? You must have been conscious, not only of your own existence, but of hers," said one of the party.

Ivan Vasilievich cried out, almost shouting in anger: "There you are, moderns all over! Nowadays you think of nothing but the body. It was different in our day. The more I was in love the less corporeal was she in my eyes. Nowadays you think of nothing but the body. It was different in our day. The more I was in love the less corporeal was she in my eyes. Nowadays you set legs, ankles, and I don't know what. You undress the women you are in love with. In my eyes, as Alphonse Karr said—and he was a good writer—'the one I loved was always draped in robes of bronze.' We never thought of doing so; we tried to veil her nakedness, like Noah's good-natured son. Oh, well, you can't understand."

"Don't pay any attention to him. Go on," said one of them.

"Well, I danced for the most part with her, and did not notice how time was passing. The musicians kept playing the same mazurka tunes over and over again in desperate exhaustion—you know what it is towards the end of a ball. Papas and mammas were already getting up from the card-tables in the drawing room in expectation of supper, the men-servants were running to and fro bringing in things. It was nearly three o'clock. I had to make the most of the last minutes. I chose her again for the mazurka, and for the hundredth time we danced across the room.

"'The quadrille after supper is mine,' I said, taking her to her place.

"'Of course, if I am not carried off home,' she said, with a smile.

"'I won't give you up,' I said.

"'Give me my fan, anyhow,' she answered.

"'I am so sorry to part with it,' I said, handing her a cheap white fan.

"'Well, here's something to console you,' she said, plucking a feather out of the fan, and giving it to me.

"I took the feather, and could only express my rapture and gratitude with my eyes. I was not only pleased and gay, I was happy, delighted; I was good, I was not myself but some being not of this earth, knowing nothing of evil. I hid the feather in my glove, and stood there unable to tear myself away from her.

"'Look, they are urging father to dance,' she said to me, pointing to the tall, stately figure of her father, a colonel with silver epaulettes, who was standing in the doorway with some ladies.

"'Varinka, come here!' exclaimed our hostess, the lady with the diamond ferronniere and with shoulders like Elizabeth, in a loud voice.

"Varinka went to the door, and I followed her.

"'Persuade your father to dance the mazurka with you, ma chere.—Do, please, Peter Valdislavovich,' she said, turning to the colonel.

"Varinka's father was a very handsome, well-preserved old man. He had a good colour, moustaches curled in the style of Nicolas I, and white whiskers which met the moustaches. His hair was combed on to his forehead, and a bright smile, like his daughter's, was on his lips and in his eyes. He was splendidly set up, with a broad military chest, on which he wore some decorations, and he had powerful shoulders and long slim legs. He was that ultra-military type produced by the discipline of Emperor Nicolas I.

"When we approached the door the colonel was just refusing to dance, saying that he had quite forgotten how; but at that instant he smiled, swung his arm gracefully around to the left, drew his sword from its sheath, handed it to an obliging young man who stood near, and smoothed his suede glove on his right hand.

"'Everything must be done according to rule,' he said with a smile. He took the hand of his daughter, and stood one-quarter turned, waiting for the music.

"At the first sound of the mazurka, he stamped one foot smartly, threw the other forward, and, at first slowly and smoothly, then buoyantly and impetuously, with stamping of feet and clicking of boots, his tall, imposing figure moved the length of the room. Varinka swayed gracefully beside him, rhythmically and easily, making her steps short or long, with her little feet in their white satin slippers.

"All the people in the room followed every movement of the couple. As for me I not only admired, I regarded them with enraptured sympathy. I was particularly impressed with the old gentleman's boots. They were not the modern pointed affairs, but were made of cheap leather, squared-toed, and evidently built by the regimental cobbler. In order that his daughter might dress and go out in society, he did not buy fashionable boots, but wore home-made ones, I thought, and his square toes seemed to me most touching. It was obvious that in his time he had been a good

612

dancer; but now he was too heavy, and his legs had not spring enough for all the beautiful steps he tried to take. Still, he contrived to go twice round the room. When at the end, standing with legs apart, he suddenly clicked his feet together and fell on one knee, a bit heavily, and she danced gracefully around him, smiling and adjusting her skirt, the whole room applauded.

"Rising with an effort, he tenderly took his daughter's face between his hands. He kissed her on the forehead, and brought her to me, under the impression that I was her partner for the mazurka. I said I was not. 'Well, never mind. Just go around the room once with her,' he said, smiling kindly, as he replaced his sword in the sheath.

"As the contents of a bottle flow readily when the first drop has been poured, so my love for Varinka seemed to set free the whole force of loving within me. In surrounding her it embraced the world. I loved the hostess with her diadem and her shoulders like Elizabeth, and her husband and her guests and her footmen, and even the engineer Anisimov who felt peevish towards me. As for Varinka's father, with his home-made boots and his kind smile, so like her own, I felt a sort of tenderness for him that was almost rapture.

"After supper I danced the promised quadrille with her, and though I had been infinitely happy before, I grew still happier every moment.

"We did not speak of love. I neither asked myself nor her whether she loved me. It was quite enough to know that I loved her. And I had only one fear—that something might come to interfere with my great joy.

"When I went home, and began to undress for the night, I found it quite out of the question. I held the little feather out of her fan in my hand, and one of her gloves which she gave me when I helped her into the carriage after her mother. Looking at these things, and without closing my eyes I could see her before me as she was for an instant when she had to choose between two partners. She tried to guess what kind of person was represented in me, and I could hear her sweet voice as she said, 'Pride—am I right?' and merrily gave me her hand. At supper she took the first sip from my glass of champagne, looking at me over the rim with her caressing glance. But, plainest of all, I could see her as she danced with her father, gliding along beside him, and looking at the admiring observers with pride and happiness.

"He and she were united in my mind in one rush of pathetic tenderness.

"I was living then with my brother, who has since died. He disliked going out, and never went to dances; and besides, he was busy preparing for his last university examinations, and was leading a very regular life. He was asleep. I looked at him, his head buried in the pillow and half covered with the quilt; and I affectionately pitied him, pitied him for his ignorance of the bliss I was experiencing. Our serf Petrusha had met me with a candle, ready to undress me, but I sent him away. His sleepy face and tousled hair seemed to me so touching. Trying not to make a noise, I went to my room on tiptoe and sat down on my bed. No, I was too happy; I could not sleep. Besides, it was too hot in the rooms. Without taking off my uniform, I went quietly into the hall, put on my overcoat, opened the front door and stepped out into the street.

"It was after four when I had left the ball; going home and stopping there a while had occupied two hours, so by the time I went out it was dawn. It was regular carnival weather—foggy, and the road full of water-soaked snow just melting, and water dripping from the eaves. Varinka's family lived on the edge of town near a large field, one end of which was a parade ground: at the other end was a boarding-school for young ladies. I passed through our empty little street and came to the main thoroughfare, where I met pedestrians and sledges laden with wood, the runners grating the road. The horses swung with regular paces beneath their shining yokes, their backs covered with straw mats and their heads wet with rain; while the drivers, in enormous boots, splashed through the mud beside the sledges. All this, the very horses themselves, seemed to me stimulating and fascinating, full of suggestion.

"When I approached the field near their house, I saw at one end of it, in the direction of the parade ground, something very huge and black, and I heard sounds of fife and drum proceeding from it. My heart had been full of song, and I had heard in imagination the tune of the mazurka, but this was very harsh music. It was not pleasant.

"'What can that be?' I thought, and went towards the sound by a slippery path through the centre of the field. Walking about a hundred paces, I began to distinguish many black objects through the mist. They were evidently soldiers. 'It is probably a drill,' I thought.

"So I went along in that direction in company with a blacksmith, who wore a dirty coat and an apron, and was carrying something. He walked ahead of me as we approached the place. The soldiers in black uniforms stood in two rows, facing each other motionless, their guns at rest. Behind them stood the fifes and drums, incessantly repeating the same unpleasant tune.

"'What are they doing?' I asked the blacksmith, who halted at my side.

"'A Tartar is being beaten through the ranks for his attempt to desert,' said the blacksmith in an angry tone, as he looked intently at the far end of the line.

"I looked in the same direction, and saw between the files something horrid approaching me. The thing that approached was a man, stripped to the waist, fastened with cords to the guns of two soldiers who were leading him. At his side an officer in overcoat and cap was walking, whose figure had a familiar look. The victim advanced under the blows that rained upon him from both sides, his whole body plunging, his feet dragging through the snow. Now he threw himself backward, and the subalterns who led him thrust him forward. Now he fell forward, and they pulled him up short; while ever at his side marched the tall officer, with firm and nervous pace. It was Varinka's father, with his rosy face and white moustache.

"At each stroke the man, as if amazed, turned his face, grimacing with pain, towards the side whence the blow came, and showing his white teeth repeated the same words over and over.

But I could only hear what the words were when he came quite near. He did not speak them, he sobbed them out—

"'Brothers, have mercy on me! Brothers, have mercy on me!' But the brothers had, no mercy, and when the procession came close to me, I saw how a soldier who stood opposite me took a firm step forward and lifting his stick with a whirr, brought it down upon the man's back. The man plunged forward, but the subalterns pulled him back, and another blow came down from the other side, then from this side and then from the other. The colonel marched beside him, and looking now at his feet and now at the man, inhaled the air, puffed out his cheeks, and breathed it out between his protruded lips. When they passed the place where I stood, I caught a glimpse between the two files of the back of the man that was being punished. It was something so many-coloured, wet, red, unnatural, that I could hardly believe it was a human body.

"'My God!' muttered the blacksmith.

"The procession moved farther away. The blows continued to rain upon the writhing, falling creature; the fifes shrilled and the drums beat, and the tall imposing figure of the colonel moved alongside the man, just as before. Then, suddenly, the colonel stopped, and rapidly approached a man in the ranks.

"'I'll teach you to hit him gently,' I heard his furious voice say. 'Will you pat him like that? Will you?' and I saw how his strong hand in the suede glove struck the weak, bloodless, terrified soldier for not bringing down his stick with sufficient strength on the red neck of the Tartar.

"'Bring new sticks!' he cried, and looking round, he saw me. Assuming an air of not knowing me, and with a ferocious, angry frown, he hastily turned away. I felt so utterly ashamed that I didn't know where to look. It was as if I had been detected in a disgraceful act. I dropped my eyes, and quickly hurried home. All the way I had the drums beating and the fifes whistling in my ears. And I heard the words, 'Brothers, have mercy on me!' or 'Will you pat him? Will you?' My heart was full of physical disgust that was almost sickness. So much so that I halted several times on my way, for I had the feeling that I was going to be really sick from all the horrors that possessed me at that sight. I do not remember how I got home and got to bed. But the moment I was about to fall asleep I heard and saw again all that had happened, and I sprang up.

"'Evidently he knows something I do not know,' I thought about the colonel. 'If I knew what he knows I should certainly grasp—understand—what I have just seen, and it would not cause me such suffering.'

"But however much I thought about it, I could not understand the thing that the colonel knew. It was evening before I could get to sleep, and then only after calling on a friend and drinking till I; was quite drunk.

"Do you think I had come to the conclusion that the deed I had witnessed was wicked? Oh, no. Since it was done with such assurance, and was recognized by everyone as indispensable, they doubtless knew something which I did not know. So I thought, and tried to understand. But no matter, I could never understand it, then or afterwards. And not being able to grasp it, I could not enter the service as I had intended. I don't mean only the military service: I did not enter the Civil Service either. And so I have been of no use whatever, as you can see."

"Yes, we know how useless you've been," said one of us. "Tell us, rather, how many people would be of any use at all if it hadn't been for you."

"Oh, that's utter nonsense," said Ivan Vasilievich, with genuine annoyance.

"Well; and what about the love affair?

"My love? It decreased from that day. When, as often happened, she looked dreamy and meditative, I instantly recollected the colonel on the parade ground, and I felt so awkward and uncomfortable that I began to see her less frequently. So my love came to naught. Yes; such chances arise, and they alter and direct a man's whole life," he said in summing up. "And you say . . ."

Alyosha the Pot

[Written in 1905. Published posthumously in 1911. This version is from the collection *The Forged Coupon and Other Stories* (1911) translated by Charles Theodore Hagberg Wright.]

Alyosha was the younger brother. He was called the Pot, because his mother had once sent him with a pot of milk to the deacon's wife, and he had stumbled against something and broken it. His mother had beaten him, and the children had teased him. Since then he was nicknamed the Pot. Alyosha was a tiny, thin little fellow, with ears like wings, and a huge nose. "Alyosha has a nose that looks like a dog on a hill!" the children used to call after him. Alyosha went to the village school, but was not good at lessons; besides, there was so little time to learn. His elder brother was in town, working for a merchant, so Alyosha had to help his father from a very early age. When he was no more than six he used to go out with the girls to watch the cows and sheep in the pasture, and a little later he looked after the horses by day and by night. And at twelve years of age he had already begun to plough and to drive the cart. The skill was there though the strength was not. He was always cheerful. Whenever the children made fun of him, he would either laugh or be silent. When his father scolded him he would stand mute and listen attentively, and as soon as the scolding was over would smile and go on with his work. Alyosha was nineteen when his brother was taken as a soldier. So his father placed him with the merchant as a yard-porter. He was given his brother's old boots, his father's old coat and cap, and was taken to town. Alyosha was delighted with his clothes, but the merchant was not impressed by his appearance.

"I thought you would bring me a man in Simeon's place," he said, scanning Alyosha; "and you've brought me *this*! What's the good of him?"

"He can do everything; look after horses and drive. He's a good one to work. He looks rather thin, but he's tough enough. And he's very willing."

"He looks it. All right; we'll see what we can do with him."

So Alyosha remained at the merchant's.

The family was not a large one. It consisted of the merchant's wife, her old mother, a married son poorly educated who was in his father's business, another son, a learned one who had finished school and entered the University, but having been expelled, was living at home, and a daughter who still went to school.

They did not take to Alyosha at first. He was uncouth, badly dressed, and had no manner, but they soon got used to him. Alyosha worked even better than his brother had done; he was really very willing. They sent him on all sorts of errands, but he did everything quickly and readily, going from one task to another without stopping. And so here, just as at home, all the work was put upon his shoulders. The more he did, the more he was given to do. His mistress, her old mother, the son, the daughter, the clerk, and the cook—all ordered him about, and sent him from one place to another.

"Alyosha, do this! Alyosha, do that! What! have you forgotten, Alyosha? Mind you don't forget, Alyosha!" was heard from morning till night. And Alyosha ran here, looked after this and that, forgot nothing, found time for everything, and was always cheerful.

His brother's old boots were soon worn out, and his master scolded him for going about in tatters with his toes sticking out. He ordered another pair to be bought for him in the market. Alyosha was delighted with his new boots, but was angry with his feet when they ached at the end of the day after so much running about. And then he was afraid that his father would be annoyed when he came to town for his wages, to find that his master had deducted the cost of the boots.

In the winter Alyosha used to get up before daybreak. He would chop the wood, sweep the yard, feed the cows and horses, light the stoves, clean the boots, prepare the samovars and polish them afterwards; or the clerk would get him to bring up the goods; or the cook would set him to knead the bread and clean the saucepans. Then he was sent to town on various errands, to bring the daughter home from school, or to get some olive oil for the old mother. "Why the devil have you been so long?" first one, then another, would say to him. Why should they go? Alyosha can go. "Alyosha! Alyosha!" And Alyosha ran here and there. He breakfasted in snatches while he was working, and rarely managed to get his dinner at the proper hour. The cook used to scold him for being late, but she was sorry for him all the same, and would keep something hot for his dinner and supper.

At holiday times there was more work than ever, but Alyosha liked holidays because everybody gave him a tip. Not much certainly, but it would amount up to about sixty kopeks [1s 2d]— his very own money. For Alyosha never set eyes on his wages. His father used to come and take them from the merchant, and only scold Alyosha for wearing out his boots.

When he had saved up two roubles [4s], by the advice of the cook he bought himself a red knitted jacket, and was so happy when he put it on, that he couldn't close his mouth for joy. Alyosha was not talkative; when he spoke at all, he spoke abruptly, with his head turned away. When told to do anything, or asked if he could do it, he would say yes without the smallest hesitation, and set to work at once.

Alyosha did not know any prayer; and had forgotten what his mother had taught him. But he prayed just the same, every morning and every evening, prayed with his hands, crossing himself.

He lived like this for about a year and a half, and towards the end of the second year a most startling thing happened to him. He discovered one day, to his great surprise, that, in addition to the relation of usefulness existing between people, there was also another, a peculiar relation of quite a different character. Instead of a man being wanted to clean boots, and go on errands and harness horses, he is not wanted to be of any service at all, but another human being wants to serve him and pet him. Suddenly Alyosha felt he was such a man.

He made this discovery through the cook Ustinia. She was young, had no parents, and worked as hard as Alyosha. He felt for the first time in his life that he—not his services, but he himself— was necessary to another human being. When his mother used to be sorry for him, he had taken no notice of her. It had seemed to him quite natural, as though he were feeling sorry for himself.

But here was Ustinia, a perfect stranger, and sorry for him. She would save him some hot porridge, and sit watching him, her chin propped on her bare arm, with the sleeve rolled up, while he was eating it. When he looked at her she would begin to laugh, and he would laugh too.

This was such a new, strange thing to him that it frightened Alyosha. He feared that it might interfere with his work. But he was pleased, nevertheless, and when he glanced at the trousers that Ustinia had mended for him, he would shake his head and smile. He would often think of her while at work, or when running on errands. "A fine girl, Ustinia!" he sometimes exclaimed.

Ustinia used to help him whenever she could, and he helped her. She told him all about her life; how she had lost her parents; how her aunt had taken her in and found a place for her in the town; how the merchant's son had tried to take liberties with her, and how she had rebuffed him. She liked to talk, and Alyosha liked to listen to her. He had heard that peasants who came up to work in the towns frequently got married to servant girls. On one occasion she asked him if his parents intended marrying him soon. He said that he did not know; that he did not want to marry any of the village girls.

"Have you taken a fancy to someone, then?"

"I would marry you, if you'd be willing."

"Get along with you, Alyosha the Pot; but you've found your tongue, haven't you?" she exclaimed, slapping him on the back with a towel she held in her hand. "Why shouldn't I?"

At Shrovetide Alyosha's father came to town for his wages. It had come to the ears of the merchant's wife that Alyosha wanted to marry Ustinia, and she disapproved of it. "What will be the use of her with a baby?" she thought, and informed her husband.

The merchant gave the old man Alyosha's wages.

"How is my lad getting on?" he asked. "I told you he was willing."

"That's all right, as far as it goes, but he's taken some sort of nonsense into his head. He wants to marry our cook. Now I don't approve of married servants. We won't have them in the house."

"Well, now, who would have thought the fool would think of such a thing?" the old man exclaimed. "But don't you worry. I'll soon settle that."

He went into the kitchen, and sat down at the table waiting for his son. Alyosha was out on an errand, and came back breathless.

"I thought you had some sense in you; but what's this you've taken into your head?" his father began.

"I? Nothing."

"How, nothing? They tell me you want to get married. You shall get married when the time comes. I'll find you a decent wife, not some town hussy."

His father talked and talked, while Alyosha stood still and sighed. When his father had quite finished, Alyosha smiled.

"All right. I'll drop it."

"Now that's what I call sense."

When he was left alone with Ustinia he told her what his father had said. (She had listened at the door.)

"It's no good; it can't come off. Did you hear? He was angry—won't have it at any price."

Ustinia cried into her apron.

Alyosha shook his head.

"What's to be done? We must do as we're told."

"Well, are you going to give up that nonsense, as your father told you?" his mistress asked, as he was putting up the shutters in the evening.

"To be sure we are," Alyosha replied with a smile, and then burst into tears.

From that day Alyosha went about his work as usual, and no longer talked to Ustinia about their getting married. One day in Lent the clerk told him to clear the snow from the roof. Alyosha climbed on to the roof and swept away all the snow; and, while he was still raking out some frozen lumps from the gutter, his foot slipped and he fell over. Unfortunately he did not fall on the snow, but on a piece of iron over the door. Ustinia came running up, together with the merchant's daughter.

"Have you hurt yourself, Alyosha?"

"Ah! no, it's nothing."

But he could not raise himself when he tried to, and began to smile.

He was taken into the lodge. The doctor arrived, examined him, and asked where he felt the pain.

"I feel it all over," he said. "But it doesn't matter. I'm only afraid master will be annoyed. Father ought to be told."

Alyosha lay in bed for two days, and on the third day they sent for the priest.

"Are you really going to die?" Ustinia asked.

"Of course I am. You can't go on living for ever. You must go when the time comes." Alyosha spoke rapidly as usual. "Thank you, Ustinia. You've been very good to me. What a lucky thing they didn't let us marry! Where should we have been now? It's much better as it is."

When the priest came, he prayed with his bands and with his heart. "As it is good here when you obey and do no harm to others, so it will be there," was the thought within it.

He spoke very little; he only said he was thirsty, and he seemed full of wonder at something.

He lay in wonderment, then stretched himself, and died.

There are no Guilty People

[Written between 1908 and 1910. Published posthumously. This version is taken from the collection *The Forged Coupon and Other Stories* (1911) translated by Charles Theodore Hagberg Wright.]

I

Mine is a strange and wonderful lot! The chances are that there is not a single wretched beggar suffering under the luxury and oppression of the rich who feels anything like as keenly as I do either the injustice, the cruelty, and the horror of their oppression of and contempt for the poor; or the grinding humiliation and misery which befall the great majority of the workers, the real producers of all that makes life possible. I have felt this for a long time, and as the years have passed by the feeling has grown and grown, until recently it reached its climax. Although I feel all this so vividly, I still live on amid the depravity and sins of rich society; and I cannot leave it, because I have neither the knowledge nor the strength to do so. I cannot. I do not know how to change my life so that my physical needs—food, sleep, clothing, my going to and fro—may be satisfied without a sense of shame and wrongdoing in the position which I fill.

There was a time when I tried to change my position, which was not in harmony with my conscience; but the conditions created by the past, by my family and its claims upon me, were so complicated that they would not let me out of their grasp, or rather, I did not know how to free myself. I had not the strength. Now that I am over eighty and have become feeble, I have given up trying to free myself; and, strange to say, as my feebleness increases I realise more and more strongly the wrongfulness of my position, and it grows more and more intolerable to me.

It has occurred to me that I do not occupy this position for nothing: that Providence intended that I should lay bare the truth of my feelings, so that I might atone for all that causes my suffering, and might perhaps open the eyes of those—or at least of some of those—who are still blind to what I see so clearly, and thus might lighten the burden of that vast majority who, under existing conditions, are subjected to bodily and spiritual suffering by those who deceive them and also deceive themselves. Indeed, it may be that the position which I occupy gives me special facilities for revealing the artificial and criminal relations which exist between men—for telling the whole truth in regard to that position without confusing the issue by attempting to vindicate myself, and without rousing the envy of the rich and feelings of oppression in the hearts of the poor and downtrodden. I am so placed that I not only have no desire to vindicate myself; but, on the contrary, I find it necessary to make an effort lest I should exaggerate the wickedness of the great among whom I live, of whose society I am ashamed, whose attitude towards their fellow-men I detest with my whole soul, though I find it impossible to separate my lot from theirs. But I must also avoid the error of those democrats and others who, in defending the oppressed and the enslaved, do not see their failings and mistakes, and who do not make sufficient allowance for the difficulties created, the mistakes inherited from the past, which in a degree lessens the responsibility of the upper classes.

Free from desire for self-vindication, free from fear of an emancipated people, free from that envy and hatred which the oppressed feel for their oppressors, I am in the best possible position to see the truth and to tell it. Perhaps that is why Providence placed me in such a position. I will do my best to turn it to account.

II

Alexander Ivanovitch Volgin, a bachelor and a clerk in a Moscow bank at a salary of eight thousand roubles a year, a man much respected in his own set, was staying in a country-house. His host was a wealthy landowner, owning some twenty-five hundred acres, and had married his guest's cousin. Volgin, tired after an evening spent in playing vint* for small stakes with members of the family, went to his room and placed his watch, silver cigarette-case, pocket-book, big leather purse, and pocket-brush and comb on a small table covered with a white cloth, and then, taking off his coat, waistcoat, shirt, trousers, and underclothes, his silk socks and English boots, put on his nightshirt and dressing-gown. His watch pointed to midnight. Volgin smoked a cigarette, lay on his face for about five minutes reviewing the day's impressions; then, blowing out his candle, he turned over on his side and fell asleep about one o'clock, in spite of a good deal of restlessness. Awaking next morning at eight he put on his slippers and dressing-gown, and rang the bell.

The old butler, Stephen, the father of a family and the grandfather of six grandchildren, who had served in that house for thirty years, entered the room hurriedly, with bent legs, carrying in the newly blackened boots which Volgin had taken off the night before, a well-brushed suit, and a clean shirt. The guest thanked him, and then asked what the weather was like (the blinds were drawn so that the sun should not prevent anyone from sleeping till eleven o'clock if he were so inclined), and whether his hosts had slept well. He glanced at his watch—it was still early—and began to wash and dress. His water was ready, and everything on the

---

* A game of cards similar to auction bridge.

washing-stand and dressing-table was ready for use and properly laid out—his soap, his tooth and hair brushes, his nail scissors and files. He washed his hands and face in a leisurely fashion, cleaned and manicured his nails, pushed back the skin with the towel, and sponged his stout white body from head to foot. Then he began to brush his hair. Standing in front of the mirror, he first brushed his curly beard, which was beginning to turn grey, with two English brushes, parting it down the middle. Then he combed his hair, which was already showing signs of getting thin, with a large tortoise-shell comb. Putting on his underlinen, his socks, his boots, his trousers—which were held up by elegant braces—and his waistcoat, he sat down coatless in an easy chair to rest after dressing, lit a cigarette, and began to think where he should go for a walk that morning—to the park or to Littleports (what a funny name for a wood!). He thought he would go to Littleports. Then he must answer Simon Nicholaevich's letter; but there was time enough for that. Getting up with an air of resolution, he took out his watch. It was already five minutes to nine. He put his watch into his waistcoat pocket, and his purse—with all that was left of the hundred and eighty roubles he had taken for his journey, and for the incidental expenses of his fortnight's stay with his cousin—and then he placed into his trouser pocket his cigarette-case and electric cigarette-lighter, and two clean handkerchiefs into his coat pockets, and went out of the room, leaving as usual the mess and confusion which he had made to be cleared up by Stephen, an old man of over fifty. Stephen expected Volgin to "remunerate" him, as he said, being so accustomed to the work that he did not feel the slightest repugnance for it. Glancing at a mirror, and feeling satisfied with his appearance, Volgin went into the dining-room.

There, thanks to the efforts of the housekeeper, the footman, and under-butler—the latter had risen at dawn in order to run home to sharpen his son's scythe—breakfast was ready. On a spotless white cloth stood a boiling, shiny, silver samovar (at least it looked like silver), a coffee-pot, hot milk, cream, butter, and all sorts of fancy white bread and biscuits. The only persons at table were the second son of the house, his tutor (a student), and the secretary. The host, who was an active member of the Zemstvo and a great farmer, had already left the house, having gone at eight o'clock to attend to his work. Volgin, while drinking his coffee, talked to the student and the secretary about the weather, and yesterday's vint, and discussed Theodorite's peculiar behaviour the night before, as he had been very rude to his father without the slightest cause. Theodorite was the grown-up son of the house, and a ne'er-do-well. His name was Theodore, but someone had once called him Theodorite, either as a joke or to tease him, and, as it seemed funny, the name stuck to him, although his doings were no longer in the least amusing. So it was now. He had been to the university, but left it in his second year, and joined a regiment of horse guards; but he gave that up also, and was now living in the country, doing nothing, finding fault, and feeling discontented with everything. Theodorite was still in bed: so were the other members of the household—Anna Mikhailovna, its mistress; her sister, the widow of a general; and a landscape painter who lived with the family.

Volgin took his panama hat from the hall table (it had cost twenty roubles) and his cane with its carved ivory handle, and went out. Crossing the veranda, gay with flowers, he walked through the flower garden, in the centre of which was a raised round bed, with rings of red, white, and blue flowers, and the initials of the mistress of the house done in carpet bedding in the centre. Leaving the flower garden Volgin entered the avenue of lime trees, hundreds of years old, which peasant girls were tidying and sweeping with spades and brooms. The gardener was busy measuring, and a boy was bringing something in a cart. Passing these Volgin went into the park of at least a hundred and twenty-five acres, filled with fine old trees, and intersected by a network of well-kept walks. Smoking as he strolled Volgin took his favourite path past the summer-house into the fields beyond. It was pleasant in the park, but it was still nicer in the fields. On the right some women who were digging potatoes formed a mass of bright red and white colour; on the left were wheat fields, meadows, and grazing cattle;

and in the foreground, slightly to the right, were the dark, dark oaks of Littleports. Volgin took a deep breath, and felt glad that he was alive, especially here in his cousin's home, where he was so thoroughly enjoying the rest from his work at the bank.

"Lucky people to live in the country," he thought. "True, what with his farming and his Zemstvo, the owner of the estate has very little peace even in the country, but that is his own lookout." Volgin shook his head, lit another cigarette, and, stepping out firmly with his powerful feet clad in his thick English boots, began to think of the heavy winter's work in the bank that was in front of him. "I shall be there every day from ten to two, sometimes even till five. And the board meetings . . . And private interviews with clients . . . Then the Duma. Whereas here . . . It is delightful. It may be a little dull, but it is not for long." He smiled. After a stroll in Littleports he turned back, going straight across a fallow field which was being ploughed. A herd of cows, calves, sheep, and pigs, which belonged to the village community, was grazing there. The shortest way to the park was to pass through the herd. He frightened the sheep, which ran away one after another, and were followed by the pigs, of which two little ones stared solemnly at him. The shepherd boy called to the sheep and cracked his whip. "How far behind Europe we are," thought Volgin, recalling his frequent holidays abroad. "You would not find a single cow like that anywhere in Europe." Then, wanting to find out where the path which branched off from the one he was on led to and who was the owner of the herd, he called to the boy.

"Whose herd is it?"

The boy was so filled with wonder, verging on terror, when he gazed at the hat, the well-brushed beard, and above all the gold-rimmed eyeglasses, that he could not reply at once. When Volgin repeated his question the boy pulled himself together, and said, "Ours." "But whose is 'ours'?" said Volgin, shaking his head and smiling. The boy was wearing shoes of plaited birch bark, bands of linen round his legs, a dirty, unbleached shirt ragged at the shoulder, and a cap the peak of which had been torn.

"Whose is 'ours'?"

"The Pirogov village herd."

"How old are you?

"I don't know."

"Can you read?"

"No, I can't."

"Didn't you go to school?"

"Yes, I did."

"Couldn't you learn to read?"

"No."

"Where does that path lead?"

The boy told him, and Volgin went on towards the house, thinking how he would chaff Nicholas Petrovich about the deplorable condition of the village schools in spite of all his efforts.

On approaching the house Volgin looked at his watch, and saw that it was already past eleven. He remembered that Nicholas Petrovich was going to drive to the nearest town, and that he had meant to give him a letter to post to Moscow; but the letter was not written. The letter was a very important one to a friend, asking him to bid for him for a picture of the Madonna which was to be offered for sale at an auction. As he reached the house he saw at the door four big, well-fed, well-groomed, thoroughbred horses harnessed to a carriage, the black lacquer of which glistened in the sun. The coachman was seated on the box in a kaftan, with a silver belt, and the horses were jingling their silver bells from time to time.

A bare-headed, barefooted peasant in a ragged kaftan stood at the front door. He bowed. Volgin asked what he wanted.

"I have come to see Nicholas Petrovich."

"What about?"

"Because I am in distress—my horse has died."

Volgin began to question him. The peasant told him how he was situated. He had five children, and this had been his only horse. Now it was gone. He wept.

"What are you going to do?"

"To beg." And he knelt down, and remained kneeling in spite of Volgin's expostulations.

"What is your name?"

"Mitri Sudarikov," answered the peasant, still kneeling.

Volgin took three roubles from his purse and gave them to the peasant, who showed his gratitude by touching the ground with his forehead, and then went into the house. His host was standing in the hall.

"Where is your letter?" he asked, approaching Volgin; "I am just off."

"I'm awfully sorry, I'll write it this minute, if you will let me. I forgot all about it. It's so pleasant here that one can forget anything."

"All right, but do be quick. The horses have already been standing a quarter of an hour, and the flies are biting viciously. Can you wait, Arsenty?" he asked the coachman.

"Why not?" said the coachman, thinking to himself, "why do they order the horses when they aren't ready? The rush the grooms and I had—just to stand here and feed the flies."

"Directly, directly," Volgin went towards his room, but turned back to ask Nicholas Petrovich about the begging peasant.

"Did you see him?—He's a drunkard, but still he is to be pitied. Do be quick!"

Volgin got out his case, with all the requisites for writing, wrote the letter, made out a cheque for a hundred and eighty roubles, and, sealing down the envelope, took it to Nicholas Petrovich.

"Goodbye."

Volgin read the newspapers till luncheon. He only read the Liberal papers: *The Russian Gazette*, *Speech*, sometimes *The Russian Word*—but he would not touch *The New Times*, to which his host subscribed.

While he was scanning at his ease the political news, the Tsar's doings, the doings of President, and ministers and decisions in the Duma, and was just about to pass on to the general news, theatres, science, murders and cholera, he heard the luncheon bell ring.

Thanks to the efforts of upwards of ten human beings—counting laundresses, gardeners, cooks, kitchen-maids, butlers and footmen—the table was sumptuously laid for eight, with silver water jugs, decanters, kvass, wine, mineral waters, cut glass, and fine table linen, while two men-servants were continually hurrying to and fro, bringing in and serving, and then clearing away the hors d'oeuvre and the various hot and cold courses.

The hostess talked incessantly about everything that she had been doing, thinking, and saying; and she evidently considered that everything that she thought, said, or did was perfect, and that it would please every one except those who were fools. Volgin felt and knew that everything she said was stupid, but it would never do to let it be seen, and so he kept up the conversation. Theodorite was glum and silent; the student occasionally exchanged a few words with the widow. Now and again there was a pause in the conversation, and then Theodorite interposed, and every one became miserably depressed. At such moments the hostess ordered some dish that had not been served, and the footman hurried off to the kitchen, or to the housekeeper, and hurried back again. Nobody felt inclined either to talk or to eat. But they all forced themselves to eat and to talk, and so luncheon went on.

The peasant who had been begging because his horse had died was named Mitri Sudarikov. He had spent the whole day before he went to the squire over his dead horse. First of all he went to the knacker, Sanin, who lived in a village near. The knacker was out, but he waited for him, and it was dinner time when he had finished bargaining over the price of the skin. Then he borrowed a neighbour's horse to take his own to a field to be buried, as it is forbidden to bury dead animals near a village. Adrian would not lend his horse because he was getting in his potatoes, but Stephen took pity on Mitri and gave way to his persuasion. He even lent a hand in lifting the dead horse into the cart. Mitri tore off the shoes from the forelegs and gave them to his wife. One was broken, but the other one was whole. While he was digging the grave with a spade which was very blunt, the knacker appeared and took off the skin; and the carcass was then thrown into the hole and covered up. Mitri felt tired, and went into Matrena's hut, where he drank half a bottle of vodka with Sanin to console himself. Then he went home, quarrelled with his wife, and lay down to sleep on the hay.

He did not undress, but slept just as he was, with a ragged coat for a coverlet. His wife was in the hut with the girls—there were four of them, and the youngest was only five weeks old. Mitri woke up before dawn as usual. He groaned as the memory of the day before broke in upon him—how the horse had struggled and struggled, and then fallen down. Now there was no horse, and all he had was the price of the skin, four roubles and eighty kopeks. Getting up he arranged the linen bands on his legs, and went through the yard into the hut. His wife was putting straw into the stove with one hand, with the other she was holding a baby girl to her breast, which was hanging out of her dirty chemise.

Mitri crossed himself three times, turning towards the corner in which the ikons hung, and repeated some utterly meaningless words, which he called prayers, to the Trinity and the Virgin, the Creed and our Father.

"Isn't there any water?"

"The girl's gone for it. I've got some tea. Will you go up to the squire?"

"Yes, I'd better." The smoke from the stove made him cough. He took a rag off the wooden bench and went into the porch. The girl had just come back with the water. Mitri filled his mouth with water from the pail and squirted it out on his hands, took some more in his mouth to wash his face, dried himself with the rag, then parted and smoothed his curly hair with his fingers and went out. A little girl of about ten, with nothing on but a dirty shirt, came towards him. "Good morning, Uncle Mitri," she said; "you are to come and thrash." "All right, I'll come," replied Mitri. He understood that he was expected to return the help given the week before by Kumushkir, a man as poor as he was himself, when he was thrashing his own corn with a horse-driven machine.

"Tell them I'll come—I'll come at lunch time. I've got to go to Ugrumi." Mitri went back to the hut, and changing his birch-bark shoes and the linen bands on his legs, started off to see the squire. After he had got three roubles from Volgin, and the same sum from Nicholas Petrovich, he returned to his house, gave the money to his wife, and went to his neighbour's. The thrashing machine was humming, and the driver was shouting. The lean horses were going slowly round him, straining at their traces. The driver was shouting to them in a monotone, "Now, there, my dears." Some women were unbinding sheaves, others were raking up the scattered straw and ears, and others again were gathering great armfuls of corn and handing them to the men to feed the machine. The work was in full swing. In the kitchen garden, which Mitri had to pass, a girl, clad only in a long shirt, was digging potatoes which she put into a basket.

"Where's your grandfather?" asked Mitri. "He's in the barn." Mitri went to the barn and set to work at once. The old man of eighty knew of Mitri's trouble. After greeting him, he gave him his place to feed the machine.

Mitri took off his ragged coat, laid it out of the way near the fence, and then began to work vigorously, raking the corn together and throwing it into the machine. The work went on without interruption until the dinner-hour. The cocks had crowed two or three times, but no one paid any attention to them; not because the workers did not believe them, but because they were scarcely heard for the noise of the work and the talk about it. At last the whistle of the squire's steam thrasher sounded three miles away, and then the owner came into the barn. He was a straight old man of eighty. "It's time to stop," he said; "it's dinner-time." Those at work seemed to redouble their efforts. In a moment the straw was cleared away; the grain that had been thrashed was separated from the chaff and brought in, and then the workers went into the hut.

The hut was smoke-begrimed, as its stove had no chimney, but it had been tidied up, and benches stood round the table, making room for all those who had been working, of whom there were nine, not counting the owners. Bread, soup, boiled potatoes, and kvass were placed on the table.

An old one-armed beggar, with a bag slung over his shoulder, came in with a crutch during the meal.

"Peace be to this house. A good appetite to you. For Christ's sake give me something."

"God will give it to you," said the mistress, already an old woman, and the daughter-in-law of the master. "Don't be angry with us." An old man, who was still standing near the door, said, "Give him some bread, Martha. How can you?"

"I am only wondering whether we shall have enough." "Oh, it is wrong, Martha. God tells us to help the poor. Cut him a slice."

Martha obeyed. The beggar went away. The man in charge of the thrashing-machine got up, said grace, thanked his hosts, and went away to rest.

Mitri did not lie down, but ran to the shop to buy some tobacco. He was longing for a smoke. While he smoked he chatted to a man from Demensk, asking the price of cattle, as he saw that he would not be able to manage without selling a cow. When he returned to the others, they were already back at work again; and so it went on till the evening.

Among these downtrodden, duped, and defrauded men, who are becoming demoralised by overwork, and being gradually done to death by underfeeding, there are men living who consider themselves Christians; and others so enlightened that they feel no further need for Christianity or for any religion, so superior do they appear in their own esteem. And yet their hideous, lazy lives are supported by the degrading, excessive labour of these slaves, not to mention the labour of millions of other slaves, toiling in factories to produce samovars, silver, carriages, machines, and the like for their use. They live among these horrors, seeing them and yet not seeing them, although often kind at heart—old men and women, young men and maidens, mothers and children—poor children who are being vitiated and trained into moral blindness.

Here is a bachelor grown old, the owner of thousands of acres, who has lived a life of idleness, greed, and over-indulgence, who reads *The New Times*, and is astonished that the government can be so unwise as to permit Jews to enter the university. There is his guest, formerly the governor of a province, now a senator with a big salary, who reads with satisfaction that a congress of lawyers has passed a resolution in favour of capital punishment. Their political enemy, N. P., reads a liberal paper, and cannot understand the blindness of the government in allowing the union of Russian men to exist.

Here is a kind, gentle mother of a little girl reading a story to her about Fox, a dog that lamed some rabbits. And here is this little girl. During her walks she sees other children, barefooted, hungry, hunting for green apples that have fallen from the trees; and, so accustomed is she to the sight, that these children do not seem to her to be children such as she is, but only part of the usual surroundings—the familiar landscape.

Why is this?